P
BRE

Marita van der Vyver is a journalist living in South Africa. She has published three acclaimed children's novels, a biography and two adult novels, *Entertaining Angels* and *Childish Things*. *Entertaining Angels*, her first adult novel, was an instant bestseller in Afrikaans, and was awarded the biggest literary prize in South Africa, the M-Net Book Prize.

Breathing Space | Marita van der Vyver

Translated from the Afrikaans
by Isobel Dixon

PENGUIN BOOKS

For Alain

PENGUIN BOOKS

Published by the Penguin Group
Penguin Books Ltd, 27 Wrights Lane, London w8 5tz, England
Penguin Putnam Inc., 375 Hudson Street, New York, New York 10014, USA
Penguin Books Australia Ltd, Ringwood, Victoria, Australia
Penguin Books Canada Ltd, 10 Alcorn Avenue, Toronto, Ontario, Canada m4v 3b2
Penguin Books (NZ) Ltd, Private Bag 102902, NSMC, Auckland, New Zealand

Penguin Books Ltd, Registered Offices: Harmondsworth, Middlesex, England

First published 2000
10 9 8 7 6 5 4 3 2 1

Copyright © Marita van der Vyver, 2000
Translation copyright © Isobel Dixon, 2000
All rights reserved

The Permissions on page 470 constitute an extension of this copyright page

The moral right of the author has been asserted

Set in 10/11.25pt Monotype Sabon
Phototypeset by Intype London Ltd
Printed in England by Clays Ltd, St Ives plc

Except in the United States of America, this book is sold subject
to the condition that it shall not, by way of trade or otherwise, be lent,
re-sold, hired out, or otherwise circulated without the publisher's
prior consent in any form of binding or cover other than that in
which it is published and without a similar condition including this
condition being imposed on the subsequent purchaser

Contents

Group Photo (1985)

Ten characters in search of an author, perhaps?

Yvette is the one seated in the middle, her hands folded protectively over her bulging stomach, her feet crossed demurely at the ankles. Something about her reminds you of Alice in Wonderland, a serious child in old-fashioned clothes, lost in her own imaginary world. As if the dark eyes under the heavy dark fringe look far beyond the camera, to something which the others can't see. As if she has second sight, someone in the group remarked when they discussed it later. Or can't see, Yvette said in her soft voice, with the same little shadow of a smile as in the photo.

Paul is the handsome man next to her, the kind every decent mother warns her daughter against, because he looks far too much like an Italian model, from the dimple in his impressive chin to the soft leather shoes he is wearing with his khaki shorts. The kind of khaki shorts you buy at an exclusive boutique rather than at a farmers' co-op on the platteland.

Philip isn't as attractive as Paul and not nearly as well groomed. His light blue denim shirt is crumpled and the expression in his eyes, the same faded blue as the shirt, is self-conscious. That's him, sitting on the other side next to Yvette, with one buttock in the air, as if he wants to leap up and run away. Well, that's his reaction to anything that makes him feel uncomfortable, Emma muttered later.

Adriaan is the guy with the pipe in his mouth and the hat with the leopard-skin band on his head. He is sitting on the mat in front of the couch, cross-legged, wearing velskoene without socks, powerful and erect like a Boer soldier posing for a formal portrait. A wounded Boer soldier – the red-brown paint splashes on his white shirt look disturbingly like blood – with a mocking curl to his lips which contradicts the seriousness of his bearing. *You're not seeing what you think you see. Be warned.*

Liane is the woman with the cover-girl smile, as lovely as Helen of Troy must have been. She had set the camera on a tripod to take the photo automatically and thrown herself down on the floor at Yvette's feet like a smug cat, her one arm draped seductively around Adriaan's shoulders, the other lying possessively on Max's knee. She obviously feels at home in front of a camera.

Max looks at her with so much undisguised admiration that the photo would later become an embarrassment to him. He is wearing jeans with a tear at the knee and a faded *End Conscription* T-shirt. Greek, you'd guess, if you didn't know him, with bushy black locks and beard and chest hair. Helen of Troy's young Greek love. They went out at school, before she became a Capitalist and he a Marxist.

Bobby sits on the arm rest above Max's head with her arms wrapped around her body as if she is cold. Small and skinny in a brightly patterned shirt which hangs loose about her and trousers with an ethnic design which doesn't match the shirt at all. She is the youngest of them all, but her grey eyes look as old as the hills and as melancholy as the sea on a winter's day.

Mila is the one with the long brown legs and the short purple dress, on the other arm rest. Blonde hair cut like a boy's, lips and toenails painted an identical reckless shade of red. Her face turned away, as if something distracted her at the moment the photo was taken, so that you can't help but admire her profile – long neck, strong chin and the kind of nose always described as 'aristocratic' – her whole bearing proud, challenging yet wary. Nervous, a perceptive observer would suspect. The way in which one hand tightly grips the back rest of the green leather couch.

The assumption of nervousness would be confirmed if you looked at Ralph, his long body draped over the back of the couch, graceful, like a leopard on a branch. Or perhaps a lion, with a bush of golden brown mane and amber eyes which stare intently at the camera. Some kind of feline predator, anyway; waiting, alert and ready to leap on its prey. So self-assured that he doesn't even have to look at his victim.

A picture which tells a story of more than a thousand words, Emma thought the first time she saw the photo. She stands behind the couch looking down at the rest of the group, her face veiled by her long, curly, orange-brown hair. She looks at them with the caring of a friend – concerned about the suppressed emotions and unspoken desires between members of the group – but also with the detachment of a writer who is beguiled by the opening scene of a story. The wrong story, she would later realize. Amazed at how misleading such a picture could be.

The only indication of the story she would eventually see – when it was too late to write it down because reality had exceeded her wildest imaginings – is the way in which one of the characters looks away. Like bloody Judas Iscariot at the Last Supper, Mila murmured through her scarlet mouth when she saw the photo again a decade later. But by that time, this particular story was only a single thread in the carpet of stories which any group of friends weaves together over a span of ten years.

ONE

Dancing in the Dark (1985)

She didn't know about love, she would later say, but she believed in lust at first sight. Inexplicable lust, she realized that Friday night, when she walked into the kitchen and saw Adriaan standing in front of the stove. With a wooden spoon in his hand and a dark blue butcher's apron over a shirt covered in paint splotches. Barefoot.

Funny that she should have noticed his feet, bare and broad and brown, the feet of a man who doesn't like shoes. And his hands, which didn't look to her like an artist's hands. Big, hardened hands, better suited to a plough than a paintbrush. And his mouth, soft and vulnerable, which contradicted the challenging look on his face. Like a wound above his chin.

Later, of course, she would look for excuses. If there's one thing worse than sleeping with a married man, she rebuked herself, it's sleeping with a man whose wife you like. But when she arrived at Yzerfontein that evening, she always added in her own defence, she didn't yet know Yvette. Indeed, she didn't even see Yvette. Although she sat only a few paces from Adriaan at the kitchen table.

Later, she thought about the play in which Harold Pinter tries to pinpoint the precise moment at which a chain of betrayal begins. For her it was the immediate recognition of her own improper desires in Adriaan's eyes. Like seeks like.

'Mila, this is Adriaan Beyers, our Great Painter,' said Emma behind her. 'And this is Mila Jordaan, whom we've told you so much about.'

'I imagined you differently,' said Adriaan, in a deep, dark voice which immediately made her long for a cup of strong, black coffee. 'I expected a raving feminist with hairy legs.'

'Careful. She's the most dangerous kind of feminist,' Philip cautioned from the kitchen door. 'A wolf in sheep's clothing.'

'You think you're dealing with a dumb blonde, then she hits you with a quote from Andrea Dworkin.' Ralph proffered his hand to Adriaan. 'Hello, I'm Ralph le Roux.'

When Yvette stood up, Mila saw the massive stomach before she noticed the rest of her. Seven months? Nine months? She wore a dress which looked like an old-fashioned dressing gown, glossy material with a pattern of huge roses – which emphasized rather than disguised the girth of the belly – and ballet shoes of black satin. No make-up, but her face had that blushing, glowing beauty found only in very young, enthusiastic nuns and smug pregnant women.

'Welcome to the West Coast,' said Yvette. 'Come, I'll show you your bedrooms.'

'We couldn't figure out who was sleeping with who, so you'll have to fight it out among yourselves.' Adriaan had turned back to the stove and was stirring something in a saucepan. The smell of cream and melted cheese hung about him like incense. 'Anyway, there are enough beds here for a brothel.'

When the other three followed Yvette, Mila amazed herself by staying behind in the room. Get away, her reason cautioned. Forget the weekend, get in the car and drive back to Cape Town. Take the next flight back to Johannesburg. But she stayed where she was, without words or will. And since she'd always thought that 'magnetic attraction' was only an expression you encountered in mediocre magazine stories – the kind you would read on the sly in doctors' waiting rooms – she couldn't explain why her feet refused to obey her reason.

'How long have you lived here?' she asked, just for the sake of saying something.

'About a month. We've loaned the whole place for a year, furniture and all. It belongs to a rich Transvaler who likes my work. He said I could pay him with paintings.'

He definitely had the build of a farmer rather than a painter, she decided, the heavy shoulders and broad chest, the strong upper arms and legs, even the tanned face of someone who prefers to work outdoors. The body of a man who enjoys food, with a hint of softness around the stomach, under the apron. He lifted the wooden spoon to his lips and tasted the sauce with so much sensual concentration that she stared at him, fascinated. She could have sworn he was sucking at a woman's fingers. The mouth of a man who enjoys much more than food.

'What are you working on at the moment? Do you have anything new in the studio? Something to sell? I'd love to . . .'

She lifted her hand, held her fingers in front of her mouth, as if to stem the tide of nervous words. He looked up from the saucepan and she suddenly saw herself through his grey-green eyes, her lips perhaps too scarlet, her dress perhaps too short. But he smiled reassuringly.

'I've been struggling to get going ever since we arrived. It's more tempting to cook and go fishing. But if you're interested, I can paint something for you. Perhaps it's just the incentive I need.'

'Unfortunately I couldn't afford one of your big paintings. I'm a journalist earning a pathetic salary, not an art collector. I just thought you might have something more . . . modest somewhere?'

'I can always show you my etchings.'

He threw the invitation down before her like a gauntlet, an old-fashioned challenge to a duel, smiling. She looked him in the eyes.

'That's not what I had in mind.'

But her voice suddenly gained a breathlessness, which only made him smile more broadly.

'That's a pity.' He shrugged his shoulders and turned back to the stove. 'Perhaps I could persuade you to pose for me. I'd do a beautiful portrait of you. Just a little one. Then you can decide if you want to buy it or not.'

'I know your portraits. The women are almost always naked, not so? And surrounded by devils or satyrs or other male monstrosities with huge genitals.'

'And you don't like that?'

'No, it's not that, it's just . . . I find it a bit too voyeuristic. I don't know, perhaps all artists are voyeurs, but with you it's more . . . exaggerated. More disturbing.'

'So you don't want to pose for me?'

'Let's just say I'm not ready for such a commitment,' she smiled, her voice now as challenging as his, like a poker player beginning to gain confidence.

'Then I suppose you won't go to bed with me either?'

She began to laugh, her self-confidence swept away with her breath, and walked to the nearest window so that he couldn't see her face. He was definitely more skilled at this game than she was. The house was built high against a hill, and the curtainless wooden window frame offered an uninterrupted view of a beach which stretched into infinity like a glistening white Milky Way, bordered by the sea which lay still and grey-blue on the left and a whole palette of green on the right, a wilderness of fynbos and hardy, salt-tolerant shrubs. She let her gaze slide slowly, caressingly across the green thickets, across the slender white body of the sand, to the soft, pale blue coverlet of the sea. Far beyond, near the horizon, a rocky island stuck out like a foot, a rough black silhouette against the late afternoon light. The sun floated like a glowing ball on the sea, partly wrapped in baby pink and powder blue cottonwool clouds, the colours muted like a delicate pastel sketch. She wondered involuntarily how Adriaan Beyers would paint such a sunset. He usually used oils, sometimes smeared as thick as butter on to the canvas, and dark, threatening colours. Not the sort of blue that soothed you, the sentimental red of Valentine hearts, but bruised blue like dark shadows under the eyes, reddish browns like scabs on wounds. How was she to reconcile those dark paintings with this apparently flippant man in front of her?

'Don't mind me,' he murmured as though he had read her thoughts, his eyes fixed on the stove, a playful smile on his lips. 'My friend Max says my problem is that I feel threatened by strong women. He says the only way I can manage this feeling is to treat them as sex objects.'

'My problem is that I don't actually mind being treated as a sex object.' She walked towards him again. She felt a desire to do something she would regret for the rest of her life. Like pressing her fingers into the mouth of this man she barely knew. 'As long as you don't mind if I do the same to you.'

'Be my guest.' He turned unexpectedly and lifted the wooden spoon to her lips. She opened her mouth and he placed the tip of the spoon carefully on her tongue. She felt the hardness of the wood against her teeth and let her tongue slide slowly over the rounded bottom of the spoon. Tried to distinguish between the different flavours of cheese: ricotta, mozzarella, and something sharper, like Roquefort. Then she closed her eyes and sucked the creamy sauce from the spoon, held it in her mouth for a moment, somewhat bitter, somewhat salty, and let it slip smoothly down her throat.

'What do you think?'

It's the most erotic mouthful I've ever been offered, she thought, and opened her eyes.

'I think I'm hungry,' she said, and looked out through the window again.

The sun had vanished into the sea. She was surprised, as always, by how quickly the sun moved across that last stretch of sky. Now the sea was dark and smooth and shiny, like petrol on tar, the colour of the clouds no longer so soft. As if someone had smeared the pastel drawing with dirty fingers. That's how Adriaan would paint the scene, she realized.

'What I don't understand,' she would say the following evening on the beach to Emma, 'is that I'm not annoyed by all his sexual innuendoes. If any other man did that . . . You know me!'

Emma laughed, her long hair wilder than usual in the wind which had come up suddenly after a day of lovely spring weather. They walked on the damp sand with the icy West Coast water spilling over their feet every now and then. Painful, like electric shocks.

'He'd be thrilled if he annoyed you. He does it to get a reaction – any reaction, negative or positive. But it's also more than that. I think the reason most women don't mind when he approaches them in such a blatant way is that they can sense that he's one of those rare men who is really completely crazy about women. He doesn't do it just to get them into bed. To stroke his ego. He doesn't have a drop of misogyny in him. I don't know many men of whom one could say that. I think he's just so intensely interested in every woman that he meets.'

'*Every* woman?'

Mila heard the disappointed tone in her own voice and quickly crouched to pick up a piece of seaweed. The beach was scattered with treasures and rubbish washed up by the waves: bleached driftwood and smooth pebbles, scraps of fishing net, shiny snakes of sea-bamboo, empty plastic bottles with illegible labels in unknown languages. The seaweed on her palm was white and brittle, like the skeleton of a small creature. She stroked it carefully.

'Well, he doesn't have the usual hang-ups about fat or thin, old or young. You know. I think he looks at every woman as a possible model.'

'So everyone is an oil painting to him.' It was meant to come out jokingly, but there was still chagrin in her voice.

The wind blew the sound of Emma's laugh away. When Mila looked up it seemed as though her friend was screaming soundlessly, her neck bent back and her mouth open, her flapping hair like flames around her head. The sun sank a lot more dramatically than the previous night, the clouds shocking pink like icing made with too much red food colouring, the texture thick and uneven, as though someone had attacked it with a fork – that rippled pattern that her mother always made on her church bazaar cakes. She wondered why everything – even a kitsch sunset – had reminded her of food ever since she'd arrived here at Yzerfontein. Behind the booming waves the water formed sharp foam tips in the wind. Like stiffly beaten egg whites, she thought, and her stomach somersaulted with hunger.

When she was small, she felt constantly guilty because she thought about sex too much. Even before she realized that it was *sex* she was thinking about. She just knew it was sinful. She always knew it was sinful. So she never discussed it with anyone. She was a shy child, a sweet little girl, it seemed. Far too shy to tell any of her friends about the wonderful tingling warmth which she felt down there whenever she thought of certain things – vague, exciting, alarming things, secret acts between bodies, naked body against naked body . . . It was a kind of masturbation, she realized later. Because she was too scared to touch herself – scared that God would see her, scared that her mother would catch her – she managed to do in her head what most of her friends probably did with their hands. She cultivated a secret garden in her imagination, a secluded corner in which she began to embroider a quilt of sexual fantasy, a sensual hiding place in which neither her mother nor any supernatural being was allowed. And yet she often had the strange feeling that God knew what she was doing (after all, her mother had always warned that He could see everything) but didn't really mind. As long as she didn't use her hands. And she didn't. Never. Well, only much, much later.

'And I thought I was special,' she said, sighing.

'You are special. That's what I'm trying to say. *Every* woman is special to him!' The unexpected irritation in Emma's voice made Mila stand up, but the expression in her friend's eyes was hidden behind the strands of blowing hair. 'I saw what happened between the two of you last night. Let me give you some advice . . .'

'Nothing happened,' Mila parried, her face glowing with embarrassment.

'Sure. Nothing except an electric current so potent it could have set the whole bloody house alight. Forget it, Mila, that's all I want to say. Don't even consider it.'

Mila folded the seaweed into her palm and felt how it crumbled under her fingers. They turned silently and began to walk back to the house. Here and there a light flickered in one of the houses against the hill. On the stoep of Adriaan and Yvette's house a dark, uncertain silhouette looked out over the beach. Adriaan, she hoped. She opened her fist and watched as the seaweed whirled away in fine fragments on the wind.

'He really should have lived in a different era,' murmured Yvette at the kitchen table, as she watched Adriaan and Emma dancing to Bruce Springsteen's hoarse voice. 'In a time when noblemen and writers and artists could conquer hundreds of women. Like Byron's Don Juan.'

Mila stared astonished at a potato peel which slipped and curled, coil upon coil, through Yvette's slender fingers like a thin, transparent snake, all in one piece, perfect. And longed intensely for her Ouma Millie, champion potato peeler, dead almost twenty years now. While the potato in her own hand felt heavier, stickier. She had apparently not inherited her grandmother's gift. All around her lay scraps of peel, strewn about like wood shavings. As if she were carving a statuette out of the bloody potato. She would much rather be dancing with Adriaan.

'And what about you?' Her voice sounded unnecessarily bitchy. 'How would you like to be married to Don Juan?'

'I already feel as though I'm married to Don Juan,' answered Yvette with a shrug.

Mila looked at her again, critically, and realized that she was beginning to like her. Against her will. That first impression of smug naïvety had faded. Replaced with the suspicion that she was dealing with a woman who had something which most people longed for all their lives. An inner source of peace, strength, self-confidence, whatever you like to call it, from which she could continually draw comfort. Not just comfort for herself, but for the people around her as well.

'I accepted long ago that he views every woman as a challenge. Not necessarily to get her clothes off – although that's probably part of the excitement. To persuade her to pose for him, I mean.' Yvette's soft voice was almost disturbingly detached. As if she was speaking of someone she didn't know personally. 'It's more like a kind of insatiable curiosity. To know more about every woman he meets.'

Every woman. There it was again. *Every woman*.

'More than what?'

'More than other men?' Yvette's dark eyes shone in the light of the candles burning on the table. The potato lay naked and pale as a baby on her palm. She let it fall indifferently into the enamel basin full of water. 'Perhaps more than she knows about herself.'

Adriaan reached out his arm so that Emma could twirl around, grabbed her around the waist with the other hand and tugged her almost roughly closer, then began to move more slowly, more sensually, till the dance became a kind of teasing tango. The two bodies began melting together, swaying hip against swaying hip, a graceful four-footed creature. Adriaan's hat with the leopard-skin band skew on his head, Emma's eyes closed as she hummed along with the music: *'I'm tired of sitting here trying to write this book. Come on, baby, give me just one look . . .'*

He dances as he cooks, Mila realized, with passion and sensuous enjoyment. Remarkably light on his feet for a man with such a heavy body. Strange that she had never been attracted to such a burly man before. But, it was more than attraction, really. It was lust in its purest form. Unexpected, unwanted, inexplicable. By this time she ought to know the symptoms.

It was part of her earliest frame of reference, that wonderful, physical feeling which she would only come to name much later. Especially on Sundays after her mother's enormous lunches, when her father vanished behind the door of their bedroom with a strange expression on his face – somewhere between joy and embarrassment, as she would later think – when she was supposed to be resting, along with her two sweet sisters. (A lot sweeter than herself, she always thought, although perhaps they also just learned to hide their sins away.) Stretched out in the sweaty twilight, the curtains drawn against the heat, the synthetic material of the thin bedspreads clinging to their bare legs, the ticking of the passage clock deafeningly loud in the silence, the smell of burnt meat wafting from the kitchen. Then she fled to her secret garden, often with the bittersweet taste of her mother's vinegar pudding still teasing on her tongue, in her mouth. That mouth had changed over the years, from a cute little gap-tooth, to the ugly embarrassment of braces, to a rebellious adolescent pout, and at last to this adult version, the vulnerability usually hidden beneath a thick layer of lipstick the colour of blood. The fantasies had also become more adult, more experienced, more daring. But the taste of guilt had stayed the same. Bittersweet like her mother's vinegar pudding.

'Isn't it just an ego trip?' she asked, after staring at Adriaan for almost a full minute in silent admiration.

'Probably, in part.' Another perfectly peeled potato plopped into the water. 'But it's also a desire to be a better artist. To capture something beneath the surface when he paints someone. To see something which can't usually be seen. Surely just as you writers try to say something which can't be said?'

'I'm just a journalist,' Mila hedged immediately. 'I don't struggle with things I can't say. Although there are a lot of things I'm not *allowed* to say any more.'

Yes. She would also have liked to have lived in another era. Another era or another country.

Unfortunately she was caught in the eighties, in the country of her birth, like all the rest of them there that weekend.

It was 1985, a year which most South Africans would rather forget, the beginning of the darkest years of the State of Emergency, detention without trial, friends who vanished, international sanctions, oppression and uncertainty and fear. Especially fear. *Angst is an Afrikaner growth industry, Time* magazine proclaimed. And it wasn't just Afrikaners who were anxious. Thousands of other South Africans were detained, physically tortured, emotionally exhausted, even ruthlessly murdered by 'security forces' who made a mockery of the word 'security'. No one was safe anymore, Mila realized.

Moreover, it was the year in which South Africans began to experience a new kind of fear, close at hand. *The Hysteria over Aids*, the front page of *Time* announced. It was what everyone wanted to believe. That the rumours of the deadly disease were exaggerated. Hysterical. Yet, suddenly, you no longer felt safe anywhere, not even in your own bed.

South Africa is drifting towards disaster, and the strangest thing about this is that it is so widely recognized, one of Mila's journalist colleagues wrote in a political magazine. *The second strangest thing is that so little real effort is being put into averting it.* As a journalist, Mila was probably more aware than her white friends in other professions of how unbearable the oppression in the country had become. As a political reporter for an Afrikaans daily in Johannesburg she had to fight a daily battle to keep the public informed. Largely in vain.

She watched sceptically as a smiling politician declared on TV that the press wouldn't be prevented from publishing information. (Ha! she thought.) And then the stiff index finger suddenly appeared alongside the face on the screen (the friendly smile just as suddenly replaced with a threatening frown) and he spoke on with the voice of a sadistic headmaster: *Dramatized versions, skewed facts and half truths will not, however, be tolerated.* 'Ha!' she exclaimed. 'Why would anyone want to *dramatize* the State of Emergency?' It was already as dramatic as a nightmare; as incredible, as confusing, and yet as painfully convincing as only a nightmare can be.

It's clear what the aim is, Ralph answered in his calm way. Twisted facts and half truths would remain the exclusive domain of the government. A government which managed to make even the advertising industry seem honest and noble, he added, with a wry smile. Ralph worked as an unwilling copywriter at an advertising agency – earning his bread and butter writing alliterative advertisements for insurance and luxury cars – while he dreamed of the Great South African Novel he would write one day. He never passed up an opportunity to mock himself or his profession.

Just as Mila and her colleagues, in their own way, joked about the shamefulness of the media. Absurd, they sighed, in the bars where they drank after work, too despondent, too depressed to sleep. When they had drunk too much – which often happened – they entertained each other by thinking up far-fetched headlines. *PW slits his wrists!* (Aha! Assonance! Alliteration!) *Pik chokes on his Coke!* (Every journalist is a frustrated poet!) *Aids alert! Cabinet contaminated!* (Etc.)

It was in this absurd time that Adriaan and Yvette decided to leave Johannesburg, to live at the sea for a year, to paint and fish, to draw and garden. Adriaan was slowly becoming known for his disturbing paintings in extravagantly decorated wooden frames. Yvette had just won a prize for the first children's book she'd illustrated. They wanted to get away from controversial exhibitions and pretentious interviews. Or so they said.

They were crazy about the big house on the West Coast; five large bedrooms and a kitchen/living-room with a fireplace big enough to stand up in.

And a different picture of the sea from every window, Yvette had written excitedly to Emma. *We live without telephone or TV and only buy the paper once a week. It's easy to forget that the country is in a State of Emergency.*

Come and visit us, she wrote to Emma and Philip and Liane and Paul, *it's the kind of house one has to share with friends.*

'Why don't you and Ralph come along?' Emma suggested one evening on the phone, after Mila had told her that she couldn't escape the smell of burning tyres and charred flesh. Not even at night in her own bed. 'There's no Emergency in that part of the country.'

'Not yet,' said Mila grimly – and prophetically.

But she didn't need much persuasion.

That was how it came about that Mila and Ralph landed at D F Malan airport one Friday afternoon in late September, where Emma and Philip were waiting for them. Philip's dusty white Golf was already packed, ready for the drive to the West Coast. The moment they passed the pay kiosks of the airport parking lot, Emma took some cold beers and a bottle of almost frozen vodka out of a cooler bag.

'To a weekend at the sea!' Ralph said, in the front next to Philip, and swallowed the beer thirstily.

'To friendship,' Emma said, and threw her head back to swallow a shot of vodka in one gulp. 'To old friends and old relationships. And new possibilities.'

The rays of sunlight slanting through the car window transformed her orange-brown hair to glowing embers. Philip watched her in the rear-view mirror, an impenetrable expression in his light blue eyes, wearing a slightly forced smile. Mila wondered fleetingly how their stormy relationship was going, but suppressed the thought and knocked back her shot of vodka as resolutely as Emma had.

'I'd like to drink to oblivion,' she said. 'I'd like to forget about the State of Emergency for just *one* weekend. That's not asking too much, is it?'

What she hadn't asked for, what she hadn't expected – and what she wasn't in the least bit prepared for – was that she would meet someone like Adriaan. That she would spend the weekend in a state of tormented lust. A sort of bodily state of emergency, she would later come to think.

*

'Liane and Paul are arriving tomorrow,' Yvette said, as they set the table for supper. 'They have to attend a charity ball in the City Hall tonight.'

'To raise money for Cape Town's street children,' said Emma, sarcastically, a stack of plates in her arms. 'Still an obscene idea to me somehow. To stuff yourself with food and dance through the night while those very street children are lying in front of the City Hall sniffing glue. But perhaps I'm just jealous because she had Errol Arendz design her dress. I'm sure she'll look fantastic and be photographed for every social page in the country.'

'Look who's talking.' Ralph arranged a knife and fork on either side of each plate Emma put down. 'I hear you were on the social pages of the new *Cape Style* yourself the other day. Along with Griet and Mart?'

'Fame at last!' laughed Emma. 'Just a pity we looked like the Three Stooges. I'm standing with these bulging cheeks, trying to swallow a piece of chicken. Mart is laughing with her mouth so wide you can see her tonsils, and Griet is glaring at the photographer as if she wants to throw her glass of wine at him. It's actually George she wanted to throw the wine at. He was standing behind the photographer making sarcastic comments about closet yuppies.'

'I should actually have been in the photo,' Philip remarked from an armchair. 'But the photographer asked me to stand to one side. Bloody cheek, if you ask me.'

'I told you not to wear that stupid green jersey!' Emma exclaimed.

'My favourite jersey!'

'His mother knitted it for him when he was at school. It was already too small when I met him and then I went and washed it in hot water. Now it's just about big enough for a ten-year-old. I swear he only wears it to punish me. It makes him look like the retarded brother in *Of Mice and Men*. Not the kind of figure *Style* wants on their social pages.'

'Ag, screw *Style*,' said Philip. 'And Max? When's he coming?'

'He has to go to a UDF meeting tomorrow,' said Yvette. 'Or an End Conscription meeting. Some noble cause.'

'The road to hell is paved with noble causes,' Ralph muttered.

'He can't help it,' Emma defended him immediately. 'He imbibed it with his mother's milk. His mother was involved with the ANC before he was born. She's a formidable woman.'

'Formidable!' Philip snorted from his armchair. 'She's a Medusa who could castrate a man with one glance. No wonder Max's dad died young. I suspect she's got Max by the balls too.'

'Stop talking rubbish, Philip! The point is that his mother went to visit political prisoners in jail and helped to smuggle people out of the country while our mothers held tea parties and discussed the next church bazaar. It must have influenced him!'

'It made him an impotent bleeding heart. That's what it did.'

Emma gave him a withering look and stood back to admire the table. The plates didn't match but it was obvious that every one was originally part of an expensive dinner service. White Arzberg with milled edges, blue Delft patterns, colourful Royal Doulton roses, even a few art deco designs with green or orange stripes. Most of the knives and forks were of heavy silver, also remnants of elegant sets from bygone days.

'As you can see, our landlord believes in using only the best in his holiday home,' Yvette said. 'Adriaan is delighted, because he believes that good food deserves good crockery. And he only cooks good food, of course.'

'Of course,' Emma smiled.

'When I think of the bargain-basement crockery my mother always kept in our beach house!' Ralph sat back-to-front on one of the chairs next to the table, his elbows on the back rest, and took a swig from his beer bottle. 'Thick brown plates you could throw against the wall without breaking them. She threw them at my father regularly and they just bounced across the floor. Come to think of it, that's probably why she bought such indestructible plates. And why she always saved her worst tantrums for the holidays.'

'Maybe it's just that holidays are exceptionally stressful,' said Emma. 'It's not easy spending twenty-four hours a day with your loved one. It can drive you to murder.'

'Relationships can drive you to murder.' Philip got up from his armchair to fill his wine glass again. 'Holidays only intensify the desire.'

'I love it when he's so romantic,' sighed Emma.

'We can go ahead and eat,' Yvette decided. 'If someone could call Adriaan and Mila?'

'Where are Adriaan and Mila?' asked Ralph.

'In his studio,' said Emma. 'I'll go and fetch them.'

'Wait, I'll come with you,' Ralph said, getting up. 'I haven't seen the studio yet.'

'Don't worry!' Emma was already disappearing down the passage. 'He's promised to give us the Guided Tour tomorrow!'

'Oh,' said Ralph, sinking back into his chair.

Yvette looked at him, her head to one side, and smiled comfortingly. 'He's probably busy sketching her.'

'I'd love to sketch you,' Adriaan said in the studio as he stuffed his pipe carefully. Mila looked up swiftly from the pile of etchings she was leafing through. Amused, he decided, a suppressed smile playing around her irresistible red mouth. 'No, it's not a pick-up line. You've already made it clear that you're not going to sleep with me. Not yet, anyway.'

She gave no sign that she'd heard the last few words.

'But you've an unbelievable profile, just standing there.' Almost Roman, he decided, the straight nose and square chin. Almost masculine, although the exceptionally long neck gave a feminine grace to the whole. And the crimson painted mouth, of course. Something androgynous about her body, too. A combination of muscle and soft curves, power and vulnerability, which he found very exciting. 'And the body of a dancer. Did you do ballet?'

'It's a sore point,' she smiled. 'I wanted to do something more practical instead, like judo or karate – self-defence rather than swan dives – but my mother thought all little girls should do ballet. And my mother's word was law. So I took ballet lessons for years, against my will.'

'One can see it in the way you stand. That straight back and turned-out toes. When did you stop?'

'Well, by fourteen my breasts had finally begun to grow and when they began it seemed as though they'd never stop; and then my mother read an article somewhere about a ballerina with big boobs who became a stripper. It gave her such a fright that she wasn't so keen on my ballet classes any more. The moment that she lost interest, my own enthusiasm flared up, of course. We had that kind of relationship. So I carried on for another year or two. Just to punish her.'

'That explains the muscular arms. I thought perhaps you were a swimmer.'

'No. I grew up in the Free State. I was scared of water. And I was always self-conscious about my arms. I wanted slender, pale, wafting arms like my ballet teacher. Mine just got stronger and browner.'

'I find that very seductive. And your hair? Were you born so blonde?'

'Do you always ask such personal questions?'

'Only when I'm really interested in someone.'

'And are you really interested in me?' she asked sceptically.

'I'm interested in most women,' he answered honestly.

'So I hear.' Accusingly?

The legs showing under her short, brightly patterned skirt were long and slender, with slim knees and shapely calves, probably the aesthetic high point of this body. Although, of course, he couldn't judge without seeing the rest of it. He wondered involuntarily what her breasts would look like. What shade of pink would he need to paint her nipples? And the skin around her navel, the hollows under her arms, the insides of her thighs?

'I can't help it.' He moved to stand behind her, looked with her at the pile of etchings which lay on the scrubbed wood table. Critically, as if it were another artist's work, a dissatisfied expression on his face. 'It's because I was a sexually frustrated teenager.'

'Me too.' She stared in fascination at one of the etchings. A strange figure with the torso of a springbok and the lower limbs of a man, a sort of inverted satyr dancing around a burning tyre. The male organs looked unsettlingly realistic, the bare feet immediately recognizable. Automatically, she looked at Adriaan's feet. 'But I was too naïve to realize it. Only later, when I looked back, I understood that it was my hormones which upset me so much.'

'I knew what I was missing out on, but I didn't have a clue how to get it. I had a hell of an acne problem so I was too embarrassed to try anything with the girls.'

She turned her head to look at him over her shoulder. He still carried the marks of those teenage pimples, the rough texture of the skin on his cheeks, but she had already decided that this too was probably part of his inexplicable attractiveness. More earthy, more sensual than smooth skin, like a piece of wood before it is sanded down.

'Later I realized that many women like this rough old face,' he said, confirming her thoughts. 'The way that they like scars on a man's body. Or tears in his eyes. Signs of vulnerability. If they hear you're an artist on top of all that, someone with a sensitive soul, the kind who'd cut his ear off because he's misunderstood . . .'

'In other words, you have no trouble seducing women.'

'With some, I do still have trouble.' He folded his square fingertips around the bowl of his pipe, caressing the smooth wood as he sucked at the curved stem. Even the way he smokes his pipe, she realized with steadily rising confusion, gave her gooseflesh. 'You never forget the knocks you get in your youth, not so? If you were an awkward teenager on the platteland, in a small dorp, a guy with problem skin who could never date the prettiest girls in the school, then a bit of self-doubt always remains . . . sexual insecurity . . . like a lump somewhere inside you. Anyway, that's my explanation for my screwing around. It has nothing to do with feeling threatened by strong women. Somewhere inside me is a sixteen-year-old schoolboy who can't believe his luck every time a woman goes to bed with him.'

Now, just look at that, he thought, amused. A confession session about his sexual insecurity. Definitely not part of his usual seduction routine. But it was as if he instinctively felt that this woman would demand more than his usual tactics. As if there were more at stake than mere seduction.

'And when did you realize . . . that you could be an object of desire?'

She smiled encouragingly, her customary journalistic curiosity more than usually aroused. Which confirmed his suspicion that he was on the right track. Most women were turned on by romantic trickery, even while they suspected they were being deceived. With the other, rarer kind you had to play open cards from the start. Sometimes, of course, you miscalculated at the classification stage. That was just one of the dangers which made this little game so exciting.

'When I stopped trying to be one of the boys. I'd never have managed it anyway. I did all the right things, like smoking Lucky Strike and playing rugby, but I also drew these weird pictures which none of my buddies could understand. Which I didn't understand myself. No one in my family had an artistic background. My father was a platteland businessman, small fry, owner of a furniture store in Worcester. My mother was a housewife who worked as a hairdresser before she got married, so all the tannies in the area had their hair done in our lounge. My older brother took over the furniture store and the second one became a hairdresser. A moffie hairdresser, by the way, for which my father still blames my mother. But their choices were basically predictable. The oldest one always tried to please my father, the second was always my mother's little darling. And then I came along – the proverbial slip up after my mother decided she didn't want any more children. And then I announce I want to be an *artist*! "As if one moffie in the family isn't enough!" My father's unforgettable comment. So perhaps that's also part of what drives me. Sexually. To show my father I'm not a moffie.'

'That's just a bit too convenient,' Mila said sceptically. 'Blame it all on Daddy.'

She was still standing with her back to him, but he had moved closer to her almost unconsciously, his body leaning forward almost against his will. When he spoke again, it was with his mouth next to her ear, his nostrils filled with her scent. That unique scent which every woman carries with her, a mixture of perfume and food and body odours, of the shampoo she washes her hair with and the cream she rubs into her hands, the cigarettes she smokes and the peppermints she sucks, the salt taste of her sweat, the musty darkness of her blood, the hidden secrets of her sex. Sometimes he wanted to sniff a woman as one sniffed cocaine, as street children sniffed glue; they were like a drug he couldn't live without. Sometimes he wondered if that wasn't the only honest reason for his seemingly endless sexual wanderlust. The scent of a woman. Different each time from all the women before.

'OK, forget it, it has nothing to do with my father,' he grinned. 'I just drew more and more and hung out with my friends less and less. I became a celibate loner – till an older woman on our street took pity on me. This artistic kid who stared at her so longingly as she worked in the garden. Her dresses got shorter every week. She knew exactly what she was doing. The way in which she bent over her dahlias, so that her panties only just showed, just a little piece of black, always black. I was almost crazily horny by the time she invited me in one afternoon for a glass of Coke.'

'And then you got more than a Coke.'

'A whole lot more. Glory Hallelujah!'

'You mean you lived out every schoolboy's fantasy?' Mila's laugh trickled from her red mouth like slow honey, a low, husky, viscous sound. She turned her body and let her buttocks rest on the edge of the table. Still close enough to torture him. 'To be seduced by a tannie!'

'Well, strictly speaking she wasn't exactly a tannie. She was in her late twenties, but if you've grown up on the platteland, any woman over twenty is a tannie. And this tannie had an itch. Her husband was a sales rep who was almost never at home. She took me in hand and taught me more over the next few weeks than the ten wildest girls at school put together could ever show me. I don't know if it was chance, but some time around then my acne also began to clear up. After that I had enough self-confidence to date girls of my own age.'

'And the tannie? What happened to her?'

'Vanished without trace. One day she was just gone. The sales rep probably dragged her to another boring little town, where she transformed the next grateful schoolboy's life. Anyway, that was the closest thing I ever had to a fairy godmother.'

'I seduced a schoolboy once,' she said with a note of nostalgia in her smoky voice.

'Looking at you, you must have driven a whole lot of schoolboys crazy.'

'I wouldn't know. I said I was too naïve to know what I was missing. I'm talking about when I was already a 'tannie'. I had this fantasy about how I'd lead this beautiful young boy out of his virginal innocence to adulthood. And in the end it was *he* who led *me* out of my naïve fantasy world. He was anything but a virgin. Schoolboys just aren't what they used to be, hey?'

Without meaning to, he lifted his hand to brush a stray hair from her forehead. She didn't look away, held his eyes locked with hers, and didn't move her body either. Just lifted her chin, challenging.

'Dinner's on the table!' Emma said in the doorway behind them.

The unexpected voice made them move away from each other hurriedly, clearly guilty. Adriaan sucked on his pipe, trying to get it to light, a nick of concentration between his grey-green eyes. And Mila felt as shakily relieved as she had last felt at school, when the bell rang before a teacher realized that she hadn't done her homework. Grateful, inordinately grateful, that she hadn't been caught out. With the firm intention of behaving better from now on.

'I read somewhere that marriage is the only adventure left to the middle classes,' explained Philip at the table, as he poured himself another glass of wine. 'If I ever feel adventurous again, I'd rather travel to Antarctica or climb the Himalayas. It's less dangerous.'

'Oh, come on, Philip,' Mila said impatiently, her eyes on Emma opposite her, but Emma was looking at the food on her plate. 'We all know you were unhappily married. You're not the only one who chose badly. Does that mean that for the rest of your life you're going to be too cowardly to attempt a committed relationship?'

'Probably.' Philip smiled apologetically. 'Once bitten . . .'

'Twice scared shitless,' said Emma, still staring at her plate, as she wound a bundle of tagliatelle about her fork.

The light of the candles which burned all around the room drew orange sparks from her hair and threw glowing shadows over her face. She looked like a figure in one of Rembrandt's shadowy paintings. Or a Pre-Raphaelite model, thought Mila, with that untameable hair and straight nose and large mouth. A Rossetti figure who has ended up in a Rembrandt by accident.

'I'm like a robot that's been badly programmed.' Philip shrugged his shoulders, a disarming gesture, but Mila refused to be won over. She shook her head emphatically while he spoke. 'I'm just not equipped for married life. I cause chaos whenever I land in a marriage.'

'Bullshit! You're *made* to be married, Philip. You can't last for more than a few weeks without a woman. Your problem is that you want all the advantages of a committed relationship without any of the disadvantages.'

'Isn't that what we all want?' asked Adriaan.

And all at once Mila was again so aware of his heavy body just to the left of her that she stayed silent, confused.

'Perhaps for some people relationships are easier than for others,' said Yvette hesitatingly. 'Or perhaps some of us are more afraid of being alone.'

'I can't believe that relationships can be easy for *anyone*!' Mila exclaimed.

'Says the Queen of Disastrous Relationships,' muttered Ralph to her right.

'Ralph's pet name for me.' Now it was her turn to shrug her shoulders apologetically. 'It's true, I have a pathetic track record. I have a problem with commitment. Even when I was married, I couldn't get it right. I mean, I tried hard, but . . .'

'How long were you married?'

The sudden respect in Yvette's voice irritated Mila so much that she stuffed a forkful of pasta into her mouth to prevent herself from saying something bitchy. It was the same old story. When they heard that you'd been married – when they realized that you were actually more than just some almost-old-maid – their respect for you grew. Because, sometime, somewhere in your life, there'd been a man who was prepared to marry you. Or because you were stupid enough to think that's what you were supposed to do. Or because you weren't brave enough to say no. She chewed her food as slowly as possible.

'Just a year,' Ralph answered for her. 'To a wonderful man.'

'But we were too young,' she added quickly, her mouth still full of tagliatelle, before Ralph could embarrass her by telling everyone how he and Stuart grew up together on neighbouring farms in Natal, played marbles and kleilat and rugby and cricket together, began wanking together in the spartan hostel room of a famous boys' school. She didn't know Stuart half as well as Ralph knew him. There wasn't enough time. 'It was meant to be a shotgun marriage, but I miscarried. And then he was killed on the border soon after that.' She could hear herself swallowing her wine in the uncomfortable silence that suddenly hung over the table. That was what always happened. In the circles she moved in, being killed on the border wasn't exactly viewed as heroic. 'The whole affair was such a fiasco that I've never had the desire to repeat it. But I refuse to become as cynical as Philip. I refuse to rule out the possibility entirely!'

'If Mr Right comes along?'

Mila looked at Yvette, puzzled, uncertain whether she meant the question seriously, but could find no trace of irony.

'No, I stopped believing in fairy tales a long time ago,' she said, and broke off a piece of bread to mop up Adriaan's cheese sauce from the plate. 'But I still think that one can find the right combination of characteristics to make a relationship work. It's like one of those combination locks. If you know the right numbers, in the right order, you can unlock it. If you get two people who are ready to compromise and commit – I'm not talking about "till death do us part" now, I mean just for the foreseeable future – then surely it can work?'

'But how do you know when you have the correct combination?' Emma asked anxiously. 'What makes you prepared to give this relationship rather than that one a chance? Doesn't love play a part at all?'

'Love,' muttered Philip.

'Perhaps it's just a confluence of circumstances,' said Mila. 'I was always so crazy about my work that I've never had the desire to have a long-term relationship again. But if this State of Emergency goes on

. . . if the government is going to make it impossible for me to do my work properly . . . I don't know, but sometimes I think, ag well, I may just as well get married and have babies!'

At that moment Adriaan brushed past her chair to turn the Joe Jackson tape over and she saw the gooseflesh spring up in her bare arms. She lowered her head over her plate, helpless against the treason of her own body, and began to suck the cheese sauce slowly from the piece of bread. Very slowly, as if she was afraid of what she'd say if her mouth were empty.

'It's a *stunning* house!' Liane cried when she appeared on the verandah the next day. She stood still for a moment, as though posing in an imaginary doorway, lovely in a white linen dress with a broad white band around her golden brown hair, a sparkle in her golden brown eyes and a sweep of light pink on her lips. Her bedraggled friends, eating a long, late breakfast outdoors, stared at her with expressions varying from open admiration (Yvette) to suppressed irritation (Philip). Then she stretched out her arms, with a heavy clinking of silver bracelets, and turned dramatically so that she could admire the view over the sea. 'Absolutely *stunning*!'

When he was younger, Adriaan recalled, he always wondered what the first line of that Carly Simon song meant – about Warren Beatty, he'd heard somewhere – about someone arriving at a party as though stepping aboard a yacht. Once he'd met Liane he stopped wondering. She was the kind of woman who never arrived unnoticed. She would always make an *entrance*. Like some supernatural being.

'You can see all the way to heaven!' As she stood there now, a vision in white, she seemed almost transparent. (Like any good actress she could turn her back on her audience without losing their attention.) Before her stretched the beach, a pure white strip which disappeared into a pale blue haze in the distance. Different shades of blue flowed together about her: the almost waveless bright blue of the sea; the deeper, heavier satin blue of the air; the misty, whitish blue on the horizon. When she turned back, she looked at the bright blue woodwork of the beach house, the shutters and the front door, and nodded approvingly. 'Bit of a Greek feel, right?'

'Just show me to a bed,' groaned Paul behind her, his face tired in an attractive sort of way, his jaw stylishly unshaven. 'I had to get up in the middle of the bloody night because my wife wanted to be here in time for breakfast!'

'Which we didn't succeed in doing because you needed six espressos and a handful of Proplus just to open your eyes!' Her breathy voice rose slightly. A little frown between her bushy eyebrows. Liane Terreblanche (née van der Merwe, daughter of a platteland garage mechanic, but that was a well-kept secret these days) in the role of the Disconcerted Spouse. 'And then you had to stand under a hot shower for another hour to wake up properly!'

'Have mercy! We were still dancing at two o'clock this morning!'

'For the sake of the poor street childen, huh?' said Philip.

'We all have to do our bit,' said Paul.

Meanwhile Liane had approached the table and begun to kiss everyone, in the French manner, a brush against each cheek and two kissing sounds which were blown away by the sea breeze.

'Don't worry, you can sleep for the rest of the day if you want to,' Yvette said reassuringly.

'He's not serious!' cried Liane, embracing Yvette.

'I am,' grumbled Paul, but his wife ignored him.

'Who could sleep on such a lovely spring day?' Liane looked up at the cloudless sky as if putting the question to an angel that no one else could see.

'Watch me,' Paul muttered, a bit more decisively, but his wife still ignored him.

'It's absolutely *amazing*!' Liane placed her hands in awe on either side of Yvette's enormous stomach. Like a fortune teller clasping a crystal ball. 'To think you've succeeded in creating a human being!'

'Well,' said Yvette with a little giggle, 'it's not *that* difficult.'

'And I hope I also had something to do with it,' said Adriaan.

'Adriaan, my darling!' She threw her arms enthusiastically around Adriaan's neck. He tried to identify her perfume, but the scent was so subtle that it vanished the minute he drew back from her cheek. 'You're becoming really famous, I hear!'

'And you're becoming even more beautiful, I see.' He held her at arms' length, hands on her shoulders. The fine laugh-lines around her eyes – so fine that you could only see them up close – were the only signs that she was almost thirty. The rest of her complexion was as smooth and bright as a clean page in a sketch book. Too bright, too smooth, he had always thought. That's why he had never had the urge to paint her. In a few years – when life had left a few more lines on that perfect skin, when wrinkles had begun to draw a picture on that clean page – he would love to paint her. 'You'll be spectacular at fifty.'

'You're the only man who can make a woman look forward to old age,' Liane laughed.

Although she didn't know Mila well, she embraced her like an old friend too. Even Ralph, whom she'd met only fleetingly before, was kissed enthusiastically on both cheeks.

'Come and eat before you unpack,' said Yvette after Paul had greeted her, in the good old-fashioned Boer way, with a proper kiss on the mouth. 'You look as though you need another cup of coffee.'

'Black and strong,' said Paul and sank gratefully into the nearest cane chair.

'Aren't you getting a bit old to dance the night away like that?' Philip lit a cigarette and looked at Paul pityingly through a cloud of smoke.

'It's not that I'm not up to it any more.' The dimple in his chin made a deep notch amongst the dark stubble. 'It's just that it takes me about three days to recover.' He picked up a mug of coffee which Yvette had poured for him and swigged it thirstily. 'But I don't exactly have a choice. I'm the one who went and married the female version of Peter Pan.'

'And how is married life treating you?' Philip's voice was heavy with cynicism. 'How long is it now? Six months?'

'Six months and six days,' Liane answered for her husband.

'And it feels like six years?'

'Sorry to disappoint you, Philip, but I've actually enjoyed it so far. But I promise I'll phone you the minute I begin to hate it.'

'Please do,' muttered Mila. 'It would make his day.'

Adriaan put on his dark glasses so that he could observe Mila unnoticed. Unlike Liane, this woman made him long for his paintbrush, all the time. She was still wearing the crumpled T-shirt she had apparently slept in (although she seemed to him more the type who would sleep in the nude), and hadn't yet put on a bra (the nipples pressed against the thin white cotton, making tempting little peaks in the material; the breasts fuller than he'd expected, despite the fact that she'd told him about her mother's fear that she'd become a stripper). Her short blonde hair was still uncombed – but her mouth was painted red again. He wondered if she slept with her lipstick under her pillow. He wondered how her mouth would look without lipstick, soft like a bruised fruit, after a night of lovemaking. He wondered how those beautiful legs would feel wrapped around his hips, the soft breasts in his hands, the long neck under his lips. She tore a croissant in half and put a piece in her mouth, turned her head unexpectedly towards him as if she felt his eyes burning her skin through the dark glasses, and then turned back quickly to say something to Ralph.

According to Emma, Mila and Ralph were 'just good friends' who'd probably slept together somewhere along the way. And yet, when he looked at their body language, he wondered if they weren't trying to hide a more intimate relationship. The way in which she cocked her head to listen to him, the ease with which he rested an extended arm on the back of her chair, the incidental contact, knee to knee, skin to skin, without embarrassment. Or does the body simply fall back, at unguarded moments, into the grooves of past intimacy? Like Liane and Max, who were in love at school, and still sometimes shared a body language which shut others out.

'I've never seen you looking so good, Yvette!' said Liane, spreading butter on a slice of wholewheat bread. 'You were obviously born to bear children!'

'Coffee?' asked Yvette with a disbelieving smile.

'You don't have rooibos tea, do you?'

'Now she's going to make us all feel guilty because she only drinks rooibos and doesn't smoke,' grumbled Emma, and lit a cigarette from Philip's pack.

Adriaan watched the three women who'd been friends since their student days, Yvette and Emma and Liane, and wondered why Liane was the only one he'd never wanted to sleep with. Never wanted to paint and never wanted to fuck. Perhaps he was afraid that seeing her next to him in bed in the sharp morning light would spoil the illusion of perfect beauty, her eyes puffy and her breath sour, afraid that he would feel as though he'd raped Botticelli's Venus. Or perhaps her beauty was just too heavenly for his more earthy tastes. Not sensual enough.

He tried to look at Yvette objectively, her dark brown hair cut in a simple child-like style, smooth and shiny, to just below the ears, with a heavy fringe which hid her eyebrows; her eyes almost impossibly large and round under the protection of the fringe, as if she were continually amazed by the world. Sometimes she reminded him of a caricature of a child's face, the nose and mouth simply two stripes under a pair of enormous eyes. The face of a child and the body of a woman, he'd thought the first time he saw her. Not the hard, angular figure of the modern clothes-shop dummy; more like a primitive fertility goddess, the breasts small and high, the hips heavy and soft. A body which left him completely defenceless. Perhaps more than ever now that her breasts swelled bigger month after month, the nipples by now as hard and brown as cherry stones, the aureola spreading like stains on a white tablecloth, wider and darker, while her hips and buttocks and belly felt like the ripe curves of a giant peach under his caressing hands. He couldn't imagine that he would ever stop painting her.

And Emma with her messy hair and wide, laughing mouth and tall, athletic body had a natural wildness which made his loins stir and his fingers itch, a fleeting quality which was difficult to capture on paper. He'd tried to sketch her several times, but he was never really satisfied with the result. He wanted to try again – after he'd painted Mila.

'I'm going to shower, if you'll excuse me,' Mila shifted her chair back and stretched her arms out, throwing her head back so that her neck seemed even longer. 'And then I want to go for a long walk through the village. Does anyone want to join me?'

'Count me in,' Liane said straight away. Just as Adriaan was about to offer to accompany her. 'I passed some houses that I'd love to see close up. It's hard to believe what monstrosities one finds in these seaside villages!'

'It's hard to believe that anyone wants to view these monstrosities close up,' Ralph commented, amused. 'It's a bit like going to a Victorian freak show, not so?'

'It's my own private perversion,' Liane giggled. 'We all have our peccadilloes. And I also saw some houses with fantastic potential!'

'Come with me,' smiled Mila, 'and show me the one with the most potential. Who knows, one day, perhaps I'll also be able to afford a holiday house on the West Coast.'

'Not as long as you remain an overworked, underpaid journalist,' said Ralph.

'Ralph wants me to sell my soul and join him working for an advertising agency,' she explained to Liane.

'Not necessarily,' said Ralph. 'There are other ways of selling your soul.'

'You're not interested in becoming editor of a woman's magazine, are you?' asked Emma. 'We're desperately looking for someone at *Palette*. The boss's alcohol problem is getting out of hand.'

'I'd also be driven to drink if I had to read stories about eating disorders and women's problems every day!' Mila exclaimed, laughing.

'*The full palette of femininity,*' said Emma with a sour smile.

'Who the hell thought up that slogan? God help me, if that's the sum total of being a woman, I don't want to be one!'

'You forgot the recipes and knitting patterns. Ag well, we can't all be glamorous political reporters. Some of us have to entertain the women of the volk.'

'Glamorous, my arse. But I swear I'd rather sell my body than become editor of *Palette*. That is, of course, if anybody is still interested in the rapidly ageing body of an overworked and underpaid journalist.'

'It's not so hard to sell your soul, my darling,' said Liane, sighing. 'I do it every time I style a cute little picture for a magazine I wouldn't have touched with a bargepole before. You get used to it.'

'I always wanted to ask you,' said Philip. 'What does a stylist actually do? Except sell her soul, of course.'

'Well, say a magazine wanted a photo of your lounge – God forbid, because I know what your lounge usually looks like – then I arrange it so that it looks more photogenic.'

'And how do you do that?'

'Man, it's like dressing a bride. Something old, something new, something borrowed, something blue. If it's really a lost cause – as your lounge probably would be – then I'd stuff it full of things which don't belong to you.'

'But then it's not *my* lounge any more,' said Philip indignantly.

'Never let facts spoil a good picture, my darling,' Liane said with an innocent expression.

'So it's all actually sleight of hand and you're a swindler?'

'Well.' That breathless little giggle again. 'That's one way of putting it. For the right price, of course.'

'If you can make Philip's lounge look photogenic,' Mila said sceptically, 'you'd have to be a real conjuror.'

'Remember to call me one day when you become editor of a woman's mag,' said Liane. 'You never know, do you?'

Laughing, Mila stood up. So slowly that Adriaan wondered if she was deliberately drawing out each movement to tease him. The way she unfolded her crossed legs, rubbed the hollow in the back of her neck self-consciously with one hand and stroked her red mouth with the fingers of the other. Then she wandered away, barefoot, with a striped kikoi bound around her swaying hips. He watched her and wondered why he always wanted to paint women with whom he'd rather sleep. As if a lifeless paintbrush on a cold canvas could ever be a substitute for living fingers on warm skin. And yet it was also a form of intimacy. He tried to comfort himself with this thought.

'It's a *stunning* day!' joked Emma, stretched out on her back on the sand, her arms behind her head and her eyes closed against the late afternoon sun. She'd pulled her long skirt up and tucked it into her her panty elastic high up on her thighs, which were muscular and sprinkled with golden freckles. 'As Liane would say.'

'And has said several times today already,' smiled Yvette, cross-legged next to her, with the glistening folds of her second-hand dress spread out about her like a bridal train. The satiny material changed colour every time she moved, from tender shell pink to sombre sea green with a whole rainbow of shades in between.

'How does she manage to have such *joie de vivre*?' Mila gazed at the sea, where Liane was diving through the waves with Max and Ralph, graceful as a dolphin, her costume a white flash in the blue-green water. 'It makes me feel old and tired just looking at her.'

'Never mind the *joie de vivre*.' Emma shifted upright and held up her hand to screen her eyes. 'How does she manage to have such a body? She's always eaten more and put on less weight than any other woman I know.'

'Perhaps it has something to do with the *joie de vivre*?' murmured Mila, her weight resting on her left elbow, a glass of champagne in her other hand. 'Perhaps her body burns all the unnecessary calories in its effort to keep up those constantly high spirits.'

'Maybe she can write a new kind of diet book,' giggled Emma. 'One of those bestsellers with a silly title, something like *Laugh Yourself Lean* or . . .'

'*A Laugh a Day Keeps the Kilos Away*,' Mila suggested.

The late afternoon sun caressed her legs under the rolled-up kikoi.

Not quite so hot that it would cause unnecessary damage to her face, she reassured herself. She had recently reached the age when the sun – formerly a generous friend – had turned overnight into a backstabbing enemy. Manufacturer of early wrinkles and marks on the skin. But after almost thirty-five years in the heat of Africa it was too late to look like a pale European rose anyway. And as Emma always said, brown cellulite looked a damn sight better than white cellulite. She rolled the kikoi up higher and sighed contentedly.

A little way from them, closer to the water, Adriaan and Philip were playing beach bats. Paul and Bobby – Max's new colleague, friend, lover, whatever – sat on the wet sand and talked, the foamy seam of the sea folding over their feet now and again. It must be an extremely serious discussion, she decided, otherwise the cold water would have chased them away long ago. Liane and Max and Ralph were leaping around so energetically that they probably didn't feel the icy bite of the waves any more.

'It can be pretty depressing to live with so much joy,' said Yvette. 'Emma and I shared a res room in our first year at Stellenbosch and neither of us was a cheerful little chickadee in the morning, so it worked out very well.'

'To tell the truth, we woke up so *bedonnerd* and bad-tempered every morning that we learned not to talk to each other before ten o'clock,' smiled Emma. 'A match made in heaven.'

'But then I ended up in a house with Liane in my second year.' Yvette's rainbow dress rustled into its next shade of green. She looked like a smug Buddha, with her crossed legs and bulging tummy, a lapful of sunlight caught in the fabric's numerous folds. 'Seven o'clock in the morning she leaped out of bed singing and tried to persuade me to go swimming in the dam with her or pick flowers on the mountain or cycle down to the sea. It was awful. And she never gave up! She still doesn't give up! She came and stood next to me in the kitchen just now and asked me quite earnestly whether I didn't want to come swimming with her tomorrow morning. "While the others are still asleep." She made it sound like an invitation to some exclusive club. Something to be grateful for.'

'Early Risers Anonymous,' said Emma, and drained the last drops of champagne from her glass.

Mila pulled the silver ice bucket closer, lifted the bottle and poured another glass each for herself and Emma, then gazed in wonder at the landscape around her. The green wilderness at the spine of the beach would probably be destroyed when the town developed further. It made her feel nostalgic in anticipation. But the blue sea would always be here, as far as the eye could see, further than human greed could stretch. Thank God. If she turned her head a bit, to the little town which clung so obstinately to the hill, she could immediately see Adriaan's borrowed holiday house with its bright blue shutters. Not because it was bigger than the other houses, but because it was a confident kind of house, a house with an unmistakable presence. Like the man who occupied it now.

Meanwhile Ralph had jogged out of the water and begun to dry himself hurriedly. She watched him approvingly, his body glistening in the low rays of sun, long and lean and hard and sinewy, the kind of body she had always found attractive. So different from a stocky man with broad feet and soft stomach.

Liane and Max were still swimming, their bodies growing smaller against the waves which were beginning to loom larger, more dangerous, but they showed no sign of fear or even simple caution. Perhaps *joie de vivre* didn't only make one thin, Mila reflected, perhaps it also made you less afraid. Perhaps she should also try to cultivate a more joyful disposition.

'What is the beauty-queen story Philip was teasing her about earlier?' she asked.

'Oh, he's been teasing her about that for years,' Emma smiled. 'She was chosen as rag queen in her first year, but then she abdicated only two weeks later. It was a helluva scandal on campus. No one had ever turned down such an honour before. But she just said it made her feel uncomfortable and that was that.'

'She was completely taken aback by all the attention,' Yvette explained. 'She didn't know how to handle it. Remember, she was quite shy in those days.'

'Shy?' asked Mila, amazed.

'It's all an act, you know, the dramatic gestures and beaming smile and the whole self-assured image. A façade behind which a shy small-town girl can hide.'

'What makes it so funny,' said Emma, 'is that it was interpreted as a feminist statement. You know, a condemnation of all beauty contests. With the result that she was viewed as the most beautiful feminist on campus for the rest of her university career. The fact that she knew fuck all about feminism didn't bother anyone. She was a figurehead, that's all they wanted, and above all an exceptionally attractive figurehead. *The pretty face of feminism.* As a sexist reporter called her in a newspaper article.'

'And all that she said was that it made her feel uncomfortable,' said Yvette, shaking her head. 'It was one of those silly little phrases which immediately captured the imagination. Like Martin Luther King's *I have a dream*!'

'Or Kennedy's *Ich bin ein Berliner,*' giggled Emma.

'Liane van der Merwe taking the crown off her head and saying: *It makes me feel uncomfortable.*'

'The irony is that the feminist label made her feel even more self-conscious than the whole beauty-queen business. When she said in an interview with a student newspaper that she didn't even know who Simone de Beauvoir was, no one believed her. Everyone thought that they'd at last found a feminist with a sense of humour. *The funny face of feminism.*'

Paul and Bobby leaped up, shocked, as a wave broke unexpectedly high, over their legs, then walked over to where Adriaan and Philip were busy taking beers out of a cooler bag. Ralph tried to lure Max and Liane out of the water by waving a beer bottle in the air, with sweeping arm movements. It seemed to work, because within moments both of them began to swim back to shore with powerful strokes. Mila watched as a blue-green mountain of water rose slowly behind them and towered above them for a split second, their bodies pathetically small, before they were lifted weightlessly to its crest. The next moment they were hidden in a thunderous explosion of foam. At first it looked as though the violence of the wave had trapped them underwater – Mila moved anxiously upright – but then two wriggling bodies appeared, in full flight, like a pair of seahorses pulling a freight of foam to the beach. The wave carried them to the wet sand, where they lay exhausted, laughing and panting.

Ralph and Adriaan immediately broke into applause. Mila's mouth hung open, speechless with admiration, because she had always been afraid of waves higher than her knees. She had always thought it was because she grew up so far from the sea, because she only stayed in their holiday house at Stilbaai once a year, never long enough to conquer her fear. Now she wondered if it wasn't just the result of her lifelong lack of *joie de vivre*.

All those sweltering Sunday afternoons on a bed in Bloemfontein. If only she could have swum in the sea instead, could have dived through foamy breakers, could have felt cold water against her skin. But she lay on a bed in a stifling room, the daughter of a father who would later become a judge and a mother who would always be stricter than the strictest judge could ever be, and she escaped from the sombre atmosphere of her parents' house by surrendering herself to her sexual fantasies. She learned to fantasize, and go on fantasizing, through her school years, through her student years, even after she had lost her virginity. Stuart was the first man she had sex with, the one and only man while he was alive. The man she married just after university because she was pregnant. The man whose widow she would become scarcely a year later. But early in this relationship she realized that she couldn't have an orgasm if she didn't fantasize. She felt guilty about it, naturally, but she persuaded herself that it was better to reach orgasm, in whatever way, than to *fake* one. And Stuart never seemed to notice that her impressive climaxes had nothing to do with his rather less impressive abilities.

Until Ralph appeared on the scene. No, that's not true, Ralph was always on the scene. She met them together, two students who'd been best friends since their school days, and initially they did everything together. Like the Three Musketeers. *One for all and all for one.* She knew from the start that she would end up in bed with one of them, that she would lay her vexing virginity like a sacrifice at the feet of one of them, but it was impossible for her to choose between them. If she were less conventional, perhaps she could have suggested they do it all together. *One for all and all for one.* In the end, Stuart was perhaps just more determined than Ralph to free her from her virginal prison. It could easily have been different. When she and Ralph finally sought comfort in each other's arms a few years later, shortly after Stuart's death (the day after the funeral, to be precise), she felt so incredibly guilty about her betrayal of her husband, so recently dead (not yet cold in his grave!) that she clean forgot to fantasize. It was the best sex she'd ever had.

It was Liane – who else? – who suggested early that evening that they take a group photo.

'Why not?' Adriaan said immediately. 'Then I can at least draw

Mila from a photo. Like a bloody caricaturist!' he added in an aggrieved tone.

'Do you mean to tell me that you haven't managed to persuade her to pose for you?' Max laughed disbelievingly. 'You're losing your touch, bra!'

'She doesn't trust me,' Adriaan sighed. 'She doesn't want to be alone with me in a studio. I've even suggested that we do it outdoors, but she won't . . .'

'Let's just say that I don't trust myself,' Mila said with a jokey smile. Meaning every word.

Meanwhile, Liane had begun to organize them, as if they were part of some elaborate flower arrangement. She used a couch of battered green leather as a base and ignored their flippant comments: Max saying that he felt like a window display, Philip asking if it was really necessary to make such a performance of a photo, Mila wanting to know if she was allowed to pucker her lips like Marilyn Monroe. Liane took a step back and surveyed her handiwork, looked at the image through the camera lens, pressed the automatic button and solemnly took her pre-ordained place between her friends.

The moment the photo was taken, they leaped apart, as self-conscious as children caught pulling faces in front of a mirror. Philip jumped up to light a cigarette, Bobby began looking for the book she was reading (*Peaceful Resistance: A Political Analysis*), Ralph and Max hurried outside to keep an eye on the fish braai, Mila and Emma walked to the kitchen area of the large open-plan living room to make a salad. Paul and Yvette were the only two who stayed sitting calmly on the couch.

'No, I'm not ready for the responsibility.' Paul went on with the discussion which was interrupted by the unexpected photo session. 'Liane feels the same. Perhaps we're just cowards.'

'Speak for yourself, my darling!' Liane called across as she unscrewed the camera from its tripod. 'I definitely don't think it's cowardly to delay parenthood as long as possible. I think it's completely *sensible*! Goodness gracious, a child isn't like an outfit that you can send back to the designer if you don't like it! Once it's there, it's there. And you must be *extremely* mature to handle something like that. I don't feel nearly grown-up enough yet.'

'I don't know if you can ever be grown-up enough,' said Yvette. 'And on the other hand, it's probably important to retain some kind of childlikeness. So that you can at least enjoy the whole adventure.'

'My wife is the grown-up and I am the child.' Adriaan had fetched a bottle of wine from the fridge to fill everyone's glasses again. 'Together perhaps we can pull the wagon through.'

He bent down, and kissed Yvette on her forehead. She looked after him in surprise as he walked outside, the hat with the leopard-skin band tilted on his head.

'I wonder what he's feeling guilty about now,' she said.

'If any of you lot want a puff of the joint outside, you'd better move it.' Emma stood in front of the sink, rinsing off a head of lettuce, gazing out through the window. 'Max and Ralph are smoking it at one hell of a pace.'

'Is Max smoking dagga?' Liane asked, stunned.

'He brought enough along to keep him stoned for the whole weekend,' said Bobby, sunk deep into a chintz armchair next to a reading lamp, her book on her lap again.

'Max?' Liane shook her head disbelievingly. 'Where on earth does he get it?'

'Scored last night,' said Bobby. 'I took him to a few seedy clubs.'

'When I knew him at school, he was such a nerd that he wouldn't even smoke a cigarette!' Liane threw her hands in the air as if to emphasize her words with the clinking of her silver bracelets. 'Now it's joints and seedy clubs!'

'I said it sounded as though he was searching for his lost youth,' Bobby said, with the shadow of a smile on her earnest face. She stared out through the window, at the crescent moon which hung low in the sky like a silver earring, beneath the hazy clouds which veiled most of the stars. 'Then he said it's never too late to have a happy childhood.'

Mila stared in turn at the serious young woman and wondered, not for the first time today, why Max had brought her along. What made him think that she would fit into this group? She was in her early twenties – a few years younger than anyone else in the company and more than a decade younger than the oldest among them – and she looked even younger because she was so slight. Probably also because her clothes were hopelessly big for her. Like a child who'd raided her parents' wardrobe, Mila thought, with a childish disregard for colours and patterns that are meant to match. Red and orange insects on the shirt, green and yellow ethnic stripes and dots on the trousers, blue-patterned socks which showed above the lace-up boots. It's never too late to have a happy childhood?

And none of the other guests knew anything about her, except that she was a postgraduate student and part-time lecturer at Max's university. His new colleague and possibly also his new lover. ('Very bright and serious about the Struggle.' That's all they could get out of Max.) And so far she hadn't revealed much more about herself, sitting apart from the group reading most of the time, sometimes discussing politics or law with Max or Paul with a frown on her face. ('*The Unbearable Heaviness of Being Bright*,' Paul remarked drily after she questioned him about his law practice on the beach, seemingly unaware of her pale feet soaking like frozen fish in the icy water. 'I'm afraid I didn't make much of an impression,' he added. 'My work is too frivolous. Not enough political credentials. But she's still young. She'll become frivolous yet.')

'Perhaps he just wanted to get away from protest meetings and politics for once.' Bobby's face was still turned to the window, her skinny arms wrapped protectively across her chest, the fingers as fine as twigs, the nails chewed to the quick. Clearly a nervous disposition. Probably too intense for her own good. 'It's very therapeutic, dancing in a darkened club like that. It can make you forget everything.'

'That sounds promising.' Philip looked up from the newspaper he was paging through. 'Perhaps I should also come dancing with you some time.'

Worst unrest in the Cape since '76, announced the headline. Mila felt her stomach tighten. In the newspaper she'd bought on the plane the day before, she'd only read the first few words of the leader. *A pall of teargas, smoke – and anger – hung over Cape Town's fringes last night after clashes between security forces and thousands of demonstrators . . .* Then she'd folded up the paper, determined to forget her work. But it couldn't be long now, she thought. It couldn't be long before the teargas and smoke and rage hung over the whole land, before the State of Emergency was extended to every corner of the country, before there was nowhere you could run to escape from the anxiety. Not even this idyllic little town on the West Coast.

'It's easier if you're stoned,' said Bobby.

'No, dagga doesn't work for me.' Philip shook his head with an expression of genuine regret. 'It makes me paranoid. And drinking doesn't help any more either. The hangovers just get worse. But I've never tried dancing before.'

'He never *wanted* to try dancing,' muttered Emma over the salad bowl, so quietly that no one but Mila heard her. 'Too scared he'd look ridiculous.'

'What do you mean?' Mila asked quietly. 'What does he want to forget?'

'I think he wants to forget about me most of all,' sighed Emma.

'What is going on in your relationship, Emma?' Mila asked, like a strict older sister. It was a role she often found herself in when she was talking to Emma. Perhaps because she'd have loved to have had a younger sister like her, someone who sometimes needed the well-intentioned advice of an older sister, instead of the boring little goody-goody of a younger sister she really had. Or perhaps just because strictness was sometimes the only possible reaction to Emma's stormy love life.

'I wish I knew!' Emma brushed her wild hair out of her eyes and sighed again. 'At first he was the hunter and I was the unwilling prey, you know, the one who wasn't ready for a permanent relationship yet . . .'

'I remember. The night you two met, at Griet's party – he followed you the whole night like a puppy dog.'

'He kept cornering me and trying to talk about politics or religion. I wanted to be frivolous and laugh and dance. That became the pattern for our entire relationship . . .' She sliced a cucumber with vicious chopping movements, smiling wryly. 'But now it feels to me as though I've become the hunter, the one who wants commitment, some security, and he . . . it's as though he's always pushing me away. If I confront him he says, no, he wants to be with me, I should just give him time to get used to the idea. But I think he's just scared of being alone. Me too, of course,' she added, shame-faced.

'But you're still young enough to get away, Emma.' Mila's voice was still quiet, almost whispering, but urgent. 'You don't have to be trapped in a relationship that's not working. Don't wait until you're as old as I am!'

'What do you mean?' Emma asked, surprised.

'I mean you're still young enough to meet someone else.' Mila kept her eyes on the bottle of olive oil in her hand, sprinkling it carefully over the mozzarella and tomato slices. 'It's harder at my age.'

Emma burst out laughing, her expression disbelieving.

'You make it sound as though you've got one foot in the grave!'

'I'm turning thirty-five soon.' Mila set the olive oil bottle down on the counter, a fraction too hard. 'Then half of my life is past. According to the Bible, anyway. The way I drank and smoked in my younger days, it'll probably pass a whole lot faster. Nowadays I'm beginning to regret the opportunities I let slip when I was your age.'

Emma stared at her silently for a few moments.

'And what about Ralph?'

'What about Ralph?'

'Are you going to let that opportunity slip too?'

'It's not that simple, Emma,' sighed Mila.

'Exactly what I'm trying to say about my relationship with Philip!' Emma threw her hands up in a gesture of helplessness, the sharp vegetable knife still in her hand. 'It's not just a case of leave-him-and-look-for-another-man! If only it were that simple!'

It was Ralph who made her realize that reality could sometimes be better than the best fantasy, thought Mila. She'd always be grateful to him for that. But it was also Ralph – or rather the circumstances in which they came to know each other's bodies, so soon after Stuart's death – who made her realize that guilt could be such a powerful turn-on. Soon she wanted more than Ralph could offer her. Not more sex, but more excitement, more stimulation, more – yes, admit it – more guilt. It was the only sensible explanation for the string of 'illicit' relationships she'd become involved in after Stuart's death. Married men, men from different backgrounds, men with different skin colours, men who were far too old or too young (the Roman Catholic judge who was older than her father; the beautiful schoolboy who made her feel like a paedophile), you name them, the less accessible the man, the greater the attraction. Sexual fires stoked by mutual feelings of guilt, secret experiences which she couldn't even share with her best friends, fantastic orgasm after fantastic orgasm, without the help of fantasy! She told herself that her work kept her too busy for a 'normal relationship'. The detachment of an illicit affair suited her better, the excitement of meetings in strange hotel rooms, the impossibility of promises . . . Till she really looked at herself in the mirror one day – painting her mouth red for another secret assignation with another unavailable man – and saw the other woman. The Other Woman. Like in one of those stupid soaps on TV, the one sexual cliché after the other, right down to the red lipstick. Never again, she promised herself, never again would she fall for a married man. Never again would she sleep with any man she couldn't introduce to her mother the next morning, proudly. A promise which drastically reduced her sex life. But she'd stuck to her word. And now, after three years of admirable self-control, she'd met a man for whom she'd gladly rip her self-control to shreds. Rip her clothes off her body. During an innocent weekend with friends. Truly, one was no longer safe anywhere.

An innocent weekend with friends, she thought. And yet, on that last night, the atmosphere had become increasingly stormy. Figuratively speaking, because outside the wind died down and the sea gradually became calm, and later the crescent moon hung so low over the smooth water that it looked as though at any moment it could splash down into it. But in the borrowed beach house everyone's feelings became flammable, as though there was electricity in the air causing one emotional thunderstorm after the other, irrational explosions made worse by the fact that no one was completely sober. Except Yvette, who remained the calm eye of the storm throughout. It became the kind of night which disturbs the equilibrium between a circle of friends in subtle ways, so subtle that the effects can only be traced years later, as a winding river on a map can be traced with a careful finger, back to its source.

'Dagga is supposed to have a calming influence,' Bobby said the next day as they carried their luggage out. 'I don't know what happened last night.'

'The less said about last night,' Mila muttered, 'the sooner we can all forget about it.'

'Did something happen last night?' Ralph asked. 'Did I miss something?'

Mila gave him a dirty look and walked back quickly to the house to fetch another suitcase.

Afterwards, when she tried to put the events in chronological order, she remembered that it had all begun with a discussion about politics. As everything in this country begins and ends with politics, she thought bitterly. Bobby and Max were speaking about the Struggle, about friends who were imprisoned, or had gone underground, about their own powerlessness to do anything about the situation. Liane made a flippant remark because she was afraid that the sombre topic would spoil the cheerful atmosphere. Max knew her well enough to give her an amused glance, but Bobby frowned, irritated.

'Can't we forget about the State of Emergency for just *one* weekend?' Liane turned the volume up and began to dance through the room with swaying hips. *You can't start a fire without a spark* . . . The theme song of the weekend, as Mila would later come to think about that particular Bruce Springsteen track. 'Let's pretend we're in a different country. Somewhere where people can be superficial without feeling guilty!'

'You mean the kind of game that people have been playing for centuries when they just don't want to know what's going on around them.' Bobby's tone was sharp, as intolerant as only the very young can be. Or the very old. 'So that later they can say, *we didn't know.*'

'That's not . . . that's not what I meant,' stammered Liane.

'That's not what she meant,' chorused Max, his voice soothing.

'For fuck's sake!' Liane cried, frozen in the middle of the room, everyone's attention suddenly on her. 'Do we really have to speak about politics every single minute? So that our credentials won't be questioned one day? So that one day – after the revolution – we'll still be tolerated here?'

'Liane . . .' sighed Paul.

'That's not what Bobby meant,' said Max, placating again.

'No, not every single minute.' Bobby's frowning, blushing face was a mask of discomfort, but her voice remained implacable. 'But one should *also* speak about politics. Amidst all the superficialities. Without feeling guilty.'

'It's different for Bobby,' explained Max. 'Lots of her friends are in jail.'

'But that still doesn't mean . . .'

'Just imagine how you would feel if most of *us* were locked up.'

'No, she's absolutely right,' sighed Bobby, and dropped her head into her hands. 'I'm a guest in this house, I don't know about your issues, I had no right to spoil this evening by confronting anyone with politics . . .'

'No, I just opened my mouth without thinking again!' Liane responded immediately. 'As usual.'

'I'm sorry,' whispered Bobby, shaking her head continually. 'I'm really sorry. I don't know what's going on with me.'

'No, I'm the one who should apologize.' Liane sank down on to the leather couch next to Bobby and threw a clinking arm around the younger woman's thin shoulders. 'I don't know what you must think of me.'

'Now they're going to argue about which of the two of them should be most sorry,' muttered Paul.

'I'm sorry, OK?' Liane bit her lip, her face twisted with remorse. 'I promise you I'm not really as . . . as superficial as I sound.'

'I know.' Bobby looked up, a shy smile lifting the corners of her mouth, gradually spreading to her eyes, her whole earnest face lit like a spotlight. 'And I'm not really as self-righteous as I sound.'

'And they all lived happily ever after!' Max called out, relieved.

But that was only the first of the arguments the night would bring.

Barely half an hour later, while Bobby and Liane were dancing to the beat of the Rolling Stones (unlikely bosom buddies after their earlier tiff), Max and Paul began arguing. Again about politics.

Mila heard the two male voices grow steadily louder, but didn't pay much attention as she was flirting with Adriaan. A seemingly innocent discussion about art in the twentieth century – but Adriaan's words fell like overripe fruits from his mouth, too heavy with erotic innuendo to stay hanging on some theoretical branch. And she devoured these forbidden fruits greedily, forgetting about everything and everyone about her, until Paul's voice cut through the room like a machine gun.

'It's easy to see poverty as an adventure when you have a wealthy mother in the southern suburbs! And a hefty inheritance sitting in the bank collecting interest!' He tried to laugh jokily, but even his laugh cracked like a shot in the sudden uncomfortable silence. 'It's a stage most of us struggled through as students, Max. You're getting a bit long in the tooth for those Marxist slogans.'

'What's the alternative?' Max lifted his bearded chin and looked Paul straight in the eyes. 'To marry a stylist and become a yuppy lawyer?'

'Ouch!' said Liane but danced resolutely on. 'That was a low blow, Max.'

'Sorry, Liane, but I just can't understand you so-called liberals with all your materialism. Or is it just plain old-fashioned greed? Soothe your conscience by voting for the PFP and hope with all your heart that the NP will stay in power, so that everything can just stay the same, otherwise you might have to share your swimming pool or your holiday home or whatever with your countrymen!'

'What *are* you talking about?' Liane stood with her hands on her hips. 'We don't have a swimming pool or a holiday home!'

'But that's what you want, not so? Isn't that why Paul is working his butt off? To make more money, to buy more things . . .'

'And you, Max?' Paul's voice was more measured now, but his attitude still tense, his body bent forward in his chair. 'What are you working for? Political credibility? What do you do with your money – or do you hand over your salary to the Struggle every month?'

Bobby closed her eyes and danced fiercely on, stamping her feet and swaying her body with her hands lifted above her head, a primitive rain dance which seemed completely out of place in this living room with armchairs covered in faded linen, a couch of torn green leather, threadbare Persian carpets and old art deco lamps with pedestals in the form of lithe silver figurines. Liane watched her, a desperate expression in her eyes, and then began to move in the same way. Initially hesitant, but gradually with more and more abandon.

'I work because I want to change things,' Max answered in a measured tone. 'Because perhaps I'll want to have children one day. Because I'd like to raise them in a country they can be proud of.'

'That's what we all dream about,' sighed Paul.

'It's time to stop dreaming and start *doing*.' A slow smile crinkled the skin around Max's dark eyes, like soft white paper. 'Otherwise for the rest of your life you'll remain a useless liberal in Never Never Land.'

'And you'd rather be a useless radical on Robben Island?' asked Paul, shaking his head, the dimple in his chin fleetingly visible, and sank back into his chair.

And then the argument was over, as unexpectedly as it had begun. While Mila was still wondering why it felt like so much more than just a difference of political opinion. As though an old, repressed animosity had unexpectedly surfaced, broken through a civilized exterior, and been just as suddenly suppressed again. While Bobby and Liane carried on their footstomping rain dance with such force that the art deco lamp next to them began to tremble on its slender pedestal.

The next outburst was one which had hung threateningly in the air for hours – although no one wanted to acknowledge the warning signs. There'd been a sense of aggression between Philip and Emma the whole day, a resentment that built up like a dark cloud while everyone pretended not to notice, as if it would blow over if they could just ignore it long enough. Philip spoke less and less and smoked more. Emma's mouth carried on laughing, as always, but her grey-blue eyes lost their brightness. After the photo session she tied her hair up high on her head, pulled tightly back from her forehead, making her look like a disillusioned nun.

It was already late, but no one showed any sign of getting ready for bed. Liane and Bobby were talking on the stoep, their heads close together. Mila couldn't imagine what the subject could be. (Peaceful resistance? Styling? Max's possibilities as a lover?) Paul and Max were sitting together in a corner poking fun at each other's politics. (This time apparently with no hard feelings.) Ralph was stretched out on the couch – drugged by Bobby's dagga – wiggling his feet to the beat of B B King's blues. The other five were gathered around the table.

'I've never been so tired in my life before,' Yvette apologized after trying to suppress a yawn for the umpteenth time. 'It's probably the body's way of storing up rest for all the sleepless nights that lie ahead.'

'Like a camel storing water before setting off into the desert,' said Emma sympathetically.

'The poor camel doesn't usually have a choice,' remarked Philip. 'Honestly, I can't understand why any rational person would willingly journey through a desert.'

'It was a metaphor, Philip,' Emma said quickly.

'An appropriate metaphor.' Philip lifted his cigarette to his lips and held his fingers nervously in front of his mouth as if to hold back his next words. 'Parenthood is as fucking dangerous as a desert.'

At once the atmosphere around the table was tense. Adriaan fiddled with his pipe, Yvette stared at her wine glass, Mila tried to watch Emma without her noticing. Emma was the only one who looked directly at Philip, her eyes openly hostile and her lips pulled back into a bitter line.

'But it can't just be dark, surely?' Yvette said softly. 'Even with a . . . with a disabled child there must still be rays of light?'

'My child isn't "disabled", Yvette,' Philip said, just as softly. 'He's a vegetable. He doesn't live, he just lies in a bed. He can't hear or see or think, he can't experience emotion, he can't do anything but lie there. I know that Emma blames me for running away – for leaving him and his mother in Pretoria – but I couldn't . . .' He shrugged and sucked deeply at the cigarette. Emma shook her head, murmuring something inaudible, but he didn't look at her. Avoided everyone's eyes. 'I couldn't bear it. I *never* want to feel so powerless again. That's what being a parent means to me. Danger, darkness, powerlessness.'

'But before he . . . before the operation . . . *before* the brain damage?'

Yvette's voice was almost pleading. Philip stared at his cigarette for a long time before he answered. It was a routine tonsil operation which did the damage. Much more than brain damage. Something went wrong, a rock tumbled into a dam and disturbed the calm surface of a seemingly happy family life. The two-year-old child went into a coma from which he never fully woke, the mother grasped at religion and longed for miracles, the father was driven to drink and depression, the marriage collapsed spectacularly. Like a building blown up from the inside. Six years later the shock waves were still rippling outwards. He shook his head slowly, his voice thick with regret.

'No. Fatherhood was never a joyful experience for me. From the start I experienced it as a frightening state of uncertainty.'

'But you experience everything in life as a frightening state of uncertainty!' Emma exclaimed impatiently.

'Perhaps. But a child only intensifies that. It's like climbing a cliff blindfolded.'

'No, Philip, you're being dishonest.' Emma's fingers shook so much that she struggled to light her cigarette. 'You're trying to deny your feelings for your child. You've been doing it for years!'

'No, it's precisely because I love him . . . in spite of everything . . . that I say that parenthood isn't worth the trouble. It's too painful. There are too few rays of light. Does that answer your question, Yvette?'

'But surely there are millions of people for whom parenthood means more joy than pain?'

'Perhaps they have a greater gift for joy than I have.'

'Why don't you give yourself another chance?'

'To do what?'

'Have another child?'

'And fuck my life up some more?'

'If only you were prepared to work through your fear!' Emma burst out. 'To *try* to work through it. You can't run away from everything you're afraid of for the rest of your life. Relationships, marriage, family, fatherhood, any form of commitment!'

'She's been trying to get me to a shrink for months,' muttered Philip, to no one in particular, and stubbed his cigarette out fiercely.

'It wouldn't do you any harm to see a psychologist,' said Mila.

'Another one!' Philip slammed his fist into the table so that the glasses shook, his face suddenly twisted with rage. 'Where's your fucking imagination? Can't you think of a more original solution? Do you want us all to become characters in an American sitcom? To start sounding like superficial idiots? *I'm OK, you're OK! Have a nice day! God loves you!*'

Emma leaped up with tears in her eyes and fled from the room. Yvette stood up heavily, groaning, and shot an accusing glance at Philip before she followed Emma. Ralph sat upright on the couch and looked at the scene around the table in confusion.

Everyone wants to know why I sing the blues, sobbed B B King in the sudden silence.

'Who wants coffee?' asked Adriaan but got no response.

'Now I'm convinced that you have to get your head read!' Mila glared at Philip as if she was looking down the barrel of a gun. 'You need more help than I thought.'

'Now you've had it, brother!' Ralph exclaimed from the couch. 'You've really pissed the ladies off!'

'Shut up, Ralph,' Mila snarled at him. 'You can't think when you're high.'

'Need some help, Philip?' Ralph grinned.

'No thanks,' said Philip with a pained smile. 'It's been a long time since I was frightened by an enraged female.'

'*I'm a brave, brave mouse*,' Ralph began to sing quietly, '*see me marching through the house, and I'm not afraid of ANYTHING . . .*'

'And what about PMT?' asked Adriaan with a mocking smile.

'*P-M-T?*' sang Ralph in a quavering voice. '*We-e-ll ... except for Pre-Menstrual Tension ... I'm not afraid of ANYTHING! I'm a brave, brave mouse, see me marching through the house ...*'

'OK, I give up, just please stop *singing!*' cried Mila, blocking her ears. Then her shoulders began to shake with laughter. 'It's not fair. It's three against one. Besides, I think it's time for bed.'

If only she'd done it. If she had only forgotten about her warm, wanton body, and climbed into her cold bed, chaste and alone, then things might have turned out differently. So she rebuked herself later. Half-heartedly. The other half of her heart knew that it had already been too late. The stone had already fallen into the dam. The first ripples had already appeared on the surface.

Philip was the only one who went to sleep. She stayed sitting at the table because she couldn't resist the temptation to have one more cup of coffee with Adriaan. She hoped that Ralph would fall asleep on the couch in his drugged state but he came to sit next to her, mocking, quarrelsome, even openly hostile. It must be the dagga, she decided. And tried to ignore him. But then came the accusation which hit her like a blow in the belly, literally making her flinch with shock.

' . . . and you use your husband's death when it suits you. As a kind of contraceptive against any form of emotional involvement.'

'What *are* you talking about?' she asked, spluttering with indignation.

'I'm talking about when you play the grieving widow because you need an excuse not to get involved in a relationship. When you want to get out of a man's bed as quickly as possible, when you get scared that you're about to lose control, when you . . .'

'That's not true!'

But even to her own ears her shrill denial sounded unconvincing.

'Or when you sleep with a married man. Then the widow act probably comes in very handy? You know he won't leave his wife, and he knows you won't "leave" your late husband, so no one needs to feel guilty.'

'It's not true!' She drew a sharp breath, struggling to calm her voice again. 'I loved Stuart . . .'

'What does love have to do with it?'

Doesn't love play a role at all?

'You make it sound as though I'm grateful my husband is dead! Because it gives me an excuse to manipulate other men!'

And then she began to cry, helplessly shocked by the unexpected attack. When she felt Adriaan's hand on her shoulder the shock was compounded by an unbearable feeling of guilt. Not just the usual guilt towards Stuart and Ralph, but also towards Yvette and her unborn child, towards Emma who had warned her not to get involved with Adriaan, towards everyone in this circle of friends whom she would upset, every person she would betray – living or dead or not yet born – if she gave in to this overwhelming urge to feel Adriaan's broad brown hand, now resting so innocently on her shoulder, all over the rest of her body too. To feel that hand stroking all over her skin. All over.

'I loved him,' she sniffed, wiping her wet nose with her fingers.

'No one's questioning that, Mila.' Ralph's voice had become more sympathetic, his amber eyes less merciless. 'No one except you.'

'But I don't know if . . . if it was enough,' she said, sighing, 'I don't know . . .'

Whether she should have married Ralph instead?

'It was enough.' Ralph reached his hand across the table to her, a gesture of *rapprochement*, a slender hand with long, sensitive fingers. The hand of a harpist, she thought as she looked at him through a mist of tears, a harpist or a lover who could play a woman's body like a harp. Why didn't Adriaan have hands like that? 'You've been burdened with survivor's guilt for years, Mila. You can't spend the rest of your life feeling guilty because you're the one who lived. It's time to leave the grieving widow act behind . . .'

'I think I need some fresh air,' she mumbled when her eyes began to fill again.

And she fled blindly through the back door, leaving Ralph's hand lying on the table like an empty glove.

Ralph-and-Mila. Mila-and-Ralph. That's how their friends said their names, she realized outside in the dark, with invisible hyphens, as people do with old married couples. It was more than a decade since Stuart's death, since that first guilty discovery of each other's bodies in the house she had shared with Stuart till shortly before. On the carpet which she had bought with Stuart barely a month earlier. She had sobbed with shaking shoulders and Ralph had tried to comfort her, pressing her head against his chest and murmuring inaudible words into her hair, and before she knew it . . . It was the first time in her life that she had literally ripped the clothes from someone's body. She had tugged at his shirt so desperately that she pulled half the buttons off. She thought that only happened in movies. Actually the whole scene was as unreal as something in a movie – until guilt settled on her bare shoulders like a damp blanket. Just moments after the most fantastic orgasm of her life. Nothing unreal about *that*.

After that she and Ralph both began other relationships, sometimes finding comfort with each other again for a while, but always fleeing swiftly from each other again. She could never explain it to anyone else. She couldn't even explain it to herself. It was always more than friendship – ever since their student days it had been more than friendship – and yet it had never developed into a more conventional relationship. At first she thought it was Stuart's shadow which hung between them, something which would vanish with the passing of time. These days she suspected that she must have some perverse character flaw, a deeply suppressed feeling of inferiority which made it impossible for her to be content with any man who really cared for her. *If he wants me, then surely there must be something wrong with him?* That kind of thing. Although she would never admit it to anyone, of course. Not while she could hide behind a sensual body and a seductive voice; not while she was viewed as a competent journalist with a sharp mind; not while she could cover all trace of doubt or uncertainty or vulnerability with her red lipstick every morning.

The moment that he walked out of the back door, he was aware of her. Even before he saw her in the dark, next to the glowing coals of the braai fire, he felt her draw him closer, steadily and confidently, like an angler reeling in a fish. She sat on the ground, her back turned to the house, her chin propped on her raised knees.

'That's how I'm going to sketch you,' he decided as he sat next to her. 'Exactly as you are now.'

'Tearful and *bedonnerd*?' she asked without looking at him.

'Moody and mysterious,' he said. 'It's an irresistible picture.'

'I'm not a bloody *picture*, Adriaan! Go and look for another model if you want to draw pictures! There are dozens of women who'd feel flattered to pose for you!'

He looked at her stubborn profile and fought the temptation to touch her face.

'Why does he upset you so much?'

'Ralph?'

'Are you lovers?'

For the first time she turned her face to him. Her mouth, which was no longer painted red, was partly open – as if she was surprised by the question, or didn't know how to answer – and suddenly so close to him that his will power snapped. She drew her breath in when his lips touched hers, but she didn't close her mouth, didn't pull her head away. He kissed her without holding her, used his lips and tongue instead of his hands. She drew a breath again, more sharply than before, and quickly turned her face away.

'Why do you do this?' she whispered.

'Because I've wanted to do this all weekend. Because it's probably my last chance to do this.'

'No, I don't mean why are you kissing me! I mean why would you want to do it to any woman? Why do you have this desire to seduce every woman you meet?'

'Not *every* woman!'

'You know what I mean.'

'Hmm.' He looked up and saw that the clouds had dispersed. The black sky was a sheet of stars, astonishingly bright above the dark coastal town. The crescent moon was so thin that it was almost transparent, shiny and brittle like a shard of mother-of-pearl. 'I also know that you're clever enough not to be content with some corny answer.'

'And what would the corny answer be?' she asked with an uneven smile, her lips still wet from his kiss, her mouth unsettlingly close to his again.

'That you're more special than any other woman. That I'm going to be in love with you for the rest of my life. That this could be the beginning of an amazing relationship.'

'And the honest answer?'

'That I believe everything I've just said. But I know from experience that it will pass.'

'I find such honesty quite erotic.' This time it was she who touched her lips against his, still without their holding each other, and brushed her breasts against his chest. He felt a thrill of pleasure which embarrassed him – as if he were still a clumsy teenager being seduced by the wife of a sales rep – when he realized that she wasn't wearing a bra. The hard nipples under the smooth material of her summer dress, through the thin cotton of his shirt, made his body react immediately, his hips strain forward with reckless desire. 'Promise me you'll always be this honest with me.'

'If it produces this reaction . . .' he murmured into her mouth and lifted his hand at last to touch her body.

Then she jerked her face away.

'Ralph . . .' He followed her startled gaze to the back door, saw a tall figure framed by a sharp light from the kitchen, a bush of hair like a halo around an invisible face. Then the figure turned and vanished into the house. Mila slammed a balled fist against her forehead and moaned in a low voice. 'Fuck, fuck, fuck, fuck, fuck . . .'

'Is it *that* bad?' he asked, dismayed.

'I swore I'd never do it again! I was never going to mess with a married man again!'

'Did you promise Ralph that?'

'No, I promised myself! But it just makes it worse that Ralph had to see it now!' He touched her shoulder to calm her down, but she shook his hand away, as if it burned. 'How long do you think he was standing there?'

'I haven't a clue . . .'

'Oh, fuck!' she said in a despairing voice. 'I need a cigarette. I'm going to start smoking again!'

She jumped up and walked away from him quickly. He saw her stand still for a moment at the back door, saw her pull her shoulders back resolutely, an enticing silhouette against the light from the house. Then she vanished inside.

It's over, he realized. Whatever it was, it was over. She would never let him get so close again. She would never let herself let him get so close again.

She blinked her eyes in the sudden bright light and saw with relief that Ralph was no longer in the room. Felt the tension flow from her shoulders, grateful that she didn't have to see the reproach on his face, not now when her resistance was so low. Somewhere in the background Tom Waits was singing, a low, gruff, melancholy sound. Liane and Max were sitting on the floor in front of the couch talking. Bobby lay in a chintz armchair, her legs thrown over the arm rest, and listened absent-mindedly to the conversation. The rest must all have gone to bed.

Then she became aware of Yvette just behind her, at the sink next to the back door, drinking water. The sink below the window – uncurtained like most of the windows in the house – looking out over the back yard. Where Adriaan was still sitting next to the fireplace.

'You're still awake?' she asked, her shoulders stiffening again.

She walked to the sink to pour herself a glass of water, too. You couldn't see the last coals glowing on the fire from here. Thank god. But she imagined she could still make out Adriaan's stocky outline in the light of the crescent moon. Perhaps only because she knew he was sitting there, she thought hopefully.

'I struggle to sleep these days,' said Yvette. 'It's difficult to lie down comfortably with this stomach.'

Mila avoided her eyes, just glanced fleetingly at her face and saw that she was staring blankly out of the window, a strange figure in a long white Victorian nightdress.

'Well, I'm ready for bed,' she said and drained the glass greedily. 'It's been a long day.'

'I wonder if Adriaan is going to sit there the whole night staring at a dead fire,' Yvette remarked, yawning, as if she were talking to herself.

Mila felt her cheeks begin to glow, again confused about what Yvette had seen. Or not seen. Yvette shrugged her shoulders and turned away from the sink. For a moment, just a moment, they looked into each other's eyes. Yvette's dark eyes wide and defenceless, Mila's light eyes pleading.

Afterwards she often wished that she could have read reproach in Yvette's eyes instead. Or even undisguised animosity. It would have increased her feelings of guilt, of course, but she was, after all, used to living with a guilty conscience. It was the uncertainty that she couldn't bear. The fact that she never knew what Yvette knew.

The next morning Mila and Adriaan parted jokingly, nonchalant under the watchful gaze of their friends.

'It may not look like it, but I'm devastated that you still refuse to pose for me,' said Adriaan when she kissed him quickly on the right cheek.

'Perhaps next time,' she consoled him. 'When we all have another decadent weekend.'

'We must definitely do this again,' said Yvette, hugging Mila, turning a little to one side because her stomach was in the way.

'Well, I turn thirty next year,' Liane announced. 'I think that's an excellent reason to have a decadent weekend!'

'I thought you wanted to hire the most expensive restaurant in town and dance on a table,' said Paul.

'Oh, that too, of course! After I've danced on a table, I mean. After I've ruined my husband's professional reputation for ever,' she laughed. 'I'm only going to turn thirty once in my life!'

'Thank God,' sighed Paul.

'Seems to me you'll have to postpone your swimming pool and beach house for a few years.' Max looked at Paul, shaking his head, his black eyes small between the laugh lines. 'Or at least until you've recovered financially from your wife's thirtieth birthday celebrations.'

'Just don't postpone it for too long,' warned Philip. 'After the revolution none of us will be able to afford a swimming pool or a beach house any more.'

'Perhaps Bobby can borrow a beach house from one of her comrades for us now and again?' Ralph suggested.

'I can't think why any of my comrades would want to lend a beach house to a bunch of spoilt whiteys like you,' said Bobby with an ironic smile.

'That's why I like her!' Max threw his arm around Bobby's shoulder and pulled her closer, laughing. 'She never stops dishing out the compliments!'

'But perhaps there's still time to convert some of you,' said Bobby with her head against Max's shoulder. 'Before the revolution.'

When they drove off in Philip's packed Golf, Mila looked through the rear window as the group of waving people in front of the house with the blue shutters shrank smaller and smaller. Until the car turned a corner and at once the whole window became blue, blue sea and blue sky, a bright blue infinity. Then she turned back, sighing, and tried hard to think of her work in Johannesburg.

On the way to the airport everyone was quiet, as though they were still uncomfortable about the previous night's eruptions. Or perhaps they were just tired. Anyway, she was grateful that she could sink away into her own longing thoughts. Adriaan's breath against her ear as she looked at his etchings. The teasing weight of his hand on her shoulder. The surprisingly sweet taste of his tongue between her lips. But in the plane Ralph suddenly grew talkative, in a laughing, nervous way. Almost as though he was the one with the guilty conscience.

Back in Johannesburg she lured him shamelessly to her bed – for the first time in almost a year – and responded to his caresses with more passion than usual. He looked at her, surprised, questioning, but said nothing. Later she realized that he probably suspected the truth.

That it was Adriaan's heavy body which she felt rock under her own uncontrolled one, Adriaan's brown outdoor hands which caressed her thrusting hips, played exploringly between her moist thighs, carefully touched her wet cheeks. Adriaan's sensual mouth in which, at last, she could press her fingers, sighing with pleasure, weeping with misery.

TWO

Spaces Tell Stories (1986)

'You mean you were serious when you said you wanted to arrange a decadent weekend?'

'Of course I was serious!' Liane laughed into the receiver. 'I'm always serious, my darling!'

Paul's eyebrows lifted almost imperceptibly as he brought her a cup of tea.

'To celebrate your thirtieth birthday?' asked Mila.

'Ja!' Liane pressed the receiver against her cheek, took the cup from Paul with one hand and blew him a kiss over the fingertips of the other. 'When Emma said the other day that you and Ralph would be in the Cape for Christmas, we decided right away that we'd simply have to persuade you to come down a bit earlier, so that you can celebrate my birthday with us. I've tracked down a stunning beach house at Hangklip and we're all going . . .'

'Wait, wait, wait!' laughed Mila down the line. 'First I'll have to see if I can get away from the newspaper earlier. It's not that easy. Everyone wants to take their holidays in December and it's kind of expected that those of us without children will stand aside, you know, so that the mommys and daddys can go away with their children.'

'That's one form of discrimination that's always made me furious! As if we childless people don't also want to see our family and friends over Christmas!'

'I can think of far worse forms of discrimination.'

Mila's voice sounded so tired that Liane realized, with a prickle of guilt, just how difficult her work must be these days. When they'd seen each other the previous year the State of Emergency was only in force in certain areas. In the meantime the government had extended it to the rest of the country and had begun to limit the press so severely that some papers, in a bizarre attempt at protest, had begun to publish blank spaces instead of articles below headlines: *Something Happens in Soweto*, above a blank square space. Even someone like Liane, who had never paid much attention to the news before, was unsettled every time she picked up a paper with such a gaping white wound. She could scarcely imagine what it must do to Mila's state of mind.

'Anyway, you've still got more than two months to twist the editor's arm.' She stirred the cherry tea with one of her grandmother's apostle teaspoons and gazed with dissatisfaction at the spacious sitting room she had so carefully decorated in shades of white. A huge sofa and a few armchairs upholstered in creamy white linen, half a dozen simple etchings in identical frames against a winter-white wall, blinds of bleached canvas in front of enormous windows which opened on to a sunny courtyard. Whiter Shades of Pale. That's what she'd had in mind, everything open and clean and light. But today the room just looked plain boring. Like a landscape under snow. 'Can't you play on his feelings?'

'What feelings?' Mila's laugh sounded as tired as her voice. 'I've never encountered a newspaper editor with feelings.'

'Tell him you have to attend a reunion!'

'A reunion of what?'

'Of our West Coast weekend. Everyone else has already said they're coming.'

'Do you think it's a good idea? We all got a bit volatile last year, if I remember correctly.'

'I'm sure some sparks will fly again,' laughed Liane. 'But it's better than a *boring* weekend where everyone agrees about everything.'

Paul looked up quickly from the paper he'd begun to read on the sofa, his eyebrows raised noticeably higher than usual. He'd taken off the jacket of his tailored suit and thrown it over the back of a chair, unbuttoned his cotton shirt's collar and loosened his dark blue tie. The wavy pattern on the tie consisted of the initials of a famous European designer, endlessly repeated. *JPG, JPG, JPG, JPG, JPG, JPG* . . . The triangle of skin which showed above the open collar was almost shockingly tanned against the snow-white cotton. Especially when you remembered that the Cape winter had only just ended. Suddenly, Liane felt as dissatisfied with her attractive husband as she did with her tasteful sitting room.

'I'd prefer a boring weekend,' Paul said, his eyes on the paper again.

'I don't know if you want to remember your thirtieth birthday as the occasion when your circle of friends split up once and for all,' Mila said at the same time over the phone.

'Ag, no, it won't be that bad!' said Liane, loud enough for them both to hear her.

She took a quick sip of tea and put the gold-rimmed cup firmly back in its saucer. Something else she'd inherited from her grandmother. Her firm determination. And maybe also her love of the luxurious, for objects which other women would probably view as unnecessary. The dogged determination of a woman born in a concentration camp, who salted away a little money month after month so that at last she could buy a set of paper-thin porcelain cups with pink roses and gold rims. So that her granddaughter could drink her cherry tea out of those cups today. A grandmother to be proud of, Liane often thought. And there weren't too many of her family members that she could be proud of. Her father with his greasy fingernails and his below-the-belt jokes, her mother with her happy-clappy enthusiasm for some charismatic sect, her brothers with their bland, boring little wives and their bland, boring little lives . . .

'Says who?'

'Well, some of our personal lives are in better shape now. Emma and Philip . . . OK, I'm not saying that they're cooing like a pair of lovebirds . . . but it looks as though they've agreed to some kind of ceasefire . . .'

'So I hear,' said Mila sceptically.

'And Bobby is also less uptight these days. According to Max she's having this red-hot affair with one of her comrades . . .'

'Didn't Max also have an iron in the fire?'

'I think he tried hard, but didn't get anywhere. Now they're just friends.'

'The older I get, the more I wonder if that's still possible.'

'What?'

'To be "just friends" with a man.' Mila's voice sounded dusty with tiredness, like a tape turning too slowly. 'Or with anybody, in fact.'

Liane swallowed her tea in flustered silence. In the background you could hear other voices, a phone constantly ringing, the soft humming of the computer, something falling with a loud bang, someone swearing impatiently. The general chaos of a newspaper office, she thought, with a sudden surge of envy, while the creamy calmness of her own sitting room irritated her more every moment. Must be pre-menstrual tension.

57

'Well, it's not easy, is it? Friendship between a man and a woman . . . between a straight man and a straight woman . . .'

'I don't even know if there is such a thing as a straight man or a straight woman any more!' Mila exclaimed impatiently.

'Well, I can't speak for *you* . . .' Her laugh sounded shriller than usual, almost frightened. 'And there are still a few straight men left in the country! I mean, if someone like Adriaan stops flirting with every woman he meets, then I'd start worrying . . .'

'According to Emma, he's so besotted with his new baby daughter these days that he's clean forgotten to flirt with the rest of the female sex.'

'Never fear, my dear, it's just a stage he's going through. I mean, he'll probably stay besotted, but he'll never allow one woman to occupy his whole heart. Even if it is his own daughter. Who looks exactly like him, by the way. It's quite uncanny to see them together!'

'Yes, so I hear.' Liane listened to the click of a cigarette lighter, Mila drawing in a sharp breath. 'And I hear that he's decided to bring the child up in the Cape. Have they found a place to live yet?'

'A stunning place on a farm outside Stellenbosch! Well, the farm is stunning, but the house is a wreck. But he says it doesn't matter. His latest idea is to begin an artists' colony, you know, a kind of Bloomsbury Set in Africa. A place where all conventional behaviour is thrown overboard.'

'Where everyone can sleep with everyone else's partners.'

'Something like that,' laughed Liane. 'You know Adriaan and his crazy schemes!'

'No,' said Mila, and drew audibly on her cigarette again. 'Actually, I don't know him at all.'

'Didn't you stop smoking?'

'I started again. I'm afraid the State of Emergency is driving me to drink and drugs.'

'It sounds as though a weekend by the sea could only do you good. You must see this house, Mila! It's on a piece of ground as big as a smallholding, completely private, with a front door ten paces from the sea. And a bit of mountain peering over your shoulder all the time.'

'Sounds wonderful . . .'

'You'll be crazy about it. And you deserve it. Any journalist who's survived the last year deserves a break!'

'Any *person* who's survived the past year in this country deserves a break. I'll do my best. I promise.'

When Liane put the phone down a minute later, she had made a decision about her sitting room. What the room desperately needed was colour. Warm shades like ochre and tangerine, terracotta walls and colourful ethnic mats, cushion covers of bright African print . . .

'I know what I want for my birthday,' she said to Paul, who looked up quickly from the creamy white sofa. 'A new image for the sitting room! All the colours of the rainbow under one roof! There's no need to look so alarmed, my darling. It won't cost that much. I'll do everything myself. I just think it's time to get away from this clinical white look. After all, we're living in a multi-coloured country!'

When Liane phoned Max about a month later, she was sitting barefoot on sheets of newspaper in the middle of the floor. Most of the furniture was covered with sheets of plastic, the blinds in front of the windows had been removed and the walls were almost completely painted – in a colour which looked less and less like the shade she'd seen in her mind's eye.

'It's too orange!' she groaned. 'I feel as though I'm trapped in one of those plastic oranges people used to stick on car aerials years ago!'

'I'd completely forgotten about those oranges,' said Max nostalgically.

She stared at the orange paint splashes on her jeans. They reminded her of the sun-filter curtains which her mother had hung in their sitting room years ago, a roughly woven transparent material which she could lie and stare at for hours, stretched out motionless on the brown corduroy couch, passive and depressed, while outside the humid heat folded over the house like a plastic bag. And the orange and white tiles on the kitchen floor, always slightly sticky under her toes when she crept through the kitchen at night to dish up leftovers from pastel Tupperware bowls, hungry because her mother's self-pitying complaints at the dinner table made each mouthful of food stick in her throat like wet cement, because night after night she would push her half-full plate away with an exaggerated sigh, because she wanted to be in the safety of her own bed when her father, drunk and foul-tempered, stumbled through the front door. Incredible how a single colour could evoke an entire atmosphere! That paralysing unhappiness which dominated her last few years in that platteland house as her parents' marriage disintegrated painfully slowly, yet absolutely irrevocably, before her very eyes.

After her two brothers had left home, her mother didn't even try to pretend that there was still hope for the relationship. Like a patient with a terminal illness who, towards the end, with a strange kind of relief, refuses all further medication. And yet, when her mother moved to the city at last, to get away from the neighbours' pitying eyes, it was with the transparent excuse that it would be better for her talented daughter to spend the last two years of her schooling in a good city school. Her talented daughter, used to being an exotic fish in an ordinary little pond, splashed around lost in a sea of children who were more talented, more exotic, more popular, more sophisticated than she was. And the memory of that last tortuous stage of her parents' relationship burned all the earlier, happier memories away. She felt like a war victim who had watched her entire past go up in flames. To this day she could still not share that episode of her life with anyone without feeling as though she were being scorched by the same flames. One day, she hoped, one day . . . In the meantime, she loved telling people about her idyllic platteland youth. Sometimes she told it with such dramatic gusto that she began to believe in it herself.

'The oranges and the lime green fur on the dashboard and the little dog with the nodding head in the back window,' she murmured. 'Whatever happened to all that stuff?'

'Probably vanished into the bottomless pit of middle-class values,' Max replied, sighing. 'Because snobs like us mocked them relentlessly. We always imagined we were better than the mechanics in Goodwood who decorated their cars like Christmas trees. Meanwhile we were as bourgeois as could be!'

'Please don't start one of your political speeches now, Max,' she begged. 'I can't take it. These orange walls have weakened my resistance!'

She heard him laughing softly into his beard, saw in her mind's eye how his black eyes grew smaller, how his face crinkled up. He'd always had an infectious laugh, a sound which began with a deep, indistinct rumbling, like an engine being turned on somewhere in his belly and growing steadily warmer, idling. But as his political commitment had become greater, that rumbling laugh had become rarer.

'Anyway, I accepted long ago that I was irredeemably bourgeois. Unlike some of my friends who imagine they're revolutionaries because they toyi-toyi with the cleaners on campus.' The laugh had warmed up properly now. 'So grant me my middle-class disappointment about the colour of my walls. I had something in the line of a Tuscan villa in mind. Now I'm stuck with the disgusting orange of the South African flag!'

'It just goes to show. It's not so easy to escape your roots.'

'It's not a joke, Max.'

'It's not a tragedy either, Liane. Sorry, but I just can't take your sitting room walls seriously. You know I've never had any feeling for "interior decoration".'

'I wish you wouldn't spit it out with so much contempt! You make it sound almost obscene!'

'If only it were. I like obscenity. No, it's not that I despise interior decorating, Liane, it's just that I don't notice it. I probably wouldn't notice if you decorated the whole house in the colours of the South African flag!'

'What about the ANC flag?' she asked sarcastically. 'Would that be subversive enough to get your attention?'

'The security police would probably force you to change your colour scheme.'

'Can they do that?'

'They can do anything,' he said in a sombre tone.

She moved her feet on the outspread newspaper, suddenly uncomfortable, and noticed the report below her bare heel. *Apartheid Barometer: Zwelakhe Sisulu, son of ANC leader Walter Sisulu and UDF president Albertina Sisulu, has been repeatedly banned, placed under house arrest, threatened with imprisonment or detained since his involvement* . . . And she sighed involuntarily because, as usual, she couldn't work up the necessary moral outrage over such unsettling news. It's not that she approved of the political leadership in the country – goodness gracious, she wasn't *that* naïve! – but it didn't *upset* her as much as it upset Max or Bobby. Sometimes she wondered if it was a form of self-protection, a shield around her heart which made it impossible for her to take the whole mess seriously. Which made the state of the walls of her house more important than the State of Emergency outside them.

Or perhaps it was simply a lack of imagination. Because the unrest in the townships never really touched her. Except on the odd day when her maid couldn't come to work. On those days she definitely felt the unrest in the dust under her fingers, saw the unrest in the creases in her clothes, smelled the unrest in the overflowing rubbish bin in the kitchen. On those days she heard the unrest in the uneasy silence which hung over the whole house, without the high whine of the vacuum cleaner or the low murmur of the washing machine, without the flood of strange black voices and incomprehensible black words which spilled constantly from the radio in the kitchen. On those days she even *tasted* the unrest, every time she poured herself a cup of tea. For some reason her own tea never tasted as good as the tea Beauty brought her.

'But now tell me about the plans for the birthday feast,' said Max in a more cheerful tone, almost as though he wanted to comfort her. 'Can everyone come?'

'Ja, it looks as though even Mila and Ralph are going to make it. Mila thought up a sob story about long-lost friends for her editor. And I decided to invite some more people to come on the Sunday, just for the day, you know, in case the rest of us aren't talking to each other by that time. Mila reminded me how volatile everyone became last year. And Adriaan has offered to cook lunch. He's planning a Tuscan menu to celebrate my new Tuscan sitting room.'

'I hope his menu is less of a fuck-up than your sitting room,' said Max. 'Who else do you want to invite?'

'Ag, probably just the same old crowd. Griet and George, Mart and Tomas, Johannes and Joe . . .'

'Any single women?'

'Oh, is that where this is leading? Actually, I was about to ask if you didn't want to bring one of your lovers along.'

'Oh no, I'd rather come on my own. Who knows, maybe I'll meet the woman of my dreams there.'

'I thought I was the woman of your dreams!'

'You are. But you're not available. That's why I wanted to know if you were going to invite any available female friends.'

She laughed, a bit too extravagantly, an involuntary defence against the unexpected tingling in her stomach. He'd only say something like that over the telephone, she thought with a feeling of resignation. Never while he was looking her in the eye. He probably felt embarrassed about the fact that he'd been so crazily in love with her at school. Let's face it, she'd often said to herself, she was just cut from a different cloth to the women he went out with these days. Such pale, spectacled, *styleless* numbers. Ag, well. Women like her were probably little more to men like Max than pretty little pools in which to admire their own reflections. Flattering to the ego, but too shallow, too transparent, to really captivate them. While a more intellectual woman (someone like Bobby, perhaps) held the fascination of a deep, dark well. Much more interesting below the surface.

'Most of my friends are just middle-class idiots like me,' she said with sharp sarcasm. 'We get more excited about a new lounge suite than about a new Emergency ruling.'

'I can't afford to be too fussy. It's been far too long since I last had sex.' Me too, she wanted to say, but stopped herself in time. There were limits to what you could say to an ex-boyfriend after all. 'Just as long as they're not dumb blondes. I'm not *that* desperate.'

'I thought you were a swinging bachelor who wrote down a new name in your little black book every week.'

'The other day I heard a remark about a little black book which gave me cold shivers. A gay colleague who studied in America said his little black book has suddenly gained a whole new meaning. That's where he ticks off the names of ex-lovers who get ill.' He rubbed his beard slowly, a scratchy sound in the receiver. 'I'm afraid Aids is going to make it harder and harder to be a swinging bachelor. One of these days the zipless fuck is going to be a faint memory of a bygone era. Like those plastic oranges we were talking about just now . . .'

She wondered if it was only because she didn't know anyone with Aids – just as she didn't know anyone who was in jail for political reasons, or for any other reason – that the growing anxiety about the disease felt as unreal as Max and his comrades' political angst. But if someone like Max got Aids – or went to jail – everything would change. Or would it? Sometimes she wondered if the brutal reality of life outside could ever scale the high walls around her house, wriggle through the burglar bars in front of her windows and touch her privileged bourgeois existence. It just didn't seem possible.

'Is it really that bad, Max? I mean for those of us who . . .' And then Mila's despondent exclamation echoed in her ears again. *I don't even know if there is such a thing as a straight man or a straight woman any more!* 'For those of us who are more or less straight?'

'I think it's a lot worse than we realize.'

'Well, then I should be grateful that I married in good time!' She could hear how silly she must sound to him, but she was suddenly in a hurry to finish off the conversation. Anxious to do something to rescue her walls before her husband walked through the front door that evening. She could already see the expression of amused disgust on his face. *Isn't it a bit . . . orange?* 'The only advice I can give you, Max, is to shave off that beard.'

'Do you think that will make me feel less horny?' he asked, flabbergasted.

'No, but it would make you look better – less like a Greek tramp – which will improve your chances of getting a woman into bed.'

'I thought I looked like a Greek philosopher,' he exclaimed, offended.

'Philosophers usually look like tramps,' she said unsympathetically. 'To bourgeois women like me, at any rate.'

'I've decided to resign from *Palette* and work from home,' Emma announced two days before the planned weekend, her voice a bit too blasé, as she struggled to push a stubborn trolley through a busy supermarket. 'Or, from Philip's home. I've decided to move in with him.'

Liane stared at her dumbfounded, the tin of olive oil she had just taken from the shelf like a weapon in her right hand.

'I've wanted to do this for a long time now,' Emma added quickly.

'What?' Liane dumped the olive oil in the trolley and tried to keep her voice even. 'Resign from your job or move in with Philip?'

'Work from home . . . write freelance articles, do proofreading, translations . . . anything to do with words. I know I won't make much money, but I'll be able to make ends meet at least.'

Her grey-blue eyes were anxious, but the firm line of her mouth warned Liane that it wouldn't help to protest. She had made an attempt to pin her hair up in a loose bun at the back of her head, but strands had already escaped and were now hanging in corkscrew curls around her face, while the bun had begun to fall lopsidedly over one ear.

'And if you can't make ends meet?'

'Then I'll go and work in the post office! I just can't sit at a mediocre magazine, writing mediocre little stories about fucking mediocre TV starlets any more! Or about the fucking love life of the British monarchy! *It's driving me fucking crazy!*'

A woman holding a toddler's hand shot a vicious glance at Emma and pulled the child away quickly, as mothers do when children stare at perverts or mad people. Liane pulled at the trolley – which was blocking the aisle so that several shoppers glared at them in irritation – and decided that it had been a big mistake to ask Emma to come shopping with her. She'd hoped that Emma would help her to choose food for the weekend – that it would be a fun outing instead of a boring chore – but Emma hadn't shown a flicker of interest in the food on the shelves. She'd wandered through the supermarket like a sleepwalker and shrugged her shoulders every time Liane asked her advice. And now this embarrassing outburst in front of the cooking oils!

'And I'll have more time to write what I actually want to write,' said Emma more calmly, an angry red dot on each cheek the only remaining evidence of her outburst.

'The Great Afrikaans Novel?'

It came out with more sarcasm than she'd intended.

Emma smiled apologetically and wiped her glowing face self-consciously. 'Ag no, I'd rather begin with Small Afrikaans Short Stories.'

'Perhaps it's not such a bad idea.' Liane tried to drum up her usual optimism as she felt herself sinking away in frustrated incomprehension. 'I mean, to break away before you get completely trapped at work. Before they seduce you with a BMW and an expense account and all the other perks which will make it much harder for you to – '

'Not bloody likely,' Emma interrupted her. 'We're speaking about an Afrikaans magazine here, Liane, not an international media corporation. A *mediocre* Afrikaans magazine.'

'I thought you loved your work!'

'I *did* love it. When I began, it was like a dream. I felt like a character in a book. Someone working at a woman's magazine! In the stupid love stories I read at school, the heroines always worked at magazines or publishing houses.'

'Did they?' Liane peered at the list in her hand and pulled the trolley in the direction of the dairy products. 'I only remember heroines who were captured by pirates and ended up in harems.'

'We obviously didn't read the same stupid love stories.' Emma laughed, the vagueness wiped from her eyes, like a sleepwalker who had woken up. 'Anyway, when I was at school, that was the height of my ambition. To live in the city one day – in my own flat – and to work at a woman's magazine and go out with handsome men.'

'Well, you have your own flat and you work for a woman's magazine. If you dump Philip, then you can even go out with handsome men.' Liane threw two kinds of cottage cheese and a big plastic bottle of milk in the trolley. Wished again that she'd come to the supermarket on her own. 'But now you want to move in with him! I can understand that you want to leave your job, Emma, I can understand that you want to write something more than magazine stories, but I simply can't, for the life of me, understand why you want to move in with Philip!'

'He asked me to,' was Emma's laconic reply.

'If he lived in the city it would still make sense. But now you want to go and sit in Stellenbosch! Who the hell is going to give you freelance work if you live there?'

'We're living in a new world, Liane.' Emma pushed her lopsided bundle of hair upwards on her head, an unconscious, pointless gesture as it began to sink down again almost immediately. Liane wished she would pin it up properly for once. 'In a decade we'll all be sitting at our computers communicating with people all over the world. Why would anyone still want to work in an office!'

'To show your colleagues your new outfit?' Liane kept her voice purposefully light, her eyes on the grocery list. 'But what happens if . . . you know, your relationship with Philip doesn't work out?'

As has already happened a couple of times, she thought as she watched her friend with a mixture of irritation and admiration. Emma had always reminded her of one of those magnificent red-haired models (Rossetti's Lizzie Siddal, in particular) who, over the centuries, had inspired famous painters (and probably driven less-famous painters mad), with the voluptuousness of her body and the wildness of her hair, her long legs and pale shoulders, freckles sprinkled like brown sugar over her face and arms. And yet she had an inexplicable lack of self-confidence – not just about her appearance, but also about her other talents – which kept her trapped in a relationship with a man who tore down what little was left of that self-confidence.

'It's not that I have anything against Philip,' she mumbled defensively. 'We all know he has his problems . . .'

'I think it's going to work this time,' said Emma with conviction, her grey eyes less misty every moment. *Radiant* was the word which struck Liane involuntarily. Although it was probably just anxious insecurity which made her eyes shine so feverishly. 'Otherwise I'd never risk it. Remember, it was always *him*, moving into *my* flat . . .'

'And moving out again.'

'And moving out again,' admitted Emma. 'But I've never sacrificed my own security before.'

'And why would you want to do that now, Emma?'

Liane stared at the block of Edam in her hand. She had done stupid things in a supermarket before, but it had never been necessary to try to prevent a friend from leaping blindly into an abyss in front of a fridge full of dairy products. It was only too obvious – to everyone except Emma – that Philip was never going to marry her.

'He's asked me to marry him.'

'What!' Despite everything she knew about Emma and Philip, she felt an unexpected excitement welling up inside her. 'When?'

'A week or two ago, but I'm still . . .'

'No, I mean, when are you going to get married?'

'I don't know,' Emma said quickly, 'I don't want to think about that now. I mean, Philip . . .'

'*Philip!*' Liane let the block of cheese fall heavily on top of the other groceries. 'Goodness gracious.'

'Exactly. Goodness gracious. That's why I don't want to be in too much of a rush. But it's the first time that he's admitted that he sees a future for our relationship. I mean, before it was always a case of let's see whether we still want to be together next week . . .'

Emma took a deep breath and raised her shoulders. Completely different from the earlier offhand shrugs. A gesture so loaded with suppressed emotion – and unsettling vulnerability – that Liane quickly looked down at her grocery list again. And still she couldn't rid herself of that welling-up of excitement. She knew her feelings about weddings were hopelessly old-fashioned, terribly sentimental and completely irrational. But she also knew there was nothing she could do about it. Just the thought of a wedding – even one as unlikely as that of Emma and Philip – was enough to infect her imagination with all the romantic clichés which she had dreamt of as a teenage girl on the platteland. Misty white veils and bunches of blushing pink roses and soothing violin music and flattering candlelight, all those dreams which had transported her from her parents' house, lifted her from the brown corduroy couch and let her float through the ghastly orange sun-filter curtains to a world where everything would be prettier and more romantic and more *stylish*. The inexorable breakdown of her parents' marriage probably affected her dreams of the future, because her imagination was always focused on the most fantastic wedding that anyone had ever experienced, never on what would happen after it.

'But then we've got something else to celebrate this weekend,' she said with a pleased little smile.

'No, not yet,' Emma parried immediately. 'It's still too soon.'

'What are you waiting for? Surely you're not going to get officially engaged?'

'With a formal announcement in the newspaper? And a posed photo of the two of us staring into each other's eyes?' Emma giggled behind her hand, her hair now completely collapsed over the one ear. 'Can you imagine anything more bizarre? *Emma, eldest daughter of Braam and Kleintjie Nel of Pretoria, and Philip, youngest son of Cecil and the late* . . . Oh fuck, I can't even remember what his mother's name was!' She shook her head, the proverbial last straw which made the rest of her hair tumble down. Now it hung like an uncontrollable trailing plant over one shoulder. Little orange ringlets clinging like autumn leaves to her forehead. 'He never speaks about her. Not about her strange life or her strange death. You know, sometimes it seems to me as if there are all these black holes in our relationship. All these subjects that we have to avoid as though we'll be sucked into oblivion if we dare to touch on them! His mother's death, his retarded child, his feelings of guilt about his ex-wife, his uncomfortable relationship with his father, his resentment towards his stepmother . . .'

'Well, it's obviously not going to be a big family wedding,' said Liane with forced frivolity. 'Thank your stars, my darling. Paul's mother insisted on inviting all her senile aunts to our wedding. And she has a whole nursing home full of senile aunts. Apparently the women in her family never die, you have to hit them over the head with a plank to get them into a coffin. Just my luck, to get an immortal mother-in-law. Anyway, it was too awful for words, they stuffed the flower arrangements under their coats and carried away bowls of left-over food in their handbags; I didn't know whether to laugh or cry!'

'No, it obviously won't be a family wedding,' said Emma, her voice filled with regret. 'Or a church wedding.'

'Just not a registry wedding!' Liane exclaimed in horror.

'I hope not. I've got this image of a proper white wedding in my head. You know, perhaps not ten bridesmaids and Mimi Coertse serenading us . . . but at least not just ten minutes at the magistrate's court. Stupid, hey?' She smiled shyly and threw the unruly bush of hair back over her shoulder. 'I mean, perhaps there won't even be a wedding. Perhaps he'll get cold feet – perhaps *I'll* get cold feet – anything could happen! Do you understand why I don't want to tell the rest of the world quite yet?'

'Do you know what you're doing to me?' Liane moaned. 'It's the juiciest piece of news I've heard in months – and you expect me to keep it a secret for the whole weekend.'

'Unless Philip . . . I mean, once he's got used to the idea . . . if he decided to say something himself . . .'

'You mean you want to give him the opportunity to spread the good tidings himself.'

'It won't be easy for him. Not after all his tirades against Holy Matrimony.'

'That was his choice,' said Liane unsympathetically.

'Perhaps I just need to hear it from his lips – in public – before I can believe it myself?'

This time it was definitely insecurity – undisguised, undiluted, frightening insecurity – which shone in Emma's eyes.

'It's not exactly a year I wish to remember.' Max raised a tall glass of champagne and surveyed his friends around the fire. 'But at least it's almost over. And we all survived it.'

'Some of us only just,' murmured Philip.

'Even more reason to drink to it,' said Max determinedly. 'Viva!'

'There were a few good bits too,' said Yvette.

'Like?' asked Max and Philip at the same time, with equally wry smiles.

'Like the fact that the passbook laws were finally done away with.'

'Too little, too late,' said Max. 'Rearranging the deckchairs on the *Titanic*.'

'Like last year, when the Immorality Act was scrapped,' said Emma, her eyes on the evening star which flickered faintly against the velvet grey dusk. 'I always thought the day when that happened – such a perverse law, trying to control so many people's most intimate emotions – I thought it would be an unforgettable day. And then it was so very ordinary. I remember walking down Long Street, on my way home from work, wondering all the time why it felt just like any other day. Why people weren't dancing in the streets.'

'Because in the end it means fuck-all.' Max gulped his champagne with a grim face. 'What difference does it make if you can marry someone because the Immorality Act has been scrapped – but you still can't live in the same house because the Group Areas Act is still in force? You can't even go swimming together because you're not allowed together on the same beach!'

'Ja,' sighed Adriaan, and scratched in the crackling fire with a piece of wood. An explosion of orange sparks hung high above the flames for a moment like a swarm of fireflies, almost motionless on this warm, still, summer evening. The sun had set only moments ago and the air was gradually becoming a darker grey. They sat on a narrow strip of beach, halfway between the double-storey house they had rented for the weekend and the high-tide mark a few metres further, while small wavelets rolled across the sand with foamy sighs. 'All that I remember of the year is the smell of breast milk in the middle of the night and nappies full of shit in the morning.'

'I tried to warn you,' grinned Philip opposite him. 'The first year of parenthood is hell. After that it gets worse.'

'Nevertheless, it's an experience I wouldn't miss for the world!' Adriaan assured him, his voice heavy with sarcasm. And yet, just beneath the sarcasm, a note of wonder threatened to break through. 'I didn't expect it to be so . . . overwhelming. Such a total onslaught on every sense! Even my imagination is beginning to crack under the strain. When I close my eyes to see a painting, I see flying dummies and melting safety pins. I feel as though I'm caught in one of Salvador Dali's weirdest nightmares.'

'We're all caught in a weird nightmare,' said Max, rubbing his dark beard slowly. 'The longer the State of Emergency continues, the weirder the nightmare gets.'

'Perhaps it's got something to do with Halley's Comet.' Yvette leaned her head back, looking for the next visible star of the evening. 'I mean everything that's happened this year. The State of Emergency here . . . the explosion of the *Challenger* in America . . . Chernobyl in Russia ... People have believed for centuries that comets cause catastrophes.'

'Most of the catastrophes in this country aren't caused by heavenly bodies,' mumbled Max, 'but by earthly arseholes.'

'Who are we talking about now?' asked Philip. 'Political arseholes?'

'Ordinary arseholes,' answered Max. 'Our oumas and oupas. Our own families.'

'I don't know about that,' said Yvette softly. She rested her chin on her knees and folded her arms around her calves. A year ago, Max recalled, her stomach was too big for her to sit like that. 'My ouma was a cheerful fat tannie in a flowered dress. I'd prefer to blame some heavenly body.'

She wore a flowery dress which looked as though it had belonged to that very grandmother. It was wide and buttoned in the front down to the waist, probably a practical outfit for someone who had been dutifully breastfeeding for almost a year. As she'd told Emma earlier that evening, in the proud tones which before she would have used to describe her best illustrations. It made Max wonder, not for the first time, what precisely happened to women's minds when their breasts began producing milk.

'And what about your family, Max?' Philip's face was hidden behind the curtain of smoke which hung heavy and still above the fire, but his voice was unmistakably challenging. Max sipped his champagne carefully. He could guess where Philip was heading, and it bored him already. 'What about your mother who smuggled ANC members out of the country? Is she less guilty than Yvette's cheery ouma who knew nothing about politics? Or is she more guilty because she knew more?'

'Because she lives in a comfortable house in a rich suburb? Because she didn't end up in jail along with Mandela?' Max balanced his glass on the sand between his bare feet and looked at his toes as he spoke. 'I don't know, Philip. And I'm not interested in the question. I was speaking about collective guilt. We're all guilty because we were born here and have benefited our whole lives from an inhuman system.'

'Collective guilt *se moer*,' snorted Philip. 'It's like that old joke about equality. Everyone's equal, but some are more equal than others.'

Max intertwined his fingers around his knees and tried to gauge Philip's expression through the smoke. In the past they could argue for hours about such questions, about degrees of responsibility and definitions of democracy. As though politics was little more than an academic subject, as clinical as mathematics, as abstract as philosophy. As though *people* weren't involved in the fuck-up. In the past, when he'd still tried to hide with Philip behind that smokescreen of scientific objectivity.

'I'm not interested in degrees of guilt,' he said quietly. 'That's academic hairsplitting, not so?'

'But that's what academics are supposed to do! If you can't split hairs you won't be able to split atoms!'

'That's why you're a better academic than I am, Philip. You enjoy sitting drinking tea with all the wankers in your department. Talking about politics as if it's an interesting plant species which you can study under a microscope. Without ever going out to dig up that plant yourself. Without ever getting your hands dirty!'

Without ever showing your face in the townships, Max thought disparagingly. Without ever seeing the clenched fists at a mass funeral, or hearing the ground rumbling under a thousand toyi-toying feet, or smelling the sweaty fear when a crowd is peppered with rubber bullets. Without ever being confronted with the fear on the other side of the truncheons and weapons, on the twisted faces of young white policemen or in the cursing orders of their anxious commanders.

'And you prefer to shout slogans with the students. Trying to tread on the Groot Krokodil's tail. Playing Indiana Jones instead of Mr Chips!'

'I just reached a stage where academic debates began to feel pointless,' said Max as calmly as possible, determined to close off the subject. Liane would be furious if her carefully planned weekend was spoiled right at the start by a political argument. And the rest of the company already looked bored with yet another pointless academic discussion. 'If you ever have the courage to creep out of your ivory tower and attend a few protest meetings – attempt some form of interaction with the political reality of the country – you'll see what I mean.'

'But haven't you become addicted to the adrenalin pumping through your body every time you go to a protest meeting?'

The curtain of smoke had shifted, so that Philip's face was clearly visible for the first time. And yet his expression was still enigmatic – a teasing smile at the corners of his mouth and a serious frown between his brows. He'd always had the ability, thought Max with frustration, to hide his feelings behind a deceptive mask.

'I'd rather be addicted to the adrenalin at a protest meeting,' said Max with a wry smile, 'than to the tea in my departmental staffroom.'

'*Hors-d'oeuvres!*' Liane called out as she walked slowly over the sand towards them, like a bride marching down the aisle, a silver tray with oyster shells and lemon slices held in front of her chest like an enormous bouquet. The yellow light from the open front door behind her shone through her long cream dress and framed her well-formed legs in a golden glow. Paul strolled behind her with a bottle of Pongraz in each hand and a sardonic smile on his lips. With superior amusement, as always, at his wife's theatrical performance. 'Just to whet your appetite for the perlemoen we're going to eat later!'

'Any sound from our bedroom?' Yvette asked anxiously.

'Just relax,' said Adriaan, scratching in the fire. 'You'll hear her from here if she wakes up.'

Even though he too, with a guilty expression, stared up at the bedroom window on the top floor now and then.

'Perlemoen too!' Emma's clear laugh hung in the air for a moment among the shooting sparks. 'Where did you get such a feast?'

'Let's just say that it fell off a lorry,' said Paul as he went to sit between Yvette and Adriaan. 'Or in this case probably from a boat.'

'Paul got it from one of his shady clients,' whispered Liane next to Max. Her drama training ensured that her whisper could be heard all the way up to the house.

'A lawyer never refers to his clients as "shady", Liane,' said Paul with a pained expression. 'No matter how shady they are.'

'I always think that if there is such a thing as heaven, it must be a place where they eat oysters every day,' declared Emma as she stared appreciatively at the oyster in her palm. 'Raw from the shell. I can't imagine that angels and other heavenly creatures would bother much with ovens and washing up.'

'On the contrary!' Adriaan squeezed a few drops of lemon juice over a shell, winkled the smooth oyster out with eager fingers and placed it like a gift on the tip of his tongue. He held the piece of flesh in his mouth for a second, unwilling to let go of the sensuality of the experience, and then swallowed it with a smile. 'My idea of heaven is precisely a place where you could cook the most wonderful food in the universe. A kind of five-star kitchen – no, much more than five stars – a Milky Way kitchen! With pots and pans and knives about which one can only dream on earth!'

'And who washes the dishes?' Emma wanted to know.

'It gets done in hell, of course! A place where lost souls have to wash dishes for ever, continually tortured by the fragrance of those celestial dishes . . .'

'My idea of heaven, at the moment, is any place where I can get a full night's undisturbed rest,' said Yvette with a suppressed yawn.

'And what are we eating for the rest of the weekend?' Emma asked.

'I'm delighted to see that you're paying more attention to the menu than you did when we were in Pick 'n' Pay together,' said Liane sarcastically. 'And seeing that we didn't achieve much more than to discuss your future plans,' she added with a dangerous glint in her eye, 'I asked the rest of them to help with the shopping. Bobby is picking up some crayfish on her way tomorrow and Mila is bringing a box of Mozambique prawns. And on Sunday Adriaan is making his famous paella!'

'Whatever happened to the Tuscan menu?' asked Max with a third oyster in his mouth. 'To celebrate the Tuscan sitting room?'

'Beware,' said Paul. 'This is the kind of conversation which causes divorce.'

'The sitting room looks stunning!' protested Liane without looking at either of them, her eyes on the flames. Her brown hair, longer and smoother than last year, shone in the firelight, the short fringe as straight as a ruler above the frowning brows. 'Even though it didn't turn out Tuscan. It's got more of a North African feel. *Casablanca. The Alexandria Quartet* . . .'

'*Orange is the colour of my true love's walls* . . .' murmured Paul. The dimple in his chin clearly visible.

Yvette dropped her head to her knees and giggled into the folds of her flowery dress.

'Ag, please Paul! The walls aren't such an *awful* orange any more! I tackled it with a sponge, created a weathered effect, like a wall that's peeling. It's the latest trend overseas.' In the dancing light of the flames the frown suddenly looked like a scar between her eyebrows, her nose longer and sharper than usual, her finely chiselled features suddenly witchlike. A startlingly attractive witch nevertheless. 'In a few years everyone's houses will look like that. Mark my words.'

'So we're eating paella on Sunday,' said Max, to save her further embarrassment.

'Seeing that we have all this seafood falling off lorries left, right and centre,' affirmed Adriaan.

'We're still going to need a miracle on the scale of the five loaves and two fishes if Liane's guest list is anything to go by,' warned Paul.

'Ag, Paul! I haven't invited more than twenty people!'

'Over and above the ten already in the house?' asked Yvette, astonished.

'And they won't all arrive,' she added quickly. 'Griet's already phoned to say that she might come without George because they're fighting again. And Louise is so depressed about her divorce that she'll probably stay in bed the whole weekend. And Mart and Tomas will probably forget or get lost or only arrive by next weekend – you know what they're like! Anyway, we can always sit outside in the sun if the house gets too crowded!'

'Don't rely on the sun,' said Paul. 'The weather report doesn't look too good.'

'I stopped relying on weather reports long ago, my darling. And the food is more important than the weather.' She turned to Max and turned on her most dazzling smile. Like a light in the dark, he thought admiringly. Click on, click off. 'I hope you reminded Bobby about the crayfish she's supposed to pick up tomorrow?'

'I wouldn't rely too much on that, either. Her head's like a sieve these days. Last week she forgot about an End Conscription meeting she'd organized herself.'

'Is that what love has done to her?'

'At this stage, of course, we don't know if it's love or just plain lust. Her lover's just moved in with her. That's why she can't be with us tonight.'

'I'd also stay at home if I could screw the night away,' muttered Adriaan, his pipe clenched between his teeth.

'Isn't it a bit soon?' asked Emma.

'It's never to soon to screw the night away.'

'No, I mean to live together! How long has this affair been going on?'

'Surely you don't expect everyone to wait as long as you and Philip before they move in any direction?'

'Well . . .' Emma dropped her head so fast that her hair fell like a stage curtain on either side of her face.

'*Well?*' said Liane and gave Philip a meaningful glance.

'Well?' Philip frowned like a child who'd been caught not listening to the teacher. 'Oh. Is that what you're talking about? OK, then I suppose I'll have to confess. I've asked her to marry me.'

'*What?*' asked Yvette, astounded.

'To protect her honour,' he added quickly.

'I'd have burst if I had to keep that secret the whole weekend!' exclaimed Liane.

'How come I know nothing about this?' asked Yvette, still astonished, and now feeling a bit insulted as well.

'Or perhaps I just gave in to her friends' emotional blackmail,' said Philip with a shrug.

'Do you mean to tell me you *knew*?' Paul stared at his wife with disbelieving admiration. 'And you managed to keep quiet about it?'

'Just for two days!' laughed Liane. 'I wouldn't have managed for much longer!'

'The age of miracles is truly not yet past!' exclaimed Adriaan.

'I don't know what the greatest miracle is,' said Paul, shaking his head. 'Philip's astonishing decision to get married – or Liane's astonishing ability to keep a secret.'

'Et tu, Brute?' muttered Max. 'Are you also deserting the sinking ship of swinging bachelors?'

'I was never on that ship,' grinned Philip. 'But I know the sinking feeling you're talking about. Remember, I spent years on a sinking marital ship.'

'And you're ready to get on the boat again. I take my hat off to you, comrade!'

'What can a man do?' Philip said, raising his palms helplessly.

'Pour the Pongraz, Paul!' Adriaan boomed, and raised his glass with a dramatic gesture. 'It's an opportunity for a toast! Or at least a moment of sympathetic silence.'

'I can't believe it,' said Yvette, still astounded, but by this time at least smilingly so.

The only one who remained staring motionlessly at the flames while further cries of surprise and congratulation flew back and forth over the fire – so exuberantly that no one heard the baby crying on the top floor – was Emma. Her face still hidden behind her glowing hair, her expression still an enigma.

It was the morning-after thirst which chased Max out of bed early, the kind of thirst which made you feel as if your tongue had changed overnight into a foul-smelling sand dune, the inside of your mouth like a beach polluted with rotten seaweed and redbait. And a hammering headache, he realized as he stumbled blindly in the direction of the kitchen, cursing himself. Philip's reckless decision to get married had allowed his own suppressed recklessness to burst through the respectable surface. And now his body was making him understand quite plainly that he was too old for such irresponsible excess.

Only when he opened the tap above the sink full of greasy dishes did he hear the whispering women's voices outside the house. He touched his arm, confused in the dark room, then remembered that he had dropped his watch next to the bed the previous night, and wondered for a moment whether he wasn't still drunk. Perhaps he was hallucinating, perhaps he was hearing the imaginary voices of mermaids or mountain nymphs. Or perhaps he was just dreaming that he was standing here in the kitchen, he thought hopefully; perhaps in reality he was still sleeping in his bed.

He drained a glass of water in one thirsty gulp and ran another from the tap. He was indeed awake, he decided, and it couldn't be later than six o'clock. Why would anyone be sitting on the back stoep talking at this time? He recognized Liane's voice as he drank the second glass more slowly. Whispering like an actress who wanted to ensure that the back row of the audience could hear. He took a few steps closer, the glass still in his hand, and heard how Mila tried to suppress her husky laugh. A seductive sound, even so early in the morning. She and Ralph were supposed to have left Johannesburg the night before to drive here through the night, but he had only expected them much later. Then he heard something which sounded like a cork being pulled from a bottle, followed by little moaning sounds and clicking tongue noises, then by a silence of intense satisfaction. It must be the baby who'd fallen from her mother's breast for a moment. That explained why Yvette at least was already awake. Mila had probably not yet slept: her whispering voice had the rushed excitability of someone who'd drunk too much coffee or sniffed too much cocaine. And Liane, well, Liane had always got up ridiculously early.

' . . . not at all ready for it!' whispered Liane. Anxiously.

'I'm ready, I realized this year.' That must be Mila. 'The problem is finding the right man.'

'And Ralph isn't the right man,' whispered Yvette.

It sounded like a statement rather than a question – which surprised him so much that he took a step closer. Somewhere at the back of his mind, in conflict with the hammer blows in his head, he felt the twinge of a guilty conscience. He'd always been fascinated by women's conversations, by what women spoke about when they were on their own. Perhaps because as a child he had never had the chance to listen to what his mother viewed as 'idle chatter'. Because his mother, unlike other mothers, didn't speak to friends about 'trifles'. When Lida Ackermann let her voice drop – or closed the kitchen door behind her – the subject was never anything exciting like sex or women's secrets. When she wanted to stop her son from hearing what she said, he immediately lost interest. It would be yet another boring political discussion. The Big P, as his reserved father called it. Sometimes joking, sometimes irritated. A friend who had to leave the country, someone who was in contact with someone in jail . . .

'Why not?' Liane sounded almost as surprised as he was. 'Wouldn't he want to?'

'It's not that he doesn't want to.' A heavy sigh from Mila. 'I don't think he *can*. I think he must have an extraordinarily low sperm count!'

Shocked silence. Now it was too late to let them know that he was standing just behind them, Max realized with a growing feeling of panic, his headache suddenly forgotten. Trapped.

'Earlier this year I did the most unbelievably idiotic thing,' admitted Mila with another heavy sigh. 'I don't know, I think the State of Emergency affected my reason – or else my biological clock began to tick so loudly in my head that I went mad – but I took my IUD out without telling him. And worked out when I was ovulating and made sure that I slept with him that night. And the previous night and the next night too. Just to be sure. And I did it for a few months. We're not talking about a moment of weakness here, we're speaking about long-lasting madness! I was just so unbelievably *gatvol* of politics, but I was too scared to leave the newspaper! What the hell do I have left in my life if you take my job away? Then I thought if I got pregnant . . .'

Another loaded silence, with the baby's greedy sucking as the only accompaniment.

'And then you didn't get pregnant,' said Yvette softly.

'No. Then I got pregnant. That's what sorted me out. I slept with another man – someone who was only in Johannesburg for a few days, one of those seventy-two-hour affairs with absolutely no hope of a future – then I got pregnant. Now I sound like a heroine in one of those fucking photo-stories! They're always such pathetic virgins who get knocked up by totally unattainable men!'

This time her joyless laugh was not a seductive sound. And her friends didn't laugh with her.

'And then?' whispered Liane.

'Then I miscarried again.'

Her voice scraped through the silence like a piece of chalk being dragged across a blackboard. He didn't hear the sucking noises any more, Max realized. It was as though even the baby was listening to her in amazement.

'Again?' whispered Yvette.

'I had a miscarriage years ago . . . when I "had" to get married.' The shuffling sound of a cigarette being pulled from a packet, a lighter which clicked a few times, followed by a deep drawing of breath. 'Jesus, I hate myself when I smoke so early in the morning. It wasn't the State of Emergency which made me crave nicotine again, Liane. It was that miscarriage. Ag, one always has to have an excuse, hey? The only good thing was that it happened so early in the pregnancy. Before I told anyone. I mean, I toyed with the idea of telling Ralph it was *his* child! Can you fucking imagine? Luckily fate foiled all my devious little plans.'

'What happened to the real father?' asked Yvette.

'I suppose he's still around somewhere . . .'

'And there's no chance that he could be the right man?'

'Ha! No, he was just another one of my totally unavailable and totally unattainable fantasy lovers. I'm going to make more coffee. Who wants . . .'

Max didn't hear any more. The scraping of her chair's legs on the stoep tiles gave him the chance to flee into the dark passage in three giant leaps, where he had to fumble around in confusion to find the knob on his bedroom door. It was with a whirlwind of emotions that he sank down into his bed again: enormous relief that he hadn't been caught eavesdropping on his female friends, deep disappointment in his own moral character – whatever will I do next, he wondered in disgust, spy on them undressing? – intense discomfort over what he had heard. And yet, in spite of everything, an inexplicable, childish excitement.

So that's what women spoke about when they were on their own. About sex and men. Just as he'd always imagined.

Bobby ate with the complete concentration of someone who has been starved for weeks, unaware that Liane and Mila, on either side of her, were staring at her in fascination. She tore off a crayfish claw, put it in her mouth and crunched it open between her teeth, pulled the strip of pure white flesh out and chewed greedily as she licked her fingers, quickly picked up her fork to spear a slice of tomato and a lettuce leaf, glistening with olive oil, and lifted it to her lips. Unaware of everything around her, even of Mona, who waddled around in front of her on uncertain baby feet and tried to grab her plate with plump baby fingers.

Liane wondered if it was love which gave her such an amazing appetite. Or perhaps just good sex, as Max suspected. Funny, but when *she* fell in love, her appetite was always the first victim. Love and cold water were all she'd ever needed, from that first, ecstatic school holiday when she'd come to know Max, up until now. Well, until she'd met Paul. She felt an unexpected surge of melancholy, wallowed in it for a few moments. Seeing that she'd been happily married for almost two years (or as happily as anyone could hope to be once the original excitement has blown over), she was probably not supposed to wonder if she would ever experience that ecstatic state again. Then her attention was distracted by the way in which Bobby wiped up a pool of olive oil on her plate with a bread crust, swallowed the crust with a couple of lettuce leaves and licked the remaining oil from her lips. It was impossible to be melancholy while a performance of such gastronomic enjoyment was played out before your eyes.

They were eating outside, a sheltered corner at the side of the house, where they could feel the heat of the sun – every time it broke through the fleecy clouds – without being disturbed by the wind which had come up unexpectedly a few hours earlier. Or perhaps not so unexpectedly. Her husband had already looked at her with those characteristic raised eyebrows a few times. *If only you'd listened to the weather report.* The possibility that her birthday dinner tomorrow might be spoiled by bad weather began to look all the more likely.

'Leave Bobby alone so she can concentrate on her food!' Mila stretched her arms out eagerly to Mona, but the child clung stubbornly to Bobby's bony knee. 'What does Bobby have that I don't have?'

'Children are just like cats,' Bobby explained with her mouth full of bread. 'The less attention you pay them, the more attractive you become to them. Just more evidence that we're basically all born perverse. They're always crazy about me because I ignore them.'

'Don't you like children?' Mila asked, surprised.

'They probably don't taste too bad with tomato sauce,' smiled Bobby. 'But I like cats more.'

'Da!' Mona had at last succeeded in getting hold of a lettuce leaf from Bobby's plate and was now insisting on feeding her. 'Da! Da! Da!'

Bobby rolled her eyes and opened her mouth obediently. Liane studied her with a professional eye to pinpoint why she looked so much better than a year ago. It wasn't as though she'd deliberately changed anything about her appearance. Alas! The same multi-coloured, eclectic clothing, style-less enough for her to be taken seriously at political gatherings; the same short, curly hair which would benefit from a visit to a good hair salon; the same wise, wistful eyes, the eyes of a much older person, hidden these days behind round wire-framed spectacles which didn't exactly flatter her either. And yet her face, without make-up as usual, had gained a rosy glow, her hair a golden sheen, her eyes an unmistakable sparkle. A year ago one could have described her as 'plain-with-potential', but now it was as though a fire had been lit somewhere inside her, an inner glow which had melted the plainness away. If she took off those stupid glasses, she'd actually look like the young Ingrid Bergman.

'Is there some ulterior motive behind all this seafood?' asked Mila, a piece of crayfish tail in her mouth.

'What do you mean?' asked Liane.

'I mean, if it's true that seafood is good for the libido, we'll be chasing each other around the furniture by tomorrow.'

'Perhaps we have overdone it a bit,' admitted Liane, giggling. 'Philip has already said if we don't braai some meat tonight for a change, he'll start getting withdrawal symptoms.'

'*Remember, I'm a boerseun from South West!*' Bobby called out in an offended tone, as Philip had earlier. '*I can't live without red meat without losing my self-respect!*'

To which Max had responded, as Philip had known he would, by declaring that South West was a wind direction. 'And seeing that your country will soon be independent,' he added, like a street preacher threatening the unconverted with the Second Coming, 'you may as well begin practising saying *Namibia*.' At which Philip, unconverted to the bitter end, just laughed. Liane had always suspected that Philip and Max's joking scorn for each other was just a way of disguising the intensity of a very old, very close friendship, a friendship which could bridge any gap in politics or personality, more like brothers than friends. But sometimes she wondered if they still belonged in the same circle of friends at all.

'Well, if I'm to take Emma's word for it,' said Mila with a mysterious smile, 'Philip doesn't need seafood anyway. They've apparently got this amazing sex life, despite all the arguments. Or perhaps as a result of the arguments. How does that song go again? The one about what a satisfied woman can do?'

Mona looked at Mila, her attention drawn away from Bobby's plate for the first time, her mouth open in a dribbly smile. 'Do-o-o,' she cooed as well.

'The next Barbra Streisand,' mumbled Bobby.

'I thought you were too young to know about Barbra Streisand!' Now it was Mila's turn to look surprised. 'I'd forgotten that these days you're also a satisfied woman.'

'Of course, we're all dying to hear more,' said Liane quickly, before anyone could change the subject.

Mona waddled over to Mila. It was astounding how much she looked like Adriaan, Liane realized again; not just the colour of her eyes and skin and hair, but even the shape of the laughing mouth, full of dormant sensual promise, the confident carriage of the sturdy little body, the way in which the fat little baby hands grasped at you as though they weren't going to let you go again.

'What do you want to hear?' grinned Bobby.

'Everything,' said Liane. 'Begin at the beginning.'

'An excellent place to start,' said Mila, her eyes on Mona.

'Where did you meet him?'

'Meet *her*.' Bobby burst out laughing when she saw the confusion on Liane's face. 'Don't tell me you didn't know!'

'It's a *woman*? I mean, not that it matters,' she added quickly. And then, flustered, 'It's just that . . . I didn't know . . . no one told me.'

That's how it felt, she remembered, when as a child she sat cross-legged with the other children, playing rotten egg. That terrible embarrassment when she realized that she was the only one in the group who didn't know that the stone had been dropped behind her back. Rotten egg. She looked at Mila questioningly, but Mila showed no surprise. And yet her smile seemed suddenly a little tense.

'Her name is Robin,' said Bobby, nibbling thoughtfully on a crayfish tail, the worst of her hunger apparently satisfied. 'Perhaps that's what made you think she was a man?'

'No . . . I can't remember if anyone said her name . . . I don't know,' stammered Liane.

The truth, she knew, was that she had simply assumed that Bobby's lover would be a man. Nothing in her attitude or appearance had made her suspect that she was . . . Well, Bobby wasn't butch, was she?

'She's English and quite a bit older than me and has been involved in the Struggle a lot longer than I have. Imprisoned and tortured and all those things. But you'd never guess it if you saw her. It's as though she radiates a peacefulness, a kind of goodness, something almost . . . angelic. Don't laugh! I don't know how to explain it without sounding corny!'

'No, I'm not laughing,' Liane said quickly.

The possibility that Bobby was in love with an angel could hardly astonish her more than the mere fact that she was in love with a woman.

'She's really amazing,' said Bobby. 'The other day I said to her that she had the heart of a saint. Then she said luckily she didn't have the hormones of a saint!'

'Ah!' said Mila, relieved. 'I was just thinking it was all getting a bit mystical for me. So you've at least got a proper sex life?'

'Not necessarily,' said Bobby with an impish smile. 'But then who wants a *proper* sex life?'

'Blessed are you among women!' Mila lifted Mona's plump body on to her lap. The child stared at her with admiring grey-green eyes, almost as her father had looked at Mila a year ago.

Liane took a bite of crayfish and chewed slowly on the soft white flesh. Which suddenly tasted like paper. Confused thoughts and strange emotions blew like leaves through her mind. Strange leaves from strange trees. It's not that she had a moral problem with . . . alternative sex. Goodness gracious, she wasn't that naïve! In the circles she moved in as a stylist, it was so common that her relatively 'normal' sex life sometimes felt abnormal. It was just that she hadn't expected it, she assured herself. That she felt caught out. Rotten egg.

'Why didn't you tell me about Bobby's lover?' Liane asked furiously, the moment she managed to catch Max alone.

He gave no sign that he'd heard her. It was as though the angry wind had wrenched the words from her mouth before she had the chance to form them properly. It had been Adriaan's idea to go for a walk along the beach, but by this time it felt more like a struggle for survival than an innocent stroll. The wind blew at gale force so that her straining body was blocked by an invisible wall with every step. Grains of sand flew like fine hail against her legs, whipping her hands, blinding her. Mila, Ralph and Adriaan were walking at the front of the outstretched line, fast and furiously, as though they were competing with each other to reach some secret destination first; Max and Liane followed a little way behind at a fairly steady pace; Bobby and Philip and Paul formed the struggling rearguard, heads low and faces grim, determined to brave the torture in dignified silence. Emma had eagerly offered to stay at home with Yvette and the baby. As anyone with any sense should have done, thought Liane resentfully. She opened her mouth to repeat her question, throwing her words into the wind with all her might.

'Why didn't you warn me about Bobby's lover?'

'What about Bobby's lover?'

She glared at him mistrustfully.

'That she's a *woman*! Why didn't you tell me?'

For a moment he looked genuinely surprised. Then his black eyes vanished in a nest of laugh lines.

'I thought you knew!'

'How was I supposed to know! Not so long ago you were still trying to get her into your bed!'

'You can probably deduce that I . . .'

His laughing mouth formed the rest of the sentence, but she could only see his lips move.

84

'What?'

'That I didn't . . .' Another bubble of inaudible words in his wind-blown beard. 'Otherwise she'd never have . . .'

'All that I know, Max, is that I felt like an absolute *idiot* when I heard!'

'Why?' He walked with his hands pushed deep into the pockets of his threadbare jeans, his broad shoulders bent forward in an off-white cable-knit jersey. 'What does it matter . . . someone's lover . . . looks different . . . you had imagined her?'

'Imagined *him*!'

'What does it matter, Liane? You're not the sort . . . to condemn the relationship . . .'

'Please, Max! Spare me the moral message! That's not what I'm talking about!'

'What *are* you talking about?'

'I'm speaking about my own stupidity! Because the possibility of a female lover didn't even cross my mind! It's like my father, who loudly declares that South Africa is the most wonderful country in the world – the only country he'll ever live in – when he's never even been anywhere else! It's so terribly . . . *bourgeois*!'

'I thought you'd made peace . . .' His eyes teasing, his lips moving soundlessly. 'Irredeemably bourgeois?'

'It's easy to say you're bourgeois! It's like saying you're fat and ugly – when you actually think you don't really look too bad. And now my nose has been well and truly rubbed in my own middle-class mentality. Now I've seen how far my bourgeois petticoat still sticks out!'

'I don't know why you upset yourself so much,' said Max, shaking his head. 'It's not important what sex Bobby's lover is . . . or what sex you thought she was.'

Because his hair was so windblown, and because he had to walk with his head bent so far forward to protect his eyes against the blast, she noticed for the first time that he was beginning to go bald. A patch on his crown where the skin was clearly visible under a thin layer of black hair. Her heart suddenly kicked against her chest.

Every time she spotted the unmistakable track of approaching age on one of her contemporary's bodies, it upset her more than when she felt the cold breath of old age on her own neck. As if she were more afraid of being left alone than of dying. As if the possibility of her own death remained completely and utterly far-fetched. Probably just another example of her lack of imagination.

She lifted her head for a moment, felt the wind hammer against her eyelids, and saw that Mila was now marching on her own at the front of the group. Her long dress flapping in the wind, walking stick in one hand, chin lifted resolutely, eyes on the horizon. Moses leading the struggling Israelites through the desert. As though she wasn't going to let anything stand in her way, not the angry wind, nor the impassable rocks which blocked the beach in the distance. If she couldn't walk further along the beach, she would simply lift her stick to divide the stormy waves.

In the meantime, the struggling rearguard had lagged even further behind. They were probably planning to turn around quietly and sneak back to the house. AWOL, like soldiers fed up with marching.

'When did you find out?' she asked when the wind had died down a little. 'That Bobby . . .'

'Well, she never really made a secret of it. I always had the idea that she wouldn't mind sleeping with a woman. Or had already done it, but wouldn't necessarily rule men out. I was always aware of a kind of ambivalence. The way in which she looked at men *and* women. I must admit that I found it quite exciting.'

'And now?' The wind had begun to rage with force again. A boxer who had just stopped to catch his breath before he tackled the next round with fresh aggression. It felt as though she had to force her voice through a choking band around her throat. 'Do you think she's decided which side of the fence she wants to be on?'

Max's smile crept slowly out from his beard to the crinkles round his eyes.

'I think she would ask why one can't be on both sides . . .'

'So you reckon you've still got a chance of getting her into bed?'

'Now that I know her better . . . she sounded more experienced than she actually was . . . like a horny schoolboy who constantly talks about sex to hide his lack of experience. Not that she constantly talked . . . you know what I mean . . . I wonder if she'd even slept with anyone before Robin . . .'

'You mean she was a *virgin*?'

'It's not impossible!'

'A twenty-four-year-old virgin?'

'Look, if you're uncertain about your sexuality . . . basically two options . . . screw everything that moves . . . or you stay completely chaste . . . hope that the future will bring clarity . . . I think she'd pick the second option . . . a total nerd at school . . . Not the sort who'd run through all the rugby players in the first team.'

'Or all the netball players,' mumbled Liane, more to herself than to Max. 'Well, that would explain why she is so completely bowled over by this *angelic* Robin! Remember that Cat Stevens song which you always sang to me? "The First Cut is the Deepest"?'

He dropped his head as if his neck had suddenly been snapped by the wind. She wished she could reach out her hand, touch his shoulder or cheek, as she could touch him long ago. A gesture of comfort, friendship, trust in this terrible wind which had turned any other form of communication into a struggle. But it would probably have made them feel even more like two stammering, clumsy teenagers.

'And how do you like sleeping with an older woman?' Liane asked when she got into bed and laid her head, as usual, on her husband's left shoulder.

'I'm getting used to the idea,' Paul answered, stroking her hair.

She looked at his profile in the light of the lamp which shone on his side of the bed, the narrow nose and strong chin with the little hollow which she loved to run her finger over, the Adam's apple in his suntanned neck, the sturdy chest under her open hand. She rubbed the few hairs on his nipples, so familiar underneath her fingertips that she would certainly be able to identify him by his chest alone were she suddenly to be struck blind. She was always glad that he wasn't a hairy man, that she could feel him like a piece of sculpture, could feel the texture of his skin, sometimes smooth and cool like marble, sometimes rougher and warmer, like unglazed clay.

'Thirty.' She rolled the word carefully on her tongue. Like a strange dish which she was tasting for the first time.

'Does that make you feel old and unwanted?'

'Not unwanted. Not while I can fall asleep on your shoulder. But old, yes,' she admitted with a little sigh.

The bedroom reminded her of a hotel room. Not the shabby platteland hotels of her youthful holidays, but the identical, impersonal, shiny rooms of a modern hotel chain. Bedspread and curtains of the same patterned material, identical bed tables and lamps on either side of the bed, the carpet that colourless colour which she could only describe as 'hotel grey'. She had always been over-sensitive to décor, she thought, dissatisfied. Colour schemes and ugly furniture could affect her mood like the moon affected other people's. Perhaps that was the only explanation for this sudden tightness in her chest. As though she were struggling to breathe.

'Didn't you say the other day that you weren't afraid of growing old?'

'It's not age that frightens me. I think I can cope with wrinkles and a sagging body and a weak bladder and all the other indignities. I'm not that vain . . .'

'On the contrary. I've always thought you were astoundingly un-vain for someone blessed with your looks.'

He turned his face to her, his brown eyes appraising and at the same time teasing under his long lashes, like a fighter weighing up his opponent. She would always remember the first time he looked at her like that, the first time he took her clothes off and explored her body, the indescribable excitement somewhere deep inside her. She stroked his stomach slowly, still as muscular as when she had first met him (perhaps even more muscular, as he worked out in the gym regularly these days), moving her hand slowly until it was under the elastic of the shorts he slept in. Each movement felt smooth and practised. But in a pleasant way.

'But I can't cope with the thought of dying,' she murmured with her cheek against his chest, his heartbeat a soothing sound under her ear. 'And I can't really make my peace with old age before I've made my peace with death. The two kind of go together, don't they?'

'Listen, Liane, do you want to make love or do you want to speak about death? I'm afraid you'll have to choose. I can't do both at once.'

She laughed self-consciously and wriggled a nest for her fingers in the bushy hair of his groin. Her hand felt at home here too, she thought, while his penis stirred under her light touch. He'd moved his arm under her T-shirt and drew a line with his index finger along her spine, making her break out in gooseflesh from head to toe. As always. And yet it was as though there was something wrong tonight, as though the excitement remained superficial, limited to her skin. She waited in vain for the usual warmth low in her belly, the moistness between her legs, the uncontrollable thudding of her heart.

'Did you know that Bobby's lover was a woman?' she asked frowning, and lifted her head from his shoulder.

'No. But I wasn't terribly surprised when I heard.'

'Why not?'

'I don't know.' His hand, which had moved from her back to her chest, grew still. 'It's probably just something you sense? Without realizing you've sensed it?'

'It seems I'm the only person in this whole group of friends who was surprised to hear it!' She couldn't keep the indignation from her voice, she realized helplessly.

'No, I think that some people just hide their surprise better than others.' He reached out his hand to switch off the light and turned his body towards her in the darkness. She could hear from his voice that he was smiling. 'Forget about it now. It's not that important.'

'Why does everyone keep telling me it's not important! Of course it's important whether you want a penis or a vagina in bed with you!'

'Why does it upset you so much?' he asked, bewildered.

'Because I didn't know! Not because she's *lesbian*, you understand, but because I'd assumed that she wasn't lesbian!'

She felt him shaking his head in the darkness. Of course he didn't understand. She couldn't even understand why she was going on like this. She only knew she was frightened, and the fact that she didn't have the faintest idea why she was frightened made it even worse. Her husband's shoulder was suddenly tense under her cheek, his penis limp next to her hand, all sexual desire clearly snuffed out. But she suppressed her disappointment and comforted herself that she wasn't in the right mood anyway.

Just before she fell asleep, she wondered if it wasn't something to do with her thirtieth birthday. If she hadn't reached the beginning of the end of her sex life. And yet, despite this disturbing thought, she dozed off without any trouble. With her head, as always, on her husband's left shoulder.

While he lay for a long time staring into the darkness.

Liane and Max burst through the front door, panting and glistening with sweat. Emma and Mila, who were drinking coffee at the counter between the kitchen and the sitting room, looked up in surprise. Ralph, breaking eggs over a mixing bowl on the kitchen side of the counter, frowned as though they were disturbing his concentration.

'Was that really necessary?' Mila asked indignantly. 'To go jogging on the Day of Rest?'

Max stumbled past her to the sink, too tired to answer, and ran a large glass of water. His black hair clung wet against his head and his hairy chest shone darkly through a sweat soaked T-shirt with a slogan in shrieking red letters: *Workers of the World Unite!* Liane fell on her back on the couch, but managed to laugh breathlessly.

'Can't you forget about your lovely bodies for just one day?' Emma pulled her packet of cigarettes closer, overcome with a perverse desire to do something unhealthy, to protest against this obscene chasing after fitness so early in the morning. 'Even if it is only to make the rest of us feel better.'

'It was Liane's idea,' said Max, greedily gulping down the water.

'Of course,' said Emma and lit a cigarette.

'She had an anxiety attack earlier this morning about The Big O.'

'The Big Orgasm?' Mila asked in amazement.

'Old Age!' laughed Liane, her breathing now a little more measured. 'I just decided that it was time I began to do something to my body. Before it's too late.'

'Then she came and pulled me out of bed to jog to Johannesburg and back quickly,' moaned Max.

'If there's anyone among us who *doesn't* need to do anything to her body,' said Emma sighing, 'it's you, Liane.'

'What's wrong with *my* body?' asked Ralph.

Emma leaned over the counter and looked critically at Ralph's tall body. He pulled his stomach in and pushed his chest out, which made him look like a puffed up pigeon. A comical picture in garish shorts which hung down to his knees and a T-shirt printed with Andy Warhol's famous image of a soup can.

'Not bad,' she said mockingly. 'But you work on your body, Ralph. You swim and row and cycle and what the hell else. You earn your body in the sweat of your brow. Liane's apparently fell from heaven. She doesn't go to the gym, she doesn't exercise, she eats what she likes, it's just not fair!'

'Exactly,' said Liane earnestly. 'I can't go on like this! I've always thought my metabolism probably works faster than anyone else's, I don't need to punish myself with exercise and diets and so on. But I got a fright when I heard myself wheezing this morning!'

'But you tried to run a bloody marathon!' Max sat next to Mila on a bar stool. 'Anyone else would have collapsed half way!'

'And if you think thirty is old . . .' Mila stared at her coffee mug like a fortune teller reading dark omens on the bottom. A dejected twist to her mouth, despite the slogan on her T-shirt: *Wild Women Don't Get the Blues*. 'You ain't seen nothing yet. That's all I can say.'

'Ag, I suppose I'll get used to it.' Liane stood up from the couch and walked over to the counter. 'Anyway, it's a *stunning* day! The prophets of doom were wrong again. The clouds have vanished, the wind's died down, the sea is glittering! I don't know what you're all doing in this stuffy house!'

'Have you forgotten about the hungry hordes who have to be fed this afternoon?' Ralph stopped stirring for a moment and lifted the bowl so she could see the creamy yellow mixture in it. 'Adriaan was worried that the paella wouldn't be enough for your extensive guest list, so I decided to make aïoli as a starter.'

'What would I do without my friends in the kitchen!' she exclaimed gratefully.

'Your male friends in the kitchen,' said Mila. 'I get the impression that most of your female friends don't spend too much time in kitchens.'

'We have other talents,' said Emma.

'Like?' asked Max sceptically.

'It's true, you know,' said Liane thoughtfully. 'If there's one thing which distinguishes my friends from my parents' friends – I mean more than all the obvious things like politics or musical taste or dress sense – it's the fact that almost all the men cook better than their fathers.'

'We don't have a choice,' muttered Ralph. 'It's because the women all cook worse than their mothers.'

'But we're better in bed than our mothers,' Mila said. 'You can't have everything.'

'Even Philip can cook eggs and read a recipe,' laughed Emma. 'His father couldn't even make a cup of tea when his mother died. That's probably the biggest reason why he married again so quickly. The poor man had to choose between death by starvation or marriage in indecent haste.'

'And Philip still thinks that death by starvation would have been the honourable choice,' Max remarked.

Emma opened her mouth as though she wanted to say something, but got no further than a mournful smile. Her hair was standing up like an untrimmed hedge about her head, the orange-brown curls far too bright against the purple T-shirt on which shocking pink angels spread their gilded wings. Quite an interesting array of T-shirts around this kitchen counter, Liane decided. Her own sweaty version, a stretched grey Calvin Klein number which had once belonged to her husband, looked utterly unimaginative in comparison.

At that moment Bobby walked in through the back door, loaded with plastic bags full of groceries, a Sunday paper clamped awkwardly under one arm. *Children Need Peace*, declared her T-shirt, the letters formed by cheerful pastel pictures of children in a variety of playful positions.

'Ah, here come the vegetables for the aïoli!' announced Ralph, and took some of the plastic bags from her hands. 'You were gone for so long that I wondered if you hadn't quickly driven back to Cape Town to see your new lover . . .'

He stopped talking, bewildered, when he saw her expression.

'Rashid's been murdered,' she said, and dumped the paper down in front of Max. Her eyelids were pink and puffy behind the little round glasses. 'They shot him in front of his own house. On his garden path.'

Max's stupefied gaze moved from her face to the report on the front page.

'Rashid Essop?' Mila asked anxiously, and began to read the report with Max.

'The lawyer in the Langa case?' Ralph put his arm comfortingly around Bobby's bony shoulders. 'Did you know him well?'

'He's a good friend of Robin's. I called her from a phone box. She's completely . . . completely . . .'

She pressed her face into the hollow under his arm and began to cry, her shoulders shaking.

'The fuckers!' Max exploded, his face white with shock above his black beard, his eyes glowing with rage. 'The bloody fuckers!'

'How many assassinations have there been now?' asked Emma in dismay.

'It just doesn't stop,' Mila mumbled, shaking her head.

'And it won't stop until we see the end of this fucking government!' Max raged on. 'Until all these fuckers have been kicked out of parliament!'

Liane was the only one who remained speechless. The only one who didn't know who Rashid Essop was. Once again the rotten egg in the circle, she realized, bewildered. It couldn't go on like this. She would simply have to open her eyes, look beyond the orange walls of her sitting room, begin to notice what was happening around her.

Just before lunch the crowded living room sounded like a noisy pub. Max stood to one side in the kitchen with his back to the fridge door, as if he wanted to protect the remaining supplies of cold beer against the plundering hordes, and surveyed the room in a detached way. The same impersonal appearance as the bedrooms, as if the furniture had all been bought on the same day in some chain store. Even the prints on the walls (watercolours of whitewashed fishermen's cottages) and the stack of books on the coffee table (big illustrated books with glossy blue-green jackets) looked as though they had only been provided to match the colour scheme.

He let his eyes wander over Liane's guests, his mood a strange mixture of frightening alienation, cynical fascination and enjoyable maudlin drunkenness. The buzzing of the voices grew louder and softer in his ears, louder and softer, like when you play with the volume controls of a radio. There must be something wrong with his ears, he thought. The news about Rashid Essop's death must have disturbed his equilibrium. He had to lean against the fridge to stay on his feet.

It wasn't grief which had made him reach for the first of many bottles of beer a few hours earlier. He didn't know Rashid well enough to be personally struck by his death. It was rage. Blinding, choking, overwhelming rage. *The fuckers.* And despair. *God knows how long it will go on.* How many more illegal gatherings did he have to attend, how many emotional trials, how many heartbreaking funerals? If he believed in God, he thought with a bitter smile, he would have stood here praying. *God, protect me from rage and despair, against raging despair, against despairing rage . . .*

'And what are you standing here smiling for?' Bobby suddenly asked in front of him.

'I'm not smiling, I'm praying.' He quickly downed the bottle in his hand and took two more beers from the fridge. Gave one to her. 'Funny, hey, but the day you decide to drink till you're pissed, it's never as easy as when it just happens.'

'Liane's spent weeks organizing this party, Max.' Bobby's grey eyes stared accusingly at him. 'Don't you think it's a bit selfish to drink yourself into a stupor on purpose?'

Adriaan's bellowing laugh rose up outside the back door. He had decided to make the paella outside on the barbecue rather than in the stuffy kitchen. Now he was playing his usual role as court jester to the group of guests keeping him company.

'Liane lives in another world.' Max waved his bottle in the air to encompass the whole noisy gathering and poured foam on his feet. 'You and I know it's not reality.'

'What is reality, Max?' Her eyes looked sadder than ever before. 'The privileged academic existence which you and I lead while we fool ourselves that we mean something to the Struggle? A brilliant young lawyer who is shot on his own garden path? The black woman who was necklaced the other day in Nyanga while a TV camera immortalized every gruesome second of her flaming death? What the fuck is reality for the man who stood behind that camera? I mean, if that's his reality, can you imagine what his nightmares must look like! What does that man dream about at night?'

'He probably can't afford to dream.'

'I don't know if anyone in the country can still afford to dream. What about the millionaire's wife who was raped and murdered last week in Bishopscourt – by the gardener who had worked for her for twenty years? What was *her* reality? Definitely not the same as the gardener's! There is no such thing as "reality" in this country. Just different versions of madness and self-delusion.'

In the newspaper with the report on Rashid's death, Max remembered, there was a quote from Bishop Desmond Tutu. He'd read the two sentences over and over again to understand them, like at night when you fall asleep over a book, the pathetic way you try to grasp a last sentence before you tumble down into your own subconscious. He couldn't process the words because his mind had got stuck on an image of a bloodied body on a cement pathway, the brilliant brain blown open in a herbaceous border, the attractive face in the soil, bloodstains on snapped ranunculus. But now it was as though a door in his memory had been thrown open, as though every word of the quote was suddenly brilliantly lit, clearly visible, unerasable. '*I believe we are a whisker from catastrophe in our country*,' the servant of God had said. '*We are on the verge of a disaster of monumental proportions*.' If the faithful began to sound despairing, then an unbelieving soul probably had no chance of escaping despair.

'What I don't understand,' he said, 'is how some people manage not to be destroyed by all this madness. People like Desmond Tutu, like your beloved Robin, like my own bloody mother! How they can simply go on, against all odds, day after day and year after year, trying to push a bloody rock up a bloody mountain!'

'I've also wondered about that.' She swallowed her beer thoughtfully, her eyes again on Liane's laughing, chatting guests. 'The Struggle probably needs angels and devils. We're the screwed-up devils, you and me, full of rage and vengeful thoughts. We need angels like them to protect us against acts of madness . . .'

'Is this the philosophers' corner?' asked Ralph, who had come to fetch another bottle of wine from the fridge. 'I don't know how you manage to preserve your dignity while this astounding superficiality rages all around you.'

'I feel as though I need a good dose of superficiality to help me through the day,' sighed Bobby.

He studied her for a moment, his expression teasing and yet sympathetic, and then gathered her into his arms, as he'd done earlier when she'd begun to cry. This time she just smiled gratefully.

'I didn't know you were such a comforting type of person, you know? A man who can make exotic dishes and hug sad women. And on top of it all, you weren't exactly at the back of the queue when looks were handed out either.'

'This could be the start of a beautiful friendship,' he grinned.

'If someone would only explain to me who all these people are, perhaps I could also start to enjoy this party.'

'Shoot. What can I tell you?' At that moment Adriaan laughed again noisily outside the back door, as if he wanted to ensure that they didn't forget about him. Ralph gestured with a jerk of the head over his shoulder as he poured himself a glass of wine. 'I don't know everyone standing out there with the cook, but the tall guy with the glasses and the short bald guy are Johannes and Joe. One is a lecturer and the other is an architect and they've been together for about ten years. Mila always says they're the most stable couple in her circle of friends. So much for the joys of heterosexuality.'

'And the dark beauty who's setting the table with Mila and Emma?'

'Sonja.'

'Heterosexual?' she asked with a little smile.

'Undoubtedly.'

'What makes you so sure?'

'Perhaps Max can tell you more. He fell for her dark beauty at one stage.'

'Nothing more than an instant in the wind,' Max defended himself from behind his beer bottle.

'You can't turn around without falling over some woman from Max's past.' Bobby looked at the beautiful Sonja with her head on one side and smiled again, this time a bit more broadly. 'And you're sure she wouldn't let herself be seduced by a woman?'

'Can one ever be sure?' asked Max. 'Just look how you've surprised us all.'

This time she surprised him with a bubbly giggle. Strange, he thought, but he didn't feel quite as unbalanced as he had a quarter of an hour ago, either. As though the mere fact of Ralph's presence had already comforted them. By this time the party was so noisy that he struggled to hear the music playing somewhere in the background, but he thought it was the tape he had given Liane as a birthday present. *Forces Favourites*, a collection of 'alternative' South African musicians protesting against national service. Liane had raised her eyebrows, a gesture which she had apparently stolen from her husband, and asked jokingly whether such subversive music wouldn't disturb her peace of mind. That's the idea, he said. Only half joking.

'OK. What's the other table setter's name? Louise? Is she the one getting divorced?'

'Another of Max's past loves,' said Ralph.

'But I've got nothing to do with the divorce,' said Max quickly.

'Good grief. Is there any woman here with whom you haven't had an affair at some stage, Max?'

'I think there's only you,' Max grinned into his beard. 'And no one can say I didn't try.'

'Do you know Griet?' asked Ralph. 'On the carpet over there, playing with Mona?'

Griet sat cross-legged while the child tried to hide under the folds of her wide skirt. They were concentrating so hard on the game that it looked as though they were trapped in a soundproof air bubble. Cut off from everything and everyone around them.

'Is she the one who writes fairy tales?'

'Yes. At the moment she's working on a book that Yvette wants to illustrate. I wonder what's happened to Yvette?'

'Probably collapsed somewhere. She's looked dead on her feet the whole weekend. I didn't realize it was so exhausting having a baby!'

'And the Beautiful People with Liane on the couch?' Max asked. 'Why are they all dressed in black from head to toe?'

'Perhaps in mourning for Liane's fleeting youth?' Ralph suggested.

Though she didn't look much more than twenty sitting there on the couch, thought Max. The only one of the extremely attractive group wearing white, a long white dress of stretchy cotton with a high neck and scooped shoulders which emphasized her golden brown arms. When she leaned forward to hear what one of the others was saying he could see the skin pull tight across the hollow of her collarbone, smooth and caramel coloured like very expensive, very fine stockings.

What is it about her? Why did he still sometimes feel – usually completely unexpectedly – as though she held his heart in her hand? There had been so many other women after her, so many more mature relationships after their clumsy puppy love. And yet she still touched him, with her breathless little laugh and her bright eyes and her stubborn optimism, in a way in which no other woman had ever touched him. Perhaps a strange kind of protective instinct. As though he wanted to protect her against the disillusionments of age. Perhaps just because he didn't want her to become as cynical and brittle as most of the other women in his life.

And yet he was haunted by the possibility that he actually wanted nothing more than a sweet little woman. A cheerful chickadee to sing away his cares and tensions. An uncomplicated, un-neurotic, inexhaustible Barbie doll.

No, he thought as he watched her, it wasn't her uncomplicated surface that attracted him. Rather the suspicion of what lay trapped underneath that surface. All the suppressed emotions, all the unbearable memories, all the damage and pain which was hidden away behind that terrible cheerfulness.

Suddenly, the woman's voice on the subversive birthday tape soared up above all the other voices in the room, heavy with emotion. *But we're still making love, we're still making war, it's not for us to even try to choose any more* . . . And then, as if she had been waiting for this cue, Yvette appeared in the passage doorway, her face glowing with excitement, with a cake which she had hidden in her room for the whole weekend. If one could call it a cake, was Max's first dumbfounded thought. It looked like an amateurish model of the Voortrekker monument, decorated with a layer of psychedelic orange icing sugar, surrounded by a fence of thirty flickering candles. Liane gave a little shriek and leaped up from the couch, then walked laughing to the table.

'We couldn't find the right birthday cake anywhere,' Emma explained. 'The shop cakes were all either terribly unoriginal or bordering on really bad taste. Then we thought, well, if we have to settle for kitsch, at least it shouldn't be a borderline case . . .'

'And here you have it,' said Yvette with a beaming smile. 'The Kitschest Cake in the World. Made and decorated with pride by a few of your friends.'

'It's absolutely *amazing*!' Liane took the disgusting cake from her in awe and placed it proudly in the middle of the table. 'How did you smuggle it into the house without me seeing? How did you get the icing so awfully orange? Is it *edible*?'

'Of course!' said Emma indignantly. 'It's what we're going to have for pudding!'

'You mean we can all have a bite of the Voortrekker monument?' Adriaan grinned from ear to ear. 'Symbol of our fucked-up past?'

'That's probably what's meant by "eating your heart out",' said Ralph as he also walked closer, inquisitively.

'You first have to blow out the candles,' warned Yvette, 'before Mona puts them in her mouth, flames and all.'

'Perhaps she can help me,' said Liane, and lifted the child on to her hip.

Mona stretched out her arms as if she wanted to dive head-first into the cake. Adriaan laughed with fatherly pride and belted out the first notes of 'Happy Birthday'. The rest of the guests, who had all gathered around the table by this time, began to sing along with varying degrees of enthusiasm, as Liane and Mona blew at the candles, cheeks bulging. In the background Jennifer Ferguson was still singing – a lot more tunefully than most of Liane's guests – on the birthday tape: *I'm still caught up with desire for a Fine Time, that is Good, and going to last a Long Time* . . . High and clear and full of yearning longing.

And at that moment Max decided, with a last twinge of his political conscience, to surrender himself to the superficial spirit of the occasion. It was just another version of reality after all, he consoled himself, no more crazy than any other version. A light-hearted weekend at the sea with his white friends, in a land growing ever darker around them.

THREE

I'll Tell You All My Secrets (1987)

He would always remember the first morning of his second marriage as a moment of hope. In contrast to the first morning of his first marriage, when he had woken up despairing in a strange hotel room, with the absolute certainty that he had made one of the biggest mistakes of his life. Everything which happened after that, Philip usually added when he told this story, confirmed the despair of that first day.

How could it be otherwise, Yvette had wanted to know. If you bake a cake with bitterness in your heart, of course it will taste bitter. (One of her cheerful fat ouma's sayings, apparently.) Relationships are like baking a cake, Yvette insisted, the ingredients you put in, the way in which you do it, determine the result. (Why did women always have to simplify things with metaphors which pre-schoolers could understand? Was it an innate ability to make metaphysical questions less abstract, to make the chaos of the universe more manageable for their children? Or was it an innate contempt for metaphysics?) Besides, the ever-hopeful Emma had added, one catastrophic relationship doesn't mean that one is doomed to catastrophic relationships for life. We're supposed to learn from our mistakes after all!

Another question. One of the Big Questions, according to him. How did women manage to remain so hopeful, in spite of everything? Even clever women. It probably had something to do with the drive to reproduce, with the necessity of bringing children into the world and carrying them through it. It would probably be impossible to force a child out of your body, with the kind of pain which he could scarcely begin to imagine, if the place you were forcing him to looked completely dark. Somewhere you had to find a ray of hope to ease your path through that pain, to prevent the darkness from swallowing you both.

Thank God he didn't need that desperate hope. He could sink down into despair whenever he wanted to. And he often wanted to. Yes, it was true, at first it was Emma's hopeful nature which attracted him, her ability to find a positive thread, and to keep tugging at it until she had unravelled the chaos around her. And yet that initially attractive characteristic had gradually become an irritation, as often happened in relationships. Indeed there was a point at which a positive attitude changed into unforgivable stupidity. When hopefulness became no more than myopia.

But that first morning of his second marriage, with his friends in a wooden house at Smitswinkel Bay – a coastal village just around the corner from Cape Town, yet so isolated that you couldn't reach it by car, but had to carry your luggage along a winding footpath down the mountainside – in that surprising isolation, he felt almost as hopeful as Emma. Yes, his second marriage did begin well.

'If I ever have a honeymoon again, touch wood,' said Liane and quickly touched the round breakfast table, 'I'll do what you've done and invite all my friends along too. It's an amazing idea. Why sit alone somewhere staring into your partner's eyes? You've got the rest of your life to do that!'

'But you're not meant to be staring into your partner's eyes when you're on honeymoon,' Adriaan said with a worried frown. 'I'm sure there must be a more pleasant way of passing the time. Yvette, what was it again that we did so much of when we were first married?'

'I'm quite prepared to refresh your memory,' said Yvette, with Mona, almost eighteen months old, bouncing on her lap. 'Now that we've eventually got you-know-who off my worn-out breast, we can start doing that kind of thing again.'

'Bottie!' shouted Mona and waved the bottle in her hand around enthusiastically. 'Not tittie Mona! Bottie Mona!'

'Wait a bit,' Philip objected. 'The conversation's gone off track here. Firstly, this is not a honeymoon, Liane. It's an ordinary long weekend. Max happened to get this house lent to him, and Emma and I happened to get married last night. Anyway, most of you invited yourselves.'

'You know I'll sink to any level to spend a weekend in the Cape,' said Ralph. 'Even if it means inviting myself to my friends' honeymoon. And now that Mila is working in parliament six months of the year, I'm the only one in this group who's stuck in Johannesburg the whole year round. I don't expect you to feel sorry for me. But you can't blame me as much as these lucky devils who live just around the corner.'

'And the rest of us didn't want to leave you alone in your misery,' said Paul. 'An unpleasant honeymoon can spoil even the most promising marriage.'

'Don't let anyone say we're just fair-weather friends!' laughed Liane.

'Although we are, of course, overjoyed with today's fair weather,' smiled Mila, admiring the panoramic view over False Bay through the floor-to-ceiling windows. 'I still say you Capetonians don't really appreciate the beauty around you. The extent of the beauty. Just look at that. It's enough to make one believe in a god again!'

She waved her arm to include the whole scene: the sea which lay below them, shining and smooth like a thick layer of oil paint, the sky tinted the same dark blue colour as the water – but with lighter strokes so that it seemed thinner and more transparent – the vague blue outlines of the Hottentots-Holland mountains in the hazy distance, subtle water-colour lines. And on the right-hand side, much closer, the fynbos of the nature reserve around Cape Point, the different shades of green melted together like spatterings of colour on an Impressionist's canvas. Like Monet's garden or Seurat's Sunday afternoon scene.

The sun which shone through the massive windows filled the room with so much bright light that Liane and Paul were both wearing Raybans at the table. Like Hollywood stars who don't want to be recognized while eating out. Hers had classic tortoiseshell frames, the lenses so dark that her eyes were invisible; his had the teardrop shape which American fighter pilots like to wear, the lenses reflecting like one-way glass on a modern building. They were, incidentally, the only two at the table who were already bathed and freshly dressed. Or probably not so incidentally. Their shirts both as unnaturally white as the evidence in washing-powder adverts, their hair with the kind of gloss you only ever see in shampoo adverts. An advertisement couple, indeed.

'I don't care what Philip says,' declared his wife next to him. *His wife*. God, he hadn't even been married a day and that sentimental possessiveness which he had always despised had already begun to creep in. If he wasn't careful, in a year's time they'd begin to sound like Liane and Paul. 'But I'm not going to let him hijack my first and hopefully my only honeymoon. I'll remember this weekend as a honeymoon. Even if it is a kind of alternative honeymoon.' The wide sleeves of her white towelling dressing gown, the white towel wrapped around her wet hair like a turban, and the fact that she was holding her head up exceptionally straight in order to keep the headdress from falling, made her look like a medieval noblewoman addressing her subjects. But the stiller she held her head, the livelier her hand movements became. She didn't realize that the wide sleeves dragged to and fro in the egg yolk on her plate. Which made the majestic portrait a little more down to earth, something that Breughel rather than Van Eyck might have painted. 'When my ouma heard that we were going to spend our wedding night with a group of friends, she just stammered sort of sympathetically that she and my grandfather also had to be quiet on their first night, because they had to sleep in the same little house as my great-grandmother! That's the most intimate thing I've ever heard her say. The very first sign she's given that she and my grandfather ever had anything like a sex life.'

'Can you imagine,' said Mila in amazement, 'binding yourself to someone for life before you've even slept together? And for that generation, "for life" really was . . . for life. No escape. The potential for disappointment was just so unbelievably great!'

The potential for disappointment is still unbelievably great, thought Philip, but he kept quiet. Determined not to be accused of cynicism this morning. Sexual disappointment is just one form of disappointment. There are so many others, which can be so much worse. But he kept quiet.

That year, 1987, when the State of Emergency was extended again, was another dark and dismal one in a country full of sunshine and light. A land of blinding white happiness and clear-sighted black suffering, Emma had written in one of her first, uncertain short stories. 'An expanse as wide as God's mercy', to quote Eugène Marais, where people murdered each other mercilessly. A place of exhausting droughts alternating with devastating flood waters, of stylish beach houses within walking distance of desperate squatter shacks, of despairing birthday feasts and hopeful funerals. A place of elegant restaurants full of fat white women swallowing diet pills and dirty streets full of hungry black children sniffing glue, of powerless political parties and powerful banned organizations. A place where angels and demons played in all the teams, Emma had written, not necessarily black against white, but often grey against grey. A place where certainties, clichés, ideals are undermined day after day.

That first weekend in May, when Emma and Philip celebrated their honeymoon, was only days before a general election (limited to the white population) which would drag the country deeper into the darkness. The official opposition party, which for decades had at least been more liberal than the official ruling party, was replaced overnight by a party which was even more conservative than the government – even whiter – with a core of fear and intolerance that was even more deeply rooted. Even blacker and more evil, one could say, except that black and evil could no longer be used as synonyms in this country. Perhaps all Conservative parties the world over had the same dark heart, Philip speculated; maybe some just hid it better than others. Perhaps some just have better spin doctors. Just look what Saatchi and Saatchi did for Margaret Thatcher. The South African Conservative Party didn't shrink from wearing its black heart on its white sleeve, though. While the government professed to be throttling its own monster child, the new opposition displayed its racism like an old-fashioned mourning band pinned to its sleeve.

While another, more radical, conservative organization, with a leader who better understood the power of imagery, carried the metaphor to its logical, literal conclusion. The Afrikaner Weerstandsbeweging displayed a mangled version of the swastika on bulging forearms in khaki uniforms. Like an obscene hand gesture. Fuck off. Later other parties in the country – and not necessarily just white parties – would behave with the same intolerance, but in the Year of Our Lord 1987 the rise of this new, shameless, whiter-than-white conservativism was the proverbial last straw, the excuse that many South Africans had long sought in order to leave the country. Even in Philip and Emma's privileged Afrikaans circle of friends.

And yet the little flames of hope continued to flicker, innumerable, unquenchable, unpredictable. The darkest hour comes just before daybreak, people told one another. *Voor in die wapad brand 'n lig.* Ahead in the wagon track a light is burning. *Vasbyt, min dae.* Hold on, not long now. The harder the times, the more easily such sayings are bandied about.

But it wasn't the darkest hour. It wasn't even nearly dawn. And Philip's flare of light had nothing to do with the political developments in the country, anyway. It was simply a brief moment after a long period of darkness in his heart, a candle lit unexpectedly which would burn itself out soon enough. Signs of a depression which would only be officially diagnosed a few years later.

'How did Max manage to get hold of this house?' asked Liane as she washed the dishes, the dark glasses still on the tip of her nose and the shocking pink rubber gloves looking like elegant accessories on her slender arms. She lifted a colourful saucer from the sink, read the potter's name on the bottom and nodded approvingly. 'Everything is in such wonderfully good taste! Not the sort of thing you'd expect from a Struggle groupie's friends!'

'Max's friends aren't all hard-line Marxists, you know.' Emma took the saucer from Liane carefully and dried it. 'The house belongs to one of his colleagues, a lecturer in the English department, if I remember correctly.'

'It's all a bit too tasteful for me.' Yvette, who was packing away the dried dishes in the gleaming white kitchen cupboards, was again dressed in an imaginative ensemble of second-hand clothing. A man's waistcoat with a back of purple satin over a long, loose, gauzy blouse and a wide gypsy skirt which made her look like part of the chorus in *Carmen*. A silver chain with bells, which she'd bound around her ankle instead of her wrist, completed the exotic picture. More than exotic, almost bizarre, in this clinical white kitchen. 'I'm constantly nervous about the damage which Mona could cause with her grasping hands. It makes me feel uncomfortable.' She caught Emma's eye and they began to laugh together. 'Why does that sound so familiar?'

'Isn't that a famous feminist statement?' asked Emma.

'Are you *never* going to forgive me for my youthful impetuosity?' Liane wanted to know from behind her dark glasses.

'No, we're proud of you!' laughed Emma. 'Who would want to be a stupid beauty queen if you could sound like a clever feminist?'

'I wouldn't really mind being a beauty queen.' Yvette looked out through the window at the small beach below them. Mila and Adriaan were standing barefoot in the shallow water, with Mona hanging like a shopping bag between them. Each time that a wave was about to break over her short little legs, they swung her high in the air. Paul, Ralph and Philip threw a Frisbee around, to the tail-wagging, barking delight of Mona's new friend, a young Labrador with heavy, clumsy paws and a glossy golden coat. A dog which had the strange name of Tat because Mona insisted on calling him Cat, but couldn't get her tongue around the 'C'. 'With a crown and a sceptre and all . . .'

'Ag, well,' Emma consoled her, 'some of us have other talents. You can draw more beautifully than any beauty queen I know. And bake a better chocolate cake.'

'I'd still like to be a beauty queen,' Yvette insisted. 'One who can draw and bake as well.'

'Talking about drawing,' said Liane, examining a plate over her dark glasses to check that she'd washed it properly, 'how are the illustrations for Griet's children's book going?'

'Well, I struggled so to get going that I began to wonder whether my creative juices hadn't all turned to breast milk. But for the last month it's been going better every day. I don't know if it's something to do with the fact that I've finished breastfeeding. But now I'm beginning to think that it might be the best work I've ever done.'

'So motherhood wasn't the end of your brilliant career after all?'

'On the contrary,' smiled Yvette, with a little tinkling of bells. 'I think it's going to become *really* brilliant now.'

'Such humility!' Emma exclaimed.

'And you, Emma?' Yvette's dark eyes had become serious again in her pale face. 'Are you managing to write now that you're working from home?'

'Yes,' Emma answered with a heavy sigh. 'The same rubbish that I wrote in the office. That's why I know so much about beauty queens. I have to interview them all the time. I don't know why we've got such an obsession with beauty queens in this country. The idea is probably that their pretty faces and trivial comments will entertain the people, but I don't know, sometimes I wonder whether such an overdose of superficial beauty doesn't contribute to the depression the whole nation is suffering from these days!'

'Can't you write a short story about it?' Liane lifted a pink glove to push the glasses back over the bridge of her nose. 'About a country full of stupid queens and people who can't laugh any more?'

'No, I'm afraid the kind of stuff that I'm trying to write these days is more . . .' Emma shook her long hair out of her face because her cheeks suddenly felt uncomfortably hot. 'I don't know what it is, but almost all my stories these days are about sex.'

'As in sexual fantasies?'

'More like sexual nightmares. But one person's nightmare is probably another's fantasy. I don't know, maybe it's my own little rebellion against the terrible pressure to be politically engaged. The greater the political fuck-up around me becomes, the more I crave the total escapism of erotica. Some people will probably consider it pornography.'

'Goodness gracious!'

'How are you going to get it published?' Yvette wanted to know, with a worried frown.

'No, I'll never be able to publish it! My ouma would die of shock! I don't know, I hope it's just a passing phase. Perhaps just an obscene reaction to all the *proper* articles I've had to write for *Palette*. There are so many things one can't say in a woman's magazine. No one ever swears in an interview. Everyone always speaks exquisite Afrikaans. If I had to interview a gang member from the Cape Flats, he'd sound like the minister's wife leading a prayer meeting. Exquisite Afrikaans without a single swear word. Not that the editor would let me interview a gang member from the Cape Flats anyway!'

'I didn't realize you felt so repressed!' said Liane in a shocked voice. 'Now I'm even more relieved than ever that you decided to resign!'

'Weren't you the friend who tried to persuade me not to work from home?'

'No, no, no, I tried to persuade you not to work from Philip's home! I didn't think that you'd ever go so far as to get married . . .'

'Me neither,' admitted Emma.

'But I'm very glad you decided to do it, nevertheless,' added Liane quickly. 'I don't know how you managed it, but recently Philip's been sounding more positive – or at any rate less negative – about the state of Holy Matrimony than ever before.'

'I don't know if I've got anything to do with it,' said Emma, drying a cup attentively. 'It's as though Philip feels relieved . . . in a strange way . . . now that the State of Emergency is driving everyone around him to despair. Like a patient who is so grateful to hear that he's not the only one suffering from an unknown, incurable disease that he immediately begins to feel better!'

'Like Robinson Crusoe must have felt when he found another person's footprint on his deserted island,' said Yvette with a sympathetic smile.

'More like Robinson Crusoe would have felt if he found that he wasn't on a deserted island after all,' said Emma. 'That the whole island was full of people just like him. All equally fucked-up.'

'All in need of a good therapist, as Max would say,' added Liane.

'You must hear Philip on the subject of Max and therapy,' smiled Emma. 'He says Max definitely has the soul of a missionary. He's been trying to turn all his friends into Marxists for years. Now he's apparently given up and decided that it's easier to convert us to Jung. It doesn't clash with our capitalist interests and it satisfies the need for a mystical experience which most of us have now that we can no longer depend on religion.'

'And Philip of course has no need of a mystical experience,' said Yvette.

'Of course not. He prefers the security of a universe without a god or belief. It makes him feel safer than faith and love and all those messy feelings.'

She shook her head and stared morosely through the window. The drying-up cloth hung limply in her hands. The three Frisbee players were now sitting on a rock talking. She watched how the sun gleamed in Philip's hair as he laughed uninhibitedly, his head thrown back, his whole posture so relaxed that he looked twenty years younger. Like the carefree student he must once have been, long before she knew him. The only memento that she had of that unknown young man was a small passport photo from the late sixties. His hair was a lot longer and thicker then, his eyes so full of excited innocence – despite the John Lennon glasses which he wore to appear more worldly-wise – his smile so full of childish self-confidence, that she wanted to cry every time she thought of the photo. Because she had never seen him smile like that. Because she didn't ever expect to see him smile like that.

'Well, I don't know about you, but Max is busy converting *me*. I . . . I think I realized for the first time that there are things which happened in my childhood . . . things which I have to work through before I can grow up.' Emma and Yvette looked at each other, fleetingly, and then at Liane. Liane looked at her hands which lay still in the water. Then she laughed, that childish, breathy sound which they knew so well. 'But I don't know if I want to grow up yet!'

'A year ago I didn't know anyone who was seeing a therapist,' said Emma, perplexed. 'OK, maybe a few arty English types, but not my good Afrikaans friends. Now it feels as though I've woken up in the middle of a Woody Allen movie. Everyone around me is either in therapy or thinking of going into therapy. Even my cheerful friend Liane!' She laughed, but it was an abrupt sound which couldn't seem to get past the lump in her throat. 'Only it's not as funny as a Woody Allen movie. It's not just about failed relationships, it's about a whole society collapsing in ruins. A failed country, not so?'

'I think it's Bobby who's persuaded Max to see a shrink,' said Liane. 'I think that's all that's keeping her together since Robin's been . . . detained.'

Detained. Funny how inappropriate the words sounded on Liane's lovely lips, thought Emma. It was as though her voice struggled, her tongue knotted, like when you try to say something in a foreign language for the first time.

'How long has it been now?' asked Yvette.

'More than two months. No visits, no letters, no news. *Nothing*. I don't think I could endure it if I was Bobby. Even if I had the best therapist in the world.'

'Not to mention Robin,' said Yvette quietly. 'There's no therapist in jail to keep her going.'

'I still can't believe it.' Liane took off her sunglasses. 'I thought that if one of my friends landed up in jail – or one of my friends' lovers – then the State of Emergency would eventually become a reality to me. You know, something which would touch me *personally*, not just reports that I read in the papers. Or don't read. And now it still feels unreal! I mean, how is it possible that we can get together for a weekend in a stunning house on a stunning beach while Robin is detained in God knows what kind of circumstances? And thousands of others like her!' She looked at them, her eyes as pleading as her voice. '*How is it possible?*'

Welcome to the real world, thought Emma as she studied the distress on her most beautiful friend's face.

'I think it will be good for Bobby to spend the weekend with us.' Yvette, with deliberate cheerfulness in her voice, bent down to pack a few plates away. 'I think it'll do us all good to be together again!'

'Actually Max wanted to bring Bobby here alone for the weekend,' said Emma. 'He thought she wouldn't want to see people. Then she said she didn't want to be alone. So it's actually thanks to Bobby that I can spend my honeymoon here.'

'Or thanks to the South African government who threw her lover in jail.' Liane laughed, embarrassed at her unexpected cynicism. 'Goodness gracious, I'm beginning to sound like Philip!' And then in the same breath, as if she couldn't wait to become her usual light-hearted self: 'But tell me about this sex bomb that Max brought to your wedding! I've been wanting to ask you all morning!'

'The *coloured* sex bomb, you mean?' asked Yvette with an innocent smile.

'No, that's not what . . . that's not why I'm inquisitive . . . I mean, Max has always had friends of all races!'

'But he's never brought one of them along to his white friends' wedding before.'

Liane looked at Yvette, perplexed by the challenging note in her voice.

'Now *you* sound like Philip!'

'She's a postgraduate student,' said Emma. 'Sociology or crimin-ology or something like that. Apparently very bright.'

'That figures,' smiled Liane. 'Max's greatest fear is a dumb blonde. This one is definitely not blonde. I'm happy to hear she's not dumb either.'

'Her father is some bigshot in the Struggle. Don't ask me who.'

'So she's got the right political credentials as well!'

'And she can dance,' laughed Emma.

'Can she ever dance! Look, I know it's racist to say that black people dance better than white people, but she danced rings around all the other people at your wedding! I couldn't stop staring at her.'

'You weren't the only one,' said Emma. 'I watched the men when she was tangoing with Adriaan. I think the temperature in the room rose about ten degrees.'

'I didn't know Adriaan could tango!'

'Adriaan can do anything,' Yvette remarked drily. 'If he has a captive audience.'

'Well, it's good that Adriaan and Paul were there to dance with her,' laughed Liane. 'Max isn't exactly an exhibitionist on the dance floor. If it was up to him alone, we might never have seen what she could do with that body!'

'No, we would have seen it,' said Emma with a wry smile. 'That's why he brought her along. So that everyone could look at her. All his white friends who could only ever dream about such sensual coffee-coloured bodies. All the so-called liberal men who were never brave enough to date a coloured girl. He wanted them to stew in their own hypocritical juices.'

'Do you think so?'

'Don't you?'

'I've never understood how his mind works.' Liane stared out of the window, her shoulders as straight as a ruler. Then she busied her hands in the sink again. 'When is he coming?'

'Probably only late afternoon. It's International Workers Day. His Marxist conscience will never let him lie around on the beach with his bourgeois friends all day.'

Emma's eyes wandered to Philip again. His dark blond hair looked lighter than usual in the sun, glistening every time he moved his head. He was explaining something to Paul and Ralph, his body language still relaxed. And all of a sudden she was in a hurry to finish up in the kitchen, to go and sit outside next to her husband, to enjoy his extraordinarily good mood. It was like an unexpected wedding present, she thought, this sudden overwhelming certainty that this was the man she loved. In spite of everything. *Her husband.*

'So he prefers to march with the workers?' asked Liane.

'Something like that. He and Bobby are both involved with the End Conscription Campaign's beach picnic.'

'A picnic!' Liane's voice leaped with surprise. 'That sounds a lot more fun than a protest march!'

'Not necessarily. It's a multi-racial picnic on a white beach. The police are probably waiting for them with truncheons and teargas.'

'Where do they get the courage to do things like that? To be teargassed and hit with truncheons for the sake of a picnic? OK, I know it's for the sake of the Struggle, not for the sake of a picnic, but still . . . Couldn't they just have a *normal* picnic – just for *one* day of the year – then they can struggle on tomorrow again?'

'I suppose it's like the sport boycott. The same argument.' Emma dropped the dried cutlery impatiently in an open drawer, anxious to join her husband. 'If normal sport isn't possible in an abnormal society, a normal picnic probably isn't, either.'

'But then everything we do must be abnormal!' Liane pulled the plug from the basin and stripped off the pink gloves. 'Even a normal weekend with friends! Normal friendship must also be impossible. And normal relationships. Normal sex, for that matter!'

'What is "normal" sex?' Emma asked.

'Ag, Emma!'

'No, I'm serious. It's something I've been grappling with recently. Ever since I began to write about sex so incessantly.'

'If we lived in Britain, we wouldn't be having this stupid conversation,' said Yvette. 'So we must at least admit that abnormal circumstances can lead to abnormal conversations.'

'But if we all suddenly woke up in Britain one morning, the circumstances there would be abnormal to us! If you come from Africa, democracy and freedom of speech and all those things aren't normal! "Normal" surely means what you're used to, doesn't it?'

She looked at them again like a scared child looking for comfort.

'No.' Yvette shook her head slowly, her voice scarcely audible, as if she were ashamed that she couldn't reassure her friend. 'Then you could say that someone who lived in an asylum led a normal life – because that's what he's used to. We don't lead normal lives, Liane. We've just got used to abnormal ones.'

'Seems I need a shrink even more than I realized,' said Liane with a tight smile. 'Could one of you perhaps refer me to someone?'

'And there the newlyweds vanish into the sunset,' Liane sighed later that afternoon on the beach. By this time she sounded a lot more carefree, more like her old self. Her body was baked to a golden brown by the sun, her hair still slightly damp after braving the cold waves with Ralph a while ago. She watched Emma and Philip as they moved over the rocks hand in hand, in the direction of the green hill behind which the sun would soon begin to sink, and gave a satisfied smile. 'Like the end of an old-fashioned movie. All that's missing is some heart-tugging music. Something like Rachmaninov!'

'The first notes of Beethoven's Fifth would probably be more appropriate,' muttered Ralph as though talking to himself. 'To suggest the threatened future of the relationship.'

'I thought I was the one who wanted to make movies.' Paul's eyebrows lifted high above his dark eyes, his impressive chin deeply notched. 'Now I discover a competitor in my own home. And a musical adviser among my friends.'

'You'd never make a movie with such a sentimental ending, my darling.'

'And all yours would end that way?'

'Perhaps not all,' she said with her chin on her knees, her bare arms folded around her raised legs. 'But that's how I would end this one. I would love to believe that they'll be happily married for the rest of their lives.'

She stared at the rocks just in front of them, where Yvette was wandering around in search of interesting shells and seaweed, her colourful gypsy outfit a bright moving spot against the blue sky. Adriaan had disappeared a few hours ago with a fishing rod over his shoulder and the eternally hopeful heart of the enthusiastic angler, convinced that he'd at least bring home an *hors-d'oeuvre* for dinner. Mona was burying Mila's feet under a heap of sand. Tat, who was under the impression that this new game had been devised especially for him, tried to dig up the lost feet again, frisky and slobbering with eagerness.

'I don't know about the rest of their lives,' sighed Mila in her *Wild Women Don't Get the Blues* T-shirt. 'But their chances of being happy are surely not much worse than those of any other couple still brave enough to get married these days.'

'Perhaps all the arguments were just teething problems,' said Liane.

'We're speaking about a few years of arguments,' said Ralph. 'Not even elephants could have such a struggle to cut their teeth!'

'What are you trying to say, Ralph?' Mila challenged. 'That they shouldn't have got married?'

'No, I'm happy that they got married! Otherwise I wouldn't be sitting here beside the sea. It was one of the best weddings I've ever been to. And it's certainly the best honeymoon I've ever had!'

'I wish we could all be less sceptical.' Mila's red mouth pouted in dissatisfaction for a moment. 'It's sad to me that we've all become so old and disillusioned. So that the very idea of a happy marriage begins to seem absurd.'

'Look who's talking!' Ralph exclaimed. 'You're more sceptical about marriage than anyone else I know. Except for Philip, of course, but he's in a class of his own.'

'And some of us do still believe in marriage,' protested Liane. 'Otherwise we wouldn't be married, would we?'

'Well . . .' said Paul.

'Well?' laughed Liane. 'Don't tell me you're unhappily married, my darling!'

'Spit it out, brother,' said Ralph. 'You're not going to get a chance like this again.'

'No.' Paul leaned back on his elbows, his eyes on the waves, but it looked as though he didn't really see the sea. 'I suppose I'm happy. Sort of.'

'That's more than most married men can say,' murmured Ralph.

'I never realized you were all such enthusiastic supporters of marriage,' said Mila, with an irritated frown beneath her blonde fringe.

'It's not marriage which bothers me,' Ralph tried to explain. 'It's relationships in general. According to my experience, you get only three degrees of comparison in relationships. Difficult, more difficult and fucking impossible. And when I think about Emma and Philip's relationship, well, then I automatically think of the third degree . . .'

'But not all relationships are cut from the same neat pattern!' Mila cried. 'It's not as though you can buy a guide book which says that if you and your partner argue three times a week and have sex three times a week, you've got a worse relationship than a couple who argue once a month and have sex once a month! We all have to make up our own pattern as we go along! And some relationships have . . . weird patterns. As you ought to know.'

He answered her accusing look with an apologetic smile, but said nothing. She dropped her eyes and began to scratch in the sand with one finger. The angry frown still between her eyes.

'Anyway, they don't argue all the time any more,' said Liane. 'I get the feeling that they've finally begun to accept each other as they are, rather than trying to play Pygmalion the whole time.' She gazed in the direction in which Emma and Philip had walked. By this time they were just two dark, bobbing silhouettes – one moment invisible behind a high rock, then again clearly etched against the sun. They weren't holding hands any more. 'You can only have one Pygmalion in a relationship. And even then it's a dicey business.'

'I don't think they'll ever stop arguing,' said Mila. 'I've got this image in my head of how one day they'll be sitting on the stoep of some old-age home whacking each other over the head with their walking sticks. Too deaf to hear each other, and too senile to remember what the argument was about anyway . . .'

She smiled at Mona, who had dumped another bucket of sand over her feet. The child crouched next to her and began to flatten the sand with her spade. The plump little body, bare except for sagging plastic pants, glowed like polished oak in the late afternoon sun. The dog, who was still under the impression that he was included in the game, grabbed the spade between his teeth and tried to pull it out of Mona's hands. When it looked as though he was going to win the struggle, Mila grabbed him by the scruff of his neck and lifted the wriggling body on to her lap, laughing.

In the meantime, Yvette had walked closer, the pockets of her gaudy waistcoat bulging with shells and other sea treasures, and observed the scene with her head tilted to one side. Then she saw Adriaan approaching from the east and raised her arm to wave at him.

'It doesn't look as though we'll be eating fish tonight,' she said, disappointed.

'That doesn't matter,' said Ralph. 'I feel like making a big pot of pasta.'

'That's the best thing about these weekends.' Liane pulled a stretched cotton jersey over her head, her body suddenly all covered in gooseflesh in her wet bathing costume. The heat had begun to disappear behind the hill along with the sun. 'That the men spend more time in the kitchen than the women. That's what I call one giant leap for womankind.'

'Have you noticed that the women still wash the dishes?' asked Yvette with a sweet smile. 'It's miraculous how quickly our magnificent manly chefs vanish from the kitchen as soon as the taps are turned on.'

'That's just because we don't want to make you feel completely useless,' said Ralph.

'How can you see from here that Adriaan hasn't caught anything?' asked Mila, gazing at the scarcely visible figure in the distance.

'By his walk,' answered Yvette, her smile now wide and pleased. 'If he's caught something, he's always got that *swagger*. Like John Wayne walking through the main street of a cowboy town.'

'That's another reason married life depresses me,' said Mila shaking her head. 'The possibility that someone could know you well enough to read your body language at such a distance.'

'Why do you have such a fear of intimacy?'

'It's not that!' She looked at Paul in surprise, but it seemed he had asked the question absent-mindedly. He was still staring at the sea, his perfect profile serious. 'It's something else. I don't know. Maybe I'm afraid of sacrificing my privacy. Remember, I'm the middle child who always had to share a room!' She laughed, her lips as red as ever, her blonde fringe almost the same colour as the sand over her feet. 'My greatest desire, as long as I can remember, was never a doll or a bike or something like that. It was always just a room of my own. Long before I heard of Virginia Woolf.'

'Pappa!' Mona cried out excitedly, leaping up quickly and grabbing Mila's hand. 'Da Pappa! Da Pappa! Tum, tum, tum!'

'No, I don't want to come now,' said Mila, 'I'm sitting very nicely here.'

But Mona pulled so fiercely at her hand that she had to get up, groaning. Her feet broke with difficulty through the weight of sand which was tightly packed around her ankles. Then she walked away with the child, hand in hand. Tat fell over his own feet in his eagerness to join them and ran in panting circles around them on the beach.

'Yet another lovely Kodak moment,' sighed Liane as she looked after them. Mona like a fat gilded cherub beside Mila's lovely legs in the low rays of the sun. 'I never knew Mila had such a way with children!'

'She said *she* didn't either,' said Yvette. 'But she must be doing something right. Mona is completely crazy over her.'

'Mutual adoration, if you ask me. Funny, I always think of Mila as this tough-cookie journalist, but it's as though her whole attitude softens when she just looks at Mona. You can almost see her knees go weak.'

'She's not that tough at all. She often comes to stay with us on the farm when she's working in parliament.' Yvette drew a tentative stripe over the sand with her toe. 'I said to Adriaan only the other day, if something had to happen to me, he should marry her. Then at least my daughter would get a stepmother she likes.'

'And what does Adriaan think of that?' Ralph asked. 'Or doesn't he have any say in the choice of his next wife?'

Yvette laughed a little self-consciously and looked over his head at the house on the hill. Her toe was still drawing lines on the sand.

'He said he wouldn't be as stupid as to marry again. Then I thought perhaps I should just ask Mila to be Mona's godmother. But I'm scared it might sound . . . as though I feel sorry for her. You know, as if I think, oh shame, she's never going to have her own child, so I'll give her a little bit of mine!'

Ralph stared thoughtfully in front of him. His mane of hair gleaming in the light of the sunset. Even the hair on his lean body – with Mila's striped kikoi bound around his hips – had the sheen of a lion's pelt.

'No, I don't think she'd see it that way,' he said. 'I think she'd feel flattered.'

'Do you think so?' She sank down gratefully on the sand next to him. 'I don't know, you know her better than the rest of us, but I get the feeling that recently she's been really confused about parenthood and . . . you know, everything that goes with it. She doesn't want to get married or live with someone, but she'd still love to have a child . . .'

'I've offered to help her,' said Ralph, his smile mocking, his amber eyes serious. 'But she said she liked me too much to saddle me with such a responsibility.'

'So perhaps a godchild would be some kind of comfort after all?'

Ralph watched the three figures in the distance. Mila had let go of Mona's hand so that she could run the last few paces to her father on her own, stumbling on her short legs. Adriaan dropped the rod on the sand, caught his daughter in his waiting arms and threw her in the air like a big golden ball.

'I think she'd be a wonderful godmother,' he said with conviction.

'How are things in the world of advertising?' Ralph grinned and threw a handful of chopped mushrooms into the pan on the stove. 'She asks sarcastically.'

'No, I wasn't being sarcastic!' laughed Emma. 'It was an innocent question!'

'There's no such thing as innocence in the world of advertising. Perhaps that answers your question.' He added finely chopped garlic, parsley, basil and a little nutmeg, and waited patiently for the mushrooms to begin to sizzle. 'No, sister, things are not looking good. But we can't all write stories to stay alive. Some of us have to think up silly slogans.'

'And some of us have to churn out silly magazine stories.' She sat next to him on a kitchen cupboard and looked at her feet, which hung a little way above the floor. 'Sometimes I think that it would have been better to work in a post office. Licking stamps rather than licking VIP's arses for interviews . . .'

'I thought you were busy with a collection of short stories which was going to rock the Afrikaans literary world?'

'In my dreams. I don't know if I'll ever have the courage to show my stories to a publisher. At the moment I don't even have the courage to show them to Philip!'

'Perhaps that's a good thing,' he said, stirring the mushrooms. 'He's the kind of critic who could scar a sensitive writer's soul for life. I know what I'm talking about. I gave him a poem to read years ago. One of the early fruits of my pen. Needless to say, his commentary destroyed all my illusions of being a poet. But perhaps that was also a good thing.'

He smiled philosophically and threw the rest of the vegetables into the pan, a mixture of cauliflower, broccoli, asparagus and green beans.

'So you became a copywriter.'

'So I became a copywriter.'

'But one day you will write that brilliant novel!' she said laughingly.

'Oh, I'm already at chapter 22! Characters, storyline, atmosphere, everything worked out in fine detail. All safely kept in here.' He tapped his head with his finger. It wasn't the first time she'd noticed what lovely long fingers he had. Precisely the hands you'd imagine a writer to have – although all the writers she had met till now had utterly ordinary hands. 'There's just one problem. The minute I try to capture it on paper, everything changes into superficial advertising copy. Like in that Simon and Garfunkel song. *All my words come back to me in shades of mediocrity* . . . I aim for pathos and all I get is bathos!'

Emma looked out through the window at the sea, glistening black under the star-strewn sky. The foam of the waves flashed bright white in the darkness but the roar of the water couldn't be heard above Bob Dylan's voice, which boomed through the whole house with the help of four big speakers. In the sitting room, Adriaan was busy explaining a complicated card game to the rest of the company. Without much success, to judge by the rowdy and argumentative commentary of his fellow players. Emma had come to sit in the kitchen because she couldn't stand card games. Or because she felt that she should display greater interest in the art of cooking, as she had remarked jokingly to Ralph, now that she was a respectably married woman. But mainly because she felt in need of Ralph's restful, calming presence.

'I realized the other day that none of my friends are doing what they actually want to do,' she said as she watched him admiringly, his long legs in faded black jeans, his black pullover with rolled-up sleeves, his hair curling in his neck, sticky from the sea, his lovely hands busy over the stove. He pulled a pot of steaming pasta shells off one hotplate and overturned it in a colander, opened the tap at the sink and held the colander under the running water. Deliberately, no hurried movements, no sign of the sweaty anxiety which overcame her whenever she cooked for more than four people. 'Or have the partners they ought to have. Except perhaps Adriaan and Yvette. But the rest of us . . .'

'It's all a bit of a fuck-up, isn't it?'

Why hadn't she chosen someone like Ralph as her life partner, for instance? It would have been wonderful to throw open her heart to such a tall, strong, balanced man, someone who would teach her to cook and spoil her, someone who wouldn't feel threatened by her pathetic attempt at writing something more than magazine articles. Why did someone as unfathomable as Philip have to conquer her unwilling heart? Steadily, slowly but surely, like a fort besieged by enemy forces. No question of love at first sight. Unwilling, rebellious, protesting. That's how she had learned to love Philip McCarthy.

'Paul has always said he'd prefer to make movies,' she said, deep in thought. 'And Liane will probably always dream about the roles she'll never play. Lady Macbeth. Hedda Gabler, Blanche in *A Streetcar* . . . And we all know that Mila would have preferred to have worked for *Time*. Or for any foreign publication which wouldn't censor her reports. And Max would love to be a Great Hero in the Struggle . . .'

'But not so much that he's prepared to go to jail or die for it,' he muttered.

'And Philip . . .'

'Is there anything that Philip would love to do? With his whole heart?'

He asked the question without sarcasm, a serious frown on his forehead. She wanted to sigh resignedly, but was shocked by the sound which escaped from her mouth. Like a faraway cry from a dark pit, full of sadness and helplessness which she wasn't even aware of.

'I think he would love to be a scientist. Someone who works with things rather than people. *Small* things. The smaller the better. I think he would love to do research about something completely obscure like the sex life of some threatened butterfly species somewhere on an island in the Pacific. To know as much as possible about as little as possible, rather than the other way around, like most of us.'

'Hmm. Perhaps that's the challenge of life after all,' murmured

Ralph as he tasted a bit of cauliflower from the pan. 'To realize what you can do and what you can't do – and to concentrate your whole being on what is within your reach. To stop dreaming impossible dreams. I, for instance, am gradually beginning to realize that I've got a better chance of becoming a really good chef than I have of becoming a really good novelist.'

'Then you're a lot further along the road of life than I am.'

'Remember, I'm quite a few years older than you are,' he smiled.

'But I'm like a child who's still dreaming about what I'll do when I'm grown up! I don't know when it will sink in that I "grew up" long ago. This is it. There's no rehearsal for this pathetic concert. You don't get another chance if you fuck-up on this one!'

'For a woman who's just got married,' Ralph said without looking at her, 'you're in an exceptionally dark mood tonight.'

'I know. Perhaps it's delayed shock. It's as if the enormity of what I've done has only just hit me. While my new spouse – for once in his life – is acting as though he doesn't have a care in the world. Just listen to him laughing over there!'

Ralph came to stand in front of her and put his hands on her shoulders. She wished that she could drop her head against his firm chest and sob her heart out. While his long fingers stroked her hair.

'Remember, there's always one consolation in life. *It could have been worse.* Some days I have to murmur it over and over again, like a mantra, just so as not to explode with frustration. *Itcouldhavebeenworse, itcouldhavebeenworse, itcouldhavebeen . . .* Last week, to give you an example, I had to translate three English adverts – one for a roll of toilet paper, one for a tin of fish and one for the Progressive Federal Party. And because I couldn't think of anything worse than toilet paper and tinned fish, I had to say to myself that it would have been worse if I'd had to translate an ad for the Conservative Party.'

'Can't you object if an advert goes against your principles?'

'All ads are against my principles. The fact that I write adverts for a living is against my principles.'

'But some must be worse than others? I mean if, for example, you had to write an advert in favour of national service. Couldn't you take a stand and say no, you can't do it, you're a conscientious objector?'

'A conscientious objector in advertising is almost as inappropriate as a vegetarian in a butchery.' He grinned as he threw the pasta back into the big pot, mixed in the vegetables from the pan and added a mugful of cream. Then he swept the pot off the stove with a dramatic gesture and held it out to her proudly. '*Voila! Conchiglie con le verdure!* Or pasta with green stuff as I call it when I'm not trying to impress anyone.'

There was something about his face, suddenly so glowingly pleased, that had always made her think of a Russian ballet dancer. The broad, sharp lines of his cheekbones and the irregular nose and the hair which swept back so wildly. And the feline grace of his tall body, of course. Which would probably also move exceptionally gracefully when making love. She felt her skin blaze with shame. She had known Ralph for years, she thought, panic-stricken. Why should she think of him in this way now, for the first time, a day after her wedding? Was fear of marriage driving her crazy? No, she decided, it had to be all those unfinished sex stories on her computer.

'I think it's time you learned to cook properly, sister,' said Ralph. 'You won't believe how therapeutic it can be.'

'And you think I need therapy?'

'Well.' He put the pot down and looked at her with a concerned expression. 'You've just braved the last adventure left to the middle classes. Isn't that what your husband said about marriage?'

'My husband,' she said in a hoarse voice.

'And an adventure is always a frightening experience. Yes, you're probably going to need therapy. And it's better to cook in your kitchen than to cry on a psychologist's couch. Cheaper, too.'

'Even if I do cry into the cooking pots?' she asked as her eyes filled with tears.

'It will just make the food that little bit saltier,' he comforted, and pulled her closer, so that she could cry with her head on his firm chest as he stroked her hair with his long fingers.

Bobby's face was filled with dark hollows in the flickering light of the candles on the round table. She stared at the fork in her hand, her little glasses slipping down her nose, as if she'd never seen a fork before. Or had never really looked at her hand.

'Bobby?'

Her shoulders jerked when she heard her name, her expression as guilty as someone who has fallen asleep during a church service.

'Are you OK?' asked Ralph. 'Or do you just not like my food?'

'No! I mean yes, I'm OK. No, there's nothing wrong with your food.' She laughed, a sad, high-pitched little laugh, and took a quick sip of wine. 'I'm just not completely . . . with it yet. It was such a *weird* day.'

'You can say that again,' said Max to her left.

'It was a weird day,' she said again, seriously. 'To hold a "picnic" while surrounded by hundreds of furious policemen trying to glare each mouthful of food from your lips!'

'I think they were more pissed off that we made them work on a holiday,' said Max, 'than over the fact that we were having a multiracial picnic on a whites-only beach.'

'But they didn't chase you away violently.' Liane leaned forward to see him better, her breathy voice anxious. 'Why not? I mean, why didn't they use truncheons and teargas like they did before? Does it mean that the police are becoming . . . more human?'

'I'm afraid you're too optimistic,' said Max. 'As usual.'

'It's got fuck-all to do with humanity,' muttered Bobby. 'Only the foreign TV cameras stopped them.'

'The last beach picnic was a fiasco for the public image of the SAP,' Max explained. 'Do you remember that photo of the little black boy being attacked with a truncheon? It was used in newspapers around the world!'

'Jesus, he couldn't even have been six years old!' Bobby burst out. 'That weeping face and the snotty nose and the skinny little legs! Just after some minister had again proclaimed, all holier-than-thou, that apartheid was dead! It made the government look even more deceitful than usual. More ridiculous.'

She shook her head so vehemently that her glasses bounced on her nose. Her plate of food was still barely touched.

'So there's really no reason for hope,' said Liane with a dejected frown.

'There's always reason for hope,' said Bobby. 'The fact that the police were more hypocritical today – to impress the rest of the world – is perhaps evidence that it's no longer so easy for them to ignore what the world thinks.'

'It's about money, as usual.' There was just enough self-mockery in Max's voice to add irony to his predictable remark. 'Remember, it's almost a year since the Americans introduced economic sanctions. We're all beginning to feel the pinch. For some people it means not being able to buy enough food for their children – for some just that they've got a bit less money to decorate their houses in Oranjezicht.' He glanced jokingly at Liane, but she stared silently at her wine glass. For a moment he looked taken aback at her sober reaction, but then steamed ahead indignantly. 'It's the only reason that the government is now suddenly declaring that apartheid is dead! And then all the lies are exposed by a single photograph of a little boy being beaten from a beach.'

Philip leaned back in his chair, frustrated because he found himself on the border between two totally different yet equally passionate discussions. It was difficult to decide which one held the most interesting possibilities – the political tirade on his left-hand side or the plea for pornography on his right.

'We need an Afrikaans porn mag!' Adriaan had just declared with his usual booming bravado. 'That's the only thing that will free Afrikaners from their sexual hang-ups! *Freedom, equality and pornography!* That ought to be the slogan of the New Afrikaner!'

'I'd prefer freedom, equality and eroticism,' said Mila disapprovingly.

'What for!' barked Adriaan. 'What's the difference between pornography and eroticism?'

Mila rolled her eyes. 'Why does this discussion feel like *déjà vu*? Why do you insist on denying the difference between pornography and eroticism?'

'Because time usually wipes out the distinction! Yesterday's pornography is today's erotica. D. H. Lawrence said what was pornography for one man was the laughter of genius to another.'

'No,' said Mila decisively. 'Eroticism is – and remains – more *subtle*.'

'*Subtle!*' Adriaan exclaimed. 'And where have you ever seen a subtle Afrikaner? It's not in our genes to be subtle! Our Dutch and French ancestors fled here because they were drop-outs and adventurers and religious fanatics. They weren't moderate enough to produce moderate descendants. And the landscape and climate have never cultivated moderation. We just don't live in a subtle environment. We're a nation of intense emotions – even if most of the emotions are repressed most of the time. We can be fucking repressed, but we're certainly not subtle! Even our repression is unsubtle!'

And on the opposite side of the table the other conversation continued, just as intensely. Just as unsubtle, Philip thought, amused. Bobby was talking again, her eyes shining with passion.

'I wish you could have seen those squealing township kids put their feet in the "white" waves of a "white" beach for the first time in their lives! At first they were a bit frightened of the sour-faced policemen, but the waves were so tempting that they soon forgot about them, and at the end they had an absolute jôl. At one stage I closed my eyes so that I couldn't see the police – just sat there listening to the screams of enjoyment – and then I began to imagine that it was just an ordinary picnic in an ordinary country . . .'

Then Philip's attention was again drawn back to the other side of the table where Paul was now holding the floor.

' . . . the front page story about next week's election in the latest *Time*? They say that P. W. Botha is fighting the campaign as a "moderate" – *with a ferocity which only Afrikaners could consider moderate*.'

'Exactly what I mean!' Adriaan cried. 'Even our so-called middle-of-the-road political parties would be considered the lunatic fringe in any more or less civilized country.'

How on earth had the conversation jumped so quickly from pornography to politics? Somehow, thought Philip, all interesting discussions in this country always ended up a political cul-de-sac. He'd known that for years. It was just the speed with which it happened these days which stunned him. While the conversation on his left had leaped equally suddenly, equally unexpectedly, from the political to the personal.

'The longer I know you,' said Bobby with a shy smile at Ralph, who was stroking her hair comfortingly, 'the more you remind me of my brother.'

'I thought you were an only child?'

'No, I had a brother. He's been dead for more than ten years, but I still miss him every day. Maybe more than ever now that Robin is . . . away.' She dragged her fork backwards and forwards on her plate. It was clear that she couldn't work up an appetite tonight. When she spoke again, her voice hung in the air, dull and dead, like a ghost voice on the radio. 'He hanged himself when he was nineteen. I was thirteen. He was my biggest hero.'

Philip felt as though a muscle in his heart had jumped, as if something which was stretched tight inside him had suddenly snapped.

The same way. The same age. He looked at her like a veteran discovering a comrade, someone who had survived the same bloody battle years ago.

'While he was in the army,' she said. 'Something happened on the border. I don't know what. I'll probably never know. Perhaps it wasn't even a specific incident, maybe it was just . . . everything. The whole experience.'

Philip didn't hear the other conversation any more. All his attention was focused on Bobby, on her sad face, her thin hands around the wine glass, her strange, disembodied voice. Remembering his own loss. Painfully intensely. To be thirteen years old and to lose the person closest to you, the very closest, without any warning, to death. At thirteen you're too old to react to grief like an innocent child, but at the same time too young to handle the loss in an adult way. Especially when you're dealing with suicide. A deliberate act which can burden loved ones with unbearable anger and unmentionable guilt. A burden which can hamstring you for life. He ought to know.

'Is that why you've got this thing against national service?' Liane moved forward in her chair, visibly uncomfortable, like most people when death suddenly comes up in a conversation. 'Why you got involved with the ECC?'

'I don't know . . . I think I would have . . . I would probably have got involved with something like that anyway,' Bobby answered hesitatingly. 'War and violence have always disgusted me. Under any circumstances. And to be forced to fight for the maintenance of a value system which goes against everything you believe in . . .'

Philip became aware of Emma's gaze. It made him feel nervous, as it always did when she looked at him like that, as if she read his most secret thoughts with inexplicable understanding. God, where did the love in those grey eyes come from? What had he done to deserve it? What was he to *do* with it?

'But you must remember that my father was a military attaché,' said Bobby with a wry smile. 'A diplomat who had to justify the South African Defence Force's perversity to those abroad. And then the army drove his own son to suicide. I suppose you could see it as some kind of poetic justice. So perhaps I'm just in rebellion against my father.'

'There's an epidemic of suicides among national servicemen these days,' said Max, scratching his black beard. 'It's worse now that they're being sent into the townships. I think the border can somehow still be romanticized. If you're brainwashed enough, of course. The classic war situation, somewhere on the front, far away from your loved ones, defending nation and motherland. But how the hell do you romanticize a Casspir in the streets of a township? What do you do with your conscience – or what's left of your conscience – when you continually have to fire on unarmed children? The number of suicide attempts among national servicemen has risen almost five hundred per cent in the last year. Five hundred per cent. In a year. What it boils down to, is that one out of ten of our proud troepies has tried to commit suicide. It's completely absurd! How the fuck do you keep an army going when your troops are more eager to kill themselves than the so-called enemy!'

If only he could blame the army, thought Philip. If he could just blame *something* – or *someone* – for what his mother did. Oh, he blamed his father for years, of course. But nowadays he wondered whether his mother wasn't a victim of the kind of despair which sometimes overcame him. Despair like a black bag being pulled over your head so that no one can see you, so that you feel as though you can't breathe, so that the darkness and the lack of oxygen begin to affect your mind. And then surely no one could blame you for what you do?

'I don't know what I'll do if the Conservative Party win lots of seats next week.' It was Yvette's soft, controlled voice which brought him back to the table. A floating plank to cling to in all this passion which was spilling over him from either side. The two conversations were beginning to sound all the more like the same conversation, anyway. *The Unbearable Whiteness of Being.* 'I don't know if I can live in a country where the government and the opposition are simply a case of right and extreme right.'

'Of course you can,' said Paul with a sardonic smile. 'We were all born into a society which seems unbearable to any moral person who looks at it from outside. We're all used to it. Like the frog which doesn't jump out of the pot when the water is gradually heated up. The question is not whether we *can* live here, Yvette, it's simply whether we *want* to live here.'

'Louise has decided she doesn't want to,' said Emma. 'She says she's *gatvol*, completely fed up with this mess. She's going to get married to her new lover because he has a British passport.'

'Louise, who only got divorced the other day?' asked Paul in surprise.

'Last year, at least. She's completely calculating about it. She says she's doing it for the passport, but at least she's more honest than Mart and Tomas, who say they're just going to live in London "for a while". "Until things sort themselves out over here," as Tomas puts it.'

'Tomas is one of those optimistic idiots who believes that we're all going to wake up one morning in a free and democratic fairyland,' said Philip, irritated. 'And then he can catch the first available flight out of London and come home with all the other exiles – to a brand new South Africa without any political or social or economic problems! It's the kind of liberal short-sightedness which really gets on my tits!'

Emma looked at him in surprise, with something like relief on her smiling face. And he wondered suddenly whether this apparently independent woman didn't need his incurable pessimism – like a ship needs the heavy weight of an anchor – so as not to drift away on the stream of her own optimism. He had always convinced himself that she was independent enough to survive without him, that *she* was the one who would leave *him* if their relationship became completely impossible, that he would never be forced to make that decision. But if Emma needed his pessimism – like he needed her optimism – then they were probably doomed to stay together. Doomed to spend their lives in mutual irritation, like two castaways on a desert island. Or like most other married couples, he thought with a desperation which closed like a fist about his heart.

After dinner the level of the conversation dropped as quickly as the wine in the bottles. Philip decided to escape outdoors, where he found Max and Bobby in a dark corner.

He looked at the glowing stub between Bobby's fingers in confusion for a moment before he realized that it wasn't a cigarette. Then this gathering isn't so stiflingly suburban after all, he thought, with a strange sense of relief. Probably the first time in his life that he was relieved to see a dagga zol.

'God save me from the suburbs,' he muttered as he sank down on the floor of the stoep next to her. She reached her hand out to offer him a puff, but he shook his head. 'No, I've already told you that dagga doesn't agree with me.'

'A pity,' she said in a detached way. 'Max and I have just decided that life is only bearable if you're a little bit stoned.'

'We were talking about loneliness and fear,' said Max, his face almost invisible in the darkness.

'Ah! Two of my favourite topics. I'd much rather talk about loneliness and fear than about rugby and dresses! Like that lot inside!'

'Are you serious?' asked Bobby.

'About rugby and dresses? Or about loneliness and fear?'

'About the conversation inside.' Bobby pulled on the stub again. 'I can see that you're an expert on loneliness and fear.'

'Is it that obvious?' asked Philip with an expression of exaggerated dismay on his face. 'And I thought I was the little ray of sunshine in this circle of friends!'

'You and your cynical jokes.' Her voice suddenly accusing. 'Why do you always have to mock everything?'

'Self-defence,' said Max. 'If you always mock other people's points of view, you never have to reveal your own, right?'

'Hey! What's going on now?' asked Philip, taken aback. 'I didn't come here to be psychoanalysed!'

'We're just trying to offer you a bit of free advice,' said Max. 'Therapy usually costs a lot of money.'

'If I wanted free advice, I'd write to *Huisgenoot*'s agony aunt!'

His mocking tone didn't quite disguise the annoyance in his voice.

'And if life becomes unbearable?' Bobby sat with her head leaned back against the wall, her eyes closed, and inhaled the last bit of dagga from the stub. 'What will you do then, Philip?'

'Alcohol remains the best crutch. Until the hangover hits you, anyway.'

'Since Robin's been in jail, no crutch can hold me up.'

The lost sound of her voice frightened him so much that for a few moments he could find no words. He saw a single tear creep slowly from under the frame of her glasses, and trickle down her cheek. He wanted to reach out his hand to touch her, but didn't know how to. For the umpteenth time in his life he wished that he could be more like Ralph. Someone who never struggled to reach out physically to other people.

'It feels as though she's dead . . . as if I'm grieving for her . . . but in some ways it's worse than when someone's dead. There's no finality, just this continual uncertainty. I don't know how much longer I can take it.'

'At least they haven't begun to murder white women in jail,' he tried to console her.

'Not yet.' Her whole cheek was wet now. 'But death is not the worst thing that can happen to a political prisoner. They can humiliate you so much that you begin to look forward to death. That's what I'm most afraid of. That they'll break her spirit. That she'll be a living corpse when they let her go one day. *If* they let her go one day.'

'Not Robin,' said Max and folded his hand over hers. 'She's been there before. She knows what to expect. She's too strong for them. She's one of the strongest women I know.'

'That's what I try to tell myself all the time.' She wiped her thin hands over her cheeks. Her nails were chewed shorter than ever these days, her cheeks hollower than before, her eyes bigger, her body skinnier. Almost like someone in a concentration camp. And the fact that she'd recently shaved her hair as short as a schoolboy made her look even more like a war victim. 'But I know that every person has a breaking point. And I'm scared . . . terribly scared . . . that they'll push her to that point this time. I never thought it was possible to love someone so much. After my brother died . . . it was as though a piece of my heart died with him too . . . a big piece. Too big. I lost the ability to really care for someone else.'

Philip remembered the emotions he'd had to wrestle with after his mother hanged herself in a farm shed. A few days after his thirteenth birthday. As though she'd just waited until her youngest child was old enough to manage without her. Of course he wasn't old enough. There are some things you are never old enough for.

'I think that's why the Struggle was so irresistible to me,' she said, still whispering, as though she didn't care whether they could hear her or not. 'If I couldn't commit myself to one other person, at least I could commit myself to the suffering masses out there . . . They always talk about the relationship problems people in the Struggle have to deal with . . . as though it's caused by the Struggle . . . but it's also the kind of people who are drawn to the Struggle. People like me who would have had problems with relationships anyway. Until I got to know Robin. She made it possible for me to feel again. And now she's gone. And sometimes the loneliness just gets so fucking overwhelming that I can't handle it!'

'I never learned to feel again.'

Philip was silent for a moment, frightened by his own voice, by this unexpected confession, and listened to the sighing of the waves, the muffled voices in the house, the singsong wailing of someone other than Bob Dylan, thank God, from the speakers. Then he told them about his mother. A subject he'd always avoided like the plague. Even when he tried to speak to Emma about it, every word stuck in his throat like a shard of glass. And now he was sitting here on a dark stoep next to the sea, astounded at how easily the words fell from his mouth. He even told them about the pathetic letter which she'd left to try to comfort him. Nothing for his older brother or sister, nothing for his father, just the last few words to her youngest son, the one who was always closest to her heart. *Because you're too young to understand.* God! As if the rest of the family wouldn't also struggle to understand!

'I'll never forget the expression on my father's face when he gave me that letter. Almost like hate . . . and fear. It was in an envelope, so he didn't know what she'd written. And I punished him by never telling him. But I was also furious with my mother for being so inconsiderate! She could also have written a few words to him. Or to her other children. All she did by singling me out was to alienate me even more from the rest of the family. She and I were always the two odd cases in the house. But I suppose if you tried to be too considerate, you wouldn't be able to commit suicide. If you thought about everyone you're leaving behind.'

He wondered who was singing with such raw emotion inside the house. Someone Emma often listened to. Although it had never felt as though the voice was wrapping barbed wire around his heart. *I'll tell you all my secrets, but I lie about my past.* He'd never paid much attention to contemporary music. Always preferred the more subtle emotions evoked by classical music. It just goes to show. The moment you begin to bare your soul to other people, you become as vulnerable as a ruin. Any emotion can blow through you like a cold wind.

'The worst of all is the loss of feeling Bobby's just spoken about. That you can be so scared of ever experiencing such intense emotions again that you lose the power to feel. I temporarily regained it after the birth of my son . . .'

He was shocked, once again, at what he was saying. Beside him, Max rummaged in the top pocket of his denim jacket and brought out another spliff. The match flame flickered over his frowning face as he lit it.

'That's why I'm so scared of fatherhood. It *forces* you to feel. But after my son . . . after he was brain damaged . . .'

No. He wasn't going to talk about this as well. About what happened to him after Mel's operation, after it dawned on him that nothing remained of the laughing, babbling little blond boy he remembered. Just an empty body which would lie on a bed for life. And a pair of expressionless blue eyes which looked only vaguely familiar.

'Then I stopped feeling for the second time,' he said, in as matter-of-fact a way as possible. 'This time apparently for ever. Who's that singing inside?'

'Tom Waits,' Max replied. 'Are you sure you don't want a puff?'

'Ag, why not,' he said sighing and took the glowing cigarette from his friend. He wondered if it was the new marriage – the strange, confusing, conflicting feelings which it evoked in him – which made him act so out of character tonight. He inhaled the dagga with a strange feeling of excitement, like the first time he'd done it, when he was still an idealistic student. Before he decided that it didn't agree with him. Neither dagga nor idealism. 'I suppose it can't really make me feel worse than usual, can it?'

But he said it with a twisted smile, because at that moment, on that dark stoep with the soothing sighing of the waves and Tom Waits' barbed-wire voice in the background, he felt better than he had in months.

Adriaan and Ralph and the child and the dog played with a flapping kite on the windy, deserted beach below the house. Emma and Mila sat on deckchairs on the stoep, sheltered from the wind, each with a book on her lap; Emma with a Salman Rushdie novel, Mila with an American journalist's report on this strange society here at the foot of Africa. But each time that Emma looked up, Mila was staring longingly at the beach, the book still open on the same page. And each time Emma saw the expression on Mila's face, her irritation rose a little higher.

The rest of the company had decided over lunch to visit the nature reserve at Cape Point. It was Liane who'd said that she'd love to see how the Atlantic and Indian Oceans flowed together – which started a drawn-out argument about where the oceans actually met. At Cape Agulhas, as Philip and Bobby and Paul contended ('because any schoolkid knows it's the most southerly tip of the continent') or at Cape Point, as Max and Yvette and Liane maintained ('because even a baboon can feel that the sea to the left of Cape Point is warmer than the sea to the right of Cape Point').

'And what about the Two Oceans Marathon which is held at Cape Point every year?' Max wanted to know.

'It's just a name,' Philip explained impatiently. 'Who the fuck would want to take part in the One Ocean Marathon?'

'What the fuck does it matter where the oceans meet!' Adriaan eventually cried out with his hands in the air, tired of the pointless argument.

In the end, those to whom it did matter decided that a drive to Cape Point would be a pleasant outing. Of course no one would change their stance. ('Of course the people at Cape Point will say it happens at Cape Point! They'll lose their jobs if all the tourists wanted to go to Agulhas!') Sometimes Emma felt as if no one in this company would ever change their stance on anything.

Mila jumped up without warning – her expression suddenly relieved, like someone who had made a difficult decision after a tortuous struggle of conscience – and disappeared quickly into the house. She came back with a beer in her hand, the green glass of the bottle misty from the cold.

'Want to share with me?'

Emma wondered why it sounded as though she wanted to share more than a beer.

'I wouldn't mind a sip or two,' she answered, her eyes on her book again.

Mila sank down into the deckchair and stretched her legs out in front of her. She was wearing the same pair of shorts as the day before. The unshaven stubble on her calves glistened like a scattering of golden glitter in the sun. She hooked her bare feet into the railing of the stoep, took a gulp of beer and gave the bottle to Emma. The book lay forgotten on the ground beside her, Emma noticed, with a feeling of unease.

'Do you ever lust after other men? I mean apart from Philip?'

The question was so unexpected that for a moment Emma could only stare at her, dumbfounded.

'Well . . . sometimes . . . it just . . . happens,' she stammered. Like last night in the kitchen, she thought anxiously. Would Ralph have said something to Mila? But surely Ralph couldn't have read her thoughts! She took a sip of beer and stared out at the sea. 'These days perhaps more often than before. Do you think it gets worse as you get older?'

'Yes,' said Mila scowling. 'I can only hope that it stops sometime. It would be awful to still be turned on by a sexy young man at the age of seventy!'

'But don't you think that when you're seventy, the object of your desire will also be . . . sort of elderly?' she asked with a tense little giggle.

'Not necessarily.'

Emma watched how the brightly coloured kite began to sink with a slow, graceful, spiral motion. Then it jerked suddenly and dived straight down – but just before it hit the sand, the wind caught it again and carried it upwards in a beautiful curve, higher and higher and higher. She caught her breath involuntarily, overcome by the excitement of the performance, like a child in a circus tent. Then she heard Mila's heavy sigh beside her.

'Why are you suddenly so worried about lust?'

'Because of me and Adriaan.'

'What about you and Adriaan?'

Emma took a quick gulp of beer to dispel the shock in her voice.

'We've got this . . . vibe between us. I don't know what to call it. A magnetic attraction. But that sounds so incredibly corny. Potent enough to set the whole bloody house alight. As you put it when you warned me against him that first time. Or warned me against myself.'

'But I thought that was over! I thought you listened to my warning!'

'Things like that don't just go away, Emma.' She took the beer bottle from Emma and drank from it with a desperate expression on her face. 'All the warnings in the world couldn't make it go away.'

'But it doesn't *look* as though you . . .'

'We've just learned to hide it better,' said Mila quietly. 'We've got more to hide . . .'

Emma reached for the bottle in bewilderment. She didn't want to hear any more. She wanted to stop her ears, she wanted to jump up and run away, she wanted to shake Mila by the shoulders.

And yet she asked, 'What do you mean?'

'Well.' Mila took a deep breath, placed a cigarette between her lips and lit it with a hand which trembled slightly. 'We don't have sex any more. Not in the technical sense of the word.'

She pulled her long tanned legs in under her body. Lifted her chin so that her profile looked proud and confident again, especially with the cigarette in the sophisticated red mouth. Like an old-fashioned movie star.

'What do you have then?' asked Emma, astonished.

'I wish I knew. Last year we began ... something. He was in Johannesburg for a few days. For an exhibition. But we decided we couldn't handle it. It was too intense.'

Emma heard Adriaan laugh – an exuberant sound which rose up above the waves and the wind for a moment – while the kite did a nose-dive into the sand again. He lifted Mona to his hip so that she could hold the string with him. Ralph picked up the kite and ran a little way with it, his hands high above his head, before letting go. The wind scooped it up immediately and carried it upwards, so high that it looked as though it was going to scrape the cottonwool clouds. Adriaan shouted something, but they couldn't hear his words on the verandah, just the deep, dark sound of his voice. Ralph stood with his hands on his hips, his tousled golden-brown hair blowing about his head, and watched the kite growing smaller and smaller. They're so different, thought Emma, so completely different. The one so thickset and sturdy and heavy, as though his bare feet didn't just stand flat on the earth, but grew out of it, like a tree; the other so tall and lean and light-footed, as though his body didn't really touch the ground. The one reminded you of a friendly bulldog, the other always of a dangerous cat. And here Mila sat beside her, attracted to both, torn between the forbidden excitement of the one and the safe familiarity of the other.

'Too intense,' Emma mumbled.

It wasn't a question. She only said it because she didn't know what else to say.

'Look, I know it wasn't the first time in Adriaan's marriage that he's slept with someone other than his wife. We all know about his escapades.'

'But you're not "someone else", Mila! You're my friend! Yvette is my friend! I introduced the two of you. I thought you'd become friends. And now you tell me without as much as a blush that you've slept with her husband!'

'Not without a blush.' Mila closed her red mouth stubbornly around the beer bottle, took a few swigs and was quiet for a while before she spoke again. 'I really agonized about this, Emma. Jesus, did I agonize. I'm not saying it so that you'll feel sorry for me, I just want you to know that I didn't just do it head over heels. It was almost a year after I'd met him that weekend in Yzerfontein. I told myself for a whole year that it would blow over, I should just be patient, one surely can't stay turned on for ever by someone you hardly know! But it didn't blow over. I began sleeping with Ralph again. Just to forget about Adriaan. I even tried to get pregnant by Ralph. But then even that was a fuck-up.'

'When did *that* happen?' asked Emma.

'But I told you?' Mila looked at her, confused. 'That morning at Hangklip?' She shook her head quickly. 'No, it was Yvette and Liane that . . .'

'*Yvette?*'

'Not about Adriaan! You're the first person I've told about Adriaan. No, I just told them about my pathetic attempt to get pregnant. Anyway, it didn't work. And then Adriaan came to Johannesburg for an exhibition and when I saw him again, after all those months, I just knew. That it hadn't blown over. That it was worse than ever.'

Emma took a cigarette from Mila's packet and lit it, frowning. She felt like someone who had been made an accessory to a crime against her will. Attracted by the adventure of the forbidden, by her desire to know more, and at the same time repulsed by the absolute certainty that it was forbidden.

'It was obviously also not the first time that I've slept with a married man. But it was never like that before. It was never . . . even nearly . . . so intense. We just couldn't get enough of each other. We shut ourselves away in my flat for four days and . . . screwed. Without stopping. I lost five kilograms because I didn't eat or sleep. It was unbearable. All we knew was there was no way that he could go on with his marriage and I could go on with my life if we didn't try to control . . . this passion. And I'm not talking about sexual passion. It was more than sex. Don't look at me like that, Emma! I know everyone always thinks it's more than sex! But we're both old enough and experienced enough to recognize the difference between sex and emotion.'

She stubbed out her cigarette and stared at her bare knees.

'That's why we got scared,' she said slowly. 'We could handle the sex. No problem. It's the emotion that was . . . frightening. We were both almost thirty-seven years old and neither of us had ever experienced something so intense. I don't mean that he doesn't love Yvette! He loves her more than he'll ever love another woman. He'll spend the rest of his life with her. What he feels for me is something else. Maybe also love. I don't know. Maybe another kind of love. But too intense to last. Like a flame which has to burn out somewhere along the line. I just don't know when. What scares me the most is the thought that it could still take many years before . . . before we can look at each other . . . like other people . . . without feeling that we're going to burst into flames.'

Her face suddenly twisted like a piece of crumpled paper. Emma looked away quickly, scared that she was going to cry, at the two men who were now standing next to each other laughing. Adriaan with Mona on his back, Ralph with the kite string in his hand, the kite still high in the air.

'So you're not sleeping together any more.'

Mila had managed to smooth her face again, blink away the welling tears, even to smile weakly.

'Sometimes I wish we could just fuck until we're sick of each other. It's still the best way to put sexual obsession behind you. But we're too scared to risk it. Now we're trying very hard to stay away from each other . . . but we don't always manage it . . .'

'Listen Mila, stop beating about the bush and answer my question. Are you two screwing or not?'

'We don't have "sexual intercourse" as it's described in the dictionary. But we can't leave each other alone either.'

'You mean you mess around like two horny teenagers?'

'I suppose that's one way of putting it . . .'

'When you visit them on the farm?'

'No! Not in Yvette's house! That would just be too awful!'

'Sorry,' said Emma with cutting sarcasm. 'I obviously don't understand the etiquette of this kind of relationship. So it's OK to have an affair with a friend's husband – as long as penetration doesn't take place? And as long as whatever does happen, doesn't happen in the friend's house?'

Mila turned her face away quickly, like someone who'd been slapped and was waiting for a blow on the other cheek. Emma shook her head and stared at the beach, where Ralph was carefully reeling the kite in. Adriaan waved to them and began to walk towards the house.

'I'm sorry. I didn't mean to sound so bitchy.' Emma was suddenly anxious to lighten the atmosphere before Adriaan reached the house. 'I think I'm in shock. I need time to process everything. Can we talk about something else in the meantime?'

'Like?' Mila said, without a flicker of interest.

'Your work at parliament? You haven't said anything about it the whole weekend. Isn't that what you've wanted to do for years?'

Mila sighed next to her. 'Yes, I've been dreaming about it for years. Perhaps just my stupid feminism again. You know, because so few women have managed it. I thought it was the best way to prove myself in the business. To sit among the boys in parliament, to hang out in the bars with them and play snooker till late. *Anything you can do* . . . you know? And now that I've got the chance at last, it's a huge disappointment. Like so many things people dream about for years. It just feels totally . . . irrelevant! A bunch of old white men in black suits sitting around talking shit. It's much more exciting to go to a meeting in a township. That's where the action is these days, that's where history is being written, not in parliament. Definitely not in parliament. I feel as though I'm watching an old elephant bull slowly dying. And it's a fucking depressing sight.'

'How long now, do you think? Before the elephant dies?'

'Some days I think it can't be more than five years. Other days it feels as though it's going to go on for ever. Like hell.' Mila stared in a detached way at the label of the beer bottle in her hand. Then she lifted her chin, brushed her fringe back impatiently and smiled again faintly. 'Like my passion for an overweight, married Casanova. While a wonderful, available man like Ralph is waiting at my back door, as it were. It makes no sense, right? But some days it feels like it will go on for ever.'

'We're going for a walk,' Emma announced casually as she and Philip strolled through the sitting room.

Too casually, it seemed. Liane immediately looked up from the French fashion magazine she was paging through.

'In this wind?'

'I don't mind the wind.'

Now Mila looked up too. She was sitting cross-legged on the wooden floor of the sitting room, studying the *Weekly Mail*.

'I thought you *hated* the wind?'

'When it blows in the city, yes. Not at the sea. Not in nature.' She had actually begun to blush, Emma realized. She brushed her hair awkwardly from her glowing cheeks. 'Look, if you want me to fill in an official application before I can go for a walk along the beach, just let me know!'

'No, I was just a bit surprised, that's all,' said Mila, amused.

'Man,' Philip said sighing, 'we actually want to go and screw somewhere in the great outdoors. Does anyone want to come along?'

'Sorry,' giggled Liane. 'I keep forgetting that you're meant to be a honeymoon couple.'

'We aren't a "honeymoon couple".' As he opened the glass door to the stoep, a wild gust of wind burst in. He closed the door again quickly. As though he suddenly had doubts about the wisdom of his decision. 'But seeing that you all insist on calling us a honeymoon couple, I'm sure you won't be offended if we try to get a bit of traditional honeymoon action out of the weekend?'

'But isn't this traditional action supposed to take place indoors?' asked Mila, her blue eyes stretched wide.

'Not when your friends are on honeymoon with you. Look, I know I have many sins and perversions, but exhibitionism has never really attracted me.'

'Well, I'm crazy about sex myself,' said Mila. 'But you have to be unbelievably horny to brave this wind!'

Emma slipped laughingly out through the stoep door with Philip, a feeling of daring like a warm hollow in her stomach. Outside, the wind caught her full in the face and snatched the laugh from her mouth. She clung to Philip's arm and stumbled forward a few paces on the footpath which led to the beach. The warmth in her stomach vanished completely.

But she pressed on resolutely because she remembered the excitement of the previous day, when they'd had sex utterly unexpectedly next to the sea, sheltered by a high rock, not far from where their friends sat on the beach. Utterly unexpectedly for her, in any case. Philip had probably had more than a romantic sunset walk in mind from the start. He wasn't a man for romantic walks. In fact he didn't like any kind of walking. Another of the many differences between them. Walking was about the only kind of exercise she'd ever enjoyed. And sex of course. He preferred sports where you had to move as fast as possible and smash a ball with all your might. Squash, tennis, cricket, that kind of thing. And sex. Of course. Probably the only way that he could release all his suppressed emotions. Otherwise he would lie still for hours reading – just the hand with the cigarette constantly being raised to his mouth, apparently independent from the rest of his body, like the arm of a robot. Or sometimes not even reading, just lying staring into nothingness, expressionless. Sometimes he even forgot to smoke. That's when she got so scared that she fled blindly, it didn't matter where to, just to get away from the despondency which hung about him like a thick bank of mist. Scared that she would also get lost in that mist.

'It's like living with a fucking wax doll!' she had accused him again recently. 'Like that model of Sleeping Beauty in Madame Tussaud's! It looks as though she's breathing, but you know she's never going to wake up!'

She had wanted to say it in a joking way, but she could hear the despair in her own voice. He had just stared at her, expressionless. No, not expressionless. Not a muscle in his face moved, but his eyes were two grey-blue wells which attracted and repulsed her at the same time, as though he were daring her to dive, to burst through the seemingly calm surface and sink to the dark bottom. But she had turned her back on him and asked if he didn't want to come for a walk with her.

'You go for a walk.' As you would say to a child: *Go and play outside for a while. The grown-ups want to talk.* 'I walked enough when I was a child.'

On the farm in South West where he had grown up. On that never-ending farm, with its relentless, desolate plains, in that relentless, desolate country. Where he had only taken her once, for an intensely uncomfortable visit to his father and stepmother. The woman he could never forgive for taking his mother's place too quickly. She had probably begun to take her place even before her death. The merry widow who had come to stay on the neighbouring farm for a few months, babbling and bubbling, plump, with heavy breasts and soft curves. While his mother grew thinner and quieter by the day. Until she was little more than a drifting shadow, a gaunt woman in a huge straw hat who wandered obsessively around the farm, a transparent vision in the terrible heat. That's why Philip didn't like walking, Emma suspected. Not because he'd walked too much, but because his mother had walked too much. Obsessively, aimlessly, senselessly. Behind all his other fears she always sensed the fear that he would become like his mother.

'None of us have idyllic childhood memories,' she consoled him time after time. 'Not even our cheerful friend Liane.'

She told him about the night when an inebriated Liane confessed to her two student friends that she'd do anything – *anything*, she declared passionately – to have her early teenage years over again. Better. Prettier, happier, more romantic. It was the first time that Emma and Yvette had ever seen her drunk. At one stage she began to cry. Her greatest fear, she told them tearfully, was that she would turn out like her father. *Addicted to drink and sex*. That's how she'd put it.

'You're far too puritanical for that,' Emma had said. 'If you're not careful, you'll end up as the oldest virgin on campus!'

And then she really began to sob. Her second greatest fear, she declared, was that she would turn out like her mother. *Frigid and fanatically religious*. The next morning she couldn't remember anything. Or perhaps she forgot on purpose. A week or two later she told them about her idyllic platteland childhood again. Emma and Yvette looked at each other and decided not to say anything. That's what they still did, every time Liane began to speak about her fairy-tale youth.

She looked at Philip beside her, his head lowered as though he wanted to charge at the wind like a raging bull, the line of his lips obstinate. She knew that intolerant expression on his face so well, when things didn't work out the way he wanted. And suddenly, without any warning, her heart was again filled with inexplicable love for this inexplicable man she had just married.

It wasn't a church wedding or a family wedding – but at least a proper celebration. She had worn an off-white wedding dress and her mother had burst into tears when she saw her. Philip had agreed that a colleague who had studied theology and lost his faith somewhere along the way could perform the official marriage ceremony at their house in Stellenbosch. His only condition was that God's name shouldn't be dragged into the ceremony unnecessarily. ('There are limits to what I'll do to please you, Emma.') The ex-theology student had viewed it as a personal challenge and succeeded in delivering a spirited sermon without ever referring to any supernatural beings. After that they had partied with their friends until the early hours and just before dawn had ventured down the steep footpath to the isolated beach house. All pissed and loaded with luggage, Emma giggling in her off-white wedding dress. The fact that no one sprained an ankle or broke a leg was probably the best possible evidence that supernatural beings were at work somewhere after all. But she hadn't yet shared this thought with her atheist husband.

And when he'd unexpectedly suggested a walk along the sea yesterday, she had looked at him in surprise and immediately, gratefully agreed. When he turned to her just as unexpectedly – the moment they had vanished behind that high rock – his breathing heavy in her ear, his hands all over her body, her surprise had been even greater. His embrace was extraordinarily urgent. Admittedly, if you wanted to do this kind of thing in the open air, within sight of your friends (apart from a strategically placed rock), you had to do it with a certain urgency. Anyway, she had found it extraordinarily exciting. The almost brusque way that he had pressed her back against the smooth rock, impatiently unbuttoned her jeans and pushed them down to her knees. The stone cold under her bare buttocks, his penis hot between her legs, the tip already moist, as though he had worked himself up while they walked, while she had clambered unsuspectingly in front of him over this high rock. He lifted her up slightly against the rock, his hands under her bottom, and penetrated her, straining, shoving, hard. Scarcely two minutes later they'd climaxed together. Perfect coordination.

'And I thought married sex was going to be boring,' she had gasped.

He just grinned and pulled up his zip.

And now they were braving this blustering wind because they wanted to repeat yesterday's excitement. Never a good idea to try to recreate a moment of unexpected pleasure. By this time they ought to know that, she thought bitterly. It wasn't as though they were two inexperienced beginners. They had always had an unusually active sex life. So active that it sometimes worried her. As though that was all that bound them together, the only glue in their relationship. That sticky mixure of semen and vaginal juices. Even during the lowest points in their relationship – and there were many low points – they could still reach breathtaking sexual heights. These days she didn't agonize about it any more. She convinced herself that any lasting relationship had to have a foundation strong enough to withstand emotional earthquakes. Their foundation was sex. Had always been sex, would probably always be sex. But sometimes, just sometimes, she wondered why she always thought of it as *sex*. *If two people love each other, surely they ought to make love occasionally? Rather than always having sex?*

But the fact that she had stopped agonizing about it didn't mean that she'd stopped longing. She had always longed for more than a 'normal relationship'. More romantic, more passionate, more uncontrollable, more . . . *more*. Probably something to do with the stories she always carried around in her head. If the greatest part of your existence takes place in your imagination, reality can begin to look terribly boring. Her relationship with Philip was at least not *boring*. But it was also not the Great Passion which she still, secretly, desired. She had realized it again that morning. That was why she was so irritated by Mila's unwelcome outpouring. Not just because she was unwillingly dragged into an intimate intrigue, but also because she felt a prickling of envy. Because she could only ever dream about the kind of unstoppable, uncontrollable, overwhelming passion which Mila had talked about.

Philip suddenly stood still and looked at her, shaking his head.

'No, look, I'm not as randy as all that.' She struggled to hear him because the wind was thundering in her ears. Struggled to see him because the sand was blowing into her eyes. Decided again that they must be crazy. 'I had an instant in the wind in mind. Not humping in a hurricane!'

'Come, let's go back,' she said immediately. 'We can have ordinary double-bed sex in the dark tonight. Like most married couples.'

Perhaps they could even manage to make love, she thought as they walked back, a lot faster, the wind now pushing them from behind. Like most married couples must manage to do *sometimes*.

'Who wants more sausage?' Max lifted up a big piece of boerewors with a barbecue fork and held it up like a tombola prize. A few drops of fat fell on the sizzling coals. 'Come on, there's lots left! Eat, for night approaches! Braai, the beloved country! Ours is not to wonder why, ours is but to drink and braai . . .' He sounded like an auctioneer at an agricultural show on the platteland.

'If you thought up all those slogans yourself,' said Ralph, 'a bright future in advertising awaits you.'

'Or in the Struggle,' said Bobby. 'We could do with something more original than "Workers of the world unite".'

'It's all the same thing, isn't it?' said Philip in a combative voice. 'The only difference between the Struggle and the advertising industry is that the Struggle's copywriters aren't much good.'

'Philip?' Max brought the piece of sausage a step closer to Philip's plate – which was already piled high with a lamb chop and a salted rib and a toasted sandwich and a gigantic potato wrapped in foil. 'You'll have to do your bit, my bra. After all you're our prime example of a carnivore. *A meat eater from South West!*'

'Namibia,' grinned Philip passing his plate to Max obediently.

'Just look at Bobby there next to you. Not a scrap of meat on her plate. That's what happens when you hang out with Communists and moffies. Before you know it, you're a vegetarian.'

'I stopped eating red meat long before I began hanging out with Communists and moffies,' mumbled Bobby.

'Speaking of Communists,' said Adriaan after he'd taken a big bite of his chop, his lips shiny with fat, 'I've always seen you as a bastard *soutpiel* – because of your English father and because you were at that fancy English boys' school – so I must admit that I was quite worried when you insisted on taking charge of the braai this afternoon. I never trust an Englishman with a braai grid in his hand, I've been to too many disastrous "barbecues" with my English friends. But you braai like a boer! Thank god!'

Max bowed his head modestly, a pleased smile on his bearded face. They were all sitting on the stoep, sheltered from the wind which had raged right through the night and was still sweeping the beach every now and again in half-hearted gusts. The sky looked as though it had been scrubbed clean, the thin fleecy clouds like transparent net curtains against glistening blue glass. The sea was also a fresher, brighter blue than the previous day. The whole scene like an old painting which has been properly dusted down for the first time in years, the colours so surprisingly bright that it seems newly painted.

'And now that I've passed Adriaan's litmus test,' said Max, still smiling, 'I've got enough self-confidence to make my Big Announcement. I'm going to leave academia.'

'Are you going farming?' Adriaan asked jokingly.

'No, I'm going to start working as an advocate next year.'

'Welcome to the real world,' grinned Paul.

'Advocate Ackermann.' Ralph looked pleased. 'Nice alliteration. Sounds good.'

'Sounds better than *comrade* Ackermann anyway!' laughed Liane.

'When did you make this earthshattering decision?' Emma wanted to know.

'I've been agonizing about it for years.' He sat down next to the table, under a broad sun-shade of unbleached cotton, and sipped his white wine. The smile had vanished and he rubbed his beard a little anxiously. 'But recently I got this now-or-never feeling. There are things happening in the country which I want to be part of, and I can't do that while I'm sitting in a sterile academic environment. I think I've finally realized that I'm a doer rather than a thinker. I'd never have become a great thinker, anyway,' he added with an apologetic shrug.

'You're going to miss the holidays,' warned Philip.

'There are lots of things I'm going to miss. Sexy female students who stare at me as though I'm the Fourth Wise Man. The one their mothers never told them about. To name just one example. But there are many people in the Struggle who need a good advocate. Of course I don't yet know whether I'll be a good advocate. But I want to at least try.'

He sounded so sincere, so idealistic, that even Philip couldn't bring himself to be flippant. Besides, it was what he also wanted to do, one day. Resign from his safe, often boring post as a political science lecturer, to venture to do something more daring, more exciting. The problem was that somewhere along the way he'd forgotten what it was that he thought he could do long ago, besides becoming an academic.

'It sounds like the right decision,' said Yvette, pleased. 'I've always thought if you no longer believe in what you're doing, you should begin something else as soon as possible.'

'Easier said,' muttered Philip before he could stop himself.

'You could also do something else, Philip.'

'Easier said,' he repeated, as he looked away, shaking his head.

But what was the use? You couldn't argue against such naïvety. You couldn't even mock it. Sometimes he felt as though he was surrounded by irrationality – Yvette's naïvety, Max's idealism, Liane's cheerfulness, Adriaan's bravado, Emma's optimism – as if his friends all lived in a fool's paradise. Although it was also possible that *he* was the fool. The idiot who still believed in the power of reason. In an irrational universe.

'Didn't you say long ago that you wanted to write?' asked Max.

'Long ago. Since then I've realized that I can't write anything that hasn't been written already. And written better as well.'

'It's not what you write,' Emma protested immediately, as he should have predicted, 'it's how you write. That's all that counts. If you're honest, if you're true to your inner voice, if you say what *you* want to say . . .'

She stopped suddenly, embarrassed, and brushed the hair from her face. Of course it wasn't the first time that they'd argued about this subject. His fear of exposing himself – as she saw it – which made him try to prevent her from exposing herself. She didn't expect him to *encourage* her to write, she'd often told him. *You don't have to bring me coffee or massage my neck while I'm at the computer.* But why must he always try to *discourage* her? That wasn't how *he* saw it, of course. But he'd stopped trying to explain his point of view to her long ago.

She saw his behaviour as chauvinistic, his lack of interest in her writing as a suppressed sense of threat. How could he say to her that her writing wasn't *brilliant* enough to threaten him? She could write – he would even admit that she wrote very well – but there was still an enormous difference between very good and brilliant. And if you can't be brilliant – if you can't be Shakespeare or Flaubert or Tolstoy – then the whole exercise becomes a waste of time. That's how he saw it.

'Unless you discard all literary pretensions,' he said as he ripped the last bit of mutton from the bone with his teeth. 'Unless you decide to write detective stories or sex-and-shopping novels, with the sole aim of making as much money as possible. Nothing wrong with that! Business is business, after all, and words on paper can be an excellent business proposition!'

'Then you may as well discard the idea of stories.' Ralph sat on the floor of the stoep with his plate balanced on his long legs. 'If you want to make money you have to write cookbooks or religious books. That's all that Afrikaners want to read. Just look at the bestseller lists! They all consist of books which tell you how to live your life – from how to be a good parent to how to be a good pet owner. We must be a fucking insecure nation to need so much advice! And the very top sellers are always cookbooks and religious books. In fact, if you could combine the two, you'd probably get the biggest bestseller ever. Something like *Prayer and Preserves*. Or *On My Knees In Front of the Oven*. Funny that no one's thought of it yet.'

'Except that *On My Knees In Front of the Oven* could be seen as a suicide manual,' giggled Emma. 'It has the same tone as *With My Wrists Over the Washbasin*.'

'No reason why an Afrikaans suicide manual shouldn't sell brilliantly, either,' grinned Ralph.

'I'd love to write a cookbook one day, too,' said Adriaan, helping himself to more meat. 'But I've got something less spiritual in mind. I think if you can combine food and sex, you've got a winning recipe.'

'*Pornographic Puddings*?' asked Mila sarcastically.

'Something like that, yes. Food which looks erotic, food you can eat in erotic ways, food you can do other erotic things with . . . A sexy version of *Cook and Enjoy*!'

'The Afrikaner way is more like *Eat Up and Be Grateful*,' said Mila.

'Forget about Afrikaners,' said Philip. 'If you want to make money, you have to write in English. Even if you don't want to make money, you may as well begin writing in English.'

He heard Emma draw a sharp breath opposite him. Another topic they argued about regularly. Her blind loyalty to a language with one foot in the grave, as he saw it. His cynical betrayal of a language which has been unfairly condemned to death, as she saw it. But Emma said nothing, to his surprise. It was Mila who turned to him, full of indignation.

'No, it's more necessary than ever to write in Afrikaans! We just have to stop using this stiff dictionary language every time we pick up our pens!' Mila leaned forward on her deckchair, her husky voice so passionate that all her friends stared at her in surprise. 'We must write as we speak. That's how the language developed, after all, when people stopped using formal Dutch to write, when they began writing in this ordinary "kitchen language". Now the kitchen language has again become the stiff language of church and state, so we have to take the revolution further.'

'And what about the more recent history?' asked Philip. 'You can't wish Soweto away, Mila.'

'Our black countrymen aren't going to wake up tomorrow and decide, *Oh, what a beautiful language,*' said Max, shaking his head.

It wasn't often that he and Max ended up on the same side of an argument, realized Philip. As opposed to Emma and her female friends who always clustered together, he and his friends enjoyed exploring different directions in a discussion. At least, *he* enjoyed it. It seemed to him that Max was growing tired of the endless arguments.

'If the Afrikaner is no longer in power, it will no longer be the "language of the oppressor",' said Mila with conviction. 'And we all know that the Afrikaner can't stay in power for much longer! Meanwhile, we ought to begin to claim back the language from all those arseholes in black suits and uniforms who hijacked it!'

'I don't understand it,' said Philip, frowning. 'I don't understand this passion for the language. I'd love to believe it's just plain self-preservation – because you're dependent on the language to earn your daily bread – but surely you could write just as well in English if you had to?'

'Of course I can write a political report in English. It's what I'll end up doing anyway. There isn't much of a future for me in the conservative Afrikaans press. But there are certain things you can *only* say in the language you absorbed with your mother's milk.'

'There are certain words and expressions which cannot be translated,' Emma agreed immediately. 'I'm crazy about the way we repeat words. *Nou-nou, kort-kort, speel-speel.* Perhaps just another example of our lack of subtlety. I mean, why say a word once if you can say it twice?'

'Afrikaans can never sound subtle,' said Adriaan. 'Not with all those guttural sounds. That's what I'd miss most if I ever lived in another country. Words like *grot, graaf, gogga* . . . '

'Then you'll have to go and live in Sweden,' said Philip unsympathetically. 'There everyone sounds as though they're constantly trying to get a fishbone out of their throats.'

'I'd miss the names of animals and plants.' Ralph brushed his long fingers through his hair and grimaced self-consciously. 'Have you ever paged through a bird guide and noticed how unimaginative the English names look alongside the Afrikaans ones? "Double-breasted" this and "white-billed" that. While in Afrikaans you get names like *kelk-iewyn* and *troupand.*'

'Well, you can't really imagine the English calling birds "wine-cup" and "wedding ring", can you?' said Philip.

'I think about it a lot,' said Emma, her voice unexpectedly melancholic. 'About what I'd miss if I had to go away.'

'What do you mean if you "*had*" to go away?' asked Bobby with sudden, sharp interest, after spending most of the meal staring sadly at the sea. 'What would force you to go away?'

'I don't know. Perhaps just the opportunity to do it,' answered Emma with disarming honesty. 'You know, if I had a job I could do something with overseas? Ag, well, it's just a kind of daydream. What would I miss if I left? In the same vein as, What would I grab if the house was on fire?'

Bobby turned her head to look at the sea again, gnawing at her thumbnail. The sun shone on the lenses of her glasses so that you couldn't see the expression in her eyes.

'And in the last few months there've been so many acquaintances and friends leaving . . .' said Emma. 'One can't help but wonder about it sometimes. I've come to the conclusion that it's not just the obvious things that I'll miss. My friends and the mountain and the sea and Afrikaans swear words . . . I think it's also all those "typical" Afrikaans things which I don't like. Braaivleis and rugby and Mike Schutte jokes and the sound of a Kreepy Krauly in a suburban swimming pool. Perhaps even boeremusiek!'

A gust of wind tugged at her hair, fanning it out like a peacock's tail, glowing orange in the sun. She had rolled up the sleeves of her T-shirt so that the freckles on her white shoulders looked like fine spatterings of paint. Philip stared at her, astounded at the way in which something in his stomach suddenly contracted, the involuntary reaction of his body to a picture he'd seen so many times before. *Is this how it feels to love someone?* Or was it just his hormones being stirred up by her hair and her freckles and her unexpected melancholy?

'I think I can live without boeremusiek!' laughed Liane behind her dark glasses. 'But it's true that you sometimes miss the weirdest things. When I was an exchange student in America, I developed an absolute craving for bean soup, the way my mother always made it. So thick that you could spread it on a slice of bread. I began to dream of my mother's bean soup. And I'd never been particularly crazy about it before. I actually thought it was a bit *common* to make soup that thick.'

147

'It's a shared frame of reference,' said Max, fiddling with his beard. 'That's what we're talking about, right? When I studied overseas, it frustrated me endlessly that I always had to explain my background to my friends. If I say something here about Esme Euverard's voice, or the day when Verwoerd was buried, or the try that Mannetjies Roux scored in nineteen-whatever, then you all immediately know what I'm talking about. When Liane tells us about her mother's bean soup which you could spread on bread, then we all know exactly what it looks and smells and tastes like.'

'And how it makes you fart,' added Adriaan seriously.

Then his face broke open in a smile and he reached his arms out to his daughter who'd appeared, yawning, on the verandah. Her face had that crumpled look of a toddler who'd just woken up, like clean laundry which still needs ironing. She rubbed her eyes with fat dimpled knuckles, apparently astonished that they hadn't all vanished while she'd slept. When his son was that age, Philip remembered, he'd looked just like that when he'd woken up. Just as crumpled and astonished. Just as laundry-fresh. He leaned over the table to reach the bottle of white wine and poured a glass while he wondered if there was anything he would really miss if he had to go and live in another country. The first thought which occurred to him, strangely enough, was that he wouldn't want to go without Emma. But beyond that? His friends, he supposed, although their irrational views often irritated him. The farm he'd grown up on. Although it was years since he'd been there. His son in an institution in Pretoria. Although he never saw him.

'That's probably why exiles and immigrants always cluster together,' said Max, 'whether they like each other or not. That need for a shared frame of reference. Someone who'll laugh at the same jokes as you.'

'Listening to you lot, I'd swear you all had one foot in another country already!' Bobby spat out the words contemptuously. 'I wonder if any of you will still be here in five years' time?'

'I'll be here,' said Philip without hesitation. 'I don't have the faintest idea what will happen in the next five years, but I don't want to miss it.'

And for the umpteenth time that weekend he was genuinely surprised to hear the hopeful note in his own voice.

FOUR

Like a Window in Your Heart (1988)

It was one of the things he'd miss if he were dead, thought Ralph. Driving through the Karoo, with a tar road stretching out ahead of you, empty and straight, and the bare, brown plains around you and the sky immeasurably high above you, higher than in any other part of the country, and the mountains only hazy blue outlines on the horizon. With the sound of a classical concert filling the whole car. With a sleeping woman next to you.

With Mila next to him.

She had curled herself up on the seat, her face turned towards him, her short blonde hair tousled, her mouth less brightly coloured than usual. The tawny red lipstick almost completely rubbed off.

They had left Johannesburg before dawn, with the aim of being at Onrus before dusk that night, still in time to go for a walk on the beach. Mila had taken a turn behind the steering wheel, but he had chosen to drive the greater part of the journey himself. It gave him an indescribable feeling of freedom, driving through this deserted landscape. Actually more than freedom, a feeling of unreality, as though he was floating weightless in space. Neither here nor there, but somewhere in between. Travelling.

That's how life ought to be, he thought. The journey should always be more important than the arrival. If you begin to feel too at home in a place, too comfortable, you should know that it's time to move on. That was one of the reasons why he wanted to leave the country for a while. His friends suspected that he wanted to go because he felt uncomfortable about what was happening in the country. How could he explain that it was *comfort* that was driving him away?

Because he felt too comfortable in his little yuppy cottage in Melville, the walls and window frames painted rose pink and lilac, a pretentious version of a holiday home in Provence, the little garden an even more pretentious version of an English country garden, the bedroom perhaps the worst of all, minimalist, decorated in Oriental fashion, a cream coloured futon on a low wooden base, a wooden slab on a few bricks instead of a table. Like the home of someone without legs, he thought sometimes. Ironic for someone who was taller than average. Or masochistic perhaps. An unconscious way of punishing himself because he felt so comfortable in this house which reminded him of the warm south of France and the green heart of England and the exotic Far East. Of everything but Africa, really.

Because he felt too comfortable in this country, where his lifestyle often made him forget that he was living in Africa. Yes, he had the obligatory African ornaments in his house – little wire bicycles and wood carvings and three masks against the sitting-room wall – and he listened to African music and he went to watch black actors in local productions. But more than that? The reason he felt so comfortable was that he had spun himself a little European cocoon, soft and familiar and reassuring, in the dangerous confusion of Africa. Like almost all his white friends – and almost all his friends were white. But a cocoon is only a temporary home. Some time or other he had to creep out of it. And the question was, where to?

Was he prepared to creep into Mother Africa's dark heart, feel her warm arms around his body, let her squeeze him tight, feel her sometimes foul breath on his face, endure her sometimes chastising voice in his proud white ears? Or would he always long for the more detached, more disinterested, more 'civilized' embrace of lovely Europe? You couldn't speak of Mother Europe. The continent was too chilly to be a mother. Stepmother Europe at most. And who said this stepmother would want him? Wasn't she already tired of all the lost stepsons from other continents who came to stand begging and dirty on her clean doorstep?

When Schubert's quartet ended, thunderous and dramatic, he immediately pressed the button to play it again. 'Death and the Maiden'. A piece of ravishing European music to help him take leave of Africa, he thought with a self-mocking smile. An ironic soundtrack for this unreal trip through the Karoo, to a small coastal town with the name of Onrus – Unrest – where he would spend a last weekend with his friends before he left the country.

Not for ever. Just for a year.

How many times had he repeated those words. *I just need some breathing space for a while. That's all.* Get away from his nagging political conscience for a while, forget about the oppression and injustice in his country for a while. Forget about Mila for a while. Although he didn't say that to anyone, of course. Least of all to her.

He looked fleetingly at her sleeping face, the fine frown lines on her forehead, the laugh lines like fine porcelain cracks around her eyes, the skin on her neck looser than when he first saw her almost twenty years ago. Almost twenty years. It was a shockingly long time to be in love with one woman. Half of his life. There were other women, of course, but she was always the one that he really wanted, the one he couldn't have, the one who slipped through his grasp.

He remembered it as though it were yesterday, that summer day in Stellenbosch when he offered her a lift on his scooter because she had stumbled out of a bookshop with a load of heavy plastic bags. Because she was wearing the shortest skirt he had yet seen on campus, over the loveliest legs he had ever seen, anywhere. Because the thought of that pair of legs on either side of his body, firmly behind him on his Vespa, was enough to give him an erection, in broad daylight, in the main street of town.

He had stopped next to her and asked her if she wanted a lift. It was the first time in his life he'd done anything like that. Usually he was too shy, usually he left such smug predatory behaviour to his best friend. Usually he simply watched in speechless admiration as Stuart – with his gleaming white smile and his witty remarks and his easy self-confidence – roped in all the prettiest, most popular, most desirable girls on campus. But that day he stopped next to an attractive blonde with a magnificent pair of legs and began to speak to her as though he played this game every day of his life.

She had looked at him, her light eyes amused below her blonde fringe, her hair a lot longer than now, her lips paler and her lashes more dramatically emphasized with mascara, just like all the girls looked in those days. And then she said, sighing. 'I've waited all my life for a prince on a white charger – and now look what I get. A presumptuous law student on a red scooter.'

'How did you know I study law?' he asked. Pleased.

'One can't exactly miss you law students.' He was so thrilled by her smile that he clean forgot about her unforgettable legs. 'The way the lot of you pose in front of the law faculty all day.'

'Perhaps I'm a prince in disguise,' he grinned. 'Perhaps this scooter will change into a white charger the minute you climb on.'

'That's the most outrageous pick-up line I've ever heard, you know?'

'And I can see you must have heard a lot. But if you don't try it, you'll always wonder whether it wasn't perhaps true after all.'

'How do you know me so well?' she asked, laughing.

She gave two of the heavy plastic bags to him, swept her long tanned left leg over the Vespa and moved in behind his back. Her one hand lightly on his shoulder, a finger only just touching his neck, the piece of skin which stuck out beneath his T-shirt. He'd never been so aware of anyone's touch before.

'You'll have to hold on tighter,' he said over his shoulder, 'otherwise this horse might throw you.'

'I'll stay on if you drive carefully.' Her husky voice so close to his ear made him think of a clarinet. Jazz, not classical music. The tone was too earthy for classical music. 'It's not far to my residence.'

The further the better, he thought. The further he could ride with her, with the sun gleaming on her bare legs on either side of his hips, the happier he'd be. If she'd asked him to drive all the way to Bloemfontein – to go and ask her father if he could marry her – he would have done it without thinking twice. At that moment he would have done anything. She was barely nineteen years old, he had just turned twenty.

He introduced her to Stuart that same day, as excited as a little boy who has caught an extraordinarily colourful butterfly. It was the first time – the first and only time in the five years they spent together at university – that he introduced a girl to Stuart. And this was the girl that Stuart married. Maybe it was because of this that Stuart married her. Because he could see how much Ralph wanted her. Because he couldn't resist the temptation to compete. As they had competed since they were kids, in every game and sport, climbing trees, horse-riding, swimming in the farm dam, athletics and rugby at school, wanking and wet dreams in their hostel room. By the time they were students, Ralph knew that it was sometimes politic to let Stuart win. That the outcome was often more important to Stuart than to him. But he would always be sorry that he hadn't tried harder with Mila. Even if it had spoiled his friendship with Stuart. He had to choose between a relationship with Mila and friendship with Stuart. And he had known for almost twenty years that he had made the wrong choice.

Mila sighed in her sleep and moved her legs. He tried to concentrate on the road, irritated by the unavoidable tenderness which welled up in him every time he looked at her sleeping body. She had managed, all those years ago, to open a door in his heart which he wasn't even aware of. Suddenly the strangest emotions had been released in him, emotions which made him feel wild and confused. His panic-stricken reaction was to try and close that door again, to hide the intensity of his feelings, to share her with his friend Stuart. He was still struggling to close that door.

He allowed the stormy sounds of the violins to spill over him and looked at the landscape flowing past him endlessly, changelessly, like a calm, dun river. Dull brown ground, dull green bushes, dull white sheep. And the astounding wideness of the faded blue heavens over everything. Always exactly the same, kilometre after kilometre after kilometre. Here and there a farm gate or a windpump, a simple homestead in the distance, rare signs of human presence in a godfor-saken scene. Was it the loneliness which moved him so each time he drove through the Karoo? Or was it just because the landscape looked so different from the lush green hills of Natal where he grew up? The attraction of the unknown?

But he was in such a melancholy mood today that even an industrial area would have moved him.

The other exceptionally clear memory he had of Mila, as clear as the day he met her, was the day she married Stuart. She wore a loose white dress with a low back because she was more than four months pregnant, because she wanted to hide her swelling stomach and focus interest on her strong, tanned back. A traditional church wedding with a grand reception because her hypocritical mother had insisted on it. A coronet of white flowers in her blonde hair and a bouquet of arum lilies in her hands. Funeral flowers, one of her mother's friends had remarked disapprovingly. Superstition, was Mila's laughing response. Less than a year later, Stuart was dead. At the funeral she had again looked like a bride, again wearing a loose white dress, this time without a bare back, of course, and put white roses on his grave. Not arum lilies. But he remembered her wedding day better than the day of the funeral. Perhaps because that was the day that his foolishness at last dawned on him.

While he was dancing with her, the ritual dance with the bride that every male guest was entitled to, her head suddenly dropped against his chest. The back of her neck a lovely, long, curved line, completely exposed between her short hair and the low back of her dress. Completely vulnerable.

'I don't know what the fuck I'm doing!' she had whispered. 'Is it too late to jump on your white charger and gallop away?'

He had been too astounded to utter a word.

'Sorry, I forgot.' She lifted her head and smiled at the dancing guests around her – as an exemplary bride should – her blue eyes misty behind a sheen of tears which she blinked determinedly away. 'There never was a white horse, was there?'

And then the music stopped and she slipped out of his arms to cut the wedding cake. He walked outside and stared at the stars and decided there was only one way to survive this evening. After that he had got so drunk that he remembered nothing else.

But there was another memory – the freshest, the clearest and the most painful – of the evening a few months ago when he had arrived at her temporary flat in Sea Point unexpectedly. His advertising agency had sent him to the Cape to meet a potential client. He had quickly tried to phone, but couldn't reach her, so thought he'd just surprise her.

He drove to her flat straight from the airport and parked in the street in front of the building. Just as he was about to climb out of the hired car, she appeared on her balcony on the second floor. It was already heavy dusk, but he could see her clearly, because the light was switched on in the room behind her. She was wearing a dressing gown – that old man's dressing gown of dark blue flannel he knew so well – and her short hair was damp as though she'd just showered. A glass of wine and a cigarette were in her hands. And then Adriaan appeared behind her. In an unfamiliar flowered dressing gown, his hair wet, too. A comical scene – the broad shoulders and stocky body in this strange woman's dressing gown, like an unconvincing transvestite – but Ralph was too shocked to be amused. Adriaan wrapped his arms around her from behind and kissed the nape of her neck. She threw her head back and rested her damp hair against his shoulder. Ralph couldn't see the expression on her face, but he knew her body language well enough to read the delight in her posture.

He had sat motionless in the hired white Toyota, staring at the two people on the balcony. Like a horror scene in a movie, something that you don't want to see and yet can't look away from. Adriaan sank down until his head was no longer visible above the low balcony wall. Perhaps he had sat down on a chair behind her. But it was clear that his hands were still caressing her body. All that Ralph could see was her torso straining backwards, the blue flannel dressing gown beginning to shift open in front, the way in which her hands gripped the wall.

After a while – probably just a few minutes, although it felt to him like hours – she turned around slowly and pulled Adriaan up by his shoulders. And then they vanished into the flat. Ralph sat in the car like a statue. Minutes? Hours? Long enough, in any case, to decide that it was time to do what he'd been threatening to do for years. One of the most important reasons he hadn't yet done it – the twenty-year passion that he'd harboured for this woman, the unbearable thought that he would have to say goodbye to her – had just crumbled before his eyes. It was time to get away, he realized. To go overseas, travel, perhaps do a creative-writing course at a foreign university. To do *something* to change his life. God knows, he couldn't translate adverts for ever, longing for his dead friend's wife.

He pressed the button on the cassette player to listen to the piece of music again and heard Mila sigh. He was startled when he saw that her eyes were open – who knows for how long – that she was lying with her head against the seat, staring at him.

'Can't we listen to something more lively for a change?'

'What do you have in mind?' He gave her the little case with the tapes in so that she could pick something else. *The Sound of Music*?

She ignored his sarcastic tone and pushed Paul Simon's *Graceland* into the cassette player.

'I like that bit where he sings *Losing love is like a window in your heart . . . everyone can see that you're blown apart*.'

'Is that what you call lively?'

'No.' Her eyes burned him like blue flames. 'That's what I call realistic.'

Perhaps she was trying to comfort him, he thought, perhaps she wanted to tell him that she knew why he was going away. On the other hand, maybe she didn't have a clue about what was going on in his heart. He gazed at the mountains, which were gradually losing their soft blue haziness, gradually beginning to look greyer and greener and more dangerous, as the horizon moved slowly but surely closer. Less like a romantic picture, he thought. More realistic.

'I've never really wanted to leave the country,' declared Mila passionately, 'but now less than ever. I don't know if I've ever been as excited about my work before!'

She had just told them – her eyes so bright you'd swear she was talking about a new lover – that she was going to start working for a new newspaper, an independent weekly being formed by a group of disillusioned Afrikaans journalists. ('A newspaper where we can write what we like, not what we have to. In Afrikaans!') The first issue would appear before the end of the year.

'And if you get banned?' asked Max, his fingers in his beard.

'They can't go on banning the truth for ever, Max. It has to come out some time or other, in some way or other. I want to be there when it happens.'

'I can't believe that an old journalist like you can still get so uncynically excited about "the truth",' said Philip, shaking his head.

'I prefer "seasoned" to "old". Call me a seasoned journalist. It sounds less . . . old.'

'And age is becoming a sore point for some of us,' said Ralph jokingly.

'But you're still young enough to be idealistic about a new paper,' laughed Emma. 'There's hope for you yet, Mila!'

'Look who's talking!' Ralph exclaimed. 'Our young friend who turned thirty just the other day!'

'Do you mean to say that I'm the only one still in my twenties?' Bobby looked in wonder at her friends around the kitchen counter. 'When did you all get so old?'

'Shit happens,' said Paul. 'It'll hit you too.'

'Now we're not just a bunch of spoilt whiteys,' laughed Max. 'We're a bunch of spoilt *old* whiteys.'

'I turn forty next year,' said Ralph thoughtfully. 'That's another reason why I want to go overseas now. In your thirties you can still get away with travelling through Europe like a bum. Everyone knows that's what young people are supposed to do. After forty you might get seen as a real bum.'

Forty, thought Bobby. There was a time, not so long ago, when she thought forty was a little way this side of death. And now her lover was forty, and one of her best friends was turning forty next year. The fact that she saw Ralph as one of her best friends these days was perhaps even stranger than the fact that everyone around her had suddenly grown so old. She had always thought of her comrades in the Struggle as her real friends. This group had been Max's friends when she'd met them three years ago. And at first she had only spent a weekend with them now and again, but as more of her comrades ended up in jail or went underground or left the country, she had become more dependent on this group's support. Especially since Robin had been put in detention last year. Those four months of loneliness and anxiety had finally driven her into this group's comforting arms. Not without a fight, of course.

'I can't believe how they can go on about their personal problems!' she'd burst out at Max one evening. Rebellious, after a stylish meal around Liane's stylish green wrought-iron table with the soothing sounds of a Mozart concerto as background music, the host and hostess as elegant as ever, the food little nouvelle cuisine portions on colourful handpainted plates. All so terribly seductive that it was easy to forget about the Struggle for a few hours. 'About their relationships and their friends' relationships and their cars being stolen and their bank managers who won't give them overdrafts. It's all so bloody petty!'

'Problems are problems,' said Max. 'Lost love between two people can be as tragic – for the two people, in any case – as lost human rights for millions.'

But it was only after Robin ended up in jail that she had begun to understand what he meant.

These days she accepted that the personal and the political in this country were as interwoven as the dough plaits of the koeksisters her mother loved to serve at posh diplomatic parties. You couldn't separate the plaits without breaking the koeksister. These days she didn't even try.

And now Robin had gone underground, continually on the run

from the security police. Sometimes it felt worse than when she had been in jail. Then she knew they couldn't see each other. Now she lived in despairing hope, always waiting for the next meeting, for Robin's next unexpected appearance.

And now Ralph had decided to flee overseas. Just when she was beginning to rely on him, just when she was beginning to realize how valuable his friendship had become to her. *Not for ever. Just for a year.* She felt her throat constrict when she heard those comforting words. *I just want to get away for a while. That's all.* Just when she needed him the most.

But when he announced that he wanted to hold a farewell weekend with his friends, she had offered her parents' beach house at Onrus without hesitation. Then it dawned on her that Max's friends had also become her friends. The whole bunch sitting here around the counter.

The same pine counter between the sitting room and the kitchen where she and her brother had spoken for hours on end so many years ago. The same uncomfortable little pine chairs with high legs and low backs, the same worn-out carpet in the sitting room and the same ghastly grey linoleum in the kitchen. Everything in this holiday home had stayed the same, a simple stone house with second-hand furniture which didn't match, so different from the grand homes her mother had created overseas, the sophisticated houses in the sophisticated cities where her father's diplomatic posts had led them. She and her brother had stayed behind in soul-destroying Afrikaans boarding schools, only visiting their parents abroad in the holidays, in strange houses which felt like window displays. With the exception of the summer holiday at the end of the year when the family went to the much-loved, familiar, reassuring holiday home.

Today she knew that this house and her brother were the two lodestars by which she had guided her life, the two fixed beacons which prevented her from getting lost in her own rebelliousness. Even after Eben's death, after she had begun to live out her rebellion in a struggle against the injustice of the government rather than the injustice of her parents, she had felt closer to him in this house than in any other place. To this day she was aware of his comforting presence whenever she sat at the kitchen counter.

This was where they had talked the most – as they dunked huge hunks of homemade buttermilk rusks into mugs of sweet milky coffee – this was where he told her about the girl in the white bikini who asked him to rub suntan oil on her back, or the gigantic bonfire which he and his friends had made on the beach the night before, or the spot where they wanted to go and dive for perlemoen that day. And she, five years younger – too young to hang out with him and his buddies – had listened to his adventures with bright, admiring eyes. And in her turn she told him about the highlights of her day. Of course never as exciting as his. And yet he had always listened patiently, his eyes perhaps not bright and admiring, but his smile tolerant, loving, sometimes proud of his silly little sister. As she told him of the skeleton of some unknown creature which she had found between the rocks, or a new path through the overgrown sand dune which she discovered by accident, or the boy who allowed her to row his canoe on the lagoon. No one else had ever listened to her with so much attention.

Her elegant mother always had made it quite clear that she would have preferred an affectionate little daughter with a pink bow in her hair, someone who would play with dolls and bake cookies quietly in the house, not this wild girl who wandered around outside on her own all day. And her father, well, no one ever knew what her father wanted. Even when he was supposed to be on holiday he carried himself like a military attaché. Even in his swimming trunks on the beach he walked around with the ramrod stiff bearing of a professional soldier, nodding his head formally at acquaintances, as if he were at a diplomatic cocktail party. And the few times that he tried to play with his children they were all equally uncomfortable. No one enjoyed it. *They fuck you up, your mum and dad.* When she heard that line from Philip Larkin for the first time, she didn't know whether to laugh or cry.

'I never ever want to be younger than thirty again.' Yvette leaned back on her bar stool, her shoulders against the wall and her hands on her stomach, which looked like a massive balloon under her loose dress, the picture of glorious contentment in her second pregnancy. 'Even if a good fairy offered to spirit us back to an earlier age tonight. I never want to experience the ignorance and confusion of my teenage years and early twenties again!'

'The older I get the more ignorant and confused I feel,' said Paul with a wry smile. 'I don't know when the so-called wisdom of age is supposed to arrive. So far I can't detect any trace of it.'

'If you can admit your own ignorance,' said Ralph, 'you're on the right track. Then you only have to accept it. That's what they call wisdom.'

'No, there are still too many missing pieces.' Paul shook his head and gulped his wine. 'I know I'm never going to finish the whole bloody jigsaw, but I still can't accept that there should be so many holes in the damn thing!'

Paul's looks were changing, realized Bobby. When she met him three years ago there was a kind of blankness in his face, a hole which could only be filled by youthful beauty. Now he was more attractive to her, because his face had at last begun to show traces of something else. Not age, she decided, something more than age. Something like hesitation, self-doubt, uncertainty. Perhaps even the first signs of that wisdom that he was waiting for.

'Perhaps it isn't a jigsaw,' said Yvette thoughtfully. 'Perhaps it's more like an inexplicable artwork. A painting which looks different each time you look at it. It's the enigma which makes it worth the trouble of keeping on looking, not so?'

'Perhaps I'm more like my wife than I like to admit,' Paul continued. 'She always says she doesn't want to be thrown into an existential crisis every time she looks at her sitting-room walls. She wants easy pictures which match her furniture. I'm probably just looking for an easy existence which matches my preconceptions.'

'We promised we'd drink a toast to her,' Emma reminded them.

'Our poor friend who can't join us because she has to work on an exotic island,' grinned Ralph, and lifted his glass in a joking gesture.

'She says it's harder than we think to style idyllic island scenes for a woman's magazine,' laughed Paul.

'I can imagine,' said Max. 'Sometimes you must have a hell of a job trying to get a good shot of waving palm trees and transparent blue sea.'

Bobby couldn't remember exactly where Liane was. Mauritius? Réunion? One of the Seychelles? In any case a fantastic break, a chance to get away, as she'd said last week on the phone. ('Away from the depressing State of Emergency!') Yet there had been a sharp tone in her breathy voice. As if she wanted to get away from more than politics.

'Well, I hope she enjoys her break,' Bobby raised her glass and wondered why she felt so sad all of a sudden. 'You too, Ralph. I hope you enjoy your year abroad.'

As long as it was just a year, she thought as her throat constricted again, so long as it was just the breathing space he was looking for. A year could be a long time, as they all knew by now, in the third year of the apparently never-ending State of Emergency. By this time it was more than a political condition; it had become an emotional state. And a state of emergency in your heart could be more dangerous than the State of Emergency outside the walls of your home.

By the winter of 1988 it felt to Bobby as though everyone in the country was caught in a net of despair. Radical freedom fighters, liberal democrats, nationalist racists, far-right fearmongers – all tired of struggling. As if only the most efficient assassins were still swimming around in the dark undercurrents, as deadly as sharks lured by the scent of blood. Mysterious gangs which removed political thorns from the government's side, with no fear of retribution. Griffiths Mxenge, David Webster, Dulcie September, an endless list of 'troublemakers' who were eliminated without conscience. And for Bobby there was a fear gnawing at her day and night, a personal fear which exceeded even her worst political ones – that Robin's name would be added to that list.

And then there were the fanatical loners who leaped about on the borders of madness, characters like the 'Wit Wolf', who bared his fangs in the centre of Pretoria. A man with the name of Barend Strydom, who later that year would pull out a gun to shoot all the black people around him. On Strydom Square – named after another Strydom – as if he wanted to ensure that no one would ever forget his horrific deed when they referred to the square.

'*Stry-dom*,' Ralph had murmured. 'What an unbelievable name! Fighting-stupidly.'

'Or perhaps *Stryd-om*,' Mila had suggested. 'Struggle behind us.'

'God knows why anyone in this country still wants to write stories,' Ralph had said. 'Whatever you can imagine has already been trumped by reality.'

It was also the year in which the government closed the few remaining paths of resistance. All the most important anti-apartheid organizations were forbidden to carry on with any business or any activities at all. *If repression stifles dissent, can absolute repression smother it entirely?* an American magazine wanted to know.

No, Bobby believed. On the contrary.

*

Long after midnight, Ralph and Bobby and Paul still sat at the kitchen counter. Ralph knew only too well why *he* couldn't sleep, why he needed alcohol to make the night shorter. (Loneliness and sexual frustration and fear of the unknown, not necessarily in that order.) He suspected that Bobby would be able to offer the same reasons. What he couldn't work out, was Paul's drunken presence among them.

Was it just because his wife was overseas that he'd thrown off his usual mantle of soberness and restraint? He looked scruffier than they'd ever seen him before, his beige polo shirt spoiled by a red wine stain on the chest, the collar skew and crumpled. Even his face looked skew and crumpled. One corner of his mouth drooped a little when he spoke, as though a dentist had just given him an injection. Or as though he'd had a slight stroke. His eyelids were puffy and his hair a mess.

Ralph had already drunk enough to begin to confess his inexplicable passion for Mila. To admit that this was the unspoken reason why he was leaving the country now. What surprised him, was the fact that neither Bobby nor Paul looked at all surprised at his admission. And he had thought he deserved an Oscar for the masterful way in which he had hidden his true feelings for twenty years.

'It's absurd to spend most of your life in a state of unfulfilled longing,' he sighed as he poured more Southern Comfort into the three glasses in front of him.

'Is there any other way to live?' Paul's eyebrows leaped high up on his forehead. 'If you stop longing . . . well, then you can just as well stop living.'

'No, I'm not talking about a vague longing after impossible things! A sports car, an annual holiday on an exotic island, a blind date with Jessica Lange . . . I'm speaking about a longing which threatens to become an obsession. The longing for someone close to you, someone who's part of your life, and yet will never be close enough!'

'I know all about that kind of longing,' mumbled Bobby.

'I thought . . . I thought Robin . . .' Paul spoke with frowning concentration, visibly struggling to roll each word audibly off his clumsy tongue. 'I thought you'd found the lover of your dreams!'

'Sure. And then my life turned into a nightmare. Now that she's not in jail any more, she has to scurry around underground like a rat – from one safe house to the other – so that the security police don't catch her again. If I want to talk to her, I have to send an indecipherable message through a long list of comrades in the vague hope that some time or other, God knows when, it will reach her. And that someone in that list isn't an informer. It's like playing Chinese whispers. And I can do nothing about it, I can't blame her, I can't rant and rave, because she's on the moral high ground! Or in the moral underground, in our case.'

'And if . . . if you could choose?' Paul asked. 'Just suppose . . . just suppose . . . she offered to leave everything tomorrow? For the sake of your relationship?'

'It's too late. She's in too deep. Even if she decided to stop it all tomorrow, the police wouldn't leave her alone. And anyway, it's completely unthinkable that she'd decide something like that.'

'But just suppose,' said Paul like a lawyer – a very drunken lawyer – talking to a stubborn client. 'Just suppose that you could go and live in another country . . . somewhere where you . . . where you would be safe . . . where you . . . where you could have a normal relationship!'

'A sexual relationship between two women won't be a "normal" relationship anywhere, Paul. Heterosexuality remains the norm.'

'No, you . . . you're avoiding my question.'

'Because I'm not sober enough to answer you! If you ask me tomorrow, I'd say no immediately, that wouldn't work, it will never work, we can't just betray everything we believe in! But tonight I'd dearly love to believe in fairy tales. That somewhere on earth there's a place where we can lead a wonderful life together, without political involvement or moral judgements from other people. Some mythical island like Lesbos!'

'I thought I was the only one struggling to sleep,' said Yvette in the sitting-room doorway.

'You're the only one with a proper excuse,' said Ralph. 'It's your big tummy keeping you awake, not your tormented soul.'

'Says who?'

She walked closer, opened the fridge and poured a glass of orange juice, an exhausted expression on her pale face.

'What about a sip of Southern Comfort?' asked Ralph sympathetically.

'No, thank you, I'd prefer to stick to orange juice.' She climbed groaning on to one of the high bar stools next to them, one hand under her stomach as though it was the only way that she could heave the added weight up from the floor. She began to laugh when she saw the concern in Ralph's eyes. 'It's not that bad! One of these days my body will be my own again, then I can do what I like and drink what I like again.'

'Not that you ever were a big drinker.' Paul's voice sounded almost accusing. Or perhaps it was just his heavy tongue influencing his tone.

'You neither.' Her dark eyes rested reproachfully on his crumpled appearance.

'Shit happens,' he said. 'We spoke just now about . . . what was it again? Oh yes, unrequited love. And I wondered . . . did I ever tell you that I . . . that I had a terrible crush on you long ago?'

'On *me*?'

'On you. At the time you and Liane were sharing a house. That was why . . . well, that was why I began to visit her . . . you know . . . really wanted to see you . . . but you were so . . . you weren't . . . I don't know. You were so bloody unattainable!'

'Unattainable? But I wasn't at all . . . I thought Liane was . . . I thought Liane was the unattainable one! To most men!'

'I must have been different to most men,' he said with a laconic smile.

'You're still different to most men,' she said reassuringly, her cheeks blushing red, her eyes brighter than usual. 'Thank God.'

'And Liane at least responded when I greeted her. You didn't pay any attention to me . . . just swept past me . . . in those weird old-fashioned dresses of yours. Pencil behind the ear . . . paint splotch on the cheek . . .'

'But you weren't . . . you weren't in my *league*!'

'Obviously not. The guys who hung out with you . . . all such pale aesthetes . . . they always made me think of children's Bible pictures. And the shit they talked about! Postmodernism and Foucault's . . . whatever . . . I didn't have a clue. Thought you were saying fuck-all this and fuck-all that. What the hell did I know? I was a boring law student who hung out on the beach . . .'

'No, that's not what I meant!'

'I tried a few times to . . . impress you . . . wanted to show you I knew something about European movies. Remember I once said something about *La Dolce Vita* . . . and then I couldn't . . . I couldn't remember the bloody director's name! *La Dolce Vita*! No wonder you thought me an imbecile!'

'No, that's not true, Paul! I wasn't in *your* league. That's what I meant. You were this suntanned Adonis who looked as though you bought your clothes in Europe. As though you had your hair cut in Europe! Every girl I knew wanted you. Until you began courting Liane. No one could compete with Liane. You were the most attractive couple anyone had ever seen. Like Robert Redford and Mia Farrow in *The Great Gatsby.* I was too shy to talk to you. You were too glamorous for me!'

'Now she tells me,' muttered Paul and drained his glass in a single gulp. 'My whole life could have turned out differently . . . if I was just . . . if I was only brave enough to ask her out.'

'My sympathies, brother.' Ralph poured the last bit of alcohol into the three glasses in front of him. *My whole life could have turned out differently. If I was only brave enough.* 'Let's drink to lost opportunities.'

'I feel terribly flattered, Paul, really.' Yvette suppressed a pleased giggle, the blush on her cheeks not quite dispersed. 'I mean, to discover that the most attractive guy on campus was my secret admirer . . . that's the kind of thing most women can only dream of . . . but surely you can't really think that the two of us could have . . . had a relationship?'

'Ag, you're just saying that . . . because I became a boring lawyer . . .'

'No, it's not –'

'If I'd gone out with you . . . who knows . . . maybe I would have had the courage to become a . . . director. A second Fellini!'

'Why didn't you become a director anyway?' she asked softly, her head cocked.

'Liane,' he answered with a smouldering, yearning expression in his dark eyes. 'She's not . . . she's not the kind of woman . . . you can't take chances like that if you're married to a woman like Liane. I knew if I became a lawyer . . . I knew I'd make enough money . . . you know . . . maybe never be a spectacular success . . . but at least not a spectacular failure.'

'But you're so well matched! Just think what an odd couple the two of us would have been. You with your smart tailored suits and me with my "weird old-fashioned dresses"!'

'I like your weird dresses. Anyway, if I'd made movies . . . I wouldn't have worn suits . . .'

'Perhaps not suits,' teased Bobby, 'but designer jeans at the very least?'

'OK, I know Liane and I *look* as though we suit each other! But you can't base a relationship . . . you can't . . . you can't build a bloody marriage on looks! We've . . . I think we've both realized it . . . in the past year. She says we must . . . she wants us to see a therapist . . . see if it can still be saved . . .' Suddenly his face looked a decade older. Deep, sad grooves around the mouth. A slackness under the eyes. 'I don't know . . . I don't know if it's worth the effort . . . to try to rescue the whole thing.'

It was so quiet around the counter that Ralph could hear the rain swishing against the windows. The soft, cosy sound of a rainstorm in no hurry to depart.

'Ag, fuck, I can't take it any more!' Bobby cried out, her voice far too loud in the silence. 'Can't someone give me some good news for a change! I mean somewhere on earth there must be relationships that still work? Japan? Iran? Please!'

'Perhaps it would be better,' said Paul with a shrug, 'if we . . . if we separated now, before there are children . . . pets . . . before the whole business goes any further.'

'But Paul, do you . . . do you know what you're saying?' stammered Yvette.

'I know,' said Paul slowly. His voice suddenly clear. His words formed carefully. 'I've been practising saying it for months. This is the first time that I've been brave enough . . . to get it right. Must be Dutch courage.'

'Ag, fuck,' said Bobby again, and stuck a finger under the frame of her spectacles, rubbing angrily at the soft skin around her teary eyes. 'If you can't give me good news, please just give me more alcohol.'

Ralph watched her, disturbed. Drunken melancholy, he decided. As he tried to ignore an unsettling burning behind his own eyelids. They'd both drunk far too much. While Paul, who had drunk with them glass for glass, was staring with dry eyes and a peculiar expression at the raindrops against the kitchen window. He looked utterly exhausted, but also infinitely relieved.

'The more things change . . .' smiled Mila as she poured a spoonful of runny batter into the sizzling oil. 'Just look at us now. The men are sitting around the TV watching rugby and the women are in the kitchen cooking. Yet another Saturday afternoon in good old South Africa.'

At this moment a jubilant yell sounded from the sitting room, as if the men around the TV set wanted to wholeheartedly endorse her statement. It was a vitally important game between Transvaal and Natal, they had informed the women. The fact that Natal was leading made Ralph's face beam as though he had personally scored each point. Adriaan was supporting Transvaal, thunderingly loudly, as usual. While the rest didn't care who won; or so they said. It sounded rather as though they felt honour-bound to kick up as much of a racket as Adriaan every time any player, from either team, began to run with the ball.

'I thought we were dealing with rational beings.' Bobby observed the men's strange behaviour with the clinical interest of a scientist studying a cage full of guinea pigs. 'Now the whole bunch of them have turned into cheering couch potatoes.'

'What surprises me more than the men's regression in front of the TV,' said Emma, 'is our feminist friend's regression in front of the stove. Just watch her toss that pancake!'

She was sitting next to Bobby at the kitchen counter, staring almost open-mouthed at the way Mila prised one pancake after another from the pan, placed them in a plate above a pot of boiling water, and without hesitation dropped the next spoon of batter in the sizzling oil. Her movements smooth and practised, as effortless as a machine.

'Can you believe it,' laughed Bobby. 'She looks like a tannie behind a table at a church bazaar!'

'My mother always cooked at the church bazaars,' said Mila. 'I probably picked up the skills without even realizing it.'

'And all these years I've viewed you as my role model,' said Emma, shaking her head. 'If someone asks me why I don't cook, I say: Because my friend Mila doesn't cook. And now you suddenly come out of the closet as a real pro pancake maker. Now I wonder what else you can do that I don't know about. Knead bread dough? Plait koeksisters? De-bone chicken?'

'I can do lots of things you don't know about,' Mila laughed. 'But they're mostly things you don't do in a kitchen.'

'More cimmanon sugar,' ordered Mona, who was sitting wide-legged on the linoleum floor of the kitchen, her mouth and hands already brown and sticky from the cinnamon sugar which was lavishly sprinkled over the pancake on her plate.

'No, you can't just lick off the sugar, Mona.' Yvette stood next to Mila, busy chopping a heap of vegetables, her voice motherly, strict. 'Eat that pancake up first, then we can negotiate about more cinnamon sugar.'

Mona looked at her mother with a cocked head and an appraising look, as if she were trying to gauge exactly how seriously this order was meant. Now that she was almost three years old, with a bush of golden brown hair through which no comb could find its way, and the sunbrowned feet of a farm child, she looked more than ever like her father. Stocky and plump with grey-green eyes, her mouth already a little less childlike, more sensual than a year ago when she still hadn't yet got all her milk teeth. But her body language mirrored her mother's. The head to one side, the speculative gaze, the mysterious little smile which suddenly hovered about her lips.

'Mila!' Her full attention now on Mila's back, her eyes like laser beams trying to pierce Mila's heart. 'Mona wants more cimmanon sugar!'

'Sorry, my precious,' said Mila without turning round, her voice filled with regret. 'Your mother says no.'

'Why do mothers always have to be such ogres?' sighed Yvette.

When Mona realized that she wasn't going to get her way, her bottom lip began to tremble dramatically. When this warning didn't work either, she burst into tears and ran to the sitting room to find comfort from her father. Adriaan plonked her on his lap and stroked her hair absent-mindedly, his attention still on the television screen. Clearly not the reaction she wanted, because within moments she clambered from his lap disappointed, by this time with dry eyes, and went to sit on the kitchen floor again, the dog like a shadow at her heels.

'If it wasn't for Mona and Tat,' Emma observed, 'we'd have an absolute separation of the sexes in this house this afternoon. Thank God she's still too young to pay attention to such divisions!'

'It's got nothing to do with age,' said Bobby. 'Some of us have spent our whole lives struggling with those divisions.' She saw Yvette's concerned expression and added quickly, 'I'm not saying that your daughter is going to turn out lesbian! I just think it's sad that we're forced to choose so young. Cars or dolls. Blue or pink. One or the other . . .'

In the meantime, Mona had pulled a piece of paper closer and had begun drawing a picture furiously. Heavy, self-assured lines in different coloured crayons. Quick straight strokes, alternating with wild, emotional zigzag lines. No wobbly stick men for this artists' child.

'Did you want to be a boy when you were little?' asked Yvette, her eyes on the razor-sharp vegetable knife in her hand.

'Not in the sense that I wanted that thing between my legs,' answered Bobby. 'It always seemed to me more of a nuisance than a showpiece.'

'I must admit I was quite jealous of my brother's little willy.' Emma supported her cheek with her hand, her hair thrown over one shoulder. She looked like an advert for some Irish product. Guinness or Aer Lingus or something like that, with the flaming mass of hair and the winter-white skin and the moss-green man's jersey. 'He could spell his name on the ground when he peed. Perhaps that's why I always wanted to be a writer. If I couldn't wave a penis around, I could at least wave a pen around.'

'I could never understand what all the fuss was about,' said Bobby. 'I must admit, I still wonder, every time I see a penis. Which is, of course, less often than the rest of you.'

'Not necessarily,' murmured Mila at the stove. 'Some of us have to make pancakes to get rid of our sexual frustrations.'

'But I was always envious of boys' freedom,' Bobby admitted. 'That they didn't have to wear dresses or plait their hair, that they could play rougher games and stay outside later, all those things. So it was an obvious choice to me, from early on. Not to be a boy, but to behave like a boy. To enjoy the same freedom. Now still.'

'But can't you enjoy that freedom without . . . without . . . I mean, without . . .'

'Sleeping with women?' Bobby smiled at Yvette's sudden embarrassment. 'I'm sure you can. But for me freedom also means the freedom to choose with whom I want to sleep.'

'I've only ever fantasized about a relationship with a woman,' Emma said thoughtfully. 'Never had the courage to do it.'

'Read the Bible to give you courage,' teased Bobby. '*Test everything and hold fast to the good.*'

'I did test it,' said Mila, 'but it just made me more confused.'

She shot another pancake up into the air, this time even higher and more flashily than before, as though she knew that everyone was suddenly staring at her.

'You tried *what*?' Emma sounded dizzy with astonishment.

'Sleeping with a woman. But I missed the hardness of a man's body. And then when I slept with a man after that, I missed the soft curves of a woman's body. Just goes to show. Life's not meant to be perfect.'

Yvette peeled a handful of carrots with great concentration. Her face showed no surprise.

'Why not?' asked Bobby. 'Why can't you sleep with men and women? If it's equally good for you?'

'No,' said Mila, shaking her head. 'It's better with men. It's just . . . I miss something . . . but well, I always miss something. Period. Whatever I do in life.'

'When was that?' asked Emma, still astonished. 'Recently?'

'Years ago,' smiled Mila. 'In my wild youth.'

'As if you're old and sober now!'

Bobby wondered why Emma's voice suddenly sounded so bitchy. Then she was distracted by the next burst of excited cries from the sitting room, before a communal *Aaaah!* washed through the house in a wave of disappointment. Only Adriaan laughed loudly, pleased that the enemy hadn't succeeded in increasing the lead.

It was as though they were sitting inside a huge shell, thought Bobby. The soughing of the rain outside and the cosy seclusion here in the house, the heavily steamed panes which made everything on the other side of the windows look hazy – the rain pulled like a glistening grey veil over the sky, the trees vague shapes, the other houses in the street only shadows – as if nothing that happened in the misty world outside could touch them in here. She couldn't remember when last she'd felt so safe.

'Anyway, I admire your guts,' said Emma, still staring at Mila's straight back. 'My fantasy will probably always just remain a fantasy. Especially now that I'm a respectably married woman.'

'Marriage is perhaps all you need to drive you into a woman's arms,' teased Bobby.

'That's possible.' Emma laughed and brushed a few loose corkscrew curls from her forehead. 'I must admit I'm amazed that we've survived the first year. It was a hell of an adjustment!'

'I wish I could say that it gets easier,' said Yvette.

She scraped the vegetable peels on to a piece of newspaper and threw it in the bin under the sink. She looked like a huge water bird on dry ground, waddling slightly, almost comical, her balance affected by her bulging stomach. She was wearing a long, loose dress in dark colours, heavy black lace-up boots and a black velvet hat pulled down low over her ears. Sometimes Bobby suspected that she dressed so strangely on purpose – as if she wanted to ensure she wouldn't be taken seriously – but on days like today she seemed blissfully unaware of her eccentric appearance.

'My mother said that it's only getting easier for her now,' said Emma. 'After more than thirty years. I think she wanted to comfort me, but it suddenly made divorce seem terribly attractive. I mean, to endure thirty years of pain and suffering just for a few years of dull contentment in your old age!'

'I don't think you and Philip will have to wait so long,' said Mila. 'One of you will have murdered the other by then.'

'Thanks, Mila. That's almost as uplifting as my mother's words of consolation.'

'On the other hand, I don't know if I'm imagining it, but it seems to me that you're enduring less pain and suffering than a few years ago. So perhaps there's hope.'

'Perhaps we just hide it better.' The sharpness in Emma's voice caught Bobby unawares again. Mila too, apparently, because she looked at Emma in surprise. 'Like some of our friends.'

'We all hide things from each other,' said Mila, turning back to the stove.

'But some of us have more to hide than others.' It was as if the two women had begun a secret conversation, as if they were suddenly speaking a coded language which the rest of the company couldn't decipher. Then Emma sighed, like someone admitting defeat, and stared at her hands in her lap. 'Or perhaps it's just the calm before the storm. At the moment we're both ignoring the Question of Children. But I won't be able to pretend for much longer that it doesn't matter. If Philip wants me to stay with him, he'll have to be prepared to raise a child with me.'

At that moment Mona leaped up from the kitchen floor – with the perfect timing of an actress who knows how to capture the spotlight – and handed her drawing to Emma with a proud smile.

'For *me*?' asked Emma, surprised.

'Emma.' Mona pressed a fat index finger on the page, indicating a few of the wild lines. 'Emma's hair.'

'Blue hair.'

'Green hair too,' said Mona. 'Purple hair too.'

'Thank you, Mona,' said Emma and kissed the child's forehead. 'I'm completely overwhelmed by the honour. One day when you're a famous painter, I can boast that I was one of your first models.'

'Is it that important for you to have a child?' asked Bobby, frowning. 'More important than your relationship with Philip?'

'Yes,' she answered without hesitation, still admiring the picture. 'If she does indeed become famous, I could probably buy myself a car with this little scribble.'

'That's something I just don't understand,' said Bobby, shaking her head. 'The urge to reproduce.'

'That's what Philip always says. It's difficult for me to understand that some people don't want to reproduce. There are only two things in life that I've ever been really sure about. The one is that I want to write stories one day, and the other is that I want to have children.'

'Well, if you're talking in the plural,' said Mila, 'you'll have to get going.'

'With Philip I can't even think in the plural,' she said with a sad little laugh. 'If only he'd be prepared to have *one* child with me! Maybe then he'd realize that it wasn't so bad. But at the moment we're definitely talking about singular.'

'Why don't you just do it then?'

'What?'

'Why don't you just go off the Pill? He doesn't have to know.'

'That won't work,' she sighed. 'Not with Philip. He'd never trust me again. I mean he won't trust me with *anything* again.'

'So you'd rather leave him?'

'I'd rather leave him.' Emma glanced quickly at the men in front of the television, suddenly worried that one of them could hear her. Although it would probably take a bomb to distract their attention from the last tense moments of the game. Paul was the only one who was beginning to look a little bored, staring now and then through the sitting-room window at the rain, deep in thought. 'Before it's too late, as you're always warning me. Before my biological clock begins to tick so loudly that I do something utterly irresponsible.'

'Wait until you're my age before you begin to talk about biological clocks and irresponsible actions.' Mila sat next to her on a bar stool, finished with the pancakes, and lit a cigarette. 'In two years I turn forty.'

'Why don't you just do it then?' asked Yvette unexpectedly.

'What?' Mila drew sharply on her cigarette.

'What you're advising Emma to do.' Yvette had taken Mila's place in front of the stove to make soup. She lit the gas under a big pot and bent forward so that Mona could blow out the burning match. From her bent position she looked fleetingly up at Mila, her dark eyes almost pleading. 'Throw your contraceptives away and get pregnant.'

'It's a bit more complicated if you don't have a steady partner!'

'No, it ought to be easier,' said Yvette. 'The man doesn't even need to know he's the father.'

'There's a four-letter word you're forgetting about.' Mila exhaled the smoke slowly as she stared out through the kitchen window. 'Maybe in the sixties you could still do something like that, but these days, with Aids . . .'

'I don't mean that you should jump into bed with a total stranger. I mean someone you know well enough to know that he doesn't have Aids. Preferably someone who wouldn't be able to claim the child, you know, like a married man. You've had affairs with married men, after all.'

Shocked, Mila looked at Yvette, who was standing calmly in front of the stove, stirring the pot with a wooden spoon. Her other hand rested on the small of her back, the elbow bent backwards.

'How would you like it if someone did something like that with Adriaan!'

'As long as I didn't know, it couldn't harm me, could it?'

'Oh, come on, Yvette!' Mila stubbed her cigarette out so roughly that it broke in half. 'You don't really believe that!'

And Bobby wondered why she suddenly felt like a confused spectator at an inexplicable play.

'I do believe it.' Yvette turned away from the stove so that she could look Mila in the eye. 'I know Adriaan has affairs with other women. I know he knows I know. I know he sometimes has the desire to discuss it with me – to salve his conscience – but I don't want to hear about it. What I don't know, can't hurt me.'

'But if you *know* he has affairs,' said Emma impatiently, 'the harm's already done! All you can do is to refuse to hear the gruesome details! To protect yourself from further pain!'

'Do you mean to say that you never get jealous?' asked Mila with disbelieving eyes. 'Never?'

'No, you both misunderstand me. I'm not saying that I'm above jealousy or possessiveness. I mean that those kinds of emotions are usually stirred up by insecurity – and I've never been insecure in my relationship with Adriaan. I know that he sometimes needs variety. That doesn't mean that he's rejecting me. I know that he'll always come back to me. He gets something from me – and I from him – a kind of certainty that we belong together. I don't know how to explain it . . .'

'It's true,' said Mila, her eyes on the steamy windows again. 'It's clear that he'll never leave you.'

'I don't know about never,' she said, looking at the vegetables simmering in the pot. A slight smile played around her childlike mouth. 'But I don't think he'll leave me for another woman. If we drift apart, it will be for other reasons. If I had an affair, for instance. I don't think he could handle that.'

The very idea of Yvette having an extra-marital affair was so strange that all three stared speechlessly at her for a few moments.

'Have you ever considered it?' asked Bobby. 'Having an affair?'

'I've never had the need to,' she answered in her open-hearted way, her head tilted under the black hat, with that mysterious Mona Lisa smile at the corners of her mouth. 'But I don't know how I'll feel in a few years' time. You never know, do you?'

At that moment exuberant cheering from the sitting room signalled the end of the match. Mona leaped up from the kitchen floor and ran to share in the jubilation, the dog as always hot on her heels. Yvette looked after them, the little smile now spread out over her whole face, her hands folded under her big stomach. Bobby wondered whether she could really be as happy as she looked. Whether *anyone* could be so happy without a strong dose of self-deception.

The beach lay deserted before them, a study in shades of grey. To the right the light grey sea with whitish-grey waves rolling slowly closer, to the left the lagoon in a deeper, shinier grey, calmer and smoother than the sea. The low sand dunes overgrown with hardy grey-green shrubs, the rocks a blackish grey, the faraway mountains a hazy blue-grey. The only sign of life was two gulls wandering calmly at the water's edge like an elderly couple.

And yet this melancholy scene made him feel better than he had all day in the house, Ralph realized. When the soaking rain had stopped unexpectedly a little while ago, he and Max had immediately decided to walk to the beach, leaving the others beside the fire with a bottle of wine. They spoke little as they walked through the quiet, wet streets of the town, as though they first had to shake off the superficiality of the afternoon in front of the television before they could have a meaningful conversation. Now the unimpeded view of the beach had apparently also released their thoughts, because Max had just begun to speak passionately about his new work as an advocate.

'That's why I understand Mila's excitement about the new paper,' he said as they walked along the path between the rocks, down to the beach. 'Truth is a slippery business – it's not something you can really ever come to grips with – but it gives you an incredible kick if your work has to do with a search for truth. Even though you know there's no such thing as "the whole truth". Even though you know there will always be gaps and differing versions. In the end, the search is more important than whatever it can deliver!'

'You make everything sound terribly noble, brother,' said Ralph with a cynical laugh. 'But I've always thought that an advocate's work is more or less like a gravedigger's. First you have to dig through a pile of lies to reach the truth – or some version of the truth – and then you have to cover everything up with Latin phrases and highflown words. Especially if the truth you dig up looks different from the truth your client tells you.'

'You mean that it's more or less the same as advertising.' Max grinned into his black beard, cut shorter and neater than before. Probably to match the dark suit and official toga which he had to wear to court these days. 'The only difference is that you use clever slogans instead of Latin phrases when you want to cover up the truth!'

'No, the difference is that we have no feelings of moral superiority about our work,' laughed Ralph. 'We openly admit that we'd do anything to keep the client happy.'

'OK, I admit that there are lots of advocates who should rather be in advertising. That's why I decided to concentrate on human rights. It's different to – '

'Duck!' Ralph shouted. 'Here comes the moral superiority again!'

'Ag, your arse! You're just bitter because some of your friends can be proud of their work!'

They walked along in silence for a while. At their approach, the two wandering gulls flew up unwillingly and hovered above them, watching, it seemed to Ralph, with resentful little eyes.

'Mila said you'd written a screenplay which was accepted by the SABC.' Max looked sideways at him. 'Why are you so modest about it? Isn't that what you've been threatening to do for years?'

'No. For years I've been threatening to write the Great Afrikaans Novel. But I realized that screenplays were an easier way to make money.'

'But that means you've now got your foot in the door? If *one* of your scripts is accepted to begin with . . .'

'I've got my foot in the door,' said Ralph seriously, 'but that can also just mean I'm going to lose my toes.'

'If your first screenplay is accepted on your first try, there's no reason . . .'

'It wasn't my first screenplay,' Ralph interrupted him. 'Also not the first time I've tried to flog this one. In the end I had to make so many changes to satisfy the powers-that-be that fuck-all of the original was left.'

'But won't it be easier next time?'

'What? To write a screenplay? Or to sell my soul?'

'It sounds as though your soul's already lost, Ralph.'

'Touché,' grinned Ralph.

It had begun to rain again softly. He threw his head back and closed his eyes, suddenly filled with an inexplicable joy at the pleasure of the moment. To be here, now, on this wet and deserted beach, to feel this drizzle stroking his face. What the hell did it matter how he earned his living?

'But I can't help but envy you,' he said after they'd walked a little way in silence. 'You *know* what you want to do in life. And you can do it without a struggle with your conscience. These days I feel like a middle-aged adolescent. I don't have a fucking clue what I want to do with the rest of my life! I've got all sorts of far-fetched ideas, like I'm going to write this novel to end all novels. But I'm also old enough to know when I'm fooling myself.'

'Well, I know what I want to do professionally, but when it comes to my personal life . . .' Max's worn-out boots made deep tracks in the wet sand. He walked with his hands in the pockets of his jeans, his shoulders hunched forward. 'I know that I don't want to stay a "swinging bachelor" for the rest of my life. But I get cold shivers, literally, every time I think of a wife and kids and all those things. The whole bloody catastrophe. Every time someone wants to know when I'm going to "settle down". I *hate* that phrase.'

'I don't think I'll ever settle down.' Ralph rubbed his damp hair, curlier than usual, and wondered, nonplussed, where that sentence came from. 'I just don't think I could do it.'

'But don't you think that's a kind of immaturity? To still feel like that at our age?'

'Probably. I just said I felt like a middle-aged adolescent. Perhaps that's another reason for going overseas now. I've reached the age where the pressure to settle down gets greater every day. Perhaps I just want to make sure that I won't capitulate in a moment of weakness.'

'You've given so many reasons for this overseas trip that no one can keep up any more,' muttered Max.

'Because I'm still trying to justify it to myself,' Ralph explained. 'I feel like a double traitor towards people like you and Mila. In the first place, because my work is totally meaningless in comparison to what you're doing. In the second place, because I'm giving up this totally meaningless job in order to leave the country.'

'But you're not leaving the country!' Max looked at him again surreptitiously, his black eyes questioning. 'Surely it's only for a while?'

'Of course!' His voice was suddenly so hoarse with emotion that it scared him into silence for a moment. Then, calmer, he said, 'Of course, it's only for a while.'

'Tell me, Adriaan,' Philip's voice was exaggeratedly formal, like a TV reporter conducting an interview with a famous artist. But the cigarette which hung rakishly from the corner of his mouth made him look more like Bogart acting the cynical detective. 'Has your work sold better since you refused to take part in that controversial exhibition in Chile?'

'Ah! You want to know if it's lucrative to be politically correct.' Adriaan smiled broadly, his elbows on the kitchen counter, his rough brown hands folded above his bowl of vegetable soup. He wore his hair longer these days – long enough to tie up in a pony tail low in his neck – which made him look more than ever like a farm hand from an earlier century. 'Well, of course there's always the possibility that I missed a unique opportunity to build up a worldwide fascist fan club . . .'

'But your conscience just wouldn't let you take part in such a "contaminated" exhibition.' Philip's eyes glittered dangerously.

'No, it's bad enough being surrounded by fascists in my own country,' Adriaan went on, ignoring the sarcasm in Philip's voice. 'I couldn't think of a single reason why I would want to go and look for the same problem in another country. But to answer your question, Philip, my paintings are indeed selling better these days . . .'

'At higher prices than ever before,' muttered Mila, dunking a piece of bread in her soup.

'At higher prices,' he agreed, his eyes on her hands. 'I don't know if my refusal to take part in a controversial exhibition had anything to do with it. I have a suspicion that most art buyers in this country wouldn't give a damn if a painting was exhibited in hell itself . . .'

'Does anyone in this country still have money left for art?' asked Emma.

'Believe it or not. Of course they can't afford the overseas stuff any more, so they have to buy what they can get at home.' He raised his palms and smiled apologetically. 'And here at home I'm a big fish in a small pond. Flavour of the month. That's all.'

'There's no need to be so modest,' said Paul. 'One can hardly open a magazine these days without seeing a photo of you or Yvette. How many interviews do you do each month?'

'This is the fifteen minutes of fame that Warhol was talking about.' Adriaan's face had suddenly become unusually serious. 'Perhaps that's all that an artist can aim for these days. What does it matter if no one knows who you are after you die? As long as *De Kat* and *Style* want to interview you, you're as famous as you're ever going to be.'

'And meanwhile, your work gets so expensive that your own friends can't afford it any more,' said Mila. 'Not that I could ever afford it. I'm just saying.'

'And Yvette's also just won a prize,' said Philip. 'It sounds as though everything's plain sailing for the Beyers family in good old South Africa. Even though you're surrounded by fascists!'

'What prize did Yvette win?' Bobby wanted to know. 'How come I know nothing about this?'

'Because you only read Struggle newspapers.' Philip slurped up a spoon of soup, still with a manic glint in his eye. 'And this is an Establishment prize.'

'A medal for "outstanding children's literature",' Adriaan answered, looking at his wife with almost possessive pride. 'From the Academy for Science and the Arts, no less!'

'For the illustrations I did for Griet's fairy-tale collection,' explained Yvette, blushing.

'It's the best work she's ever done,' boasted Adriaan. 'I think it's brilliant!'

'Well, I don't know about "brilliant" . . .' murmured Yvette with her eyes fixed on her plate. 'But I must admit that the fairy tales really inspired me.'

'That's wonderful,' said Bobby. 'Congratulations!'

'It's true, what Philip is saying,' declared Adriaan. 'The Beyers family is doing well. We can pay the rent – for the first time in our lives – we're going to have another baby soon and our daughter looks radiantly happy at her new pre-school. Even our dog looks radiantly happy! We're all so happy that we can't sleep at night! It's hell for a little Calvinist family, all this worldly happiness. We keep expecting to be zapped at any moment. That some catastrophe is going to hit us because we've forgotten that life is actually meant to be a vale of tears.'

He tried to hide his smugness behind a jokey tone, but didn't quite succeed. What he did disguise incredibly well, Ralph decided, was the relationship between him and Mila. He'd been watching them carefully since the night before in the hope that he would catch them out in some way, detect some crack in the wall of feigned indifference between them, intercept a furtive glance or a semi-accidental touch. Like the way Adriaan had stared at Mila's hands just now. For a moment, just a moment, Ralph felt the perverse, painful pleasure of a masochist. Before the ludicrousness of the situation dawned on him. Adriaan had looked at Mila's hands as he would look at any other woman's hands, like an artist wondering how he would paint them. It would be much more suspicious if he suddenly stopped looking at her. No, Ralph realized, he was not going to catch them out. They were like two professional poker players – so practised that they'd even learned to control their body language – playing the most important game of their lives.

'And what are you going to do about your prize?' Philip asked Yvette. 'Seeing that the Academy is now also this "contaminated" organization? Establishment, Broederbond, conservative, all the swear words in the Struggle's book?'

It was obvious that he wanted to pick a fight. Yvette looked at him with her head to one side, her big eyes completely innocent. Alice in Wonderland.

'What would you suggest?' she asked quietly. 'That I give out a pompous press release to say that my politicial conscience unfortunately does not allow me to accept such a contaminated prize?'

'Or you could use your acceptance speech to shit on your audience from a dizzy height,' grinned Philip. 'Like Breyten Breytenbach did with the Rapport Prize.'

'Just don't expect the audience to give you a standing ovation,' warned Emma. 'Only a poet can succeed in shitting on an audience in such beautiful language that they applaud him.'

'Or you could announce that you're giving your prize money to the UDF,' Philip suggested. 'Like that other writer did.'

'As a faithful supporter of the UDF I suppose I'd have to second that,' said Bobby.

'Or you can do what artists have done for centuries when they've received official recognition,' said Max. 'Take the money and run.'

'As a faithful supporter of capitalism I'd second *that*,' said Paul with a gleaming white smile. 'Forget about principles. You can't buy food with principles. Grab the money.'

'It's not money,' giggled Yvette. 'It's just a medal. I don't know what the UDF would do with a medal for outstanding children's literature. I don't know what I'm going to do with it!'

'Perhaps you can turn it into a big earring,' suggested Mila. 'That's what I wanted to do with the stupid medal the army sent me after my husband's death. In the end I threw it in the sea. My small gesture of personal protest.'

'An earring!' Yvette smiled, pleased. 'Then I can wear it as a form of protest if I ever get an official prize again!'

'Perhaps I can base a big anti-establishment work of art on it!' cried Adriaan enthusiastically. 'A collage of useless medals and army dog tags and Youth Group certificates and insurance forms and junk mail and all the other crap we get buried in daily!'

'It's probably the best way to cope with the absurdity of everyday life,' said Emma. 'To turn it into art.'

'Or to joke about it,' said Philip, again with a cigarette hanging skewly from the corner of his mouth. 'To refuse to take it seriously.'

'Sometimes you don't have a choice,' said Bobby softly. 'Sometimes everyday life forces you to take things seriously.'

'Then there's only one way to escape.' Philip lifted his glass as if to propose a toast. '*Sex, drugs and rock 'n' roll.*'

'My wife always says money is the only reliable escape.' Paul's expression was vaguely amused, as always when he spoke about his wife. As if he'd forgotten what he'd said the night before. 'You can buy your way out of any mess.'

'And you, Paul?' Yvette asked, her voice suddenly urgent. It was clear that she hadn't forgotten the previous night's confessions. 'What do you think?'

'Sometimes I think that money isn't a bad escape route,' he admitted. 'Sometimes I think it's just another kind of jail. On the other hand, if you have to be in jail, a money jail is probably not a bad choice.'

'Why would one *have* to be in jail?'

'We're all in one kind of jail or another, aren't we? Something which keeps us where we are?'

'But we can all escape somehow. That's what this discussion is about, isn't it?'

'I don't have a clue what this discussion is about any more,' said Adriaan, bewildered.

'About escape routes,' grinned Paul. 'What's *your* escape route, Yvette?'

'Imagination,' she answered. 'That's all you need to survive reality.'

'And if reality becomes so ghastly that it begins to affect your imagination?' Mila asked.

'*Sex, drugs and rock 'n' roll,*' said Philip again.

'I don't have much experience of drugs and rock 'n' roll, Philip. I suspect you don't either. But I admit that sex can make you forget everything.'

'For a while,' said Ralph, his voice sharper than he'd intended.

'For a while.' She smiled at him, teasing. 'But we're only talking about a moment's breathing space. There's no way to flee for ever. If you dream, you have to wake up again. If you get drunk, you have to

181

get sober. If you want to travel overseas, some time you have to come back home.'

'Not necessarily,' he said wistfully. 'It's theoretically possible to spend the rest of your life travelling.'

'Then it's not an escape any more, Ralph; then it's a way of life. Like a gypsy or a bum. And gypsies also need to escape sometimes to make life bearable.'

Her eyes burned into him as he stared uncomfortably at his wine glass. He couldn't get away from the heat of those blue flames, he realized. He'd never get away from them.

'Dance,' said Bobby opposite him. 'That's the best escapism in the world. Safer than sex and drugs, cheaper than travel, easier than art. If you follow Yvette's advice and use your imagination, you can even do it without music!'

'Didn't you say we were maybe going to dance tonight?' asked Max.

'If you're up for a real platteland disco in a genuine platteland hotel?' Her eyes shone excitedly behind the lenses of her round spectacles. 'The music is totally unpredictable – anything from Sonja Heroldt to the Grateful Dead – and the people are – how shall I put it without sounding snobbish . . .'

'Peasants?' asked Adriaan eagerly.

'Well, not the sort you'd encounter in a trendy club in Cape Town. These are people who'd sakkie-sakkie to Led Zeppelin.'

'Sounds fantastic!' Adriaan exclaimed, immediately carried away by the idea. 'Let's go sakkie-sakkie!'

'I think the last time I did that sakkie-sakkie ballroom stuff was at my wedding,' said Mila, astonished.

'Then you'll have to practise first!' The next moment he'd pulled her from her high bar stool and began to spin her across the kitchen floor, singing: *'Ken jy tant Mossie se sakkie-sakkie-sakkie boeredans . . .'*

Even now, as they danced – Mila's body limp with laughter, Adriaan's stiff back and pumping right hand a parody of an enthusiastic boeremusiek dancer – there was no sign of the secret intimacy between them.

Ralph stared at them, dazed. He had thought he knew her better than he knew anyone else in the world. For almost twenty years he'd played the role of friend and confidant and sometime lover; for almost twenty years he'd tried to make peace with the fact that he would always love her. And now he realized that he didn't know her at all. If she could hide something like this from him, a secret relationship in such a small circle of friends, he'd rather not know what else she'd hidden from him in the last twenty years.

It made him feel as though the earth had been pulled out from under his feet, as if he were spinning somewhere in space, weightless. Not pleasantly weightless, like when he had driven through the Karoo, but weightless like something that doesn't exist any more. Not between here and there, just nowhere.

And despite all that had just been said in this kitchen about escape routes and breathing space, he couldn't think of a single way to shake off this sense of being totally lost, non-existent.

'I'd forgotten how good it feels to dance with a man who can dance!' declared Emma, out of breath as she fell into the chair next to Ralph. 'Philip always treads on my toes till they're raw!'

Paul followed her off the crowded dance floor, his tanned face shiny with sweat, his smile gleaming white in the flashing of the disco lights on the low ceiling. A group of teenage girls formed an admiring guard of honour against the wall as he walked by. Sometimes it must be a real pain to be so attractive, Bobby mused, too exhausted from dancing to speak. Never to just disappear in a crowd. On the other hand, perhaps you get so used to turning heads that you don't notice it after a while. Paul didn't show any sign of self-consciousness or arrogance in the hall of this small-town hotel where he was definitely the most attractive man – and possibly also the best dancer – that some of the people had ever seen.

'Probably a good thing . . . that Philip isn't here.' Panting, Max grabbed at a bottle of beer on the low table between them and took a few thirsty swigs. He'd also just returned from the dance floor where Bobby had made him leap around for more than half an hour. 'He's got a way of . . . watching you when you dance . . . as though he's thinking you're behaving like a total idiot. But he wouldn't deign to tell you so.'

'It's all an act,' smiled Emma. 'He'd give anything to be able to dance with total abandon. But he's too self-conscious, he can't switch off his head, he's always too busy analyzing his own behaviour. He just pretends that he prefers not to dance.'

When Yvette said that she'd rather stay at home with Mona, Philip had immediately offered to keep her company. It wasn't necessary, she'd assured him, she couldn't dance with this stomach of hers, anyway. Well, he'd said, he couldn't dance with these feet of his, anyway.

'I think it was a great idea to come here,' said Paul. 'Otherwise we'd just have got drunk at the kitchen counter again.'

'Speak for yourself,' said Emma. 'Some of us went to bed early last night!'

'And some of us don't need a kitchen counter in order to get drunk,' mumbled Ralph as he poured another glass of whisky from the bottle in front of him, his eyes glazed and his tongue heavy.

He'd already drunk more than half the bottle on his own, Bobby realized. Over and above the wine he'd drunk during supper.

'I think it's time you got up from that chair, Ralph,' said Emma. 'Can I reserve you for the next dance?'

'I don't want to dance,' he said. 'I want to drink.'

'Not even to Abba?'

'Especially not to Abba.'

'Then you should have stayed at home with Philip and Yvette,' said Emma unsympathetically.

Mick Jagger's sensual voice suddenly moaned over the loudspeakers. Emma turned determinedly to Ralph. 'Come, it's time to get some exercise.'

'It's too late for exercise,' he mumbled. 'I'm far too drunk to dance.'

She shrugged her shoulders and looked at Max.

'Give me a chance!' said Max pleadingly. 'I haven't got my breath back yet!'

'Is there anyone in this hall who's not too tired to dance with me before "Honky-Tonk Woman" is over?' she shouted, her hands cupped like a megaphone over her mouth. 'It's my all-time favourite Rolling Stones number!'

'Why don't you go and dance with Adriaan and Mila?' asked Ralph.

'I'd clean forgotten about Adriaan and Mila! Have they been dancing ever since we got here?'

'Without stopping. Un-fucking-exhaustible. They're somewhere there in the middle of the crowd.'

'Well then, all you lazybones, I'll see you later!' And she began to press through the crowd with swaying shoulders.

'Well, she's in a good mood.' Max gulped his beer and looked sideways at Ralph. 'Unlike some of us.'

Ralph gave no indication that he'd heard him. Just drained his glass like a wounded soldier who has to brave an operation without an anaesthetic, someone drinking with the sole purpose of dulling the pain. Bobby watched him with concern. She had seen him pissed a few times – last night, for instance – but never drinking so desperately. Slumped into his chair, his shoulders drooping, his whole body limp. Only his eyes moved constantly, wandering restlessly over the dancers. She couldn't leave him alone now, she decided when Max and Paul stood up to buy another drink at the bar counter. He looked as if he needed a guardian angel to get him through this night. Not that she'd ever seen herself in the role of any kind of angel. That was Robin's field, she thought.

'Is leaving that difficult for you?' she asked, frowning.

He looked at her confused, as though he'd forgotten that she was sitting next to him.

'Is that why you're drinking like this?' she asked again. 'Because you have to say good-bye?'

'Because I have to say good-bye.' His voice sounded hollow, as though he was just repeating her words to grasp what they meant. And then, after staring sightlessly ahead for a few minutes, he muttered, 'I wonder what's happened to Mila and Adriaan.'

'I thought they were on the dance floor.'

'They were, but I think they've disappeared.'

'Where would they vanish to?' she asked, laughing. 'They . . .'

The expression on his face pinched her voice tight in her throat. Something between despair and rage, a terrible mixture. And suddenly something clicked in her mind. Like when the row of symbols on a fruit machine suddenly appears in the correct order and hundreds of clinking coins are spat out. *Adriaan and Mila. Of course.* That explained the tension in the kitchen, between Mila and Emma, between Mila and Yvette. It explained Ralph's determined drunkenness, his restless eyes, his despair and his rage. It even explained his decision to run off overseas.

Then she heard Mila's husky laugh behind her. She swung round guiltily.

'Gosh! It's pouring out there!' Mila exclaimed, her short blonde hair pressed damply against her head and her arms folded tightly across her Fair Isle jumper.

'You're crazy to be outside in weather like that!' Her voice sounded far too upset. 'We were getting worried.'

'I had to get cigarettes.' Mila pulled the jumper over her head when the steaming humidity of the dance floor hit her. 'Adriaan came with me. Where are the others?'

'Max and Paul have gone to buy more drinks.' Bobby jerked her head in the direction of the bar counter. Where Mila could probably also have bought cigarettes. 'Emma's dancing. And Ralph is busy drinking himself into a stupor. As you can see.'

Mila looked at Ralph with a worried expression. She put her hand on his shoulder, but he avoided her eyes, staring morosely in front of him.

'Won't you come and dance?'

'Ask someone else, Mila.'

'I don't want to dance with someone else, Ralph. I want to dance with you. Please?'

Adriaan had appeared behind her, smiling, but the smile stiffened when he heard the pleading tone in her voice. He looked at the awkward way in which she held her hand on Ralph's shoulder, as if she didn't know quite how it got there.

'I'm not in the mood for dancing tonight,' mumbled Ralph.

'Fair enough.' She drew her hand away slowly and let it fall limply at her side. 'Then I'll just have to drag Max or Paul away from the bar.'

She gave a forced laugh and walked away, her back straight.

'What do you think?' Adriaan's heavy voice suddenly sounded gritty with uncertainty, but he made a mock bow in front of Bobby. 'May I have the honour of a dance with you?'

'Not now, Adriaan. I'd like to stay with Ralph for a while.'

'That's not necessary,' said Ralph, even more curtly than before.

'I know. But I want to.'

Ralph glared at her, his tawny brown eyes glinting with suppressed frustration. Then he stood up, a clumsy movement, knocking his stool over with a heavy thud, and stumbled to the door of the hall, the whisky bottle still in his hand. Adriaan gave a step forward as though he wanted to stop him, but then stood still and stared after him with a helpless twist to his mouth. Bobby's gaze flew back and forth between Ralph's disappearing back and Adriaan's powerless expression.

'Perhaps he just wants to take a pee,' consoled Adriaan. 'Perhaps the fresh air will do him good.'

'Perhaps not,' said Bobby. 'I think one of us should go and see.'

'Leave him,' said Adriaan. 'If the cold out there doesn't chase him back inside within five minutes, hopefully it will drive out his demons.'

But Bobby shook her head, jumped up and walked in the direction in which Ralph had vanished. So anxious to follow him that she didn't even think to grab her anorak from the back of her chair. The moment she walked out of the door, the cold made her gasp. The rain fell in slanting gusts, hit her in the face and streamed over her hair as though she was standing in a shower. She hesitated for a second, wondering whether to fetch her anorak, but then she saw Ralph on the other side of the street, his T-shirt already so wet that it clung to his body. He weaved purposefully between a few parked cars, steadier on his feet than a little while ago in the dance hall. As though the rain had instantly washed away his drunkenness.

She ducked her head between her raised shoulders and jogged over the road to follow him. As she walked over a stretch of open ground, slipping in the mud which clung to her shoes in heavy clods, shivering from the cold, she saw that he'd already crossed the next street and turned right, in the direction of the sea. She felt his name form in her mouth, but she knew it wouldn't help to call out to him. He'd never hear her in this pouring rain. She couldn't even hear the throbbing dance music in the hotel hall just behind her. And what would she shout to him anyway? *Come back, you're crazy to be outside!* No, she decided, all that she could really do was to follow him at a safe distance. Make sure that he didn't do anything completely stupid.

He walked as though he knew exactly where he was going, so fast that it looked as though he'd break into a run at any minute. Or perhaps it was just the steep slope of the street – the street that led to the harbour, she realized. What the hell did he want to do in the harbour? Everything around him was dark, deserted. Pools on the wet tar reflected the dull lights of a few street lamps. No sign of life, the noise of the hotel now far behind them. The only café in this part of town was already closed for the night. The café where Mila had supposedly gone to buy a pack of cigarettes. A little way in front of her Ralph's dark silhouette turned for a moment into a three-dimensional person as he walked through the light pool of a street lamp, his hair in sopping strings at his neck. Then he faded to a fleeing shadow again. Of course he was running away, she thought angrily. *Coward*. Tonight from the dance hall, soon from the country. *Fool*. Away from Mila, away from Adriaan, away from rage and despair, away from all the other emotions that he couldn't bear. *Foolish coward*.

By this time he'd reached the harbour. He jogged past a few big fishing boats, vague shapes rocking and groaning on the dark water, in the direction of the narrow pier with the flashing red light at the furthest point. *No. It couldn't be*. The pier would be even wetter and more dangerous than usual, with the rain pouring down and the waves thundering over it. White fountains of spray shooting high into the air, sometimes vaulting right over the wall, sometimes sinking back halfway, pouring down on the glistening surface.

'Ralph!' she screamed as hard as she could, and began to run to catch up with him. 'Ralph, come back!'

It would be perilous to chance the pier now – even for a gymnast used to balancing on narrow beams. To attempt it in Ralph's drunken condition was completely crazy. Her heart thumped so anxiously in her chest that she didn't hear the waves any more, or her own voice screaming his name over and over again. But he jogged faster, further away from her, straight to the pier.

It was a kind of suicide, she thought with a terrible feeling of *déjà vu*. Perhaps not premeditated, perhaps not as purposefully as her brother had done it, but nevertheless a form of suicide. *No, no, no*.

She was now only a few paces behind him, so close that he *must* hear her if she screamed loudly enough. She opened her mouth again, but felt the scream freeze in her throat, because he was already standing on the pier. Hesitating a split second, as though he suddenly realized what he was doing. Then he walked onwards. Apparently fearless. If he was startled by her voice now, he would slip. She could see the whole scene playing itself out in front of her eyes, melodramatic, in slow motion. How he would struggle for a moment or two to keep his balance – and then the inevitable tumbling down. His body disappearing into the stormy sea, his head reappearing between the foaming waves a few times, a hand vainly reaching into the air. She began to walk purposefully to the wall, her eyes fixed on the moving silhouette in front of her. He looked as small as a marionette against a wave which towered frighteningly high in the dark air just a little way ahead. Small and vague, because she was blinded by tears, blinded by the rain and the spray. Her legs shook and her teeth chattered, with cold, with fear, with despair. She didn't know if she'd ever been so afraid in all her life. She didn't know if she would be able to do something to help if he fell into the water. She only knew she wanted to be close to him if it happened, that she had to try to help him, even if it was the last thing that she did. It was a thought which ripped a hole in her stomach. She'd always been a strong swimmer, but even a champion swimmer would be powerless against the violence of the waves breaking on this wall tonight. And yet she knew that she would leap after him. Into the whirling, pounding, foaming waves. Even if it was the last thing that she did.

Then she was also on the pier. She moved carefully, inch by inch, as if she was walking on a fresh layer of snow. Remembered all at once the first winter holiday that she and her brother had spent in Europe, how they had stormed outside yelling when it began to snow, how she had clung to him giggling to keep her balance and yet had landed on her bottom time and time again, her body limp with laughter and her fingers frozen stiff. A wave broke unexpectedly in front of her – she screamed before she could stop herself – and a curtain of white foam was flung across the sky. For a moment she couldn't see Ralph at all. When the curtain was pulled away again, she realized that he had begun to run. Straight to the flashing red light on the furthest point of the wall. Like a long-jumper who was going to attempt the jump of his life. The sound that burst from her throat was raw, an animal shriek that broke through the darkness around her, louder than the rain and the waves and her panting breath and her thumping heart. But Ralph didn't stop running.

At the last possible moment, just before he would have plunged off the end of the wall, he flung out his right arm, reaching straight out through the air, and grabbed with his other arm for the base of the flashing red light. His momentum was checked so suddenly that his body rocked to and fro for a few seconds, swaying over the drop, while the whisky bottle flew out of his right hand, soared through the darkness in a perfect bright arc, and disappeared into the stormy sea below.

Bobby ran the last stretch till she reached him, threw her arms around his body from behind, pressed her face between his shoulder blades, felt his drenched T-shirt against her cold skin, and cried until her shoulders shook. He just stood there, motionless, but she felt his tense muscles gradually begin to relax beneath her arms. Like ropes being untied all over his body. Until his hands at last hung limp and open and helpless at his sides.

When he turned around his face looked like a sheet of paper which had been ruthlessly erased. All the emotions written on it, the rage and the despair and all the other unbearable feelings. All that remained were dull signs, illegible marks, a kind of messy, crumpled emptiness.

'What the hell do you think you're doing!' The terrible relief replaced by a terrible anger. 'What the fuck did you come here for?'

'I could ask you the same question,' he answered with a twisted smile.

'I was afraid . . .' She took a deep breath and hugged him again, this time with her cheek pressed against his chest. Closed her eyes, suddenly so tired that she wanted to fall over, and said softly. 'I was scared. That's all.'

'I wanted some fresh air.' He rubbed her wet hair which was plastered to her head. 'I came to throw a bottle into the sea. That's all.'

'Let's go back,' she said.

But she stayed standing there, her head against his chest, too tired to move.

'Come,' he said, and took her hand. As though he was the sober one. And led her slowly, carefully back along the slippery pier.

When she eventually felt the firm cement of the harbour under her feet again, her knees collapsed. She sat flat on the ground and began shivering uncontrollably. But he pulled her up, determined and firm.

'Come,' he said. 'You'll get sick if you don't get rid of those wet clothes soon.'

'It's a bit late to think of that now!' she burst out again.

But she was too tired to feign indignation, too tired and too relieved. She walked silently back to the hotel with him, her body numb with cold, her brain dazed by the intensity of the emotions she'd experienced in the last half hour. When they arrived in the dance hall like two drenched castaways, Mila stormed at them, her face as pale as wax.

'Where have you been?' Her mouth a raw wound, pulled skew by tension and relief. 'What have you been doing?'

'She was desperate to go looking for you,' said Adriaan behind her. 'We just about had to tie her up to keep her here.'

The rest of the group had also clustered around them.

'Do you really think it's a good idea to go swimming on a night like this?' asked Paul with his usual sardonic smile.

'Swallow,' said Max and pressed a glass of whisky in Ralph's hand. 'You look as though you need it.'

But Ralph shook his head and gave the glass to Bobby – who drained it without hesitation.

Emma just stared at them dumbfounded, her grey eyes wide with shock.

'We'll have to get you home,' Mila decided with an anxious frown. 'Where are your car keys Adriaan? I'll take them home, then the rest of you can come later with Max.'

'I don't know about the rest of you,' sighed Adriaan, 'but this platteland disco is getting too heavy for my sensitive urban soul. I can only handle so much drama in one night.'

'Yes, let's go home,' said Emma with an uneven smile. 'If I hear another Abba song, I'll scream.'

The others apparently felt the same, because everyone began to pull on jerseys and jackets and coats. Only Mila stood motionless, staring at Ralph.

'What did you do outside, Ralph?' she whispered.

'I went to throw a bottle in the sea.'

'Why?' she whispered. 'Why have you been in such a destructive mood all night?'

The conversation suddenly sounded so personal, so private, that Bobby dropped her eyes, embarrassed. She stared at the pool which had formed around her feet. No use putting her anorak on now. It didn't look as though Ralph and Mila realized that she could hear them. It was as though they were suddenly completely unaware of their surroundings.

'You said long ago that I had a self-destructive streak,' Ralph said with a shrug.

'Like most people,' said Mila. 'But you've always suppressed it better than most people.'

'Some things can't be suppressed for ever.'

'Does it . . .' Mila swallowed heavily, her voice pinched so tightly in her throat that Bobby struggled to hear her. Still staring at her wet feet. 'Does it have anything to do with me, Ralph?'

He didn't answer, just gave her a heartbreaking smile.

'I'm sorry,' she said in a hoarse voice. 'I mean, if anything you did tonight has anything to do with me, I'm sorry. If it's got nothing to do with me, I'm still sorry. I didn't mean to hurt you, Ralph. I didn't mean to hurt anyone . . .'

'I know, Mila.' And then he turned away from her, threw his arms up in a dramatic gesture and declared with a voice full of bravado, loud enough for the rest of the group to hear him, 'I don't know what the hell happened to me tonight. I only know that in a few hours I'm going to have the worst hangover of my life!'

'And probably double pneumonia too,' said Mila in her normal smoky voice as they moved towards the door. 'And this is a man who plans to fly to London in a few days!'

With a hole in his heart, thought Bobby. The hangover and even the possible pneumonia would pass quickly, but she wondered how long it would be before his heart would be whole again. Just for a year, she murmured, like someone praying. Just for a year.

FIVE

When Will These Things End? (1989)

'I'm glad you came before the others,' said Yvette, when Mila appeared on the stoep with the tea tray. 'There's something I want to talk to you about.'

Her eyes remained on the baby at her breast, his busy mouth exactly the same browny pink as the aureole he was suckling on like an anemone, the skin of his cheek translucent white with light pink and blue undertones, mother-of-pearl smooth under her stroking fingertips. Small sucking sea creature. His eyes closed, as though the light, even after seven months, was too bright for him, as though he was still dreaming about the dark waterworld in which he was formed.

But something in Mila's posture caught Yvette's attention. The way she suddenly stiffened before she put the tea tray down on the cane table, a moment of suppressed tension as she bent forward. Just a moment, then it passed.

'It's about Pablo,' she said quickly.

'About Pablo?' Surprise in the blue gaze, relief in her husky, low laugh. 'What do I know about babies!'

'No, it's about . . . I wanted to ask you . . . I mean I wanted to know if you'd be at all interested in being his godmother. No obligation! Not at all. I just wanted to discuss it with you first. Give you the right to refuse before I ask someone else.'

Mila was suddenly very busy pouring tea. They were sitting on the stoep of the dilapidated Victorian house outside Stellenbosch where Yvette and Adriaan had lived and worked for the last three years. One of the little coloured panes in the diamond-shaped windows on either side of the stoep was broken and a ray of transparent sunlight fell through the hole on to Mila's hands, which moved nervously between the teapot and the two cups. The rest of the panes threw glowing red and blue and green reflections on to the cool cement floor. Mila pushed a cup of tea over to Yvette.

'I don't know what to say.'

'I won't be offended if you don't want to . . .'

'No! It would be an honour! It's just that . . . well, I don't know if

I'm such a good choice . . . I don't actually know what a godmother is supposed to do. Can one go to the library and take out a book on it?' She smiled awkwardly. 'I don't know if I deserve the honour, Yvette.'

'You don't have to deserve everything on earth, Mila. Sometimes things just happen.'

'And sometimes things get out of hand,' Mila said quietly.

But Yvette's attention was again distracted by her son, by his smooth black hair which slipped through her fingers like wet seaweed. Where did all this water imagery come from? With Mona it was different. Mona had been a warm, lively baby from the start. Like holding a bundle of sunshine, she had thought in wonder that first day. While Pablo had aimed at the dark side of her heart from the very first moment. Leaped into the deep end of her love. Her little merman. With Mona, her feeling was less intense. Not less loving, of course not, just . . . different. Perhaps because it was her first experience of motherhood, woven with the insecurity and tension of all first experiences. The second time it was full surrender at first sight. Her heart overflowed, there was no room for fear. Or was it different because he was a boy? This was the only uncertainty that sometimes gnawed at her heart. She knew that her own mother loved her sons more than her daughters. She would hate to send her own daughter out into the world with this knowledge.

'I actually wanted to ask you to be Mona's godmother,' she tried to explain. 'But I agonized about it for so long that it became too late. I mean, by that time you'd already developed such a good relationship that it was unnecessary. Mona views you as a kind of fairy godmother anyway.'

'Why?'

She looked at Mila uncomprehendingly.

'Why did you agonize about it for so long?'

'Ag, you know. Indecision's my second name,' she answered with a self-conscious laugh.

'Oh, I thought it was perhaps because . . .'

'The Great Procrastinator. That's what my mother always called me.'

Mila was quiet for a moment, pulled her feet back from the red reflection on the floor and crossed her legs. The tips of her black patent leather shoes were as sharp as pen nibs, the rest of her outfit just as nonchalantly elegant. Black polo-neck sweater, short red wool skirt and black winter tights; a pair of gigantic silver crosses in her ears – the kind of jewellery which would never be worn by a woman lacking self-confidence. Yvette was suddenly uncomfortably aware of the fact that she was still trying to hide her body, seven months after her child's birth, in the same shapeless pillowslip of a dress she had worn during the last weeks of her pregnancy.

'And what does Adriaan think about it?' asked Mila, looking out over the rolling lawn, to the blue mountains in the distance.

'Oh, he thinks that the whole idea of godparents is old-fashioned and unnecessary. Like having your child christened, he says. And yet in the end he did agree to have the children christened. I still don't know if it was just to please me or because actually deep down in his heart he wanted it himself. With Adriaan one never knows.'

'But he doesn't mind if I become his son's godmother?'

'No!' she laughed. 'Why should he?'

'Well. It's quite a commitment, isn't it? It means that for the next twenty years I'll be part of your life!'

Yvette stared at her son's pearly cheek. She couldn't pretend any longer that she didn't know what Mila was talking about. Or was trying to talk about. Indeed, the subject had lain between them for years now, like a rock, as big as a rock and as heavy as a rock, but they pretended it wasn't there because neither of them wanted to tackle it. To talk it out of the way.

'You're part of our lives anyway, Mila,' she said with a resigned sigh. 'With or without Pablo.'

'Perhaps I should admit that I don't actually like little boys,' warned Mila. 'I mean, they're completely irresistible until they're about five years old, but soon after that they begin to irritate me. When they get those knock knees and crew cuts and start acting like miniature versions of their fathers. You know, all the aggression and the bossiness and the obsession with their little willies. I find it extremely boring. I don't know, maybe it's because I never had brothers, perhaps boys frightened me when I was little. I don't have a clue how their minds work. It's only when they're about eighteen that I begin to find them irresistible again. In a different way, of course.'

'It's OK, Mila. I didn't really expect you to agree. I just wanted to . . .'

'No! It's not that I don't want to do it! I think perhaps it's exactly what I need. You know, to learn to like little boys. I'm sure that Pablo would be irresistible at any age!'

'I suppose the ideal would be to choose some kind of relay team,' said Yvette thoughtfully. 'Then you only need to take him on for the first five years, when he's at his cutest for you. And then perhaps Emma could play godmother for the next five years – just think of the stories she could make up for him – and then Liane or Bobby. And then you could have him back when he's twenty. Irresistible all over again,' she added with a satisfied little laugh. 'Perhaps even help show him the ropes sexually.'

'By twenty, my dear Yvette, he'll have known the ropes for a long time already.'

'Too true. Well, then you'll just have to borrow him from Bobby or Liane at sixteen. Adriaan is always boasting about how he was seduced by an older woman when he was a schoolboy. I'm sure he wouldn't mind if his son followed in his footsteps.'

'When he's sixteen,' said Mila sombrely, 'I'll be in my mid-fifties. That's not "older", Yvette. For a sixteen-year-old schoolboy that's ancient! On the other hand, if he can survive Liane and Bobby as godmothers, he'll probably turn out weird enough to be turned on by geriatric sex.' She began to shake with laughter. The heavy silver crosses in her ears swayed rhythmically with her. 'No, I'd better take him on for the full twenty years. If I fuck up, then at least it will be a consistent fuck-up. That sounds better to me somehow than four different godmothers who can fuck you up in four different ways.'

'Well, if you put it that way . . .' Yvette looked at Pablo, who had fallen asleep in the meantime, his mouth still resolutely locked on her nipple. As if nothing, not even his dreams, could match up to this pleasure. 'What do you think? Would you like to hold your new godson?'

'And if he begins to cry?' Mila asked with an anxious frown. 'I don't have a milky nipple to stick in his mouth.'

But she stood up and took the baby carefully from Yvette. Her hands, which usually moved so gracefully, suddenly looked clumsy. Almost too big against the little sleeping body which moved, agitated, in unfamiliar arms. His eyes fluttered open slowly, like a butterfly opening two velvet brown wings. Mila stiffened, held her breath, but he just stared quietly at her, his eyes hazy behind a veil of sleep. When his eyelids again fell drowsily closed, she sighed with relief.

'Well? How does it feel?'

'Like the last words in *Casablanca*.' Then Mila looked up, the wonder on her face replaced with anxiety. 'I hope this doesn't mean that I have to give up smoking and drinking and swearing!'

'Ag, no.' Yvette smiled reassuringly. 'How does that song go again? *Don't go changing . . .*'

'*I love you just the way you are*,' grinned Mila.

'If there's one thing that you may well have to give up – just temporarily of course – it's such attractive jewellery. Babies are like jackdaws, they can't resist bright things. And if Pablo were to grab those crosses, he could tear your earlobes to shreds.'

'Glad you warned me,' said Mila, touching her right ear protectively.

'Are they Indian?' Yvette asked.

'Native American,' Mila answered proudly. 'Ralph sent them to me last Christmas.'

Native American. Yvette bit her lip in contrition. That's what happened when an exhausted mother of two young children tried to talk to an energetic career woman. A neglected, politically fossilized mind in conversation with a busy, stimulated brain. A plump, pear-shaped breastfeeding body compared with a pair of slender ballerina legs which have never been disfigured by the varicose veins of pregnancy, a flat stomach which has never been stretched out all marshmallow soft and saggy, a pair of firm breasts which have never been attacked by a baby's greedy mouth. In a few years there would probably be a fashionable new word for Native American. And she'd probably be caught out again. She'd always be a step behind.

No wonder her husband couldn't resist this woman. Not that he could ever resist any woman. But none of his previous affairs had made her feel this threatened. It was time she admitted it to herself. She felt, for the first time since she'd married Adriaan, as if she'd been weighed and found wanting. Was it that she had changed? Grown older and more vulnerable?

Or was his relationship with Mila really different from all the others?

She stood up quickly, took the baby from Mila's arms almost brusquely, and vanished into the house.

After she'd put the sleeping child down – actually just an excuse to get her emotions under control – she came to sit outside next to Mila again. Mila said nothing, just stared silently in front of her, drinking a cup of cold tea. On the other side of the expanse of lawn, deep green after three weeks of winter rain, the farm dam glistened in the late afternoon sun between the bare skeletons of a row of poplar trees and the grey-green shade of a clump of blue gum trees. In the distance rose the majestic blue peaks which had still been covered with a layer of snow a week ago. For the last few days the sky had been cloudless and the sun yellow and warm, melting the snow and baking the muddy ground dry. It looked as though it was going to be a lovely weekend.

Like a special birthday present, thought Yvette, such mild sunny weather in the middle of the Cape winter. Not that she ever minded the cold, damp winters. They suited her pale complexion and her unathletic body and her preference for indoor activities. Africa's sweltering summers had always made her feel like a European tulip in the Kalahari desert. It must be something to do with her mother's Irish ancestry – ever since she was little she had painted pictures in shades of green that she would never, ever see in the country of her birth. As though somewhere in her subconscious she cherished a memory of the variety – and the seductiveness – of landscapes so green they hurt your eyes.

But she realized that most of her friends would fade away without regular doses of sunlight. Max, who looked as though he was born on a Greek island and raised on a fishing boat; Mila, with her legs which were always coloured an even golden brown and her fringe which was always bleached a streaky blonde; Liane, who sometimes created the illusion that she was covered in a layer of honey from top to toe; Paul, who boasted the sultry features of an Italian model even in the heart of winter. Her husband, too, of course, with his hands of warm brown clay. And her daughter, with her father's hands, her father's skin.

It was for their sake that she was happy about the promise of sunshine. Something to make the weekend more enjoyable. Something to offer them, over and above the chance to get together again for a while.

She still couldn't explain why she wanted to have a party this year in particular. She'd never been the sort who believed that birthdays had to be celebrated with fireworks and a cast of thousands. That was more Liane's style. Even when she turned thirty, two years ago, she didn't bother with Liane's plea for a large-scale party. ('It's such a milestone in any woman's life, my darling! Whether you're in ecstasy or agony about it, it's still an occasion!') She had just shrugged her shoulders and quietly turned thirty. But for some reason she wanted to turn this very ordinary birthday – not a *milestone* – into a social occasion. Perhaps it had something to do with the new baby. With the realization of her own mortality which had slowly begun to take root in her mind since the birth of her first child. Or with her father and mother, who had looked so unexpectedly old when they recently came to attend the christening of their new grandchild. Or with her father-in-law, who was disappearing into the fog of Alzheimer's. Or with Adriaan's expression, like a little lost boy, when he tried to find his father in this fog. Perhaps it was just a case of raging against the dying of the light. Heaven alone knew.

All she knew was that she wanted to celebrate the beginning of her thirty-third year properly. It was a kind of spiritual milestone after all, as she had remarked to Adriaan, only half in jest. (Christ was thirty-three years old when he died, right?) 'Aha!' Adriaan had cried out triumphantly. 'I knew your mother's Catholic beliefs would catch up with you one day!' Ag, well, she'd said, hopefully her agnostic father's cynicism would protect her against the worst damage.

'There seems to be such a lack of cheerfulness in our circle of friends,' she said wistfully. 'Perhaps that's one of the reasons I want to give a party.'

'And you think a party will create more cheer?' Mila raised her eyebrows and lit a cigarette. 'Of course there's always the possibility that it could feel more like a funeral than a party.'

'One can always hope, not so?'

'You'd stand in front of the gates of hell and hope, Yvette.'

'Well, Liane was wild with excitement when I phoned her.'

'Not that it takes much to get Liane excited.'

'She sounded like a teenager being invited to her first evening party.'

'And I assume she immediately asked you if she could spend the night.'

'Always afraid of missing a moment's fun!'

'I don't think that's what she's afraid of.' Mila blew a thin stream of smoke through her red lips and shook her head slowly. 'I know what it's like when a relationship begins to fall apart. Anything is better than being alone in each other's company.'

'I thought things were going better with them,' said Yvette, shocked.

'I think things are worse than ever.'

'But weren't they in therapy?'

'Therapy can't work miracles. Oh, of course she hides it fantastically well. She didn't study drama for nothing. Paul is the one struggling to keep up the act. I don't know why he bothers. I mean, is there anyone left in the country who can boast a relationship that works?' She spat the question out with so much bitterness that Yvette stared at her in dismay. 'How many happy couples do you know these days? You can count them on one hand, not so? I hear that Emma and Philip are also getting divorced. OK, they were never a fairy-tale example of a happy couple, but there was a time when I thought they were going to make it work after all . . .'

'Are they getting divorced?'

'She's moved in with Bobby. Looking very hard for a place of her own. So I'm afraid . . .'

'But their relationship has always been a series of dramatic storms. That doesn't necessarily mean it's over!'

'The difference is that this time there wasn't a dramatic storm. She simply packed a case and moved out. Without a scene. I think it eventually dawned on her that she was never going to persuade Philip to try out the adventure of parenthood with her. About bloody time, I'd say.'

'So he's prepared to give her up rather than have a child again?'

'And she's prepared to give *him* up. That's probably what they mean in the divorce court by "irreconcilable differences".'

Yvette realized that she'd been shaking her head constantly. *You're in denial, honey.* As her motherly therapist remarked each time she sat and shook her head almost unconsciously like that. *No, no, no.* It wasn't denial, she wanted to shout each time, it was disillusionment. She couldn't deny that her husband had had an intense relationship with one of her friends. (Had perhaps even begun it again.) It was just that she didn't have the faintest idea what to do about it. If she could only behave like a character in an old-fashioned melodrama! Brandish a blade, draw blood. Hers or someone else's. But words were the civilized Westerner's only weapon. And if words let you down? If you couldn't *talk* about something?

'I've invited both of them to the party,' she said with a worried frown. 'I hope it doesn't cause problems . . .'

'It's not your problem, Yvette.' Mila stubbed out her cigarette with a vicious twist of the wrist. 'If they can't handle being at the same party, one of them must go home. Or both of them.'

'That's why I can't stand it when a relationship in my circle of friends breaks down! It affects so many other people. No matter how hard you try not to take sides – to treat both fairly – it's almost inevitable that in the end you'll lose one of the two as a friend!'

'Don't torment yourself. Think of it as a process of natural selection. Old friends are like old clothes – all those outfits you no longer wear, but can't throw away because you feel sentimental about them. Or think you might need again one day. Sometimes you have to throw away the old to make way for the new.'

'You know I can never throw away old clothes,' said Yvette with an embarrassed smile. 'I can't even throw away my grandmother's clothes. How the hell am I to learn to cast off old friends?'

'It takes practice. Like everything in life. I ought to know. I've had enough practice casting old lovers away!'

Yvette looked swiftly away from Mila's pained smile. Stared across the lawn to the blue gum trees, where her husband's stocky figure had just appeared. He was carrying his daughter on his shoulders, their hair exactly the same colour, like two jars of honey held against the light. The Labrador at his legs also honey-coloured, but lighter. The late afternoon sun made the child look like a gilded figurine in a religious procession, a plump idol carried at shoulder height through a crowd. So different from her mother and her baby brother, with their dark seaweed hair and their pale underwater skins. Her father bent forward to lift her from his shoulders. The moment her feet touched the ground she began to run. There wasn't much speed in the three-year-old body, her paces still too short and her arm movements too wide, but she stormed at the stoep like a little toy tank, climbed the steps, stumbling with haste, and threw her arms out wide.

'Hello, Mamma!' she called excitedly. 'Hello, Mila!'

She hesitated for a moment, as if she didn't know who to hug first. Then Yvette made it easier for her by turning to Mila. Mila moved forward on her chair, stretched out her arms and caught the charging body.

'What have we here?' Adriaan climbed the steps with big paces, his black gumboots splattered with mud and his grey pullover crusted with dry paint, and looked disparagingly at the teapot on the table.

'Why are you two sitting here drinking tea like two old tannies? It's long gone time for sundowners!'

'We were just waiting for you to come and lead us astray,' said Mila as the child clambered eagerly on to her lap. Her red boots made dusty marks on Mila's red skirt, but she didn't seem to notice. 'Gosh, but I missed you so! If you ever walk that far again, you must take me along, OK?'

'Well, seeing that no one missed me,' grumbled Adriaan, 'I suppose I can fetch a bottle of wine.'

Mona stared in fascination at Mila's earrings, giggled excitedly when Mila shook her head to make them swing back and forth, and reached out a fat, dirty hand to carefully touch one of them.

'Do you want a drink, my dear wife?' asked Adriaan, when he came back out of the house with a bottle of red wine and three glasses.

'Just a little one, my dear husband.'

He didn't ask Mila. Just poured out a glass and gave it to her almost absent-mindedly. And something in this simple gesture, so loaded with mutual knowledge, so full of hidden intimacy, upset Yvette so much that without warning her eyes filled with tears. She turned her head away, distressed. What was going on with her?

'What do you hear from Ralph?' he asked, sinking into the cane chair between them. 'Is he still hanging around in London?'

'Ja, but he's finished with his scriptwriting course, and it sounds as though he's beginning to long for home. He's hanging out with South Africans incessantly these days, even people he hardly knew here, like Mart and Tomas. I always think that when the "exiles" begin to cluster together like that, you can bet they're feeling homesick.'

'What about Louise?' asked Adriaan. 'Has he looked her up yet?'

'You've always had a soft spot for Louise, hey?' said Mila with a teasing smile.

'I must admit I admire the way that she gets what she wants,' laughed Adriaan. 'Like marrying a boring Brit just because she wanted a British passport.'

'Surely not just for the passport,' protested Yvette. 'I got the impression that she quite liked him!'

'Don't you think a marriage needs a bit more commitment than "quite liking" someone?' asked Mila with a sharp edge to her voice. 'What the hell happened to love?'

'One of the Great Questions of the late twentieth century,' murmured Adriaan. 'What the hell happened to love?'

'I'm serious, Adriaan.'

'Me too.'

He swept his hand across his hair, bound as usual these days in a loose plait low in his neck. Yvette turned her eyes away from her husband and stared wistfully at her daughter. The child had clambered off Mila's lap and begun to unpack from a tattered box a collection of dolls and teddy bears in varying stages of decay. *What the hell happened to love?* Indeed.

'Perhaps it's all part of the so-called end-of-the-millennium syndrome.' It sounded as though Mila was talking to herself. Her eyes rested somewhere between the glistening dam and the blue mountain peaks on the horizon. 'Everything is changing so constantly ... everything around us is so awfully temporary ... I just don't think it's a good time for steady heterosexual relationships.'

'What makes you think that homosexual relationships are any better?' asked Adriaan.

'I don't know. Maybe it's just because Johannes and Joe are still the most stable couple in my circle of friends. And Bobby and Robin ... every time I saw them together, I thought, OK, it *is* possible, there are still relationships which work ...'

'And then Robin opened a letter bomb,' said Adriaan. 'So what's the moral of the story?'

'I feel despair every time I think of it,' said Yvette with an involuntary shudder. 'Not just because such a thing can happen in this country, but because it can happen *now*. Just when it looked as though things were getting better at last ...'

'What things?' asked Mila indignantly. 'What are you talking about? The State of Emergency has just been extended again!'

'I know, but the hunger strikes in the jails did work, in a way. I mean, almost a thousand political prisoners were released. And there's less violence, not so? When did we last see a necklace-murder on TV?'

'Heaven help us if that has become the measure of normality,' said Mila sarcastically.

'I'm not talking about normality, Mila. We all know we're not living in a normal country. I'm just talking about improvement. Even a slight improvement!'

'Because a few weeks have gone by without someone being burned alive?' asked Adriaan mockingly.

And suddenly it felt to her like the worst betrayal he had ever committed against her. To take Mila's side now. To be sceptical and pessimistic when she so desperately wanted him to be hopeful.

'And what about all the people who've gone mad with hate?' Mila asked. 'What about the "Wit Wolf" who wanted to ensure "the survival of the Boer nation"? The bastard stood in court the other day and *smiled* when he was found guilty of murder! Does that sound to you like a society in which things are going better?'

'Mila, I'm just an ordinary housewife and my only . . .'

'You're anything but "an ordinary housewife"!' Mila exclaimed impatiently.

'Whatever! The point is that I don't sit in parliament every day and I never go into a township! Except the few times that my char misses her train and I have to drop her off at her home in fear and trembling. So the only way that I can find out what's happening in the country is to read what you and your colleagues write. And what you write . . .'

'What we write is a pile of shit! It's only a tenth of the truth. The rest is forbidden.'

'Even at the *Vrye Afrikaan*?'

'Even at the so-called *Vrye Afrikaan*.'

It looked as though Mila had wiped her mouth with a cloth soaked in vinegar.

'I thought you could write what you wanted . . .'

'Oh, I can write some things that I couldn't write a year ago. I can use English words and swear words in reports. I don't know if that can necessarily be called a giant leap for Afrikaans journalism. And every day I can try to piss as close to the line as possible – as Ralph always put it – but the line is still there. And there is no way I can break through that boundary, Yvette.'

Yvette stared speechlessly at her. A year ago she was so uncontrollably excited about the new newspaper. The only independent Afrikaans newspaper in the country. *The truth has to come out some time or other, in some way or other. I want to be there when it happens.* And now this despondency at the corners of her lovely mouth, the tiredness in her blue eyes. Is this what disillusionment looked like? It was an expression which had become a kind of brand in her circle of friends. Perhaps she saw it today for the first time because she'd discovered it in her own mirror in the past year. Perhaps the warning signs had been flashing before her eyes for years while she stared unseeingly at the world around her. Alice in Wonderland. As her friends thought of her. Well, she had news for them, she thought with a bitter taste in her mouth. Alice has grown up. Alice doesn't live here any more.

Sleeping Trinity. That's what she'd call this illustration. Father, Son and Daughter – precious, precious, precious – together in a bed in the soft morning light. A quick sketch, just a few lines on paper, brushing like fine drizzle against a cheek. Watercolour to capture the shadows on the sleeping faces, the smooth dark head of the baby lying in the crook of Adriaan's left arm, the sunlight dancing over his muscular right shoulder and creeping through his daughter's curls.

Of course she and Adriaan often complained about their lot, this complete lack of privacy in their marital bed. Pablo still spent the best part of the night between them so that she could feed him in bed, and at the age of three Mona still climbed out of her own bed in her own room every night and crept in next to her father. And yet it filled her with an ecstatic joy to gaze at them like this in the morning. The three most precious people in her life. It was often the most spiritual moment of her day. Her form of morning prayer.

She slipped quietly out from under the duvet and looked back one last time at the sleeping trio. Lot's wife who couldn't get away. Walked slowly to the bathroom next to the bedroom and bent over the basin to wash her face. Suddenly saw her own image in the oval full-length mirror diagonally opposite her. An old-fashioned portrait, framed in wood, of a ghost woman in a long white nightdress.

She turned to the mirror, fascinated – without even turning off the tap first, as if she was afraid that she would lose this sudden objective view if she hesitated for a moment – and stripped the nightdress over her head with a single impatient movement so that she stood naked in front of the mirror, her face still unwashed and her eyelids swollen with sleep. Stared at her body as though she was about to sketch a self-portrait, at the full hips and plump thighs, the bush of black pubic hair against the snow-white stretched skin of her stomach, the breasts small and high, and yet so much heavier than usual, like two of those plastic bags full of milk you could buy in supermarkets. That's all that they were these days. Milk bags. And yet, objectively viewed, they still looked attractive. Or not repulsive, anyway. The nipples two pinky brown nut-shells. Soft black hair at her armpits, which she usually left unshaven in the winter, hard black stubble on her calves which had to be shaved again.

This is the body that Adriaan loves, she assured herself. This is the landscape he had felt at home in for more than seven years – despite all his expeditions to other, more alluring landscapes. She had forgotten long ago about the few other men who had explored *her* before he took such complete possession of her; not just of her heart, but apparently also of her memory. The weight of someone else's hands on her hips, the texture of someone else's tongue in her mouth, the size, length, weight of another man's penis. It was as though Adriaan had conquered the realm of her entire erotic experience, the slightest memory of any of his predecessors ruthlessly wiped out, with only his body as a weapon. As if he had even taken over her imagination. She couldn't even begin to imagine that she would ever surrender her body to another man again.

She couldn't imagine life without Adriaan. That was the terrible truth. Even an unsatisfactory existence with him had to be better than existence without him. Wasn't that what love meant? Or was that simply another way of describing cowardice?

Sometimes she wondered if it was her parents' fault that divorce was so unthinkable to her. She had grown up in one of those rare homes where a man and a woman visibly loved each other, were clearly crazy about each other's company, openly attracted to each other's bodies. She had always thought it was the greatest gift that any parent could give a child, but these days she wondered . . .

'My mother and father hate each other with an overwhelming hatred!' Adriaan had exclaimed the previous night at the table, while they ate with Mila. 'That's all that still keeps them together, I suspect. Hatred can be a lot more addictive than love.'

'When I was small, I thought my parents loved each other,' said Mila thoughtfully. 'That's what I was taught, at school, at church, everywhere, that parents love each other. I simply accepted it, without question, as I accepted so many other things.' She had smiled, melancholy, her eyes on her wine glass, as if she were talking to herself. 'Now that I look back on their relationship, I can find no evidence of love. They had sex every Sunday afternoon – at least, I think that's what they did when my father closed the bedroom door with that strange look on his face – but they did it with a terrible sense of duty. As they did everything in life – baking rusks every Wednesday or mowing the lawn every Saturday – without any passion. No fiery arguments, but also no unexpected embraces. Everything was planned, each emotion under control, as cold-blooded as two bloody crocodiles!'

'Your father was a judge,' Adriaan reminded her. 'You have to be pretty cold-blooded to send someone to the gallows.'

'No, he only became a judge later. Just before I went to university. I'm talking about when I was little, when he was just an ordinary advocate. Or do you think all advocates are cold-blooded bastards too?'

'Not if I look at Max,' he muttered. 'His problem is that he's too much of a bleeding heart.'

'And my mother!' she exclaimed, without any interest in his answer, simply getting a series of rhetorical questions out of her system. 'What the hell was her excuse? Why did she never show any emotion? You would swear her make-up would crack if she smiled too quickly!' Her laugh was a sharp, grating sound, no trace of the usual husky seductiveness. 'Even now that my father has cancer, she refuses to show any emotion. My father has completely changed since he got ill. Thank God. He even cries in front of his daughters. But the Iron Lady remains the Iron Lady. In-fucking-vincible. To the end.'

Yvette thought of *her* mother, an emotional extrovert who had often embarrassed her five children by bursting dramatically into tears at each school concert or prize-giving or sporting event. She remembered how the other schoolchildren had giggled and whispered, how her ears had flamed as she stared out straight in front of her, as if she had nothing to do with the blubbering woman next to her. *I don't know her. I don't know her. I don't know her.* Until the cock crowed – and long after that – she would deny the woman who had brought her into this world. A kind of betrayal of which Mila, of course, knew nothing.

'Have you ever thought that you might take after your mother?' asked Adriaan.

'What exactly do you mean, Adriaan?' said Mila, in a dangerously quiet voice.

'Just that you also try to hide your emotions behind your make-up. Your whole appearance – *femme fatale*, successful career woman, cynical journalist – all those masks you hide behind.'

'So you think I'm a cold crocodile.'

'No. Your salvation is that you never get it quite right. There's always a kind of vulnerability which shines through. Even the red lipstick can't quite cover it.'

She had stood up quickly to collect the dirty plates. He watched her with a strange smile. Yvette felt her heart contract, like an anemone, and heard the rushing of the sea in her ears.

'You should see my mother!' he cried, laughingly, as if he wanted to console her. 'You should hear her and my father bickering! Even now, as the poor old man gets more senile by the day. Sometimes I wonder if he didn't deliberately decide to become senile, as a last resort, to get away from the endless squabbling. When I was younger, it drove me mad. I decided that I would never get caught in such a relationship. Now I drive Yvette crazy because I refuse to argue with her. The moment an argument flares up, I think: God help me, here we go. And then I run away.'

Usually to another woman, thought Yvette.

'In other words, we're all doomed.' Mila held a stack of dirty plates as though she wanted to throw them at him. 'Either we're going to repeat our parents' mistakes or we're going to make even bigger mistakes because we're reacting against our parents' mistakes.'

He leaned back in his chair and laughed at her.

'Of course! Just look at history! It's an endless repetition of fuck-ups, generation after generation after generation!'

'And there's no such thing as free will,' she added sarcastically.

'Never heard of it.'

'Ag, come now, Adriaan! You don't really believe in predestination and all that crap! You can't be that much of a Calvinist!'

'I'm no more of a Calvinist than you are, Mila.'

'I refuse to believe that history has to be repeated endlessly.' Mila carried the plates away, shaking her head, and began to pack them in the dishwasher. 'Especially not such sordid bits of domestic history.'

'It doesn't always have to be sordid,' said Yvette. 'My parents set me a wonderful example. But sometimes I feel that I . . .'

'Yvette is the only person I know who grew up in a fairy-tale marriage!'

'Not a "fairy-tale marriage", Adriaan.' She took a quick sip of wine, hurt by the annoyance in his voice, and turned to Mila to explain. 'My mother was a city kid. English speaking with an Irish background, someone who was educated in good Roman Catholic schools, and rebelled against the tyranny of the nuns her whole life long. To no avail, because she's still Catholic to the bone. My father was an Afrikaans farm boy who went to a tiny little school and was brought up strictly Calvinist. In his second year at medical school he renounced all forms of religion. He's a doctor, he thinks like a scientist, he always tries to hide his feelings, he likes being alone. She's a potter, she thinks with her heart, she bursts into tears three times a day and she can't cope on her own at all. Their personalities are worlds apart – and yet they've got the closest thing to a happy marriage that I've ever encountered. Except in fairy tales, of course.'

'Do you realize how lucky you are?' Mila asked with envy in her voice, still on her haunches in front of the dishwasher. 'You're the only one among us who has a map to follow, some kind of guide when it comes to relationships, a sort of picture in your head of how it ought to be. The rest of us have to stumble around in the dark. We don't know what we're aiming for or how the hell we're going to get there. Christ, Yvette, all I know is, I don't want to end up like my parents!'

Yvette said nothing, just shook her head. These days she suspected that her parents' exemplary marriage had left her unnecessarily vulnerable. Utterly defenceless against the onslaught of modern marriage.

She was startled to see Adriaan in the doorway of the bathroom behind her, embarrassed to be caught like this – stark naked in front of a full-length mirror, examining her wrinkles and fat rolls – and she jumped back quickly. Her first reaction was to grab for her nightdress, but she had stripped it off so recklessly that it had fallen beyond her grasp. Adriaan followed her agitated glance to the bundle of crumpled white cotton lying on the floor next to his feet, a teasing smile on his sensual mouth.

'What a pleasant surprise! A naked woman in my bathroom!'

He stepped forward quickly and took her hips in both his hands, pulling her close to him, till her breasts brushed against his chest. The boxer shorts which he wore at night felt ominously hard against her stomach. It had never taken much to arouse him in the morning, she remembered with a paralysing feeling of nostalgia. Long ago, before they woke up with children in the bed every morning. He stuck the tip of his tongue in her ear and licked slowly, like a cat, at the whorls and spirals of the shell. While his one hand stroked the curves of her back and came to rest just above the groove of her buttocks – always one of his favourite parts of her body – and his other hand slid in between her thighs, his fingers caught for a moment in the bush of hair, and then with a practised movement slipped further down, coming to rest at precisely the right spot. Where she was already waiting for him, wet and wanting him, she realized, amazed. Everything happened so quickly that she hardly had time to gasp for breath. Only when his naked penis pressed against her stomach like the barrel of a gun did she manage to protest weakly.

'No, Adriaan, not here . . .'

'Why not?' he asked, pressing her backward firmly. To the basin, where the forgotten tap still ran.

'Mona could wake up any moment now.'

'We can be finished by the time she's awake. Don't you remember the quickies we used to have in the mornings? You could have an orgasm while brushing your teeth!'

'That was long ago,' she protested, overwhelmed with nostalgia, her legs weak with desire.

'Not *that* long ago.'

He lifted her buttocks to the edge of the basin. She wriggled off straight away and fumbled with one hand behind her back to turn the tap off. Something practical, she thought, if she only could concentrate on something practical, perhaps she would be able to rein in this completely unexpected lust.

'She always wakes up with you, Adriaan! You know I always say you are like two – '

'If I could just get you to shut up for a second,' he whispered in her ear, 'we could already be halfway.'

'OK, but just not here . . . I can't here, next to the children . . . any other place . . .'

'Any other place?' He stepped back a bit, but held his hands firmly on her hips. Almost as she'd seen him hold a struggling fish. Almost as proud of his catch. 'Come. I know where.'

He pulled her out through the bathroom door, past the sleeping children in the double bed, through the bedroom to the passage. What would they do if Mila suddenly walked out of the guest room? Standing here like two horny teenagers without a stitch of clothing between them!

Adriaan!' she whispered urgently. 'Have you gone completely insane?'

'Yes. Completely insane with lust for my wife.' He pushed her into their daughter's room, pulled the door closed behind him, and led her to the low children's bed covered in teddy bears and soft toys. 'Seeing that she occupies our bed every night, surely we can borrow hers for once?'

He swept the toys off the bed and pulled her down with him on to the duvet. On to the cotton cover she had herself painted full of plump pink cherubs. Beneath the ceiling on which he'd painted a playful version of Michelangelo's famous creation scene – with himself in the role of Creator, an amused twist to his lips and a golden brown plait falling over one shoulder, his sturdy farmer's fingers stretched out to his daughter's stubby toddler's hands. Mona had the same posture as Adam in the original painting, but she was laughing with a wide-open mouth. And Yvette soared high above them, a beaming guardian angel.

Now Yvette lay on her back and stared over her husband's shoulder at the angel with the familiar face and began to giggle helplessly. He hushed her by pressing his tongue into her mouth. Usually she hated it when he kissed her in the morning, because his breath smelt sour, because her breath smelt sour, because . . . But all that she was aware of at that moment was an almost forgotten tide of sensual pleasure welling up inside her. Like long ago, she thought, amazed, before the children were born. Before the bed became too full at night and they became too tired by day.

Before everything which had happened in the last few years.

Bobby's eyes. That was the first thing Paul noticed when he walked into the kitchen, and after that for a while he could see nothing else. As if he was blinded by the expression in those dull grey eyes, duller than ever, greyer than ever, framed by the round glasses. God, he thought, the eyes of a woman who has left the earth. Who has been to hell and back and hasn't yet found the words to describe the experience. Her eyes had always looked melancholy, but now that superficial melancholy had been replaced by a bottomless grief. So painful to see that he turned his head away involuntarily.

While Liane, as always, acted more courageously.

'Bobby, my darling, come here so that I can give you a hug!' she cried out, walking straight to her and enfolding her slight shoulders in a smothering embrace. 'I'm so terribly sorry about Robin . . .'

She looked smaller and thinner than before. Not that she ever had much fat on her, but now she was really little more than a bundle of bones under a T-shirt which hung about her like a sack. Or like a flag, yellow, green and black with the words AFRICAN NATIONAL CONGRESS spelled out in challenging capital letters on her chest. As if she had wrapped herself in a political banner to forget about her personal loss.

'How are you coping?' Liane kept her hands on Bobby's shoulders and studied her face, concerned. 'What are you doing to keep going?'

And Paul was again amazed at his wife. Everyone knew she was an excellent actress – and yet no one could accuse her of acting now. Her concern was so obviously sincere that Bobby stared at her in confusion. Clearly more used to meaningless words of comfort than to the kind of sympathy which demands a reaction.

'Well, I get up every morning and I shower and dress . . .' She tried to keep her voice jokey, but her mouth began to quiver. 'Like we all do . . .'

Then Liane did something which surprised her husband even more. She bent forward and kissed Bobby on the forehead, an almost motherly gesture of comfort, as though she was kissing a child's sore spot better. Bobby looked away quickly, her grip on her emotions now completely undermined.

'Yes, with the rest of us things aren't too hot either, hey?' Liane looked at the group in the kitchen with a rueful smile: Adriaan standing in front of the stove cooking, Mila at the basin scrubbing pots, Yvette and Emma sitting at the table buttering bread rolls. 'I went to an astrologer the other day, would you believe it, and she said . . .'

'I would believe it,' muttered Adriaan.

'She said it's all to do with the planets,' she went on unperturbed. 'All the personal and political upheavals we're struggling with these days, Uranus or Jupiter or something like that, I can't remember the details. I know you think it's ridiculous, Adriaan, but I'm telling you, this woman was absolutely amazing! I learned more about myself in one session with her than in all the months I was in therapy!'

'What did you learn?' asked Mila.

'That I'm not actually as nice a person as I'd always thought.' She sat on the empty chair next to Yvette and brushed her hair out of her face with the usual clinking of her silver bracelets. 'Of course, Paul says he could have told me that ages ago. Without the help of the stars.'

'Some time or other we all have to realize that we aren't as nice as we'd like to be,' said Yvette in her serious way. 'Maybe that's what is meant by "growing up".'

Liane looked at the young ginger cat who came to rub against her legs and bent down to pick him up on to her lap. Another action which surprised Paul. Usually she didn't pay much attention to pets. Sometimes he wondered if he'd ever really know her. Sometimes he suspected that this was the main reason he still stayed with her. Her continual unpredictability. He couldn't imagine, for example, how she would act if he were to leave her. Sometimes he was afraid that she would behave like a character in a melodramatic play – hysterical weeping and suicide threats – and at other times he was convinced that she would be too proud for such a performance. No, he thought, she would maintain her dignity. But the point was that he didn't know. And there was no way of finding out without leaving her.

'Oh well, I've always said that I wasn't ready to grow up,' she said as she stroked the cat's head. 'Anyway, you couldn't have picked a better time to have a party. It'll do us all good to be frivolous for a change!'

'Easier said than done,' sighed Emma. 'All the parties I've been at in the past few months felt more like political meetings. Everyone sitting in a circle talking about the latest issue of the *Vrye Afrikaan*.'

'Glad to hear my newspaper is adding to the cheerful atmosphere among my friends,' said Mila, scrubbing a pot so that the foam flew.

'Don't worry, we're going to have an old-fashioned kind of party.' Adriaan turned away from the stove and wiped his hands on his bright red apron with a black slogan across his broad chest: *Cooking Up a*

New South Africa. No escape from the Struggle, thought Paul, even in the kitchen. 'We're going to play dance music and drink plonk and get roaring drunk. Like we did when we were young and horny.'

'Well, some of us are still young,' said Liane, hands on her hips, coquettishly.

'And we're all still horny,' muttered Mila.

'Speak for yourself,' said Emma. 'I've renounced sex. Been living like a nun for weeks.'

'Then you must be the horniest of us all,' said Mila.

'No,' said Emma and pulled her pack of cigarettes closer. 'I live out all my sexual frustrations in the stories I write. The pen as surrogate penis.'

'Isn't that what you always aimed at?' asked Yvette.

'You mean ever since I saw how my brother waved his willy around to spell his name in pee?' The moment she lit her cigarette, the cat jumped off Liane's lap and came to brush against her ankles like a street child begging for a cigarette butt. She looked at him with a surprised frown. 'Isn't this cat a bit weird?'

'Well, his name is Woof, so he probably has a bit of an identity crisis,' said Yvette. 'Perhaps I should take him to a cat psychologist.'

'Or to Liane's astrologer,' suggested Adriaan.

'What is it with your daughter that she can't distinguish between cats and dogs?' asked Liane laughing. 'Isn't *that* a bit weird?'

'This time we can't blame Mona,' said Yvette. 'It's Adriaan who began calling the cat Woof.'

'To spare the dog's feelings!' Adriaan cried. 'Just think how he would have felt if he had to realize that all this time he hasn't actually been a cat!'

'Sometimes it's a relief to realize that you aren't what you thought you were,' said Bobby with a little smile. 'Just ask me.'

It was the first time that she'd opened her mouth since Liane had embraced her so fervently. And yet her eyes remained two black holes in her face.

'We're talking about something a lot more traumatic than sexual orientation,' said Adriaan. 'How would you feel if you had to realize that you belonged to another species?'

'Sometimes I feel as though I do belong to another species,' she replied.

Paul turned his head away. Afraid that those holes would suck him in if he looked at her any longer. He leaned against one of the kitchen cupboards, a vantage point from which he could view the whole company, like a director overseeing a movie scene. The kitchen reminded him of his ouma's farm kitchen: the back door which opened on to the yard, the giant fireplace in the corner and the big wooden table in the middle of the floor. But his tidy grandmother would have had a fit if she could see this floor, strewn with everything from toys and shoes to magazines and pet dishes, with a few unrecognizable, presumably organic products in between. Like the object near to Bobby's left foot, which could possibly be a dried-up apple core – but also possibly something worse. And suddenly he longed for the clean black and white tile floor and gleaming steel surfaces of his wife's new 'industrial kitchen'. Perhaps less cosy than this higgledy-piggledy farm kitchen, yet far better suited to his tidy character, which he probably inherited from his grandmother. If this floor was an example of what was meant by the adventure of parenthood, he thought gloomily, it was yet another reason for avoiding it.

He looked at Yvette, who was sitting diagonally opposite him, still spreading butter on a heap of bread rolls, her hand movements as calm as her face. Dressed in flowered velvet, something between a dress and a dressing gown, as usual an outfit that no other woman in the room would wear. *Just imagine I'd married her.* The sudden thought almost made him jump with fright. And yet for years he'd cherished the unspoken idea that she would make him happier than Liane. Because she was softer and quieter, more tolerant, less judgemental. More maternal.

'Emma, my darling, how on earth do you manage to look so good?' Liane wanted to know. 'I thought I'd find you in sackcloth and ashes! And here you sit as though someone has snipped you out of the latest issue of *Cosmo*!'

She did indeed look better than when they'd last seen her with Philip. Thinner and trimmer and neater, her hair shinier and shorter (still a flaming bramble bush of hair, but now at least a pruned one) and her lips painted almost as carefully as Mila's.

'Isn't it absolutely disgusting?' asked Mila from the sink. 'She could at least have the decency to *look* as though she's suffering.'

'Ag, I cut my hair and had my face massaged and began going to the gym,' said Emma nonchalantly. 'Don't you know the old saying? Looking good is the best revenge.'

Her laugh sounded just a bit too high.

'So tell me, Liane, how are the plans for the new shop progressing?' asked Yvette quickly.

A transparent attempt at changing the subject, because Liane phoned her almost every day with the latest snippet of news about the development of the shop. That's how she spent her evenings these days, glued to the phone for hours on end, providing drawn-out progress reports to everyone she knew. But he couldn't complain, thought Paul. Otherwise they would have to sit and talk to each other.

'Oh, I'm wild with excitement about the whole venture,' answered Liane. 'But I'm still looking for the right name. I want something original. Obviously. Just not one of those pretentious French names which no one can pronounce properly!'

'So what are you looking for?' asked Mila. 'An indigenous name?'

'Just not ethnic,' she said with an attractive wrinkle of her finely chiselled nose. 'Ethnic is even worse than French. No, I'm looking for an utterly ordinary English name. Well, not ordinary, either. You know what I mean.'

'Why not an Afrikaans name?'

Liane rolled her eyes and shook her head.

'I don't have anything against Afrikaans, Mila. Perhaps I don't feel quite as strongly about the issue as you do, but I've got nothing against it. I just don't want to sound like a blooming housewives' co-operative!'

'Aren't there already enough shops hawking bric-à-brac?' asked Adriaan with an innocent expression.

'I'm not going to hawk bric-à-brac!' she cried out indignantly. 'I'm going to sell designer pieces! Anything which contributes to a feeling of beautiful living, from beautiful butter knives to beautiful bedding! And I'm going to tell my clients how and where and with what they can use any purchase. So they get free advice on top of it.'

'Sounds rather like my dad's furniture store in Worcester,' said Adriaan, tipping a third bottle of red wine into an enormous pot. 'He was always dishing out unsought advice to his customers. "Brown couches don't go with pink flowered cushions." That kind of thing.'

He stirred the contents of the pot with a wooden spoon and added a handful of unpeeled garlic cloves. A load of golden fried chicken pieces were being kept warm in two other pots and an astounding quantity of button mushrooms lay on the counter next to him, ready to become part of the party dish. The self-confidence with which he tackled this large-scale cooking process – joking all the while with his friends – fascinated Paul.

'I don't mean to be funny, Adriaan, my darling, but I particularly want to protect my clients from furniture stores in Worcester.'

'Ah! So you want to protect South Africans from their own bad taste. What a noble idea!'

'Perhaps it's my calling in life,' laughed Liane.

'Sounds to me like a dictatorship.' Adriaan leaned over to the table, took the butter knife out of his wife's hand and scrutinized it critically. '*No, my darling, I'm afraid that this little knife doesn't quite match the painting on that wall. Get rid of it!*'

'Of what?' asked Yvette. 'The knife or the painting?'

'Both!' declared Adriaan. 'Everything which doesn't contribute to Beautiful Living!' He put the knife down and looked at Liane with a teasing smile. 'That's what we're talking about, not so?'

'And like any decent dictator,' added Paul, 'she's convinced that she's doing it all for the sake of her subjects.'

'Ag, come now, Paul,' said Liane, suddenly irritated. 'You don't care a fig whether I play dictator somewhere else, as long as I just leave you in peace!'

'Ah!' said Adriaan. 'So that's why you were so eager to give her the money to open a shop.'

'To *loan* her the money,' said Paul. 'One day, when she's a successful business woman, she can pay it back. Perhaps then I can finally make that film I've always dreamed about.'

'And if the movie flops, perhaps she can keep you?' Yvette's brown eyes teased him from across the table.

'Let's just call it a contingency plan.'

'I don't know about you,' Bobby burst out, her voice so passionate that everyone looked at her in surprise, 'but I don't want to live in a world where everyone's sugar spoons match their lounge suites! It'll be fucking boring! Rather give me bad taste!'

'Hear, hear!' Adriaan boomed. 'Viva Bad Taste!'

The way that Liane suddenly began to laugh, that breathy, little-girl laugh, completely without resentment, overwhelmed Paul for a moment. It's not that he didn't love her any more, he realized again. That wasn't the problem.

He would never forget the first few months of their romance. What an enchanting discovery she was to him, from her slender sunbrowned toes to the lemon scent of her shiny brown hair. How he had marvelled at the knobs of her ankles and the whorls of her ears, the pink transparency of her fingernails and the soft down at the back of her neck. How proud he was to sit with her in a coffee bar, to see her dark eyes light up when he walked into a room, to hear that breathless laugh on his pillow the first time he woke up next to her. How grateful he was that she had chosen him above all the other men who had admired her from afar.

And how astounded he was later to hear that she had experienced the same emotions. Perhaps that's how all lovers felt. Amazed. Proud. Grateful. And yet, he'd thought, if you were something special – as she undoubtedly was – surely you had to *know* it?'

She was still something special. Still, by far, the most beautiful woman he knew. Probably even more desirable than when he met her a decade ago, like a green fruit which has gradually become soft and juicy and completely ripe. He was still proud of her when they sat together in one of the trendy restaurants she so often dragged him to. Grateful for the years that she'd spent with him.

But it wasn't enough any more. It was never enough, but it had taken him years to admit it to himself. And after that admission, he had still sat with her for months in a marriage counsellor's stuffy office. With the absolute, indisputable certainty in his heart: It's just not enough.

It wasn't that Paul disliked parties. It was just the first few hours which got him down. He always wished that he could lie down and sleep somewhere while the first few guests arrived and stood around uncomfortably, making small talk. While everyone drank as quickly as possible so that they could be bold enough to brave the dance floor the moment the music was turned up loud enough. Or perhaps just to build up courage for the more honest, more dangerous conversations which awaited them later in the night. He wished, in other words, that someone could wake him up when the party was in full swing, when the first bottles of alcohol were emptied and the initial awkwardness had disappeared.

But as he'd been here since early afternoon, he was expected to do his duty now. To stand here like an awkward host in the dark shed next to the house – to make the first few guests feel at home – while he himself felt more ill at ease than anyone else. The women were still busy blow-drying their hair or polishing glasses or carrying piles of plates, or whatever it was that had to be done before such a carefully orchestrated social occasion. It had been so long since he and Liane had given a party that he'd forgotten the feverish activity which preceded a celebration like this.

And now he stood here with his wine-glass and his grimace, between a bunch of guests he didn't know from a bar of soap. Some of them he'd seen in magazines or newspapers. Not on the social pages where Liane and her many superficial acquaintances so often stood and beamed, but on artistic photos next to unreadable reviews or profound interviews. Serious artists, mostly dressed in black, some of them with unusual hairstyles in all the colours of the rainbow. There were some whose gender remained a mystery to him. The enigmatic figure just behind him, for example, ostensibly a man with a shaved head, a tattoo on a sinewy arm and black jeans with holes at the buttocks, had just begun to talk in a soft, feminine voice. Her/his companion was someone with long, loose blonde hair and the finely chiselled features of an angel in a medieval painting, dressed in a black leather jacket and black Levi jeans and black Doc Marten boots. A lovely young man with slightly feminine hand gestures? An attractive young woman with a slightly masculine attitude? God knows.

He looked away, disturbed, and listened to Dollar Brand's piano playing over the speaker next to him. He felt as though he was trapped at a conference of vampires. The only person with a tanned skin among all these pale artists in black clothes, in a dark shed which looked like a Gothic cathedral, with flickering candles casting dancing shadows against bare walls. Even the few black guests looked pale and bloodthirsty to him.

Luckily, he hadn't worn his snow-white cotton shirt and neatly ironed khaki trousers. He would have felt like the pathetic Brad in *The Rocky Horror Picture Show*. Liane had given the outfit one glance and had shaken her head ruefully.

'No, my darling, that's not right for this occasion. You're going to look like a boring lawyer from Oranjezicht.'

'But I am a boring lawyer from Oranjezicht!' he'd argued. 'What do you want me to do? Borrow one of Adriaan's hats and wear a pair of odd socks?'

'You know what I always say. When in doubt, wear black. If it's not the right choice, you can always go and stand in a dark corner and melt into the background.'

So he had put on his black jeans and a black polo-neck jersey. But even in the weak candlelight he could see that his black outfit was less faded and crumpled than any of the other outfits around him. Not completely authentic.

It was with enormous relief that he noticed Max in the doorway. Not in black, thank God. Almost unrecognizably neat, in fact, in a tweed jacket over a white T-shirt (without a slogan), his face as clean and white as the shirt, the rough black beard gone. The primitive caveman look could apparently no longer be reconciled with the black advocate's gown.

Max walked up to him with a broad smile, arm in arm with a dark exotic beauty, and greeted him with the three-part African handshake.

'Howzit, my bra?'

'Is that how you greet your colleagues at the Bar?'

'No, only comrades and potential comrades deserve such an honour. I know that your heart beats in the right place. Even though you try so hard to hide it beneath your yuppie outfits.'

'Speaking of yuppie outfits. What happened to the T-shirt with the Communist slogan? *Workers of the World Unite?* What was it again?'

'Ag, once you've proved your credentials in the Struggle, you don't need to display them on your chest any more,' said Max in an exaggeratedly modest way.

'And you prove yours in the high court these days? Far away from the dangers your comrades in the townships have to face?'

'The ever sceptical Paul Terreblanche,' grinned Max, and turned to the woman next to him. 'Have I introduced you to the ever beautiful Rehana Abrahams?'

'Not yet had the honour.'

Max's taste in women these days displayed the same development as his dress sense, Paul decided as he shook her manicured hand. This one was certainly not your usual 'Struggle groupie', as Liane liked to refer to Max's companions, with that spiteful crinkle to her nose. He wondered what Liane would say about Rehana Abrahams. She was wearing black (of course), but it was a black dress which undoubtedly came from a designer shop; the neckline just low enough to be daring without being vulgar; the material clinging at her stomach and hips, but not so clingy that you could see the line of her underwear. Of course it was also possible that it was the kind of dress you wore without underwear.

'Come, let's get something to drink,' Max suggested, his hand on Rehana's elbow, and began to steer her between the other guests, clearly proud. 'So long, comrade,' he grinned over his shoulder.

'So? What do you think?' Bobby had come to stand next to Paul without him noticing, small and silent, like a night creature brushing past in the dark. He couldn't see her eyes, but her voice sounded lighter than it had been in the kitchen earlier. Lighter and emptier. 'How does Max manage to seduce such a stunning woman? What does he have that we don't have?'

A balloon filled with bravado, he thought. And yet he was grateful that she was speaking again at least. It was better than the silence she had wrapped about her like a blanket this afternoon.

'Do you know her?'

'Not well enough.' Her gaze still fixed appreciatively on Rehana Abrahams. 'I find such sultry beauties utterly irresistible. Max too, apparently.'

Almost as though she was trying to imitate Adriaan. When she looked up at him, he realized that her eyes also looked different. Shallower, the black holes not so fathomlessly deep any more. The pupils unnaturally enlarged. His eyebrows lifted involuntarily.

'I'm glad to see that you're in a better mood.'

'It's wonderful what a little bit of dagga can do.' She giggled like a little girl, just for a moment, then her face grew serious again. 'Well, not a little bit. I had to smoke three gigantic joints before I was courageous enough to brave this party.'

'Perhaps I should have smoked with you. I don't feel very courageous, either.'

'I've brought an emergency supply.' She tapped her denim jacket's top pocket. She hadn't changed her outfit – or even combed her spiky hair – for the party. Just pulled on the faded denim jacket over the ANC banner. 'Just scream if you can't bear it any more.'

He wished he could ask her how she managed without screaming. How she endured everything that had happened to her recently without constantly drugging herself. But he didn't feel brave enough for that, either.

'And what does the beautiful Rehana Abrahams do for a living?' he asked, to steer the conversation back to safer waters.

'Oh, she's got some high position at some big chain store. Personnel. Tries to persuade the white bosses in her charming way to appoint more black managers.' Again the little giggle, quickly suppressed. 'Old Max wouldn't be seen dead with her if her work wasn't PC, would he?'

'Isn't she PC enough just because she isn't white?'

'Wake up, bro.' She looked up at him, a whole head shorter than him, and raised her eyebrows in the same sceptical way as his. 'The Immorality Act was scrapped a long time ago. Hadn't you realized that it's no longer a novelty to be a "mixed" couple?'

'Not in the circles I move in,' he said. 'Not among the boring lawyers of Oranjezicht.'

'On the other hand, Max is so hopelessly horny these days that he'd screw anything, PC or not. Even a dumb blonde who works for the National Party. As long as his friends in the Struggle don't get to hear about it.'

'Wasn't he always fairly . . . amorous?'

'It's getting worse.' She leaned closer to him, lowering her voice dramatically. 'I think he's going through a mid-life crisis.'

'Like all of us.'

'You always forget that I'm not as ancient as the rest of you old fogeys,' she said accusingly.

It's true, thought Paul. Especially now that her eyes looked older than ever before. Older and sadder than everyone else's eyes put together.

Later, when the party was in full swing, he was still standing to one side watching his friends dancing. Usually he and Liane were the most enthusiastic dancers – often the first to begin and the last to stop – but tonight he just couldn't work up the necessary enthusiasm. Dancing was like reading a novel. You needed some kind of suspension of disbelief, otherwise you couldn't get carried away. And tonight he was watching the bizarre ritual through the eyes of an unbeliever.

A bunch of intelligent adults moving to the beat of pulsing, deafening electronic music – 'She Drives Me Crazy' by a pop group with the absurd name of Fine Young Cannibals – bodies swaying, faces blank, eyes glazed. Some of the dancers looked rather uncomfortable, as if they realized how ridiculous they must seem to an onlooker, but most of them had simply surrendered to the ecstasy of the moment. Like Bobby, who stood on her own and jerked around, head back, mouth slightly open, like an idiot.

Liane was dancing with the androgynous angel figure, but they weren't looking at each other, were apparently deliberately ignoring each other. Perhaps she felt self-conscious because she didn't know whether she was dancing with a man or a woman. Her sexual antennae had never been as well developed as she would have liked.

Max, on the other hand, couldn't keep his hands off Rehana's gyrating body. Not that it could be easy trying to catch hold of her, because she swayed like a snake twisting up out of a basket, blissfully unaware of Max staring at her like a hypnotized victim.

Then he saw Adriaan and Mila. And his disbelief was immediately dispelled. It wasn't what they were doing individually, it was the perfect co-ordination between the two bodies which took the breath away. They barely touched each other, but it was as though they were bound to each other by invisible puppet strings. When her hip swung out to the right, his hip followed a split second later to the left, almost a mirror image. No, not puppet strings, electric wires. As though the air around them crackled with electricity. Something in their movements, or perhaps just the atmosphere of suppressed passion, reminded Paul of two Spanish dancers. Adriaan was actually far too sturdy to suggest the switchblade body of a male flamenco dancer, yet he seemed miraculously lighter and leaner. And Mila's long scarlet dress swept dramatically around her ankles with each sensual sway of her hips. This was what dance ought to mean, thought Paul, this passion and grace and sensuality.

'Now you can see why I don't really dance any more,' said Yvette to his left, her voice thin and her smile stiff. 'Just look at the competition.'

'But you used to be a good dancer at university!' protested Emma to his right.

'No. I loved dancing, but I was never . . . in Mila's league.'

'Mila isn't *such* a great dancer,' he tried to reassure her. 'I've also danced with her. It's just the combination . . .'

'Exactly,' agreed Yvette, making him want to bite his tongue. 'And they're an unbeatable combination.' She shook her head slowly, an expression of resigned sadness on her face. 'It's obvious they've had an affair, isn't it?'

'Affair?' he asked, astonished.

And yet, underneath the astonishment, somewhere deep inside, it was as though he could hear a key turn. A forbidden door being unlocked.

'Didn't you know?' Her eyes stretched wide, too black against the white of her skin, too big above the mouth which had folded closed like a flower. 'I thought everyone knew.'

Of course he should have known.

'No,' he said softly. 'I didn't know.'

'Oh . . .'

She turned her face to Emma, the eyes still impossibly wide, impossibly black. Emma recoiled, startled.

'Well . . . Mila told me . . . but that was long ago . . . two or three years . . . I can't really remember . . .' She cleared her throat, adding almost pleadingly, 'She didn't tell anyone else. I don't know why she told me. I didn't want to hear it!'

'No need to *tell* anyone,' said Yvette, staring at her husband and her friend on the dance floor again.

'But it's been over for ages, Yvette,' said Emma quickly.

'Does it look to you as though it's over?'

'Well, they wouldn't dance like that if there was still something between them, it's too obvious, they would have tried harder to hide it, they would have been more careful . . .'

All in one breath, growing weaker and weaker towards the end, like a punctured tyre losing air.

'I don't know. All I know is what I see in front of me. And what I see in front of me is that there is still . . . something between them. Not necessarily an affair. But something in the air around them, like static. I mean, even if I were blind I'd be able to *feel* it. Or do you think I'm paranoid, Paul?'

While he shook his head slowly, trying to gain a few seconds to think of an honest yet diplomatic reply, he felt Emma stiffen next to him. He followed her gaze to the door of the shed and saw that Philip had just arrived. It was clear, even at this distance, that he was drunk. Unsteady on his feet, his eyes bleary and confused, like someone who has woken from a nightmare and isn't sure where he is. Then, as if guided by a radar, he turned his head straight towards them.

'I think it's time we danced.' Emma tugged his hand urgently. 'Please!'

Not that he needed much convincing. At this moment he'd do anything to escape from Yvette's merciless questions. From her resigned smile and her pale face. And from Philip, who was moving purposefully in their direction, the bleariness in his eyes suddenly replaced by an almost maniacal gleam.

And now they left her here to cope with Philip on her own, thought Yvette as she stared after them. Not that she could blame them for fleeing so quickly. What else did you expect when you confronted your friends, without warning, about your husband's infidelity?

At your own birthday party.

Suddenly she wanted to shrink with humiliation, curl up somewhere in a corner to cry. The words had simply come out of her mouth before she could stop herself. That was her only excuse. And yet she knew it was no excuse. That was what happened when you tried to build a wall around your feelings, when you tried to dam them up day after day, week after week, month after month. Sometime or other, that wall would break.

'How're things?' Philip asked.

'I don't think it was such a good idea to have this party,' she said.

'Too late for regret now,' he said with a grimace.

She crossed her arms and looked at him with her head to one side. His dull blond hair was even thinner, the grooves around his mouth deeper, his general appearance messier – his denim shirt was half unbuttoned and hung loose over his crumpled trousers – but he was still an attractive man. He had always had this slightly decadent intellectual attractiveness. It was just that the decadence was threatening to get out of hand these days.

His eyes roved restlessly over the guests. When he saw Emma dancing in Paul's arms, he looked quickly down at his hands. 'I think I need a drink.'

'Do you really think so?' She sounded like a strict schoolteacher, she realized. 'What made you decide to come?'

'You invited me.'

'Yes, but . . .'

Why only now? she wanted to ask. The first guests would soon begin to go home. But something in his expression, the godforsakenness which glimmered in his eyes for just a moment, stopped her words short.

'I was sitting drinking at home,' he replied with a shrug. 'And then I thought, ag, I can just as well go and drink at my friends' expense.'

And with these words he walked away to pour himself a drink. She looked around her quickly, looking for more lively company, and smiled with relief when she saw her friend Griet.

'Hey, great to see you,' she said, giving her a quick hug. 'Where's George?'

'Don't ask.' Griet twisted a strand of blonde hair around her forefinger. 'I came on my own.'

'Did you fight?'

'Not a week goes by these days that we *don't* fight. If you ask me, it's the state this country is in that's affecting everyone. You know, all the anxiety and uncertainty and the whole fuck-up.'

'But we've been living with anxiety and uncertainty for years . . .'

'But we can't go on like this. Things fall apart, the centre cannot hold, you know. Even the government realizes it. The sports boycott, economic sanctions, the stupid war on the border . . . Why do you think so many political activists are being murdered these days? Bobby's lover, the guy from the trade unions who was shot in his car last week . . . Even the idiots at the top are desperate! How can anyone have a normal relationship in times like these?'

'But people have always had relationships . . . in ghastly circumstances. In wars and revolutions and concentration camps. What's wrong with us whiteys here at the foot of Africa? Why do we have one of the highest divorce rates in the world?'

'Guilt,' said Griet sombrely. 'Guilt by association. Or do you have a better explanation?'

'Maybe there's a wicked fairy who's cursed all relationships . . .'

'Nice try,' smiled Griet. 'I thought I was the only idiot who could believe such crap.'

The music had jumped from First World to Third World, from the Rolling Stones' wailing guitars to the African Jazz Pioneers' booming brass section. The pairings on the dance floor had also changed: Mila and Bobby stood talking with Philip, Adriaan was dancing with Rehana, Max with Emma, and Paul with Liane. Paul and Liane moved with the kind of co-ordination you only get after years of practice, but without a trace of the smouldering passion which characterized

Adriaan and Mila's performance. Like a bored married couple, thought Yvette. Another bored married couple. She took a deep breath and pulled her shoulders back.

'I'm going to ask my husband for the next dance,' she announced. 'I may not be Ginger Rogers, but bloody hell, he's not Fred Astaire, either!'

And she walked towards Adriaan like a soldier to the battlefield – her step firm and her head held high – determined to give her all to win him back. Even if it was only on the dance floor.

It hadn't been *that* bad after all, she decided the next morning in her untidy kitchen. Even untidier than usual after her husband had made coq au vin for about fifty people. But she wasn't going to clear up now. She was going to drink a quiet cup of coffee before the rest of the house woke up. She and the two children and the cat and the dog were the only creatures showing any sign of life.

She threw a handful of coffee beans into the grinder and lifted her daughter on to her lap. Mona struggled to turn the handle, but Yvette knew by now that any attempt to offer assistance would only lead to an unpleasant confrontation. So she simply held the grinder still and tried to think about something else as the aroma of ground coffee beans tantalized her nose. The baby viewed the drawn-out process from his rocking chair on the kitchen table. Quite a sight, so clean and innocent in a pastel blue romper between the empty wine glasses and overflowing ashtrays and general debris of the party. Woof was curled up in a pool of sunlight on the windowsill and Tat was gnawing at a bone in the corner next to the fireplace. A peaceful early morning scene, despite the state the kitchen was in.

No, it hadn't been that bad. After she had plucked up her courage and asked her husband to dance, the rest of the evening went better. Perhaps just because she felt less helpless, less like a character who has to watch as she's written out of the story. And now, thank heavens, it was all over. Everything except the clearing up. Surely she now had at least a decade's grace before she would have to organize another party like that again.

'Do you think it's possible to hurry your daughter up a bit?' Emma's voice was a hoarse caw. Her hair stood up in an untidy orange bird's nest and her face was as crumpled as the T-shirt in which she'd slept.

If she'd slept at all. 'I don't think I've ever needed a cup of coffee as much as at this moment.'

Yvette thanked Mona with a kiss and stood up quickly to switch on the coffee machine. She knew a woman in need when she saw one. Emma stumbled to the nearest chair and sank down shakily.

'Hungover?' asked Yvette after they had sat in silence for a little while, listening to the gurgling of the coffee maker.

'Hungover and penitent,' mumbled Emma, her elbow on the table and her cheek squashed against her hand. 'I can't believe I did it. Jesus, I can't believe I could be such an idiot!'

'You're not the only one who drank too much,' Yvette said comfortingly. 'I didn't even realize that you . . .'

'I slept with Philip again,' Emma interrupted her. 'I actually allowed him into my bed again. Your bed. One of the beds in your house.'

Here we go again. That was Yvette's first thought. With a kind of exhausted resignation.

'I know what you're thinking. The same old pattern as before. But I promise you . . .'

'No,' lied Yvette, 'that's not what I . . .'

'This time it's different, Yvette! I'm *finished* with him! I've already gone to see a lawyer, I'm going to sue for a divorce, it's all over. *Over and out. Schluss. Finis.*'

'Mona wants porridge,' said her daughter, who was sitting at the end of the table drawing. 'Mona's hungry.'

'How can it all be over if you – '

'A moment of weakness. That's all. I drank too much, I didn't think what I was doing, I felt sorry for him. He overwhelmed me in the dark! My body simply took over! My brain knows it's over, but the message has apparently not yet reached my body . . .'

'Or your heart?' asked Yvette and poured two mugs of coffee.

Emma looked at her pleadingly, her head propped in both hands. What does she want? thought Yvette, suddenly moved. *Forgiveness?*

'Mona wants porridge, Mamma,' her daughter repeated, this time in a higher, whining tone. 'Mona is dying of hunger!'

'She's inherited her father's talent for exaggeration,' said Yvette as she carried the mugs of coffee to the table. She put a dummy in Pablo's mouth, because he, too, had begun to make fretful little noises, and turned back to a kitchen cupboard to take out a box of cornflakes.

228

Relieved at the distraction that the children provided, because she honestly didn't know what to say to Emma. 'Are you also hungry?' she asked instead.

Emma shook her head and gulped greedily at the coffee.

'I am!' Liane walked into the kitchen, dressed like Emma in a T-shirt and tracksuit pants, but less crumpled. 'I'm hungry for the kind of breakfast my mother used to make on Sundays! Bacon and egg and toast and fried tomatoes and – '

'That's not on the menu today.' Yvette cut her short, poured milk over a bowl of cornflakes and plonked it down in front of her daughter. Irritated, as always, at her friend's early-bird cheerfulness. 'There's not a single clean pan in the house, so you'll have to be content with coffee and rusks. Unless you want to begin washing dishes?' she added threateningly.

'Dishes!' Liane gave an exaggerated squeal of disgust. '*Zut alors.* Well, I suppose I'll have to force down a couple of dozen of your homemade rusks.' She opened an old-fashioned blue and white striped cake tin and took out three chunky rusks. Then she froze and looked at Emma in concern. 'What's wrong, my darling?'

'This is how normal people look when they wake up in the morning,' muttered Yvette.

'No, this is how a woman looks when she's consumed by regret and self-reproach,' said Emma, sighing, her head again in her hands. 'I behaved like a slut.'

'Who was the lucky man?'

'Philip.'

'Well!' giggled Liane in surprise. 'There are worse things that can happen to a woman than being seduced by her own husband!'

'Not if her own husband is on the point of becoming her ex-husband.'

'Ag, come now, Emma. Surely you're not really going to get *divorced*!'

'Yes,' said Emma, determined. 'We are.'

'Even now that you . . .'

'Especially now that we . . .'

'I don't understand . . .'

'I don't, either.' Emma looked as though she was going to burst into tears. 'But we're definitely going to get divorced.'

'What does *divorce* mean?' asked Mona, with a spoonful of cornflakes halfway to her mouth.

Emma looked at the child in confusion, as though she had completely forgotten about her presence, and took a quick sip of coffee.

'I'll explain later,' said Yvette. 'First finish eating.'

'What can I say?' Another breathless, nervous laugh from Liane. 'Except that I don't know how on earth Philip managed to . . .' She glanced at Mona and lifted her eyebrows in a meaningful way. 'I mean, when I saw him last, he could scarcely stand on his own feet . . .'

'He didn't need his feet to do what he did last night.'

'But most men . . .'

'Philip is different from most men.'

'Even when he's completely pissed?'

'Even when he's completely pissed.'

'Goodness gracious! I can't help but wonder why you want to leave him.'

'Probably because I want something more from a relationship than a man who never struggles to get a stiff cock.'

'Nevertheless, it's something to be grateful for.' Liane kept her eyes on the rooibos teabag which she had just dunked in a cup of boiling water. 'A man who never struggles to . . . get an erection.'

'What does that mean, Mamma?'

'What?'

'*A rection.*'

'Oh,' said Yvette, relieved that the child hadn't latched on to Emma's more obscene description. 'I'll explain later, my love. Come, first eat up your food.'

'*A rection, a rection, a rection* . . .' mumbled Mona, to make sure that she remembered the difficult word.

'How are you going to explain that one?' asked Emma, suppressing a smile.

'Next time I'm going to ask *you* to explain,' threatened Yvette. 'Keep that in mind for the rest of this conversation.'

'I don't know what happened to our sex life.' Liane sank down at the table and stared despondently at her tea cup. 'Paul and I were never . . . well . . . as active as you and Philip,' she added, stammering and blushing, 'but there was always . . . you know . . . some degree of action. But these days our bedroom feels to me like . . . like Mars! No sign of life!'

'I thought . . .' Yvette swallowed heavily. 'Didn't you see a therapist?'

'Ag, therapy. Postponing the inevitable. That's all it boils down to.

It's like that glue you try to mend broken porcelain with. It looks as though it works, but when you've washed the plate a few times, it always falls apart again.'

Her hands lay in her lap like two dead birds. Liane, who always spoke with Italian gestures, flying fingers and clinking bracelets.

'I used to think, if only I could get Philip to a therapist . . .' Emma stood up quickly to pour another cup of coffee, her back turned to them as she spoke. 'Now it's too late, anyway. I'm not going to allow last night's madness . . . I refuse to let a moment of drunken lust ruin the rest of my life!'

When had they all become so terribly disillusioned? Yvette wondered. Perhaps the seed was already sown a decade ago, during those carefree evenings they'd spent in student bars – three clever, attractive, privileged girls for whom the future seemed almost blindingly bright. And now they were sitting here in a dirty kitchen – three women with disillusioned eyes – in a country which was falling apart around them. One was in the process of getting divorced, one sounded as though she was soon going to get divorced and the third clung to a faltering marriage with desperate stubbornness. The only person at the end of the twentieth century who still believed that love endured all, understood all, forgave all. If she lost this foolish belief, she lost everything. And, God help her, she wasn't brave enough to face life with such disillusionment.

It turned into a lovely winter's day, with a cloudless, bright blue sky and soft sunshine which melted on the earth like butter. Yvette packed a picnic basket – cold sparkling wine and cheese and bread, black olives and sun-dried tomatoes and homemade green-fig preserve – and led her guests to the dam with the determination of the Pied Piper of Hamlin. Where they now lay or sat next to the water, in the sun or in the thin shadows of a few bare willow branches, some still hungover after the party and others simply tired.

Mona, the only active member of the company, darted here and there with a butterfly net, in search of fairies in the long grass. To make her task easier, she had disguised herself as a fairy: in a fancy-dress costume of pink chiffon and pink ballet shoes, a pair of cardboard wings (which Adriaan had quickly devised) fixed to her back. Yvette sat to one side under an umbrella and watched the life-size fairy and her lazy friends with a little smile. The peacefulness of the scene, the play of light and shade on the faces of the still figures, the lushness of the grass and the glittering of the water reminded her of something painted by Manet. Something like *Déjeuner sur l'herbe*. Except that no one was naked of course.

Mila and Rehana sat closest to her, their feet in the water; Emma lay just behind them on her back with a big straw hat over her face; Bobby leaned back against the rough trunk of a willow tree a little way off, her sad eyes hidden behind dark glasses. On the far side of this group sat Liane, shining white like a supernatural being in a man's white shirt and white trousers, her silver bracelets glittering in the sun. Max and Adriaan looked like two dark devils next to her. Paul lay with Yvette under the umbrella, his mood unusually sombre. No trace of the usual sardonic smile about his lips.

'No, I wouldn't be able to work from home,' explained Rehana, moving her feet slowly in the water. 'I need the stimulation of the office. That buzz you get between a group of workers. Like bees in a hive.'

She was still wearing the elegant black dress she had worn the previous evening. Obviously she hadn't expected to spend the night here. And yet she looked surprisingly at home among a group of friends she had met barely twelve hours earlier.

'And if the stimulation becomes an irritation?' Mila asked, thoughtfully stroking her new godson's dark head, a black stain against her purple T-shirt. He was sleeping comfortably in a sling at her breast. 'If your colleagues begin to scream at each other and the boss is constantly throwing tantrums and the secretary is having a nervous breakdown?'

'Sounds to me as though there's a lot more melodrama in a newspaper office than I'm used to,' laughed Rehana.

'Perhaps just bigger egos than you're used to. It's amazing how precious people can become once their names start appearing above their reports.'

'I thought they were all comrades in the Struggle,' said Rehana, disappointed. 'So busy fighting for democracy that there wouldn't be time for petty office politics.'

'Ha! I wish you could see how malicious the arguments between these so-called comrades can become!'

'That shouldn't surprise anyone,' said Bobby behind them, her bony body still hidden under the yellow, green and black folds of her oversized T-shirt. 'Sometimes the tension becomes so unbearable that you just have to lash out. And then it's usually the ones closest to you who suffer. Colleagues, family, lovers . . . Robin and I also did it to each other.'

Her almost translucent bare feet, as small as a child's, reminded Paul of the day that he met her. The same pale feet like two frozen fish in the icy seawater. Then she was so unbearably serious about the political rights of millions of people whom she didn't know. Now she was so unbearably heartbroken about her own personal loss, about the death of one person whom she'd loved, that he yearned for that day.

'I know there are excuses for the storminess,' said Mila, 'but I also know that I can't cope with it for much longer. I feel as though I have to get away, for my own sanity, get some breathing space, otherwise I'll become just another crazy journalist. And then I'm worth fuck-all to the Struggle, anyway. But I also know that I won't be a freelance journalist. I don't have enough self-discipline to work from home.'

'You don't need discipline,' mumbled Emma, her face hidden under the big straw hat. 'Just desperation.'

'It's different for you, Emma. You're busy working on a book. At least that gives you a reason to get up in the morning!'

'Not a reason. Just an excuse.' Emma's voice was sombre. 'I've been working for almost three years on a bunch of short stories. And it feels to me as though I'm not making any progress at all.'

'That's not true,' said Bobby. 'You've been writing like a woman possessed sinced you moved in with me.'

'Desperation. I have to keep writing, otherwise I lapse into self-pity. And I don't feel cheerful enough to write the usual light-hearted stuff for *Palette*. Now I get rid of all my frustrations in my tormented short stories. But I still don't know if they're good enough to be published.'

'The one you gave me to read the other day,' said Bobby, 'was bloody brilliant.'

'Do you really think so?' She peeked out quickly from under the hat, like a tortoise sticking his head out of his shell. 'Philip didn't think so. He said . . .'

'What the fuck does Philip know?' asked Mila angrily. 'I can't believe he actually read one of your stories!'

233

'He didn't finish it. He said I couldn't write about a lesbian relationship if I hadn't slept with a woman.'

'What the fuck does Philip know about lesbian relationships!'

'That's why I gave it to Bobby to read. To tell me if I sounded like a fake.'

'Oh,' said Bobby, injured. 'I thought it was because you respected my literary opinion.'

'Of course I respect your literary opinion,' laughed Emma. 'Especially now that you've said that my story is brilliant!'

'But I already told you last week that it was well written!'

'*Well written* is not the same as *brilliant*, Bobby.'

'And you're obviously not satisfied with anything less than brilliant. I'll remember that if you ever give me another story to read.' Bobby looked at her, a saucy smile fanning across her face. 'On the other hand, if you were prepared to sleep with a woman for once, you wouldn't need to use me as a bullshit detector. Just think of the trouble you could spare yourself . . .'

'Bobby sounds a whole lot better than yesterday, hey?' said Yvette, pleased. 'Perhaps the party spread a bit of cheer after all.'

'She looks better too, thank God,' said Paul, who was leaning on his elbow next to her. 'I couldn't look at her at all yesterday. I can't stare such undisguised pain in the face.'

'I can't even begin to imagine how she must feel. None of us has the faintest idea what's going on in her heart . . .'

'Do we ever have an idea of what's going on in someone else's heart?' he asked with unexpected sharpness.

She looked questioningly at him, but he stared past her, past Bobby and the other women, to Liane who was sitting cross-legged between Max and Adriaan. Her head bent over the Sunday paper on her lap, the shadows of the willow branches dancing on her hands.

'I just can't take it any more!' Liane looked up from the paper, a sharp frown between the perfect arcs of her eyebrows. 'Will these things never end?'

'Isn't that a David Kramer song?' said Adriaan thoughtfully. 'When will these things end?'

'What things?' asked Max.

'All these things!' Liane threw her hands up in the air. The silver bracelets tinkled musically. 'Another guy from Swapo shot dead in South West!'

'Namibia,' said Max patiently.

'Namibia,' she said obediently. 'At his own front door. It just doesn't make sense! The country will be independent in a few months! Everyone knows that Swapo will win the elections! What does it benefit the South African government to murder Swapo supporters at this stage? It's like a naughty boy taking pot shots at a flock of birds, because he's frustrated with his father!'

'Exactly.' Max looked at her in surprise. Surprised that she was so upset by something she'd read in the paper. Perhaps even more surprised that she was reading the paper at all. 'It's a kind of malicious pleasure that's born out of powerlessness.'

'I know you think I'm naïve, Max, but . . .'

'Of course you're naïve.' It was still odd to see his white smile without the black frame of the beard. His mouth looked smaller than before, more vulnerable. 'In certain areas, at least.'

'But most people have a basic grasp of morality, don't they? And the people who do this kind of thing . . . they must also have had it . . . but they lost it somewhere along the way . . .'

'We're talking about professional assassins, Liane. A secret division of the security forces specializing in dirty tricks. It's their *work*. They do it for *volk* and *vaderland*. *The end justifies the means. You can't make an omelette without breaking eggs. All's fair in love and war.* Every cliché in the – '

'But surely the war is over!'

'Says who?'

'The border war?' she asked, bewildered. 'I mean, if Namibia is becoming independent . . . then surely it must be over?'

'It's not over, Liane. The border has just moved. It's not in Namibia any more. It's all around us. Between us.'

'Ja,' murmured Paul, and sipped his glass of sparkling wine slowly.

When he looked at his lovely wife in her shining white clothes, he didn't know how he would ever find the courage to tell her. He shook his head and stared at the bubbles in the glass. 'I'm going to ask Liane for a divorce.'

'When?' asked Yvette softly, without any surprise in her voice.

Without looking at him. As if she wanted to make it easier for him. Like confession in front of a priest whose face you can't see.

'As soon as I've plucked up the courage.'

'It doesn't help to delay the agony, Paul. She knows something is wrong . . .'

'I know. But she doesn't yet know *what*.'

'And you?' Still without looking at him. 'Do you know?'

'Yes.' Another sip of champagne. To win time. 'I've met someone else.'

Her head jerked up. Disbelief on her pale face.

'It's not what you think.' He put the glass carefully down on the blanket, next to the picnic basket, and stared at the glistening dam. He wished that he was wearing his dark glasses. 'It's a man.'

Her mouth opened and closed wordlessly. An old-fashioned little mouth, like a heroine from one of those classic black and white movies he loved to watch, lips that moved without a sound. Just piano music, which in this case would have been thunderingly dramatic.

'Are you . . . do you mean to tell me . . .' she stammered finally.

'Yes. I'm attracted to a man. *My name is Paul Terreblanche and I am gay.*' He tried to say it jokingly, but his voice crept uncertainly over his tongue. 'Isn't that how one's supposed to come out of the closet?'

'How long . . . have you known?'

'Probably all my life. Somewhere in my subsconscious. But I've always suppressed it . . . not even admitting it to myself . . . until a year or two ago.'

He sat with his legs pulled up, elbows on knees. Yvette looked at his folded hands, the fingers tightly interlaced, and remembered Liane's limp, lifeless hands this morning in the kitchen. Also tried to think back further – last year, five years ago, ten years ago – to see if there were any signs which she could possibly have missed. As she had missed so many other things. *Alice in Wonderland*. At university there were indeed some men who had sneeringly referred to him as a 'moffie' she remembered. But she had thought they were just jealous because girls found him irresistible. The lovely tanned body, the well-groomed black hair, the self-confident manner with which he wore his clothes. Surely it was ridiculous to question someone's masculinity just because he was better dressed than other men! She had always detested the almost obligatory macho chauvinism of the average Afrikaans male. The kind who were immediately suspicious of any more refined member of the species; treating any son who wanted to play the piano rather than rugby like a potential queer. She had always refused to fall into that trap. So what was she to say to this man sitting helplessly next to her?

'And now?' she asked. 'Why are you prepared to admit it now?'

'It's not that I *want* to admit it. Believe me. It's going to hurt too many people. Remember, my father is a dominee! My mother believes that it's a sin in the eyes of God and the congregation. And I'm not even talking about what it's going to do to Liane . . .' He smiled sadly as he looked out over the dam again. 'I thought if I could bluff everyone for the first thirty years of my life, I could probably do it for the next thirty years. I thought it was better to keep everything as it is, just go cruising now and again, then no one need get hurt. But then I met someone . . .'

Someone who became more than just a one-night-stand almost immediately. Whether it was enduring enough to be called love, he didn't yet know. But it was already more than he had ever felt for Liane. More passion, more desire, more unbearable longing. It was already enough to make impossible the lie that his life had become. That's all he knew.

'And Liane suspects nothing,' she said, shuddering.

'I always thought that she was the thespian among us.' He stared at his interlocked fingers. 'Now I realize that I've been acting all my life. And I can't do it any more, Yvette. I just can't play this role any more.'

Yvette felt her eyes fill with tears. She couldn't take it any more, she thought hopelessly. If she wasn't careful she was going to become a blubbering idiot like her mother.

'Pappa!' Mona stood breathlessly behind Adriaan, the cardboard wings rather skew by this time, the butterfly net hoisted high above her shoulders. 'There's a fairy on your hat!'

'Wait, let me catch him for you!' Adriaan grabbed at his hat with an open hand – a second before she would have hit him over the head with the net – and stretched his closed fist out to her. 'Here he is!'

'It's not a boy!' she cried, upset. 'It's a girl! Stupid!'

'Who's your "stupid"?' he exclaimed, pulling her down on to his lap and tickling her. The homemade wings made it difficult to hold her wriggling body down. She giggled in a high, helpless, almost hysterical tone. 'Say "Sorry, Great King", otherwise I won't stop.'

'No!' she shrieked, giggling. 'No, no, no!'

'*No, Great King!*'

'Stupid!' she cried the moment he let her go. 'Stupid old Pappa!'

She jumped backwards quickly, still giggling, so that he couldn't catch her again. One wing was torn and hung limply against her back, but she hadn't realized it yet.

'Sometimes I long for the good old days,' said Adriaan with a dramatic sigh, 'when children were seen and not heard.'

'You're stupid because you don't know anything about fairies! Fairies are always girls! Boys can't wear dresses! Boys can't fly!'

'Says who?' asked Paul with a wry smile.

But Yvette didn't hear him. She was staring at her sunbrowned husband and her daughter who looked more and more like her father every day, at her seductive blonde friend who was stroking her baby son's black hair absent-mindedly, at the rest of her friends who were relaxing here next to the dam. Overwhelmed by an ominous feeling, an instinctive realization that she was experiencing the end of something. Much more than the end of a few relationships, she thought, more like the end of an era. The end of innocence, she decided, as her daughter burst into heartbreaking sobs over her broken cardboard wing.

SIX

Freedom is Just Another Word (1990)

And then things ended. Or in any case, changed completely, irrevocably. By the autumn of 1990, when Emma, heavily pregnant, invited her friends to spend a weekend with her on the West Coast, they were living in a different country from the one in which Yvette had celebrated her birthday scarcely eight months before. Another country, another world, thought Max that Friday night, next to the moonlit lagoon at Churchhaven, wondering at how quickly everything had happened in the end. After so many years.

Because it wasn't just in South Africa that everything had changed when the prison gates swung open for Nelson Mandela and an astonished, moved, overwhelmed nation saw the tall, lean, grey-haired man's first steps to freedom. A month later, Max and Bobby and Ralph – and Mila, along with other journalists from around the world – were among the jubilant crowd in the capital of the former South West Africa when a brightly coloured flag with a saffron yellow sun was hoisted for the first time in the independent state of Namibia. Everywhere in Southern Africa an intoxicating atmosphere of optimism hung in the humid late summer air like the scent of over-ripe fruit.

And meanwhile, in wintry Berlin, The Wall had fallen, broken down piece by piece by the people who had had to live on either side of it for thirty years – a bloodless, joyful process which astounded the rest of humanity. In Prague, the so-called Velvet Revolution, once again bloodless, astounded humanity again. *Days of miracle and wonder*, as Paul Simon sang.

Until the Christmas Day killing of a dictator and his wife in Romania reminded humanity that bloodletting was always the rule, rather than the exception, when the winds of change blew through history.

'A last weekend of freedom,' Emma had said to Max over the phone. That's what she wanted to celebrate, before her child was born in a month's time. 'Once the baby's here, I'm going to be busy for a long time to come. Perhaps never really free ever again.'

Her excited tone couldn't disguise the note of anxiety in her voice.

'That's one way of looking at it,' he consoled her, 'but of course you can also view it as the first weekend of freedom in a democratic country. Without political freedom, personal freedom isn't possible anyway.'

'Sorry, Max,' she sighed, 'but you ought to know by this time that I can't look at the world through that wide-angle lens of yours. I can't see the "whole political scene"; I only see little images within the bigger picture. My eye works more like a zoom lens. When I write, I always focus on the little bits of personal history. The little stories which aren't part of the grand narrative in the history books.'

'So you're not busy writing *War and Peace*?' he said in mock disappointment.

'Oh no, there are enough megalomaniac male writers who can tackle that,' she laughed.

'And when can we eventually read the long-awaited book?'

'Soon,' she answered anxiously. 'In a month or two. That's something else I want to celebrate this weekend. If I can get permission from the Cultural Desk, of course,' she added jokily.

'I'll have to speak to my comrades,' he replied, smiling.

'Just warn them that it's not Struggle literature. I can't write about the capital letter struggle, Max, just the one we have to fight in our own minds . . .'

He could almost hear her shrugging her shoulders, apologetic.

'That's the kind of book which needs to be published now, Emma,' he assured her. 'Freedom also means freedom to write what you like.'

'Do you really think so?' Now openly anxious. 'That each one of us has been freed in all areas just because Nelson Mandela isn't in jail any more? I mean, say we get a new government and they – '

'We will get a new government.'

'But what if it's just a case of white bullies being replaced by black bullies? What guarantee do I have, as an exceptionally white woman who writes and speaks in Afrikaans, that I'm going to have the freedom in the New South Africa to say and write what I like?'

'The new leaders know what it means to be caught on the wrong side of the censorship laws,' he reminded her. 'That ought to be enough of a guarantee.'

'You have a lot more faith in humanity than I have, Max. Your mother always taught you that all people were created equal. I was brought up to believe I was a member of a chosen master race. I had to realize on my own that my brain was poisoned – but sometimes I wonder whether my soul hasn't been irreparably damaged too. I still struggle to believe that most people are basically good. That any nation which has been oppressed for a long time will necessarily have the decency not to oppress another nation. Look what the Israelis are doing in Palestine these days! And what about our Afrikaans ancestors, who were thrown into concentration camps thirty years before the Jews were? That didn't exactly produce a tolerant nation!'

'I don't necessarily believe in people's basic goodness, either, Emma,' he said with a sigh. 'But till the day I die, I'll cling to the hope that I might be surprised.'

'Me too.' Her sigh hung like a scarcely audible echo of his in the receiver. 'Otherwise I probably wouldn't want to bring a child into the world.'

And now they were sitting with Bobby on the silvery white beach, under a black firmament in which stars swam like glittering fish, bewailing the fact that so many of their friends weren't in the right frame of mind to celebrate the birth of a new country with abandon. Liane's characteristic *joie de vivre* was badly damaged by Paul's 'betrayal' (as she still insisted on calling it), while Paul had moved in with his new lover and apparently felt too guilty or too embarrassed to make contact with his old friends. Philip had made a half-hearted attempt to persuade Emma not to go ahead with the divorce – after she realized that she had got pregnant on the night of Yvette's birthday party – but she had told him (after much soul-searching and wringing of hands) that she couldn't imagine living with him again. With or without a child. Philip's only visible reaction was to give himself over to alcohol with even more cynicism than before. For months he had been hanging out, night after night, with other single men in noisy bars and childless, womenless houses, regularly falling into bed drunk, and just as regularly waking up with a hammering headache. During these extended bar sessions, he liked to tell whoever would listen that his ex-wife had stolen his semen, that he wanted to set up a petition to ensure that the rare crime of semen theft would be viewed in a serious light in the New South Africa. Then he would collect the signatures of a few amused bystanders, on cigarette boxes or serviettes or any available piece of paper, which he would lose by the end of the night. When Emma heard this story, she didn't know whether to laugh or cry. The way she'd often felt when they still shared their lives.

But the crisis which had hit Adriaan and Yvette made the rest of this circle of friends' problems seem trivial. Divorce and sexual betrayal, extra-marital pregnancy and drunkenness were definitely not to be taken lightly, but, in a way, they were like the ingredients of a soap opera. Adriaan and Yvette had, it seemed, ended up in a classical tragedy.

Their son, Pablo, had drowned shortly after Christmas.

Adriaan had been standing with the one-year-old boy on his shoulders, looking out over the sea, on an apparently safe rock, when he was pulled off by a freak wave. Down below in the foaming, whirling water he lost his grip on the child's foot. After the waves had thrown him on to the surrounding rocks time and time again, he at last managed to pull himself out. Bloody and half-conscious and completely crazed because he could no longer see the child in the water. He wanted to dive into the waves again, even though he knew it would be not only useless, but also life-threatening. Possibly precisely because he knew it would be life-threatening. Anything would be better than telling his wife that he had let their son drown. The only thing that stopped him, he told her later, was the expression on his daughter's face. She had stood a little way back on a rock and watched the whole drama in silent horror. Pablo's body was only found two days later. Mona didn't utter a word until many days after that.

'And he's going to blame himself for the rest of his life,' said Max. 'The more Yvette tries to persuade him that it wasn't his fault, the less he believes her.'

He lay on his back with his hands folded behind his neck, stunned by the brightness of the stars. As if you could reach out your hand to pluck them like glistening fruit from a heavenly tree. And yet it was just this brightness, this apparent proximity, which emphasized their inaccessibility. Immeasurably far from here. Completely untouched by anything which happened on this planet.

'Yvette thinks it's her fault,' said Bobby next to him, her chin propped on her knees and her arms wrapped around her legs. 'Because she said he should take the children out of the house that day. Because she wanted to work on an illustration. It's crazy, of course, but it doesn't help to tell her that. I had the same kind of irrational feelings of guilt about Robin . . .' She wrapped her arms more tightly about her legs and stared at the silvery-grey water of the lagoon. 'They say it's a normal part of the grieving process . . . denial, self-reproach, rage . . . all those emotions you have to work through before you can eventually reach some kind of acceptance.'

It was exactly a year since Robin's death, Max realized. And it was the first time he'd heard Bobby speak willingly about her feelings. Till now she had been so resolutely silent that he had begun to wonder whether she hadn't got stuck in the so-called denial phase.

'And you, Bobby?' Emma leaned back on her elbows, her bulging stomach a mountain over which she could barely see, her voice hesitating. 'Have you reached some kind of acceptance?'

'I accept the fact that she's dead. That I'll never see her again. But I can't accept the *way* that it happened.' Her voice became quieter and quieter, shrinking with every word to a barely audible whisper above the lapping of the water on the beach. 'I don't know if I'll *ever* be able to think about it without anger.'

'But would it be easier for you if she'd died in a different way? I mean, let's say it was a car accident . . . say a drunk man crashed into her . . . wouldn't you feel the same anger?'

'How the hell should I know? All I know is that I can't cope with the way she . . . with the way that they blew her into pieces . . . you know, as if they wanted to make sure that nothing of her remained. Not even a body to mourn over. Sometimes I think if only they'd shot her instead . . . like so many other activists . . . if only there was a proper body to bury! But it probably wouldn't have been easier. Now I comfort myself with the thought that at least she didn't die a slow, torturous death. It happened so fast . . . a split second . . . she probably didn't even realize that her last moment had come.'

Max put his arm around her shoulder and stared with her at the water.

'What do you *do* with such terrible anger?' asked Emma, when it began to feel as though the silence was reaching to the stars.

'For the first few months, I thought up the craziest revenge fantasies.' She was now talking with her thumbnail between her teeth, gnawing it down even more. 'It was indescribably lonely in that bed . . . it still is. I still can't lie on her side of the bed. Anyway, I lay there and fantasized about how I would torture them. The bastards who made the bomb, the bosses who gave the order, the whole vile mob, all the way up to the politicians responsible for all the shit in this land! How I would hang them by the feet like dead birds and send electric shocks through their balls and pull their skin from their bodies excruciatingly slowly . . . I was mad with rage! And do you know what brought me to my senses in the end? Realizing what Robin would have thought of such barbaric bloodthirstiness. The disgust I would see on her face if she were to hear about my lust for revenge. She was the least violent person I knew.'

'Yes,' said Max. 'She would have forgiven anyone anything. Even the bastards who killed her.'

'That's what I try to think of these days. Every time I want to sink into anger.' She stuck one of her fingers under the frame of her glasses and wiped her eyes quickly. 'But it's not easy. It's not easy to follow in the footsteps of a bloody angel!'

They heard a car approaching, from very far away. No other signs of human activity. No other noises of any kind, just the low, sighing lapping of water and the high, monotonous chirping of crickets in the shrubs around the beach house.

'I think that's Ralph.' Emma cocked her head to try to identify the sputtering noise of his old Combi's engine. 'He had to go for dinner with some bigshot at the SABC . . .'

'Sucking up,' said Max. 'That's how he put it.'

'But he's already signed the contract for the TV series,' said Bobby. 'What does he still have to suck up for?'

'He says a scriptwriter can never suck up enough,' smiled Emma. 'I think he wants to work a few new ideas into the storyline – and the powers that be aren't very open to new ideas. As we can all see every time we turn on the TV.'

'I'm glad he's back home,' said Bobby. It was the first time in weeks, realized Max, that he'd seen that rare, glowing, smile. 'I have to admit that I thought he wasn't going to come back. And it's wonderful that he's decided to live in the Cape. I don't know what it is about him – maybe just because he reminds me so much of my brother – but sometimes I think that if I didn't have this strange preference for women, I would have fallen for him in a big way.'

'Me too,' said Emma.

'Have you also developed a preference for women since moving in with Bobby?' asked Max, in mock amazement.

'I've always had a preference for women,' she answered, laughing. 'I just don't necessarily want to sleep with them.'

'No, we all know you prefer lovers who make you feel inferior,' said Bobby sarcastically.

'I can't help it,' said Emma thoughtfully. 'I'm just not used to supportive, unselfish men. My father has been a giant baby his whole life long. And my brother probably inherited that chauvinism. It's terrible to see how his new wife spoils him! I sometimes feel as though I want to take her by the shoulders and shake her! And the man I married, well . . .'

'Perhaps you need to give yourself a good shake, sister,' said Bobby.

'I'm trying my best, comrade. Ouch! The baby's just kicked!'

'She obviously thinks you should pull yourself together, too,' said Bobby. 'Remember, you have to be a role model for her, otherwise she's also going to fall for a giant baby one day. And I'd never forgive you for that.'

'Is it a girl?' asked Max.

'Bobby has decided it's a girl.'

'I *know* it's a girl,' said Bobby. 'I can see that you're carrying completely differently from those two silly women in the class who're expecting boys!'

'She goes with me to pre-natal classes,' Emma explained. 'She's offered to help me through the birth.'

'Well, it's obvious that Philip isn't going to fulfil his paternal duties. And I always wanted to be a father,' said Bobby with a cheeky smile.

As the approaching headlights bored two holes through the darkness, Max began to shake with laughter. He could hardly imagine what a strange picture these two women must make among the more traditional couples on the floor of the pre-natal class. Emma, who was almost twice as big as Bobby (even when she wasn't pregnant), with those long legs and massive stomach and untameable bush of hair, stretched out in Bobby's frail arms, pressed against Bobby's little finch body, between those birdlike legs. Groaning and moaning and huffing and puffing together – or whatever it was that you were supposed to do in these classes. When the car stopped next to the beach house, he was still laughing.

'It's not *that* funny,' said Bobby, somewhat offended. 'I do it better than most of the real fathers in the class!'

'It's true,' Emma agreed. 'She's a born father.'

At that moment, Ralph called through the darkness to them.

'Wait, I'll come and get you!' Bobby shouted, and jumped up. 'I'd love to hear what you think of fatherhood!'

'*Let this cup pass from me!*' cried Ralph.

'Are you talking or praying?'

'I'm giving you my opinion on fatherhood! Hubris!'

'And what do you think of female fathers?'

'Certainly can't be a worse fiasco than male fathers,' called Ralph's disembodied voice in the dark.

'My sentiments exactly,' murmured Emma.

Max looked at how Bobby flew off over the sand and melted into the dark sky.

'She sounded really excited,' he said, amazed. 'It's the first time since Robin's death that she's sounded really excited about anything.'

Yvette stared through the car window at the dull grey bushes next to the road, the sea deep blue on the left, the sky a cloudless cupola over the wide, deserted landscape. When they had lived here on the West Coast, she remembered, she used to tell her friends that the surroundings reminded her of a Greek island. The heat and the hardy vegetation, the dusty dirt roads leading to isolated bays and pure white beaches, the limewashed fishermen's cottages against a sky the colour of laundry blue. Now everything seemed to her unmistakably South African. As dull and deadeningly boring as everything in South Africa seemed these days.

'It's a beautiful day,' she said, sighing.

Adriaan drove silently on. Kathleen Ferrier sang Mahler's *Kindertotenlieder* through the speakers next to them, an old recording he had been listening to with masochistic obstinacy in the last few weeks.

'Pappa, Mamma says it's a beautiful day!' exclaimed Mona from the back seat.

'I heard,' Adriaan said curtly.

Yvette's heart shrank for the sake of her child. It was difficult enough for her, an adult, to understand what was happening to her and Adriaan. Why they tortured each other so, with every sentence and every silence between them, why they could offer no comfort to each other, why they had hardly touched each other for months. How was this four-year-old child to understand what was happening? All she knew was that her baby brother was swallowed by a giant wave. And that everything changed after that.

She sighed again, and Adriaan looked sharply at her. She looked away guiltily, to the sea which was now only a narrow blue strip behind a rise. *Fuck it, Yvette, I just can't take your sighing any more!* he had shouted a week ago. At his wit's end.

'If the weekend seems such a punishment to you,' said Adriaan, 'perhaps it's better to turn back now.'

'No, Pappa!' Mona cried in a high, anxious voice. 'You promised you'd build me a sand castle.'

'No, we're not going to turn around,' said Yvette determinedly. Without sighing. 'We need this weekend. It will do us good.'

'And you *promised*!' Mona cried again.

It will do us good. How many times, since Emma had invited them, had they murmured these words to each other? Like a magic spell which would change everything. *It will do us good to get away for a while.* Out of a house where every room, every piece of furniture and every plate of food reminded them of a dead child. *It will do us good to be among other people for a change.* People who lead normal lives, people who laugh and argue, people who are good to each other. *It will do us good to go to the sea again.* Because the sea had become a horror to them.

Mona had begun to cry heartbreakingly when she saw a beach for the first time after Pablo's death, but Adriaan and Yvette could only stare speechlessly at the waves, crushed by their feelings of guilt. By this time, it was clear that Mona, with her childish surrender to her emotions, had progressed much further than her parents along the long road back to what psychologists would call 'a normal emotional life'.

'I'm not cross with the sea any more, Mamma,' she had recently explained. 'Oupa says there are good waves and bad waves. It was a nasty old monster wave which took Pablo. But most waves are good waves. That's what Oupa says.' Ironic that it was Adriaan's father who could reach out to his grandchild through the fog of his senility, could articulate and exorcize her fear, while her parents were so busy battling their own monsters that they could offer her no comfort.

Also a good thing that Churchhaven was next to a lagoon rather than the open sea. There would be no bad waves, Yvette comforted herself, just lapping water and soft white sand to build castles with.

'I hope you're right,' muttered Adriaan with his eyes on the road.

'You're the one who said it first,' she reminded him. 'Ag, *come on, Yvette, it will do us good.*'

'Then I can only hope that I was right.'

This time he was the one who sighed heavily. She looked at his profile, the square forehead with the horizontal frown lines which had been etched deep into his tanned skin in the last few months, the wiry brown hair which was interwoven with silver threads these days, the fleshy nose and the wide mouth, which suddenly looked more vulnerable than ever to her. She looked at his strong shoulders and wondered when they had become so bowed. She looked at his broad hands on the steering wheel. And tried to remember when last those hands stroked her body.

Three hours later she was standing on the stoep of a simple limewashed beach house with a thatched roof, a stone's throw from the almost motionless blue water of the lagoon, busy setting the table. The tablecloth was a colourful length of fabric which Bobby had bought in Namibia the previous week – printed with the smiling face of the new leader of the country – but Yvette smoothed it with her fingers without looking at it. Her eyes continually wandered to her daughter on the beach, the tanned child and the golden dog next to each other. Like a Hockney painting, the lonely figure next to the glistening water, the bright light, and the strange emptiness of the scene. They were digging a hole as big as a grave next to the water, the child with a plastic bucket and the dog with his paws. For the rest of her life, Yvette thought sadly, she would probably be the most watchful mother she knew. Too scared to let her remaining child out of her sight for a moment.

'No, look, Ralph, it can't go on like this!' Emma said, carrying a stack of plates to the table. 'If you don't tell me something about your TV series now, I'm going to die of curiosity. I don't know why you're so bloody modest about the whole affair!'

'Well, if it was a great work of literature, I would probably be less modest,' said Ralph, following hot on her heels with a tray full of glasses.

'Ha! Who the hell cares about great literary works these days?'

'Look who's talking,' grinned Ralph. 'I hear via the grapevine that the whole publishing industry is buzzing with news of a great work by an unknown young talent, soon to be published.'

'For a moment, I thought you were talking about someone I know. But I'm afraid I don't know any "young" talent.'

She looked like a caricature of a paunch-bellied American farmer. The smug posture, hands on the hips, with denim dungarees stretched tight over the full stomach, the long hair bundled into a baseball cap, the good-natured smile on the freckled face. The self-satisfaction of pregnant women, thought Yvette as she stared longingly at the massive stomach.

'Ag, you know when people speak about writers, anything under forty is viewed as young,' said Ralph. 'These days I fall into the category of "middle-aged male scriptwriter". That just doesn't sound as sexy as "young female short-story writer".'

'You've hit the nail on the head! Sexy is the word that counts. It has nothing to do with great literature, Ralph. All that the publishing industry still gets excited about today is sex. This young talent you're talking about apparently described a few sexual positions that hadn't been covered before in Afrikaans.'

'Ah! So you finally scraped together the courage to show your erotic stories to a publisher!'

'Well, it's not as though the stories are all "dripping with semen". That was what Philip said when he read one of the early ones.' She laughed again, this time a little embarrassed, as she arranged the plates on the table. 'I've been moving in a different direction recently. I've been writing more about the consequences of erotic encounters.'

'You mean you've been writing about pregnancy and children?' asked Ralph, amused.

'No, I mean the less visible results of sex. The pangs of the heart rather than the pleasures of the flesh . . .'

'What are we talking about now?' asked Ralph with a suspicious frown. 'After pleasure comes pain? And other moral tales by Emma Nel? Where does the sudden whiff of Calvinism come from?'

'No, man, Ralph, it's got nothing to do with Calvinism! It's just – '

'Everything that Afrikaners do,' Ralph interrupted, 'has something to do with Calvinism.'

'OK, but that's not what I mean. It's just that I went through a phase where all my stories turned out erotic in one way or another, however hard I tried to keep them decent. And then, one day, I decided: To hell with this, if I can't write anything that is "decent" enough to be published, then I may as well write as I like. And the moment that I began writing for myself, you know, without continually thinking about publication, then the erotic element faded . . . and then all these other "forbidden" subjects began to simmer in my subconscious. And I don't mean subjects which are forbidden by law. I'm talking about things which I had forbidden myself to write about before. Things which were too difficult to express in words. Things which frightened me . . .'

Yvette arranged the last few knives and forks on the table as she tried to pretend that she was interested in the conversation. She had realized in the last month that her friends had begun to treat her like her parents' generation treated their maids. Not rudely. No, her mother would never let a rude word slip past her lips when she spoke to a servant. But when her female friends came to visit, they would talk about the most intimate subjects while the black woman moved through the room like an invisible apparition. It was as though her friends didn't see her any more, Yvette realized with horror. Was it possible that grief could make one invisible?

'Like boundaries in relationships,' Emma went on. 'That's something which fascinates me. I mean those vague, shifting borders, for example, between sexual passion and violence . . . you can bite your lover till he bleeds while you're having sex, but you can't bite him the next morning in a rage . . . Or between "normal" jealousy and the kind of jealousy which drove Othello to murder Desdemona. Or between healthy sexuality in a family, a father who likes to dry off his little daughter's bare body, and a father who crosses the line to incest. Do you know what I mean?'

Yvette's attention had wandered to her child again. Now she was trying to fill the hole in the sand with water – a painfully slow process, because the water had to be carried carefully, step by step, from the lagoon in the toy bucket. By the time she reached the hole, half of the water had already spilled. And the remaining half was sucked up by the sand almost immediately. Like poor old Sisyphus, thought Yvette, longing to go and help her.

'I think I began to write that erotic stuff precisely because it was so difficult for me . . . because I had to challenge myself to go further with every sentence, you know, not to shrink back . . . So it's probably logical that the next step should have been to tackle something even more difficult. More frightening.'

'When I hear you talk like that,' said Ralph with a resigned smile, 'I understand why I'll never be able to write anything more serious than adverts. Or screenplays, which sound like adverts, anyway. It's all to do with courage, right?'

'I don't know. I think courage is sometimes just a euphemism for desperation.'

'And what are you going to call the book?'

'Well, I'd like to call it *Border Stories*,' she said with a sudden twinkle in her eye. 'But my publisher says there's already a whole genre in South African literature called "border stories". And you have to be male to take part. Preferably quite macho too.'

'I should think so,' grinned Ralph. 'The border war is, by definition, the last bastion of testosterone in our literature! Heaven help us if women annex that too.'

'No, not annex,' she said with a sweet smile. 'Just add a feminine touch. Like hanging up lace curtains in a bar.'

'And the next thing you know, the bar is full of women! And what must the poor men write about then? Labour pains and menstrual cramps?'

'What do *you* write about?' she asked, laughing. 'You still haven't given me a clue!'

'I'm afraid you won't respect me any more,' he said, his eyes chastely lowered and his feet crossed at the ankles, a parody of virginal innocence.

'Try me.'

'Promise you won't laugh.'

'On my Voortrekker word of honour.'

'OK. Here it comes. I'm being paid a shitload of money to write a politically correct script about a fairy-tale street, somewhere in the New South Africa, where four happy families are neighbours. White, black, coloured and Indian, of course. We just can't get away from the official race classifications of the Old South Africa, hey? Anyway, my instructions are to show how cultural differences can be bridged with humour. Humour which will be understood by the "average South African", mind you. Whoever that mythical figure might be. So we're not talking Monty Python here. More like Leon Schuster. In the end, of course, they're all good mates and the white family's daughter marries the coloured family's son while the Indian mother offers to make the wedding dress and the black family takes care of the catering for the reception. Or something along those lines. The finer details still have to be worked out. The only condition is that the closing episode has to be so positive that it will solve each and every racial problem in the country. You promised you wouldn't laugh!'

But Emma threw her head back with such abandon that the baseball cap fell off and a wave of orange hair broke over her shoulders, and she laughed from the depths of her massive stomach. Even Yvette began to giggle, her hand pressed over her mouth and her eyes stretched wide. Amazed to hear this almost forgotten sound in her own head.

And while they enjoyed their Greek lunch on the stoep later, she listened in wonder to her husband's laugh. Admittedly, not the same exuberant laugh as long ago – like booming church bells spreading good tidings, she'd always thought – but still loud enough, determined enough, to be announcing something.

It was Emma's idea, as hostess for the weekend, to have a Greek meal. Seeing that everyone was always saying the West Coast reminded them of the Greek isles, she explained. Seeing that everyone would rather be in another country, anyway. No! Max and Bobby had protested straight away. They didn't want to be anywhere else but the New South Africa! Sorry, Emma sighed. She was so used to wishing that she was in another country that she'd clean forgotten about the New South Africa.

Adriaan laughed, and piled his plate obscenely high with moussaka from the bowl Ralph had brought along. For the first time in weeks his eyes seemed to Yvette more green than grey, a glittering green like fresh leaves, rather than the lifeless grey of dead branches. This was another man, she thought, astonished; not the one who had driven here a few hours ago. It wasn't just the heavy sombreness which had vanished, it was as though even his appearance was miraculously altered, as though the wrinkles on his forehead had faded and the grey threads on his head had diminished. Or perhaps it was just the huge umbrella which cast such a flattering shadow over his face, she decided more soberly. There was something in his bravado – fluctuating between hesitation and exaggeration, something which probably no one else would notice – which made her suspect that he was making a painful effort to hide the gaping wound in his heart from his friends.

'OK, I was wrong,' he said to Liane, who had come to sit between him and Max at the long table. 'Your shop is definitely not in the same league as my father's platteland furniture store. My father would have given his eye teeth – he would have given my mother, for that matter – to have as much free publicity as you've had!'

'I must say, it's going better than I hoped,' said Liane with a smile which she struggled to keep modest.

When a woman was as pretty as Liane, you couldn't imagine that she could get any prettier. You waited instead (albeit subconsciously) for the day her beauty would begin to fade. But Liane's beauty showed no signs of fading. On the contrary, as she sat there now, she looked lovelier than ever. Perhaps it was just the obvious self-confidence she'd acquired since she'd been living on her own and managing her own shop, Yvette speculated. Since she featured in the press as often as a budding film star.

'By now every magazine in the country has run an article about Liane Terreblanche and The Style Shop! What's your secret?' Adriaan wanted to know. 'Do you bribe the editors? Do you sleep with the journalists?'

'My darling, there are no limits to what I'll do to get publicity for my shop.' She laughed lightly. 'Unfortunately most journalists in this field are female.'

'Unfortunately?' asked Bobby, eyes innocent behind her round glasses.

'I can always help out if you're looking for someone to sleep with them,' said Max, spreading a layer of pink taramasalata on some pitta bread.

'I would think you've already got your hands full, Max.'

'What on earth makes you think that?'

'Well, it sounds as though you're trying to lure a specimen of every possible population group to your bed. *The United Nations of Max Ackermann's Bedroom.*'

'Isn't that what's meant by "political liberation"?' His eyes as innocent as Bobby's now.

'One would swear you'd never heard of Aids!'

'One would swear you'd never heard of condoms! Don't you remember those little balloons we called FLs when we were at school?'

'I never used those little balloons when I was at school,' laughed Liane. 'Don't you remember how innocent I was?'

'To my regret, yes.'

His face had been beardless for more than a year, but at weekends, when he gave up the battle against stubble, the skin about his mouth was shadowed, making him look like a traditional cartoon baddie. The kind who was usually pictured with a mask over the eyes and a sack of loot over the shoulder. But it was the first time that Yvette noticed how much of the stubble was silvery white these days. And, for the first time, she wondered whether it wasn't just vanity – rather than professional dignity, as she'd assumed – that had made him shave the beard off a year ago. Especially in the light of Liane's hint about his active sex life. Although heaven knows what gave Liane the right to lecture him on morality.

'And why are you looking at me so critically, my darling?'

'Just looking,' said Yvette, her cheeks hot. 'I like your new hairstyle.'

'Thanks. Me too, actually. It's all part of the New Liane in the New South Africa. New job, new husbandless life, new effortless hairstyle . . .' She brushed her fingers self-consciously through her cropped hair, almost as short as Bobby's, but obviously better cared for. And she laughed lightly again. 'Of course, it's also part of an extensive Plan of Revenge. As Emma said last year: Looking good is the best revenge.'

'And just see what I look like now,' laughed Emma, her hands splayed out over her stomach.

'You look stunning! Your hair is glossy, your eyes are sparkling, your complexion is glowing . . .'

'My bladder leaks, my back aches, my feet are swollen. And I'm dying for a cigarette. The minute the baby's born, I'm going to smoke a whole packet of Lexingtons. Talk about *after-action-satisfaction*. If they ever make one of those ads again, they can replace one of those glamorous sportsmen with a woman who's just been through labour!'

'Don't forget about the champagne,' grinned Bobby.

'Do I look to you like a woman who would forget the champagne?'

'She's packed two bottles of Moët et Chandon in her hospital suitcase,' Bobby informed them. 'When I complained that it was too heavy – seeing that I'm the substitute father who has to carry the bloody case – she took the two baby-care books out.'

'Ag, I can always borrow a baby book from one of the more exemplary mothers,' said Emma with a shrug. 'I've got a feeling that I'm going to need alcohol more than advice on how to wind the baby.'

'Well, I obviously have no idea how you feel – not having been there myself – but you look scandalously good,' declared Liane. 'I don't know how you do it! Yes, you too, Yvette, when you were pregnant last time, you looked like an advertisement for happy motherhood . . . like an . . . advertisement . . .'

Yvette saw the sudden flush of embarrassment on Liane's high cheekbones, heard the confused hesitation in her voice, and looked away quickly to where Mona was playing on the stoep. When she was pregnant last, she thought with a heart which felt like a wet sponge. *Happy motherhood.*

'It's not as easy as it looks,' said Emma, and took hold of Yvette's hand, unnoticed, underneath the table.

It was as though this unexpected touch wrung out the wet sponge, as though the water had to stream out somewhere. When had someone last touched her so sympathetically, she wondered, as a flood of tears dammed up behind her eyes. Why couldn't she hide her feelings better? Her mouth began to quiver so uncontrollably that she couldn't get a word out. Why couldn't she be more like her husband? She leaped up and fled from the table.

'Sorry, sorry, sorry . . .' mumbled Liane, with both hands in front of her mouth.

'What's wrong, Mamma?' called Mona, her voice high and anxious.

'Mamma's sad,' she heard Adriaan say as she disappeared into the house. 'Come sit on my lap.'

'Is she sad about Pablo?'

'Yes. And about lots of other things. Come sit with me?'

'Why?' The little voice now more controlled, but still shaky. 'Are you also sad?'

While she could still clearly hear her husband and her child – while the tears still streamed down her cheeks – she ran a glass of water from the kitchen tap. She could see almost nothing in the dusky living room. The wooden shutters in front of the windows were pulled closed against the sharp sunlight outside, the unfamiliar furniture shadowed into ghostly shapes. Then her eye was drawn by a faint reflection in a mirror on the opposite wall. Her fingers tightened around the glass. She saw a stranger with dark, oily, unkempt hair, circles like fresh bruises under staring eyes, the pale shiny skin of a feverish patient, and a small mouth which was pressed together so despairingly that the lips had all but disappeared. A few pieces of charcoal and a sheet of paper, she thought longingly. That's all she needed for this shocking illustration. Self portrait, Churchhaven, 1990.

'Yes, I'm also sad,' she heard her husband admit. 'Will you come and make it better?'

'Why aren't you crying then?' her daughter asked suspiciously.

But she still climbed on to his lap. Yvette heard how he pressed her to him, groaning.

'People can be very sad without crying,' he said.

'But you never cry!' she said. 'And Mamma cries all the time!'

Yvette tried to swallow the lump in her throat along with the water. Somewhere in her head she heard her own little-girl voice – the same anxious, accusing tone. *Why does Mamma cry so much?* Because my heart is so full, her mother had usually replied. *Why is Mamma's heart so full?* Because I love all my children so unbearably much. *What does 'unbearably' mean?* You'll understand one day, Yvette.

And now she understood, thought Yvette, her cheeks wet again.

'What news of Paul?' Max asked Liane as the two of them sat, wet, on the beach. 'How's life treating him these days?'

She stared ahead of her as though she hadn't heard him, her eyes on the sand castle Adriaan and Emma were building with Mona. A highly unlikely sand castle – as one would expect with Adriaan as architect – a slender tower with irregular holes and inexplicable bumps. Like something dreamed up by Gaudi on one of his off days.

Adriaan and Mona's torsos were bare, both with equally brown pot-bellies. Emma's black bikini covered only the essential bits of flesh at either end of her bulging stomach. Almost like a photo of a naked woman's body on which a censor from the Old South Africa had stuck three black strips. She reminded Max of a highly pregnant version of Botticelli's Venus. The milky white body, with the long red hair streaming over her shoulders.

It was the first time since school, she had admitted earlier, that she'd been brave enough to wear a bikini in public. Which made Max wonder yet again whether he would ever understand women's strange relationships with their mirror images. Emma's long, generously endowed body, with that light sprinkling of freckles, had always been extremely attractive to him. But she had always thought that she was too big to be alluring, her bone structure too heavy, her hips not narrow enough, her buttocks not flat enough. And now that she was eight months pregnant, her body bigger than ever, she paraded on the beach with the confidence of a supermodel – in a minuscule bikini, breasts bulging out of the top, buttocks barely covered by the pants. No, Max decided, this was no demure Renaissance Venus. This was a more primitive kind of goddess, like those clay figures of fat fertility goddesses from earlier civilizations. An unsettling kind of sensuality. He wasn't sure that a man was supposed to find his heavily pregnant friend's exposed body quite so sexy.

'I don't know,' Liane answered at last, when he had already forgotten his question, and ran a hand through her hair. Cut so short that it was already almost dry, while a string of droplets still glistened against her chest like a silver chain. About four fingers from the hollow in her neck. 'He phones me now and then to hear how things are going. And then I tell him how fantastically well the shop is doing. He doesn't have to know about my personal life. And I don't want to know about his. And seeing that he gave me the money to start the shop, I suppose he could be called the father of the baby. Until I pay him back, anyway . . .'

'But you don't have to pay him back, do you? I thought he said . . .'

'I don't have to, but I want to. Every cent. With interest. He tried to bribe me, Max. That's what he did. He thought he could buy my approval!'

'Approval?'

'Of his decision to come out of the closet. As if I wouldn't care about the humiliation. As long as he paid me enough! It makes me feel like a prostitute!'

'But it's not as though he rejected you personally. It's just that you're the wrong sex . . .'

'It feels worse than a personal rejection, Max. I mean, if it was my boring personality or my rusty intellect or my fading looks which put him off, at least I could do something about it! You know, get a face-lift or enrol for some course to make my life more interesting! But it's my sex. Which I can do sweet fuck-all about. It's the worst form of betrayal I can think of.'

'That's not how you should think about it, Liane, it's . . .'

'Who the fuck are you to tell me how I should think, Max!'

He looked at her, surprised, not used to swear words from her lovely mouth, even less used to the high, sharp tone of her voice, reminding him of a bitter old woman. For the first time, he wondered how she would sound thirty years from now. Her determined *joie de vivre* perhaps completely evaporated by then.

It was such an upsetting thought that he looked away quickly, to Ralph and Bobby, who were playing beach bats at the water's edge, as determined as two champions battling out the finals at Wimbledon. At first glance, it looked as though Ralph's tall sinewy body ought to give him an unfair advantage, but Bobby smashed the ball with a power one didn't expect from her slender arms, and intercepted Ralph's shots with an agility only found in someone who was slightly built. Her red-patterned shorts flapped like a skirt around her knees, far too big for her, like most of her clothes.

In the meantime, Adriaan had broken off from adding the finishing touches to the grotesque sand castle and now stood next to Emma with his stomach pushed out. Mona, who apparently had to be the judge of the pot-belly contest, stared open-mouthed at the two bulging stomachs above her head. A few strands of hair blew across Emma's face and twisted like orange snakes through her laughing mouth. Medusa rather than Venus, thought Max. A lovely, laughing Medusa.

'Sorry,' said Liane next to him. 'I didn't mean to sound so bitchy. It's obviously becoming a habit. Each time Paul phones, I change into this queen-size bitch! I can't help myself, you know; it's as though the mere sound of his voice triggers this nasty button somewhere inside me. I can hear how I'm driving him further and further away, how each time he sounds a little cooler than before . . . a little more scared . . . but I just can't stop. It's like a boil that's been lanced – a meanness in my character I've hidden behind a nice smile my whole life long – and now it's threatening to poison my whole self-image. I'm not really such a horrible person, am I?'

'No.' Her pleading voice moved him unexpectedly. 'You've just lost a little of that famous joy de veever.' He pronounced the French words wrongly on purpose, a clumsy attempt to make her smile, but it didn't work. 'And I'm sure it's just a temporary loss.'

'I'm not so sure of that,' she said without looking at him. 'I don't think I'll ever be able to play the role of Pollyanna with conviction again.'

'You'll get other roles,' he said reassuringly. 'An actress of your calibre will always get other roles.'

'What? *Who's afraid of Virginia Woolf?* I don't want to be remembered as a bloody bitch, Max!'

'Would you rather be remembered as a Cheerful Chickadee?' She laughed at last, but it was a shaky, struggling sound, without joy. '*Il n'y a pas d'amour de la vie sans désespoir de la vie.*' This time he did his best to pronounce the French words correctly. 'As Camus said.'

She glared irritably at him.

'Max, I don't know if you make your multi-coloured lovers weak at the knees when you philosophize in foreign tongues, but I understand fuck-all. Speak to me in plain Afrikaans. Or shut up.'

'It means something like, "You can't really enjoy life without sometimes despairing about life." It's something I've been thinking about a lot lately.'

'Why?' Her voice sounded suddenly concerned. 'Do you despair about life?'

'No, on the contrary, it's been years since I was so hopeful. One can't be anything but hopeful about what's happened in the country recently. I was astounded by the absolute . . . euphoria which hit me the day Mandela was released. I stood there on the Parade in Cape Town, among all the thousands of other people who waited for the whole day to hear him speak for the first time, and when he eventually arrived, it was as though something . . . faith or hope, or whatever . . . spilled over me in such waves. I was completely overwhelmed by the intensity of the emotion. And I suspect that it had something to do with the intensity of the despair which I've sometimes felt over the last decade. There were some truly dark days in the Struggle . . .'

'I didn't realize that you ever despaired. You always sounded so sure that everything would be all right one day. You and Bobby . . .'

'No, I never thought that *everything* would be all right. That's just too much to ask. But I did believe that things would improve. That some day we would have a more democratic government in a more democratic country. It's just that there were days when I didn't believe that it would happen in my lifetime . . . When it felt as though the despair was being pulled over my head like a plastic bag . . . as though I couldn't breathe . . .'

'I never allowed myself to feel despair. I carried on like an ostrich and kept my head in a hole and told myself that it wasn't so bad. One could still live in this country. One could still eat in good restaurants and listen to good music and . . .'

'And help other people to decorate their houses,' he added jokingly.

'And help other people to decorate their houses,' she said with a laconic smile. 'And, hopefully, I can go on doing that under a new government, otherwise . . .'

'Otherwise?'

'I suppose I'll have to make sure I can get away.'

'That's not an option for me.' He shook his head emphatically. 'I *belong* here on the southern tip of Africa. For better or for worse.'

'I wish I could feel one-tenth of your commitment!'

'I wish I could have one-tenth of your hedonism!'

'My hedonism-that-was.'

'It'll come back. You'll see. Now that you've discovered the dark side of your personality, you'll appreciate the light side more than ever.'

'You mean now I'll *really* become frivolous and superficial?'

At that moment, Ralph threw his beach bat down and jumped up in the air with outstretched arms, clearly the winner. Bobby laughed at him, stripped off her shorts and ran into the water. As exuberant as a schoolgirl in her black Speedo.

'Look at Bobby, and you'll see what I mean,' said Max. 'She went through hell last year, and yet it's as though she's lighter than ever this weekend. Not more superficial, just . . . lighter.'

'But isn't it easier for her to accept Robin's death now that things in the country are eventually beginning to change? Now that she can see all the sacrifice wasn't for nothing?'

'In one way perhaps it's easier,' he replied thoughtfully. 'But I think she misses her more than ever, now, precisely because of all the changes. Wishing that she was here to experience everything. It's probably just a question of time. I don't think that it heals all wounds . . . but it probably brings a kind of acceptance . . . even if it's just an acceptance of the fact that certain wounds will leave scars for life.'

She stared at the lagoon in silence for a while, watching Bobby and Ralph cleave through the water with powerful strokes. They swam until they grew small in the distance. Then began to float calmly on their backs.

'And Ralph?' she asked. 'Do you think the time overseas healed his wounds? Or drove out some of his demons?'

'Good question. I had lots of time to watch him last week. We drove up to Namibia together, you know. And spent almost every evening celebrating together . . .'

'Why does it sound to me as though the Independence Festival was just an excuse to party all week?'

'You're just sour because you missed it!'

'Ag, no. At the moment, I'm not exactly in the mood for parties.'

'That's like saying the sun isn't exactly in the mood to shine,' he grinned. 'No, you'd have been crazy about it, Liane. It was an incredible experience, as though the entire nation was high for a week. No one slept. Everyone partied day and night.'

'Everyone?' she asked sceptically. 'What about all the white South West Africans who believed that the end of civilization had dawned?'

'They don't count any more. Anyone who still wants to call himself a South West African has had history pass him by.'

'Tell that to my racist cousin in Windhoek. Or my conservative uncle in Swakopmund. They'll call themselves South West Africans till the day they die.'

'Like all the white Zimbabweans who still talk of Rhodesia. All the white dinosaurs who refuse to adapt to Africa. They're all going to die out, Liane, the whole lot of them.'

'You're talking about my entire family,' she said, her head bent, her fingers fidgeting with the sand between her feet. 'I don't necessarily like them – in fact, I think my cousin is an absolute arsehole – but they're still my family.'

'We've all got white dinosaurs like that in our families,' he sighed. 'We can't be responsible for their sins.'

'We've just been talking about you,' she said to Ralph, who had jogged up, dripping, to pick up his towel. 'I was asking Max whether your sojourn in foreign lands had driven out at least a few of your demons.'

'Demons?' he asked with exaggerated astonishment, as he dried himself quickly. 'What demons are we talking about?'

'The whole shebang,' she answered.

He spread his colourful towel out next to her, sat down with a sigh and picked up the packet of cigarettes which lay under his T-shirt. 'Well, I started smoking again, so that's one demon that hasn't been exorcized yet.'

'But you stopped *years* ago.'

'*Years* ago,' he confirmed, and lit a cigarette. 'But it's one of the things that I learned to accept over there. That I'm basically a lazy sod who needs crutches like cigarettes or alcohol to keep me upright.' He inhaled the smoke with an expression of perverse pleasure, slowly, deep into his lungs, before he blew it out again reluctantly. 'I also accepted that I would never write the Great South African Novel – so I could just as well start making money writing a politically correct TV series. And that I would, alas, never live with Mila and two cute little kids in a cute little house in the suburbs.' The wistful expression in his eyes contradicted the light-hearted tone of his voice. 'So I may as well follow Max and become a swinging bachelor.'

'Isn't it a bit late in the day to start swinging?' Liane asked.

'Not if I steal Max's Little Black Book for all his ex-lovers' phone numbers,' he grimaced. 'Anyway, that's my plan for the future in a nutshell. To make more money and seduce more women and be more like my friend Max. Without attending protest gatherings, of course.'

Max watched Adriaan drape a piece of limp sea-bamboo over the already extravagantly decorated tower of sand. Emma lay on her back, her stomach rising like a hillock, her hair spread like a peacock's tail about her head, while Mona arranged pieces of seaweed and broken shells in the orange curls.

'And Mila?' asked Liane. 'What does she think about your new plans?'

'Frankly, my dear, I don't give a damn,' said Ralph with a resigned smile. 'No, I'm afraid all that Mila cares about at the moment is the young Scandinavian she picked up in Namibia last week. He's with her in the Cape at the moment.'

'Is she bringing him with her tomorrow?' Liane asked, suddenly all ears.

'She's scared that it'll spoil the atmosphere if she drags a foreigner along. You know, then we all have to stop talking shit in Afrikaans and try to conduct civilized English conversations. But I think she'd love to show him off. He's quite a dish.'

'If you like gigantic Vikings,' said Max indifferently.

'Who doesn't like gigantic Vikings?' asked Liane, giggling.

'A tall slob with long blond hair and a windswept beard. Looks as though he's just sailed around the world single-handed.'

'He's cool,' said Bobby. 'Even I looked twice when I saw him the first time.'

She had just got out of the water and hunched down next to them, shivering with cold, her towel folded around her shoulders. Without the round-framed glasses, and with her wet hair plastered against her head, she looked even younger than usual. Not a day older than eighteen.

'How did they meet?' asked Liane, her curiosity now properly whetted. 'What was a Viking doing in Windhoek?'

Max gave her a dirty look, irritated by this sudden giggling eagerness to hear more. After she'd spent the last half hour sitting next to him with a face that wouldn't have been out of place at a funeral.

'He's the cameraman for some European TV crew,' said Ralph. 'The whole world's media was in Namibia last week.'

'Now that's what I call good news!'

'That he's a cameraman?'

'No, man, that for once she's having an affair that she doesn't have to hide! She's always involved with . . . the wrong men.'

'I'm sure Yvette's even more delighted,' murmured Ralph.

'But isn't that whole affair . . . ?' A note of alarm in her voice. 'It was over long ago, wasn't it?'

'Ja. And I didn't smoke for *years*.'

'What are you trying to say?'

'Nothing. Just thinking of the proverb about old love which never dies. As my comrade Max can confirm,' he added in a teasing tone.

'I don't think that Mila's affair could make any difference to Yvette's mood,' said Bobby thoughtfully. 'I don't think anything can really touch her at this stage.'

'It definitely touched her when I reminded her of her dead child!' Liane exclaimed. 'I felt like an absolute criminal!'

'I mean that nothing except her dead child can really touch her now,' said Bobby quietly.

'I expected Adriaan to go and comfort her,' said Liane, shaking her head. 'I mean, *I* don't know how to comfort her. But then he just sat there . . .'

'He doesn't know how to comfort her, either,' Bobby tried to explain. 'It's one of the most awful things about such grieving . . . you build a jail out of your own grief . . . and no one can get close to you . . . not even the people you love the most.'

'But he could at least have tried!'

'Perhaps he's tried so often that he's given up.' Without the usual protection of the spectacles, her face looked naked, vulnerable. 'I did the same when I was mourning Robin. I pushed people away from me until they gave up. I was so overwhelmed by my own pain, I was like a wounded dog. If someone wanted to touch me, I tried to bite their hand off. It's a wonder that I have any friends left at all,' she added with a sheepish smile.

Adriaan stepped back a few paces and stood wide-legged, hands on his hips, to admire the completed sand castle. The posture of a farmer looking out over his farm with possessive pride. Max and Ralph looked at each other and began to clap hands dutifully.

'The fragile male ego,' sighed Liane.

'Fucking fragile,' sighed Bobby.

'I also helped, hey!' shouted Emma, still flat on the sand, with seaweed and shells in her hair. 'I just can't take a curtain call right now! It's too hard to get up!'

'Me too!' shouted Mona. 'I helped the most!'

'Not to speak of the female ego!' laughed Liane. That familiar breathless, happy laugh, Max noted with immeasurable relief.

'Are you sleeping?' Yvette looked up from the bed, surprised. Surprised and at the same time disappointed. She had heard someone turn the knob carefully, push the door open and hesitate a moment as it creaked unexpectedly loudly. Thought it was Adriaan. Hoped it was Adriaan.

Bobby's voice sounded scared, she realized with shock. She couldn't see her clearly in the dusky light of the room. From outside, through the closed shutters, her daughter's voice floated in, high and excited. The dog answered the exclamation with an eager bark. Then her husband's booming voice. Even from such a distance it was an impressive sound.

'Ja,' she tried to say, but her voice couldn't scrape past the lump in her throat.

Bobby pulled the door closed behind her and came to sit on the bed. So light that the mattress barely dented.

'I remember,' she said hesitating, her voice little more than a whisper, 'after Robin . . . everyone always wanted me to talk about how I felt. I didn't want to talk. And yet I wanted to. Perhaps I couldn't. I don't know. It was weird . . .'

'Ja,' sighed Yvette. 'It's weird.'

'But now I've begun to talk at last. And it's as though I can't stop. Now it's *really* weird.' She glanced at Yvette quickly, smiled awkwardly, and stared at her feet again. 'So you can relax. I don't mind if you don't want to talk. I just came to exploit you because I want to talk.'

'Talk,' whispered Yvette. 'I'm listening.'

'Ag, you don't even have to listen. It's just . . . easier . . . in a way . . . to talk to you than to anyone else here this weekend. I don't know how you feel . . . but I remember how I felt last year . . . and I know that the death of a child must be even worse than the death of a lover . . . I want to tell you something that I haven't told anyone else. It's a stupid little thing, but it almost drove me crazy, the first few months after Robin . . . died.'

Even after a year, Yvette noticed, she hesitated for a split second before she linked those two words together. As though Robin and death equalled a sum her mind still couldn't process. How long would it be, she wondered despairingly, before she could speak about Pablo's death without feeling as though she was standing swaying over a deep, dark pit? She couldn't afford to vanish into that pit. She wouldn't have the will power to ever climb out again. She waited silently till Bobby spoke again.

'We had a fight, that last morning, because I said she was more committed to the Struggle than to our relationship. I said she took me for granted. She simply accepted that I would play second fiddle while she played Joan of Arc. And she said that I was selfish and childish. Her last words – the last words I ever heard her say – were, "You're still a spoiled little white girl!" And then she closed the door behind her. With great self-control. I would have slammed it with a hell of a racket, of course. And then she was gone. And I never saw her again. And you know what my last words to her were? "Fuck off, Robin." I don't know if she heard or not, because she was already out of the door and I didn't say it very loudly. Half muttered it out of sheer hopelessness. I'll never know if she heard it or not. That's the worst of all. But it's the last thing I ever said to her. *Fuck off, Robin.*'

'Perhaps I should be grateful that Pablo's entire vocabulary consisted of about ten words,' said Yvette, as though she was talking to herself.

'At least I don't have to torment myself about his last words. All he said was, "Tata, Mamma."'

'Do you know how it troubled me that she died with such a low estimation of me? I mean, I *know* I'm selfish and childish, but surely no more than anyone else! But it wasn't good enough for her. She wanted me to be better than other people. That's the trouble with living with a bloody angel!'

'It doesn't count, Bobby. Things that you say to your lover in anger can never be counted against you. If I think about everything I've said to Adriaan . . . That's unfortunately one of the first things you learn when you love someone. Exactly what to say to hurt that person the most. How to do the most damage with the least effort.'

'I know. Of course I *know* that. With the rational part of my mind. But you can't think rationally when you're suffering from shock. And the state of shock lasts much longer than you realize . . .'

Yvette thought about the morning she'd held her son for the last time. As usual, her thoughts wanted to veer away from the sheer drop which suddenly yawned in front of her, but it was as though Bobby's sympathetic presence somehow gave her the courage to look into the abyss. That morning, she'd asked Adriaan to take the children out of the house so that she could work on an illustration. Well, it was a threat rather than a request. And she didn't really want to work. All she wanted was a day on her own. A day of silence and privacy. A day without children. That's all.

Bobby spoke on, but she wasn't listening any more, heard only a soft murmuring in her ears. Almost like the sea during that holiday – the rumbling she lay listening to each night – those two weeks in the hired beach house which changed her life for ever. She had looked forward to it so much – more than she'd ever looked forward to a holiday – because she and Adriaan had been too busy and too tired for the last few months to pay any attention to each other. She had had to finish a series of illustrations for a children's storybook, and Pablo was teething – with difficulty – keeping her awake at night, and Mona was particularly demanding during the day because she didn't get enough attention from anyone in the house. Adriaan painted literally day and night in preparation for the most important exhibition of his life. His MOB Exhibition, as he jokingly called it. *Make or Break*. It was a tense, exhausting, awful time. All that kept her going some days was the thought of that family holiday at the sea.

Of course, she had expected too much. In her depressed state, she had built up a ridiculously romantic, unrealistic dream image. Of intimate conversations she and Adriaan would have beside the braai fire while the children played sweetly at their feet, of lingering moonlit dinners followed by nights of passion while the children slept like angels, of early morning rambles along a deserted beach while the children . . . No, she hadn't thought about what they would do with the children in the morning. It didn't matter, in your dreams you didn't have to worry about such details.

But not even in her worst nightmare would she have been able to imagine the horrors of that holiday. Not just the tragedy with which it ended, but the disillusionment which had grown in her like an ulcer, from the very first day. Adriaan had walked out of the front door every morning before sunrise, fishing rod over the shoulder, and only returned at sunset, burnt raw by the sun, tired of being buffeted by the wind, fed up with struggling against the heavy rod. Too exhausted to talk to her or play with the children. So exhausted that soon after supper he would fall asleep on the couch, often still fully dressed. And the next morning he would walk off again with the rod over his shoulder. Away from her and her ridiculous dream of a romantic holiday, away from the children who had to be looked after and kept busy, away from the house which had to be cleaned and the food which had to be cooked and the dishes which had to be washed, away from the whole filthy reality of a family holiday which began to feel more like a jail sentence every day.

Until she'd put her foot down that morning, too furious to brook any opposition. 'You're taking the children with you today, or I'm packing up and driving home. Then you can enjoy the last few days of your "family holiday" on your own!'

He was completely taken aback by the anger which had simmered inside her for days. 'But I go fishing to relax!' he'd exclaimed, bewildered. 'That's what one's supposed to do on holiday!'

'Exactly,' she'd hissed. 'And I haven't relaxed for a moment since we arrived.'

In the end he had left sulkily, annoyed by her blatant emotional blackmail. Well, that was how he saw it. With his daughter holding his hand, skipping with excitement, and his son snug in a sling on his back. 'Tata, Mamma,' Pablo had said, dribbling, curling and uncurling his fat fist, his head dark against Adriaan's broad back. 'Tata, Mamma.'

'What drives me crazy,' said Yvette in the middle of one of Bobby's sentences, 'is not what I did or said, but what I *didn't* do. If I'd only hugged him that last morning! If I'd just held that soft little body one more time . . .'

She stopped talking as suddenly as she had begun, afraid she would sound sentimental. Actually, she should have hugged all three of them that morning, she thought, so tightly that none of them could ever escape. Because it felt as though she had lost them all.

But she'd been so relieved to have a day on her own that she hadn't even watched them leave. And only two of them came back.

She didn't remember much of the first few hours after Adriaan had walked into the house again. She didn't remember what he'd said – but she would remember for the rest of her life what he looked like. Like one of Bosch's horrific hallucinations, Goya's frightening phantasms, Picasso's twisted figures in Guernica. A nightmare image made up of parts of all the most unsettling paintings she had ever seen.

The hopelessness in his eyes, the way he opened and closed his mouth without a sound, the tears and the blood running down his cheeks. He'd got a deep gash on his forehead while he was in the water, but the blood was fresh, bright red and fresh, because he smashed his head, continually, crazily, against the kitchen wall. His whole body was full of cuts and scrapes and bruises. Most of the wounds would heal after a week or two, but the despair in his eyes would probably never disappear completely. He had learned to hide it, but now and again, unexpectedly, she saw it again like a layer of oil on a pool of seawater. Just a sudden darkening of the grey-green surface. Then she knew that the nightmare was far from over.

Again she heard the soft droning of Bobby's voice in her ears, the sharp shriek of a seagull over the water, the exuberant shout of one of her friends on the beach. She must get up, she realized, she must get up and go outside. She couldn't lie and grieve in a dark room for the rest of her life. There were people outside in the sun, people who loved her, people who were waiting for her. Or perhaps they weren't waiting any more.

It was this unbearable thought which gave her the will power to get up quickly, walk to the window and push the shutters open almost roughly. The room was immediately flooded with blindingly bright sunlight. She had to blink her eyes a couple of times before she could see the little group of people on the beach. They were all there, she realized, her friends, her husband, her child. Even her tail-wagging dog. She turned to Bobby who was watching her with concern.

'Do you know what I want to do now? I want to have a glass of cold wine on the beach. Are you coming?'

'That's the most seductive offer I've heard in a long time,' said Bobby with an eager smile.

'Shame.' Yvette turned back to the window so that Bobby couldn't see her face. 'Sounds as though your love life is almost as boring as mine.'

Late that Saturday night, four of them sat on the stoep with a bottle of Southern Comfort, listening to Janis Joplin, who sounded more alive than ever on a CD Ralph had brought back from overseas. And closer than ever, as though she was singing on the beach just in front of them. Her voice almost bloody with raw emotion. '*Freedom's just another word for nothing left to lose*,' Ralph and Max sang along, both of them a little tipsy.

Earlier in the evening, Emma had announced that she was going to bed early, as befitted a responsible mother-to-be. Besides, it was extremely boring, she explained, sitting there like a Sunday School teacher watching her friends happily getting pissed.

'Ag, no, Emma, stay with us a bit longer, please?' Ralph pleaded. 'One glass of wine surely won't do much harm!'

'I already had a glass of wine while we were eating.'

'You're becoming a martyr, you know? And no child wants a martyr for a mother.'

'I promise you, Ralph, the minute this child is born, I'll become my normal sinful self again.'

'Sin is like any other activity. If you don't practise it regularly, you can forget how to do it.'

'No, I don't want to do anything to spoil this pregnancy,' she said determinedly. 'I'm probably not going to get another chance.'

And with these sober words she and her unborn child went off to bed.

Yvette took the opportunity to excuse herself from the conversation as well. She'd never really been part of it, anyway. More like a ghostly presence among them, an invisible phantom, making everyone feel slightly uncomfortable. A strange thing happened to Adriaan's face as his wife walked out of the room – like a mask being ripped off. Suddenly his expression was defeated.

'I'm afraid I'm going to fade as well,' he mumbled, apparently too tired to open his mouth properly.

For a moment, it looked as though Ralph was going to protest, but he just nodded wordlessly when he saw the plea in his friend's eyes.

'That's good,' Liane said after Adriaan disappeared. 'Yvette needs him.'

'If you ask me, he needs her more,' Bobby said, her eyes wise, melancholy.

Now there were only four of them sitting on the stoep – Max, Ralph, Bobby and Liane – and since three of them had just attended the Namibian independence celebrations, the meandering late-night conversation continually turned back to the subject of political liberation, in Africa and elsewhere. Until Liane cried out that she just couldn't understand why they were all so excited about the New South Africa. The three of them stared at her, speechless.

'OK, I know that for millions of people it's going to be wonderful to vote for the first time and get houses and water and electricity and all those things – but that's not what I'm talking about! I want to know what difference it's going to make to *our* lives – I mean us "spoiled whiteys" – except that morally we'll feel better living in a democratic country. I mean, is anything, practically, going to improve for us? Will we have better schools? Or better hospitals or roads? No, I'm serious!' she exclaimed when Ralph laughed as though he couldn't believe his ears. 'I want to know, because if it is so, then I'll rejoice with you! But I can't just sit here rejoicing when actually I'm dead scared because I haven't got a clue what will happen!'

'None of us knows what will happen,' said Ralph, trying to placate her, after taking a swig from the bottle of Southern Comfort. 'We're all a little scared because we don't know what to expect. But surely it can't be any worse than the past year?'

'Of course it can! That's exactly my point! OK, I know I sound like a typical racist, refusing to share my privileged lifestyle with the rest of the people in the country. But you ought to know me well enough to know that's not what I mean. I'm no *more* of a racist than any other white person in this country.'

'No, Liane, I don't understand what you mean at all,' said Bobby with an angry frown.

'I mean, we're all pumped full of racism from the day we're born. It's like a cancer, Bobby, it's in our marrow. For all that we know, it's in our genes by now! The Afrikaner's Struggle is not the struggle for democracy and liberation of the masses and all those wonderful political ideals, it's the struggle against our own racism. It's the . . .'

'Liane, you can't –'

'No, wait, let me finish,' she said, holding her arm up in the air.

A bare arm, Max realized, for the first time this weekend, without the usual heavy silver bracelets. He wondered if this was part of a conscious paring-down process, like the new short hairstyle; if these bare arms and fingers (even the wedding ring and engagement ring had vanished) were another element of what she, with so much sad pride, called the 'New Liane'. The new, more serious, more disillusioned Liane, he thought, with an unexpected welling-up of nostalgia for the old, more cheerful, more superficial friend he had known since his schooldays.

'It's something I've wanted to say for a long time, something that must be said, but we're all too scared to say it. I just can't wake up one morning and decide, right, now I'm not a racist any more, now I'm never going to have a single racist thought, ever again. Not even when a rude black taxi driver tries to push me off the road! Because that's the hardest of all, isn't it? To keep even your thoughts pure?'

'Well . . .' said Ralph, taking another swig of Southern Comfort.

That was one thing he had to admit, thought Max with grudging admiration. She had always had the ability to cut through theoretical lectures and ideological debates, to get to the practical heart of the matter, with the kind of fearlessness which made most other people recoil in fright. Or perhaps it wasn't fearlessness, just ignorance. Like the child who dared to say that the emperor was naked.

'Sure, all three of you have progressed much further along in this struggle than I have. And even I've learned to hide the slightest trace of any lingering racism. Like a cancer patient trying to hide all visible signs of the disease behind make-up and a wig. But what I want to know, my darlings, is what about that bit of the disease which remains in your marrow. What do you do if you feel it stirring somewhere inside you? Or don't you feel even the slightest stirring any more – not even when you're alone behind the steering wheel?'

'OK, I'll admit that you may have a point,' said Bobby, still staring ahead of her with a frown, at the lagoon which shone blue-black in the moonlight. 'But you're exaggerating, as usual.'

'What do you expect?' Liane's breathless laugh made all three look at her in surprise. 'I studied drama. Exaggeration remains the best way to gain the attention of an unwilling audience!'

'Good. Now that you have our full attention,' said Max after he had taken another mouthful from the bottle, 'what do you actually want to say? That we don't have the right to get excited about the possibility of a democratic country? Just because somewhere deep inside us some traces of racism might remain?'

'No,' she said impatiently. 'I got side-tracked. As usual. Racism is only *one* of the things which scares me. Because we all know that it's not necessarily an Afrikaner disease. Sure, we Afrikaners suffer from it more than most people, but you're going to encounter it everywhere. What about the so-called "reverse racism" you get in America these days?'

'So you're scared of reverse racism if we get a black government?'

'I'm scared of lots of things, Max,' she answered with a deep sigh, and took the bottle from him. 'I know I'm a spoiled white woman who has to accept that my standard of living is going to be drastically lowered. That's OK, I'll be able to cope with it, as long as I can comfort myself with the thought that most people in this country are going to get a better deal this way. But what do I do if the new leaders are just as power-hungry as the bunch we have now? If we have a corrupt black government and most people stay poor and hungry and unemployed? We've been saddled with a white dictatorship for forty years. I don't know about you, but I definitely don't have any desire to live under a black dictatorship for the next forty years!'

'We won't get a black dictatorship,' said Bobby with conviction. 'The leaders in the Struggle are people who *believe* in democracy. In democracy and freedom and all those "wonderful political ideals" which you spoke about just now!'

Liane looked at her like a child who'd heard that Father Christmas didn't exist, but still longed to believe in him. Ralph sat with his eyes closed, as though he didn't want to hear any more, as though he only wanted to listen to Janis Joplin now. The bottle held like a sleeping baby in his arms.

'And what about the ordinary people, Bobby?' Suddenly she sounded too tired to argue any more. 'I don't know the leaders, I just look at the people around me, people of all races. And what I see, every day of my life, is intolerance and hatred and aggression. And bad road manners!' she added with a joyless laugh. 'What difference does it make if the leaders behave like angels and ordinary people stay . . . ordinary people?'

'Ah,' sighed Ralph with the bottle of Southern Comfort at his lips again.

It was ironic, realized Yvette when she woke the next morning, that she and Adriaan were the only surviving 'couple' among everyone here this weekend. Ironic that the only double bed in the beach house was automatically offered to them. Because here they lay like two strangers forced to share a bed, ramrod stiff and uncomfortable at the furthest edges of the caved-in mattress, scared that they might roll closer to each other by accident. Might accidentally touch each other.

But how could they admit to their friends that it had been weeks since they'd shared a bed? That Adriaan slept in his studio these days, and she with Mona in her bed full of teddy bears and dolls, under the duvet cover which she had painted long ago with fat cheerful cherubs, under the ceiling which Adriaan had decorated long ago with his amusing creation scene. Such a light, lovely, playful child's room, she had thought then. How could they explain to their friends that the double bed in their own bedroom had become forbidden territory? Like a battlefield from a recent war, still strewn with land mines and bombs. Memories which could explode at any time.

She lay with her face pressed deep into the cushion, trying to ease a blinding headache. As Adriaan always did when he woke up with a hangover – except she knew this headache had nothing to do with alcohol. It was a pain which made her wake groaning at least once a week, as though an invisible vice had been fixed around her head in the night and screwed tighter and tighter, a pain which made her want to scream as nothing except labour pains had ever made her scream. She knew it had to be psychosomatic, a physical manifestation of an emotional crisis. She didn't need a damned therapist to tell her things which she'd already worked out on her own. As she had snapped at Bobby the night before.

'I don't understand how your mind works,' Bobby had said,

bewildered. 'You saw a therapist before, didn't you? And now that you really need it, you refuse to get professional help!'

How could she explain to Bobby that it took all her will power just to struggle through every day – for the sake of her husband and her remaining child – to get up and make breakfast and tidy the house and fulfil all her daily duties? While she clung to the illusion of family life with constantly growing despair? She simply couldn't afford to devote too much attention to her wounded emotions. To unwrap the bandages and take a closer look at the bloody mess. Who was going to comb her child's hair while she poked around inside herself? But it was impossible to explain to someone like Bobby, someone who could mourn on her own after a loved one's death, without feeling responsible for a husband or a child or the whole precarious structure of a 'normal family', without constantly trying to limit the damage. So she had just said that she didn't feel ready for therapy. She would get to it some time. Which was, in a way, an honest reply.

After all, you can't describe your own drowning while you're still drowning. All you can do is to cling to a piece of driftwood and hope that you'll survive. So that one day, when everything is over, you can tell the story.

And sometimes it felt almost as though the worst was over. As though she was drifting towards some safe beach, not too far away. Like yesterday, when she had walked out of the oppressive room with Bobby to drink a glass of wine at the water's edge. Suddenly she had felt almost carefree, almost happy, almost content. A feeling which was almost strong enough to carry her through the rest of the day.

Until Adriaan followed her to the bedroom last night. He lay down next to her and reached his hand out to her, hesitatingly. It was the first time in weeks that he had tried to touch her. She had thought that her heart would rejoice if this were to happen again. She had thought that her whole body would wake up, singing, if his fingers stroked her neglected skin. She had thought . . .

And then nothing happened. Absolutely nothing. She lay there like a corpse, her heart apparently as dead as her hormones. Maybe it was fear which paralysed her, fear that she would start to cry, that he would realize how precarious her grip on her emotions had become. Or a delayed form of anger, because he had made her wait for this touch for so long, because she had spent so many yearning nights on her own, because maybe he was only touching her now because they were forced to spend the night in a bed together. Or perhaps her heart and her body had indeed died slowly in the last few months.

It was the first time in weeks that they'd had sex. If you could call it sex, she thought afterwards, a few desperate male convulsions on top of a numbed female body. More like necrophilia.

Anyway, it made her realize that the worst was far from over.

She lifted her head as carefully as one would pick up a priceless porcelain jar. As she tried to scrape together the energy to stretch her arm over her husband's sleeping body, to reach the plastic container of pills on the bedside cupboard, her daughter shifted restlessly on the camp bed below the window. She slept on her stomach, in exactly the same position as her father, one leg stretched out and one leg pulled up high, her face turned to the left, away from the double bed, her hair like a layer of golden-brown autumn leaves that had blown over the pillow in the night. Both their hands were folded into fists; his tighter than hers, more angry.

She sank down with a moan into the pillow. The memory of the overflowing joy which a similar scene had given her before – her husband and her two children together in a double bed, sleeping, happy, safe – was almost as painful as the screws slowly drilling through her head. She closed her eyes tight – against the pain which banged in her head, against the memory which hammered at her heart – but she couldn't stop the tears which dripped from her tightly closed eyes. She cried hopelessly, her face pressed into the pillow to smother any sound, until the pillowcase felt as wet as a facecloth against her cheeks.

The moment that Mila walked into the house, the atmosphere changed in an almost unnoticeable and yet unmistakable way. She was wearing a dress which looked long and demure from the front, but which from behind could only with a great deal of imagination be called a dress. Her back was bare and a split in the soft material stretched from her ankles to her thighs. It was as though her mere presence sent shock waves through the room, the seductive clothes and the slender dancer's body and the husky sensual voice, the whole exciting package.

'And here you're all sitting in the New South Africa.' She stood with one hand on her hip, the other one on Mona's head, and viewed the company with a teasing smile. 'And it still feels like the Old South Africa, hey?'

'Not to me!' protested Rehana from the floor, where she was working on a complicated jigsaw puzzle with Adriaan. She'd arrived a couple of hours earlier, on her own.

'Of course not,' Mila said. 'I'm talking about us threatened palefaces!'

'Not to me, either!' Max exclaimed. 'I smell freedom in the air!'

'You smell garlic and basil,' Ralph remarked drily. 'Forget about freedom for a while and chop those herbs. I'm going to need them soon.'

Max gave him an indignant look, but picked up the vegetable knife and went ahead with his humble task. Ralph had loudly offered to give him a free cooking lesson – an offer which he couldn't refuse without scandalizing the women. He had no desire to learn to cook, but he knew it was what sensitive New Age men were supposed to do. He just couldn't understand why Ralph had to turn a simple process into such a long-winded operation. He was making ratatouille, but to Max it looked like an unnecessarily complicated vegetable stew.

Mila sank to her knees to admire Rehana and Adriaan's jigsaw. 'Ah! Something to keep Mona busy!' Adriaan had exclaimed when he found the dusty puzzle box on a shelf in the beach house that morning. While even Max could predict that a four-year-old child would quickly lose interest in a seascape consisting of five hundred minuscule pieces of cardboard in different shades of blue. By this time, Mona had fetched her play dough and begun to build a herd of multi-coloured monsters next to the boring seascape-in-the-making. While Rehana and Adriaan were so engrossed in the puzzle that it looked as though they were going to spend the rest of the day on the floor.

'Good to see you again for a change,' Mila said to Rehana. 'Glad you could make it.'

'Into the New South Africa?' asked Rehana with a sparkle in her dark eyes.

'To Churchhaven,' smiled Mila. 'With Emma's directions, that's quite something.'

'Don't tell me you got lost!' Emma cried.

'Why do you think I'm only arriving now?'

'Well, I thought you were probably struggling to tear yourself away from the young Viking.'

'It's got nothing to do with the young Viking.' Mila's laugh was as seductive as a slow striptease, thought Max. 'Though I might well have ended up in his native land if I'd followed your directions.'

'But it's the easiest road in the world! Johannes, Joe and the rest got here all right! You drive straight from the city till you get to the . . .'

'Remember, I don't know this part of the world as well as you lot who grew up here.'

'That's got nothing to do with it! You just turn right once in the direction of the sea and – '

'Left in the direction of the sea!' Max and Ralph shouted simultaneously.

'I rest my case,' said Mila, arms folded across her chest.

'But you can *see* what side the bloody sea is on!'

'It's OK, Emma,' Ralph consoled her from the stove. 'We all know that you can't differentiate between left and right. It's a good thing that you write fiction and not guide books for tourists.'

'And I must admit, I wasn't really concentrating on the road,' said Mila. 'Before I knew it, I'd already passed the turn-off . . .'

'Well! I would also have problems concentrating if I had a young sex slave hidden in my flat,' said Liane from the stoep door.

She stood with her hand on her hip and a teasing smile on her lips – an unconscious echo of Mila's posture a few minutes earlier – but she looked a great deal less elegant than usual. Her new short hairstyle, clearly not yet combed, stood straight up on her head, a variety of laundry pegs were clamped to various places on her clothes, a piece of lime-green material hung over one shoulder and some lavender serviettes were stuffed down the front of her shirt collar. She was setting the table outside, an apparently simple task which she had tackled as though she was in charge of the décor for an opera. She had brought along a whole collection of table linen and serviette rings and other accessories from her shop, which were now being tried in different combinations, with Johannes and Joe as advisers. Bobby had been sent outside to keep a watchful eye on the spectacle – to make sure that she left some space on the table for food.

'I don't know if you'll believe me, Liane, but my thoughts don't *only* revolve around sex,' said Mila as she sat down next to Emma and Griet at the kitchen counter. 'And I'm not hiding the man away. I left him at home because he needed the rest.'

'That's the problem with young lovers,' Adriaan remarked from the floor. 'They have the passion, but they can't stand the pace. They just don't have the stamina of us older men.'

Mila glanced at him, a knowing smile on her red lips.

'And what about you?' Liane shifted in next to the counter as well, her curiosity overpowering her devotion to the art of table decoration. 'Don't you also need the rest?'

'I'm old enough to have stamina, my darling,' said Mila. 'But listen, let me make something clear, before you start treating me like a paedophile. The man isn't *that* young.'

'How young?' asked Emma.

'Well, he's at least thirty,' answered Mila, lighting a cigarette.

'But that's not young!'

'How do you expect me to feel now, Emma?' She sat with her bare back to Max, which made it difficult for him to chop the basil without slicing his fingers. 'I'm turning forty at the end of the year. When my mother was forty, she was old and cold and over the hill.'

'Well, you're obviously none of the three.' Rehana had torn herself away from the jigsaw and was also sitting on a high bar stool next to the counter. 'So relax.'

'I've heard that a younger man can make you feel about ten years younger,' said Liane. 'As if you've had a face-lift and a tummy-tuck and a liposuction job all at the same time!'

They all burst out laughing together – that high, suppressed, almost hysterical laughter of a group of women busy with 'girl talk'. Ralph squeezed his eyes shut, as though his ears were hurting, and shook his head ruefully. Although Max suspected that he, too, with great enjoyment, was listening to the conversation. It was as though the women around the counter had suddenly turned into a conspiratorial teenage gang, their heads close together and their voices childishly excited. He tried to move the bread board with the basil leaves discreetly closer, painfully aware of the dirty apron around his body and the blunt vegetable knife in his hand. He just didn't have Ralph or Adriaan's ability to wear an apron with such self-confidence that it became an erotic object. He wondered whether it was innate talent or a technique that could be mastered with a little practice. If he ran around his flat now and again with an apron on. Probably all he needed to lose the last vestiges of his masculine dignity.

'Well, either you're going to feel as though you've had plastic surgery,' giggled Mila, 'or you're going to realize that you need it.'

'Why don't you try it yourself?' suggested Griet to Liane. 'You're a free woman, after all.'

'Where the hell am I to pick up a young lover? I can't go and hang out in shady bars!'

'No, those days are long gone! We're living in a new decade. Apparently, the Health and Racquet Club is the best pick-up joint these days.'

'The Wealth and Faggot Club?' Liane raised her eyebrows. 'I don't mean to be nasty, my darling, but with my recent history I'm particularly fed up with moffies.'

'You're not going to get away from moffies anywhere,' said Mila unsympathetically, 'unless you go and shut yourself up in a cupboard.'

'I'll encounter a whole horde of them there,' sighed Liane. 'Hiding in the closet.'

'What I want to know,' said Rehana, 'is where you get the energy. I mean, when I get home in the evenings, I'm so tired that I can't even stroke the cat. And you manage to entertain a young lover!'

That was the problem with getting involved with an ambitious young career woman, thought Max, looking nostalgically at Rehana. Probably the most important reason why their fleeting relationship hadn't worked out. Nothing to do with 'cultural differences' as some of his friends would like to believe. They were just too tired after work in the evenings, too stressed and too irritable to work on their relationship as well. And yet he was grateful that she hadn't, like so many of his other short-lived partners, disappeared from this circle of friends. It was still a joy to watch her, the exotic slant of her dark eyes, the lips which were almost too wide for the narrow face, the hair which fell so smoothly over her shoulders.

'Perhaps you should follow my example and leave your job,' Mila suggested casually.

'You've resigned?' Emma exclaimed, loud enough to draw the attention of the rest of the company.

'Can you believe it? The Namibian independence was my last newspaper story. I wanted to tell you straight away, but you're all so damn inquisitive about my sex life that I haven't had the chance to get to my professional life.'

'I don't believe it!'

'I'm still struggling to believe it. I've been threatening to do it for so many years, and now that I've actually made the leap, it's a bit of an anti-climax. Perhaps I'm just disappointed that the sky hasn't fallen on my head. The South African newspaper industry hasn't collapsed in ruins. The *Vrye Afrikaan* can exist without me.'

'And what are you going to do now?' Ralph was so amazed that he didn't even realize that the peppers were burning on the stove.

'Well, they owe me more than a month's leave, so what I'm going to do first is take a good holiday. I'd like to travel a bit. I'm thinking of freeing the young sex slave in my flat from his chains and black leather outfits and showing him a few nice places in the country.'

'That'll be a change of scenery, at least,' Adriaan observed. 'It sounds as though he hasn't seen much more than a few nice places on your body so far.'

'And then?' asked Ralph. 'When the scenic tour is over?'

'Then I'm going to earn a huge salary,' she said smugly. 'I've had an offer that I can't refuse. Cape editor of a new glossy magazine by the name of *Thina!*'

'*Tina?*' asked Liane with a puzzled frown. 'Like that teen magazine in the seventies?'

'No, man, *Thina!* Like in "*thina lusapo lwayo*". A line from what will probably be our new national anthem,' she added, because Liane was still staring at her uncomprehendingly.

'Are you going to work for a Xhosa magazine?' asked Liane, really puzzled now. 'But you can't speak any black languages!'

'Well, at least I know the words of our new anthem. Which is more than I can say for some of my friends.'

'Cut the crap, Mila,' said Ralph. 'Who are the sponsors of this magazine? The National Party?'

'Ralph! Good grief! I haven't sunk that low yet! OK, I admit, it's lower than snake shit to exchange a pathetic salary at a Struggle newspaper for a fantastic salary at a glossy magazine. But I still have some principles!'

'And where does the fantastic salary come from? Is there anyone in the country – except political parties and crooks – who has enough money left to begin a black glossy magazine?'

'It's not a black magazine,' said Mila. 'It's an ordinary English magazine with a politically correct name. Well, OK, probably not so ordinary. The idea is that it should be more stylish than *Style*, more cosmopolitan than *Cosmopolitan*, more catty than *De Kat* . . .'

'A local version of Andy Warhol's *Interview*, then?' asked Ralph, arms folded, a sarcastic lilt in his voice.

'Something like that,' she answered with a deep sigh. 'And don't ask me who's going to read it, because I haven't a fucking clue.'

'If you send free copies to all your friends,' Emma said reassuringly, 'you'll have a readership of about twenty.'

'I *know* that it all sounds terribly far-fetched. But, according to market research, there is a need for a more upmarket, more trendy, more politically correct local magazine. For white and black readers. Perhaps not quite *Interview*, Ralph, perhaps just a more pretentious version of *Huisgenoot*. But it's the first time in my life that I've been offered a decent salary. I think I have the right to be a little bit excited!'

'How the mighty are fallen.' Shaking his head, Ralph turned back to the stove to rescue what was left of the peppers, a pleased grin on his face. 'Not that I can throw stones. Just look at my brilliant career!'

'Ralph, I'm getting really fed up with the way that you're always running yourself down!' Emma cried. 'One would swear you think there's some heavenly Ladder of Literature with Struggling Novelists beaming on the top rung and Rich Scriptwriters wailing and gnashing their teeth at the bottom. It doesn't work like that! It doesn't matter if you write novels or screenplays or fucking fairy-tales, as long as you write them *well*!'

'You tell him, Emma!' laughed Mila.

'Hear, hear!' Adriaan stood up to fetch another beer from the fridge. 'And at this point I would like to propose a toast to all of you writers. To our charming hostess's first book and our busy cook's first TV series and our sexy journalist's first editorial position. Oh, yes, and our beloved Griet's next fairy tales. May all your pens bear much fruit!'

'You've forgotten about our struggling lecturers' next boring academic papers,' said Johannes from the doorway, drawn by Adriaan's loud speech.

'Not to mention all the notes we poor advocates have to make,' said Max.

'And all the invoices we poor shopkeepers have to write out,' said Liane.

'Perhaps we should just say: *Let's drink to everyone who has ever picked up a pen!*' suggested Rehana.

'Perhaps we should just say: *Let's drink!*' said Adriaan, and raised his beer bottle like a freedom salute.

Yvette was lying on the bed with a damp facecloth on her forehead – not quite awake and not quite asleep – when she heard a soft scratching at the door. Almost like the sound the cat made at home when he wanted to come into a room. Then the door slowly opened and she heard Mila's voice. As hesitant and nervous as Bobby had been the day before. They entered as though this was a terminal patient's hospital room, she thought. Her head so sore that the thought didn't even upset her.

'I hear you're feeling miserable,' whispered Mila. 'I've brought you some of my migraine tablets.'

'I've already swallowed handfuls of pills,' she mumbled. 'It makes absolutely no difference.'

'This stuff is magic!' Yvette stared for a moment, unimpressed, at the two white pills on Mila's palm and closed her eyes again. 'I've been getting the most awful migraine attacks for years. I promise you, by this time I've tried every pill on the market, and these are the only ones that help. You'll see!' Her voice was so urgent that Yvette opened her eyes again and lifted her head reluctantly. Mila sat down next to her on the bed, passed the glass of water on the bedside cupboard to her and watched her swallow the pills. 'Just you wait a bit. You'll begin to feel better quite soon.'

Yvette nodded resignedly and waited for Mila to leave the room. But Mila stayed on the bed, not saying a word. Until at last she reached out her hand and began, almost absent-mindedly, to stroke Yvette's arm. Yvette jerked her arm away and saw Mila's cheeks redden with embarrassment.

'Sorry,' she said miserably. 'I'm not used to being touched any more.'

'It's OK.' Mila swallowed audibly and intertwined her fingers on her lap, as if she were scared that her hands would wander to Yvette's arms again of their own accord. 'There are a few things I also have to apologize for.' Here it comes, thought Yvette, with a strange detachment. Here it comes at last. 'I know you know about . . . about me and Adriaan. I can't tell you how many times I've wanted to tell you I'm sorry.' Something which she had waited for for so many years, thought Yvette. And now she was in so much pain that it hardly touched her. 'But I've always had the feeling . . . even after we ended the thing . . . that it wasn't really over. You know, like a fire that you can't really put out. And I had the feeling that one can't be forgiven for a sin you're still committing. Even though I wasn't . . . physically doing it . . . it was still in my head. You know, the idea that it could flare up again.'

Yvette lay quiet for a long time. She wondered if she was dreaming this conversation. Why did it feel so unreal?

'And now?' she asked at last. 'What made you . . . ?'

'Because it's over,' said Mila quickly, and looked pleadingly at her. 'I don't expect you to throw your arms around me, Yvette. I don't know if you . . . if one can ever really forgive something like this. I just know that it's over.'

'How do you know?' Her voice suspicious. How else? After so many years.

'Because things have happened . . . are happening . . . in your lives for which I blame myself. Which make me feel so guilty that I wouldn't dare to get involved with Adriaan ever again. It's not rational, I know, but perhaps it's good. I don't mean good that it happened, but good that I feel so terribly guilty about it. It shocked me out of my selfishness. It blasted away all my pathetic excuses. It forced me to look at my own life honestly. And I didn't like what I saw.'

'What are you talking about?' she asked, squeezing her eyes tightly shut.

'About Pablo's death,' Mila answered in a dull voice. 'And what it's done to you. Is doing to you.'

'How the hell can you take responsibility for my child's death?' she cried, her voice raw with emotion. 'Who the hell do you think you are?'

'I said it wasn't rational! I can't help it, Yvette! I feel guilty about it. Perhaps not responsible, but guilty. As though my sins were so terrible that they had to be punished in a terrible way . . .'

'Don't you think it's a little bit presumptuous to try to claim the leading role in this drama?' Now her rage burned like a blowtorch. As though she could control it, could hold it away from herself, direct it cold-bloodedly at Mila. 'Don't you think if anyone was to be "punished" in the process, it would be me and Adriaan?'

'That's not what I mean,' Mila murmured pleadingly.

'What *do* you mean then?'

'I don't know . . . I don't know how to explain it . . . without sounding presumptuous . . .'

'You're still a bloody Calvinist, aren't you?' The rage was gone, she realized, as unexpectedly as it had come over her. And suddenly she felt lighter than she had in weeks. Maybe just because, surprisingly, the headache felt lighter. She even managed to pull the corners of her mouth up, a shaky attempt at a smile. 'Guilty you are born, and guilty you will die.'

'I can't help it.' Mila's smile wasn't exactly convincing, either. 'There are generations of guilt in my genes.'

'I only want to know one thing.' It was as though the relief was spilling over her in unstoppable waves, as though she was about to drift away in a sea of infinite relief, completely carried away by the emotion. 'Perhaps it's unfair to ask you, but I think I do have the right to know. When did you . . . stop?'

'We tried a few times,' Mila answered, staring at her entwined fingers. 'But we finally stopped when you were expecting Pablo. OK, as I said, on a certain level . . . in my imagination or wherever . . . it felt as though it was never really over. But for all practical purposes that was the end. When you got pregnant.'

Then she had tortured herself unnecessarily for almost two years, Yvette realized. And yet not. She could sense that it hadn't really been over then. Perhaps it would never really be over, she thought with a strange feeling of tenderness for her friend sitting here with her, for her husband sitting out there with his friends. Still so overwhelmed with relief that the thought didn't really upset her.

This time she was the one who reached out her hand to stroke Mila's arm. And Mila didn't pull her arm away, but stayed motionless on the bed, while tears of remorse, sorrow, relief dripped slowly down her cheeks. Motionless, almost breathless, like a weeping statue.

SEVEN

It's Hard Being a Man (1991)

Emma's blonde daughter sat on the carpet in front of the fireplace, tearing a roll of toilet paper to shreds with almost vandalistic delight. Mona, nearly six years old, stared in horror at the destructiveness of the one-year-old baby she had treated like a cute living doll for the last few days.

'She doesn't show much respect for paper.' Yvette viewed the scene with some amusement from the couch, the piece of colourful knitting in her hands completely forgotten. 'One would never guess her mother was a writer.'

'It's probably because her mother is a writer,' said Emma without looking up from her book. 'I think she already suspects on some unconscious level that it's the only thing which will ever come between us. A piece of blank paper which has to be filled with words.'

'You realize that this is the type of problem she'll be discussing with her therapist one day? *It all began with my mother* . . .'

'Oh, no! I'm not going to fall for that kind of emotional blackmail! She can take out her frustrations on the toilet paper. Just as long as she learns to distinguish between paper which can be torn and paper which must be treated with respect. Till now, she's never, touch wood, torn up a book or a magazine. I'm quite proud of her.'

Quite. What a lie. She was so proud of this child that her heart often felt as though it would burst right out of her chest. She sat in an armchair next to the fire, her legs curled up underneath her, and tried hard to concentrate on the latest Booker Prize winner. With one eye still on the baby – that squint all reading mothers have to learn. But now and again she forgot about the book completely and stared in wonder at her daughter. As pretty as a baby in an advertisement, she often thought, with those wide blue eyes and rosy cheeks and chicken-fluff hair. Although her own judgement was completely unreliable, of course. Beauty is in the eye of the beholder, she regularly reminded herself. And if the beholder is an admiring mother, even the ugliest baby looks lovely. And yet she knew in the depths of her proud heart that Sasha, even objectively viewed, was an enchanting child. The kind who constantly gets compliments from strangers. Usually, she just smiled modestly when a woman in a supermarket or a fellow mother in a park admired her baby – but she often wondered whether they couldn't hear how her proud heart strained to break through her ribs.

'I still remember how we struggled to teach Mona not to scribble on walls,' said Yvette, her eyes again on her busy hands. She was knitting an item of clothing for Sasha, but Emma couldn't work out exactly what it was meant to be. All that was apparent at this stage was that it was definitely not going to be a traditional baby outfit in pastel pink. The dominant shades were cherry red and watermelon pink and aubergine purple, more suitable for a food painting than a little jacket or jersey. 'She saw how Adriaan and I painted walls – and floors and ceilings and furniture, you know what our house looks like – so of course she wanted to do it, too. If she'd done it only at home, it would still have been OK – there aren't many white walls left anyway – but she began to decorate the walls of our poor unsuspecting friends' houses too.'

'I remember,' laughed Emma. 'Didn't she tackle Liane's passageway?'

'Liane was one of the few people who was accommodating. She gave her a bunch of washable felt-tip pens and said, "Scribble away to your heart's content, then your mother and I can chat in peace." Our other friends were less taken with the idea. In the end, we solved the problem by giving her free rein in her room. We said she could do what she liked with her own walls – and then the terrific desire to draw vanished just like that. So at least we knew it wasn't an uncontrollable creative urge which overwhelmed her every time she saw a white wall. More like an uncontrollable rebelliousness because everyone was always telling her she wasn't allowed to do it. Of course, Adriaan saw the whole affair in the best possible light. He said great art always begins with disobedience. You first have to learn to say *no* before you can create. I said, so long as he remembered that juvenile delinquency also begins with disobedience. I mean, how the hell are you supposed to bring your child up if you teach her not to listen to you?'

'If you ask me, that's a typical absent-father theory!' said Emma indignantly. '*Great art begins with disobedience*. Sure. But meanwhile, someone has to teach the kid to eat vegetables and go to bed on time every night!'

'He wasn't absent, then,' said Yvette with an apologetic smile.

'Perhaps not officially. But you were always the one who had to maintain everyday discipline, not so? While the Great Artist locked himself in his studio to create Great Art! I know I sound bitchy, but at the moment I'm extremely irritated by the whole phenomenon of the absent father!'

'But surely, in your case, it was your own choice?' said Yvette, hesitantly.

'Is anything ever really your own choice? You're confronted with a certain set of choices – usually not a huge variety – and you can't choose the best one because you don't have the foggiest idea what the best one will be, so all you can really do is avoid the worst one. In my case, that was obviously to stay married to Philip and raise the child under the same roof as him. But that doesn't mean that it's great to bring up a child on my own!'

Mona carefully tried to take the toilet roll out of Sasha's hand, but Sasha shrieked indignantly and Mona pulled her hand back in fright. It was clear that she'd forgotten how possessive her little brother had been at the same age; how determinedly babies can cling to seemingly unimportant objects. Emma wondered if the child remembered anything about her brother. Except the name, which she sometimes murmured in her sleep.

It was clear that Mona had inherited her mother's eccentric dress sense. This morning, she was wearing a blue and red Spiderman suit and one of Adriaan's old hats. The one with the leopard-skin band, which she always kept close to her these days.

'There's another reason for my bitchiness,' Emma admitted. 'I'm jealous of men. Jealous of their ability to divide their lives into such neat little compartments – work, sex, children, relaxation – each thing in its little pigeonhole, the borders all clearly marked. With me, there's no question of such borders. There's no way I can separate my responsibility towards Sasha from my obsessive desire to write. No way I can lock myself in a room to create Great Art. Whatever I want to create has to be done with a child on the hip and a porridge spoon in the hand, and it definitely won't be Great Art. But, well, I'm not even aiming for greatness any more. I'm only too grateful if I write three paragraphs a day. And I know I can't complain, because the alternative is to go and work in an office again, and leave my child in someone else's care, and that's completely unthinkable to me. But sometimes – just sometimes – I'd like to have the luxury of a pigeonhole. To forget that I have a child for once, so that I can write with complete commitment.'

'I felt like that after Mona was born,' Yvette reassured her. 'Do you remember, I couldn't draw a single picture I was happy with for a whole year? It was as though I was unconsciously waiting for this unproductive phase to pass, to start working again like in the old days, before Mona. And then it struck me one day that I would *never* again work like I had before she was born. It was a scary realization – and yet in some ways liberating. That was when I decided to begin illustrating Griet's fairy tales.'

'And the rest, as they say, is history,' smiled Emma. 'A *Star is Born*.'

'That book saved my life,' Yvette said earnestly. 'It gave me back my self-confidence. But after Pablo died, I stopped working again for a long time, and this time the psychological block was much worse, because it had nothing to do with self-confidence or lack of time or anything like that. I actually had too much time – one child less can make a huge difference to a mother's productivity – but I couldn't even pick up a pencil without bursting into tears. I felt so terribly guilty . . . if it wasn't for my work, my son might still be alive . . . if I hadn't used my work that day as an excuse to send the children away with Adriaan. For almost a year I didn't draw anything, not even practice sketches which I could tear up later, like after Mona was born. Absolutely nothing! That was when I began to knit so frenetically,' she added with a laugh which stuck somewhere in her throat. 'That was my only creative outlet.'

Emma stared at the fire, too ashamed to look her friend in the eye. What did she have to complain about? She had won an award for the book she'd published last year. And her baby sat at her feet, beautiful and glowing with health. Alive.

'What got you going again?'

'I don't know . . . I still can't explain it properly . . . but the moment Adriaan moved out of the house, it was as though the creative floodgates were opened again. The ideas literally streamed out of my imagination. So fast that my fingers could scarcely keep up. It was weird. I think the problem was that, for a year, I was paralysed by the fear that our marriage wouldn't survive the crisis. And when the worst actually happened – when I realized, OK, now I haven't only lost my child, I've also lost my husband – then it was as though in some strange way I felt ... relieved. Like a remorseful criminal being sentenced. Now you know where you stand, you can work off your guilt and get on with your life.'

'Why do you use words like "sentence" and "criminal"? You didn't do anything wrong!'

'It's probably this mixture of Calvinism and Catholicism in my blood. On the one hand, I have feelings of guilt which I can never get away from; on the other hand, the Catholics believe you can buy forgiveness. You know, Father forgive me for I have sinned, and then it's a case of three Hail Marys and off you go. So when Adriaan left me, I immediately saw it in that light. As though I'd paid for my guilt and could go ahead with a clear conscience. Turn over the proverbial new leaf.'

'And the affair with Tomas?' Finally a chance to ask what she'd been burning to ask for days. 'I mean, that's part of the new leaf, isn't it? Didn't that also help to open the creative floodgates?'

'Well ... perhaps yes ... a little ...'

Yvette blushed like a lovestruck teenager, held her index finger in front of her mouth and gestured with her eyes towards her daughter on the carpet. Although the child didn't show the least bit of interest in the conversation; she had begun to page through a coffee-table book in another vain attempt to distract Sasha's attention from the toilet roll. Sasha ignored the book and stared frowning at her fat little hands, at the soft paper which was being crumpled and torn between her fingers, an expression of determined concentration on her face. If she could only focus that kind of attention on a less destructive task one day, thought Emma with extravagant maternal pride, she would go far.

'Do angels use toilet paper, Mamma?'

'Um,' said Yvette, caught off guard by the question. Then she saw that the book was open on a full-page print of a baroque painting. Plump white angel flesh everywhere. 'I don't think they need it.'

'Not even when they poo?'

'Well ...'

'What do they do with their dirty bums?'

'They probably wipe them on the grass ... like dogs?'

'Is there grass in heaven then?'

Yvette looked helplessly at Emma.

'This is waiting for you too,' she said. 'Be warned.'

'Or perhaps they wipe it off on the clouds,' Mona suggested. 'Then the clouds go black from the angel poo. And then Jesus makes it rain to clean the clouds again.'

Yvette began to laugh, a soft, bubbling, infectious sound which moved Emma unexpectedly. It was difficult to believe that this woman had been in such a despairing state last year that her friends wondered whether they would ever hear her laugh again. At one stage she had looked like someone who had been locked in a dark cellar for weeks, her skin sallow and unhealthy, with a lifeless sheen like candle wax, her hair oily and unkempt, her eccentric outfits replaced by a grey chain-store tracksuit, which hung looser about her week by week as the soft plumpness melted from her bones. And now she was sitting there on the couch with shiny black eyes and shiny black hair and a blush to her cheeks, as colourful as a flower garden in a South American waistcoat with complicated embroidery. An earring in the shape of a twisting green snake swinging from one ear. The old Yvette, Emma thought gratefully. Or a phoenix who looked even better than the old Yvette.

Another woman who had crept like a butterfly from the cocoon of a broken marriage. What was it that made so many women blossom after they were forced to give up a relationship? She remembered how she had tried to laugh off her own metamorphosis two years ago as revenge. She knew there had to be a more valid reason, but she still couldn't explain it. Butterflies crept out of cocoons because they couldn't do anything else. That's all.

'Stop it now, Sasha!' Mona suddenly sounded like a despondent little housewife, a frustrated expression under the hat which had sunk down low over her eyes. 'Look how you're messing up the house! It looks like a pigsty!'

'It looks like a pigsty anyway,' said Yvette resignedly. 'Another few pieces of paper on the floor won't make much difference.'

The beach house where they had been staying for the last few days did indeed look as though it had been hit by a hurricane. The floor was strewn with dolls and flippers and books and baby bottles, the furniture draped with damp towels and clothing, the dining-room table invisible under newspapers and children's drawings. And in the kitchen, the unwashed dishes were piled high. It was difficult to believe that nine living creatures – five adults, two children and two dogs – could cause so much chaos. In such a short time.

If Mila and Liane were here, things would never have got so out of hand. Not just because both of them were by nature neater than any of the present guests, but also because they were respectively the owner and the decorator of this chaotic residence. But Mila and Liane were only arriving the next evening. And Paul, the only other person for whom it would be impossible to live in such chaos, couldn't be with them because he had been living in Johannesburg with his lover for the last few months. In a painfully tidy house with a painfully tidy garden, according to Adriaan, who had also moved to Johannesburg recently. Perhaps that was a good thing too, thought Emma, because Adriaan's presence would have upset more than just the house. The same could be said of Philip, but no one had seen him for a year now. As far as she knew, he was still busy with his year's sabbatical at an American university.

And yet it was easy to forget the state of the house each time you looked outside through the wide windows. It was a beach house in the original sense of the word, built literally on the beach, right next to the sea, on solid pillars which were anchored deep in the soft sand. ('A house with legs!' as Mona had shouted excitedly when she saw it for the first time.) The window frames at the front were filled from morning till night with a constantly shifting seascape, changing according to the tides and weather patterns, the angle of the sun and the moon, the play of light and shade on the water. And although the weather had been pretty miserable for the last few days, Emma wasn't bored for a minute while she could sit next to the fireplace and watch the crackling fire and the stormy waves in turn.

This was the house where Mila had spent her summer holidays as a child. After her father's death the previous year she had inherited it, to her astonishment. Her two sisters, who made it quite clear that they would have sold the ramshackle old building, were consoled by large sums of money. ('Makes you think of King Lear and his three daughters, hey?') So Mila had asked Liane to do the house up a little more stylishly. When Emma heard this, she thought back with painful nostalgia to breakfast on a stoep long ago – blue sky and blue sea and blue shutters – and their good-natured joking about the day when Mila would be editor of a magazine and would offer Liane work. *Who knows, perhaps one day I'll also be able to afford a beach house.* Now she was, alas, the Cape editor of a glossy magazine and the proud owner of an inherited beach house. Now she could even afford Liane's stylish advice.

'But you aren't allowed to get rid of the basic furniture,' Mila had warned. 'There's a lot of unnecessary crap which can go – little ornaments and silly pictures and kitsch ashtrays, which my sisters will probably want for their kitsch houses – but the furniture must stay. However ugly it may look to you. It's my "memory bank". That's all I ask.'

Liane had carried out this instruction – which would have made most interior decorators groan, because the furniture was really hideous – with her usual enthusiasm. She had changed the whole boring look of the house by painting the walls in bright colours, lightened the heavy atmosphere by replacing the dark curtains and old-fashioned bedspreads with gauzy muslin hangings and lengths of unbleached cotton, and finished it off by scattering a few brightly coloured cushions about and hanging a few modern posters on the walls. Unrecognizable, Mila had sighed contentedly, and yet as familiar as the back of her own hand.

The question was whether she would recognize it if she were to walk in now, thought Emma anxiously.

'We'll have to do something about this mess,' she said with the determination of a general on the eve of a great campaign. 'Before Mila and Liane arrive tomorrow.'

'Ag, it's not that bad,' said Yvette with forced optimism. 'Surely there must be a vacuum cleaner somewhere in one of the cupboards?'

'Can I hold the vacuum cleaner?' Mona asked. 'Can I, Mamma?' She pressed her hands together beseechingly. 'Please can I hold it?'

'I don't know what I did to deserve this,' said Yvette, shaking her head, 'but my daughter is crazy about housework. Give her a broom and a scrubbing brush and she grins from ear to ear. A vacuum cleaner is enough to inspire religious ecstasy!'

'Please, please, please,' Mona was still pleading.

'It's probably what the feminists call regression,' murmured Emma.

'It's what I call completely unfair!' exclaimed Yvette. 'What did I fight for all these years! To see my only daughter turn into an enthusiastic *Hausfrau*!'

*

'Here's a monster!' exclaimed Max, bending over a rock pool, and tapping with his chisel at a gigantic shell. 'The mother of all oysters! What do you think, Bobby?' He held up his find triumphantly. 'Do you think you can cope with this beauty?'

'Don't dare me,' said Bobby from the next pool. 'You know I can eat more oysters than is good for any human being.'

'Ag, come now!' Max pressed his diving knife into the mouth of the oyster, wiggled the top shell deftly loose and held the bottom half with the piece of juicy sea flesh out to her like a gift on a tray. The shell was big enough to cover his whole palm. 'Live dangerously.'

'But I can't keep on gobbling them up as fast as we can take them out! Poor Emma's mouth has been watering ever since we left this morning. We can't go home empty-handed!'

'There's no question of empty hands!' called Ralph, from another rock pool, and raised his bucket to show her how many he had gathered already. 'And there's lots more where these came from.'

'Oh, well then.' She clambered over the rocks and took the shell without further hesitation. 'Force yourself, doll.'

'And we can come and fetch more tomorrow for our weekend guests,' said Max.

'Tomorrow, we have to help clean the house,' she said after she had swallowed the oyster greedily. 'For our weekend guests.'

'But men aren't supposed to do housework!' cried Max indignantly. 'Men are meant to collect oysters! To go out and hunt!'

'These days, I wonder more and more about what men are really supposed to do,' said Ralph as he hauled himself up on to a rock. 'Are there any guidelines left?'

'I wouldn't know, comrade,' sighed Max. 'Things are becoming more and more mysterious to me.'

'Perhaps you should read a few women's magazines,' Bobby suggested.

'*You* don't even read women's magazines,' mumbled Max, getting out of the water too.

'I don't need to,' said Bobby smugly. 'I *understand* women.'

Max stared at the two dogs chasing each other on the beach. Ghostly shapes in the trails of mist which clung to the rocks and hung low over the sand. One was Mona's four-year-old golden Labrador, the other the young collie dog he'd got for himself three months ago. A man must have a dog, he declared to his friends. The only statement about masculinity he could still make with a measure of certainty, he added jokily.

'Perhaps I should subscribe to *Pastel*.'

'*Palette*,' grinned Bobby.

'*Palette*, *Sarie*, *Rooi Rose*, the whole shebang. If that doesn't help me to understand women . . .'

'At school, the gender roles were crystal clear to me,' said Ralph as they walked back over the rocks to the beach. 'The girls talked about make-up and clothes and tried to stop the guys from going too far when they messed around. The guys smoked and drank and talked about rugby. And tried to go as far as possible, of course.'

'To me, the make-up and clothes were almost as boring as rugby,' said Bobby. 'I always felt as though I fell between two stools and landed flat on my bottom.'

'No, I felt safe in that prescriptive set-up,' said Ralph. 'I knew the rules and tried to follow them as best I could. It was only at university that things got confusing. When I realized that some girls weren't impressed with smoking, drinking, rugby-playing macho guys. Usually the very girls I most wanted to impress. That was the beginning of the end.'

'Of what?' asked Bobby sceptically. 'You didn't stop smoking or drinking. And you're still crazy about rugby. The only difference is that, these days, you look guilty whenever you have to admit it.'

'Exactly. I've become one of those pathetic guys who watches rugby on the sly.' He peeled his wetsuit from his body, suddenly shiveringly aware of the cold, and grabbed quickly at a towel. 'I always have to pretend that I've switched the TV on by chance when there's an important match on – otherwise my female friends might think I'm a typical Afrikaans macho man. And then my whole carefully cultivated image would be screwed!'

He pulled a thick jersey over his head and sat next to Bobby on the damp sand. She threw her weatherbeaten denim jacket over her shoulders and began to rub her hair dry. The mist around them was so thick that it looked as though they were sitting in a steam room, everything hazy and white. Max threw a piece of sea-bamboo to the dogs, who floated through the white haze a little distance from them, and laughed with possessive pride when the young collie grabbed it away in front of the Labrador's nose.

'Ja,' Ralph continued, 'as Lou Reed sings: *It's hard being a man. I can't stand it any more, more, more . . .*'

'Especially if you have to work so hard at your image,' said Bobby. 'And so she forces me to eat my own words.'

'So what exactly did you do to change your image?' Bobby peered at him over the rim of her round-framed glasses. 'Begin reading sensitive love stories? Study articles on menstruation? Take cookery classes?'

'I already began to cook at school. But I'd rather have died than admit it to my mates. Just as I wouldn't admit that I liked classical music. As I said, the rules were clear, I just tried to follow them. The problem was that I learned to like classical music before I learned the rules. My mother's influence. Us kids all had to play at least one instrument, and at weekends on the farm we had concerts with my mother and father. Like the bloody Von Trapp family! There was no way I could tell the guys in my class about those embarrassing musical evenings. Only Stuart knew. The guy who later married Mila. But he was like a brother – and even more embarrassing things happened in his house – so we kept each other's secrets.'

Stuart's greatest secret was even worse than he'd suspected. His father was one of the most respected sugar farmers in the region, his mother one of the prettiest girls in the country in her day. Ralph secretly thought that she also had to be one of the clumsiest women in the country. No other woman in the district stumbled over her own feet or fell down stairs or walked into doors quite so often. Not that he ever saw any of these accidents happen, just the bruises and dark scabs which regularly showed on her body. Until one day he heard a few neighbours talking about her 'drinking problem'. ('On the booze again . . .'; 'Isn't it awful. A woman who has everything in life . . .'; 'Yes, but we mustn't judge . . .') He was shocked, of course, but still relieved to find an explanation for her frequent injuries. He never discussed it with anyone, and simply accepted that he would carry his bosom buddy's secret to the grave.

Only at university did he realize that for years he had kept the wrong secret. One night when Stuart was drunk he grabbed a girl roughly by the shoulders and after that, in a pathetic maudlin state, confessed to Ralph that he would shoot himself rather than become like his father.

('*A fucking wife-beater.*') Only then did it dawn on Ralph that it was Stuart's respected father's violent moods which so regularly left those marks on his mother's body.

Of course, that contributed to his dismay when Stuart decided to marry Mila. After all, he couldn't warn his best friend's new wife (with whom he was still passionately in love) that her husband was a potential wife-beater. But he did decide one thing. If he ever saw those familiar bruises on Mila's body, he would beat up his best friend himself.

And then Stuart died; so young that perhaps there just wasn't time for him to turn into a wife-beater. To this day, he didn't know whether Mila ever discovered her very proper in-laws' guilty secret.

'I had to hide secrets from my schoolfriends, too,' said Bobby, next to him. 'Like the fact that not one of the boys in the first rugby team did anything for me. While there was this long-legged girl in the first netball team who aroused the strangest feelings in me . . . Charlene van Niekerk. I wonder what happened to her.'

'Probably a mother somewhere in the suburbs,' murmured Max.

'No. Somehow I can't see her with baby bottles and slippers somewhere in the suburbs.' Her lenses were so covered with droplets that she probably couldn't even see the sea, thought Ralph. He hadn't realized that it had begun to rain again. 'Perhaps something like an air hostess or a travel agent?'

'We'd all like to preserve a romantic illusion of our first love,' said Max sympathetically.

'Which shouldn't be too difficult in your case. Your first love still looks as good as she must have done at school.'

'Better,' said Max with a crooked smile.

'And she never became a boring suburban mother. I must admit, at one stage I thought she was going to become just another swinging socialite – and if there is one thing that depresses me more than suburban housewives, it's swinging socialites – but then suddenly she transformed herself into a businesswoman. I hear she's going to open a branch of her shop in Johannesburg one of these days!'

'And in Pretoria.'

'She's quite something, isn't she?'

'She always was,' said Max. 'Quite something.'

'What did she see in *you*?' asked Bobby with genuine amazement. 'Weren't you a bit of a nerd?'

'A bit!' grinned Max. 'That's a bit of an understatement. All I was interested in was trying to get the highest marks in the history of the school. I didn't smoke, I didn't drink, I didn't play rugby. My mother always brainwashed me about the dangers of contact sports. That was another one of my problems. I wasn't just a nerd, I was a nerd with a weird mother on top of it all. A white woman who entertained black men in her home. Even at a so-called liberal English boys' school that was something out of the ordinary. So I hung around on the fringes of school life. There's always this kind of no-man's land where you find the cleverest and the stupidest and the weirdos, all the odd cases. Until I met Liane. She was so completely and utterly unattainable that I didn't even try to impress her. In fact, I tried hard to ignore her. But we holidayed in the same building, she with a friend's family on the top floor and me with my weird mother on the bottom floor, so we kept bumping into each other on the staircase. And of course, that was exactly what impressed her, the fact that I didn't seem the least bit interested. She was probably fed up with schoolboys who turned into stammering idiots the minute they came near her. Anyway, it was a tactic I have learned to use on beautiful women, with great success,' he added smugly.

'Ah. I knew you had to have some secret,' said Ralph. 'It can't possibly be your looks or your personality which make all the most beautiful women in the Cape fall for you.'

'Of course it doesn't always work,' laughed Max. 'But with Liane, it worked like a charm. And when the rumour went through the school that I'd swept this absolute stunner off her feet, my reputation changed overnight. Suddenly, I wasn't a nerd who had to be avoided like the plague, but some kind of Don Juan. They probably thought that if I could seduce Liane, I could seduce any girl. But they also reckoned that it couldn't be my looks or my personality which did the trick. That's how the story of my big dick started.'

'So *that's* your secret,' said Ralph.

'It's a legend!' Max brushed a hand over his damp black hair, suddenly a bit embarrassed. 'It's a silly story thought up by a bunch of stupid schoolboys who couldn't believe that the size of your brain could be more important than the size of your cock!'

'But surely every legend contains a grain of truth?' Bobby's face was serious, her eyebrows raised, but her grey eyes glittered behind her wet lenses. 'I mean, the schoolboys must have seen you without your clothes on before they spread the story?'

'Well, I wouldn't say that I have a small cock,' he answered, now thoroughly embarrassed. 'But it's not an ostrich either!'

And with these words he stood up quickly, whistled for the two dogs playing on the rocks and began to jog away over the sand. The dogs followed him with wagging tails and a few exuberant barks, the sounds quickly smothered by the swirling mist.

'It seems that even a big cock doesn't make it easier to be a man,' said Bobby, watching him go.

'The problem is that you always have to pretend that you're not aware of it,' Ralph explained, 'otherwise your friends feel threatened.'

'Do you feel threatened now?'

'No,' he answered seriously. Before he added with an involuntary grin, 'But he said it wasn't *that* big, after all.'

Liane burst breathlessly into the kitchen. 'Well, here we are, earlier than expected, but Mila's new BMW drives like a dream. She says that every time she gets into the car, she decides that it was worth selling her soul.' She smiled swiftly at Emma and Yvette, who were making a salad at the sink. 'The other two have gone to the café quickly. I just wanted to come . . .'

'Two?' asked Emma, rinsing a lettuce off under the tap.

'That's what I wanted to warn you about,' she said, still breathlessly. 'We brought Philip along.'

'Are you out of your fucking mind?' cried Emma.

'Well, it sort of . . . happened,' explained Liane with an anxious frown. 'I bumped into him in town this morning. He's just back from his sabbatical in America and he looked so happy to see me that I invited him to join me for a coffee. Then I told him that we were coming to Stilbaai this weekend and he sounded so inquisitive about how everyone was – not at all his usual sarcastic self, I'm telling you! – and before I knew what I was doing . . . Well, I don't quite know how it happened, but I asked half jokingly: "Why don't you come along, then you can see for yourself?" And he said: "Why not, I don't have any plans for the weekend." What could I do, Emma?'

'You could have thought before you spoke, Liane.' Emma left the lettuce in the sink and lit a cigarette with shaking hands. 'For a change.'

'Ag, come now, Emma, it can't be that bad!' Liane exclaimed, her expression pleading. 'I think the year in America has done him good! He hated the Americans, obviously, but I get the impression that something of their philosophy has rubbed off on him. That positive thing. Perhaps it's infectious.'

'*Positive?*' asked Yvette, crumbling a block of feta cheese. '*Philip?*'

'Well, he's not exactly going to sing *The Sound of Music* when he walks in here, but he sounds less cynical, less negative, more . . . I don't know, perhaps he was just in an exceptionally good mood this morning, but he was really delightful company!'

'He could always be "delightful company", Liane. He's clever, he's witty, he has a wonderful sense of humour . . . Fuck, I was married to the man, I ought to know!' She drew deeply on the cigarette and shook her head. 'But in the last year or two, all his excellent qualities vanished the minute he was near me. We just don't bring out the best in each other. I can already see what's going to happen. We're going to start fighting and spoil everyone's weekend. It's a fuck-up, Liane. It's a mega fuck-up.'

'Relax, Emma. It won't be so bad. You'll see.'

'Not so bad! All I want is a peaceful weekend! Without drama, without tension, without having to watch my words all the time in case someone bites my head off! And now two of my best friends turn up with my ex-husband in tow! Without warning. After I haven't seen him for a year. How would you feel if I'd suddenly dragged Paul in here?'

'Well . . . I probably wouldn't have thought it was a fantastic idea.'

'For fucking sure you wouldn't have thought that!'

'But in the long run it might have been good,' said Liane pleadingly. 'To break through the aggression and the bad vibes for once. To meet each other in a relaxed situation, among friends . . .'

'What the fuck makes you think that a forced weekend with my ex-husband is going to be a "relaxed situation"!' Emma threw her hands up in despair. 'I don't understand it. I just don't understand it. I know that you've always had this naïve belief that everything will work out if everyone just does their bit, Liane, but I honestly can't understand why Mila didn't stop you. At least she's – '

'You too,' said Liane accusingly. 'You also believed that everything would work out.'

'And look where it got me!' Emma exclaimed with a bitter laugh. 'I kept on believing that my relationship with Philip would work out long after everyone around me had lost hope. And now I have to bring up a child on my own and I'm so tired – so tired from morning till night – that I can't even imagine I'll ever have a relationship with another man again! Not to mention ever writing another book. No, Liane, I don't believe that things will "work out" any more. I screwed up. I wised up.'

'Mila said you'd blow your top,' said Liane, shamefaced. 'That's why she pretended to drive to the café. She said I'd invited him so I had to tell you.'

'And Philip? What does he think about the fact that he's obviously not welcome?'

'Emma, the fact that you don't want him here doesn't mean that he's not welcome.' Liane lifted her chin and looked her straight in the eye. 'The rest of the people in this house aren't only *your* friends. We're supposed to be friends to both of you.'

'And they say that the advantage of friends over family is that you can choose your friends!' Emma felt her cheeks grow hot as the truth of Liane's words dawned on her – but she couldn't just let go of her anger. By this time it was like a wave she had to ride till it broke against something. 'Sometimes I wonder if my judgement didn't leave me in the lurch when I chose some of my friends!'

'I wouldn't be surprised,' said Liane. 'You didn't show very good judgement when you chose a father for your child!'

'None of us can boast good judgement when it comes to our love lives.' Yvette had rescued the lettuce from the sink and plucked at the leaves as though she was tearing up an unwanted letter. 'I got married to a bloody Don Juan, and you to a bloody . . . Oscar Wilde, and you to . . . well, to Philip! So I suggest we stop throwing stones and be grateful that our friendship has at least been more durable than our marriages!'

'Oscar Wilde?' asked Liane, astonished.

'Perhaps we should first see whether our friendship survives the weekend.' Emma felt the corners of her mouth lifting, almost unwillingly. The wave had broken. The rage was gone. 'My ex-husband's mere presence is apparently enough to turn me into a hysterical shrew. I can't predict how I'll react if I have to *speak* to him.'

'Oscar Wilde.' Liane began to giggle. 'I'd never thought of it like *that* before.'

'It can't really be worse,' mumbled Yvette, also with a crooked smile, her hands more careful with the lettuce now. 'I'd forgotten about redheads' infamous tempers.'

'It *can* be worse,' said Emma threateningly. 'And it has fuck-all to do with my hair. You know I've dyed it since university.'

'You dye your hair?' Liane's eyes were round with disbelief.

'Don't tell me you didn't know, Liane!'

'No! I got to know you with red hair and I'd always assumed that you were born a redhead!'

'Well, it was always reddish, but more . . . mousy-red. So I thought if I had to have red hair, at least I'd have proper red hair.'

'So you made it psychedelic orange,' said Liane.

'It was never mousy,' said Yvette. 'No woman with mousy hair can throw such terrible tantrums.'

'You think you know someone after fifteen years,' Liane remarked, deflated. 'And then you don't even know what colour her hair is.'

'Listen, Yvette, I've tried very hard to be decent.' Mila stood at the sink, her hands in the sudsy water, her husky voice ominous. 'I reined in my raging journalistic curiosity and didn't ask you straight away about this hot affair between you and Tomas I've been hearing so much about over the grapevine. I hoped you'd say something yourself. But you're as silent as a damned sphinx. So now I'm just going to ask you.'

Yvette's dark eyes slipped, startled, to the window, as though she wanted to flee outside, to the yard where the rest of the company was still sitting in a cosy circle around the fire. It was a cold moonless night, almost too cold to be outside, but after Max had braaied the galjoen and the yellowtail, he'd thrown more wood on the fire and stoked the flames up high again. Now everyone sat as close as possible to the heat, unwilling to exchange the feeling of companionable hardship for the comfort of the house. Emma and Yvette had come inside because they were worried that they wouldn't hear if the children woke up. Mila had followed them, ostensibly to wash the dishes, but it was clear that she was simply looking for an excuse to ask Yvette about her new relationship.

'And Mona is in bed,' said Emma mercilessly. 'So you can't use her as an excuse again.'

'I don't use her as an excuse,' Yvette said quickly. 'It's just that . . . it's better if she doesn't . . . if she doesn't hear too much. She's very vulnerable at the moment. She refuses to believe that Adriaan has gone. She imagines that he's busy somewhere with an exhibition or something. Just a temporary thing. She firmly believes that one night he's going to walk in through the kitchen door again. Probably with Pablo in his arms. And then everything will go on as before, the whole little nuclear family happy together again, as if the last year and a half was just a nightmare.'

'I wouldn't be so surprised if he did decide to come back after all, you know?' said Mila, her eyes on the suds in the sink.

'I don't know,' said Yvette, carefully drying a plate. 'I don't even know whether I want him to come back. A few months ago, I would have done anything to lure him back, but now . . . I'm ashamed to admit it, but I'm rather beginning to enjoy my freedom. I'm enjoying the affair, at any rate. It's the first time in years that I've felt attractive again. I don't know if I'm prepared to give it all up and turn into Adriaan's dowdy little wife again.'

'You were never a dowdy little wife, Yvette,' smiled Mila. 'Not with your way of dressing.'

'No, in the last year I got dowdy. Dowdy and desperate.'

'But now you're looking better than ever,' said Emma, packing away some dry plates. 'So obviously the affair is doing you good. I can't understand why you're ashamed to admit that you're enjoying it!'

'It's more complicated than that . . .'

'Isn't it always?' murmured Mila. 'Just ask me. I can write a thesis on complicated affairs.'

'I still love Adriaan. I'll probably always love him. But I also know that he neglected me . . . that he simply accepted that I would be there when he came back from his . . . adventures. And for years I convinced myself that it was OK, as long as I knew in my heart that I was the woman he really loved, but now I don't think so any more. I mean, I think he still loves me, but it's not OK any more . . .'

'He still loves you,' said Mila, staring out of the window.

'But it couldn't go on like that, Mila. My self-confidence had grown too shaky. My whole view of life had grown too shaky. The further he drifted away from me, the more desperately I floundered after him. But after Pablo . . . I don't know . . . it was as though I didn't have any energy left to flounder any more. I had to let him go and try to save myself. And then Tomas turned up from London . . . for the first while we looked for nothing but comfort from each other . . . talking non-stop about our broken marriages. And then the comfort gradually changed into something more . . . but it happened so slowly that we hardly realized it . . . I mean, there were no earth-shattering emotions when we slept together the first time. It just gradually got better.'

'Naturally,' said Mila. 'Sex is like any other sport. It takes practice.'

'No, I don't just mean the sex, Mila! I mean the whole relationship. I'm enjoying it more and more. All the attention he gives me, the flowers and the chocolates and the romantic messages he leaves on my answer-phone and the Shakespeare sonnets he sends me and the – '

'Shakespeare sonnets?' Emma stared at her in surprise. 'I didn't know Tomas was so romantic!'

'Me neither,' laughed Yvette. 'But Mart always said that he likes acquiring new interests. Projects he attacks with total passion and then drops the minute something else captures his attention. So I'm probably just his "project" for the moment. But I don't mind. It actually makes it easier if I know it's only temporary.' She was quiet for a moment, drying a few knives, suddenly visibly uncomfortable again. 'But I must admit . . . it worries me that he isn't officially divorced.'

'Ah,' said Emma. 'Morality rears its ugly head.'

'No,' she said quickly, 'it's not that. I mean, I don't feel guilty that I'm having an affair, because my husband has had affairs his whole life long, but I feel guilty that I'm . . . having an affair with Tomas. Because he's married to someone I know.'

'But they've been separated for almost two years!' Mila exclaimed. 'He came back to South Africa and Mart wants to stay in England. There's no chance that they'll get back together!'

'What worries me, Mila, is that back then I couldn't understand . . .' She crumpled the dishcloth like a piece of paper, her eyes downcast, her cheeks flaming. 'Well, I couldn't understand how . . . how you could be so unfeeling as to have a relationship with a friend's husband. And now I've done the same thing!'

'It's not the same at all! For god's sake, Yvette, you and Adriaan were together when I began to mess with him. Or he with me. Whatever. Anyway, it's something completely different to go out with a man who happened to sleep with one of your friends a few years ago! Especially if she's in another country!'

'I don't know how Mart feels about it,' said Yvette in her quiet, stubborn way. 'Perhaps it will make her uncomfortable if she sees me again. Perhaps it will make me uncomfortable.'

'You'll probably never see each other again,' Emma reassured her as she put the last knives and forks away in a drawer. 'It doesn't look as though she's ever coming back to South Africa.'

'So why not leave the guilt to those of us who have more to feel guilty about?' Mila pulled the plug and watched as the dirty water gurgled away, a strange smile about her mouth, painted as carefully red as ever. 'Enjoy the affair, Yvette, that's the only advice I can give you. Enjoy it while it lasts.'

Emma was jerked awake by the scream – the same high, heartbreaking, blood-curdling sound – but this time she wasn't as frightened as the first night it had happened. Earlier in the week she'd leaped up in alarm and stormed into the room next to hers. Yvette was sitting up in bed, in the weak circle of light cast by the bedside lamp, rocking her daughter in her arms. She looked at Emma with despairing eyes and said she should go back to sleep. There was nothing she could do. It was only a nightmare.

Only a nightmare.

A dream which could make a child scream like that, Emma had thought, must be worse than anything she could imagine.

The next morning at the breakfast table, Yvette had stammeringly explained that Mona regularly had these screaming nightmares. It had begun a few months after her little brother's death – in the beginning only now and then – but after her father had left, it had got worse. About once a week. At least once a week.

Sorry, she had said, she should really have warned them. But she'd thought that perhaps it was only the memories at home which tortured the child so much. She'd hoped it would get better if she could sleep in another house for a change.

For the rest of the week she had indeed been sleeping better. Perhaps because the fresh sea air and the daily walks in the rain and the constant playing with Sasha made her fall into her bed exhausted every night. Too tired to be troubled by nightmares.

But now it had happened again. She couldn't just leave her memories – like her toys or her cat – at home.

Emma lay in the dark and listened as Yvette tried to comfort her daughter, smelling her own daughter's warm body in the hollow of her arm and stroking her downy soft baby hair. It was so dark that she could hardly see the child's profile on the pillow. And suddenly she felt again that familiar, suffocating fear which had overcome her in dark rooms ever since her own childhood. As though she couldn't breathe. Her hand brushed searchingly over the low cupboard next to her bed, felt around carefully until she reached the bedside lamp. Not to switch it on. Just to feel the switch under her fingers. The comfort that she could drive away the darkness with the slightest movement. If she wanted to.

That's what she'd done as a child to reassure herself. Lay like that with the switch under her fingertips for hours. Her pride as the oldest child had usually kept her from switching on the light; her little brother and sister must also have been afraid of the dark sometimes, but never as panic-stricken as she was, she was certain of that. Her pride and her refusal to let her father see how scared she was. He had little patience with nervous children. He had little patience, period. He was a maths teacher who was bitterly hated by the children in his class. Later he became a school principal who was bitterly hated by all the children in his school. She knew. She was one of those children.

Her only defence against him, the only way in which she could make the other children understand that she was different from him, was to become one of the naughtiest children in the school. But at home she didn't oppose him. It was as though she had to save all her strength for her daily rebellion at school. In front of the other children. Like a stage performance, really.

And at night she lay in her bed, shaking with fear.

Even when she was little, she couldn't seek solace in her parents' bed like other children. Her father had always refused to allow children in his bed. If she had nightmares – as she regularly did – her mother got up quietly, sat on the edge of her bed and stroked her hair until her breathing calmed again. Over the years the nightmares gradually vanished, but the fear of the dark had always continued to plague her.

And there was nothing she could do about it – except to lie like this, with her hand on the light switch. Now, in the dark, she thought of how her mother had often come to sit on her bed of her own accord late at night. While Emma pretended to be asleep – her hand still on the switch – and her mother pretended she didn't know that Emma was pretending. That was the kind of relationship they had always had. Still had now.

There were so many things they didn't talk about. Emma's book, for instance. Her mother was an Afrikaans teacher – with a far greater gift for teaching than her impatient husband. Someone who was able to cultivate a love of literature among promising pupils. But her enthusiasm for Afrikaans writers was apparently limited to dead white men. Well, perhaps a few elderly female poets as well. Corpses and grannies, thought Emma, that's what her mother liked. The younger generation of writers made no impression on her. Or perhaps they did. Perhaps they made her too hot under the collar.

All Emma knew was that her mother was quite proud when the book was awarded a literary prize last year. (She belonged to the generation who still believed in the prestige of literary prizes.) And that she had decided that Emma's father should rather not read the book. And perhaps a good thing, too, thought Emma in her dark bed. Fingers still wrapped around the switch. There were a few people whose opinion of her work she would rather not hear. They had too much emotional power over her. Her father, her mother, her ex-husband . . .

Philip. She wondered if Mona's heartrending scream had woken him. He had always been a restless sleeper – except when he had drunk too much, and spent the night in an almost unconscious state. But tonight he hadn't drunk too much. She had to admit that he had behaved himself extraordinarily well, beyond all expectation. She had thought that the fish braai would be a catastrophe – such a forced togetherness – but everything had gone surprisingly well. There were the usual political arguments, of course. What was a night in Africa without a dose of politics? It helped, at least, to avoid the personal.

'A year ago,' Philip had said in his argumentative way, 'everyone was so excited about the so-called New South Africa. And now it's just the same fuck-up as the Old South Africa. Crime and violence and mutual distrust wherever you look. What makes you think it will ever stop?'

'You can't judge,' said Bobby. 'You've been out of the country for a year.'

'You've been in Disneyworld for a year!' declared Max, throwing a few more logs on the fire. 'You've got used to a sheltered existence at an American university. Not that your existence at an Afrikaans university was ever anything other than sheltered. But I can imagine that Africa would feel a bit rough now.'

'No, it's precisely because I've been away for a while that I can judge now. It always helps to view a situation from the outside – to cut through the crap, as they say in "Disneyworld" – and this desperate enthusiasm for African democracy looks more than ever like a load of crap.'

'No one ever said that everything would work out overnight.' It was clear that Max was struggling to be patient. Clear that Philip still had the inexplicable ability to upset him more than any of his other friends. 'But no one can doubt that things have changed irrevocably. Just think of all the awful laws they scrapped last month! The Group Areas Act, the Population Registration Act, the Native Land Acts . . .'

'But the National Party is still in power. The whites still live like kings – just look at us, sitting around a cosy little fire in Darkest Africa – and the blacks are still fucked. So what has actually changed?'

Emma stared intently at Philip, convinced that he was playing devil's advocate, but the dancing flames threw shadows across his face and his expression was as unfathomable as usual. That was one of the things which had broken her will when they were married. That his face, unlike hers, unlike most people's, often gave no indication of his feelings. On the contrary. He would tell you the most hilarious story with a sombre expression – and a heartbreaking one with a mocking smile.

'Perhaps nothing has changed for us here around the fire,' said Yvette. 'But for our children, for your daughter who's lying inside sleeping, Philip,' she added slowly, throwing each word at him like a small, sharp stone, 'things changed dramatically when the schools were opened up this year. They don't know that anything has changed, thank god, they can sit in a classroom with children of all races, from the start. But I realize it every day when I drop my child off at her nursery school.'

'The fact that . . . my daughter will soon sit in a crowded classroom and be prepared for life by overworked and underpaid teachers, doesn't necessarily excite me.' Emma wondered if anyone else heard the hesitation before he said 'my daughter'. 'That's unfortunately what democracy means at school level, Yvette. It's not just a case of cute coloured faces in every classroom.'

'Do you always have to be such a fucking prophet of doom?' Bobby asked, shaking her head.

'Not in the least! Our own Christian National school education was so astoundingly inadequate in preparing us for life – and yet we all managed to survive, somehow. So I'm confident that our children will also survive their school days. Somehow.'

'Do you know that the emigration figures last year were the lowest in thirty years?' Bobby asked. 'That means that *something* has changed, Philip. Something in people's minds. And, to me, that sounds more important than all the laws which are scrapped and all the schools which are opened!'

'Temporary euphoria,' Philip said. 'Wait until we see this year's figures, then we can talk again.'

Ralph looked up quickly. 'I hate to align myself with Philip, but I hear that thousands of our returning exiles are quite disillusioned. There are some seven thousand of them who haven't found work yet.'

'Welcome to the circle of the scoffers,' Philip grinned, and clapped Ralph on the back.

'He who laughs last . . .' muttered Max, staring at the flames.

'And I hear that in the past two years there were almost six hundred suicide attempts in the army,' Philip said. 'That's the New South African army, mind. Sounds to me as though the soldiers are still just as fucked up as they were in the Old South Africa.'

'Of course the soldiers are fucked up,' said Max, irritated. 'But not as badly as a few years ago. Believe it or not, six hundred suicide attempts in two years is a dramatic improvement!'

'Can you believe it,' Philip mumbled in mock surprise. 'Only in Africa, hey?'

It was bad enough that her husband had remained an enigma to her until the last day of their marriage, thought Emma in her dark bed. But it was even worse to admit that his thoughts were *still* as obscure to her as this moonless night. No question of the wisdom of hindsight. No question, so far, of any kind of wisdom.

She could, for example, not imagine what he would be thinking about now. If Mona's scream had woken him. And it *must* have woken him. Suddenly, she wished that she could go and talk to him, sit next to him on the bed, simply sit next to him, without touching him, and try to explain a few things to him.

'Did you hear that scream, Philip?' she would ask him. 'That's why I didn't want to stay married. That's why I thought it was better that our daughter should grow up without a father from the beginning, rather than lose him after a few years. Because she would have lost you. We both know that. You would probably have done it differently from Adriaan. You wouldn't have gone away: you've already fled from a family once. You would have stayed on in your own house and driven us away from you. As you drove me away from you before this child was born. And then she would have had to learn to live without you. And perhaps also woken up screaming in the night . . .'

And what would his response be to this? She didn't know, she thought hopelessly. She just didn't know.

'Will you tell me Pablo's story, Mamma?' asked Mona in the room next to hers, her voice calm at last, just a little shadow of a sob still lingering about the last word.

'Shhh,' cautioned Yvette. 'We don't want to wake everyone.'

As if anyone could sleep through that scream, thought Emma. She could hear them clearly, because her bed was separated from Yvette's only by a thin internal wall. And it was so dark that she couldn't see the wall, so it felt as though they were lying in the same room.

'Please, Mamma,' begged Mona.

'One day, not so long ago,' began Yvette, 'there was a little boy with hair like soft black seaweed, and eyes which swam in his little face like two dark fish. He had a sister who – '

'You forgot about the ears!' Mona's voice rose high with dismay. 'Ears like small pink shells!'

'Shh. And ears like small pink shells.'

'Don't change the words.'

'Sorry. I won't do it again. Shall I go on?'

'He had a sister who loved him very, very much . . .'

'He had a sister who loved him very, very much, and a Pappa who loved him *and* his sister very much . . .'

Emma wondered if she should block her ears. She felt guilty about listening to such an intensely personal story. Or perhaps just cowardly, because she knew that the ending could only be heartrending.

'They were two very special children, their mother said, because the brother was as soft as a drop of water and the sister was as warm as a sunbeam, and when they played with each other, it looked like it does when the sun shines on the water, enchantingly beautiful . . .'

Yvette was quiet for so long that Emma wondered if the child had fallen asleep again. But then the little voice floated through the wall again, the tone high and cosseting, as though she was speaking to one of her dolls.

'Don't worry, Mamma. You don't have to tell the story any more. Don't cry . . .'

Almost as though mother and daughter had switched places.

When Ralph took his coffee mug to the stoep early the next morning, Philip was already standing there watching the sun rise over the sea. The sky was cloudless for the first time that week, he noticed immediately, the sea as smooth as a mirror. The waves only tiny specks of foam.

'I thought I was the only one awake,' he said. 'I forgot that you also grew up on a farm.'

'Did your father also turf you out of bed if you tried to sleep late?' Philip gazed at the horizon, his elbows propped on the verandah railing. '*Come, come, come! Do you want to lie here like a lazy kaffir till the sun gets up?*'

'Even weekends and holidays,' Ralph confirmed. '*Are you going to stay in bed all day? Like a bloody old woman?* My father was always more sexist than racist.'

'The old bastards,' muttered Philip. 'What's going to happen to them in the New South Africa?'

'What's going to happen to *us* in the New South Africa?' Ralph sat astride the railing and blew thoughtfully on his coffee. 'They're going to be dead in a few years. We're going to suffer for the rest of our lives from the consequences of their misdeeds.'

'Like waking up early on a Saturday morning?'

'If only that was all!'

'But I hear that the New South Africa isn't treating you too badly.'

'As long as I keep churning out PC TV scripts,' sighed Ralph. 'My worst nightmare is that this terrible pressure to be politically correct all the time is going to crack me up. That I'm going to wake up a raving racist one day.'

'A local version of Kafka's *Metamorphosis*,' grinned Philip. 'Why don't you write a story about it?'

'No, I'll leave stories like that for more gifted writers. I've found my humble *métier*.'

The sky over the sea was flecked with pink, an unimaginable variety of shades, from the softest salmon pink to the brightest watermelon. If only he had the words to describe this, thought Ralph. *If only he had the words*. His heart's desire, always.

'At least the payment isn't so humble, right?'

'Ag, well. It pays the bills,' he said jokingly. 'What about you? Do you still have dreams about writing something some day?'

'I don't think I ever really wanted to write. It was an interesting game. Looking for an idea for the perfect story. That one masterpiece which would change Afrikaans literature for ever. But every time I got an idea – and I had a whole lot of them – my desire to write vanished immediately. And now my ex-wife has rather upstaged me.'

'How do you feel about her book?'

'Now you sound like a bloody psychologist, Ralph,' said Philip with a disparaging snort.

'No, I'm really interested in hearing what you think! I mean as an intelligent reader, not as a resentful ex-husband.'

'Well, the intelligent reader thinks it's better than the resentful ex-husband thought it would be.'

'And is that all you're prepared to say? About a book the critics are raving about?'

'The critics rave too easily in this country. And if they don't rave, they dish out blows below the belt. I thought she was too young to handle it. Both the low blows and high praise. I thought she could be a writer one day, but that she had to get more experience first, you know, lose that charming naïvety of hers. But I probably underestimated her will to be a writer.'

'What about her ability to write?' asked Emma from the doorway behind them.

They both swung round in surprise. She stood there with her child on one hip, in a dressing gown of white towelling, with a white towel twisted like a turban about her wet hair. As she had looked on the first morning of her marriage, Ralph remembered suddenly.

'Don't worry, you don't have to answer,' she said with a quick laugh.

'No, I'll tell you what I thought . . .'

'I don't know if I really want to hear!'

'I thought you sounded older and less naïve than I remembered. And that makes you a better writer than I remembered.'

'I'm older than you remember, Philip. And even Snow White would be less naïve if she had to live with a man like you!'

'Well, then I'm glad I could do my bit for Afrikaans literature,' he grinned. 'If you hadn't lived with me, the book probably wouldn't have been as good.'

'If I hadn't lived with you, the book probably wouldn't have existed. One needs a kind of desperate drive to finish something like that. You made me desperate enough.'

'Are you thanking me or insulting me?'

'Let's just call it a grateful insult,' she answered with a wry smile. 'Do you want to hold your daughter?'

'What makes you think she'll come to me?'

He looked at the child in alarm, as downy blonde as a chicken in a sleeping suit of soft egg-yolk coloured cotton. Her eyes the same shade of blue as his.

'Oh, she's a real politician.' She took three steps closer and pressed the child unceremoniously in his arms. 'She'll pose in anyone's arms.'

Sasha looked as though she was going to burst into tears, despite her mother's assurance of social adaptability. Her blue eyes grew even wider and her lower lip began to curl like a soft pink leaf. Philip looked at her in bewilderment for a moment. Then he stretched his eyes in the same anxious way and tried to push his lower lip out as far as possible. The pink leaf froze. She stared at him in surprise. When he did it a second time, she pulled her lip back and rewarded him with a cautious smile. The third time she laughed open-mouthed, and stuck out her fat hand to touch his curling lip. Philip looked worriedly at the bright threads of spit dangling from her jaw.

'If you dribble on me,' he said threateningly, 'I'm giving you straight back to your mother.'

'Ma-ma!' said Sasha, still laughing, still dribbling.

'Pa-pa!' said Philip, pulling a face again and pointing to himself. 'It's time that your frame of reference was extended a little.'

Emma's laugh sounded like a sigh of relief. As long as she didn't expect Philip to turn into an exemplary father all at once, thought Ralph, concerned. She viewed herself as less naïve these days – but at this moment she looked to him very much like Snow White after the dwarves have announced that she can live with them.

Ralph was busy filling two chickens with eighty garlic cloves when Liane came to stand next to him in the kitchen.

'I'm sure you know what you're doing,' she said with that charming crinkle of her nose, 'but aren't we all going to . . . stink terribly for the rest of the weekend?'

'Well, if you view the heavenly scent of garlic as a "stink", you're probably going to have a problem.'

'Paul always teased me about being so sensitive to food smells,' she said with a sheepish laugh. 'Funny, he was never someone who could endure body odours, but garlic and cabbage and that kind of smell never put him off.'

'You're speaking about him as though he's dead,' he said, not looking at her.

'Sometimes it feels as though he's dead. I don't hear from him at all since he moved to Johannesburg. It's my own fault, of course. I didn't exactly encourage him to phone me. But in the last while . . . I don't know what it is, but I miss him . . . just to hear his voice again . . .'

She brushed her hand across her hair quickly, still short and boyish, but not quite as bare about the face as a year ago. Lighter in colour, too, he noticed. Gold sunstreaks which looked so natural that they had to be the handiwork of an exceptionally skilled hairstylist. Still a stripped version of the old Liane, but at least a softer, more natural version of the so-called new Liane who had made her appearance a year ago. Liane van der Merwe, as she introduced herself these days, her despised maiden name now proudly reinstated.

'Why don't you phone him?'

'Embarrassment,' she replied with a shrug. 'False pride. Fear. Whatever. But you saw him last month when you were in Johannesburg, didn't you?'

'Yes.' He added the last garlic clove to the rest. 'He invited me to his house for a drink.'

'What does his house look like?'

He burst out laughing. Surprised at the question – and even more surprised at his surprise. Of course it would be easier for her to ask about her husband's house than to ask about his heart. The inside of a house was, after all, a terrain in which she felt at home. The inside of a soul a far more alien field of experience.

'Impressive,' he replied. 'Everything black and white, very art deco, with old black and white movie posters against the walls . . .'

'Perhaps it was those disgusting orange walls in our sitting room which drove him away, after all,' she said with a melodramatic sigh.

'Ag, no, your colourful sitting room is a lot more interesting than that forced two-tone look. I mean, even his clothes were black and white! I felt so out of place in my multi-coloured T-shirt that I almost asked him if I could borrow something from his wardrobe. So that I could also match the décor.'

'I wonder what he'd say if he could see the sitting room now,' giggled Liane. 'I painted it again the other day, you know. It's no longer orange, it's lime green. With blue accents.'

'I think he'd run away screaming,' said Ralph, amused. 'Like the figure in Munch's painting.'

'Has he become so camp?' asked Liane, shocked.

'No, that's not what I mean. On the contrary. His lover claims that he tries to play Rock Hudson.'

'Did you meet his lover too?'

'Yes.' He moved the casserole with the chickens to the oven, not sure what she wanted to hear. 'He's a director . . . so, naturally, we spoke about screenplays . . .'

'It's kind of sad to me, you know?' she said, her eyes on the floor. 'That Paul has had this secret desire to make movies his whole life long – and now he's sleeping with someone who makes movies. Almost as if he's accepted that that's the closest he'll ever get to his dreams.'

'We all have to compromise on our dreams.'

'That doesn't make it less sad.'

He washed his hands under the tap and looked sideways at her. She leaned against one of the kitchen cupboards, her hands pressed into her trouser pockets. As if she was afraid that her usual dramatic hand gestures would betray her emotions.

'Sure. But I don't think he views it as a compromise. I think he views his previous life as one long compromise.'

'*Sure*.'

It was as though her facial muscles had pulled together involuntarily, in a flash, scarcely a split-second, before she had everything under control again. It made him feel like a heel, as if he had given her an unexpected blow in the stomach.

'Anyway, he gets all this inside info about a subject which has fascinated him for years. And a shared passion is supposed to be an advantage in a relationship, after all. A kind of guarantee that you'll always have something to talk about.'

'We also thought we'd always have something to talk about.' She looked so sad that he wished he could hug her. But she was not the kind of woman who was easy to hug. There was a cold pride in her – or maybe just a fear of being pitied – which had always kept him at arm's length. 'I mean, the sex was never stunning. With hindsight, of course, I can understand why not. The poor man must have closed his eyes and thought of England every time we . . .' This time it was a bitter laugh, dripping from her mouth like aloe juice. 'But it never mattered very much, because we had a stunning friendship. But in the last few months before he left . . . after he had met the director . . . the gap between us grew bigger and bigger. In the end we had nothing left to say to each other.'

That was what Paul had said, too, Ralph recalled. That the worst of all was the silence which hung over them like a shroud in the end. And he had looked just as sad as she did when he'd said it.

His partner had looked at him in concern and put his arm comfortingly around his shoulder. And after that, almost absently, run his hands through Paul's short black hair while Paul began to fidget on the black leather couch, visibly uncomfortable. Riaan had talked on enthusiastically about one of Fassbinder's more obscure films, apparently blissfully unaware of any discomfort in the room.

'Just relax for a bit, Paul,' he'd suddenly said with a cheeky smile. 'By this time your friends all know you're sleeping with a man.'

'But is it really necessary to drape yourself over me every time someone comes to visit?' Paul had asked with barely suppressed annoyance.

'It's your own fault, sweetie pie. You know I get rebellious when you behave like Mary Poppins.' Riaan had looked at Ralph, shaking his head, palms raised in a gesture of exaggerated incomprehension. 'It happens every time someone from his previous life turns up. Then he suddenly becomes all prim and proper. Christ, as though it wasn't enough that the poor man spent thirty years in the closet! You would think he'd enjoy behaving outrageously for a change. Mince around a bit to shock his straight friends. But no, the minute a baby maker walks in here, it's as though someone's stuck a rod up his arse to keep his back straight!'

'If I was in the habit of flapping around the house screaming,' said Paul with his characteristic sardonic smile, 'I would probably have done it when we had visitors too. But you know that's not my style.'

'No,' Riaan said. 'Rock Hudson is more your style.'

'I thought that's why you fell for me. Because I act so deliciously straight?'

'I always forget he's a lawyer.' Riaan's luxurious moustache quivered with good-natured indignation. 'He'll never let you win an argument!'

It could hardly be labelled an argument, thought Ralph. Arguments in relationships usually made him cringe – both as participant and as observer. The venom, the disillusionment, the terrible ability to punish each other with words. While this amusing exchange made him feel more like a spectator at an interesting tennis match. Perhaps they were still too much in love for venom and disillusionment, he thought. But then he remembered that the relationship had started more than two years ago. Perhaps it had nothing to do with being in love, he realized. Perhaps this was a really mature relationship. Two people who were happy to be together, lucky to be together, with enough life experience to realize it. An exceptionally rare species.

'You'll probably be able to be friends again one day,' he said to Liane. 'But you first have to get the divorce over and done with. I mean, I know everyone says that people get divorced too easily these days, but no one could accuse *you* of haste. What are you waiting for?'

'Ag, I was completely crazy the first year after he left. I was so angry that I didn't want to communicate with him at all – not even through a lawyer. And he didn't really have reason to rush me. I mean, it's not as if he could marry his director! So I thought I'd just wait until the worst of the anger was over. Until I could speak to him without exploding. And now it's been so long since I last spoke to him . . . I don't think I'd know what to say any more . . . and I don't want to send him divorce papers out of the blue . . .'

'Why don't you just send a normal letter? Write and tell him you're not angry any more and you want to get the divorce sorted out and you hope you can be friends again one day. Something like that. I'm sure he'll appreciate it.'

'I don't have your way with words, Ralph,' she said, pouting. 'To me it's a scary experience, writing a letter.'

'I don't know if it's going to make you feel any better, Liane, but to me writing a shopping list is a scary experience. I always have to edit everything, compulsively, until it sounds like a bunch of slogans. Buy brown bread! Remember more milk! I'll easily scrap something on my grocery list, doesn't matter how much I need it, just because it doesn't alliterate!'

'Goodness gracious.' She ran her fingers through her hair and smiled sheepishly. 'Well, I know I'll have to do something. It can't go on like this. I mean, if even Emma and Philip can spend a weekend together in the same house – without biting each other's heads off – then there has to be hope for all of us!'

'Honestly, I can't believe you're turning forty,' said Emma, admiring Mila's slender body in black lingerie. 'There isn't a slack muscle in sight!'

'Come on, there's no need to exaggerate,' said Mila – but she sounded pleased with the compliment. She turned to the mirror behind the bathroom door and viewed herself critically. 'I'm definitely getting a belly. Unavoidable, I suppose, with all the hours I sit in front of a computer these days. When I was still a political reporter I got a lot more exercise. Like running from rubber bullets and following toyi-toying protestors,' she added with a smile which hovered somewhere between irony and nostalgia.

'Well, you have to pay some kind of price for the glamorous job you're doing these days!' laughed Emma as she stripped off her jeans. 'With the salary you earn, you could afford a tummy tuck soon, anyway. Not that I think you need it, though. Look at me if you want to see what a belly looks like!'

She moved her T-shirt up, and took hold of her stomach with both hands. Not an appetizing sight, she decided. And she was seven years younger than Mila.

'Well, you have to pay some kind of price for motherhood,' said Mila teasingly. 'And a slight paunch doesn't seem too high a price to pay for all the joy you get from your child.'

'If only it was just the slight paunch,' sighed Emma. 'Unfortunately there are also the varicose veins and the sagging breasts . . .'

She pulled her T-shirt over her head and looked over Mila's shoulder into the mirror. Her body was long and milky-white with fine freckles, her underwear a sporty combination of sober white cotton, panties which covered her stomach up to the navel and a bra which was chosen for support rather than appearance. Mila's smaller, thinner body was a lovely bronze colour (even in the middle of winter), and her underwear a seductive black set of fine French lace, the panties from behind just a thin string between her buttocks, the bra cut so low that it scarcely covered her nipples. You only had to compare their underwear to see that they had a fundamentally different approach to the body. To Mila, her body was clearly still a gateway to pleasure, an impressive construction which had to be well tended and regularly polished. To Emma, these days her body felt more like an old-fashioned castle gate which had to resist the constant onslaught of enemy hordes, as though her daughter's seemingly innocent little body was a dangerous battering ram. There was never time to titivate. Every item of clothing had become part of an armoury, easily washable, non-iron, manufactured from material resistant to baby spit and baby snot and baby vomit and baby shit. Underwear of fine black lace just didn't meet those requirements.

'Ag, Emma, most women's bodies take a knock with pregnancy,' Mila consoled her as she loosened her bra. 'And in your case it doesn't look as though the damage is irreversible. Work out for a few hours a week in the gym and you'll get all your muscles back.'

Emma looked at the breasts which sprang out of the bra like bouncing balls, surprisingly big for someone so finely built, but apparently resistant to gravity. Her own breasts had vanished without trace after a few months of breastfeeding. All that remained were these two empty bags which she tried to bolster with supportive bras. As if that would make them full again. As if anything would make them *bounce* again.

'I *hate* gyms,' she said. 'I tried it after Philip and I split up. I found it unbelievably depressing. All those sweating suckers admiring their bodies in mirrors.'

'How about jogging?'

'Please! That's even worse! It makes me feel like a wobbling bowl of jelly!'

'Swimming?' Mila suggested hopefully. 'You can't wobble if you're in the water.'

'No, drying my hair is too much of a struggle.'

'This is beginning to feel like Twenty Questions. Why don't you make it easier for me, Emma? Is there any form of exercise you approve of?'

'Well, I like walking . . .'

'We're making progress,' said Mila sarcastically.

'But I'm afraid walking isn't going to do anything for these slack tummy muscles!'

Meanwhile Mila had tested the temperature of the water with her hand and closed the taps, satisfied. They had decided to bath together because the ancient geyser wasn't up to the hygienic demands of eight adults and two children.

'I can't believe that you think it's more important to *decorate* the house than to replace the geyser!' Philip had exclaimed that morning, disgruntled after shivering under a cold shower.

'It's more important for my soul,' Mila explained. 'I mean, cold water is a nuisance, but I can live with it, if I must. That's more than I can say of the ghastly wallpaper my mother attacked the bathroom with. Shells and fish in snot green and a strange rosy colour which a friend of mine always describes as "pussy pink".'

'It was bad,' Liane agreed. 'It made you understand Oscar Wilde's last words. *The wallpaper and I are fighting a duel to the death. One of us has to go.*'

'You could have tortured political prisoners by forcing them to stare at that wallpaper!' Mila exclaimed.

Now she sank gratefully into the warm water – her eyes on one of the walls which Liane had painted bright blue after disposing of the hated wallpaper – lifted the glass of gin and tonic she had put within easy reach earlier, and listened with a satisfied smile to the tinkling of ice cubes against the sides of the glass.

'I suppose I really can't talk. The only physical exercise I've ever enjoyed from the very first moment is sex. Apparently all I have a natural aptitude for.'

'Sex? What's that again?'

'The most pleasurable thing which two people can do when there's nothing else to do.'

'Ah. Now I remember why it's been so long since I've done it. It's like tennis. You need a partner, right?'

'Not necessarily. It's like tennis. You can play against the wall. Metaphorically speaking.'

'Then it isn't tennis any more,' said Emma, laughing. 'Then it's playing against the wall.'

'Still a form of exercise.'

'Only your hand gets exercise. And what would I do with muscular hands?'

'Wouldn't it help you to write better?' Mila asked, her eyes innocent.

'I'll think about that next time I masturbate.'

'I thought we were talking about tennis!'

Emma bundled her hair on top of her head, pinned it with two laundry pegs and climbed into the water with Mila. The old-fashioned claw-footed bath was large enough for them to lie fairly comfortably head-to-toe, although Emma couldn't stretch her long legs out completely. She stared at her pale kneecaps, which stuck out above the water like two icebergs.

'I've been celibate ever since I got pregnant,' she said, scowling. 'That's a chunk of two years from what are supposed to be the best sexual years of my life. And sometimes it feels as though I'm going to spend the rest of my life in an exhausted and frustrated celibate state. I honestly don't know how any single mother ever finds the time or energy to begin a relationship again!'

'I wouldn't be able to do it,' said Mila, leaning her head back against the rim of the bath, her long neck a graceful arch above the water.

'What? To be a single mother or to be celibate?'

'Either of the above. I think I've at last begun to accept that I'm going to remain childless. I'm not brave enough to do it on my own. And the men I'm meeting at this stage of my life are either irresponsible toy boys with whom I definitely wouldn't want to raise a child, or very responsible divorced men who already have their own children and don't want any more. Fair enough. My head's accepted it. It's just my damned womb which sends out a desperate SOS every now and again. Like an animal sensing that the end is in sight.'

She closed her eyes. The line of her mouth – which was still painted red, even in the bath – was so sad that Emma stared at her kneecaps again.

'Well, Griet had a child by a toy boy,' she tried to reassure her.

'Griet would have had a child by a gorilla,' said Mila impatiently. 'Let's face it, Emma, she was desperate after all her miscarriages. I'm not desperate. I can live without a child. It's just my fucking uterus which won't listen to reason! Every time I see a newborn baby, it's as though my whole lower body contracts, as if all my reproductive organs are staging a rebellion. Sometimes I wonder if I shouldn't just get the whole damn lot cut out. Perhaps a hysterectomy would make everything easier!'

'I wouldn't be able to live without a child.' Emma sipped her gin and tonic thoughtfully. 'I knew that even when I was still a child myself. I'm not talking about the usual dreams of a mommy and a daddy and two little children. The thought that I might not get a husband was never as upsetting as the thought that I might never have a child. Strange, hey? How you can sometimes sense your future long before it happens. And now, of course, it's more unthinkable than ever to live without a child. If I think that something might happen to Sasha . . . like Pablo . . . my mind just freezes. My mind, my imagination, my heart, everything. So what the hell does it matter that I don't have the body I had before my pregnancy!' She laughed resignedly, balanced her glass on the rim of the bath and began to lather her body. 'If I ever get a lover again, he'll have to accept me, flabby muscles and all. Or pay for plastic surgery. Sounds a more attractive option, anyway, than sweating in a gym every day.'

'Would you do it?' asked Mila, inquisitive. 'Have surgery?'

'Probably not. Not because of a lack of vanity, mind you, but because of a lack of courage. I'm simply too scared of operations.'

'Because of . . . what happened to Philip's child?'

'No. I've always been scared of anaesthesia. The way you lose consciousness, the absolutely helpless state you find yourself in for a few hours . . . It's probably just another manifestation of the Great Fear. My fear of the dark, my fear of anaesthesia. I guess all my hang-ups have to do with my fear of death. That final loss of consciousness . . . and the darkness after . . .' She sat upright so quickly that a wave of water splashed out on the floor. 'And you? Would you have plastic surgery?'

'If you'd asked me a few years ago, I'd have said, *of course not*,' answered Mila with a wry smile. 'I've always said that women must learn to accept their age. Not necessarily with dignity – who the hell wants to grow old and dignified? – but with courage and an adventurous spirit and a kind of defiance. *Fuck youth. Who needs it?* But it's easy to be fearless about old age when the mirror reassures you that you're still young and pretty. Now that my mirror is beginning to sing a different tune, I'm getting more and more scared . . .'

'But you look fantastic for . . .'

'Just don't say I look fantastic for someone of my age!' she cried holding her hand up in the air. 'That's one of those horribly insulting compliments! *For a fat woman you sweat remarkably little.* That sort of thing.' She began to shake with laughter, her breasts jiggling just under the surface of the water. 'I know that I still look reasonably OK, Emma. I can hide the frown lines on my forehead under my fringe, and the lines around my mouth, well, as long as I smile, no one can see them. But I know that I'm going to get wrinkles which I won't be able to hide – not under my hair or my smile – wrinkles which will spread across my face like branches. And I don't know how I'll cope with that. I really don't know, Emma.'

'One probably copes by looking in the mirror a little less,' said Emma. 'Perhaps looking more into your soul? I had a pug-ugly schoolteacher who always used to say: *Girls you must concentrate on The Inner rather than The Outer.* Then we'd giggle uncontrollably, because if you looked like her, you honestly didn't have a choice!'

Mila stared at the glass in her hand, her lovely red mouth disconsolate. 'I've always found The Inner more frightening than The Outer.'

'Like most attractive women.'

'Not you?'

'I've never been able to see myself as attractive,' said Emma with a shrug. 'Except perhaps when I was pregnant. Then I rather liked my body. Apart from the last month or two.'

'You did look good. I remember. But you look even better now.' Mila watched her over the rim of her glass as she rolled an ice cube around on her tongue. 'I've always thought you were the most attractive of all my female friends, you know? If I was a man, you'd be the one I'd want to sleep with.'

Emma was so surprised that she couldn't utter a word. For a few moments, the clicking of ice against Mila's teeth was the only sound in the room.

'If you don't get out of that bath soon,' Ralph called from the kitchen, 'you're going to miss my famous garlic chicken!'

'Ag, come on, Ralph,' Mila shouted back, 'your garlic chicken isn't *that* great!'

'If you don't eat with us,' he shouted threateningly, 'the garlic fumes will drive you out of the house later tonight!'

'Now that's what I call culinary terrorism,' mumbled Mila, and swallowed the ice block. 'Another bizarre crime for the New South Africa. Along with semen theft.'

'Perhaps we should finish up,' said Emma uncertainly.

'Why? He's just jealous because he can't lie in the bath with his buddies!' Her laugh came from deep in her stomach, low and sensual. She took another sip of gin and tonic and shook her head ruefully. 'Most Afrikaans men long for bodily contact with other men! Why do you think rugby is so popular!'

'I don't think my father is going to like your explanation,' said Emma.

'Of course not. Most men aren't even aware that they have this desire. But it must be difficult for someone like Ralph. He's one of the most touchy-feely men I know. And I mean that in a nice way. The way he'll rub your head or throw an arm around your shoulder. You know what I mean. But he's always suppressing this side of his character. If he touches men too much, it makes them uncomfortable, and if he touches women too much, well, that's almost more dangerous than touching men these days. Before you know it, you're charged with sexual harassment.'

'And he's too old to play rugby,' said Emma jokingly.

'Precisely,' grinned Mila. 'So of course he would have liked to bath with his friends. Or perhaps to share a bed with a friend sometimes, you know, like women can share a bed, without ulterior motives.'

She lay back again, her eyes on the ceiling. Made no motions towards getting out of the bath. She hadn't even soaped her body.

'You once said something that I've always wanted to ask you about,' said Emma. 'And now that we're incidentally talking about shared beds . . .'

'Is anything ever incidental?' Mila opened her eyes, big and blue and almost as innocent as Sasha's, and smiled enigmatically.

'You said you'd slept with a woman. I mean sleep . . . with ulterior motives.'

'You mean sleep . . . as in stay awake?'

'Yes,' answered Emma, increasingly convinced that Mila was enjoying her obvious embarrassment. 'Was it just once? Out of curiosity?'

'No. More than once. Out of lust.'

'Do you mean that you get lustful when you look at women?' She sounded far too shocked, she realized, and did her best to keep her voice level when she continued. 'In the same way as when you look at men?'

'Well, I don't get turned on *that* easily!' Her teeth flashed between her red lips for a moment. 'But a certain kind of body is attractive to me. Doesn't matter if it's male or female. It has something to do with length, slenderness, a hint of muscle – just a hint, nothing obvious – a naturally athletic appearance. Like the Viking I met in Namibia last year. That's why still to this day I can't understand why I was so terribly attracted to Adriaan. He's the exact opposite of everything I'm talking about now. Short and broad, with a paunch. Oh well, they say the heart has its own reasons, so the hormones probably have theirs, too. Anyway, that's why I find you attractive. You're the right type. You have that naturally athletic body. Apparently a bit wasted on someone who hates all forms of exercise.'

'I've never seen an athlete with such flabby stomach muscles,' protested Emma with a nervous giggle.

'Adriaan taught me that a paunch can be quite sexy. You don't need to look so frightened!' She laughed again from somewhere deep inside her body, such a round, rich, infectious sound that Emma couldn't help smiling with her. 'I've caused enough problems in this circle of friends by messing with someone's husband. Can you imagine what a catastrophe it would be if I tried to seduce someone's wife?'

'Well, I'm no one's wife,' giggled Emma. 'And it's been so long since I was seduced by anyone that the possibility sounds almost attractive.'

'What's going on in this bathroom?' This time it was Max who called them from behind the closed door. 'You sound like two high-school girls in the back of the school bus!'

'You're the most inquisitive man I know, Max!' Mila called back. 'What two women do in a bath has got absolutely nothing to do with you!'

'Well, whatever you're doing, you'll have to finish up! Philip says Sasha's nappy smells so bad he can't take it a minute longer!'

'Can't he change it?' Emma asked.

Although the mere suggestion was enough to make her giggle all over again.

'He says he can handle a wet nappy, but a nappy full of shit might frighten him off any further paternal duties for ever!'

'They just can't stop threatening us.' Emma stood up sighing and pulled a towel closer. 'Well, let me go and fulfil my maternal duty.'

'You asked for it.'

'I asked for it.' She looked at Mila, who lay back totally relaxed, as though she wanted to spend the rest of the night in the water. 'Perhaps we can continue this interesting conversation another time.'

'Perhaps,' said Mila, with that enigmatic smile again. 'Who knows, maybe one day we'll end up in the same bath again.'

Later that evening Ralph sat with Bobby and Emma on the stoep which looked out over the dark beach. Bobby had rolled a joint – with the excuse that she wanted to smell something other than garlic for a change – and now the dagga fumes hung about them even more pungently than the garlic. But Emma shook her head when Bobby offered her a puff.

'I can't be stoned when my baby wakes up in the middle of the night,' she said with a sigh.

'The joys of motherhood,' murmured Bobby and passed the joint to Ralph.

'Well, seeing that I'm not a father yet,' he said, and sucked purposefully on it.

'Yet?' Emma looked across at him. 'Do you have plans to become a father at some stage?'

'What do you mean? That I should pull up my socks because time is running out?'

'No. You men don't have to worry about biological clocks, after all.'

'No, I can probably wait till I'm eighty and produce a kid or two just before I keel over,' he said jokingly. 'One way to become a father without accepting any of the responsibilities of fatherhood.'

'I was just asking,' said Emma seriously. 'I always thought you'd make a good father.'

'That's what my mother always says.' He inhaled the smoke from the joint slowly. 'I don't know. There was a time in my life when I took it for granted that I'd have a child some time. But now I'm almost forty-two. Nothing can be taken for granted any more. I only wish that someone would explain that to my mother. She still wants to know – every time she sees me – when I'm going to make her a grandmother.'

'But her other children made her a grandmother ages ago!' said Bobby.

'Of course. My oldest sister's children are old enough to make her a great-grandmother soon. But that doesn't make any difference to her desire to see me with a baby in the arms as well.'

Before I die, son. That was the emotional sting in the tail of all her hints in the last few years. When he heard it for the first time, he had burst out laughing. But a few months ago she'd got cancer. Now it wasn't so easy to laugh away her wish.

'My mother also plagued me with hints like that,' said Bobby with a sad smile. 'Probably driven by desperation because I never brought any potential sons-in-law home. And because she doesn't have any other children to nag. But when Robin died . . . shortly after that . . . she stopped. I think it was when it at last dawned on her that she would never see me in a wedding dress. My reaction to Robin's death was just too extreme. She couldn't bluff herself any longer that we were just "good friends".'

'Did she ever speak to you about it?' asked Emma.

'About me being gay?' Bobby began to laugh so violently that she choked on the smoke she'd just inhaled. 'I can't imagine that she'll ever do that! My father even less!'

'But didn't you ever have the desire to confront them with it? Wouldn't it be liberating for you? For all of you?'

'Do you know, Emma, I've already . . . hurt them so much with my political activities . . . and in the end it didn't really make any difference at all. I mean, all our political arguments didn't help us to understand each other. So how would it benefit any of us if I forced my sexuality on them too? It's just another thing which they won't understand. I don't know, perhaps I'm suffering from battle fatigue, but I don't want to fight with them any more. I had Sunday lunch with them recently, and it felt so unbelievably relaxed – so normal, I thought the whole time – as I had always thought it ought to be when you went to your parents' for Sunday lunch.'

'They can't really argue with you any more, can they?' Ralph threw his arms about her shoulders. 'Everything that's happening in the country these days confirms what you've believed for years.'

'Not necessarily,' she said with a sour laugh, her eyes on the glowing cinder between her fingers. 'The fact that the ANC and Inkatha are still murdering each other is further evidence, according to my father, that black people aren't capable of governing this country democratic-ally. He laughs at me when I say that the bloodthirstiness is probably being incited from outside. It's just black barbarity, he says. But I can't even get angry any more when he says things like that. It's as though all my rage against him has vanished, as if for the first time in my life I can look at him and my mother with something like tenderness. They *still* believe that they were right – that God was on their side and all that crap – but they're like Hansel and Gretel, lost in a dark forest. Everything around them has changed suddenly, all the old certainties have disappeared overnight, and now they have to try and cope in some way in this alien environment. It breaks my fucking heart!'

'I don't think we should underestimate our parents' ability to cope.' Emma listened with her head to the side, her hair thrown over one shoulder. A heavy curtain which hung almost to the floor when she sat cross-legged and bent forward like this. 'We're talking about a very basic survival drive. *Adapt or die*. I look at my own parents . . . and it's as though they're suffering from amnesia, as though they just can't remember that they were ever racists . . . And then there are all the other things that they had to get used to in the past year . . . the fact that their daughter wrote a book which has been labelled porno-graphic by a few church ministers and moral guardians . . . and now she's raising an illegitimate child on top of it . . . it's really amazing how well they're coping with it all. My father still hasn't read the book, but if one of his conservative friends dares utter a word of criticism – also without having read it, of course – he shuts him up immediately by saying that ordinary people should hold their tongues about things like literature, which they know nothing about anyway. Sometimes he sounds almost proud of me.'

'And how does he feel about his illegitimate grandchild?' asked Ralph, blowing out the last bit of smoke and crushing the stub out under his heel.

'He did his best to persuade me to stay married until the baby was born. To avoid the "scandal". And I actually seriously considered it. Not because of the so-called scandal, but because I still clung to a shred of absurd hope that Philip would be converted if only he could see the baby. I don't know what I expected. That he would fall to his knees and confess that he'd always really, deep in his heart, wanted to be a father?' Her laugh hung in the dark air for a moment, thin and sad, before she went on. 'But in the end I realized that I was fooling myself. And then it just felt hypocritical to stay married. It's something my father will never understand – that you can rebel against hypocrisy. It's the glue which binds his whole existence, holds all the broken pieces together. Maybe his whole generation's existence. And now the illegitimate baby is winning his heart anyway.'

'Well, she is a charmer,' said Philip behind them. 'And that doesn't mean that I'm "converted". I'm just saying.'

He had come to stand quietly in the doorway, as unnoticeably as Emma had appeared in the same place this morning. It was as though they were continually sneaking up on each other, thought Ralph. As though they were burning to talk to each other, but were too scared to begin a discussion, as if they could only fan the flames of existing conversations. In such a clumsy, moving way.

'I said it was an absurd hope.' Emma lit a cigarette, her head bent over the match flame, her face again hidden behind her hair. 'I suppose any kind of faith is absurd. But I always believed that some time or other you would realize that life wasn't as impossible as you made it out to be. Now I've discovered that sometimes it's even more impossible than you made it out to be.'

'There's nothing like a child to make one grow up fast.'

'Do you mean that I was childish before I had a child?'

'No. But you were more . . . bright-eyed.' Not the slightest trace of mockery in his voice, Ralph noticed, surprised. Although nothing that happened this weekend between Philip and Emma could surprise him more than the mere fact that they were both here, socializing together. 'More optimistic, more believing, more . . . like a child. A very nice child, I must add. Nothing wrong with being childlike. The problem was that you expected me to turn into a child again, too. Believe in fairy tales again. Fairy tales like *The Happy Marriage* and *The Adventure of Parenting*. Jesus, Emma, I couldn't pretend that I was Peter Pan in Never Never Land!'

He took a gulp from the whisky glass he had brought with him, bent forward over the railing and stared at the dark, rushing waves, his back turned to them now.

'No, you were never Peter Pan,' said Emma. 'But I also couldn't pretend that I was Morticia in The Addams Family.'

Philip's back began to shake with laughter.

'And now?' Ralph stroked Emma's hair, fascinated by the soft, thick, sheep's wool texture under his fingers. 'Now that you also don't believe in fairy tales like *The Happy Marriage*? What do you believe in now, Emma Kolêma?'

'Probably in other fairy tales.' She let her head fall against his shoulder, her voice very quiet. Philip turned around and watched her, but it was too dark to see his expression. And even if he could see it, Ralph thought resignedly, it still wouldn't offer any clue to his feelings. 'If you told me two days ago that Philip and I could spend a weekend together in the same house without driving each other to drink and desperation, I would have thought: now *that* was a nice little fairy tale.'

EIGHT

You Can't Always Get What You Want (1992)

Two T-shirts, two pairs of underpants, shorts, jersey, a pair of flip-flops and a swimming costume. He didn't actually like swimming, but one had to do one's bit. If everyone wanted to lie on the beach, he would lie with them. Towel, toothbrush, comb. For the hair he had left to comb. It had become so thin so fast in the past year that he got a fright each time he looked in the mirror. Not that he liked looking in the mirror, but he had to when he shaved. Razor? No, he wasn't going to turn into Hagar the Horrible if he went without his razor for a weekend. And it freed him from looking in the mirror. What else?

He looked at the small pile of clothes and other essentials which lay next to the weathered sports bag on his bed. Surprised, as always, by how little he really needed. And the older he got, the less he needed. Perhaps that was the only art of ageing. To gradually distance yourself from everything unnecessary, so that in the end very little remains to say farewell to. To travel lighter each year, so that death can blow you away without any effort. As you would blow the dust from a piece of furniture. Pfffff.

What else? A book at least. That's what he would find the hardest to leave behind. Already he bought fewer books than in the past, went to the library more regularly or borrowed from friends, but still. Certain books you just wanted to own. And the hundreds he already owned were his best friends. How did you get rid of your friends?

The next question was which one to take. The four he was reading at the moment all lay on the bedside cupboard, next to an overflowing ashtray, three dirty coffee mugs and a glass with the remains of last night's whisky, in which a dead gnat floated. And a framed photo of Mel at the age of two, a laughing boy on a swing, just before the operation. He had only put the photo on the cupboard a few months ago. Only after the child was dead – or after the shadow which had lain almost motionless in a bed for nearly eleven years had finally melted away – could he again look at the child he remembered. A little blond boy who had laughed easily.

But the question, he reminded himself, was which book to take along for a weekend with his friends at Franskraal. An old novel by William Styron, a new biography of Camus, an autobiographical work by Rian Malan, or the latest offering from one of his most productive political-science colleagues which he felt obliged to read. Styron, he decided without too much soul-searching. *Lie Down in Darkness*. Few novelists could write with such conviction about the dark night of the soul.

He had known this darkness from his youth, but it was only recently that he was officially diagnosed as suffering from depression. Last year, after his brain-damaged child's death, his spirit had become so dark – much darker than ever before – that he was forced to seek help for the first time. And he got it – glory hallelujah, as Adriaan would say – in the form of a small pill which controlled his moods. Quite ironic that he, who had always been so scared of any kind of drug, now wandered through life more or less permanently drugged. On prescription from his GP, whom these days he called – with a little bit of mockery, but not without gratitude – Doctor Feelgood. On the other hand, if you viewed alcohol as a drug, he'd been a drug addict for twenty years.

He threw the book down next to the little heap of clothes on the bed and looked around the room in a detached way. Tried to remember if he'd forgotten anything. Realized, in the same detached way, that the room was beginning to look like a hermit's cave. The bed which was last properly made three days ago, the newspapers strewn over the floor, the dirty clothes thrown over a chair and the musty smell in the air – a combination of old smoke and sweaty socks and cold coffee. And he wondered, completely unexpectedly, what Emma would say if she walked in here now. Not that she would ever have won a prize for neatness at school, but she had at least managed to maintain some kind of order when she lived in this house. As long as all unwanted articles were out of sight, shoved in a cupboard or hidden under a bed, she was more or less satisfied. *What the eye cannot see, the heart does not grieve over.* That was her motto when it came to housework. Strange, because as far as the rest of her existence was concerned, it was precisely those things which she couldn't see which upset her the most. All the emotions which he had metaphorically shoved in a cupboard. She would always insist on forcing open the door, looking at the mess, trying to light up the darkest corner with the little flashlight of hope she always carried with her. Until the batteries ran down and she packed a suitcase and vanished.

But he didn't want to think about that now. He didn't want to think about Emma, he didn't want to think about Mel, he didn't want to think of anything except a weekend of hedonism. He zipped up the sports bag, ready to leave as soon as Max arrived. It was the first time in years that he'd done something like this. Borrowed someone's house and invited a few friends to spend the weekend with him. Usually, he just fell in with his friends' weekend plans. And for the last few years he'd been so depressed that even the most seductive weekend party couldn't lure him from his house. But that was before Doctor Feelgood shoved a prescription for Prozac in his hand.

And yet, when he jerked awake in the early morning hours and couldn't fall asleep again, it wasn't so easy to make his thoughts march through the darkness in his head like disciplined soldiers. Things sometimes got out of hand. Mutiny against General Prozac. Then he was tortured by thoughts about wasted opportunities, lost chances, things long gone. À la recherche du temps perdu.

His first marriage wouldn't have lasted, anyway; he was convinced of that. The tragedy which struck the child made it impossible for the parents to carry on with the pretence of contentment. Because by then it had been a performance for a long time. Two actors with nothing to say to each other, forced to play the happy couple. That was why his second marriage was so stormy. He had refused to play-act ever again, fake contentment, suppress dissatisfaction. With Emma, he was intensely happy sometimes, perhaps more often intensely unhappy. But at least there was some emotion involved in the whole affair. It had made him feel alive, not just pretending to be alive. And these days, he knew that his unhappiness had had more to do with his own moods than with anything that had happened between them. Who knows, if he'd looked for help sooner, if he'd surrendered himself to the doubtful mercies of modern medical science, if he'd only . . .

This was the kind of self-reproach which tortured him in the early hours of the morning.

As useless as the speculation about his son's wasted life. If they had only taken him to another hospital to have his tonsils removed, if another doctor had performed the operation, if another anaesthetist was on duty. Reproach which could drive a parent mad. In the first year after the operation, he had constantly hung over the precipice of madness. Only the numbing effect of alcohol could drive away the reproach. Madness which had to be fought with madness. Like snake venom which can only be neutralized by more venom.

If he could only believe in heaven, he thought sometimes. He wouldn't be able to wait to get there. To ask God what the aim of this nasty game was. To let a child lie for almost twelve years in an institution, as still as a plant, and then one day, like a bored gardener, to pull that plant from the earth. *Give me just one reason, God.* Then he might be able to believe again that reason played a part in the universe.

The official cause of Mel's death was complications due to one of the numerous chest conditions he had suffered from. Because he couldn't cough, he could never get rid of the phlegm in his lungs. The medical staff tried to suck it out by pushing a kind of hosepipe down his throat. A hideous business, Philip had thought when he saw it for the first time. But it was even more hideous to see how the child struggled to breathe when his lung became so full of mucus that it sounded as though he would drown. A soft rattling sound which made Philip realize where the phrase 'death rattle' came from. Except that this death rattle kept on, year after year after bloody year.

The clearest memory of the last time he saw his son was the silence. The overwhelming silence which roared in his ears when he held the cold body, much smaller than any other thirteen-year-old, more like the body of a six-year-old child. The terrible, shattering finality of that silence.

'Yes, yes, yes,' said Max as he walked in through the front door, his black and white collie panting from the heat next to him. 'Howzit, my bra?'

'When are you going to learn to greet your friends properly?' Philip asked from the kitchen, where he was packing a coolbag of beer.

'When I turn forty,' grinned Max. 'I'll regard it as an official birthday resolution.'

'Isn't that quite soon?'

'No, hang on, I've got at least two years' grace!'

'Grace for what?' asked Philip, passing him a cold beer.

'Ag, you know, for that last bit of pleasure before old age overcomes me. To play the swinging bachelor for old-time's sake. When I'm forty,

I suppose I can just as well get married. What else remains?' He walked to the sink to run some water for his dog and staggered in mock astonishment when he saw the stacks of unwashed dishes. 'Except to turn into a middle-aged slob!'

'I was a slob long before I became middle aged.'

'Well, you obviously need a woman to stop things from getting completely out of hand. Even if it is only a char to come and wash the dishes now and again!'

'And you'd rather marry some unsuspecting woman and turn her into an unpaid char?'

'No, I'd rather wait patiently for the woman of my dreams,' said Max jokingly. 'In the meantime, my dog will keep me company, I hope.'

He put a square plastic dish down on the floor and watched as Tula slurped up the water. Only then did he twist the beer-bottle cap and take a few thirsty gulps himself.

'As long as you remember that the woman of your dreams tends to turn into the woman of your nightmares as soon as you put a ring on her finger.'

'My worst nightmare is that I'm going to become as cynical as you when I grow up one day,' said Max, shaking his head ruefully.

But Philip's thoughts had unexpectedly made an about-turn. Back to that forbidden territory. Mel. Mel's pointless life. Mel's disorienting death.

When the phone rang late that night and he heard his ex-wife's voice – his first ex-wife's voice – he instinctively knew it had to be the message he had waited for for so many years. Not that he had looked forward to it. He knew it would make the crust around his heart crumble. But it was still with a kind of weightlessness that he had listened to her. A strange, long-lost calm in his head. Even when she tried to slip her dose of religion in, he hadn't reproached her as usual.

'It was God's will,' she said, her voice as hollow as an old mine tunnel, as if all the emotion had been dug out by the patience with which she had waited for a miracle, for almost twelve years. Just a dull echo of grief hanging in the darkest corners. 'We have to accept it.'

What could he say?

When he met her, she was no more religious than any other woman he knew. On the contrary, he had boasted to his friends (joking, as usual, but with genuine admiration just below the surface) that he had at last met a rational woman. A scientific researcher at his university, a cool blonde with ice shards in her blue eyes, a lovely woman who could think like a clever man. The discovery that she was also fairly cool sexually, he viewed as a challenge, of course. Somewhere behind that icy blonde beauty there had to be a spark of lust which he could fan into flame, a glimmering of sensuality warm enough to melt the ice in her eyes. Even if it was only in bed. For years he had searched patiently for that spark, but she had always remained an ice queen.

After Mel's operation, it seemed for the first time as though the ice was melting. Unfortunately, not in the way he wanted it to. She was melting away in despair, he realized, and he was powerless to help her. Until she had grabbed at religion – as desperately as he had grabbed at alcohol – to get a grip on life again. She had begun to believe, praying and glowing, that her son would be saved by a miracle. He had watched the dramatic conversion in astonishment and continued to believe that it would blow over as soon as she had enough energy to face reality. To admit that no one – not even a supernatural being – could do anything about the child's condition. She had been far too rational her whole life long to suddenly surrender to irrational faith. Or so he thought.

Meanwhile he had fled – from a house which had become as cold as a church, from a marriage which not even prayer could rescue, from an existence in which he was continually reminded of a child who was no longer alive and yet was also not dead – fled from Pretoria and came to look for a new life in Stellenbosch. Where Emma had swept him off his feet, mainly because she was so different from Erna. Perhaps it was just the hair, but from the start she had made him think of a dancing flame. Prophetic, he thought later. To live with her was like walking on glowing coals. Mostly painful, but you could forget the pain in moments of ecstasy. Sexual ecstasy on the whole. After he had had to lie for so many years in a bed of snow, it was rapturous to feel his body burst into flame every time she opened her legs for him.

Meanwhile, the ice queen had also met someone else, a recently converted scientist, like her, who joined her charismatic church. They had marrried within months, apparently because sex outside marriage was against their new principles. Philip wondered if he ought to warn the poor man that sex within marriage was also against her principles. But the new husband must have had something else – apart from faith – which he didn't, because the marriage quickly produced two children. Healthy, blonde, laughing, living children. And more were planned. God willing.

'God was good to us,' she had said that night on the phone. 'To you, too. He gave you another child to comfort you.'

'Without asking me whether I wanted another child,' he reminded her.

Not impatiently or intolerantly. As you would state a scientific fact, he thought.

'But surely you're not sorry that you've had another child?'

He could almost hear her eyes widen in incomprehension. The ominous crack of a thin layer of ice. The water underneath deadly cold.

'That's not the point, Erna.' Perhaps a fraction less patiently. Just a fraction. 'I love my daughter as I love my son. Not because they've been "given" to me, but despite the fact that they've been "given" to me.'

'Oh, Philip,' she'd sighed. 'I'll never understand you. But I'll keep praying for you.'

Perhaps, he said to himself, you should be grateful for every scrap of support life offers you. Even if it is in the form of your ex-wife's prayers.

When he put the phone down, he was still extraordinarily calm. No sign of the frightening emotions that were supposed to overcome a parent when a child died. He had had almost twelve years to wrestle with these emotions, after all. Disbelief and denial, despair and rage, guilt and self-reproach, and all the others. Now that the child had died at last, he consoled himself, the worst was over.

But when he saw Mel's body the next day, when that awful stillness thundered in his ears, his chest began to heave unexpectedly. Something you could probably have called sobbing, except there were no tears to dissolve the sound. As he listened in bewilderment to these unearthly noises, it dawned on him that there was one emotion which he had avoided for twelve years. Grief.

Ordinary, extraordinary, essential grief.

*

'You're in an exceptionally cheerful mood,' said Philip as they drove over Sir Lowry's Pass in Max's old blue Toyota; False Bay like a glossy blue and green bedspread thrown open beneath them, the sea satin-smooth on this sweltering summer day. Max had switched on the car radio and begun to whistle along with some mindless pop song, the corners of his mouth pulled up in an equally mindless smile. 'Is the Bar treating you that well?'

'Ag, man, I'm always blown about by the winds of political change.' The smile had now spread to the crinkles at his eyes. 'After the negotiations collapsed last year, things began to look dark and miserable again. But now – with Codesa on the go and the referendum next month – now I smell optimism in the air again.'

'Isn't it just bullshit that you're smelling?' Philip asked. 'The same bullshit as with the previous referendum?'

'No, the previous referendum was a completely different matter! It was about a limited measure of power being handed over to a limited part of the population. The kind of question to which you couldn't possibly answer yes *or* no without sacrificing your principles. This time the question is a lot clearer. The white population must decide whether they want democracy. Yes or no.'

'I understand the question, but I don't understand your optimism.'

'It would be self-destructive to vote no! No nation can be that stupid. Not even the bastards who've fucked this country up for forty years.'

'I think there are a lot of white people in this country who would choose self-destruction above black rule,' said Philip as they drove over the saddle of the pass. 'Because black domination just means a slower form of self-destruction to them, anyway. So I can only hope your optimism bears fruit, Comrade Ackermann. Otherwise we're talking blood in the streets.'

'Perhaps that's what whites in this country need,' said Max. 'For the blood in the streets of the townships to spill over to Voortrekker Road and Church Street. If that doesn't wake them up, nothing will.'

He fiddled with the radio knob because the reception had worsened now that they were driving on the other side of the mountain. Once again began to whistle determinedly along with a cheerful pop song. *Don't Worry Be Happy.* Philip stared frowning at the road which twisted between dark green pine forests like a black snake, irritated by the whistling next to him and even more irritated by the ridiculous song.

'And what do you think about the referendum next month?' Liane noticed Yvette's surprised expression, but kept her voice casual, as though she was talking about a new carpet in her sitting room. 'Do you think it's going to work?'

'Well, it depends on what you mean by "work",' Yvette replied hesitantly. 'It sounds as though there's a good chance that the result will be positive. But there are a lot of people who are not going to be happy with a positive result.'

'My father always says, if you want to see the shit hit the fan, you must try to drive the Afrikaner into a corner.' She glanced quickly in the rear-view mirror at Mona, who was playing with a Barbie doll on the back seat of the old Mercedes, Tat's golden body asleep next to her. 'Sorry, that's how my father talks.'

'It's not just Afrikaners who frighten me. Sometimes it feels to me as if all the worst racists from all over the world have come to seek shelter here on the southern tip of Africa. As if it's become a last stand for intolerance. There's nowhere else they can flee to, is there?'

'How far can rabbits hear?' Mona wanted to know out of the blue. 'From here to the car in front of us? Or from here to the mountain?'

'I thought now that she's going to school,' sighed Yvette, 'she would save her impossible questions for her teacher.'

'I did ask the teacher,' said Mona impatiently. 'But I don't think she really knows about rabbits. She said that a rabbit can hear as far as a dog. So why are its ears bigger than a dog's, then?'

'Sounds as if teachers aren't quite the all-knowing heroines they were in my day,' smiled Liane.

'Mothers even less so,' mumbled Yvette. 'Her father taught her never to merely accept what adults tell her – because our generation was taught to swallow all the rubbish that adults shoved down our throats – and now I'm the one who has to deal with the consequences. It's impossible to answer her questions, they only lead to further questions which are even more impossible to – '

'But what do you think? Why are rabbits' ears so big?'

'Why don't you ask Liane?'

'No, wait a minute!' Liane cried out, alarmed. 'What do I know about rabbits?'

'What about little angels? That's one of her favourite topics. Do angels get colds if they go to sleep with wet wings? Who cuts their hair? Do they have tonsils?'

'Goodness gracious!'

'One of these days you'll probably also have to answer questions like that,' said Yvette with a cheeky smile. 'You may as well begin practising.'

'I don't know,' said Liane, her eyes on the road. 'Perhaps it won't be necessary.'

'Have you decided to skip the adventure of parenthood?' asked Yvette, surprised.

'It's not a question of decision.' She looked in the rear-view mirror at Mona, who was holding her naked Barbie by the back and gracefully swooping and turning and diving her through the air, a cross between an angel and a bird of prey, the doll's stiff plastic breasts jutting forward. 'It's something I've always postponed. With every excuse in the book. I'm still too young, I'm still too immature, I still want to do too many things. And then I woke up one morning, a few months ago, and I realized, goodness gracious, I'm thirty-five years old. Do you remember that Pink Floyd song, you know, from *Dark Side of the Moon*? *No one told you when to run, you missed the starting gun.* When a woman is thirty-five, she ends up on the dark side of the moon. Before she knows it, she's lying like a wilted lettuce on a grocer's shelf. Long past her sell-by-date . . .'

'I can't believe my ears! You sound like my mother!'

'Oh, yes, that's another of the tragedies of the older woman. At thirty-five we all turn into our mothers.'

'You sound as though someone has hit you over the head, Liane,' said Yvette in a cross voice.

'It's age which has hit me over the head. You wouldn't understand,' she said with a superior smile. 'You aren't thirty-five yet.'

'I'm turning thirty-five soon!' Yvette cried indignantly. 'And I feel better about myself than I did at twenty-five! To tell the truth, I feel better than I did at any age!'

'Just goes to show what an affair can do, hey?'

'The affair is over.'

'Oh, no!' Liane exclaimed, disappointed.

'It's OK.' A casual shrug of the shoulders, her face turned away. 'I knew it wouldn't last. That was why I enjoyed it so much. And now that it's over, it's a bit like thinking about one of those feel-good movies. You know? The feeling stays with you long after the movie is over.'

'But why couldn't it last!'

'It lasted longer than a year. That's long enough. Especially these days.'

'Not for me. I have this old-fashioned romantic streak in me . . . ' She smiled apologetically, stared for a moment at her hands on the steering wheel. Even her fingers had grown old. Frightening. 'I thought my marriage was going to last for ever. I just can't imagine ever falling in love again if I'm not sure that it's going to last for ever.'

'One can never be sure, Liane. Sometimes you know from the beginning that it's not going to last. Like with Tomas. But the opposite . . . even after many years . . . '

'That's why I don't want to fall in love again.'

'It's got nothing to do with what you want.' Yvette looked at her with a wry smile, her eyes sympathetic. 'It comes like the proverbial thief in the night. Hits you when you least expect it. Just wait, you'll see.'

'I can't see how it could ever happen again.' With a sigh which exploded between them. 'I don't think men are interested in me any more, Yvette.'

'Because you're thirty-five years old?' asked Yvette, amused.

'No. Actually ever since Paul and I split up. I never get asked out like other women. I mean, I know straight men are scarcer than hens' teeth in Cape Town, but most of my divorced friends pick up a date at least once in a leap year. I never get dates!'

'And what about the Greek businessman who phones you so incessantly?'

'He doesn't count,' said Liane impatiently. 'He's an absolute creep. Like the arsehole actor who asked me out last year. He spent the whole night transported, gazing at my right shoulder. I thought perhaps he was psychic, that he saw an angel or something peering over my shoulder, until I realized that he was staring at his own reflection in the window behind my head the whole time. Now there was a creep de luxe for you! You can't call such fiascos dates!'

'Oh, that's how it works,' laughed Yvette. 'If they're creeps, they don't count. Well, then most women I know get very few dates indeed.'

'But where have all the nice men gone? Never mind nice. What has become of all the normal men I'd love to date? Why hasn't one single non-creep asked me out since my divorce?'

'What is the difference between hope and wish?' It was Mona on the back seat again. She was dressing her Barbie in a bizarre outfit – a glistening gold evening dress along with flippers and a baseball cap – probably to match her own unpredictable sartorial sense. It was the hottest day of the year, but she had insisted on wearing a pair of red gumboots and a black velvet hat with her summer dress. 'Is hope better or is wish better?'

'I hope a nice man asks me out. I wish a nice man asks me out. No, my darling,' said Liane, 'both of them sound equally useless.'

'If I say I hope Pappa comes back,' Mona asked, 'is it better than to say that I wish Pappa comes back?'

Liane felt her laugh being pinched tight in her throat. She glanced quickly at Yvette, who shook her head with an almost imperceptible twitch at the corners of her mouth. Used to her child's impossible questions.

'What do you think, Mamma?'

'I think wish is a bit stronger than hope.'

'But is it better?'

'What do you think? Is it better to be stronger?'

'I think it's better,' answered Mona uncertainly.

'Well, then.'

'That's a tactic that I must remember,' said Liane. 'This way of yours of asking another question if you can't think of an answer.'

'Just in case you have a child one day?'

'How the hell can I have a child if I can't even get a date!'

'I think it's what they call the beauty-queen syndrome.' Yvette noticed the indignant look which Liane shot at her and began to laugh. 'No, I'm not mocking you! It's one of those silly things you read in a magazine and can't get out of your head. Apparently, the prettiest women are often asked out the least, not because men aren't interested in them, but because the men kind of accept that they'll be booked up a year ahead. So they don't even try. Except the creeps who don't have the sensitivity to consider possible competitors. And in the end the poor beauty queen sits at home alone night after night, while everyone thinks she has this fantastic social life.'

'Why does that sound so familiar?' sighed Liane. 'So I may just as well forget about being asked out on a date in the next five years, at least by any man whose child I'd like to have.'

'That's not what I said. Besides, it's not as though you have a deadline in five years' time. Lots of women only have children after forty!'

'It's not an option which excites me. I'd hate it if my child's friends thought I was her grandmother.'

'With your looks, Liane, it's more likely that your grandchild's friends will think you're her mother. And medical science is progressing so fast these days, grannies are going to be having children again in a few years' time. I must admit, it makes me quite nervous. My mother always said that five children wasn't enough. She's quite capable of aiming for half a dozen in her old age.'

'Mamma, Tembisa says a rainbow is just a hallusion.'

'Illusion. Optical illusion.'

'Tembisa?' asked Liane.

'They sit next to each other in class. They hold hands on the playground. It's a wonder that they haven't started grafting together yet.'

'Is she . . .?'

'Tembisa Khumalo from Kayamandi,' answered Yvette with a broad smile. 'As I said, the children are living in a different country these days.'

'And Mona is aware that she . . .'

'That they look different? Well, she's green with jealousy about Tembisa's hairstyle.'

'She's got these little plaits all over her head!' Mona cried, aggrieved. 'And Mamma says I can't make my hair like that too!'

'Does that answer your question?' grinned Yvette.

'But if a rainbow is just a hallusion . . .'

'Here it comes again,' muttered Yvette. 'Another impossible question.'

'What about Noah and the ark then?'

'Noah and the ark is a story, my love. People always make up stories about things they don't understand. Why is the giraffe's neck so long? What happens to the sun every night? All the stories I tell you every night . . .'

'But Noah is in the Bible!' the child protested. 'Then they're lying in the Bible!'

'Now that's what I call a raw deal,' mumbled Liane. 'To be thrown into a religious crisis at the age of six.'

'Some of the most beautiful stories on earth come out of the Bible. That doesn't mean that someone lied to you. There is always more than one explanation for every possible thing. Some people will tell you a rainbow is an optical illusion and other people will tell you the story of Noah and his ark. You can decide for yourself what you want to believe.'

'I like the story more,' said the child after pondering for a moment.

'That makes two of us,' said Yvette, satisfied.

A few hours later, Liane was sitting on a broad wooden balcony, watching a silver full moon rise slowly into the blue-grey sky. It was a balmy summer night, so windless that the candle flames scarcely flickered, the sea as smooth as an ice rink below them. The sounds which floated out from the double-storey house were calm and reassuring: the radio playing quietly in the sitting room; the clink of steel against glass in the kitchen, where Ralph and Mila were making supper; Yvette reading a story to Mona in one of the bedrooms, her sweet voice becoming louder and softer, higher and lower, as she portrayed the different characters. Liane picked up her wine glass and sighed contentedly. Sometimes, life in Africa wasn't so bad after all.

'How do you feel about Paul's visit tomorrow?' Philip, next to her, asked. 'Doesn't it make you a bit tense?'

She glared at him suspiciously. His expression seemed genuinely interested. But she knew him well enough to know that you couldn't necessarily trust his expression.

'Well, I could probably ask you the same thing about Emma's visit.'

'We just can't get away from our exes, can we?' he grinned.

'There are a lot of things we can't get away from,' she said.

'But Emma and I have already proved that we can spend a weekend with our friends without driving anyone to murder.'

'And Paul and I have yet to prove our credentials?'

'No,' he answered earnestly, 'you were never such an explosive combination. Or perhaps you just had better manners. Never hung your dirty laundry out in public.'

'No,' she said sarcastically. 'We hid it away in a closet.'

'I was just wondering how you get on these days. A year ago you were still refusing to speak to him.'

'It's going a bit better now that we're officially divorced. Well, actually, a lot better. I took him out for dinner last time I was in Johannesburg. It felt almost like the old days. I dragged him to a trendy restaurant and he pretended to hate it.'

'I saw him in December,' said Bobby, who had been staring silently at the moon till now. 'When he was on holiday in Cape Town.'

'Then you must have met The Director too?'

There it was again. That touch of bitterness. It wasn't so difficult to talk about Paul any more, she could keep her voice calm and control her emotions; but the minute it came to the other man her voice refused to play along.

'Yes,' answered Bobby. 'He looks like a nice man. Don't you think so?'

'I haven't met him yet.'

'You haven't wanted to meet him yet,' said Max to her left.

'OK, I haven't wanted to meet him.'

Her gaze rested on him reproachfully. In the bright moonlight, his scalp shone as white as a gravestone through the thin layer of hair on his crown. Death slipping irrevocably closer, she thought with a strange sense of calm. Why didn't it make her feel anxious tonight? All she felt at this moment was an inexplicable tenderness. Not just for her oldest friend, who was growing older before her very eyes, but for all her friends who were having to make peace with their own mortality. They were reaching an age when the thought of it could no longer be postponed.

'You'll like him,' said Bobby.

'You know, Bobby, the more everyone tells me how nice he is, the less I want to meet him. It's so much easier if you can despise your successor.' With a self-mocking laugh on her lips, a last touch of bitterness on her tongue. 'If only Paul had fallen for the male equivalent of a dumb blonde – then I'd be able to shrug my shoulders and say, oh well, it's his loss. But this Riaan sounds too good to be true! I can only come a poor second compared to him!'

'I've always thought it's better if you're able to admire your successor,' Philip consoled. 'At least it says something about your ex-partner's judgement.'

'Easy for you to talk,' muttered Liane. 'Your only successor is a cute blonde baby.'

'One of these days Emma's going to have a man in her life. And if it's someone I can admire, then I'll wish her everything of the best.'

'That's quite a tall order,' said Max. 'Is there *anyone* you admire? Apart from a bunch of dead philosophers?'

'Well, there are also a few dead artists . . . dead statesmen . . . dead sportsmen . . .' Philip shrugged his shoulders and hid his smile in his wine glass.

'It still doesn't feel fair to me,' said Liane, aggrieved. 'All I ever wanted was a nice man. And when I eventually get a nice man, I find out that all *he* ever wanted was a nice man too!'

'You can't always get what you want,' said Max sympathetically.

'I can introduce you to a dozen nice women,' smiled Bobby.

'One of these days I'm going to be desperate enough to accept your offer!'

'It oughtn't to be so difficult to find a nice man,' said Max. 'There are two of us sitting on either side of you.'

'Goodness gracious. An incurable philanderer and a man who only likes dead people. What do you call it again? A necrophiliac? Sorry, Max, I'm crazy about the two of you, but you aren't normal! Not to mention nice!'

'I'm not an incurable philanderer!' protested Max. 'I'm an incurable romantic!'

'And I am the nicest necrophiliac you'll ever meet,' grinned Philip.

'How will I ever find the woman of my dreams if I don't test every possible candidate?' asked Max.

'Your offer sounds more and more attractive by the minute, Bobby,' said Liane.

'So when are we expecting the contingent of ex-partners?' asked Bobby.

'Sometime tomorrow,' said Philip. 'And they probably won't stay too long. Emma actually didn't want to come at all, because she's busy on a new book which is making her completely *bedonnerd*. But when she heard that Paul was coming to the Cape for a court case, she offered to bring him here.'

'I still think she's doing it just to get me back,' said Liane. 'Because I dragged you along to Stilbaai last year without warning her.'

'She's not a woman who forgives and forgets easily,' sighed Philip.

'Is there a woman anywhere on earth who forgives and forgets easily?' asked Max, his eyes fixed innocently on the moon.

'Ag, I'm sure it will be OK,' said Liane with more optimism in her voice than she felt in her heart. 'One never knows. Maybe next year we can even invite Adriaan to join us for a weekend at the sea!'

'And then our little circle will be complete again!' Max cried out mockingly.

'Adriaan is such a famous TV personality these days that you can't take him anywhere without being besieged by a horde of fans,' said Philip indignantly. 'I looked him up when I was up there for Mel . . . after he died. Thought we could sit in a bar somewhere and get drunk slowly, like in the good old days, but we were constantly interrupted by young girls wanting his autograph!'

He bent forward to light his cigarette at one of the candles on the table. The flame flickered for a moment over the frown between his eyebrows and lit up his high, bare forehead. He had also grown much older, Liane realized. Even Bobby had turned thirty last year. Funny how you can look at your friends for years without noticing any changes, and then, suddenly, one full-moon night, everyone seems tired and middle-aged to you. Probably because she felt so tired and middle-aged herself these days.

'I can imagine that he rather enjoys the attention,' smiled Bobby.

'I think he's gradually beginning to get fed up. The problem with fame is that you can't switch it off if you want to sit and talk shit in a bar with an old buddy one night.'

'I've never seen his TV programme,' said Bobby. 'I hear it's very entertaining.'

'It's the best thing on TV,' Liane assured her. 'You should watch it sometime.'

'My TV was stolen,' said Bobby. 'I had one of those break-ins that's supposed to only happen in nightmares. Everything was stolen, even the food in my fridge. They made a fire on my sitting-room carpet and peed on my bedding. I haven't had the energy to buy another TV. It feels as though everything I buy will only be stolen again, anyway.'

The sigh which slipped from her mouth sounded forlorn. Liane looked at her in concern, so small in the big cane chair, her knees pulled up under her chin. Barefoot, her legs pale and thin under blue-patterned shorts and a T-shirt which hung about her body like a loose dress. When was she ever going to learn to buy clothes in the right size?

'I still suspect that the security police had something to do with it,' said Max, shaking his head.

'Why should the security police want to bother with me, Max? My only claim to fame was that I was Robin's lover!'

'Why should they have wanted to kill Robin, Bobby? She wasn't such a big figure in the Struggle. There were a lot of people who were more dangerous for the so-called security of the state. I think it's because white women like you are the ultimate traitors to them. Everything they don't want their own wives and daughters to become. You aren't just "for the kaffirs", you're also "against men". You reject everything that they cling to, the whole shebang, from racism to patriarchy. The way your flat was vandalized was just too spiteful for ordinary burglars.'

'We'll never know, will we?' said Bobby with a heavy sigh. 'Anyway, it made me realize that I should probably give up the old flat. That was the third burglary in two years.'

'So you're also going to live in a big house with a high wall and an alarm system?'

'Like all my white friends.' She gave him a cross look. 'Your new house also looks like a fucking fort!'

'Anyway, if you ever get a TV set again,' said Liane with a forced laugh, 'you must make a point of watching Adriaan's talk show. It's a lot funnier than any sitcom. He gets a bunch of weird guests to talk about art or food – but somehow or other the discussion always ends up at sex.'

'That ought to surprise no one,' said Philip. 'It remains his greatest passion.'

'And a bit of late-night titillation on TV can only do the volk good,' said Max.

'And the volk are crazy about it,' giggled Liane. 'One of the women's magazines called him "one of our foremost freedom fighters" the other day! In the same breath as a few ex-political prisoners! Because he makes us laugh at sex. In our own sitting rooms.'

'It seems the whole country has suddenly gone sex mad,' said Bobby with a displeased expression. 'Porn magazines springing up everywhere and sex shops on every second street corner. I thought we were fighting for political liberation. Now it seems as though we only got sexual liberation. Not that I have a problem with sexual liberation. But in the meantime, the townships are still burning. The politicians wag their tongues incessantly without doing anything about it – and the nation grabs at porn to forget about their despair!'

'What happened to all your optimism about the New South Africa?' asked Liane.

'Probably vanished along with all the belongings in my flat,' answered Bobby with a miserable laugh.

Max drew a sharp breath, as though he wanted to say something, but then just shrugged his shoulders and stared at the sea, which shone in the moonlight like spilt milk.

And here was her husband, walking over the beach. Her ex-husband, she corrected herself immediately. Strange how difficult it still was to get used to the idea. Every time she saw him again, it was as though her thoughts did a backward somersault, over the last year or two, as if she suddenly found herself in the past again. And yet, now that she viewed him at a distance, it was clear that he wasn't a married man. It was clear that he was gay, she realized with a sense of shock.

Or was she imagining it? Because she thought that gay men should *look* gay?

She tried to see him through the eyes of an outsider, any of the other people on the beach, someone who didn't know him. His body language hadn't changed. Thank god. She would hate it if he suddenly minced across the sand with pinched buttocks and limp wrists. And his clothing was almost boringly tasteful, as always, no tight shorts or black leather caps or shiny chains or anything outrageous. Not even an earring. White T-shirt and khaki trousers and dark glasses. All that had actually changed was his hair, which was cut a lot shorter than before. But that was the fashion these days. Not just among gay men. And his face, which had become a bit thinner, his cheekbones a bit sharper. But he looked undeniably different from the two men on either side of him.

He had always looked different, she realized with longing. That was why she had fallen for him.

He walked between Philip and Max, a fraction shorter than Philip and half a head taller than Max. Philip looked pale and thin next to him, his bare forehead shiny and his dull blond hair bleached in the sharp sunlight; Max even darker and sturdier than usual. A black haze over his shirtless chest and muscular legs. Almost as hairy as the collie next to him.

'He looks good, doesn't he?' said Mila next to her.

Liane looked quickly away from the three men who were now only a few paces from them. Why did she feel as though she had been caught red-handed? She still had the right to look at her husband after all! *Ex-husband*. A lightning flash of relief. Followed by a dull rumble of loss.

'He always did look good.'

'Too true.' Mila's smile flashed white below her sunglasses, her face glossily smeared with an excessive layer of suncream. Essential camouflage, she had declared, for a woman who wanted to hide her age for a few more years. Although the body in the purple swimming costume looked as attractive as always, the legs still long and lean and tanned. It was just the skin around the knees which was beginning to get a little looser. But it was only when you sat right next to her that you noticed it. 'He doesn't need a woman to take care of him.'

'Obviously not.'

'No, I just mean that . . .' Her voice suddenly guilty. 'Some men fall apart so visibly when there isn't a woman in the house to ensure that their clothes get ironed, you know, or that their hair gets cut now and again. Just look at Philip. He's beginning to look really seedy.'

'Well, he doesn't have much hair left to cut. And that terrible T-shirt he's wearing wouldn't have looked any better if it were ironed.'

They were sitting next to the river because the two children were still too small to brave the waves in the open sea. Ralph was playing with Mona in the deeper water and Sasha was splashing about near the bank. She was wearing a kind of life-jacket disguised as a swimming costume – bits of foam rubber under the elastic red material – which made her look like a blow-up doll. Emma, who had arrived with Paul earlier that morning, sat with outstretched legs next to her daughter in the shallow water; Yvette was a little way off, as watchful as a soldier on guard, her back stiff and straight. Mona had learned to swim two years ago – shortly after her brother's death – but Yvette would probably never relax while she was in the water. Any water. When Mona was a teenager, Yvette would probably still want to sit next to her when she bathed.

And you could hardly blame her, thought Liane, remembering the holes which were gouged out in her eyes after Pablo's death. As though the pupil had suddenly overflowed, an inkwell tipped over, staining the whole iris black.

Bobby lay on her stomach on the other side of Mila, without her glasses, her nose so close to a paperback that it looked as though she was sniffing the pages rather than reading them. A biography of a freedom fighter whose name Liane, as usual, didn't recognize. Even when Max and Philip spread their towels out beside her, she didn't lift her head. Paul stood hesitating, looking uncertainly in Liane's direction.

'Come and sit here with us!' called Mila. 'I want to ask you about life in Egoli. I miss the place more than I expected to!'

'Here in the Fairest Cape?' cried Philip in joking disbelief across Bobby's back.

'Here in the Fairest Cape,' answered Mila without joking. 'The pace is sometimes just too slow for me. I miss the excitement of Johannesburg. There's that urgency in the air, something you can almost smell the minute you get off the plane.'

'That's just the sweat of anxiety you're smelling,' grinned Philip. 'Because everyone is scared that their cars are going to be hijacked. Or their shirts stolen from their backs.'

'Come, let's ignore our local Cassandra,' said Paul as he settled down next to Mila. 'I agree with you. Johannesburg is exciting in a way that Cape Town can never be. So what if the excitement is caused by fear. At least you feel you're still alive. Here beside the sea you could easily turn into a potato.'

'My favourite state,' sighed Philip. 'As numb as a potato.'

Paul pulled his T-shirt over his head and leaned back on his elbows. Liane stared at the familiar chest, her fingers throbbing with desire. Just to touch him. Just to stroke that chest one more time, the skin as warm and smooth as glazed clay under her palm, explore the small tussocks of hair around the nipples, the tip of the nipple a hard grain between her thumb and finger. She felt his eyes rest on her, a suspicion rather than a certainty because she couldn't see through his dark glasses, and turned her head quickly in the direction of the river. A quiet storm in her heart. Thunder and lightning. And a wind which howled with longing for something which could never be again.

'Another fucking perfect day in Africa,' mumbled Ralph when they wandered back over the long beach to the house later that afternoon. The sea a glittering sheet of metal to their left, the river behind them a bright blue python trying to swallow the sea, the sand dunes to the right a mysterious jungle of low milkwood trees and dense green thickets. Salt, which hung in the air like pollen, clung stickily to their damp hair and made their tongues scrape drily against their teeth. The sun oppressive, as though they carried it on their heads like a heavy load. 'How did you get hold of this house?'

'My mother's family has come here on holiday for years,' Philip answered. 'I also spent a few summer holidays here when my mother was still alive. When my father married again, his new wife persuaded him to buy a caravan – one of those so-called luxury numbers which looks like an ugly suburban house inside – so that they could have a holiday in a different place every year. A different, overcrowded, noisy, common caravan park every year. Holidays in hell. That's how I remember it. I went along twice and then simply refused to do it again. Christmas alone on the farm wasn't exactly a jolly affair, but it was paradise in comparison with Christmas in a caravan park!'

'My father also flirted with caravan holidays for a few years,' said Ralph, 'but my mother is such an incurable snob that she couldn't bear it. She wouldn't rest until my father bought her a beach house in Ramsgate. Big enough for her to scream and throw plates without the neighbours hearing.'

'Was it really that bad?' asked Philip, amused. 'The plate-throwing, I mean?'

'Well, of course I exaggerate a bit to make the story sound better,' Ralph admitted with a guilty smile. 'But my mother really did throw plates. And books and bunches of keys and . . . actually anything that was close at hand. No knives, thank God. Fortunately she had absolutely no ball sense so she never hit anyone.'

'In our house, nothing was ever thrown around. Not even accusations. There were just these icy silences which could last for days. Sometimes it made me long for screaming voices, flying objects, doors being slammed . . . anything to break the silence . . .'

'My mother should have been an opera singer. But she was always worried about what the other farmers' wives would think of her if she didn't behave as properly as they did. So it was only on holiday that she sacrificed her self-control, threw the kind of tantrums a prima donna would have been proud of. I think that's what she misses most now that my father is dead. Not his company, he was never a great conversationalist, just the fact that he was such an imperturbable target for her tantrums. He allowed her to work out her rage and then simply went on as though nothing had happened.'

'And you?' His tongue felt heavy in his mouth. The thought of the cold beer waiting in the house became a torture which made every pace seem too short. The heat hung like a veil about his face, a haziness in front of his eyes and a friction against his cheeks and nose, which were already burned red. 'What do you miss about your father?'

'Those caravan holidays,' answered Ralph with a nostalgic smile. 'I don't think he could bear to be trapped in such a confined space. It was the idea rather than the reality which enticed him. I inherited that from him, I think; the ability to be seduced by an illusion.'

Philip glanced sideways at him and saw that he was staring at Mila's legs. She walked a little way ahead of them, between Bobby and Paul, her limbs as lovely as ever in cut-off denim shorts.

'A caravan holiday can only be a fantasy if you're blind and deaf. And preferably have lost your sense of smell, too. I can still smell those ablution blocks! I hated sharing a bathroom with a bunch of strangers.'

'Sounds to me as though you've displayed misanthropic tendencies ever since your youth.'

'Last night I was called a necrophiliac,' smiled Philip. 'Now I'm a misanthrope. It gives me such a nice, warm feeling to know my friends appreciate me so much.'

'It's because you Namibian farmers own such obscenely big farms. Of course you're going to be a misanthrope if you never see other people!'

'And the necrophilia, doctor? Where does that come from?'

'What is there to screw in that wilderness? Except sheep and corpses?'

'Look, I don't mind the idea of screwing sheep, but I was never so desperate that I wanted to try a dead sheep. Anyway, from what I hear, your family farm isn't such a humble smallholding either.'

'The question is whether there will be anything left of it if my brother and brother-in-law get their way,' said Ralph, suddenly serious. 'The minute my father died last year, they began plotting to sell parts of it off from under my mother.'

'I think my father has already accepted that he's the Last of the Mohicans. My brother has made it quite clear that he can't handle such a large piece of land. Or doesn't want to. I wouldn't be surprised if he sold the whole lot off as soon as the old man keels over.'

'How long has the farm been in the family?'

'Four generations,' said Philip. 'And yours?'

'Five. It's the end of an era, right? High time, I guess. But if your father and your father's father and the whole lot before them all lie on a piece of land . . . I've always accepted that I'd also be buried there.'

'Jesus, no; the last place I want to end up is among my bloody ancestors! Rather wrap me in sailcloth and dump me in the sea. Leave me in the veld where the vultures can pick my bones clean. Burn me and let the wind blow my ash away . . .'

'Sounds as though you've thought of a whole range of options.'

'I often think of death,' said Philip, his head bowed, his eyes on the damp sand between his bare toes. 'It's my way of appreciating life more.'

They walked a little way further in silence, as if the sun had even burned their tongues by this time. The beach was fairly deserted around them, apart from the gulls and terns and other sea birds which were landing and rising continually next to the water, landing and rising, like planes at a busy airport. Here and there a group of barefoot people wandered along the tidemark, but the noisy part of the beach lay far behind them. Dozens of brightly patterned towels and colourful umbrellas and screaming children and scolding parents; babies and toddlers splashing about in the river, older children and adults in the sea; a bored lifeguard on a high scaffold watching the swimmers in the waves. Liane and Max, who still had more energy than most of their friends put together, were still in the sea. The heat had long ago driven the rest of the company back to the cool shelter of the beach house.

'And did your father's death bring you any personal liberation?' asked Philip, his voice unexpectedly urgent, as if the answer was absolutely vital.

'Well, I still can't sleep late over the weekends,' answered Ralph with a joyless laugh. 'I still hear him somewhere in my head. *Come, come, come, do you want to lie under the blankets like an old woman all day?* No, brother, I'm afraid they fucked us up for life.'

Paul leaned over the balcony railing, a glass of white wine in his hand, and stared at the bright light of the sinking sun on the water. His forehead frowning, his mouth zipped tight in a sad line. It must be difficult for him to be back among his old friends, Liane realized. Such a fleeting return to a former life. Not enough time to adjust before moving on again.

'Ralph and Mila are trying to persuade Emma to spend the night,' she said carefully, testing his reaction, but he remained staring motionlessly ahead. Still the profile of a classical statue, the chin chiselled from stone, hard and angular, with the soft dent in the middle. 'She says she can't, because she promised you she'd drive back tonight . . .'

'It doesn't matter to me,' he said casually. 'I don't have anything on in town tonight.'

'But won't it be uncomfortable for you to spend the night with me . . . I mean, under the same roof?'

Stammering and blushing and angry with herself because she suddenly sounded like a nervous schoolgirl.

'Will it be uncomfortable for you?' He turned his face to her, that familiar mocking smile at his mouth, his eyebrows two high black bows against his forehead. 'Are you afraid that I'll lose all control and come creeping into bed with you?'

'Of course not!' Now she blushed in earnest. Tried to hide her embarrassment with a quick quip. 'It's been so long since I had someone in my bed that I wouldn't know what to do anyway!'

'I can't believe that it's a problem for you to get someone into bed,' he laughed.

'Well,' she said, torn between the desire to confess and the urge to protect herself against her ex-husband's pity. 'Let's just say that potential lovers aren't exactly beating a path to my door.'

'But you don't seem to notice the most likely potential lover.'

'Who are you talking about?'

'Max, of course. He's been mad about you for almost twenty years.'

'No, it's not . . . it's just . . . I mean, that's not to say that he wants to *sleep* with me!'

'Listen, Liane, I've been watching the two of you for years. I'm going to admit something now that I would never have admitted while we were married. I was jealous of him. Sometimes I picked fights with him – about politics, religion, whatever – just because I felt threatened.'

'Well, that's pretty ironic.' She had to swallow a few times to get her voice even again. 'You being jealous of another man. And then you ran away with another man yourself.'

'I know,' he said with a weak smile. 'But I was in denial. Like you and Max still are. I watched you both again today. You still have that way of shutting everyone else out if you begin to talk earnestly. I know that you don't do it consciously, that's precisely why it used to frustrate me so much. I mean, if your wife flirts with another man on purpose, you have the right to confront her, but this thing between you and Max was always more subtle than flirtation. It's clear that there's an attraction, but you're so used to suppressing it that perhaps you're not even aware of it any more.'

'No!' she said quickly, defensively. Perhaps too defensively. 'If there is an attraction . . . OK, I'll admit, there is probably something . . . but it's a kind of longing for something which is past, lost youth, lost innocence, call it what you like. Max isn't in love with me, Paul. He's in love with the naïve sixteen-year-old schoolgirl I used to be long ago.'

'But there's that little part somewhere inside you – well, perhaps even a large part – which will always remain that sixteen-year-old schoolgirl.'

'But we can never have such an innocent relationship again! It's like Adam and Eve longing for the Garden of Eden! We never even had sex, but there was an intensity of feeling which I never again . . .'

She stayed silent, bewildered, and sipped her wine quickly.

'Which you never again experienced with anyone else.' He nodded thoughtfully as he stared at the sea. 'That's exactly what I'm talking about.'

Below the balcony, behind the roofs of the two rows of houses, the water lay glistening, grey-blue and still. Almost unnaturally still, as though the waves which broke foaming over the rocks hung motionless in the air for a moment. Here and there she could see the silhouette of an angler, and on the closest rocks a few children bent over a pool, but even these human figures looked motionless in the dazzling late-afternoon light. As if she were looking at a photo rather than a movie, a moment of fleeting time caught like a butterfly in a net.

'If I went to bed with him now, it would probably just spoil our friendship.'

'Perhaps.' His gaze unexpectedly challenging. 'Perhaps not.'

She turned her face away, back to the sea which now no longer seemed motionless. It was just an illusion, she thought. A hallusion.

'Goodness gracious. I never thought my ex-husband would try to persuade me to sleep with another man!'

'*Goodness gracious.*' The dimple like a hole in his chin. 'I don't know anyone else who uses that expression like you do. So old-fashioned and innocent. Without mockery or irony. Like a Victorian heroine.'

'Goodness gracious,' she said giggling. 'Who the hell wants to sound like a Victorian heroine? I'll have to do something about my image. Do you have any suggestions for more trendy exclamations?'

'No.' With an expression in his dark eyes which made her heart leap with sudden joy. Then there was still something left, she thought gratefully. Something of the wonderment with which he used to look at her in the past. 'I'd hate it if you suddenly began to say something like "what the fuck", just to sound trendy.'

'I'd like it if you'd stay over tonight,' she said with a pleased smile. 'There are still lots of things I want to talk about.'

'Like?'

'Ag, you know. Everything and nothing.' She licked her top lip and tasted the salt of her own sweat. Although the sun had begun to sink, the heat still hung almost tangibly in the air. Not the slightest breeze from the sea, not a leaf stirring, just this oppressive humidity. 'I don't have to ask you whether you're happy, because I can see that you are.'

'As long as you remember that even in the Garden of Eden there was a snake in the grass.'

'Now you sound like your father,' she teased. But then she saw how his mouth folded back sadly again. For her, still the most beautiful mouth in the world. 'What's wrong?'

'Aids,' he muttered.

'Aids?' she muttered after him, her heart suddenly icy cold, despite the heat which clung stickily to her skin.

'Riaan tested positive.'

'For Aids?' Her voice was thin with shock.

'HIV positive. It'll go over to Aids sometime. Unless medical science finds a cure very quickly.'

She stared at him dumbfounded, too upset to utter a word.

'I'm OK,' he answered the question which she couldn't ask. 'I mean, physically OK. Negative. Whether I'm psychologically OK enough to handle this catastrophe . . .'

He raised his shoulders helplessly. She took a quick gulp of wine, something to flood the shock from her voice, to melt the sudden shell of ice on her heart.

'How long have you known?'

'Almost a year.'

'I don't believe it ... I thought you were this glowingly happy couple ...'

'That's what I keep saying to myself. *I don't believe it*. You're the first person I've told. I don't want ... I don't want to tell the others yet ... Riaan isn't ready to share it with the world. There's still such a bloody stigma attached to the whole thing! He's scared that he won't get work, scared that producers will think he's going to keel over behind the camera or infect the whole cast ...'

It was as though her heart grew colder with every word. While her cheeks glowed even hotter. Ice cold and fiery hot at the same time.

'It's strange,' she muttered. 'I always thought that Aids was something which would never touch me personally. Firstly, because I was safely married, and then ... well, because I haven't had much of a sex life since we split up ...' She shook her head, too upset to look at him, intensely aware of his breathing beside her. Her hand just touched his bare arm on the railing, his skin a shade darker than hers. 'Just as I thought earlier that this country's politics would never really touch me. I thought that I could hide away behind my white skin. Behind the burglar bars on my windows. Refuse to read the newspaper and keep *decorating* people's houses.' She pronounced the word with as much scorn as Max did. 'But then Robin ended up in jail. And then she was murdered ... and then I saw what it did to Bobby ... and I began to realize that I couldn't escape. I couldn't get away from anything which happened in this country!'

She drained her glass in one gulp, turned to her ex-husband, who was looking at her with an expression of unbearable sadness on his lovely face, and embraced him before she realized what she was doing. He let his head drop to her shoulder and breathed in the sweaty sea smell in the hollow of her neck, a greedy sniffing sound which reminded her suddenly of the first few months of their relationship, how he would press his nose into her neck and sniff at her like that, laughing. Now, of course, he wasn't laughing.

She began to rub his bent head slowly. His hair shaved so short that the stubble tickled her fingers. Grateful, despite everything, for the unexpected chance to hold this beloved body again.

*

Everything that happened afterwards, that night, she would later ascribe to the fact that she was suffering from shock. Shock and confusion, nostalgia and longing, tenderness and sorrow. And drunkenness. The unexpected recklessness with which she had drained the glass of wine on the balcony carried her through the rest of the evening. Luckily, she wasn't the only one who was overcome by recklessness. It was one of those rare occasions when a group of people who knew each other well enough and long enough not to be surprised any more, still managed to surprise each other. Even to astound each other. Walpurgis Night, Philip had muttered. No, less Germanic, Ralph had grinned. More Dionysian.

Everyone had too much to drink. A bit too much, like Yvette, who, for a change, wasn't pregnant or breastfeeding; or far too much, like Liane, who had last been drunk at university. Philip drank with his usual determination, Emma with a kind of resignation. If you can't beat them . . .

And there was other muti, too, apart from the dagga which Bobby had brought along as usual.

Paul lured Liane and Max to one of the bedrooms, shook a heap of fine powder out of a plastic bag, divided it into a few narrow lines with the tip of a knife and rolled up a ten-rand note. 'Take a walk on the wild side,' he said with a crooked smile. Liane was shocked, but her curiosity quickly got the better of her. She watched her ex-husband, fascinated. The rolled-up note held nonchalantly in front of his nostril, the other nostril pressed closed with the fingers of the other hand, and a deep, grateful sniff. What had happened to the boring Oranjezicht lawyer? Then he looked at her, as challenging as earlier on the balcony. She met the challenge, took the ten-rand note from him, and tried to pretend that it wasn't the first time she'd done something like this. Not really a convincing attempt, because she had to sniff three times before the line of powder disappeared, and then she almost began to sneeze. Her nasal cavity numb, as though a dentist had injected her in the wrong place. A moment of panic before she remembered that she could still breathe through her other nostril. She smiled with relief and offered the note to Max.

Only the following day did she realize that Paul's magic powder had played a part in what happened later. And that Paul, like any magician worth his salt, knew exactly what he was doing.

After that they danced. Even Philip danced – another of the evening's surprises – with an embarrassed grimace fixed on his face like a mask. The music was the kind most of them had grown up with: the Rolling Stones, Led Zeppelin, Pink Floyd, the Doors. *Unbelievably old fashioned!* As Bobby had shouted with her hands in her hair. Then she had fetched a case full of tapes from her car and announced that it was time their musical taste was broadened. Whether they were ready for it or not. Listen to something new for a change!

'No!' Ralph cried out in horror.

'I'm using "new" in the broadest possible sense, Ralph. As in anything that's been written in the last twenty years at least.'

'Nothing written after the seventies has ever turned me on.'

'Aha! That's the first unmistakable sign of old age!'

'But I *am* old,' he said with an innocent expression.

'Intolerance towards new things.' She stood with her hands on her hips in front of him, comically small and cross, and glared at him over her glasses. 'It's a sign that you're busy turning into a dried-up old stick.'

'*Que sera, sera,*' Ralph declared, unmoved. 'I'm afraid the day that John Lennon was shot, my interest in pop music also died.'

'I'm not talking about "pop music"! Pop music is Michael Jackson and Madonna. There's a lot of other stuff happening. Rap and rave, jungle and grunge, hip hop and techno . . . Have you ever listened to any of the new stuff?'

'Just on my car radio, when there's absolutely nothing else to listen to.'

'Well, just listen to this!' she cried out triumphantly.

And a recording of an unearthly racket began to play, screams which sounded as though they came from doomed souls in hell, accompanied by moaning electric guitars and sadistic keyboard sounds.

'Now I understand for the first time why my father says that pop music is demonic,' muttered Paul.

Most of them simply kept on dancing – by this time they would have danced to nursery rhymes – but naturally not with the same enthusiasm as the Rolling Stones had elicited.

'OK,' Bobby announced resignedly, 'if you want old-fashioned music, then let me play you proper old-fashioned music!'

And then she blasted them with a crackly recording of the Osmonds. Which made even the most determined dancers – Liane and Paul, Max and Mila – laugh so much that they could scarcely stay on their feet.

Despite the ridiculous boisterousness in the house, the two little girls slept sweetly. Mona wasn't disturbed by nightmares and Sasha didn't wake up with a wet nappy. As if it was meant to be that all the adults should be completely irresponsible for once.

'I'm glad we decided to stay over,' said Emma when she fell down on the couch next to Philip, exhausted from dancing. She lay with her head against the backrest, her skin shiny with perspiration and her cheeks pink. Small corkscrew curls clung damply to her forehead. 'I've worked so hard in the last while, I've completely forgotten what it feels like to drink too much and have fun!'

'It's unlikely that I'll ever forget how to drink too much,' said Philip, watching her with an uneven smile. It was the first time today that she was relaxed enough to start talking to him spontaneously. Till now she had rather obviously tried to avoid him. 'But it's unfortunately not always fun.'

Liane and Paul were still dancing, as graceful and inexhaustible as always. Two bodies which scarcely touched each other and yet moved instinctively together. Or perhaps it wasn't instinct, thought Philip, just habit. How would he know? Dance remained a dark secret to him. Not only how the body managed it, but also how the head allowed the body to do it. Such a total surrender to a primitive state. Like an extended orgasm. Not that Liane and Paul looked primitive. On the contrary, their movements were almost too controlled. More like two actors having sex in front of a camera.

That was probably how they had been in bed, too. Two skilled actors playing a heterosexual couple. Bobby was the one who danced with frightening abandon, spasms which rhythmically jerked her thin body, as if she was in a state of religious ecstasy. Max also moved less self-consciously than usual, swinging his arms and stamping his feet as though he was toyi-toying in a protest march, probably more drugged than he realized. The music was Latin-American, a pulsing, hypnotic rhythm which made Philip think of pictures of half-naked carnival dancers in Rio de Janeiro. He wondered why his thoughts had suddenly taken such an erotic turn.

'It's weird to see them dancing like that.' Emma stared thoughtfully at Paul and Liane, admiration in her grey eyes and sadness about her wide mouth. 'Like a time-warp. Odysseus returning to Penelope –

who has waited faithfully all these years, after Calypso has enchanted him.'

'With Riaan the Director in the role of Calypso?'

Amused by her still insatiable hunger for stories. This ability, which had often irritated him when they were together, of transforming everything around her into fiction.

'Hmmm. And Johannesburg as the enchanted island.'

She leaned forward again, her elbows on her bare knees, her long summer dress tucked up into the elastic of her panties. An old habit, something she did almost unconsciously when she got hot, something he'd found almost unbearably seductive when he first got to know her. The mass of hair bundled on to her head and pinned with two laundry pegs. As she'd always done when they'd bathed together. Something he didn't want to think about now.

'But in this story Odysseus has just popped in for a quick visit,' he reminded her as he stared at her kneecaps, glistening with perspiration, like her face. 'Come to see if Penelope is still OK. Before he goes back to Calypso.'

'Of course,' she sighed. 'It's just a myth that two people who've been divorced for a long time can live happily together again.'

'And even the myth wouldn't have had a happy ending if Odysseus had discovered somewhere on his travels that he was gay.'

'And yet,' she said in a longing voice. 'There must be some couples who *belong* together. Like Odysseus and Penelope.'

'Or Romeo and Juliet,' he said sarcastically.

He looked at Liane, who was now dancing in Max's arms, with a lot less restraint than she had with her ex-husband. As though Max's drugged exuberance was infectious. Paul had pulled Yvette, laughing and protesting, out of an armchair and begun to sakkie-sakkie with her to the beat of a samba. An odd couple, if there ever was one. Paul had put on clean clothes after coming back from the beach – the only one among them who'd taken the trouble – a navy blue polo shirt and another neat pair of khaki trousers. Like a stylish businessman on a golf outing. Yvette's dress looked as though it was cut from an old patchwork quilt, glossy pieces of satin and flowered cotton. Cinderella dancing with the prince after the ballgown had disappeared. Bobby lay flat on her back on the floor, panting with exhaustion. Her T-shirt clung to her thin body, wet with sweat, her breasts so small that she had never needed to wear a bra, the nipples two dark points against the white cotton. Philip looked away, flustered. When even his lesbian friends began to turn him on, it had to be time to do something about his sex life.

'Or like Yvette and Adriaan,' said Emma thoughtfully. 'Mila said he was quite upset about her affair with Tomas.'

'Of course. He's the one who's supposed to have affairs, not her.'

'But it shows that the feeling is still there, not so?'

'Jealousy should never be confused with love. They're separate emotions. Sometimes they go hand in hand. Sometimes not.'

'But surely you're not jealous of *me* any more?' She looked over her bare shoulder at him, her eyes searching. How well he remembered the freckles on that shoulder. Sometimes he had tried to lick them off, like a layer of brown sugar. 'I mean, say I had an affair with Tomas. You wouldn't be half as furious as Adriaan was.'

'If you had an affair with Tomas, I'd definitely be furious. I've always thought he was a prick.'

She sank laughingly against the backrest and lifted her feet on to the couch, so that her dress fell back even more, her thighs now completely bare.

'Well, that's not Adriaan's problem. He's simply green with jealousy. And I think that in this case jealousy definitely has something to do with love.'

Her bare thighs were disturbingly close to him. So close that he could see the fine network of little purply blue veins under the pale skin. He remembered how she'd hated those veins, afraid that she would develop horrid varicose snakes like her grandmother. He assured her that it was just because her skin was so thin and white that her veins showed through – even on her feet you could follow the shallow veins with your finger – and besides, he found it quite attractive: traces of mortality, vulnerability, imperfect humanity. 'I'm completely aware of my own imperfection!' she had cried out, aggrieved. 'I don't want to be reminded of it every time I wash my feet!' Strange how much he remembered tonight. Things he thought he'd . . . Well, actually for the last few months now. It was as though his son's death had lifted a lid somewhere in his subconscious. Some kind of rubbish bin in which he'd always stuffed everything he couldn't handle. And now the memories were crawling out like worms: memories of his son, of his ex-wife, of his mother and father and his youth on the farm. Sometimes, especially in the early hours of the morning, when the darkness lay like a dead weight on his chest, he was afraid that he would never be able to close the lid again.

'Do you really think so?' he asked sceptically. 'Or do you just hope so?'

'Both,' she answered without hesitation. 'I think that Adriaan and Yvette belong together. And I hope with all my heart that they get together again, sometime, somehow. Somewhere in this circle of friends there has to be a relationship which lasts! Two people who can grow old together!'

'Why?' A little surprised by the passion which the subject had aroused in her.

'Because I don't want to lose my last shred of romantic idealism. I've got just about fuck-all left!'

'And you think you'll get some of it back if Adriaan and Yvette decide to grow old together?'

'Well, who else is there?' she asked with a bewildered expression. 'It's clear that you and I are never going to live under the same roof again. Same with Paul and Liane. Ralph and Mila never openly shared a bed anyway . . .'

She threw her head back against the couch and closed her eyes wearily.

'No use crying over spilt milk, Emma. There's always the possibility of a new bottle.'

'To be found where?'

'Who knows?' He listened in horror to his cheerful voice. 'Max said only yesterday that he was still waiting for the woman of his dreams.'

It was as though they'd suddenly swapped roles, he thought in dismay. What had happened to her everlasting optimism? What the hell could he do to wipe the confusion from the corners of her wide mouth?

'Max could have had the woman of his dreams long ago,' she mumbled without opening her eyes. 'If only he wasn't so bloody PC that he tried to censor his dreams. He thinks he can't sleep with a woman before he's toyi-toyed with her!'

'Well, I think Liane is passing that test,' grinned Philip.

Emma sat up in surprise. Stared open-mouthed at Liane, who was toyi-toying with Max, arm around his waist, waving her free arm around in the air with a clenched fist, her head thrown back, laughing ecstasy on her beautiful face.

'Now then,' said Emma when she got her voice back. 'That just goes to show what drink and drugs can do to a nice, respectable girl.'

When she opened her eyes early the next morning – as early as always, despite her fuzzy brain – and looked straight into a bare male shoulder, she pinched them tightly closed again. For a single, panic-stricken moment she wondered what the hell she'd done the previous night. Then she remembered. Which did nothing to lessen the panic.

She peered cautiously through her lashes, as if she hoped that the tanned shoulder in front of her nose would have vanished, an optical illusion caused by a brain unused to drugs. Alas, it still lay there, as solid as a mountain. Tangible proof of madness.

She wasn't used to waking up next to strange men. She wasn't used to waking up next to any kind of man. What did you do, what did you say, how did you hide your embarrassment? She drew a deep breath to still her hammering heart. Honestly, the last time she'd experienced this level of panic was as a student, just before her practical drama exam.

But this shoulder didn't belong to a strange man. She hadn't yet worked up the courage to look at the rest of the body. Her gaze had frozen on the shoulder, on the dark skin, the bit of muscled forearm she could see without moving her startled eyes, the black hair on the chest below the shoulder. She knew this body, she tried to comfort herself. And yet, she thought, her skin feeling as if it was being pricked by innumerable fine needles, it was as though she had only just got to know this man.

The passion with which he had taken possession of her body a few hours ago, the hunger with which he had bitten her, the thirst with which he had sucked at her. Unquenchable, unslakeable, unassuageable. His lips on her face, his teeth against her neck, his mouth over her nipples, his tongue in her navel, on the insides of her thighs, the backs of her knees, the small of her back, even the soles of her feet. There wasn't a single spot on her body that he hadn't explored with an eager, greedy, skilful mouth, she thought as her body began to throb with desire again. Her skin beginning to glow with longing, her breathing quickening. The urge to have him again, to feel him sink away in her, dissolve, melt together, suddenly so overwhelming that all her fear disappeared.

She shifted upright, leaned on her elbow and stared shamelessly at his splayed-out body. He lay on his back, the crumpled sheet twisted around his calves, a hint of a smile about his sleeping mouth. One single look at that mouth – the memory of all that he could do with it – and her self-control vanished as completely as her fear. A woman without fear and without self-control, she thought, as she began to stroke his penis, is a dangerous, dangerous woman.

His eyes flew open at once. For a moment, he looked shocked to see her face hovering above him. Then he sighed with relief.

'I thought it was all a dream.'

'It was,' she whispered. 'You're still dreaming. When I click my fingers you'll wake up and remember nothing.'

'Keep your fingers right where they are,' he mumbled with a languid smile, his teeth white against the black stubble around his mouth, his eyes sunk away in happy wrinkles.

He had already hardened under her hand. Desire swept through her like a veld fire. She'd never been so turned-on in her life, she realized with ever-increasing amazement.

'I've got something better in mind,' she said.

'I can't think of anything better,' he moaned.

'I'll show you,' she said, and slid further down on the crumpled sheet.

She crept between his legs and pressed his penis into her mouth with an urgency which astounded her. She had never really enjoyed sex, it dawned on her. She had thought she enjoyed what she thought was good sex. Now she felt like someone who had kept a poster of a famous painting in her house for years, completely happy with the imitation because she had never seen the original art work. Now that she had experienced the genuine article she would never, ever be content with the poster again.

Half an hour later – their mutual lust temporarily satisfied – the panic hit her once more. Her breath, never properly regained, was taken away all over again.

'It can't work,' she panted.

'It feels to me as though it's working,' he groaned.

'I'm not talking about sex.' She realized that her knees were still clamped tightly around his hips. As if she never wanted to let him go. She rolled quickly off his body, on to her back, and stared with him at the unfamiliar ceiling. A welcome breeze stirred the curtains in front of the open windows and blew a cool draught over their perspiring bodies. The sun was barely up, the light in the room still hazy, dark shadows lingering in the corners. 'I'm speaking about . . . the rest.'

'What rest?'

'You and me . . . we can't . . . we just can't . . .'

'Why not?'

'We know each other too well!'

'Since when has it been a disadvantage to know your lover well?'

Lover. Just the sound of the word in his mouth was enough to melt her resistance again. She felt as though she was drowning, struggling to keep her head above water, not to sink away into this warm, seductive, comforting feeling of ecstasy.

'OK, let's say it works for a few weeks . . . and then what? What happens when it's over? Then we've fucked-up a twenty-year friendship. For a few weeks of good sex.'

'If the sex of the last few hours is anything to go by,' he smiled, 'I'm willing to take the chance. Fuck friendship.'

'I'm serious, Max!'

'Me too, Liane.' He rolled on to his side, propped up on his elbow to look her in the eyes, but she stared resolutely at the ceiling. One look at that mouth and her last shred of resistance would evaporate. 'I've been waiting twenty years for this day, you know? I've always wanted to be your lover rather than your friend . . . but you were so damn prim and proper when you were younger that it was completely impossible to get you into bed . . . and then you went and married Paul. So I never really had a choice. It was friendship or nothing.'

'Paul and I split up more than two years ago. If you were really so eager to get me into bed, you could have made a move long ago.'

'Are you blaming me because I didn't leap on you long ago?' he asked in surprise, and began to laugh softly. 'I was scared, Liane. I didn't know if you'd have the slightest desire to sleep with me. You never gave me any indication. I mean, when I sat next to you on the beach yesterday, I would have fallen over in astonishment if someone had told me that I would wake up next to you this morning! So I was scared to make a move. Scared that I would spoil the friendship. And then I wouldn't even have had the consolation of having enjoyed a good fuck in the process.'

She refused to laugh with him. But she allowed herself to look at him at last. Her gaze now openly accusing.

'You were so busy seducing every other woman in the Cape that you didn't even realize I was available, Max.'

'I've slept with other women for years because I couldn't sleep with you, Liane.'

He reached out to her forehead, brushed her fringe away with his fingertips, the touch so unexpectedly tender that she squeezed her eyes closed again. Scared that he would see the welling-up of longing in them. The desire to give up the battle, to ignore the flashing warning lights in her mind and simply follow her heart. Her heart and her hormones.

'And if we . . . .' she said with closed eyes. 'I mean, just say we decide, OK, let's see what happens . . . and we promise each other we're going to try to stay friends . . . doesn't matter what happens . . .'

'You're taking the words right out of my mouth.'

'Do you think we can, just a little bit longer . . . even if it is just for today . . . pretend that nothing happened?'

'You mean I mustn't touch you in front of Paul?'

'No, it's got nothing to do with Paul,' she said, a fraction too fast. 'I'm talking about everyone in the house. I just can't cope with everyone's comments. I'm still feeling too . . . too vulnerable.'

'I don't know how you're going to hide it. Your neck looks as though you've been attacked by a vampire. But you'll probably be able to wear a scarf or something . . .'

'In this heat?' she asked, her fingers flying to her neck in alarm.

'Perhaps you can pretend you've got the cold shivers,' he grinned. 'You know, like a junkie with withdrawal symptoms.'

'It's not funny, Max.'

But she began to laugh helplessly with him.

'It's going to be awfully difficult for me to keep my hands off this body.'

His fingers slid from her face to her breasts, making her nipples stiffen and her arms come out in gooseflesh, sending a thrill of pleasure down her spine. She wanted him again, she thought helplessly.

'Max,' she pleaded, without knowing what she was pleading for.

'I'll do my best, but then you must first give me another chance.'

'To do what?' she moaned as his mouth closed over her breast.

'To show you what good sex is,' he said when he lifted his head from her breast. 'Till now I've just been doing warm-up exercises.'

'Goodness gracious,' she giggled. 'I'm kind of glad now that I didn't sleep with you when you were eighteen. All the years of practice with other women has turned you into a champion.'

'Is yesterday over for ever?' Mona wanted to know at the breakfast table.

'For ever,' confirmed Yvette with a forkful of scrambled egg halfway to her mouth. 'Unfortunately.'

'But tomorrow there will be a yesterday again.'

'The child sounds like a philosopher,' muttered Philip. 'Beware.'

'Yes. Today is tomorrow's yesterday.' Yvette saw the confusion in the child's grey-green eyes and tried again. 'When it becomes tomorrow, we look back to today, and then we call it yesterday.'

'And the day after tomorrow?'

'That's today's day-after-tomorrow and tomorrow's tomorrow.'

'I never realized it was so complicated!' exclaimed Bobby.

'And what comes after the day-after-tomorrow?' The child was like a puppy with a bone, refusing to let go. Her father's stubbornness, Philip decided. She observed her mother with a cocked head and an appraising look. 'Is there always a tomorrow?'

'As far as I know,' answered Yvette with a patient smile. 'Eat your food up first, then you can think up more questions.'

'Tomorrow and tomorrow and tomorrow!' Sasha shouted in delight, as if she had discovered a new nursery rhyme. She sat on her mother's lap and banged her spoon against her plate. 'Tomorrow and tomorrow and tomorrow!'

'And this one sounds as though she wants to follow in Shakespeare's footsteps,' grinned Ralph. 'How does that quote go again?'

'*Tomorrow, and tomorrow, and tomorrow, creeps in this petty pace from day to day ... and all our yesterdays have lighted fools the way to dusty death*.' Emma's eyes were unusually serious above her daughter's bouncing blonde head. 'One of the most moving sentences in English literature.'

'*King Lear?*' asked Ralph.

'*Macbeth,*' answered Liane, as befitted a former drama student. 'It's the monologue which ends with: *Life's but a walking shadow, a poor player that struts and frets his hour upon the stage and then is heard no more . . .* '

'*A tale told by an idiot,*' Philip recalled, '*full of sound and fury signifying nothing.*'

'Jesus,' sighed Emma. 'To be able to write something like that!'

They were eating a late breakfast because most of them had struggled to get up after the previous night's revels. Some of them still had their pyjamas on, and nobody looked exactly rested. Except the two children, of course. Paul and Liane were, as usual, the best groomed: Paul in another of his apparently infinite collection of pure white T-shirts; Liane in a cream-coloured dress with a patterned serviette knotted around her neck. Probably a new trend from Paris, to wear serviettes as accessories. And yet even *her* face showed signs of a lack of sleep – shadows under the eyes and two tired lines around the mouth.

She probably had more reason than anyone else to look tired, Philip decided with some measure of sympathy. Except for Max, who looked like a living scarecrow, the bottom half of his face covered with uneven black and white stubble, the top half unhealthily pale, the skin under his eyes slack and baggy, the eyes bloodshot. The temptation to tease him was almost irresistible. Philip bit on his lower lip and viewed the rest of the company. It didn't look as though anyone else suspected anything. Liane kept her eyes deliberately away from Max. Too deliberately, thought Philip, but it seemed he was the only one who noticed. And if he hadn't walked past Max's room by chance early this morning, she would have been able to fool him too.

He had jerked awake, somewhere between four and five, as often happened at home, and knew straight away that he wouldn't sleep again. The intoxicating heat in the dark room only worsened his feeling of anxiety. He couldn't switch on the light to read because Ralph was lying fast asleep on the bed opposite his. After rolling sweatily around for more than an hour he had decided, in desperation, to go for a walk beside the sea. He had slipped silently out by the back door and stood still for a moment to inhale the salty sea air. It was already dawn, the fleecy clouds in the east stained bright pink, a hint of a sea breeze stroking his glowing skin like a cool hand. And then he heard the creaking bed in the back room. As though a bunch of naughty kids were using the mattress as a trampoline. A moment of confused astonishment as he walked closer. And then he realized what he was listening to. By this time he was close enough to hear the smothered cries and other background noises, too.

He had turned away quickly and walked to the sea. Well, he had thought, surprised and amused. Then Max had finally succeeded in getting the woman of his dreams into bed. And seeing that it had been a very long time since he had heard such sounds in his own bed, he couldn't help but feel a little envious.

His train of thought was disturbed by his daughter, who clambered on to his lap uninvited, grabbed a slice of toast from his plate and tried to push it into his mouth.

'Eat!' she commanded. 'Yum-yum!'

Philip opened his mouth obediently.

'The way to a man's heart . . .' joked Mila.

'Not Philip's heart!' snorted Ralph. 'I've served him food which would melt the heart of a king – and then he eats it just as dutifully as he's chewing that piece of bread now.'

'I didn't realize you were trying to win my heart,' said Philip.

'Half the pleasure of cooking is seeing others enjoying the food!' Ralph exclaimed. 'Just look how Max is relishing that scrambled egg!'

'If you gave Max a tin of bully beef and a piece of mouldy bread this morning, he'd have gobbled it up just as greedily. The man has had a hard night.'

Max raised his head from the plate and glared suspiciously at Philip.

'We've all had a hard night,' he said with a grimace. 'Madness takes its toll.'

'*Midsummer Night's Dream*,' said Liane with her eyes on her plate.

'No,' said Max, '*Rocky Horror Picture Show.*'

'I know,' she giggled. 'I mean the whole atmosphere last night. I wonder if the heat had something to do with it. We were all a bit mad.'

'Some perhaps more than others,' said Paul, his smile gleaming white.

'Perhaps some needed it more than others,' she said with an innocent shrug.

She hadn't been a drama student for nothing, Philip thought, watching her over his daughter's blonde head. The child had begun to chew on the toast crust herself, but now tried to get the remaining scrambled egg on his plate into a spoon so that she could feed him some more.

'I suppose we have to accept that we're getting too old for sex, drugs and rock 'n' roll,' he said with a resigned sigh. 'We're no longer today's children.'

'Speak for yourself, my darling!' Liane cried out crossly.

And he laughed, pleased that he had at last provoked her to behave a little less like a prissy schoolgirl.

'Are you yesterday's children?' Mona asked.

'Well, I wouldn't put it quite like that,' replied Yvette.

'Of course you are!' Bobby pushed back her empty plate and poured herself another cup of coffee, her eyes bright behind the little round glasses. 'Anyone who refuses to listen to any music written in the last twenty years has to be halfway over the hill!'

'We did listen to your music last night.' Emma stood up laughing and began to stack the empty plates on top of each other. 'We even danced to your music!'

'But you still prefer the Rolling Stones,' said Bobby accusingly.

'It's only rock 'n' roll,' said Ralph with a smile that stretched wider each moment, 'but we like it.'

Philip watched them all with an unexpected tightness around the heart. *A tale told by an idiot, full of sound and fury, signifying nothing.* And he remembered the question which he had asked himself two days ago in his untidy bedroom, as he packed his little pile of clothes for the weekend. How do you rid yourself of friends? There were so many things to relinquish, he thought sadly, but friendship remained the hardest.

NINE

Fire, Every Hour (1993)

'Liane!' said Paul, pleased to hear her breathy voice over the phone. 'This is a nice surprise!'

'I'm afraid it's not so nice,' she said softly. 'I've got bad news, Paul.'

'What?'

Riaan, who was lying on the couch, looked up, concerned, when he heard the sudden alarm in Paul's voice.

'Philip is dead.' And the breathy voice cracked, like glass, on the last word. A high, sharp, broken sound. 'He drove his car off a cliff late last night.'

'Where?' he asked, and sank into an armchair, stunned.

He stared into Riaan's eyes for a moment, registering the anxious gaze in a detached way.

'On Chapman's Peak.'

'One of the most beautiful roads in the world,' he murmured.

As Liane used to say when they drove over the winding mountain road between Clifton and Llandudno; the sea stretched out spectacularly blue and bright on the one side, the high overhang and rough crags like a majestic wall on the other; the car as tiny as a child's toy against the bulk of the mountain and the expanse of water.

'If you have to die,' she said in a dull tone, 'I suppose it's better to do it in a beautiful place.'

But it was dark when he died, thought Paul. He wouldn't have been able to appreciate the beauty.

'How did it happen?'

'No one knows. The car is completely burned out. The last people who saw him said he was . . . very drunk. Drunk and depressed.'

Then he would definitely not have appreciated the beauty, thought Paul.

'When is the funeral?'

Riaan's eyes stretched even wider. He shifted upright on the black leather couch and the checked knee blanket which Paul had thrown over him fell on to the floor. The bloody old-woman blanket, as he called it. With a resentful smile on his face, so bony and angular now, the luxurious brown moustache shaved off, the skin between nose and upper lip a white stripe across his face. Which was also growing whiter by the day.

'No, there isn't going to be a funeral. Apparently he told Emma recently he didn't even want a memorial service. He said we must just hire a beach house somewhere and scatter his ashes over the sea. On condition that no one says anything sentimental about him. Or refers to any supernatural beings.'

'Like when he got married,' Paul smiled involuntarily, a weak flicker of a smile. '*Don't mention God.*'

'Unbelieving to the bitter end.'

'*He who knows most believes least.* I read that one night on Teledata. Between the police report and the price of goats.'

'Anyway, Emma is organizing a weekend at Franskraal, seeing that it was his favourite seaside town. I think she needs to organize something to keep her busy. It's a hell of a blow for her, but she thinks she's not supposed to grieve because they've been split up for over four years.'

Paul said nothing, just stared at Riaan, but it was as though his face had suddenly gone out of focus. A hazy white circle against the black leather of the couch. How long was it since he and Liane had split up?

'We'd really like you to be there, too.'

'Where?' he asked, confused. 'Oh, you mean at Franskraal.'

'Or wherever the ashes are going to be scattered.'

'When?'

'Well, we're trying to organize a weekend that suits everyone, so it will probably only be in a few weeks' time. Is there any chance you could come?'

How could he explain to her, with Riaan sitting in the same room, that he couldn't go away now? It wasn't as though his partner had become an invalid overnight. Riaan was completely capable of looking after himself. But he still couldn't go away. Each moment they spent together was too precious now.

'I'll see what I can do,' he replied. 'It's difficult . . . at the moment . . .'

'Riaan?' she asked, concerned. 'How is he?'

She had stopped referring to him as The Director. Since he had told her about the illness last year – then only a looming thunder cloud, now a full-scale storm – her aloofness had changed to total compassion, caring, support. The same about-turn change of heart which had often amazed him when they were married.

'He's sitting here on the couch opposite me. If I don't say good-bye now and tell him what's happening, he's going to burst with anxiety.'

'OK,' she said quickly. 'Call me if you want to talk. Please.'

'I will.' And then, just before he rang off, he remembered. 'How's the pregnancy going?'

'I always knew it couldn't be as easy as my girlfriends made it look,' she said resentfully. 'But I honestly didn't know that it was going to be this bad.'

'Your friends weren't expecting twins.'

'No,' she said with a melodramatic sigh. 'Ain't I lucky?'

When he put the phone down, he saw that his hand was shaking. But it was as though the news hadn't really hit him properly. Not yet.

'One of our oldest friends had an accident last night.' Even now that he heard the words from his own mouth, it still didn't feel real. He shrugged his shoulders helplessly and went to sit next to Riaan on the arm rest of the couch. 'Philip.'

'The difficult guy who was married to Emma?'

'The difficult guy,' he confirmed as Riaan took his shaking hand. 'Who was married to Emma.'

That was how Riaan knew most of his friends, he realized with sudden regret. As you would 'know' a famous literary character without ever having read the book. Don Quixote – the mad guy who charged at windmills. Anna Karenina – the adulterous woman who leaped in front of a train. Philip McCarthy – the difficult guy who was married to Emma. And now Riaan would never have the chance to get to know Philip as a three-dimensional person. It was this mournful thought which made the news sink in at last. And Riaan didn't have much time to get to know any of his other friends better. At once he knew he had to go to Franskraal. He'd spend the weekend with his friends, he decided, and he'd take Riaan with him. Even if he had to carry him on to the plane.

Of course it wasn't so easy to convince Riaan. An hour later they were still sitting on the couch together, Riaan with his head resting wearily on Paul's shoulder.

'Don't even think for a moment about not going, Paul,' he said almost threateningly. 'But I don't belong there. They're *your* friends. It's *your* life.'

'Precisely. It's my life and you're part of my life.' He shook his head, uncomprehendingly, wearily. 'You've always blamed me for hiding you away from my old friends! Now you refuse to get to know them better!'

'I wanted to get to know your friends because I was inquisitive about you, because I wanted to know as much as possible about your previous life. You were like a jigsaw with lots of missing pieces. I wanted to track down a few of the lost pieces, try to fit them in at the right places, that's all.'

Hadn't he, once, also compared his life to a jigsaw puzzle? All the lost pieces. And someone had said that it wasn't a jigsaw, it was more like an enigmatic painting. There weren't holes in the painting, it was all there. It was just that you usually didn't understand it.

'Remember how I used to tease you because you were so prim and proper?' asked Riaan with a nostalgic smile. 'The few times that I saw you with one of your old friends. *Mary Poppins.*' His eyes on his hands which lay still and white on his lap. As lifeless as the hands of a statue, thought Paul as he intertwined his tanned brown fingers with Riaan's pale ones. Startled to feel the cold skin against his warm palm. 'But I never really blamed you. I accepted that there were things that you weren't yet . . . ready to share with me . . .'

'I was like someone who had just escaped from jail. So relieved to be free that I had no desire to see any of my old friends. I'm talking about the first year or two. I didn't want to see anyone who would remind me of my own . . . stupidity.'

'You're being too hard on yourself again.' Riaan stroked his hand absent-mindedly. Who was actually comforting whom? Paul wondered. It had been one of the most liberating revelations of this relationship, that from the very first moment their roles were interchangeable. 'You've been forced into a role since childhood.'

'Rubbish. We all get forced into roles. You were always brave enough to see the falseness and reject it. I clung to the safety of hypocrisy for a lot longer.'

Paul stared anxiously at the neat sitting room, the sober black and white colour scheme, the nostalgic black-and-white movie posters against the wall. In this room, in this house, with this man, he had been happier than ever before in his life. Barely three years, he thought hopelessly, in a lifetime of cowardice and hypocrisy. And now they had to live every remaining hour in the shadow of death. It wasn't fucking fair.

'I want you to come with me,' he said pleadingly. 'I know that it's not going to be easy. I mean, let's face it, we're not talking about a frivolous weekend at the seaside, we're talking about a kind of wake. I have to say good-bye to one of my oldest friends. And perhaps to lots of other things too. I need you, Riaan. I can't do it on my own.'

Riaan sat upright, took Paul's chin in his hand, looked earnestly into his eyes.

'OK, let's face it,' he said quietly. 'Let's be completely honest. I'm not the handsome hunk you fell in love with any more.' A shadow of a smile at the corners of his mouth – if he'd still had a moustache, it would have quivered gently now – but his eyes stayed dark and sad. 'I'm sick. And I'm vain. I don't want your friends to remember me . . . to meet me . . . as this weak and sick moffie. It's unfair to you. It's unfair to me. How does that song go again? *I'm not the man I used to be . . .* '

'You're still the man I love,' said Paul. 'More than I've ever loved anyone else. *In sickness and in health.* Jesus, Riaan, isn't that what love is meant to mean?'

'I don't know,' Riaan observed drily. 'I never had to stand in front of an altar and listen to the marriage vows.'

'I can't remember a single word my father said the day he married me and Liane. I was too panic-stricken because I knew deep down that I was making a terrible mistake. But I tried to tell myself that this was probably what all men felt when they stood in front of the altar . . . Anyway, there was no way I could understand that kind of promise then. *Till death do us part.*' He tried to keep his voice calm, but he was powerless against the passion which still broke through. 'It was only when I met you, Riaan . . . that I began to realize what it meant . . . and that was before you got sick.'

Riaan said nothing, just sank back into the couch and closed his eyes. Paul stared at his face, so pale and so tired, but still the most beloved face on earth. He wanted to shake him by the shoulders. He wanted to fold him into his arms. And he realized that at this moment, in spite of everything, he didn't want to be anywhere else but in this house, with this man.

'Look, if I wanted to go and boast about my lover's looks, I'd go and rent a pretty young boy for the weekend!'

'Not a good idea,' Riaan warned with a weak smile. 'It would only confirm all their prejudices about gay men's superficiality.'

'My friends aren't like that!' he exclaimed indignantly. Before he realized that Riaan was teasing him. He shrugged his shoulders and smiled sheepishly. 'They aren't a bunch of medieval witch-burners, Riaan. They're my friends.'

'Will we be able to share a bed?' The sadness in Riaan's eyes was replaced by a twinkle. 'Or will we have to creep around in the dark like we did when we visited your parents?'

'My father is an old-fashioned dominee. You can't expect that he'll ever offer us a bed to share. But you rather bowled him over when you began to talk theology with him. He still can't believe your knowledge of the religions of the world. And you won my mother's heart when you cooked for her. So I'd say it was a successful visit. Even if we had to sleep in separate rooms.'

'I must admit that the whole idea of sneaky sex in a pastorie was quite exciting.' The familiar, cheeky grin on his face was suddenly so moving that Paul quickly looked down at their intertwined fingers. Riaan noticed it – as he noticed every change of emotion – and ruffled Paul's hair with his free hand. Brusquely, almost brutally, as if he could brush away all their anxiety. 'What are we going to do about supper? Are you going to punish me with one of your experimental dishes again? Or shall we phone for a pizza?'

'Let's phone for a pizza.'

Paul burst out laughing when he saw the relief on Riaan's face. It was an incontrovertible fact that meals in this house had deteriorated along with Riaan's health. Paul made a brave effort, about once a week, to master something more adventurous than scrambled eggs on toast, but the result hardly ever measured up to his partner's high standards.

'But I'm not going to phone until you've promised that you'll come with me for the weekend,' he said threateningly.

'You sound like my mother!' Riaan cried in disbelief. 'She always bribed me with food!'

'Just shows you how desperate I am.'

'Well . . . if you promise that you won't be as macho as Margaret Thatcher just to impress your straight friends.'

'I'll borrow my ex-wife's clothes and walk around like a drag queen!' Paul promised. 'Anything to keep you happy!'

'Ag, no, that won't be necessary,' said Riaan with a happy smile. 'You know that dresses have never really turned me on.'

'You've got to give Philip credit for one thing,' said Mila three weeks later in Emma's cramped sitting room, as she admired the angelic blonde child on the floor. 'He created a work of art when he made this child!'

'She's a freak show,' said Emma, in mock irritation. 'I can't take her anywhere without being followed by cooing tannies.'

'I don't know how you managed it.' Mila shook her head over a cup of rooibos tea. 'I mean, you know I've always thought you were attractive . . .' She popped a chocolate biscuit into her mouth to hide her smile. 'And Philip isn't . . . wasn't an unattractive man. But I never imagined that the two of you could produce something like *this*!'

Sasha lay on her stomach a little way from them, busy with a jigsaw puzzle, bare feet swinging through the air and long blonde hair falling on either side of her serious face. As if she had already, like her mother, learned to hide behind her hair. Rosy cheeks and a bright pink blossom for a mouth.

'She looks like Philip's mother,' said Emma thoughtfully. 'The other day, when I went to help pack his things away, I came across a few photos which he'd never shown me. Of his mother as a child. I got goosebumps when I saw the similarity. I don't know why he never told me . . .' She shrugged her shoulders and drained her cup, her wide mouth suddenly sad. 'I can only hope that she hasn't inherited her grandmother's tortured spirit too. Or her father's tortured spirit, for that matter.'

'How is she coping?' Mila asked.

'I don't know. She hasn't shown any sign of trauma yet. She saw so little of him really . . . it's not as though there's suddenly this gigantic gap in her life . . . but a parent's death probably always leaves a hole somewhere inside you. Even a parent you barely knew. She'll probably become aware of it later on. I wonder sometimes if she'll remember anything about him. I mean, she's three and a half now, so it's theoretically possible. But it's probably just as possible that she'll forget everything.'

'Perhaps it would be easier in the end if she doesn't remember him too clearly.'

'I don't know. Perhaps she'll miss him more if she remembers nothing about him. Memories can be a kind of comfort. I think that's all that's kept me going in the last few weeks. The good memories I have of him . . .'

'And the bad ones?'

'Funny, I always thought there were ten bad ones for every single good one. But his death has wiped out all the bad memories. Like wrong sums wiped from a blackboard.'

'I felt like that after Stuart's death,' Mila remembered. 'I couldn't believe that I was ever unhappy with him. But after a while I began to see the wrong sums again . . .'

She stared over the coffee table – a weathered yellow-wood chest packed with piles of battered paperbacks – at the child's swinging feet. More stacks of books on the windowsills and above the fireplace and in the kitchen and even in the bathroom. This whole minuscule dolls' house of a cottage always reminded Mila of a cosy second-hand bookshop. Overcrowded and dusty and apparently chaotic, but with a kind of order within the disorder, an atmosphere of calm and peacefulness which clung to the furniture along with the slightly musty smell of old books. A home where a child would never hear two adults screaming at each other, that was the idyll that Emma wanted to create here.

'At the moment, it feels to me as if he fucked everything up by dying!' Emma burst out unexpectedly. 'All my careful plans to ensure that this child wouldn't miss her father one day! I used Adriaan and Yvette's relationship as a kind of justification for my decision not to stay married. Those awful nightmares Mona had after her father left . . . and now Adriaan is back with his family . . . and this child has lost her father. For ever!'

She grabbed a packet of cigarettes from one of the piles of books and held it out to Mila. Jerked her hand back in alarm, her grey-blue eyes suddenly guilty.

'Sorry, I keep forgetting you aren't allowed to. Since Philip died, I've been puffing like a chimney. I know it's not an excuse, but . . .'

'You don't have to look for excuses, Emma. If there's anyone who understands the craving for a cigarette, it's me.'

'That's why I feel like such a heel, smoking in front of you.' She lit the cigarette quickly, as if she was scared she would lose her nerve. 'Isn't it a torture for you to watch me fucking up my lungs like this?'

'It's not so bad any more,' said Mila, and put another biscuit in her mouth. 'It's been almost a year now. I still get cravings, but then I just raid the fridge again. As you can see, I've picked up almost ten kilos.'

'You could do with a few extra kilos,' said Emma quickly.

'I don't know how I'll cope if I ever get a lover again who smokes.' She smiled self-consciously when she heard the melancholy note in her voice. 'Sex always made me crave a cigarette. The better the sex, the stronger the craving. Probably the Calvinistic belief that one sin always leads to another . . . from dance to sex to smoking to . . . who knows? Murder and robbery, if I was to take my mother's word for it. But it was always one of life's little pleasures, lying in a lover's arms, sweaty and exhausted, sharing a cigarette in the dark. One of the things I'll miss when I'm dead. As Ralph always says.'

She didn't know how she'd cope if she ever got any kind of lover again, she thought, whether he smoked or not. Where would she ever find the courage to undress in front of anyone other than a doctor? Even in the doctor's surgery it was a torture. She just wasn't brave enough to confront the shock in someone else's eyes when she took off her lovely black lingerie. Bared the scarred body under the smooth satin and imported lace.

'Philip always said he was the last of the Great White Smokers.' Emma sucked anxiously on the cigarette, her eyes hidden by a veil of smoke. 'Now I'll probably take over the baton from him. And the greater the pressure from all sides – the more politically incorrect it becomes – the greater my desire to carry on becomes. I know it's perverse . . .'

Sometimes she dreamed of a blind lover. Someone who could never look at her. But blind people see with their fingertips. She wouldn't be able to hide her body from his fingers. No, she thought, she would have to find a blind man without hands.

'How are things with Adriaan and Yvette?' The leaps she had to make in her subconscious, from one slippery stone to another, so as not to be swept away by her whirling stream of thought. From sex to Adriaan, of course, from Adriaan to Yvette, of course, and then? 'I mean, now that they're back together?'

'Don't you see them any more?'

'As little as possible. I'm scared to . . . I don't want to open up old wounds . . .'

Emma held the cigarette in front of her mouth like a shield. Her eyes questioning, searching, perhaps even suspicious. Mila wondered if she shouldn't just eat the last biscuit in the bowl.

'It's as though he's never been away. Mona follows him like a shadow, the dog follows Mona like a shadow, and Yvette is plump and pregnant again and as happy as can be.'

'I heard about the pregnancy . . .'

She was alarmed by the longing in her voice. It could have been her. It had been her. But it didn't work. It would never have worked. And now she knew that it could never happen again. She would never be able to have a child.

'Adriaan said you persuaded him to go back.'

'That's a bit of an exaggeration! He was like someone standing on the edge of a swimming pool. You could see he was burning to be in the water. He just needed a little push. Not even a push, just a tap on the back.'

'And you decided to give him that tap.'

What else could she do? She had got breast cancer, a disease which could be exacerbated by pregnancy, by the oestrogen released by the body. *Just my fucking luck.* As she had said to her GP. Just when it looked as though she could at last have a successful pregnancy, as though it wouldn't all end in a miscarriage, then she had to choose between her own life and the life of an unborn child. It wasn't really a choice. They removed the foetus. After that they removed her uterus too. To make sure that it wouldn't happen again. She was too shattered to mourn her lost child or her lost fertility. Too busy grieving for her breast. It was the loss which lay closest to her heart, literally and figuratively. Her left breast.

'I just told him that Yvette really wanted him back. This affair that she had with Tomas made him feel incredibly insecure. Pathetic, if you think . . . about everything *he* did. The fragility of the male ego astounded me once again.'

'You said years ago that you didn't know if you would ever be able to look at him without feeling as if your whole body was bursting into flame . . .'

'It's not so bad any more. Not for ages. There'll probably always be a spark, but well . . .'

Abortion. Hysterectomy. Mastectomy. For months she had counted off her losses like rosary beads. At night in her bed, by day in front of her computer, afternoons after work when she walked on the Sea Point Promenade, weekends when she walked in Kirstenbosch or on Table Mountain. She had begun to walk obsessively. Mumbling like an old madwoman. *Abortion, hysterectomy, mastectomy.* A litany of unbearable, unthinkable, destructive losses. Her unborn child, her uterus, her left breast. And the only man she ever really wanted, even though she knew she could never have him, perhaps *because* she knew she could never have him. The only one whom she could grow to love so much that she wanted to spend the rest of her life with him, even though she knew it would never work.

'And still you sent him back to Yvette.'

Mila heard the admiration in her friend's voice and reached in confusion for the last biscuit.

'Please don't make me into some kind of saint!' she warned with a forced laugh, and licked the crumbs from her lips. 'I mean, *I* wasn't much use to him any more. These days the mere thought of a sexual relationship – with anyone – is enough to make me break out in a cold sweat. I'm afraid that's all that's left of the fires of lust. Just icy sweat!'

'You'll get a lover again, Mila.' Emma leaned forward and stubbed the cigarette out vehemently in an ashtray balancing precariously on one of the piles of books. 'You've always had an absolutely perfect body. The fact that it's not perfect any more doesn't mean that it's repulsive!'

How would Emma know? She hadn't seen what this body looked like now. She hadn't shown it to her yet, she couldn't show it to anyone, apart from doctors and nurses. She couldn't even look at it herself without starting to cry. If only she hadn't been so indecently proud of her breasts before! If only the remaining breast wasn't so lovely! It was the contrast which she couldn't bear, the difference between then and now, between what had been and what remained. Between the right-hand side, full and round and firm as a balloon, and the shocking emptiness on the other side, flat and hard, with that horizontal scar. Like a line crossed through a misspelt word.

'There we are!' Sasha leaped up, pleased with herself, the puzzle completed, and flung herself at her mother. 'It wasn't even difficult!'

'That's because you're so clever, my love,' said Emma, and embraced the little body with a beaming, soothing smile.

And suddenly Mila felt completely shut out. There was such an intimacy between mother and daughter that it made anyone else feel like an outsider. In this vulnerable state it was too much to bear. The thought of everything she'd lost was too awful. It would never have worked, she tried to comfort herself. She would never have been able to bring up a child on her own. Her friends would have realized who the father was. It would have broken Yvette's heart. It would have broken her own heart. What was left of her heart. It would never have worked.

'Philip carried a photo of her in his wallet.' Emma's eyes looked guilty again, as when she'd lit the cigarette a few minutes ago. 'Another thing I only found out after he died. Did you also – after your husband's death – feel as though you came across all sorts of things you'd rather not have known?'

'Of course.' With her fingers in front of her mouth, as though she was scared she would say too much. 'That's the survivor's lot.'

The letter which fell unexpectedly from a file of policies and personal documents, a few sheets of paper which fluttered to the floor as innocently as white birds. Actually, it should have exploded like a bomb, she thought afterwards. It was a letter to his mother, three thin sheets on which he'd spilled his heart out. Telling her how ashamed he was that he'd known since he was little that his father hit her; begging her forgiveness for not doing anything to protect her. For pretending, like all the other people around her, that he didn't know what was going on. Perhaps his courage failed him before he could post it, perhaps he only wanted his mother to read it after his death, perhaps he simply forgot about it. It was also possible that he had hoped his wife would find it some day. The only way he would ever share this secret with her.

She was crying by the end of the first sentence. The last page, where he admitted that he was afraid that he would also become like his father, turned to an illegible mess before her misty eyes, her tears washing the ink right off the paper. She would never be able to give such a revealing letter to her proud mother-in-law anyway, she consoled herself. She would never be able to look at her well-off, respected, hypocritical father-in-law without feeling revulsion and disgust. She deliberately cut off all remaining ties with them.

It was Ralph who told her last year that Stuart's father had died of a heart attack. 'Probably a relief for his mother,' he'd said over the phone. 'I don't think she liked the old bugger much.' She had always suspected that he also knew his friend's secret.

'That must be the greatest humiliation of death,' she said thoughtfully, her eyes again fixed admiringly on Sasha who was trying to plait a strand of her mother's hair with clumsy toddler's fingers. 'That it lays bare all your secrets. From the dirty socks you hid in the bottom of your cupboard to all those passionate letters from long-forgotten lovers. A good reason to springclean your house every few months, perhaps. To get rid of all the embarrassing evidence. In case of sudden death.'

'No, Jesus, Mila, that sounds like my mother who always said we couldn't go to bed with dirty feet! Just in case we died in the night!'

'I don't care about dying with dirty feet. But I must admit I can never get to sleep if my vibrator is lying out in the open next to my bed.'

'Because you might die in the night?' asked Emma, astonished.

'Well, just think of the humiliation! To expire next to an . . . artificial phallus! A plastic penis! How pathetic!'

Shortly before the plane landed in Cape Town, Paul touched Riaan's shoulder carefully to wake him up. His eyes fluttered open, his expression confused for a moment, as though he had slept so deeply that he didn't know where he was. Then he smiled, that beloved smile, so rare these days, which caught on Paul's heart like a sharp hook, tearing out a small piece of flesh each time. One of these days it would all be in shreds.

'I had a wonderful dream,' he said, stretching in the cramped seat. 'I dreamed that we were running on a long, white beach, you and me, without a stitch of clothing. With the sun sinking behind us. A golden glow over everything.'

'Sounds like the kind of movie scene which usually makes you want to puke,' said Paul.

'That's precisely why it was so wonderful. I didn't look at the scene like a director. I was part of it, feeling the wind in my hair, smelling the sea. I didn't stand to one side as usual and scream "Cut!" OK, I admit that somewhere inside me I could hear a little voice shouting "Kitsch! Kitsch!", but I decided, fuck that, I'm going to enjoy it, kitsch or not!'

'I only hope you're not going to start acting in your own movies, like Woody Allen,' grinned Paul. 'It doesn't sound as though you'll display much judgement if you end up on the other side of the camera.'

'It was only a dream,' laughed Riaan.

Paul felt the plane's wheels bump hard against the ground and listened to the high scream of the powerful thrusters as the massive machine gradually came to a standstill. For him the most exciting moment of any flight. While Liane had always sat next to him, white-knuckled, because she'd read somewhere that most aviation accidents happen during landing. He had always viewed this as one of those typical half-truths which she could work herself up about so unnecessarily. Like the time an astrologer warned her that a relationship with another man could spoil her marriage. ('I have no desire to have a relationship with another man! I'm married to a stunning man!') A few months later Paul had to tell her that he was in love with another man. ('The fucking astrologer was right! How come I couldn't see it from the start!') Perhaps, thought Paul, he should have a look at some statistics about aircraft accidents after all.

It was going to feel strange to introduce Riaan to her, he realized when he stood up to get their overnight bags down from the locker. It was going to feel strange to introduce Riaan to the whole lot of them. To spend a whole weekend with them. Like in the old days. While everyone knew the old days were gone for ever. Philip's death had wrenched a link out of a chain. The rest of them could come and go, bring new lovers and children and pets along, but the chain would never be whole again. This weekend was going to be different from any previous weekend. It was only dawning on him now.

'Ready for action, cowboy?' he asked as cheerfully as he could.

'If this was a movie, I'd be screaming "Cut!" now.' Riaan looked tired, dark sickle moons on the soft skin under his eyes, even though he'd slept right through the flight. And anxious, a nervous trembling at the corners of his mouth. 'Fade out to the next scene. A week later.'

Perhaps it hadn't been such a good idea to bring him along after all, thought Paul, suddenly overcome with doubt. But he smiled reassuringly.

'And then you'd have missed all the action!'

'You know I was never one for action movies.'

'I know.' Paul stood behind him in the aisle and rubbed his shoulder comfortingly. 'You prefer naked men running in slow motion on a beach.'

And suddenly he did something which astounded him. He bent forward and kissed Riaan on the neck, on the bit of white skin sticking out between the black T-shirt and the dark hair. Out of the corner of his eye he saw the indignant expression of the grey-haired woman on his left. He turned around and looked challengingly at her, until she turned away in confusion. She looked like his mother, he realized with a slight shock, when a TV programme didn't meet her unyielding Christian National preconceptions. The same stingy mouth, pursed like an old-fashioned money bag, the flaming indignation on the little round cheeks, the excited glint in the wide-stretched eyes. When he turned back to Riaan, he was rewarded with an amused smile.

'I know I asked you not to behave like Mary Poppins,' said Riaan. 'But I didn't mean for you to carry on as though you're in a Gay Pride parade.'

Paul smiled proudly at him. All his doubts allayed. For the moment, at least.

'You're still the best thing that's ever happened to me, you know that?'

As soon as he walked into the arrivals hall he spotted Liane among the crowd. And she took his breath away. As lovely as a full moon. As big as a circus tent. Her shiny brown hair longer than it had been in years, her body heavier than it had ever been. She was wearing a wide white dress which made her look like an enormously fat bride. Max like a bashful groom beside her, black jeans and sloganless white T-shirt, grey-black hair cut shorter and more stylishly than before, a trendy salt-and-pepper goatee about his mouth.

'Advocate Ackermann!' he called out. 'You've been attacked by a stylist!'

'In more ways than one,' grinned Max, and hugged him a little clumsily. 'We've reached a kind of compromise. She has the right of veto over my appearance and the décor in the house. As far as the rest is concerned, I'm the boss.'

'That's more than I could ever say,' laughed Paul.

'He drags me along to boring political meetings and I drag him along to boring art exhibitions,' said Liane with a beaming smile. 'He forces me to read the *Mail* and *Guardian*, and I force him to read *Vogue*. Or at least to look at the pictures.'

'Now that's what I call a balanced couple,' said Paul. 'You should have got together years ago.'

'We had to get rid of you first,' Max reminded him.

Paul tried to hug Liane too, but the massive stomach made it difficult. He took a step back and stared dumbfounded at its girth.

'It's not funny, Paul Terreblanche.'

'Are you sure there are only two of them inside there?'

'It feels like seven,' she sighed. 'But the doctor assures me that I'm not going to make the cover of *Time*. It's just an exceptionally big and boisterous pair of twins.'

He turned to Riaan, who had introduced himself to Max, and threw a proud arm around his friend's thin shoulders. Perhaps a little too possessively, he realized. As if he was in a Gay Pride parade.

'And this is Riaan the Director.'

'Delighted to meet you at last.' With that smile which lit up her face like a torch. 'I must admit that I thought Paul was a bit crazy to leave a stunning woman like me for a man he hardly knew. Now I can see he would have been crazy not to leave me.'

The poor man didn't have a hope in hell of resisting her, Paul realized with relief. The breathy voice, the unforgettable face, the natural charm, it was all still there. But something else had been added, a soft contentment which he had never noticed before. Like a sharp stone which has been washed smooth by years in flowing water.

She was probably the next best thing that ever happened to him, he realized.

Mila would remember this weekend as two days and two nights in a bell jar. She had never felt so lonely and alienated in all her life. Among her oldest and dearest friends, but caught behind glass, thick glass which distorted everything. She could see them, but only just. And they could definitely not see her. They saw an attractive woman with short blonde hair and the legs of a dancer, her body not quite as slender as a year ago, her lips not as carefully painted, but still attractive. Perhaps even exceptionally attractive – for her age. They admired her, as always, told each other that she was handling her illness and its consequences amazingly well. They couldn't see the scars under her clothes. And she would never let them see her heart.

Perhaps it was a good thing that everyone was so overwhelmed by their own personal joys and sorrows. New relationships, old relationships, pregnancy and illness, life and death. No one realized that she wasn't really there.

Perhaps also because of their personal circumstances, they spoke less than usual about politics. And yet it was once again a year full of astounding developments. A faraway queen on a faraway island called 1993 her 'annus horribilis'. And most of her former subjects in her former colony at the foot of Africa unfortunately had to agree with her. Like a never-ending ride on a life-threatening rollercoaster, frightening heights of hope alternating with dizzying descents to depths of despair, shame, rage. By the time that Philip died, scarcely eight months before the first democratic elections would take place, the dream of a peaceful future had begun to look like a mocking mirage. Trembling in the distance, apparently close but always unreachable, in a wilderness of assassinations and township killings and cold-blooded attacks in bars and sports clubs. Even during a church service.

Long ago, Mila thought almost nostalgically, she'd realized she wasn't safe in her own house any more, in her own bed, not even in her own body. But she had always believed, although it had been a long time since she'd stopped believing in churches, that she would feel safe in a church. Safe in the arms of Jesus. Ha!

'Meat!' declared Adriaan, when his daughter asked what they were going to eat. 'We're going to eat meat for the whole weekend. In memory of our friend Philip.'

He stood outside next to the impressive braai area, a broad stone chimney above a solid cement slab on which a fire was already burning high. His friends sat near by around a plastic table, next to a well-manicured lawn and a few flowerbeds. On the roof of the double-storey house, a TV antenna. The boere always take the suburbs to the sea, he had remarked scathingly when he arrived. Most of the others already knew the house, the same wooden beach house in which they'd spent the weekend with Philip last year. When Adriaan was still in Johannesburg.

'Did Philip like meat a lot?' Mona asked.

'He couldn't live without meat without losing his self-respect,' Adriaan answered, turning the grid in the fire to burn it clean.

'What does that mean?'

'It means that he was crazy about meat.'

The child looked earnestly up at him. At the age of almost eight, she had left her plump toddler's body behind. Her legs were now longer and thinner, her brown hands had lost their dimples. But she was still a miniature portrait of her father. The same vulnerable mouth – the similarity more striking now that she had lost her milk teeth – the same challenging posture as she stood there next to the fire. Little round belly under a white Victorian nightdress with a frill around the neck, hands on hips and bare feet planted firmly on the ground. Like a stubby little tree.

'But won't he get meat in heaven?'

'I hope so,' said Adriaan. 'I think his idea of heaven was something like a gigantic steak house. Lined with shelves full of good books.'

'And an endless supply of alcohol and cigarettes,' added Ralph, smiling.

'Cigarettes are bad for you,' Mona informed him with a disapproving look at the cigarette between his fingers.

'Cigarettes are bad, alcohol is bad, meat is bad . . .' sighed Adriaan. 'Sometimes life is bad for you, my loveliest daughter.'

'I'm your only daughter,' she giggled.

'That means you'll always be my loveliest daughter.'

She threw her arms around his hips and pressed her face against his soft stomach, her smile so delighted that Mila felt her eyes burning with sudden envy. She stared at her outstretched legs, her calves smooth and rounded underneath a short summer dress. She had read somewhere that a woman's legs are the last part of her body which she can show off when she gets older. A good thing that she was blessed with nice legs, she thought with the bitter taste of self-pity in her mouth, because there was not much else left. When she looked up again, the child was skipping away over the grass in her long white nightdress, wafting in the twilight as though her bare feet didn't quite touch the ground.

'Where does all the religious passion come from?' asked Ralph, amused. 'I thought today's postmodern children didn't believe in heaven.'

'Oh, but they do. In a postmodern way.' Adriaan watched her as she began to play with Sasha and the dog, a little way off. 'It's no longer a place with golden streets and harp music. More a case of angels on roller blades and rap music.'

'And the anti-smoking campaign?'

'At school,' said Adriaan, shaking his head. 'They're brainwashed about other things than in our day. But they're still brainwashed.'

'A good thing, too,' muttered Mila. 'Stop them before they get hooked.'

'No, hell, Mila!' Adriaan exclaimed. 'You're honestly beginning to sound like a bloody convent miss! Weren't you the one who always believed in sex, drugs and rock 'n' roll?'

'No, that was Philip. And look what happened to him.'

Mila watched the two girls taking turns to throw a stick to the dogs. Max's collie caught it first every time – grabbing it enthusiastically from under the nose of the older and slower Labrador – and carried it arrogantly back to the children. Tat looked as though he wasn't really enjoying the game. It was probably beneath the dignity of a proud middle-aged dog to compete with such a cocky teenager. But he played along, in a half-hearted way, to keep Mona happy. Perhaps she should get herself a dog, thought Mila. So much easier than a child.

'I hear you've even become a vegetarian!' Indignation in Adriaan's dark voice. Which suddenly made her think of strong, black coffee again. Funny how indelible first impressions could be. How certain memories could gnaw at your heart, years later – sounds, smells, tastes – when you thought the worst was over. Long ago. 'How could you betray your past like that!'

'It's not so difficult,' she mumbled into her wine glass. 'I just think of the burnt meat my mother dished up every Sunday. But I'm not really a vegetarian. I'm just trying to lead a healthier life. Perhaps it's a bit late, but, well . . .'

'It's never too late,' Bobby reassured her. 'You can share some of the soya sausage Zelda and I brought if you don't want Adriaan's boerewors.'

'Ag, no!' exclaimed Adriaan. 'Surely you can't expect me to braai that bloody artificial meat of yours!'

'We can do it ourselves,' said Bobby, unconcerned.

'Just tell me one thing, Zelda.' Adriaan turned to Bobby's new girlfriend and smiled seductively. 'Did you eat this plastic sausage before you met her? Or does she force you to do it?'

'Well, she persuaded me to try it.' Zelda's laugh was a spontaneous, sparkling sound which immediately made Bobby smile with her. 'She can be very persuasive.'

'She must be fucking persuasive if she can talk you into eating plastic.'

'It doesn't taste that bad, you know?'

Bobby watched her with a face glowing with pride. Her mousy brown hair was cut more neatly than usual, Mila observed, looking less as though a litter of hungry mice had gnawed at it. Her T-shirt and shorts were the same patterned *mélange* as before – and yet she no longer looked like a child who'd raided her parents' wardrobe. Perhaps because she'd also gained a few wrinkles. Or just learned to buy her clothes in a more appropriate size.

'It must be true love,' muttered Adriaan, shaking his head.

'Or perhaps I just don't know any better,' laughed Zelda. 'My father is a fisherman on the West Coast, so I grew up eating bokkems. We were too poor to afford meat. All we ever had were soup bones and pale, tough stewing meat.'

'My mother could afford decent meat,' sighed Mila. 'But she couldn't cook it without fucking it up.'

'You'll taste the best meat of your life this weekend,' Adriaan promised ceremoniously. 'I'll regard it as a personal challenge to lead you back to the kraal of the carnivores!'

It was clear that Zelda had fascinated him from the minute she'd walked into the house, so young and spontaneous and sensual, with a wide, voluptuous, laughing mouth, her skin as soft and smooth and dark as chocolate ice cream. The fact that she preferred women to men probably added to the fascination. He would never change, thought Mila as she watched him with a strange tenderness, the broad bare feet under Indian trousers of thin white cotton, the strong shoulders under a T-shirt with a print of an Edward Hopper painting. A group of loners in a chill, cold bar. Loneliness and alienation. Perhaps that's what they'd recognized in each other's eyes from the first, she thought. Not lust, but a reason for lust. A condition which could be temporarily – only temporarily – alleviated by sex. And the absolute certainty that you're going to be lonelier than ever afterwards. Even more alienated than before.

'I see that at least we're not only getting dead animals to eat,' observed Ralph as Max appeared at the back door with a bowl of olives and sun-dried tomatoes, a bottle of wine uncomfortably clamped under his elbow. He put the bowl down on the table and began to open the wine. 'How's the Merry Widow?'

'In her element,' grinned Max. 'It sounds like a conference on motherhood in that kitchen. They're jabbering on about birth and babies. And she's the one with the most experience, so they're all hanging on her every word.'

'Is that what you call Leslee?' asked Mila disapprovingly. '*The Merry Widow*?'

'Well, she's a widow,' said Ralph with a shrug, 'and she is surprisingly merry for a woman raising three children on her own. I can't exactly call her the Melancholy Widow, can I?'

'Careful,' said Max, 'our resident feminist scents blood.'

'Feminist my arse,' said Mila. 'I was just wondering whether you called me the Merry Widow behind my back too. Or in my case probably the Moody Widow!'

'I don't do it behind her back! It's my pet name for her! My pet name for you was the Queen of Disastrous Relationships. Don't you remember?'

'How could I ever forget such a flattering nickname?'

He smiled at her, but his amber eyes looked wide and sad under his sweeping hair, reminding her of the cowardly lion in *The Wizard of Oz*. She had lost him too. Not that she ever had him. But she could have, if she'd wanted. If she'd only known what she'd wanted.

'Not that I have much of a track record to boast of,' said Ralph. 'At least you were always brave enough to try. I simply decided in advance that no relationship would work.'

'But this time it's different,' she reassured him. 'You were brave enough to invite the Merry Widow along for the weekend. That's a helluva jump for an old loner like you.'

'Sure,' he said uncertainly. 'It's a kind of test. If she doesn't like my friends, it won't work. I'm too old and lazy to make new friends.'

'Do you hear that, Zelda?' grinned Bobby.

'I hear,' laughed Zelda.

'Don't worry if you're not crazy about them straight away,' said Bobby. 'I also thought they were a bunch of spoilt whiteys at first. But they grow on you.'

'Ah!' said Ralph. '*That's* how I must put it to Leslee!'

Even without Leslee, realized Mila, she would never have slept with him again. She couldn't bare her body to someone who had known it when it was unscathed. All that was left for her was the eyeless, handless lover of her dreams. Dreams which woke her night after night with damp cheeks and throbbing loins. Her body, which had never listened to reason, still refused to do so.

'Doesn't anyone want to fetch the meat from the kitchen?' asked Adriaan. 'The fire is almost ready.'

'Don't look at me,' said Mila. 'I can't cope with all that womb-talk. That's why I came to sit outside with The Boys.'

'You don't have to give a speech,' said Adriaan. 'Just grab the dish of meat and run.'

'I'm afraid it's infectious.'

'Motherhood?'

'Not the condition. The obsession with talking about it.'

'And you, Bobby?' asked Adriaan. 'Surely you're not afraid of being infected!'

'No, but it's against my principles to fetch meat for my friends. Makes me feel like a pusher.'

At that moment Yvette appeared at the back door, a huge dish of meat held like a sacrifice in her arms.

'Ah!' said Adriaan. 'My wife could always read my thoughts!'

'Not that it ever prevented him from thinking precisely what he wanted,' said Yvette as she approached them.

She looked at the two girls, who were playing on the lawn outside the circle of light. Mona's nightdress a white blob in the darkness; Sasha, who was wearing a more conventional nightie with pictures of Minnie Mouse, almost invisible against the blue-black sky. Just the blonde head bouncing backwards and forwards like a big ball. They were throwing the stick to each other now, the collie jumping up excitedly to grab it out of the air. Tat lay with his head on his paws and watched the game like a bored babysitter.

'Sometimes *your* thoughts are also written on your face,' teased Adriaan while he arranged the meat on the grid. 'At this moment, for instance, you're thinking it's time to get the children to bed.'

'I only allow you to read my responsible maternal thoughts,' said Yvette. 'The exciting ones I keep to myself.'

He glanced fleetingly at her, his expression doubtful, before he laughed loudly.

'Ag, let them play for a little longer! It's Friday night, we're at the sea, they're enjoying it so much . . .'

'If they don't get into bed soon, they're going to be tired and grumpy tomorrow, and then they'll spoil everyone's day.'

'My practical wife.' He pulled her in under his arm and looked at her with a proud smile. 'What would I do without you?'

'You managed quite well for almost two years,' she reminded him. 'And became a famous TV star in the process.'

'But I sacrificed everything to come back to you! Fame, wealth, young girls asking for my autograph . . .'

She tipped her head up to look at him, her eyes impossibly big under her dark fringe, and smiled disbelievingly. Her growing stomach was not really noticeable yet, her body only a little plumper than usual under a loose dress with purple and red flowers, but her face already had that self-satisfied glow which pregnancy had always given her. Mila watched them, the picture of a happy couple, and tried to ignore her longing, protesting heart.

'I need your advice,' said Emma when they were eating around the long table in the living room later, the balcony doors thrown open wide to welcome the darkness and the rushing sound of the sea. 'About the scattering of the ashes. I'm not sure how to do it.'

Her smile apologetic above the piece of meat in her hand.

'Us neither,' Ralph said. 'What did Philip say?'

'He didn't exactly give a list of instructions. It was just one of those remarks of his. Half joking, but probably serious. He just said he'd like it if his friends scattered his ashes somewhere over the sea. And got drunk in his memory.'

'The second part shouldn't be too difficult,' said Adriaan.

'And, of course, that no one was allowed to say anything senti-mental.' She stared at her plate, troubled, a messy ponytail fixed high on her head hanging sideways over one cheek. 'But how do you speak about a dead person you loved without sounding sentimental? And we all loved him . . .'

'Strangely enough,' mumbled Max.

'If there's a certain percentage of alcohol in your blood,' said Mila in her practical way, 'you can't help being sentimental. Philip drank quite enough to know that. So I think deep in his heart he actually wanted us to get all maudlin about him.'

'Perhaps,' sighed Emma. 'I thought we should do it tomorrow morning.'

'Get maudlin?' asked Adriaan. 'On an empty stomach?'

'No, get the scattering of the ashes over with. If it's OK with all of you.'

'The quicker, the better,' Liane agreed. 'Let's face it, my darling, it's not something any of us are looking forward to.'

'And that gives us the rest of the day to drink,' said Adriaan.

'But where?' asked Emma.

'Here in the house of course.'

'I don't mean where we're going to drink, Adriaan. I mean where we're going to scatter the bloody ashes!' She swept the ponytail back, clicking her tongue impatiently. Circles like bruises under her eyes, her skin pale and uncared for, her broad mouth jaded. Paul wondered when last she'd had a proper night's sleep. 'We can't just walk down to the beach and empty the box in between a bunch of people in swimming costumes! Imagine, you're sitting quietly with your little family under an umbrella, and the next moment the breeze blows bits of a dead person on to you.'

'It's almost irresistible,' said Adriaan, slowly beginning to shake with laughter.

'What about the rocks here in front of the house?' Yvette suggested.

'He wanted us to throw him in the sea.' Ralph put a bone in his mouth and ripped the meat off with his teeth, a swift movement which reminded Paul of a predator. Years ago he could hardly look at Ralph without thinking of a wild cat. Now there were only brief glimpses of that wildness. The cat had grown tame, like all of them. 'Not in a rock pool where children can pee on him and tiddlers can eat him.'

'He's going to be fishfood anyway,' said Bobby with a philosophical shrug. 'Does it matter what kind of fish eats him?'

'I think so,' reasoned Liane. 'I can only speak for myself, but I would prefer to be swallowed by something more . . . glamorous than a tiddler.'

'What do you have in mind?' asked Max, snorting into his wine glass. 'Crayfish? Salmon?'

'Well, I rather like those Japanese fish which all the Johannesburg yuppies keep as pets these days . . .'

Paul saw that Riaan was struggling not to laugh out loud.

'Please remember to dump her in a yuppie's fish pond one day,' said Max.

'We were discussing Philip's ashes,' Emma reminded them. 'We can decide what's going to happen to the rest of us later!'

'I say we do it from the rocks,' said Bobby. 'We can try to get as close as possible to the sea and scatter the ashes directly into the waves, then we needn't worry about tiddlers eating him.'

'How do you think I'm going to clamber over those rocks with this body?' Liane asked indignantly.

'Ooops,' said Bobby. 'I forgot about your delicate condition.'

'Delicate isn't the first word that comes to mind when I look at that stomach,' said Paul.

His ex-wife glared at him. Leslee smiled sympathetically, but her eyes were amused behind the black-rimmed glasses which kept reminding him of Nana Mouskouri. That was probably how she approached her work as a psychologist, he realized: with a professional mixture of sympathy and irony.

'Where's your thirst for adventure?' exclaimed Adriaan. 'What about the poor Voortrekker women who walked barefoot over the Drakensberg? Some of them must have been pregnant, too!'

'If you ask me, the poor Voortrekker women needed a good shrink,' said Liane.

'All I want to know,' mumbled Emma with a weary expression around her mouth, 'is how we're going to get Philip into the sea. It shouldn't be *that* difficult.'

'It was always difficult to get Philip into the sea,' Max reminded her. 'He was never a great swimmer.'

'Are you sure you understood him correctly?' asked Ralph. 'He didn't perhaps say we should scatter his ashes over a vineyard? It would be much more appropriate if he could end up in next year's Cabernet Sauvignon.'

'He said he wanted to be in the sea! Don't ask me why! I never understood how his mind worked anyway!'

'Perhaps just to evoke this absurd conversation,' muttered Paul.

'OK, on a point of order!' Adriaan banged the handle of his knife on the table. 'Let's wait till high tide, then the lame and the lazy among us don't have to struggle over the rocks . . .'

'I beg your pardon! I'm not lame or lazy, I'm building the population of –'

'Shut up, Liane, otherwise we're never going to reach any kind of decision.'

'Democracy in action,' said Bobby, amused.

'Democracy is a wonderful idea,' said Adriaan, 'but it's a helluva time-consuming process. Sometimes you need a steamroller like me . . .'

'They should have had you at Codesa!' grinned Max. 'We'd have had an election ages ago!'

'Did the talk show make you so bossy?' asked Bobby.

'He always tended to take over a conversation,' said Yvette. 'On TV they just paid him to do it.'

'Look, it's almost full moon,' Adriaan went on as if he hadn't heard them, 'so the sea ought to come up quite high. Almost to street level. In fact, if we're lucky, there'll be a strong enough wind blowing from the land, then we can just scatter the ashes from the balcony!'

'I wish he was here to hear us,' said Mila with a melancholy smile, her lovely mouth without even a dab of lipstick tonight.

'Me too,' said Emma as she stared sightlessly at the darkness outside the balcony door. 'I miss him.'

When he walked to the kitchen early the next morning, she was already sitting on the balcony. As if she hadn't slept at all, he thought, when he saw the tired lines around her mouth. The circles under her eyes by this time more like tattoos. He'd only wanted to fetch a glass of water and creep in next to Riaan's sleeping body again, but there was something in the way she sat, curled up so small in a deckchair, which forced him to sit down next to her.

'We can't do it,' she said anxiously. 'It won't work.'

'We can't do what?' he asked with a smothered yawn, not quite awake yet.

Unlike his ex-wife, who used to leap out of bed each morning as if she were afraid that the day would run away from her, he had always needed time to wake up properly. Riaan had been more like Liane – almost as eager to catch the day like a great golden ball – but these days he went to bed earlier every evening and got up with more difficulty every morning. As if he were practising for the endless sleep which lay ahead.

'Scatter the ashes! Look how the wind's blowing!' That's what had woken him, he remembered, a window banging in the wind. 'In the wrong fucking direction! Right off the sea! It will blow everything back into our faces!'

'Perhaps it will die down later.'

'Does it look to you like a wind which is going to die down soon?'

The sea looked like a dark, crumpled sheet full of crumbs, little white waves everywhere. Huge white waves breaking violently over the nearest rocks. Foam blown through the air like strands of white hair.

'Perhaps we can do it tomorrow.'

'And if the wind keeps on blowing?'

'Oh, well, then we'll just have to have another weekend at the sea . . .'

'No! I want to be finished with Philip! I thought I was finished with him, but then the bastard decided to die! And now he's back in my house, in a box full of ash, and I don't want him there any longer!'

She swung her legs off the chair, leaned forward with her elbows on her thighs and her hands folded over her arms, and glared at the little cardboard box next to her bare feet. So small and drab and inconspicuous that he hadn't even noticed it. And suddenly it jerked him wide awake, the thought that this was all that was left of his friend Philip. Smaller than a shoe box. And behind this thought, another more horrible, completely unbearable thought pushed its way up. Soon this was all that would remain of Riaan. The realization broke like a wave over his consciousness, sweeping the last bit of powerless denial away along with any possible words of comfort for Emma. He lifted his head and stared wordlessly at the windblown sea.

'I've been grieving about him day and night for three weeks, you know?' Her voice now more controlled, a trace of resignation about the wide mouth, even the shadow of a smile. 'It's as though his death wrenched all stability out from under my feet. I feel as though I'm drowning in a sea of emotions I can't cope with. Emotions which I thought . . . which I thought I'd left behind long ago. But enough is enough. I want to say farewell and get on with my life. I was working on a novel . . . about a couple like us . . . well, obviously not exactly like us, you know what I mean. But I'm sure now it's going to become a completely different story from the one I began . . . more honest, I think. Better, I hope. I can't wait to carry on writing, to see what's going to happen, but I can't do it before I say good-bye. I need some kind of ritual . . . We always reach for rituals when we can't handle emotions, don't we? That's why this silly scattering of the ashes is so important to me. It's a way of forgiving him . . . of going ahead . . .'

'Are you still angry at him?'

'I'm furious!' She looked at him quickly, guiltily, the circles under her eyes the same bruised colour as the sea. 'Not about what he did when he was alive, that's not that hard to forgive, but about the way he died . . . I think it was a cowardly form of suicide. To get drunk and drive off a cliff.'

He drew a sharp breath. Shocked, he realized, not at her words, but to hear her speak a thought he had kept resolutely suppressed till now.

'Do you think he did it deliberately?'

'I don't think "deliberately" is the right word,' she answered in a detached way. 'I think he was so depressed that he couldn't even put his shoes on deliberately. Since his father died a few months ago . . . strange, I always thought his son's death would send him off the rails . . . but it was his father's death he couldn't handle. Someone like Leslee will probably tell you there was too much unfinished business between them. I don't know. But I don't think he planned it. I mean driving off the cliff. I think he did it on impulse.'

'But it could also have been an accident.' He sounded as though he was trying to convince himself, he realized, his voice suddenly more anxious than hers. 'I mean, he didn't leave a note behind or something, did he?'

'Philip wasn't the kind for notes, Paul.' Her feet now on the chair again, knees under her chin, the long hair on either side of the face, just the nose sticking out. Her voice had grown softer, almost nostalgic, almost amused. 'He never wrote a single love letter. Too scared of being accused of sentimentality. I think he would have felt the same about a suicide note . . .'

'So there was no message? Except that we should have this week-end?'

'Even that wasn't really a message. We were speaking about his father's death . . . his stepmother tried to turn the funeral into a Greek tragedy . . . you can imagine what he thought of that. Then he said when *he* died one day . . . you know, the way one talks sometimes . . .

it sounded as though he simply wanted to give his friends an excuse to get together again. I don't think he would have minded if we didn't actually scatter the ashes.'

'I don't think he would have minded if we flushed them down the toilet, Emma. This kind of ritual is a comfort to the living. It has nothing to do with the dead.'

'I know,' she sighed. 'But I don't want to flush my ex-husband down the toilet. Just think what it will sound like if one day my daughter asks what happened to her father.'

After that he couldn't sleep again. He lay next to Riaan and stared at his thin body, but it was as though the room was gradually shrinking, walls moving closer to each other and the ceiling sinking lower and lower, until it felt as cramped as a coffin. Or a little cardboard box, he thought in panic. Gasping for breath. Ash in his lungs.

He leaped up and fled from the house, without even washing his face or brushing his teeth, just pulling on last night's sweater, still smelling of smoke, over his crumpled tracksuit pants. Wandered aimlessly through a few deserted streets and stared at the ridiculous names of the beach houses with a growing feeling of alienation. *By-the-C-Side. Ag-Pleeze-Daddy. Take Five. Hang Ten.* God knows why Afrikaners had such an irresistible urge to disfigure their holiday homes in this way. Perhaps something to do with a rural past, the longing to be master of the farm, claim a piece of earth by naming it. He and Liane had sometimes driven slowly through coastal towns, just to laugh at the names. To convince each other that they – son of a platteland dominee and daughter of a platteland garage owner – were more sophisticated than the rest of their nation. This morning, he didn't find it funny. There were some things you just couldn't get away from, he thought. Your past, your memories, your death. The death of a loved one.

Riaan's lovely, sickly body. The hard angularity of the ankles and wrists, the strong, sinewy arms and legs, the curve of the shoulders and the length of the back, smooth and tensed under his palm when they made love, the vertebrae like the links of a priceless necklace under his fingertips, the secret dark depth between the mounds of the buttocks, the precise weight of the penis when it grew hard and heavy under him, above him, against him, in him. The endless, unforgettable desirability of this body. A hunger which even a deadly disease couldn't still. A thirst which even death couldn't slake.

When he unexpectedly came across the little café, a sign of life in the deadly silence of the sleeping town, he walked gratefully through the door. He had begun to feel as though he was wandering through one of those ghost towns in an old cowboy movie. An ominous atmosphere as the hero nervously fingers his gun, the suspicion of enemy eyes behind blind windows. He'd probably seen too many of those movies as a kid. The enchantment of the dark bioscope – in contrast to the brightly lit respectability of a pastorie – the sensual luxury of a velvet seat against his bare legs in boys' shorts, the seductive smell of popcorn and Pepsi and cheap women's perfume. The guilty excitement of earthly pleasure after a whole week of angelic virtue. Irresistible. He didn't care which movie was showing, he just wanted to be there. For some reason it was almost always a cowboy movie.

At ten, he was crazy about John Wayne and Clint Eastwood. He thought that all the boys in his class felt like he did. Later, he realized that there was a difference. The other boys wanted to become their cowboy heroes; he wanted to marry them. But he had quickly swept this episode into a dark corner of his memory, like so many other things which should have warned him that he was different. Only in the last few years had he been brave enough to investigate all the dark corners, illuminating them with the bright light of hindsight, and sometimes he was astounded by what he discovered. Like rummaging around in a dusty attic and finding a forgotten toy, suddenly overwhelmed by memories you weren't even aware of. It was in the same sinful bioscope that a man touched his genitals for the first time. The shock of the big, sweaty hand on his bare, hairless leg. Wriggling fingers pressed into his shorts. The shame and the guilt afterwards. Not because it had happened but because he had enjoyed it.

The discovery – and the suppression – of his own sexuality had become interwoven somewhere in his subconscious with his passion for movies. Perhaps even the cause of it, the reason why for years he had dreamed of becoming a director. Movies became a gateway to secret desires and exciting urges, to sensuality and sex and sin, to everything he couldn't get in the pastorie.

He walked through the café deep in thought, staring with unseeing eyes at the shelves full of sweets, pictures of different kinds of ice cream on a freezer, colourful cold-drink cans behind the glass doors of a fridge, and wondered what he'd actually come here for. Felt in the pocket of his tracksuit pants and realized that he had enough change for a newspaper. A headline on the front page immediately pricked at his conscience, but he ignored it and turned to the weather report. As he stood in the doorway of the café, the wind cold in his face and the pages of the newspaper flapping in his hands, he read that it would probably be windy for the rest of the weekend. Even a possibility of rain tomorrow. Where did this sudden surge of gratitude come from? He hadn't realized how frightening the prospect of scattering the ashes had become to him. Ever since he'd noticed the little cardboard box next to Emma's bare feet.

When he folded the newspaper again, he couldn't help but read the report on the front page. A young American student taking her black friends back to their homes in a Cape township had been stoned and stabbed to death by a group of residents. *Because she's a settler.* Because she was white. Paul stared, dazed, at the beach house opposite him, a few windblown shrubs on a mangy lawn, name plate next to the front door. Of course. *Kannieklanie.* Can't-Complain. What was going to happen to all the white sinners in this country? All the beach houses with ridiculous names, all the carefree weekends at the sea, all the braai fires and fishing rods? We're not all like that, not all of us, he thought with a desperation which closed like an icy fist about his heart.

'You look as though you've seen a ghost.'

He jumped at the sound of Mila's husky voice. She must have walked up while he was in the café. Standing suddenly next to him, dressed in black Lycra cyling shorts which emphasized her well-shaped legs, muscular calves and slender ankles above a pair of imported trainers. Grey sweater with a hood which hung down her back, a lot more tight-fitting than the over-large denim shirt in which she'd hidden her body the previous night. His eyes dropped involuntarily to the soft curves of her breasts. *Breast. Singular.* His eyes jerked back to her face. It looked completely normal, he thought with hot relief on his cheeks, impossible to see which one had been removed.

'Worse than a ghost,' he said and showed her the front-page report. 'I feel as though I've seen the future.'

She took the newspaper from him and began to read the article. The full mouth again as colourless as the previous night. She'd lost more than a breast, he realized as he watched her. It was as though the sauciness had vanished from her. That cocky attitude, as Liane had called it, always admiringly. The challenging expression in the blue eyes, the confident tilt of the chin, the shoulders pulled so proudly back. She didn't look like a dancer any more. She looked smaller than before, as if the pain of the last year had made her shrink. So much smaller and older and more vulnerable without her red lipstick that he put his arm around her bowed shoulders. A clumsy gesture of comfort which made him feel embarrassed. When she looked up again, her eyes were cloudy. Mud in blue water.

'It just never stops, does it?'

'How the hell are we going to have a democratic election next year! If we keep on killing each other, at this rate, there'll be no one left to vote!'

'What happened to your famous sardonic detachment?' she asked with a skew smile on her pale lips.

What happened to your famous commitment, Mila? Was it her work at a glossy magazine which had gradually doused her flaming idealism? Or was it the shock of the illness which had suddenly extinguished the flame?

'Life pulled me closer,' he said with a shrug. 'Shit happens.'

'Don't you want to walk with me?'

'Where to?'

'To the river mouth.'

'I don't want to leave Riaan alone for too long,' he said uncertainly. And then, with a pathetic attempt at his famous sardonic smile: 'He doesn't feel at home among the barbarians yet.'

'He's coping very well. I watched the two of you last night. It's you that I'm worried about.'

He looked away from her searching eyes, at a few children who had begun to play in front of a house a little way down the street. The town had finally begun to wake up. Perhaps that would alleviate his feeling of alienation.

'Come,' said Mila, with a pleading note in her voice. 'It will do you good. I have to walk every day now, otherwise I feel like a junkie who hasn't had her fix.'

'Isn't it less time-consuming to jog?' he asked as they walked in the direction of the long, narrow beach.

'Especially for someone who may not have much time left?'

The sarcastic tone made him bite his lip. Embarrassed and at the same time delighted by this spark of irreverence. Still cocky after all, he thought gratefully.

'No, I was just thinking about what Liane always said about exercise. Something you have to get behind you as quickly as possible so that you can enjoy the rest of your day. I never thought about it like that. I enjoy going to the gym. It's not a sacrifice to me, it's more like a hobby.'

'That's why your body still looks so good,' she mumbled. 'I was also proud of my body . . . too proud, I suppose . . . probably far too vain. But in the last while . . . well, I wouldn't say that I'm ready to let the temple collapse completely, I don't want to become a living ruin, but it's just not so . . . essential. I don't walk for my body, I do it for my soul. I concentrate more on the soul these days,' she added with an apologetic smile.

'What does it do to your soul?' he asked, staring at his bare feet.

'Walking? It gives me a kind of silence.' She folded her arms across her chest, hands on her shoulders, head bowed. Something in her attitude reminded him of a nun. A humility which he had never noticed before. Or perhaps it was just the lack of sauciness which he was suddenly seeing in a new light. 'There are so many questions and fears and regrets and other unpleasant thoughts in my head, that I need this silence as much as oxygen. A calm space in between all the noise.'

'Sounds as though I should go walking more often,' he said with a wry smile. 'My head is a blur of white noise these days.'

'That's why I said I was worried about you. I recognize that noise when I hear it in someone else's head.' She was quiet for a while, frowning, searching for the right words. 'It's terribly difficult to die, Paul. Or to think that you're dying. Like I thought last year. But it's just as difficult, in a way, perhaps harder . . . to see someone you love slowly dying.'

'It's the most difficult thing I've ever . . .'

He bit off his sentence because his voice had begun to tremble. They were now only a few houses from the beach, the strip of white sand stretched out as straight as a runway in front of them. A few other wanderers and three dogs drifting in the distance, dark ghosts in the misty morning light. The sea still that bruised colour behind the choppy waves.

'On the one hand you feel as though you're dying too because you have to work through all the emotions with him . . . and on the other hand you know that you're going to stay behind alone. And it's a terrible knowledge . . . that the worst still lies ahead . . . when the other one isn't there any more. When his pain is over, yours has hardly begun.'

Where did she get this knowledge from? he wondered. Suddenly not capable of choking a word out past the lump in his throat.

'I've been working in a hospice for a few hours a month,' she explained. 'Death guidance, they call it. But it always seems to me that those left behind to go on living need more guidance than the dying.'

'Isn't it awfully . . . depressing? Seeing people die all the time?'

'I learned last year . . . to look death in the face. Perhaps I want to force myself not to look away again. To work through the remaining fear. That's the selfish reason.' With her fingers in front of her mouth to disguise an awkward smile. 'The less selfish reason is that hopefully I can help a few other people . . . not to look away . . .'

'How do you do that?' His voice rough with desperation.

'Do you ever talk about death? You and Riaan. I mean directly, without trying to protect each other, about what lies ahead?'

The question caught him so off-guard that he almost stumbled. He wanted answers, he thought in panic, not more questions.

'It's still too early,' he pleaded. 'I mean, we can't shy back from the practical side of it all, there's business to be organized, finance and insurance and wills and things like that. And I'm a lawyer, I'm good at that. But regarding the rest . . . I'm afraid we're not ready to spell it out. He's still too healthy. I mean, he's not yet critically ill! He can still go away for a weekend! He can still . . .'

He stopped abruptly because he could hear how pathetic his excuses sounded. Stared dejectedly at the wet sand under his feet.

'People always feel like that,' she said quietly. 'It's as though you're scared you'll call death closer if you speak about it. Let sleeping dogs lie. But if you know you're dying, you have a need to talk about it. I remember . . . when my father got cancer, he tried a few times . . . but I was too cowardly – *Ag, no, Pappa, you're going to be with us for a long time to come* – And when I got cancer myself, the same cowardice struck my friends . . .'

'But you're OK now?'

'Well.' Her arms folded over each other, apparently involuntarily, to form that protective cross over her chest again. 'I don't know if "OK" is the right word.'

'I mean, you're in remission, aren't you? You've won the battle?'

She stared at the river mouth at the furthest tip of the beach for so long that he almost stopped breathing. Opened her pale lips a few times, then closed them again, as if she'd lost her voice. The wind blew colder than ever against his cheeks while he waited for her reply.

'Temporarily,' she said at last. 'Any victory over death is always temporary.'

The rest of the windy day passed painfully slowly, like a movie in slow motion, a play in which nothing happens. *Waiting for Godot*, Mila thought a few times. Everyone was so aware of the box of ashes that the whole weekend began to feel pointless. They had come here to dispose of the ashes. And now they were prevented from doing so by circumstances beyond their control.

By midday the wind was blowing so furiously that even the children didn't want to go outside. Which only worsened the atmosphere of frustration and boredom. Trapped in a big wooden house whose many rooms were gradually beginning to shrink around them, until it felt as though they were scraping and bumping against each other, as if their bodies filled the house to bursting point. Like poor Alice after she had drunk the magic potion.

The only solution, according to Adriaan, was to drink their own magic potion. Soon after he'd switched on the stove to cook lunch, he took the first of many wine bottles from a case on the kitchen floor.

He'd actually wanted to braai again (in memory of the deceased) but the wind had forced him to change his menu. So now he would make an old-fashioned mixed grill, he announced as he tied an apron around his broad waist. A lovely fatty festive meal, like in the platteland cafés of his childhood. Chops and sausage and eggs and bread.

'A cholesterol orgy!' cried Bobby, her eyes widened in horror.

'As a special concession, I'll allow you to make a big bowl of salad,' said Adriaan.

'As long as you don't put any soya sausage in it,' said Zelda with a mischievous smile.

'I knew you had the soul of a carnivore!' Adriaan exclaimed. 'In just seven days, baby, I'll make you a man-eater too!'

'Forget it. Been there, done that, got the scars to prove it.' Zelda sat on a high bar stool and laughed at him with bright black eyes. 'Female flesh is softer and sweeter.'

'Can't argue with that,' Adriaan conceded smiling, opening a bottle of Meerlust Rubicon.

'Isn't it a bit early to start drinking?' asked Emma with a concerned frown.

'Not if we want to fulfil Philip's last wish.'

Ralph moved closer to examine the contents of the case on the kitchen floor and whistled admiringly through his teeth.

'Meerlust. Buitenverwachting. Kanonkop. Rust en Vrede . . .' he said shaking his head. 'Whatever happened to the days when we got drunk on good old Tassies and box plonk?'

'If we have to drink in honour of our dead friend, we may as well do it in style,' said Adriaan, and pulled the cork from the bottle with a flourish.

'Philip didn't really bother with fine wine,' Emma reminded him. 'Quantity was always more important than quality.'

'Well, none of us has his capacity.' Adriaan sniffed the cork and poured a little wine carefully into a glass. Each movement exaggeratedly respectful, like a pretentious waiter wanting to earn a good tip. He held the glass up against the window, admiring the colour. 'If we don't drink good wine, we'll be horribly drunk by tonight.'

'I thought that was the whole idea,' mumbled Max from behind an open newspaper.

A photo of a smiling girl with long blonde hair on the front page. The murdered American student. *Because she's a settler.* Mila turned her head so that she couldn't see the newspaper, stared out of the window at the sky full of fat, woolly clouds.

'And good wine won't make us drunk?' asked Riaan, amused.

'The destination is the same,' grinned Adriaan, 'but the journey is more enjoyable.'

'Since when have you been such a connoisseur?' asked Emma.

'Since I could afford to be one.'

'Seems that Johannesburg was good to you.'

'Well, I sold more paintings than here. People have more money.'

'And your fame as a TV star probably helped,' said Mila, more sarcastically than she'd intended.

'Johannesburg turned him into a snob,' said Yvette with a teasing curl to her mouth. And endless forgiveness in her eyes. 'Someone who drinks only estate wine and wears only designer underpants.'

'Which designer?' asked Liane inquisitively.

'I'll show you my underpants later,' said Adriaan with a suggestive smile. 'Then you can tell me whether they meet with your approval.'

No, thought Mila, nothing would ever change him. And she couldn't decide whether the thought made her feel relieved or depressed.

After lunch, the mood was more relaxed. Perhaps the good wine had a positive effect after all. More than half the company decided to take a nap, while a few stayed at the table to play cards and keep on drinking.

Mila had no desire to lie alone in a room, but she wasn't too keen on the silly card game, either, so she stretched out on the couch in the living room. Tried to read a new Afrikaans novel, as dutifully as she had tried to read the Bible as a child, because she believed that every responsible Afrikaans speaker had to do *something* to ensure the survival of the language. As had always happened with the Bible, her eyes began to close almost immediately. After a few minutes she gave up the fight. This was why she'd never got further than Exodus, she remembered as she drifted off. In the background, softer than the laughing voices around the table, a tape by a Dutch singer played over and over. Or so it seemed to her as she floated in the borderland between waking and sleeping, weightless, almost carefree. A wonderful, safe place which she remembered from her childhood. The comfort of chatting adult voices remaining on earth while she rose up in a dream balloon. The unshakeable certainty that everything would be exactly the same when she returned.

You walk to the kitchen, sang Stef Bos in a strange, familiar language, so close to her own language, *you ask what I want*, words like glistening bubbles floating through the air with her, *coffee or tea*, and she wondered what she wanted, *and I think, I want fire*, yes, she thought, that's what she wanted, all her life. But there was no fire in this mournful day, she thought as she sank back to earth. The wind had blown out the flames. All that remained was ash.

If only Philip hadn't been so depressed, if he hadn't drunk so desperately, if he hadn't driven over the mountain pass that night, then she wouldn't be lying on this couch. If only Emma had been able to open up her fearful heart to another man, her ex-husband's death wouldn't have hit her so hard. If only Riaan had been more careful when he'd been in America long ago, then Paul wouldn't have looked so lost. If she had only checked her breasts more regularly – instead of just admiring them in the mirror – she would have discovered the ominous lump sooner. So small, really. So un-ominous. As she had told herself when she first felt it.

She could get the breast built up again. Ask a plastic surgeon to play Pygmalion – to create a body part for her from transplanted skin and silicone and whatever modern science had to offer – but she wasn't ready for that yet. She still had to accept that the breast would never look exactly like the other one again. That it was possible that she could lose the other one, too.

If, if, if. If she could only imagine that someone would ever be able to love this body again. If not, why should she go to all that trouble for a breast that would never again be touched by a lover's hand?

It was as useless as burned wood, she reproved herself as she sank away into black sleep. Burned bones and burned skin. Ashes. And still she longed for fire, with her whole heart and her incomplete body.

Every hour.

But by suppertime a miracle occurred. Or something which by this time felt like a miracle.

They ate earlier than usual, a stew of fresh waterblommetjies which Ralph had brought along, slowly cooked with a little wine and the rind of a lemon and an awful lot of meat. (In memory of the deceased.) Ralph began cooking too soon because he was afraid he wouldn't be capable of doing it if he drank any more. And when he announced that the food was ready, they decided they might as well eat.

It wasn't even fully dark when they sat down at the long table, but the atmosphere was already a great deal more boisterous than during the midday meal. Tongues well oiled by Adriaan's fine wine. And yet it felt to Mila as though the exuberance sprang from despair, as though they were raging against the dying light outside. Howling at the moon. Perhaps it was just her own unsettled mood. Perhaps everyone at the table was as happy as they would ever be. A thought which left a sour taste on her tongue. Or perhaps it was just the waterblommetjies she was tasting.

'Are you planning to make a respectable woman of her sometime?' Paul asked Max, his voice a lot lighter than that morning on the beach. 'Or are you going to raise the twins in sin?'

'That's quite a cheek,' snorted Max. 'From someone living in sin himself.'

'It's not my fault that the church won't marry moffies,' said Paul. 'If I could, I'd have dragged him to the altar long ago.'

'He would actually love to have his father perform the ceremony,' said Riaan. 'Like the last time.'

'It was the last time which made me decide to wait a bit longer this time,' Liane explained, looking at a fork laden with meat. 'I don't know if I want all that spectacle again.'

She had been exceptionally quiet all day, her mouth a tired line above the majestic stomach, her legendary *joie de vivre* apparently drained by the life growing inside her.

'Was it *that* bad being married to him?' asked Riaan, amused.

'I'm not talking about the marriage – we had our moments – I'm talking about the wedding. We had this immense wedding, invited the world and his wife, including all Paul's senile aunts – and he's got lots, as you probably know – we had the wedding car and the wedding cake and the boring speeches and the whole traditional catastrophe. Everything I wanted when I was little. And I hated every moment of it.'

'I thought you enjoyed the wedding!' exclaimed Paul with a wounded frown. 'You looked as though you were enjoying it!'

'I studied drama, my darling.'

'Why did you never tell me? All these years I thought I had to pretend that I had such a fantastic wedding because my wife enjoyed it so much!'

'There were lots of things we never told each other,' she sighed. 'Anyway, these days I think that any show that begins with such an extravagant bang will almost inevitably end with a whimper. I want to cry every time I see the page in the newspaper with all those beaming newlyweds. Now I understand why my mother cried so uncontrollably at our wedding. I thought it was because she was so overjoyed that I'd found a decent man from a religious family. Now I think it's because she knew about the disillusionment that lay ahead.'

'Do you understand my problem?' Max asked Paul. 'She's become too cynical for respectability.'

'It's not that I don't want to marry again.' She was talking to Riaan, Mila noticed, rather than to Paul or Max. A kind of camaraderie had sprung up between her and Riaan, the strange conspiratorial understanding you sometimes find between two women who both know a man intimately. As she had sometimes experienced with Yvette, Mila remembered, long ago. 'I just don't want to make such a fuss about it. Funny, I always thought there was nothing as sad as a registry wedding. Now I think it's actually quite appropriate that Max and I slip into a magistrate's office one day and get the whole business over and done with as quickly as possible.'

'She's been saying that ever since she got pregnant,' mumbled Max with a full mouth. 'But every time I say OK, let's do it, she's got an excuse . . .'

'Ag, my darling, we'll do it sometime.'

'Hopefully before the twins are old enough to get married themselves.'

She put her knife and fork down on her empty plate and looked at him with bright eyes. A spark of the usual cheerfulness illuminating the lovely face.

'My whole life long I've been such an old goody two shoes! I'm enjoying behaving like a scarlet woman for a change! It's the first time in my life that I'm brave enough to – '

'Listen!' exclaimed Emma from the other end of the table.

'I don't hear anything,' said Adriaan with a frown.

'Exactly!' Emma leaped up and ran to the balcony, threw the french doors wide open and stared at the sea in delight. 'The wind has died down!'

'Wragtag, so it has!' exclaimed Adriaan.

'So we'll be able to scatter the ashes tomorrow, after all,' said Yvette, relieved.

'Not necessarily,' said Bobby. 'I don't want to be a prophet of doom, but here at the coast the wind sometimes dies down at night. And then rages again the next morning with renewed vigour.'

'Why don't we do it now?' asked Emma.

'In the dark?' asked Yvette.

'It's not that dark!' Emma was still standing at the balcony door, her eyes suddenly pleading under the wild bush of hair. 'Look, it's almost full moon!'

'Goodness gracious,' said Liane. 'It was bad enough when you expected me to scramble over those rocks in broad daylight! How the hell am I going to . . .'

'No, we don't have to scramble across the rocks. We can do it on the beach. There won't be any other people around at this time of night!'

'Perhaps that's not a bad idea,' said Paul.

'I agree,' said Adriaan. 'Let's do it.'

'What about the children?' asked Yvette.

She looked worriedly at the two little girls sitting on the carpet in front of the television, hypnotized by a Walt Disney video. Mona was wearing her long white nightdress again and Sasha – who had insisted on looking like Mona – a white T-shirt of her mother's which hung down to her feet.

'I'll stay with them,' Leslee offered. 'I feel a bit uncomfortable anyway, not having known Philip . . .'

'No, I want Sasha to come with us,' said Emma. 'It's her father's ashes after all.'

'They must both come along,' said Adriaan. 'We can't protect our children against death.'

'Do they understand what's going on?' asked Mila.

'We tried to explain to them,' said Emma with a helpless shrug. 'I don't know if they understand. I don't even know if I understand!'

'It's OK,' said Leslee quickly. 'It's probably the right thing to do. I was just looking for an excuse . . .'

'We all feel a bit uncomfortable, Les,' Ralph assured her with his arm wrapped around her shoulders. 'Even those of us who knew him.'

They drove down to the beach in two cars, eight adults and two children and two dogs in Adriaan's red Microbus, the remaining four in Bobby's silver Citi Golf.

'An alternative car for those of us who practise alternative sex,' Zelda joked when Paul and Riaan climbed in with her and Bobby.

'It's a pity there isn't a car for those who practise no sex at all,' mumbled Mila as she waited to climb into the crowded Microbus. 'I would have had a lot more space around me.'

'Just you and me really,' smiled Emma next to her. 'And the children and the dogs.'

'My dog has an active sex life!' Adriaan cried from behind the wheel. 'Which is more than his master can say these days.'

'I always forget that you've also been celibate for ages,' said Mila to Emma, her tone almost accusing. 'It's because you don't have that typical curl to the lips.'

'What curl?'

'That sourness that women get if they go without sex for too long. I'm beginning to notice it on my own mouth these days.'

'It's just because you don't wear lipstick day and night that your mouth looks different to you now,' said Emma with a nervous laugh.

An almost feverish gleam in her eyes, Mila noticed, even in the moonlight. The little box pressed close to her chest.

It was a strange little procession which braved the deserted beach, the sand gleaming white under their feet, the sea glossy and dark next to them, the waves thundering in the unusual silence around them. Emma at the vanguard between Ralph and Adriaan, who was holding Mona by the hand, with Sasha clinging to Mona's hand in turn, both children skipping with excitement at the unexpected outing. In the second row Liane followed, her long white outfit like a tent about her gigantic waist, arm in arm with her ex-husband and his lover. In the next row Max walked between Leslee and Yvette – Leslee chic in black from the frame of her spectacles down to her belted trousers, Yvette as colourfully patterned and flowered as always in a floating, chiffon, negligee-like outfit. And right at the back, Mila, between Bobby and Zelda. The two dogs ran back and forth in high spirits over the wet sand.

Mila stared in fascination at the small feet on either side of her own bare feet, which suddenly seemed unnaturally long and thin to her, like something painted by El Greco. Bobby's slender toes almost as white as the sand, Zelda's plumper and as dark as the sea. Then the procession came to a hesitating halt and they all clustered around Emma. Now she could no longer stare at her friends' toes, Mila realized with suffocating panic in her chest. Now she had to touch those ashes.

Emma unfolded the top flap of the box, stared at the contents for a moment, and then looked up in bewilderment.

'What now?' Her voice thin, her eyes pleading again. 'Has anyone here ever done anything like this?'

'I scattered my husband's ashes over the sea,' Leslee admitted.

'That's why I was afraid of coming along. I was scared I'd start to cry ... I *know* I'm going to cry ... and then you'd think me a drama queen for carrying on like that about someone I didn't even know.'

If only she could have scattered *her* husband's ashes, Mila thought. If, if, if. Burned wood, burned bones. Now he lay there in a family cemetery on a farm that she would never visit again.

'Should I hold the box and then you all walk past me?' Emma wanted to know. 'Or should I send it around? Like a communion tray?'

'I don't think Philip would have bothered about details like that, Emma,' said Adriaan with a comforting smile, and took the box from her.

He held it in front of her and she put her hand in with a sigh. Picked up a fistful of ash, turned away quickly, gripped her daughter's arm, and dragged the surprised child with her to the waves. 'Are we going to swim?' Sasha asked, the little voice high and excited. 'In our clothes?' A few paces further, where small waves broke over their ankles, she stopped and threw the ashes over the water with a sweeping arm movement. Sasha looked anxiously up at her mother, who stood staring motionlessly at the sea. The only sign that she hadn't turned into a pillar of salt was the long, dark, curly hair which began to flutter in a light breeze.

And all at once this simple picture moved Mila more than anything anyone had said or done the whole weekend. The anxious profile of the little girl, her long hair silver in the moonlight; the motionless back of the mother, her feelings – as always – hidden behind that impenetrable hedge around her head. The absolute finality of the moment.

Meanwhile, Adriaan had also taken a handful of ash and passed the box to Ralph, who passed it on to Liane, who passed it to Max, and so each one had a chance to reach in an uncertain hand and take out a closed fist of their friend's ashes. When Bobby dumped the box in Mila's hands like an unwelcome present, she realized that there was no one left to pass it to. Only she and Leslee were left standing on the wet sand, the others were all in the shallow water, in almost unseemly haste to get rid of the ashes, and surely she couldn't leave Leslee with the remains of a man she hadn't even known. Especially after she'd confessed that she was afraid of being reminded of her dead husband. Perhaps she should take it with her?

She looked indecisively at her friends in the water. Ralph threw the ash over the waves with the same wide motion of the arm as Emma; Liane sprinkled it in front of her like a plump farmer's wife feeding corn to her hens; Paul simply opened his palm and waited for the sea breeze to blow it away. Riaan stood as still as Emma next to him. Heaven knows what was going through his mind. Bobby clung to Zelda's shoulder as though she was afraid of being blown away with the ashes. Yvette bent down and let Mona blow it off her palm.

A vague memory stirred in Mila's heart, the child with puffing cheeks blowing out the candles on a birthday cake, Liane's kitsch cake in the shape of the Voortrekker monument. Philip had also been there, slightly uncomfortable as always on festive occasions, hiding behind his mocking smile. And now the child was blowing his ashes away, as she had blown out those birthday candles, with the same uncomprehending innocence. From fire to ash.

She felt her eyes burn with tears which could no longer be checked and pressed her hand quickly into the box. Astounded by how little ash still remained on the bottom. Even more astounded by the gritty texture, rougher than fireplace ash, braaivleis ash, cigarette ash, any other kind of ash she could think of. Almost as though she could feel minuscule pieces of bone between her fingers. She stared in dismay at her fist, which became mistier and mistier before her tear-filled eyes. When she looked up, she saw that Leslee was also crying, her cheeks shining wet under the heavy frame of her glasses. And she reached out blindly to this woman she hardly knew, completely overwhelmed by the desire to comfort someone, to be comforted, to press a soft body to her, feel warm breath against her face, warmth against warmth, skin against skin.

They cried wordlessly on each other's shoulders, Mila with the almost empty box in the one hand and the little bit of ash clutched tight in the other. They cried about Philip, and about Emma and Sasha, and about their own husbands who had died long ago, about opportunities which were gone for ever and dreams which would never come true. Sometimes you just had to cry, thought Mila, mourn and howl, weep and wail, about the uncertainty of life and the certainty of death. Because the fire with which you were born could turn to ash in front of your eyes.

TEN

The Sun is the Same (1994)

'Come, let's show you the house,' said Yvette, with possessive pride almost bursting the seams of her soft voice. 'It's the first time since we've been married that we haven't lived in a rented house. High time, probably, after twelve years.'

She walked ahead of Bobby and Zelda down the broad passage which led from the living room to the bedrooms. The baby on her plump hip had inherited her dark brown hair, but in a curlier, more uncontrollable form, the texture more like her father's and sister's hair. A sudden clear memory unpicked something in Bobby's mind: Yvette standing on the stoep of their previous house, the rented ramshackle Victorian place, with the dark head of her baby son against her shoulder. She thought she'd completely forgotten what Pablo looked like – after all, she'd only seen him a few times in his short life – but all at once the image of the pale little face with the big chocolate-brown eyes and the small round mouth rose up so clearly in front of her that she wanted to squeeze her eyes shut.

'Have you been married *that* long?' asked Zelda in amazement.

'Well, we had . . . a breathing space of almost two years,' Yvette explained quickly, over the baby's curly head. 'But early next year we'll have been officially married for twelve years. And I think the time on our own did us good. We don't have to wonder one day what it would be like if we weren't together . . .'

'You mean, you saw the Exit sign and decided to walk on by.' Zelda's voice held a heavy weight of respect. 'That takes some doing.'

Yvette smiled over her shoulder – somewhat laconically – and walked in through the first door.

'Or perhaps we'll be sorry precisely because we let the opportunity to escape slip through our fingers. One never knows what the future holds, does one?'

This child was completely different from Pablo, Bobby decided. Not just the texture of the hair and the strange greeny-brown colour of the eyes – as though a painter had mixed the green and the brown of Adriaan and Yvette's irises on a palette to create a striking new

416

shade – but also her whole bearing. If it was possible for a baby of ten months to look exceptionally observant, then this little girl managed it. Pablo had had Yvette's dreamy eyes – a misty expression which made you feel that he was never really part of the world in which he had lived for such a short time – while Frida looked almost preternaturally aware of everything around her. The way in which she continually tilted her head, like her mother, but as though she already saw more, in the first year of her life, than her mother ever would.

'This is where the two of you are sleeping, so you can leave your luggage here. It's my room with a view.' Yvette pulled the cord on a big white blind to conjure up a breathtaking view of a blue and green landscape. Green vineyards and blue mountain peaks sharply etched against a sky which was stained an even deeper blue on this cloudless summer day. The last day of 1994. An unforgettable year, Bobby had already decided, not just on a political level – so many wishes which had been granted – but also in her personal life. Wishes which had been granted. Wishes, she thought in amazement sometimes, which she hadn't even been aware of. 'A room of my own. For the first time in my life.'

The room was a combination of a study and an artist's studio, bookshelves covering two walls from floor to ceiling and a big work table full of papers and pens and other drawing equipment in the middle of the floor. Colourful striped carpets, and a plump sofa-bed covered with a length of cotton on which Yvette had painted bright splatterings reminiscent of an Impressionist flower garden. In fact, the whole space evoked the image of a garden rather than a room, the bright colours and the flooding sunlight. Even the free-standing fireplace, with a graceful, slender chimney of black iron, looked more like a modern sculpture in a park than something one was meant to make fire in.

'You always said your dream house would have a fireplace in every room,' said Bobby with a smile.

'In the end I couldn't manage it in every room. Too many chimneys. Adriaan and the architect were afraid the house would look like an old-fashioned factory. But I've also learned to tailor my dreams to reality. Things never work out *exactly* as you want them to.'

'That's what I keep telling Madam here next to me,' remarked Zelda drily. 'If you don't dream such impossible dreams, you can always be surprised by small felicities along the way.'

'I've also learned not to expect too much!' Bobby protested. 'It comes with age. Whether you like it or not.'

'It's a sad day when the baby in your circle of friends begins to talk about age,' said Yvette.

'I'm not the baby any more,' Bobby reminded her as they walked to the next room. 'Zelda is six years younger.'

'But I was born old,' laughed Zelda. 'Like this Frida-child.'

Frida was cutting her new teeth against a rubber toy, shining trails of spit hanging out of her mouth, watching them with wise, all-knowing eyes.

'This is Mona's room,' said Yvette. 'Emma and Sasha slept here last night.'

Another floor-to-ceiling window with a green and blue view, grass-green walls and patterned blue bedding to match the view, dolls and teddy bears next to a computer and cassette player on a small desk, a portable TV set in the corner, picture books and children's clothes and video containers strewn over the floor.

'All these electronic gadgets,' said Zelda in astonishment. 'So different from the way I grew up.'

'And you've only just grown up,' teased Bobby.

'I would never have been able to have a room like this, anyway. Not with five children in the house and a father who worked on a fishing boat.'

Without any bitterness or blame in her voice. Bobby looked at her with uncomprehending admiration, as she'd often done in the last year. What had she done, she sometimes wondered, to deserve such an angel in her life once again?

'I also come from a home with five children,' said Yvette sympathetically. 'Never knew the luxury of my own room. Not that we were poor! I mean, I could never afford my girlfriends' outfits . . . that's why I began wearing second-hand clothes in high school . . . I knew I couldn't compete with the other girls, so I decided to develop an alternative style. But I had all the perks of my skin colour. Good schools, holidays by the sea – not every year, but at least every now and again – an extra car for my mom to ferry us around in – bit of a crock, but at least it got us where we wanted to be – even a full-time "maid". Like all the other kids in my class. Of course there were only white children in my class . . .'

'My mother worked as a "maid" when I was little,' said Zelda.

'And my father only bought his first car after I left home. Also a bit of a crock. But somehow I remember my childhood as quite idyllic. We didn't need holidays at the sea, because we practically lived in the sea. And all of us were equally poor. When the boats came back empty, everyone went to bed hungry. It was only in high school that I became aware of . . . injustice. But I never developed Bobby's kind of political passion. Which of course she can't understand.'

'Of course not,' said Bobby. 'If I was coloured, I would have been furious all the time!'

'You were furious all the time anyway,' smiled Zelda. 'Until pretty recently.'

'She's taught me not to take myself so terribly seriously,' said Bobby.

'You've still got a lot to learn, my love. You still get far too worked up every time you page through a newspaper.'

'The difference is that these days it's the New South Africa that upsets me. So I've lost my self-righteous edge. I'm not sure whether I'm fighting on the side of the angels any more.'

'Are there still any angels left?' asked Yvette with a wistful expression.

'I'm afraid that the last one is standing in front of us,' grinned Bobby. 'My little chocolate angel.'

This woman was so different from Robin, in so many ways, that Bobby sometimes couldn't believe that she'd fallen in love with her. The complete lack of political passion (or political pretension, as Zelda preferred to describe it), the light-hearted, laughing personality of a radio presenter who could talk with ease to any listener. 'My West Coast accent sounds white enough,' she always joked. 'What they can't see, certainly can't hurt them.' And in the last few months she'd also blossomed into a TV presenter. 'Now I'm suddenly the right colour for the box!' Her spontaneous, guilt-free sensuality, the way in which she could gobble up a bar of chocolate or listen to a piece of jazz music with closed eyes or stretch out lazily like a cat while Bobby's fingers stroked her bare skin.

Not that Robin had been unsensual, thought Bobby with a stab of guilt. But she could never give herself over to her own pleasure so completely, she was always more eager to please her lover than to be pleased herself. As if, somewhere in the back of her mind, she was already working out a reward for the pleasure you were trying to give her. While Zelda was a lover who could give and receive with equal pleasure and equal eagerness, fully present in the moment, with you. There.

And yet, sometimes when she looked at her, she wondered if Robin hadn't sent this dark angel to her. To complete an unfinished task, to protect her against her own moody personality, to drive away the hate and rage and impatience and intolerance.

Perhaps just to teach her to laugh from the depths of her stomach again. Something which she had last done with her brother.

After they'd admired the other rooms – Frida's exuberant nursery in shades of orange and red; the master bedroom with a wooden bed as big as a ship drifting on a blue carpet; the round bath with a view over a cool interior courtyard full of purple hydrangeas; the fireplace, indeed, in the bathroom – they ended up on the stoep which hemmed the house in on three sides. There lay Emma, in a hammock between two pillars, Adriaan next to her in a rocking chair, a white sheet stretched like a sail over the vine above their heads because the vine shoots were still too young to provide enough shade. The ginger cat lay splayed out, his white stomach turned upwards, in a pool of sunlight near Adriaan's bare feet. The golden Labrador was on the lawn, watching over the two girls who were squealing in a round plastic swimming pool. Such a cosy scene of domestic happiness, thought Bobby. Like something out of an advert. Too good to be true.

It was unthinkable that any other two people could have built this house on this smallholding. 'Big enough for the whole family and the dog and the cat.' As Yvette had just described the bed in the master bedroom. With that proud, possessive tone in her voice. 'I had to sleep on my own for long enough.' And just look at the way that Adriaan was sitting there, legs stretched out in front of him and arms folded behind his head, as if he was born on this stoep and wanted to die here. Home.

And yet. It could so easily have been otherwise.

On the other side of the lawn, in the shade of a pepper tree, Zelda's two woolly mongrels had grabbed each other by the throat. Nothing to worry about, Bobby knew by now, it was just playfulness. 'They're our children!' said Zelda in mock indignation, if anyone dared ask why she hadn't chosen a prettier, more pedigreed pair of dogs. 'If Bobby and I could have two-legged children, they would have been basters too.' And Bobby had to admit reluctantly that these ugly, affectionate, brown mongrels had burrowed their way deep into her heart in just a few months.

She hadn't realized it was so easy to love two animals. Was it a suppressed parental urge after all? And yet she had never felt the least desire to have children. She hadn't even wanted to have pets. But Zelda had arrived at the house one day with the two woolly mutts . . . Funny how love had always caught her unawares.

'I want to lie here for the rest of the year,' sighed Emma from the hammock.

'That gives you another . . . fourteen hours,' said Adriaan, checking at his watch.

'I can't believe this is the arse-end of the year. To think that tonight, in six years' time, we'll be celebrating the end of the millennium! The year 2000!'

'How do you celebrate something like that?' asked Adriaan, frowning. 'How the fuck do you rise to the occasion?'

'Perhaps we should deal with tonight's party first.' Yvette smiled soothingly and gave the baby to Adriaan. 'There's still a lot of time to decide what we want to do at the end of the millennium.'

'Not really,' muttered Adriaan. 'Just look how the last six years have flown.'

Bobby caught the quick, guilty glance between them. Pablo was born exactly six years ago, she remembered. In the festive season, as Yvette had complained at the time. 'Show me a mother with a newborn baby who has the energy to celebrate any kind of festival!' A year later his drowning – also in the 'festive season' – had turned their lives into a nightmare. Now they had a new baby, a new house they'd built themselves, and, it seemed, also a new kind of happiness. But you could never get away from your memories, thought Bobby with a tightness in her throat. No happiness would ever banish the longing for her brother or for Robin. And it was always worse in the so-called festive season.

'What about a cup of tea?' asked Yvette hastily.

'What about a bottle of bubbly?' Adriaan suggested.

'Do you think it's a good idea to start drinking now?'

'It's always a good idea to start drinking!'

He bounced the child on his knee until her exceptional seriousness was driven away by a crowing laugh. Her mouth wide open to display her four teeth; the bottom two already perfectly formed, the top two still breaking through the dribbling gums. The source of the huge wet spot on Yvette's orangey-red cotton dress. A straight shift with a fairly sober flower design, almost inconspicuous enough to be worn by any other woman. It actually looked as though she might have bought it in an ordinary chain store, Bobby realized, amazed.

'At our age, we have to begin to practise moderation, Adriaan,' she remonstrated.

'Moderation's arse,' he said scornfully.

'I'm just saying. Otherwise we'll all be asleep by midnight . . .'

'I wish I could greet every new year asleep. I hate the fuss people make at midnight. But I'm bloody inquisitive to miss it,' he added with a grin.

'That's how I feel about death,' said Emma from the hammock. 'I would love to die in my sleep. But I'm kind of scared I'll miss something if I'm not fully conscious.'

'I think I should bring the champagne, after all,' said Yvette, half-alarmed. 'If we're already talking about death, we'll need something stronger than tea to see us through the day.'

'The prospect of a New Year's party always makes me morbid,' sighed Emma. 'All that desperate merriment . . .'

It was still strange to see her without the glowing orange veil around her head. Her hair was still curly and as thick as sheep's wool, but she had suddenly stopped dyeing it a year ago. It was now an ordinary dark blonde, fair, with a hint of a reddish gleam when the sun fell on it, apparently the shade she was born with. Without the grey, of course. It wasn't a symbolic gesture, she said, merely chance that soon after Philip's death she had become too lazy for the whole bothersome colouring process. 'Or perhaps I was just inquisitive about what I actually looked like. What had happened to me in the meantime. Underneath the flamboyant mask.' She seemed happy with what she had discovered, but her friends still struggled to get used to the new, paler Emma.

'Will she come to me?' Zelda asked Adriaan.

'Frida? I don't know, you can . . .'

But by this time she had already reached out her arms and swung the child on to her hip. Frida looked a bit surprised, but didn't make a sound, just weighed her up with that shameless gaze in her green-brown eyes. Zelda stared back just as shamelessly.

'Come, I want to introduce you to my canine children.'

'She doesn't like water!' Adriaan shouted as she walked in the direction of the little round swimming pool.

'I won't let her go close to the water,' Zelda assured him, over her shoulder.

'Ever since she was born, she screamed louder than other children when you bathed her,' Adriaan explained, embarrassed about his sudden panic. 'And we've never been able to get her close to the sea. I don't know, perhaps Yvette and I unconsciously forced our own neurosis on her . . .'

'They fuck you up, your mum and dad,' Bobby mumbled sympathetically.

Funny how comfortable Zelda looked with the child on her hip. Her well-endowed body hidden away in loose denim dungarees, her smooth brown arms wrapped lovingly around the baby.

'She would have made a great mother,' said Emma, reading her thoughts.

'Please don't encourage her,' said Bobby. 'She's already persuaded me to take on two of the ugliest dogs in the country . . .'

'That's one of the greatest fuck-ups of this whole parenting business,' said Emma. 'That most people on earth reproduce as a matter of course, without ever wondering if they really want to do it, or *can* do it; and then you get people who think carefully about the whole issue, who can take care of a child emotionally and financially, and they never get a chance to do it.'

'What are you trying to say?' asked Bobby suspiciously. 'That I'm preventing my partner from fulfilling her natural role?'

'No, I was thinking of someone like Mila, really. Or even Ralph.'

'Ralph gets more than enough chance to play father now he's married to the Merry Widow,' said Adriaan. 'Probably more than he ever wanted to.'

'But they're not his own children . . .'

'I don't think he's up for having his own as well,' said Bobby. 'The other day, he told me that when he takes the children's cat to be fixed, he's going to ask the vet if he couldn't quickly sort him out too.'

'A vasectomy?' asked Emma in surprise.

'It's the sensible option,' said Adriaan. 'Three children are quite enough for any home.'

'Especially for a man who's lived on his own for more than twenty years,' said Bobby. 'He probably feels as though he's ended up in a nursery rhyme. *There was an old woman who lived in a shoe.*'

'The poor man probably needs therapy,' said Adriaan. 'Luckily he was clever enough to marry a shrink.'

'Sometimes I wonder whether he didn't marry Leslee . . . to help him forget Mila,' said Emma thoughtfully. 'Not that I think he doesn't love Leslee! It's just . . . he carried a torch for Mila for so many years . . .'

'The ways of love are indeed mysterious,' sighed Adriaan.

He suddenly sounded so miserable that Emma and Bobby both looked away uncomfortably, to the round swimming pool where Mona and Sasha were moving round and round in a circle, turning the water into a wild whirlpool. The little bodies as smooth and glistening as seals, their hair plastered flat against their heads, soaking wet. Bobby also looked at Zelda, who was lying on her back on the grass, laughing, while Frida bounced on her stomach and the two mongrels tugged at her trouser legs. How had she grown to love this woman so much, she wondered, for the umpteenth time. She wished she knew how to comfort Adriaan.

'Have you met the new man in her life yet?' asked Emma.

'Who? Mila?' asked Adriaan. As though he didn't know exactly who she was talking about. And when Emma nodded, 'The old Belgian guy?'

'He's not so old!'

'He's at least ten years older than she is,' grinned Adriaan. 'That means he's not so young, either.'

'He's the best thing that could have happened to her. She thought no man would ever be interested in her again. And now she's got this — '

'I don't know how she could think that!' Adriaan interrupted her, almost brusquely. 'She was always more than just a great body.'

'Sure. But her body was important to her. Perhaps more important than mine is to me. I mean, if I had to sacrifice these withered old tits . . .' Emma laughed, self-consciously, brushed a curl out of her eyes. 'OK, I know it would still be terrible, but somehow it wouldn't be such an *outrage*. Mila had the most beautiful breasts of any woman I've ever known.'

'And I never persuaded her to pose in the nude for me,' he said, with a sigh which conveyed a whole lifetime of unfulfilled wishes.

424

'But now she's met a man who's crazy about her,' said Emma. 'With or without breasts. And suddenly, she's looking as sexy and self-confident as the old Mila!'

'I told her she'd still be sexy at seventy.' Adriaan stared over the lawn, his grey-green eyes cloudy. The long, soft line of his lips as vulnerable as a fresh wound. 'It's not looks which make a woman sexy, it's an ability to enjoy sex. That's why some of the most beautiful women on earth are as unsexy as dishwater. They've never acquired that ability. While Mila will never lose it. With or without breasts.'

'Here's the champagne.' Yvette had appeared quietly in the doorway with a tray. Bobby glanced at her quickly, wondering if she'd heard Adriaan's paean to Mila, but the dark eyes in the pale face revealed nothing. Just a shadow of a smile on the small child-like mouth. 'Perhaps it's time for a toast.'

'Let's drink to old people and things which pass,' said Adriaan sombrely.

'And to youth and the future,' said Yvette firmly.

'For just once in your life, could you try to be a little less optimistic?' Adriaan pleaded. 'Just to make the rest of us feel a bit better?'

An hour or so later, Liane and Max had arrived with their wriggling twins, along with Ralph and his instant family, and suddenly the whole house was so full of children and animals that Adriaan had an overwhelming desire to escape.

All he needed was some breathing space. A little time to calm his restless spirit. He had no idea where this restlessness came from. Probably something to do with another year passing. So many things that were past for ever.

So he announced that he was going to drive to town to buy more beer, asking Ralph and Max whether they wanted to come along. Ralph leaped up, as eager as a schoolboy who wants to escape the classroom. And it didn't take much effort to convince Max to leave his squirming sons in their mother's care for a while.

'Where does this sudden sexism come from?' Liane asked indignantly. 'Why are only the men invited?'

'I have a need for a bit of male bonding,' said Adriaan. 'I'm completely overwhelmed by the female sex in my home.'

'Tell me about it!' laughed Liane. 'I know how it feels to be an oppressed minority in my own home! I'm living in a testosterone factory these days!'

'Well, then you ought to be happy that I'm trying to lower the testosterone levels in the company.'

'If it's about male bonding, you're welcome to take Nelson and Alexander along.'

She looked in amusement at her dark-haired sons, who had recently celebrated their first birthday, waddling on the short, sturdy legs they'd inherited from their father, together trying to tear a stuffed elephant apart. This was shortly after they'd taken turns whacking each other over the head with a plastic truck. 'Thank god they aren't girls,' she'd commented earlier. 'Those thick rugby-prop legs would have been a disaster on a girl!' Not to speak of that bloodcurdling thirst for destruction, Adriaan thought in stupefied silence.

'As soon as they're eighteen,' he promised solemnly, 'we'll take them along.'

'Roll on 2011,' sighed Liane. 'I can't wait.'

If they haven't beaten each other to a pulp by that time, he couldn't help thinking.

'So,' said Max as they drove to town in Adriaan's red Microbus. 'The first democratic New Year's Eve in the history of South Africa. That's quite something.'

'Something what?' Ralph asked from the back seat, his voice argumentative. Suddenly reminding Adriaan of Philip. It hit him unexpectedly these days, this intense longing for a friend who had been dead for more than a year. In the first few months, he hadn't really missed him. It was as though he was constantly expecting to bump into him somewhere, that thin, slightly clumsy figure in a crumpled shirt, with the pale, mocking eyes, the cynical curl to his lips. But by this time it had dawned on him that he would never see him again. 'Something surprising? Something disappointing? Something frightening?'

'All those things,' said Max. 'And more.'

'But it actually means fuck-all,' said Ralph. 'We know what "democratic" means – in theory – and we know what New Year's Eve means. In practice. Especially the morning after. But what exactly does a democratic New Year's Eve mean? Are we all going to get exactly equally drunk? Or speak precisely the same amount of shit?'

'Sounds as though you're already practising for the shit-talking part,' sniggered Max.

'Words mean fuck-all most of the time,' said Adriaan from behind the wheel, his voice impatient. 'For most people. Except when they're trying to fill in *Huisgenoot's* crossword puzzle.'

'Some of us still have to earn our living with words,' sighed Ralph. 'Because we can't do sums or draw pictures.'

'Ag, come on, Ralph. I don't know anyone else with your flair for words,' said Adriaan. 'You're the only person I know who can use words like "pathos" and "bathos". Preferably in the same sentence, so that people realize you know the difference!'

'What is the difference between pathos and bathos?' asked Max, frowning.

'Pathos is the evoking of sympathy or sadness. Something which you often found in the Old South Africa. And bathos is pathos which has become ridiculous. An anti-climax. Something we unfortunately see more and more of in the New South Africa.'

'Why do you suddenly have such a problem with democracy and the New South Africa? We don't need another Philip McCarthy among us!'

'The last day of the year is supposed to be a day of reflection. I can't help but remember how excited we all were eight months ago, about the election. Even Philip would have been excited. He would have hidden it, but he would have been excited. Now the euphoria is over and we're realizing that the New South Africa hasn't been born yet. We're still dealing with the labour pains.'

'The labour pains have hardly begun,' mumbled Adriaan. 'The election wasn't the birth it was the . . . infection. No, what do you call it again? The fertilization?'

'The conception.'

'Ah! Conception! I think I'm getting a premature form of my father's Alzheimer's.'

'It's got nothing to do with Alzheimer's,' said Ralph unsympathetically. 'That's what happens if you despise words. You lose control of them, they evade you.'

'I don't despise words! They're just not my strong point. I was always better with my fingers than with my tongue. No, that sounds a bit obscene. See what I mean. I sometimes wish I could communicate with pictures. Like playing Pictionary for the rest of my life!'

He wound the window down to relieve the stuffiness in the car. They'd got caught up in a traffic jam the minute they'd driven into town. Idling vehicles and impatient drivers wherever you looked. The hefty man in the bakkie behind them played his hooter like a keyboard.

'I know what you mean,' said Max thoughtfully. 'The first few months after the election were like the beginning of a pregnancy which the whole of humanity had longed for. Now the whole business has become a reality. And the most difficult part is still to come.'

'And you can't go and sit somewhere else and wait for the bloody baby to be born, like some old-fashioned father,' said Adriaan, shaking his head. 'You have to be *there* while it happens.'

'I don't know if I have the stomach for the whole bloody business,' said Ralph.

'You don't have a choice, my bra,' grimaced Max. 'You've had your chance to escape. What made you decide to come back, anyway?'

'From England?'

'I've also wondered,' said Adriaan. 'At the time we all thought that we'd seen the last of you.'

'Me too,' Ralph admitted, and rubbed his mane of hair awkwardly.

Still the most hair – with the least grey – even though he was the oldest of the three. Adriaan watched him in the rear-view mirror; a little enviously, he had to admit. In the past year, his own hair had given up the battle against the grey. And he had noticed that Max no longer tried to comb what was left of his hair over the bald spot at the back of his head.

'But in the end the lack of danger got me down,' said Ralph, resignedly. 'I mean, the average Londoner's greatest fear is that he won't be able to squeeze on to the next Tube train. I missed the fear and loathing of this place.'

'Just goes to show,' grinned Adriaan as he parked the car. 'We're fucked for life. We may as well stay here, with all our fucked-up friends.'

After they'd bought a few cases of beer, they ended up almost automatically in the bar next to the bottle store, none of them in a hurry to go back to the house. It was a plain, old-fashioned bar, the kind in which, until recently, only men were allowed. The smell of tobacco and alcohol rose up from the shabby carpet, an atmosphere of disillusionment hung in the stuffy air. No other customers, no one behind the counter, just a grumpy waiter in a crumpled uniform watching them from a dark corner. They ordered three cold beers and took the first few foaming sips in appreciative silence.

'It's peaceful here,' said Max with a contented sigh. 'I'd forgotten how good it feels just to sit. To stare straight ahead and think about fuck-all. Like a potato!'

'Like you did before you had a wife and kids,' said Adriaan teasingly.

'Yes, comrade,' said Max sombrely. 'Like I did before I had a wife and kids.'

'Ja,' said Ralph, shaking his head. 'Nowadays it's a case of never a dull moment. Sometimes I hanker after the dull moments of my former life.'

'Does one ever get used to it?' Max looked at Adriaan, his black eyes almost pleading over his beer glass.

'To the "joys of fatherhood"?'

'And everything that goes along with it. What it does to your self-esteem when you realize you've become everything you used to laugh at. A pathetic bourgeois citizen who spends weekends sitting in a child-friendly restaurant with his little nuclear family, choking down hamburgers! And fighting with his wife about who's going to do the damn nappy run tonight!'

'Wait until they get older,' warned Ralph. 'Then you have to watch a so-called child-friendly video every Saturday night. I knew Hollywood was a shit-factory, but I had no idea of the kind of crap they dish up for children.'

'Welcome to married life.'

'Take me to your leader,' grinned Ralph. And then, with a sudden guilty expression: 'Most of the time I rather enjoy it. It's just one helluvan adjustment when you've slept alone for decades – except for the odd fling along the way – to share your bed every night. Not just with a woman, but also with a five-year-old who wants to protect his mother against the "intruder", and three fat cats lying on your feet like dead weights.'

'It's amazing how quickly one learns to screw next to sleeping children and animals,' Adriaan consoled him.

'My biggest problem is in the morning, when the two older children also creep into bed. Then I lie there with my morning glory and sex on the brain and it's just kids and cats as far as the eye can see.'

'And no way to get out of bed with your stiff cock without exposing the children to obscenity.' Adriaan shook his head sympathetically and washed his smile down with a mouthful of beer.

'The little girl is crazy about me, not half as threatened as her two brothers, but that makes everything even more difficult. She's got this childish way of rubbing up against me in the mornings. Absolute agony if you've woken up with an erection. Makes me feel like Humbert Humbert in *Lolita*!'

'And what does your resident shrink say about that?'

'Oh, she reckons it's a good thing for the children to encounter our sexuality "in a natural way". Easy for her to talk. I'm the one with the interesting body part which is going to be examined like a guinea pig in bloody biology class!'

'Didn't you say that you'd never settle down?' asked Max.

'I married for the oldest reason in the book,' said Ralph, and sipped at his beer, embarrassed. 'To have regular sex.'

'And like every fool who ever married for that reason,' said Adriaan, 'you'll realize soon enough that you had more regular sex before you were married.'

'Leslee was scared of setting a bad example for the kids. She might be a modern Jungian, but deep in her heart she remains an old-fashioned boeremeisie. So it was always such a fuss trying to have sex without the children realizing that in the end I decided: fuck this, I may as well get married.'

'And now it's still a fuss to have sex without the children realizing,' laughed Max.

'If I remember correctly,' said Ralph, 'you didn't have a burning desire to settle down, either.'

'Ah, well, if you've been in love with the same woman for as long as I have . . .'

'I was,' said Ralph with a wry smile, which made Max stare at his beer glass in confusion for a moment.

'Well, if she'd got pregnant . . .'

'So you got married for the second oldest reason in the book,' said Adriaan quickly, before the conversation got too serious. 'A bun in the oven.'

'Two buns in the oven,' grinned Max. 'Except that the buns were already well out of the oven before my fellow-cook agreed. I had almost given up hope that it would ever happen, and then, on the morning of my fortieth birthday, she asked me what was the best present she could give me. I said to drop the kids off somewhere so that we could sleep all day. I saw that she looked a little bit disappointed, and then she said no, it's something I always said I'd do when I turned forty. But I was so tired because the twins hadn't slept the whole bloody night that I just lay there staring at her blankly. Then she lost her temper and said if I didn't get out of bed immediately and drive to the nearest magistrate's office with her, she'd change her mind. So I almost fucked up my only chance to get married because I was too tired to think of anything except sleep.' He scratched his goatee, with a shamefaced smile, and stared at the bottles behind the bar counter. 'It's now almost a year later and I'm *still* too tired to think of anything except sleep.'

'The first year of fatherhood is enough to fuck up any relationship,' Adriaan assured him.

'And after that it gets worse,' sighed Ralph. 'To quote our friend Philip.'

'I don't think the twins have slept right through a single night since they were born. I mean both of them together. One night the one will sleep, the next night the other. You would swear they discussed it before we put them to bed each night, *OK, tonight it's your turn to give the old folks hell.* As if they've plotted to prevent us ever reproducing again!'

'Do you want to?' asked Ralph, surprised. 'Reproduce again? After all you've just said?'

'Well, I always wanted to have a daughter. Probably because I missed having a sister.' He drained his glass quickly and raised his hand to order another beer. His mouth suddenly weary. 'But I'm afraid the Terrible Twins have put Liane off any further childbearing. She says motherhood doesn't come naturally to her.'

'Show me a woman to whom motherhood comes naturally,' said Adriaan. 'It's fucking hard work. Why do you think they call childbirth labour?'

'She says her friends all make it look so easy. Emma even makes bringing up a child on her own look easy. So at the moment she's struggling with a huge inferiority complex about her role as mother.'

'That's quite ironic,' smiled Ralph. 'Leslee was in tears the other day because she thinks she's been neglecting the children ever since I appeared on the scene. She says she has to spread herself so thin between me and the children and the house and her work that she's beginning to feel transparent. And then she mentioned Liane as an example of someone who manages to be a successful businesswoman *and* keep a happy relationship going *and* raise two children. And on top of it all, she looks as though she's just stepped off a Paris catwalk. That's how Leslee sees it. Oh yes, and then there's her house, which always looks stunning. Another thorn in my poor wife's flesh.'

'I wonder if it would help if I told Liane that? And you can tell Leslee that her role model actually thinks she's a big flop. And then hopefully everyone will feel better.'

'No,' said Adriaan, 'they won't feel better, they'll be the hell-in with you. Women view discussing their insecurities with your friends as a serious breach of trust.'

'But they discuss our insecurities with anyone who'll listen!' Max exclaimed indignantly. 'From their hairdressers to their gym instructors!'

'They've got the patent on it. Listen to me, I've been in this game longer than either of you. By this time, I've got a good idea of what a married man can and can't do.'

'Not that you ever paid much attention to the rules,' snorted Max.

'I've turned over a new leaf. My New Year's resolution is to never again sleep with anyone apart from my wife. Except when I really have no choice.'

'Wasn't that your New Year's resolution about ten years ago?' asked Max sceptically.

Adriaan wiped away the moustache of foam which the new beer had left on his upper lip and sighed resignedly.

'It's my resolution every year. But I believe it's like giving up smoking. Each time you try, you're a little more determined than before.'

'I'm afraid that motherhood doesn't come naturally to me,' said Liane with a dramatic sigh. 'It's a battle I have to wage every day.'

She was sitting on the stoep of Yvette's new house, her eyes hidden behind dark glasses with small round lenses, staring miserably ahead of her.

'What makes you think it ever comes naturally?' asked Yvette in amusement.

'Well, just look at Leslee and Zelda . . .'

Leslee and Zelda sat cross-legged on the lawn, in a circle with half a dozen children, busy playing rotten egg. Frida all serious on Zelda's lap, the twins wriggling about on either side of Leslee, Emma's daughter with wet blonde hair and a sky blue bikini between Leslee's two little ones, Oscar and Kathleen. Mona skipped around the circle with a tennis ball in one hand and a bored expression on her face. She had already made it quite clear (several times) that she was too old for these 'baby games'. Each time in a loud voice meant to reach Leslee's oldest son under the pepper tree. But the eleven-year-old Dylan sat with his nose in a *Mad* comic, utterly unaware of the longing gazes she occasionally aimed in his direction.

'I don't like children's games,' said Liane with a moody pout. 'Even when I was a child, I didn't like children's games! If I had to make a list of the greatest horrors in my life, this rotten egg game would probably be up there in the top twenty. Rotten egg and aeroplanes landing and the fear of suddenly waking up one morning colour-blind . . .'

'I thought we were meant to be colour-blind in our new rainbow nation,' Bobby mumbled.

'Not if your work is decorating the rainbow nation's houses and offices.'

'Oh yes. Like Adriaan says, your shops have become the Gestapo of Good Taste.'

'So I hear,' said Liane with an unexpected giggle.

'So if the Führer suddenly becomes colour-blind, we can all fuck up our houses as much as we like? No one to threaten us with banishment if we arrange orange cushions on red couches?'

'Orange and red can work perfectly well together, my darling. Just look at Yvette's dress. You just have to know how.'

'And you can show everyone how?'

'I'm not presumptuous, Bobby! I know I've got a natural feel for colour and shape. Just as I *don't* have a natural feel for children and children's games!'

She shook her hair – which fell smoothly, golden brown, down to her shoulders again these days – laughingly out of her eyes. Still a face to take the breath away. Despite the new wrinkles around the eyes and the slightly drooping appearance of the once-perfect mouth. As elegant as ever: a skirt of cream-coloured linen with a broad leather belt, slender tanned feet in leather sandals, bronzed shoulders in a sleeveless white shirt.

'How is it possible for the mother of two children to stay so clean?' Emma had asked earlier. 'Do your children never touch you with their dirty hands? Do they never wipe their snotty noses on your clothes?'

'I always carry a change of clothing along. I have to drag this gigantic bag full of nappies and bottles and baby equipment anyway, so I usually pack a clean outfit too.'

'No, hell, that's too much trouble!' Emma had exclaimed. 'I'd rather just wear patterned dresses which don't show the dirty marks. When my child leaves home one day, I'll try to be elegant again. On the other hand, even before I had a child I was never exactly the epitome of elegance.'

'I always thought that messy look of yours was part of your charm. As though you'd just had sneaky sex in the back of a car.'

'Ha!' Emma laughed. 'I should be so lucky!'

'If you knew what you know *before* you got pregnant,' said Yvette as she watched the game on the grass, 'would you rather not have had children?'

'That's a completely unfair question!' exclaimed Liane. 'Now that they're here, I can't imagine what it would be like to live without them! OK, my life would be a lot calmer. But I wanted to have a child, I wanted to know what it felt like to be a mother, I was far too inquisitive to miss this experience. I just didn't realize . . . I thought that this mythical maternal instinct I'd always heard about would help me over all the obstacles . . . you know, make all the fear disappear. I've waited for more than a year for the fear to disappear.'

'It never disappears,' sighed Yvette. 'I think it gets worse. When they're small, you're afraid of physical dangers . . . that they'll stick their fingers into a power socket . . . or drown. You know. But as they get older, the dangers become more abstract. Harder to control. It's impossible to protect them from all life's knocks.'

'I don't know what I expected of motherhood. I only know that I didn't expect fear to be the dominant emotion. Fear and exhaustion.'

She watched as Nelson (or Alexander) grabbed the tennis ball from behind Sasha's back and tried to run away with it, in the direction of the stoep, as if he wanted to bring it to his mother like a present. Mona pursued him, caught him as he protested loudly, and carried him kicking and screaming back to the circle on the lawn. The moment she put him on Leslee's lap, the other half of the twins leaped up, grabbed the ball and ran to the pepper tree. When Zelda's two dogs tried to snatch the ball out of his hands, Tula sprang up growling to protect him. Which made Zelda jump up, with Frida still on her hip, to prevent a full-scale dog fight. The one with the ball burst into frightened tears – which made the one without the ball scream even louder – and Kathleen jumped up to go and comfort him. Even Dylan forgot about his comic for a while and stared in stupefaction at the chaotic scene on the grass.

'It just doesn't work with the twins!' Mona shouted in frustration. 'They're too little to understand the game!'

'Or perhaps they just don't like rotten egg,' Liane speculated. 'Perhaps they take after me more than I'd thought.'

'Now I understand why there were always identical twins in those old-fashioned farces,' Yvette observed in amazement. 'It's a guarantee of continual action.'

'Or continual chaos,' said Liane.

Alexander wriggled himself loose from Kathleen's grasp and waddled on short legs over to his mother on the stoep. Liane reached her arms out – a tired, resigned gesture – and lifted the sniffing child on to her lap. Which made his brother on the grass struggle even more furiously than before to escape from Leslee's arms.

'You can let him come as well!' Liane called out.

'Can you hold both of them at once?' Leslee asked, concerned.

'I don't usually have a choice,' Liane replied with a miserable little laugh.

'I don't know how the hell you do it,' said Bobby in astonishment, the newspaper forgotten on her lap.

'If you have to, you have to,' mumbled Liane, while her other son also clambered on to her lap.

Two pairs of dirty, bare feet treading on the cream skirt. Two dirty, wet faces pressed against the white top. (She was going to need that extra change of clothes soon.) And the mother's patient smile above the two dark heads.

'I'll never forget how panic-stricken I was when I had to hold them the first time,' she mused. 'These two floppy bodies which were suddenly dumped in my arms. I just sat there with an idiotic grin on my face – trying to hide the panic – while Max recorded the historic moment with his video camera. The so-called glowing mother. And I felt like an actress with stage fright. As though I'd been shoved onstage to play a role, but didn't know the words or even what play I was in! A recurring nightmare from my days as a drama student. Except that this time I knew it wasn't a nightmare. *This is real life, baby.* That's all that went through my head. The only words I knew in this unfamiliar play. *This is real life, baby. What now?*'

'Ow?' echoed one of the babies on her lap.

'Ow!' the other one answered. 'Ow?'

'Ow!'

And so on. Enjoying a conversation in their secret twin language. Both of them smiling by this time. Angelic innocence in the big brown eyes. Butter would never melt in those pouting mouths.

'I still wonder.' Liane's voice sounded tired. '*What now?* Or is this my lot for the next twenty years?'

Bobby looked at the beautiful face with the drooping mouth and wondered what to say. And found she had no words of comfort. *This is real life, baby. Things never work out exactly as you want them to.*

Adriaan was standing in front of the stove, with a wooden spoon in one hand, wearing a butcher's apron, when Mila appeared. Like the first time he'd seen her, he suddenly remembered, bemused by the clarity of the memory. She walked into the kitchen with a tall, unfamiliar man behind her – as she had that first time – but, once again, he hardly noticed the man because he couldn't keep his eyes off her. She had aged visibly, of course, as they all had over the last decade. But her hair was just as blonde, a little longer in the neck and softer around the face than ten years ago, and her mouth was just as red. Or as red again, he thought with relief, because a year ago it had seemed that she had locked away her lipstick for good. And the gaze in her blue eyes was as challenging as ever.

Like seeks like. That was what she had thought that evening at Yzerfontein, she had admitted to him long ago. Unfortunately, like can't always live with like. That was the lesson they had to learn the hard way. But it was a basic law of nature.

Like seeks like.

'This is Adriaan Beyers, the Famous Painter.' The voice also just as seductively low and smoky. Even though she hadn't smoked for ages. She turned to the man behind her and pulled him closer. He was as tall as Ralph, even taller, with a head of silver hair that was just as unruly. 'And this is Herman Krabbe, the Famous Belgian ... Beloved.'

Suddenly she looked as self-conscious as a teenager introducing her first boyfriend to her parents. He wondered if she was aware of the similarity between Ralph and Herman. Her first love and now, who knows, perhaps her last. She had always said that this was the kind of body which attracted her, tall and slender and athletic. He was the exception, with his bullish shoulders and his broad chest and his paunch.

'What does he have that I don't have?' he joked, to hide his unexpected emotion.

'Height,' she answered, just as jokingly, to hide who knew what. 'And good manners.'

'What's wrong with my manners?'

'What manners?'

'Pleased to meet you,' said Herman with an easy handshake and an unmistakable Flemish accent beneath his careful Afrikaans words. 'Mila's told me a lot about you.'

Like what? he wondered for a moment. Before he began to laugh jovially.

'As long as you remember she's a Famous Journalist. It's her work to lie convincingly. Speaking about work, Mila, what made you decide to give up your glamorous job?'

'Oh, one day I just realized that I was paying more attention to my hairstyle than to my writing style,' she replied with a shrug. 'I suppose it's unavoidable, working for such a trendy magazine. No one reads the bloody thing anyway, they just buy it because it looks good on their designer coffee tables.'

'Which they probably bought from one of Liane's shops.'

'Exactly. My whole life had begun to revolve around artistic pictures and stylish parties. And when I got ill ... the pictures and the parties began to seem all the more irrelevant ...'

She looked away quickly, at the sky which hung like a bright blue cloth behind the high window, holding her hands in front of her mouth in that familiar, protective way. He turned back to the stove and stirred the wooden spoon through the vegetable mixture in the pan. Breathed in the scent of olive oil and garlic. These days he found some food odours almost as stimulating as certain female scents. Yet more proof that he was growing old.

'But I hung on because I didn't know what else to do. I mean, it's probably a bit presumptuous to look for a new job when you've just heard that you've got cancer.'

She leaned her buttocks against the table opposite him so that the slit in her skirt fell open to reveal a slender knee. She didn't wear such short little dresses any more, but this slit was even more seductive. Giving you only a glimpse of forbidden goods. Making you curious to see more. He wasn't *that* old, after all.

'But now she's well enough again to be a "real" journalist,' said Herman, his hand proudly on her shoulder.

His eyes also on the bare knee, Adriaan noticed.

'Well, let's just say that I feel less frivolous now that I work on a serious news magazine. Not that I think there's anything wrong with frivolous glossies. We need some frivolity in this country!'

'Perhaps now more than ever.'

'But I don't have the right personality to be the editor of a glossy. I've always struggled to work up the necessary cheerfulness.'

'You did well enough to fool most of us.'

'I even fooled myself,' she admitted. 'If it wasn't for the election, I would probably still be sitting in *Thina*'s glamorous offices, with my four-inch heels and my French manicure and my perfect hairstyle. It was the excitement of the election which made me realize what I was missing. "Real" news. Hard news. Even bad news. Politics and power. That always turned me on. I tried to deny it for a while, because politics had become so unbelievably depressing. But the election changed everything.'

'Although the news hasn't necessarily got any less depressing,' said Adriaan as he took the pan off the plate and began to grate a block of Parmesan cheese over the vegetables. 'Sounds as though some dark days still lie ahead.'

'Sure, the honeymoon is over, and it'll get worse before it gets better, and we're all still going to have a bloody hard time of it, I know all that, Adriaan. But it's not the same country any more! You only have to look at the new MPs. When I think of the old white men with their dark suits and their dour faces, sitting there all those years!'

Her low voice suddenly rough with passion. Like long ago, he remembered, when she had been so excited about the new Afrikaans newspaper she was involved with.

'OK, I agree it's great that nowadays we're governed by a bunch of women in colourful dresses. Not to mention the men in colourful dresses,' he said teasingly. 'At least we can look at their outfits when they're talking shit on TV. Because in the end they're going to talk shit, too. You know that as well as I do.'

'Politicians are politicians,' she said, with that thick, creamy laugh of hers. 'They've always driven me to despair.'

'And yet she finds them irresistible,' said Herman, shaking his head.

As if it was just another of her exceptional qualities. The man was clearly besotted.

'Perhaps I'm irresistibly attracted to despair, my love. You always say we Afrikaners always look for the dark cloud behind the silver lining.'

Adriaan stared at her, unsettled. Remembering the deathly misery which had hung over her voice last year. The desolation about her pale mouth. And now she could laugh with scarlet lips again. *My love.* Funny how the two little words echoed somewhere inside him. As if there was a hollow that he wasn't even aware of.

'Hey! Hello!' said Emma at the open window. 'I didn't know you were here already!'

She pushed the sash window higher up and swung her long legs over the low sill. Her feet were bare and her hair clung in wet corkscrew curls against her head because she'd just been swimming in the river near the house.

'Ah!' said Adriaan. 'Here's our Famous Author at last. So famous that she has to climb through windows these days to escape her fans.'

'It's to escape my child. She lectures me every time I light a cigarette.' She sat down on the table next to Mila and took a packet of cigarettes out of the pocket of her cut-off denims. 'It's hell to be a parent in the nineties. It's not the children who smoke on the sly any more, it's the parents. My daughter is turning into a New Age health freak before my very eyes. And she's not even five!'

'And you're becoming rich and famous before our very eyes,' said Mila. 'And you're not even forty!'

'Till now, I've seen absolutely nothing of my legendary wealth,' said Emma, and sucked at the cigarette anxiously. 'I just sign the contracts my agent in London sends me.'

'*My agent in London!*' giggled Mila. 'How blasé she sounds!'

'I'm not blasé! I'm still in a state of shock! I almost killed myself trying to get this novel written. And suddenly a dozen foreign publishers want to translate it. That's the kind of good fortune an insecure writer can only dream of. It's not meant to happen in real life.'

'And Hollywood wants to make it into a movie?'

'Can you believe it? They'll probably fuck it up. Ralph always says Hollywood has the opposite of the Midas touch. Everything they touch turns to shit.'

'But it'll help you to sell a few books,' Herman consoled her.

'He's a businessman.' Mila looked at her new love with a proud, teasing smile on her lips. 'Always thinking of the bottom line.'

'Is there anything else to think of?' asked Herman with an innocent smile.

'Well, there is Everlasting Fame,' said Adriaan, stirring a few beaten eggs into the mixture in the pan.

'Or at least the fifteen minutes of fame you always talk about, right?' Emma blew out a thin stream of smoke. 'I reckon I'm in the thirteenth minute of mine. Perhaps a minute or two of injury time left. Then everything will be back to normal again.'

'Your fame has hardly begun!' Mila exclaimed. 'Your life is never going to be normal again, Emma. Once Hollywood is done with you, they'll know your name in the streets of Japan and Yugoslavia! Or what remains of Yugoslavia.'

'Or what remains of my name,' muttered Emma. 'Once Hollywood is finished with me.'

'And which actors are going to play you and Philip?'

'It's not me and Philip! I've created two fictional characters who have certain things in common with me and Philip!'

'I know, I know, I know!' Mila ducked behind her outstretched hands. 'I know the woman is ten times more neurotic than you and the man is ten times less fucked up than Philip was – and he doesn't die in the end – but I just can't help thinking of you and Philip when I try to imagine what they look like.'

'Well, I can assure you that Hollywood won't let them look like me and Philip. They probably have something in the line of Julia Roberts and Richard Gere in mind. And it doesn't matter a damn whether the woman in the book is at least ten years older and plainer than Julia Roberts and the man ten times less attractive than Richard Gere! In Hollywood, unattractive couples obviously don't exist. I get so depressed when I think about it that I want to get completely pissed.'

And with these words, she jumped off the table and went to the fridge to fetch a bottle of sparkling wine.

'Well, one of these days you'll be able to afford to get drunk in style. Moët et Chandon instead of local bubbly! Have you thought about what you're going to do with all the money?'

'I prefer not to think about it until I see it in my bank account. If I ever see it in my bank account.' She stared so miserably at the bottle – as if she suddenly couldn't remember what to do with it – that Herman took it from her and began to work the cork loose. 'Ten years ago I gave up a steady salary in the vague hope that one day, maybe, who knows, I could make a living from my stories. That I could choose how I wanted to live, where I wanted to live, rather than just fucking ahead every day because I didn't have a choice. And now that it seems as though it may, in fact, be possible to choose for the first time . . . now the choices make me so scared that I want to keep everything exactly as it is. I feel as though I've been sitting in jail for years . . . dreaming every day about what I'd do when I was set free . . . and now that the jail doors have finally swung open, I just want to scurry back to my safe little cell!'

The cork shot with a bang against the ceiling. Emma watched, frowning, as Herman poured the pale liquid into four glasses. Took the cigarettes from her pocket and quickly lit another one.

'You don't *have* to make any dramatic changes,' said Mila quietly.

'I know. It's just that . . . you know, I've always dreamed that I'd be able to live in another country one day . . . but it was never more than an impossible dream. How the hell would an Afrikaans writer survive in another country? But now that my work is being translated . . . and with the movie contract . . . suddenly it's not so impossible any more. My child's father is dead. I don't have a man in my life. What's keeping me here? Apart from fear and cowardice?'

'Friends? Family? Roots?' Mila stared abstractedly through the broad window, the champagne glass in front of her mouth. 'That impossibly blue sky out there, the blue mountains below the sky, the blue sea behind the mountains . . .'

'South Africa doesn't have a monopoly on blue, Mila.'

'On *that* blue?' asked Herman, also looking at the sky. 'Perhaps it does.'

'Oh, well. Hopefully the new year will bring new insight. Or new courage at any rate.' She took a big swig of sparkling wine, as though she wanted to wash away the anxiety in her grey eyes, and lifted the corners of her mouth in a wide, unconvincing smile. 'Meanwhile, I'm burning with curiosity about what we're going to eat tonight. It smells gorgeous.'

'Well, I'm busy with *farcis provençaux*,' said Adriaan, in his most pretentious French accent, as he carefully spooned the mixture from the pan into a variety of hollowed-out vegetables. 'Stuffed vegetables, in plain language. I suppose we can't keep ignoring the growing number of vegetarians in our midst. Unfortunately, it's not just our children who are becoming health freaks, it's our friends too.' He grinned at the dirty look which Mila shot him and wiped his hands on the apron. 'But it could also be Leslee's *gigot au pistou* that you're smelling. Buttersoft leg of lamb, fresh from her father's farm, stuffed with basil and garlic. That's for the privileged among us who still know how to appreciate meat. And Ralph has offered to make his famous bouillabaisse. Oh yes, and Mila is in charge of the pudding.'

'Mila?' asked Emma, astonished.

'Crêpes Suzettes,' grinned Adriaan. 'She has that church bazaar talent for making a huge mountain of perfect pancakes, remember?'

'And then Adriaan pours liqueur over it and lights it dramatically and pretends it's French cuisine,' laughed Mila.

'So we're going to brave the new year with an enormous festive meal,' said Herman, clearly pleased.

'Another good Afrikaans habit,' said Mila. 'Never miss a chance to eat too much.'

'Oh, and there's a whole array of salads and cheeses as well,' Adriaan said.

'But we'll never be able to eat all that food!' Emma exclaimed.

'We're getting some outside help. There'll be about twenty of us around the table. Without the crowd of kids.'

'Who are the other people?'

'Griet and Jans, Johannes and Joe, Rehana and Sipho . . .'

'Sipho?'

'The new love of her life.'

'I hear they're getting married soon,' said Mila.

'Amazing,' mumbled Emma. 'That there are still rational people who want to get married.'

'Who else? Oh yes, Mart! The election lured her back from London. And she's apparently bringing a new lover along. Or perhaps he's just a friend. I'm not sure.'

'But Tomas isn't invited?' said Mila, her red mouth teasing.

'I don't have any objection to his presence! But Yvette said it wouldn't work. Especially if Mart brings her new lover.' He scooped out the last of the vegetable mixture and smiled apologetically. 'Perhaps she's just afraid I'll punch him if I let my jealousy get the upper hand.'

'Surely you can't *still* be jealous of Tomas!' cried Mila indignantly.

'I'll always be jealous of Tomas,' he said, smiling.

But she looked at him as though every secret in his heart was written like a headline on his face. Of course he had no right to be jealous. Just as he had no right to long for this woman with the red lips and the husky laugh. And yet.

The heart has never paid much attention to rights. The heart will always have its own reasons.

A few hours later, the kitchen was as busy as an airport arrivals hall. Mila and Adriaan were frenetically frying pancakes, Ralph and Yvette were cooking the seafood soup, Leslee was keeping an eye on the leg of lamb with basil in the oven, Emma and Liane and Zelda were making salad, and Herman was keeping everyone's glass topped up. Bobby came to sit on the stoep, ostensibly to help Max look after the twins, but really because the bustle of the kitchen had got too much for her.

'At times like this, my background as an only child catches up with me,' she admitted as she stretched out in a cane chair. 'After my brother died, I got used to silence and space around me.'

'I know. I was also a spoilt only child.' Max sat flat on the floor between his sons, who were playing tug-o-war with a battered teddy bear. The one on the right jerked the toy unexpectedly from his brother's grasp. The one on the left stared at his empty hands, astounded for a moment, before his whole face began to crumple like paper, creased forehead and quivering mouth, everything suddenly skewed. Max pressed one of the teddy bear's legs into his hands again. Quite mechanically, Bobby noticed, as though he carried out such fatherly duties completely unconsciously these days. 'Now, of course, it feels to me as though I'll never have silence and space in my life again.'

'Where are all the other children? Can't they help entertain the twins?'

'I think they've fled as far as possible from the twins. I would, too, given the chance.'

'Please tell me it's not really so bad!'

'It's not really so bad.' With a resigned smile in his grey-black goatee. 'But it would have been easier if I'd been younger.'

'Do you think you'd have had the patience to sit here and play referee to such an idiotic game ten years ago?'

'No. But I would have had the rashness to say fuck the teddy, whack each other black and blue if you want to, some time or other you'll have to start fighting your own battles.' A smile unfolded slowly while he listened to the music from the house, murmuring lyrics along with the singer. '*The sun is the same in the relative way, but you're older and shorter of breath and one day closer to death . . .*'

'My brother was crazy about this song.'

'But it's probably a bit old-fashioned for you,' he said teasingly.

'I would have preferred Nirvana,' she joked along. 'But I'm also getting old enough to start appreciating old music.'

He stared at the trees on the edge of the lawn, dark green foliage against the bright blue sky, longing in his black eyes.

'I remember I once said that one of my greatest fears was that everything would be exactly the same in ten years' time. The same political fuck-up, the same personal longing for something else, the same frustrating feeling that nothing would ever really change. But I don't think I was prepared for such dramatic changes.'

'Are you talking about your personal life? Or about politics?'

'Both,' he replied with an apologetic smile. 'It's not so easy to be a white man any more. And it's fucking difficult to be a sensitive, non-sexist New Age father of a pair of Neanderthal twins!'

And once again she scrabbled around in vain in her store of comforting words. *A luta continua.* She could so easily reach for slogans before. *We shall overcome*. Was it that she had changed? Become too cynical for slogans? *Wild women don't get the blues. Don't worry, be happy. Have a nice day*. Or had all those slogans never really offered any comfort anyway?

As she stared wordlessly at her dear friend, Paul came around the corner of the house. Cool and stylish in khaki trousers and a light linen jacket. As elegantly poised and pale as Dirk Bogarde in *Death in Venice*. As though he had carried his passion for movies so far that he had turned into a movie character himself. She could almost hear the theme music, the heart-tugging Adagietto of Mahler's Fifth Symphony.

'The Great Gatsby,' muttered Max next to her, as though he could read her thoughts.

'Where's everyone?' asked Paul, as he walked towards them, smiling.

'In the kitchen,' said Max. 'Where else?'

She leaped up to kiss him, held him close perhaps a moment too long, suddenly uncomfortably aware of the fact that his partner had died less than six months ago.

'If you know what's good for you,' warned Max, 'you'd relax out here with us for a while. It's a madhouse in there. Talk about too many cooks!'

'Didn't Adriaan say it was going to be a light supper?' Thank god the sardonic smile hadn't vanished, thought Bobby. But his eyes were hidden behind very dark sunglasses. As dark as night. 'Now it sounds more like the usual Babette's Feast.'

'You know Adriaan,' said Max. 'He can turn a plate of scrambled egg into a performance.'

By this time, the twins had lost interest in the teddy bear. Max tried to entertain them by bouncing one on each knee, as they banged their fists against his chest and grabbed at his ears and crowed with pleasure every time his face screwed up in pain. Paul sank into the nearest chair and viewed his friend with an expression of concerned horror.

'When I saw them last,' he murmured, 'they weren't so . . . active.'

'I can't remember them ever being anything but active,' grimaced Max. 'Even before they were born. Sometimes they carried on so much in Liane's tummy that we could've called in the riot squad.'

'They look more like you than her.'

'To our disappointment, yes. We hoped they would inherit her fantastic looks. And my brilliant brain.'

'Nothing wrong with your looks. Or Liane's brain! She's making more money than any of us these days!'

'So far, it doesn't look as though they've inherited anyone's brain. We suspect that they're genetic throwbacks. From a more primitive time when aggression and a drive to conquer were the most important male characteristics.'

'As far as I can tell,' mumbled Bobby, 'they're still the most important male characteristics.'

'Anyway, they're a hell of a blow to my reputation as a sensitive man,' sighed Max.

Paul turned to Bobby, his eyes still invisible behind the dark glasses. 'And how is the new love?'

'Not so new any more. We've been together almost two years now.'

How long had he and Riaan been together? Four years? Five? And now a lifetime of loneliness stretched ahead of him. She remembered the first year after Robin's death. The feeling that there was a hole in her heart which nothing or no one could ever fill. That everything would gradually leak out, all remaining emotion, the last bit of hope for something better. And now there was only a tiny, tiny crack remaining.

'And you?' she asked carefully. 'How's life treating you?'

'Sometimes I think I had a bloody raw deal. To be in the closet for your whole life, and when you eventually meet someone who gives you the guts to come out, he gets Aids. At other times I think that a few days of intense happiness with someone you love can make up for a lifetime of mere . . . existence. And I got a whole lot more than just a few days.'

'I thought so, too. After Robin's death. *This is it. One can't expect more than a certain percentage of happiness in one's life – and I've had mine with her.* I didn't think I could ever be as happy with someone else. And now . . .'

'But are you just as happy with Zelda?' He leaned forward, his elbows on his knees, his voice suddenly urgent. 'Or is it just a compromise? Rather half unhappy with someone than completely unhappy on your own?'

'No,' she answered slowly. 'I'm not *just* as happy. But I'm happy in a different way. Sometimes even more happy. Other times more unhappy. Of course. It's never exactly the same. But I'm also not exactly the same person I was ten years ago. My needs have changed.

If I had to meet Robin now . . . as I am now, as she was then . . . I'm not sure it would have worked out so well . . .'

She stopped talking, confused. Suddenly feeling as though she'd betrayed her dead beloved. But the eagerness with which he listened to her, still leaning forward, the unfamiliar, unsardonic – grateful? – little smile on his lips, the hint of a dimple in his chin, made her suspect that at last, for the first time today, she'd said something that could, in some way, comfort someone else.

'Has anyone got any original New Year's resolutions?' asked Adriaan at the head of the long table on the stoep. Actually, two tables pushed together to make enough space for twenty guests. They had been eating for almost two hours, and as the dishes – and bottles – grew emptier, the tongues grew looser, the laughter louder, the general atmosphere more frivolous. 'I mean, something less boring than living more cautiously or making more money.'

'It's never boring to make more money!' Liane cried out indignantly.

'A subject she knows a lot more about these days than the rest of us,' teased Paul, who was sitting between her and Yvette at the foot of the table.

'It's only boring when other people make more money!'

'She still believes she can buy herself an escape route,' grinned Max, opposite Bobby. 'Though now it's a bit more expensive, as she has me and the twins to drag along.'

'An escape to where?' asked Jans, further down the table.

The lenses of his glasses so dirty that he probably couldn't see his plate, his chin covered in stubble and his clothes crumpled. Thank god, thought Bobby. Thank god her friends hadn't all turned into middle-aged models. At least there was still Adriaan, with his hat and his plait and his bare feet – even though he wore designer underpants these days – and Yvette, in an antique hand-embroidered silk dress – even though she looked almost elegant tonight, not half as eccentric as years ago – and Zelda, dear, lovely Zelda, who had refused to wear anything smarter than her usual dungarees over a sleeveless vest. It was clear that, next to her, Adriaan could hardly keep his hands off her bare, dark shoulders. And she wondered in bewilderment where the sudden, sharp stab of jealousy came from.

'Doesn't matter,' said Liane. 'It's not where you're going to, it's how you get there. And I like travelling in style.'

'But you don't really like travelling,' said Yvette, amused.

'I don't mean it literally, my darling! I'm talking about my journey through life!'

There was no chance that Adriaan would ever seduce Zelda, Bobby assured herself. And yet. He must have some smouldering secret, something which drew women like moths to the flame, otherwise Mila wouldn't still cringe every time those grey-green eyes scorched her. Like now. The way she darted her eyes over to Herman, lifting her glass to him, smiling almost desperately. Like a small, frightened creature looking for protection.

'If she wasn't so afraid of flying,' Max explained to Sipho diagonally opposite him, 'she would have fled to London long ago.'

'Another frightened white woman?' asked Sipho, his black eyes mocking her.

'Perhaps,' admitted Liane with a smile which would disarm anyone. 'But seeing that I can't get to London, I've decided to make the best of what I've got here. That's my New Year's resolution. To be more positive about Africa.'

'Good for you!' Sipho's laugh was mellow.

'All of Africa rejoices, I'm sure,' muttered Max.

'Are you still scared of flying?' asked Paul in amazement.

'More scared than ever, my darling. But now it's got nothing to do with my fear of technology. Ever since I flew with Nelson and Alexander I've discovered a whole new level of horror.'

'Is Nelson named after Madiba?' Rehana asked.

Still an astoundingly sensual woman, with that generous mouth, those black eyes. Max was probably thinking the same, because he stared at her in admiration every now and again, with a nostalgic smile. Which wasn't lost on Liane, who responded with an occasional irritated glare in his direction. What does one *do* with jealousy? wondered Bobby as she noticed Adriaan's hand on Zelda's shoulder again.

'Max reckons so,' Liane replied before her husband could open his mouth. 'But I had Admiral Nelson and Alexander the Great in mind, really.'

'Entirely fitting,' grinned Ralph. 'They have the inborn belligerence of great warriors.'

'And it certainly can't harm Nelson to have a politically correct name,' said Rehana with a cheeky smile.

Yvette, the one person in the company who had had enough reason to be jealous for life, leaned back in her chair, completely relaxed. She was the one who had – with unusual bossiness – forbidden partners to sit next to each other tonight. Now Bobby wondered if she didn't want to be as mischievous as her husband, just for once. Scratch open a few suppressed emotions, create a bit of drama, make the meal more interesting. So that she could watch the whole affair with that secretive little smile at the corners of her mouth.

Her husband, stroking Zelda's shoulder sensually and staring at Mila with an unfathomable expression in his eyes. Mila, pretending to be oblivious of Adriaan's attention, but struggling to hide her discomfort. Herman, talking enthusiastically to Mart about London – where he had also lived for a few years – without noticing Mila's desperate gaze. Max, struggling to tear his eyes away from Rehana, blissfully unaware of Liane's obvious irritation. Jans, trying to involve Sipho in a political discussion, not realizing that Sipho didn't want to let his bride-to-be – and her white ex-lover – slip from his gaze for a moment. Ralph, sitting next to Mila, laughing, but looking longingly at Leslee on the other side of the table every now and then. Or perhaps guiltily. Joe, leaning across Yvette to flirt openly with Paul, while Johannes was deep in a literary conversation with Griet. Emma and Charl – Mart's companion – talking like old friends, heads so close together, voices excited. You would never guess that they'd only just met for the first time.

Bobby suddenly wished that she could write a story. *New Year's Eve 1994*. No, that was too unimaginative. *You Can't Always Get What You Want*. That's what she'd call it. Or perhaps something like: *Wild Horses Couldn't Drag Me Away. Sparks Will Fly. No Satisfaction.* Funny that she could only think of Rolling Stones' songs. Perhaps she had indeed grown old enough, as she had jokingly declared this afternoon, to appreciate old music. Old music and old friends.

What would she have done without the people around this table?

'My New Year's resolution,' said Emma about an hour later, as if Adriaan's question had only just reached her, 'is to be less fearful. I've

449

decided that 1995 is the year in which I'm going to shake off my absurd fear of the dark. And hopefully a few other fears as well.'

'You don't seem to me like a frightened woman!' said Charl, surprised.

'Oh, but I am!' she said with glittering grey eyes. A hurricane of hair about her head, as usual. Charl looking at her in fascination. 'I'm scared of the dark, I'm scared of relationships, I'm scared of dying, I'm scared of living . . .'

Something's happening here, thought Adriaan as he watched them. By now, he had established in his unsubtle way that Charl and Mart weren't lovers. 'Just friends,' both had parried quickly. Too quickly? But it was too late to stop anything, anyway. Charl had fallen for Emma like a ton of bricks. As things looked now, he'd be lying at her feet, literally, by the end of the evening. And Emma glittered, her eyes, her smile, her whole face, as she had last glittered during her honeymoon weekend.

'And how are you going to conquer these fears?' asked Mila. 'Are you going to spend all of your prospective fortune on therapy?'

'No,' said Emma. 'I'm going to close my eyes and jump. I'm going to force myself to switch off all the lights in my house at night. That's a start . . .'

'And the other fears?'

'We'll just have to see.'

'Perhaps you should close your eyes and jump into a relationship,' teased Zelda. 'Doesn't look as though that should be too difficult.'

And Emma blushed like a schoolgirl. Irresistible, thought Adriaan, as he dished up the last helping of Leslee's equally irresistible leg of lamb. The other guests' appetite for meat was apparently satisfied; most of them were already eating salad or cheese. Some had pushed their plates to one side and were dancing in the moonlight. Liane and Paul at the forefront, like long ago, gliding over the stoep floor like two graceful swans. After all these years, thought Adriaan with an unexpected surge of nostalgia, they still danced like an old married couple.

'My New Year's fear . . .' Bobby's eyes stretched wide and she giggled into her glass of wine. 'I suppose you could call that a Freudian slip. My New Year's resolution is to be less serious. To laugh more. I want to be lighter!'

'If you get any lighter,' warned Ralph, 'you'll rise up and float away!'

'That's the whole idea,' smiled Zelda.

'I'm not talking about physical weight,' said Bobby. 'I know I don't have enough meat on my bones!'

'Enough for me, my sweet,' Zelda consoled her.

'And once again I want to know what the plan of action is.' Mila stared at her wine glass, her face almost inappropriately serious for this flippant conversation. 'I mean, it's easy to say that I'm going to conquer my fear, I'm going to face life with a lighter spirit, blah, blah, blah. But how are you going to *do* it?'

'I could probably start by reading the newspaper less often.' Bobby raised her shoulders casually. 'That would instantly reduce the chances of wanting to burst into tears ten times a day.'

'You can always read fairy tales,' Griet suggested. 'A lot more entertaining than newspapers.'

'Are you talking about your subversive adult fairy tales?' asked Bobby sceptically.

'All fairy tales are subversive,' Griet replied. 'Little Red Riding Hood and Snow White are seriously undermining as role models for any modern girl.'

'Or you can watch TV more often,' grinned Ralph. 'Nothing like a good old soap to make you feel as light as a bubble.'

'Believe me, Ralph, I'm not *that* desperate to have a lighter spirit.'

'Not that the writing of soapies does much to lighten *my* spirits,' said Ralph, shaking his head. 'It's still a damn depressing business.'

He looked at Leslee, who had begun dancing with Sipho, her smooth black hair shining in the moonlight, her skin almost blindingly white against her dancing partner's dark face. Beside them, Max was swinging Rehana around. Her swaying body looked as seductive as ever, Adriaan noticed. Behind them Joe and Johannes and Yvette and Griet, all in a thronging circle. *Gimme hope, Joanna.* A protest song from the Old South Africa to help them dance bravely, hopefully, into the New South Africa.

'I see you're still running yourself down,' said Emma. 'I thought that now you're sleeping with a shrink, you'd begin to like yourself more!'

'I'm not running myself down!' Ralph protested. 'I'm just laughing at myself a little! I think that this whole so-called rainbow nation of ours ought to make a communal New Year's decision not to take ourselves so seriously.'

'But why are you so . . .' Before she could say any more, Charl had pulled her out of her chair and was leading her towards the dancers. She shook her hair out of her face and called laughingly over her shoulder. 'I don't know why I always fall for such bossy men!'

'Good luck, Emma Kolêma,' said Ralph quietly and raised his glass to her retreating back.

'This meal is now really falling apart,' declared Mila. 'Don't you think it's time for your flaming pancakes, Adriaan?'

'They're your pancakes,' he said. 'My only contribution is setting them on fire.'

'You were always good at lighting fires,' she said with a joking twist to her lips. And sadness in her eyes.

'We all have our humble talents.'

'Well, it's almost midnight. If we want to have the pancakes on the table before next year, we'll have to get going.' She turned to Ralph, held her hand out gallantly and smiled seductively. 'But first I want to dance with my oldest and dearest friend. Before his wife claims him for the rest of the evening.'

Why hadn't she asked *him* to dance? Adriaan wondered as she walked away with Ralph. Her hips – fuller than before, but no less attractive – swaying in a narrow black dress with a low back. Actually only the top third of the strong, muscular back was exposed. And the back of the long neck of course. Not half as daring as some of her outfits in the past, he thought. Again flooded by a wave of nostalgia.

He had always viewed himself as a fairly good dancer, but with her he'd sometimes felt as if he was leaving the earth, as if gravity no longer sucked his broad feet to the ground. As if he could do anything, could move his sturdy body in any possible way, as if he was floating weightless in water. As if he could keep on for ever without getting tired.

When he'd had sex with her, he'd felt the same.

He remembered her best in that old blue dressing gown of her father's, the contours of her body desirable under his hand, under the soft flannel.

'Such an unsexy item of clothing for such a sexy woman,' he had reproached her once.

'Somehow I don't see myself in a see-through pink negligee,' she'd remarked drily. 'I'd feel like Miss Piggy in the *Muppet Show*. Besides, my father always said a woman should leave something to the imagination.'

'You can also leave too much to the imagination.'

'Not with your imagination, Adriaan Beyers. You could undress even an Eskimo woman with your eyes.'

Yes. He remembered a dusky evening on the balcony of her Cape Town flat, light years ago, her short wet hair and her warm damp skin under the flannel dressing gown. They had made love the whole afternoon. No, not love. This was after they'd tried not to have sex for more than a year. The result was an insatiable hunger for each other's bodies. A shameless, violent hunger. They bit and scratched and jerked each other around mercilessly. But when they stood under the shower afterwards, the lukewarm water slowly soothed all the aggression away, massaged the sore muscles and the bruises, until at last their wet mouths were filled with loving whisperings. He made her bend over, her buttocks soft and smooth under the caressing cascade of water and entered her from behind, this time carefully, terribly carefully, so as not to hurt her again. And he was rewarded with one of the most memorable orgasms of his life.

Afterwards, she had poured wine for them, lit a cigarette, and stood on the balcony staring at the sea. In her beloved blue dressing gown. He wanted to be with her – it was as though he could never be close enough to her for long enough – but he didn't want to prance around naked in the open air. So he pulled on a ridiculous flowered gown, an old-fashioned nylon thing which the owner of the furnished flat had forgotten on a hook behind the bathroom door. He had stood behind her and kissed her long neck, and his hands immediately found the familiar pathways across her body.

It was meant to be nothing more than an affectionate caress, the flannel a safe shield between his fingers and her skin, but by this time he ought to have known that any caress between them would always open the floodgates. The almost panic-stricken way she used to gasp for breath when his fingers folded over her breast. Sometimes he could swear her breasts were more sensitive than other women's, the skin thinner, the nerve endings more exposed, the nipples live power points.

Electrical wires running straight to her loins. He had listened to her shallow breathing and pulled the dressing gown up, sliding his hands between the lips of her groin. The flood gates were already open. He couldn't stop.

He never wanted to stop.

He had sunk down on his knees, his forehead against the small of her back, just above the curve of her buttocks, and pressed his fingers deep inside her. She had gripped the balcony wall with both hands and her body strained backwards while it began to move around his fingers. They gave themselves over completely to this slow, erotic dance, she in her men's dressing gown and he in his borrowed old-woman's wrap. He hoped he was kneeling low enough so that no one could see him from the street. But he couldn't really care.

With his left hand he had stroked her legs – wondering, as always, at the contrast between the firm outsides of her thighs and the silky softness inside – as his right hand kept dancing inside her. Slippery-soft muscles contracting and relaxing around his fingers, contracting and relaxing, contracting and relaxing, as regularly and rhythmically as the sea. Until her movements suddenly lost all their rhythm and her body began to shudder uncontrollably.

'Now I'm hungry all over again,' she had whispered, turned quickly round, pulled him up by the shoulders urgently and guided him inside.

He made love to her again, to his astonishment. And this time it was indeed love. Or so he thought.

'Why didn't you ask *me* to dance with you?' he asked when they were standing alone in the kitchen, his heavy voice purposefully light.

She looked up from the dish full of pancakes she had made earlier. And then looked down at her hands again quickly. Folded another pancake in half, and then in half again, forming a neat triangle.

'Probably because I was afraid.'

'Surely you can't still be afraid of me!'

'I was never afraid of you, Adriaan,' she said seriously, her eyes invisible behind the blonde fringe. 'I'm afraid of myself. With good reason, I should say.'

'Are you happy with Herman?' he asked as he mixed melted butter and sugar in a glass bowl.

Her mouth fell open, bewildered. Definitely not the right time for this conversation, he scolded himself. A stolen moment of seriousness in the middle of a light-hearted New Year's Eve meal.

'Yes,' she said quietly. 'Believe it or not.'

And yet. Everything which had happened between them in the last decade had happened in stolen moments. Moments of honesty, he sometimes thought, in a lifetime of dishonesty.

'It's not difficult to believe. He looks like a good man.'

'He's more than good to me, Adriaan. He . . . well, I can't really say he saved my life, because I had to do that myself . . . but I think he saved my soul. I was becoming a bitter, self-pitying, cynical old woman. I thought I would never have a relationship which worked. And then I met this tall, gentle man with a strange accent . . . and I told him about my illness . . . and it didn't frighten him. He really seemed to understand my fears, and my lack of self-confidence, and how I struggled to cope with the disintegration of my body. And that gave me courage to show him my body at last. *Months* after I'd met him. He was unbelievably patient with me. I got the feeling he would have waited *years* if necessary. And even that didn't frighten him away. I think not even death will frighten him, you know?'

'I'm glad, Mila.' He stirred the juice and the grated rind of three lemons into the butter mixture, his eyes on his hands. 'I'm sorry I couldn't be the one who made you happy, but I'm really glad that you are happy.'

'You made me happier than anyone else.' Her smoky voice was now very close to him, so close he didn't dare look at her. 'Unfortunately, also unhappier than anyone else.' She laughed, a heartbreaking little sound which made him wish he could block his ears. 'I told you a long time ago that the whole thing was too intense for me. The high points were too high . . . and the low points too low. With Herman, things are more moderate.'

'You know what I think of moderation!'

'Healthier.'

'Long ago you said, screw health.'

'Perhaps I shouldn't have tempted fate.' Another quiet little laugh, tearing a shred from his heart. 'I'll never again live as recklessly as I did before, Adriaan. I got too much of a fright when I got sick.'

In the meantime, he'd added orange liqueur and brandy to the mixture in the glass bowl and turned to the stove to cook the syrup in a big saucepan. Stood a few moments with his back to her, listening to the pulsing music outside on the stoep – Yvonne Chaka Chaka, he guessed – and trying to calm his unsettled emotions.

'I wish,' he said with a sigh, 'we could have met each other under different circumstances. In another life!'

'Perhaps we will.'

'You know I don't believe in that metaphysical crap.'

'Pity. It can be quite a comfort.' She shrugged her shoulders and passed him a few pancake triangles. He lowered them carefully into the simmering orange syrup. Concentrated on this simple task. 'All I know, Adriaan, is that I'll never be able to build a relationship on the ruins of another relationship. Not in this or any other life.'

'You didn't ruin my relationship with Yvette, Mila. You probably saved it.'

'Ha!'

She spat the word out with so much bitterness that he looked at her, shocked, the egg-lifter still in his hand.

'If you hadn't persuaded me to come back, I'd probably still be in Johannesburg. Too proud and too jealous to try again.'

'I merely snatched the log from the flames, Adriaan, that's all. After I had helped light that fire, my eyes wide open.'

'I don't know about wide open eyes. Love is supposed to be blind.'

'I don't know about love.' Her voice was suddenly sharp with sarcasm. 'I only know about lust.'

'It was more than lust, Mila.'

Accusingly. And at the same time defensively. More than brief lust – otherwise it would have blown over ages ago, like all his other affairs – and yet also less than life-long love. Otherwise they wouldn't be having this stolen conversation in a house he shared with another woman.

'Well, whatever it was, it wasn't enough!'

Is it possible to feel life-long lust for someone?

'Just now you said it was too much . . .'

'All I know, Adriaan, is that you were always in love with Yvette, above and beyond what you felt for me. That I couldn't bind you to me in any way! That I couldn't even tell you that I was pregnant! That you never . . .'

'You were pregnant?'

'Oh, fuck! I didn't want to tell you! Not like this! You can't just

456

blurt out something like that over a dish of pancakes! It's not the right fucking time!'

She slapped herself on the forehead with her open palm, a useless, powerless gesture which reminded him of the first time he'd kissed her. When she saw Ralph's silhouette in the kitchen doorway. *Fuck, fuck, fuck.* There was never a right time for them, he thought. Not for anything.

'I would have told you some time or other, Adriaan.' Her hands now in front of her mouth, her voice twisted into her fingers, as if she was talking into a handkerchief. 'Probably in the near future. But not tonight . . .'

'Did I make you pregnant?'

'Twice.'

'*Twice?*'

Stay calm. Concentrate on the fucking pancakes. He had to keep his hands busy, otherwise they'd begin to shake. They were shaking anyway. He struggled to hold the egg-lifter properly.

'The first time was after the first time we slept together . . .'

'The first time,' he repeated, stunned.

'Well, somewhere in the course of those first few days . . . when we had sex day and night . . . I got pregnant. I didn't use contraception because I'd been trying to get pregnant for months. With Ralph,' she said quickly, embarrassed, apologetic. 'Without any success. By the time you arrived in Johannesburg, I had begun to accept that it wasn't going to happen, that I must have some fertility problem . . .'

'And then it happened.' His voice sounded as shaky as his hands felt. 'What did you do?'

'I didn't need to do anything. I had an early miscarriage.'

Her voice still smothered in that invisible handkerchief, her hands now hanging limply at her sides.

'And the second time?'

'The last time. When we had that last fling. After you'd left Yvette. After I swore that I'd never sleep with you again. After I told *Yvette* that I'd never sleep with you again! So I decided to say nothing . . . to anyone . . . because I thought it would probably end up in a miscarriage, anyway. And yet there was still . . . this desperate part of my heart . . . which knew that it was my last chance to have a child. A woman of forty isn't meant to get pregnant just like that. After a last fling with an ex-lover who's also halfway over the hill himself! It was this part of my heart which kept hoping . . . that the pregnancy would work this time. I dreamed that I would be able to raise the child on my own . . . never tell anyone who the father was . . . I almost convinced myself I'd be able to pull it off. But I also had nightmares. That the child would look exactly like you. Like Mona. That all our friends would know who the father was straight away, the moment they saw him. That Yvette would know the moment she saw him. Funny, it was always a boy. In my dreams and in my nightmares.'

By this time he had sunk down on to the nearest chair, his legs too weak to pretend that he cared about the pancakes any more. Mila had taken the egg-lifter from him, standing with her bare back to him, placing a few more triangles in the pan.

'And then you had another miscarriage?'

'No. Then I got cancer. Just when it began to look as though the pregnancy would work out. My friends probably thought I was picking up weight because I stopped smoking. Ralph was the only one who knew. Not that you were the father. Just that I had a reason to stop smoking. I had to tell someone . . . and he's my oldest friend . . .'

The shoulder raised apologetically again, the head bent further forward, the angle of the bare neck more vulnerable than ever.

'Why didn't you ever tell *me*?'

Careful, terribly careful to keep even a shadow of blame from his voice.

'Well, this time you were in Johannesburg and I was in Cape Town . . . just the opposite of the previous time . . . and we had already decided that it was better if we didn't contact each other. We both knew you wanted to come back. Back home.'

That's how he would remember her for the rest of his life, he thought. With her back turned to him, while every word from her invisible mouth tortured him, the scent of pancake and orange in a cloud about her. Outside on the stoep, somewhere in another world, Bruce Springsteen's voice growled into the night. Another life, he thought, with a sense of yearning. *Dancing in the Dark*. His friends' laughter audible now and then above the music. *You sit around getting older, there's a joke here somewhere and it's on me.*

'Anyway, when I discovered the lump in my breast, the doctors basically gave me an ultimatum. Pregnancy is the last thing you can afford when your body can't cope with oestrogen. So I had an abortion.'

'I'm sorry. I'm sorry I didn't . . .'

He stopped talking because he couldn't think of anything to say. Wished that he could lock himself into his studio now. Paint that back and that neck.

'*Voilà!*' She turned around at last, two worn dishcloths in her hands, the dish of hot pancakes held high in front of her. As though she was offering him a gift. On her face, the bravest smile he had ever seen. 'Crêpes Suzettes.'

'Perfect timing,' he said as he heard the excited laughing voices rise up once again above the music. The clock on the wall next to the fridge pointed to midnight. 'For once in our lives,' he added, wryly.

'Happy New Year,' they said simultaneously, suddenly embarrassed, shy of each other.

He stood up and reached his arms out to her, realized too late that she was still holding the dish and simply touched her shoulders clumsily. The pancakes a steaming barrier between them. He kissed her swiftly on the cheek. The scent of orange in his nostrils for a moment, as sweet and sharp as nostalgia.

'Get the matches,' she said teasingly, her voice now light, almost floating. '*You can't start a fire without a spark.*'

He poured the rest of the syrup over the crêpes and lit the dessert. When he looked up, she smiled at him – comforting? conspiratorial? or perhaps just as she would smile at any friend? – before she turned around and carried the flaming dish outside. He watched her bare back as he stood silently next to the kitchen table. Just a moment, he thought, he needed just a moment to sort himself out. To catch his breath. To try to fix the usual jovial smile on his face.

Then he walked outside, where all of his friends thronged excitedly around the table, impressed by the dancing blue flames in the dish. Found his wife's dark head among the bunch – with an inexplicable feeling of relief – and heard at the same time, to his surprise, his daughter's voice rise high and enthusiastic above the hubbub. Saw her standing on the other side of the table between Dylan and Kathleen – all three should have been sleeping ages ago – her cheeks pink and her eyes glistening above the blue flames. It wasn't the new year which was inspiring her, he realized as she grabbed Dylan's arm, laughing. And he suddenly remembered what Yvette had said that afternoon. He hadn't really been listening, too busy cooking, but the sad tone in her soft voice had remained with him. *I think our daughter is in love for the first time*. It wasn't possible, he thought in confusion. She was born only the other day.

'Blow out the flames, Mona!' he called out, as cheerfully as he could. 'Before all the alcohol burns away!'

She bent over – without loosening her grip on Dylan's arm – and blew over the dish. As eagerly as she had recently blown out the candles on her birthday cake. Nine flickering flames. He wrapped his arms around Yvette from behind, sniffed deeply at the scent of her smooth hair, saw the happiness flare up in her dark eyes as she looked over her shoulder at him. Always a new flame somewhere.

'I hope it's a good year for you, my loveliest wife.'

'I'm your only wife,' she giggled, exactly like her daughter. 'And I'm sure it will be a good year.'

As optimistic as ever. In spite of everything.

Group Photo (1995)

It was Liane – who else? – who insisted that they take a group photo again. Although most of them, on this first day of 1995, after a celebration which had lasted most of the night, felt anything but photogenic. Twenty years older and plainer and wearier than ten years ago.

But what Liane wanted, Liane usually got. Her ex-husband and her present husband both knew her well enough not to quibble. They were the first two to sit down meekly on the red couch.

She ordered Yvette to move in between the two men – again, like ten years ago, the centre of the photo – and tried to arrange the rest around the couch. Tried, and gave up half way, because the group continued to grow as lovers and children and stepchildren and even dogs were dragged in.

'Goodness gracious!' she exclaimed. 'I'm a stylist! Not Cecil B. de Mille tackling a movie with a cast of thousands!'

'Let *me* do it.' Paul leaped up to come and stand behind the tripod. 'I always wanted to know what it would feel like to be Cecil B. de Mille.'

'Sit down, Paul,' she commanded him. 'If everyone's going to leap up, I'll never get this photo taken.'

'I'm not your husband any more,' he grinned. 'You can't boss me around like that.'

'That's my lot in life these days,' muttered Max, with half of the twins on his lap.

She rolled her eyes and went to sit obediently on the couch. Picked up the other half of the twins and waited patiently for Paul to press the automatic button on the camera and take his place on the arm rest next to her. The usual dazzling smile on her face.

So, on the photo you see three exemplary parents in a row: Liane and Max on either side of Yvette, each with a dark-haired baby on the lap. The twins in identical white shirts with navy blue sailor collars – specially dressed for the photo and looking unusually demure. Frida like a little barbarian between them, dressed in nothing but a disposable

461

nappy, although her eyes are so old and serious you would swear she was wearing her Sunday best.

Something about Yvette, maybe just the old-fashioned pinafore dress, still reminds you of a dreamy child. And yet an older, less innocent child than Alice in Wonderland. *Dorothy from Kansas!* As Emma cried out when she noticed the red satin shoes. With Ralph behind the couch – of course – in the role of the Lion. A much tamer lion than years before, his golden mane still an impressive sight, but his attitude definitely less predatory. More like a peaceful ginger cat, with his five-year-old stepson under one arm and his other arm draped almost possessively over Leslee's shoulder. Leslee, slender and sober in black, black hair and black-framed glasses. Nana Mouskouri in the role of the courageous lion tamer.

Adriaan could probably be described as the messy Scarecrow. Old straw hat on his head, faded T-shirt and over-large shorts, barefoot. Cross-legged on the floor in front of Yvette – the saucy red shoes against his right knee – his tanned labourer's hands on his nine-year-old daughter's shoulders. As if he wants to prevent her from leaping up and running away. Mona is leaning forward to keep a watchful eye on Dylan, sitting on the furthest edge of the row in front of the couch; his mouth sulky, his thin arms wrapped protectively over his knobbly knees, his whole attitude a picture of pre-adolescent boredom and embarrassment. His eight-year-old sister next to him looks like a seductive little Lolita with an arch gap-toothed smile. The promise of an exceptional future beauty just beginning to blossom.

Bobby and Zelda sit on either side of Adriaan, each with a woolly mongrel on her lap. 'Well, seeing that everyone's children are in the photo,' Zelda had said, at which Mona immediately leaped up to fetch Tat. But the Labrador had wandered away, bored, just before the camera flashed. Only his golden tail is visible in the left-hand corner of the photo.

Zelda laughs with a wide open mouth, teeth glistening white against the milk chocolate skin, while Bobby also smiles a lot more cheerfully than in the last group photo. Or perhaps just more determined to look cheerful, in the light of her New Year's resolution. The eyes behind the round glasses are still grey and wise and a little wistful.

Paul, on the arm rest next to his ex-wife, has apparently changed the least of them all. The same sultry attractiveness, the smouldering eyes and the model's chin, seemingly not a day older than when the last group photo was taken. Remarkable, because his life path had probably wandered the furthest from the direct, predictable highway to success which had stretched out ahead of him then. Dorothy's brave Tin Man, Emma decided when she studied the photo, the one who couldn't cry because his tears would make his shiny, well-oiled body rust. The one who thought that he didn't have a heart, and in the end discovered his heart after all.

Mila sits on the other arm rest, next to Max, and, just like last time, she doesn't look at the camera. Her arms crossed in front of her chest, her hands on her bare shoulders in a sleeveless red dress, her face only slightly turned away this time. Her gaze resting on something below her, perhaps Yvette's smooth fringe or Frida's curly hair, perhaps Adriaan's heavy hands on his daughter's shoulders. And yet the little smile on her red lips looks content. Herman stands behind her with a proud hand on her graceful neck, tall and slender and athletic, the kind of body she'd always liked.

Emma also stands behind the couch, a whole head taller than Leslee, with her hair hanging about her face like a home-made Christmas wreath. No longer flaming orange, but still not the kind of head which would vanish in a crowd. Her daughter, at almost five, still as blonde and blushing as a doll, held tightly in her arms. The man who stands next to her is the surprise of the photo. Looking almost as uncomfortable as Philip had the last time.

'The surprise of the decade!' Adriaan had exclaimed when he bumped into him in the kitchen earlier that morning. 'Emma has a sex life again!'

'I feel like a gatecrasher who accidentally lands up on a family photo,' he mumbled as they waited for Paul to set up the camera. 'When the family looks at the photo in ten years' time, no one can remember his name.'

'I'm sure Emma will remember your name,' grinned Ralph. 'As a farmer will always remember the first proper rain after a long drought.'

'You make me sound like a bloody nun!' Emma accused him.

'You were turning into a bloody nun,' Max remarked. 'I don't know what this guy did to break through your invisible chastity belt. But I think he deserves a medal.'

'What is a chassity bell?' Sasha asked from her mother's hip.

'Perhaps the time was just right,' Yvette speculated. 'The prince arriving at precisely the right moment to rescue Sleeping Beauty.'

'I know how you feel.' Bobby looked over her shoulder at the newcomer and smiled sympathetically. 'Ten years ago I was the odd one out among this lot.'

'And she was odd, believe me,' Paul said as he took his place on the arm rest.

'And then we couldn't get rid of her,' Liane added laughing. 'So perhaps in ten years' time, you'll be part of our next group photo!'

'We'll have to see,' Charl grinned and ran his fingers nervously through his light hair.

'We'll have to see who of us will still be here in ten years' time,' Mila said quietly, her eyes already downcast, like on the photo.

'We'll have to see who of us will still be here tomorrow,' Emma said, looking uncertainly at the man next to her for a moment, and then smiling resolutely for the camera.

If you hadn't seen that fleeting uncertainty, you would have described the smile as glittering.

Acknowledgements

This story, which grew over more than thirteen years and at last took shape on three continents, would not have been possible without the help and support of various individuals and institutions.

I want to thank the South African Foundation for Creative Arts for an international bursary allowing me to take part in the International Writing Program at the University of Iowa in the USA, where I was able to draw on the experience and encouragement of other writers from around the world. Thank you, too, to my editors and publishers in Cape Town and London for the confidence they had in the story even before it was complete, and to my agents in London, Carole Blake and Isobel Dixon, for their continuing enthusiasm and patience.

Thank you, in a painful, personal way to my mother, Yvonne van der Vyver, and various friends who shared their experiences of life-threatening diseases such as cancer and of the death of loved ones with me; especially my friend Zelma Muller, who, on her death bed, was still intensely interested in the progress of this story in which she had believed from the start.

As usual, it is the people who are closest to my heart who deserve the most thanks. My son, Daniel, for all the hours I would rather have spent with him than in front of a computer, my family and friends, who helped to babysit – or to cook unforgettable meals – while I was working on the manuscript in France, and all the rest of my friends whom I neglected so terribly while I wrote this story about friendship.

And to the Frenchman who hates to be thanked, nevertheless, for his heart and for his food: *Merci*.

Cape Town
January 1999

Glossary

Ag – exclamation, used by English and Afrikaans South Africans alike; like 'oh', but pronounced very like the Scots 'och'.

Afrikaner Weerstandsbeweging (AWB) – Afrikaner Resistance Movement: a far-right white organization, which uses a version of the swastika as its symbol.

bakkie – light delivery vehicle, pick-up.

basters – bastards, mongrels; also used to denote people of mixed race.

bedonnerd – bad-tempered, moody.

boer – literally, 'farmer', but used to denote an Afrikaner.

boeredans – literally, 'boer dancing': a popular type of partnered dancing, a less formal version of ballroom dancing. See '*Ken jy tant Mossie . . .*'

Boeremeisie – boer girl; used jokingly here to denote traditional, old-fashioned values or characteristics.

boeremusiek – boer music; refers to a type of folksy dance music, usually involving an accordion.

boerewors – literally, boer sausage, but used to denote a type of spicy mutton sausage popular in South Africa.

Boerseun – boer boy; used jokingly here to denote traditional, old-fashioned values or characteristics.

bokkems – dried Cape herring.

bra – brother, similar to the US 'bro'.

braai, braaivleis – barbecue, barbecue meat.

Broederbond – the Brothers Union: a formerly secret Afrikaner male-only society with Masonic overtones.

Buitenverwachting – fine Western Cape estate wine; the estate name means 'beyond expectation'.

Casspir – armoured vehicle, used by the South African army; much in evidence in townships during the State of Emergency.

Codesa – Congress for a Democratic South Africa: the negotiating forum at which the terms of the 1994 elections and the new constitution were hammered out (slowly).

dagga – marijuana.

dagga zol – marijuana cigarette; spliff.

dam – in South Africa, dam is used to describe a small lake as well as a water-retaining structure.

dominee – minister, here probably in the Dutch Reformed Church.

dorp – little town; commonly used in South African English.

ECC – End Conscription Campaign

Egoli – name given by black mineworkers to Johannesburg; literally 'place of gold'.

Emma Kolêma – character in a traditional song.

Esme Euverard – Afrikaans female radio personality.

Free State – the Orange Free State: one of the provincial divisions of the Old South Africa.

fynbos – Euphorbia: name for an extensive group of plants found in the Western Cape.

galjoen – blackfish, *Coracinus capensis*.

gatvol – fed-up; literally 'arse-full'.

gogga – any type of insect, creepy-crawly; commonly used in South African English; the 'g' sounds are strongly guttural.

graaf – spade; the 'gr' sound is strongly guttural, the 'r' rolled.

Groot Krokodil – literally, 'Great Crocodile': pejorative name for former South African President P. W. Botha.

grot – cave; the 'gr' sound is strongly guttural, the 'r' rolled.

jôl – rave; a good time.

Kanonkop – fine Western Cape estate wine; the estate name can be translated as 'Cannon Hill'.

kelkiewyn – literally, 'wine-cup'; bird name.

'*Ken jy tant Mossie se sakkie-sakkie-sakkie boeredans . . .*' – Literal translation of old song: '*Do you know Aunt Mossie's sakkie-sakkie boer dancing . . .*'; see *sakkie-sakkie* and *boeredans*.

kikoi – rectangular cloth of striped cotton, worn sarong-like around the hips; worn traditionally by African men, though not historically in South Africa.

kleilat – old children's game, using clay (klei) and a stick or lathe (lat).

koeksister – traditional South African confection made from plaited dough, deep-fried and soaked in syrup.

kort-kort – literally, 'short-short'; very soon, quickly.

kraal – pen, fold, corral.

Kreepy Krauly – suction device to clean swimming pools.

Leon Schuster – popular South African comedian.

Madiba – term of endearment for Nelson Mandela.

Mannetjies Roux – famous South African rugby player; his first name is a nickname meaning, literally, 'little man'.

Meerlust – fine Western Cape estate wine; the estate name is of German origin, but could be interpreted as 'More Desire' in Afrikaans.

Mike Schutte – South African boxer, about whom jokes are made on the basis of his supposed lack of intelligence.

Mimi Coertse – Afrikaans opera singer.

moer – literally, 'nut' (on a bolt): an equivalent of 'cunt', commonly used in strong expressions; 'se moer' literally means 'your cunt', but is less strong than the English equivalent, more like 'your arse'.

moffie – gay man, effeminate man.

muti – witch doctor medicine, magic potion.

net-net – literally, 'just-just': only just.

nou-nou – literally, 'now-now': soon.

NP – National Party.

ouma – grandmother, granny.

oupa – grandfather, granddad.

pastorie – minister's (dominee's) house; vicarage, rectory.

perlemoen – abalone, mother-of-pearl.

PFP – Progressive Federal Party.

platteland – literally, 'flat land'; refers to rural areas, away from the urban centres; used in South African English.

Pongraz – well-known South African sparkling wine.

Robben Island – island off the coast of Cape Town where political prisoners (most famously Nelson Mandela) were detained.

rooibos tea – literally, 'redbush tea'; popular South African tea without caffeine and low in tannin.

Rust en Vrede – fine Western Cape estate wine; the estate name translates as 'Rest and Peace'.

sakkie-sakkie – traditional partner dance; a relaxed type of ballroom dancing, still popular in South Africa, more commonly in the Afrikaans community.

SAP – South African Police.

Sonja Heroldt – Afrikaans singer, often jokingly referred to because of her sweet voice, squeaky-clean reputation and cloying lyrics.

South West – South West Africa: country to the north-west of South

Africa, on the west coast of Africa; formerly a South African Protectorate and the subject of dispute, now independent and called Namibia.

soutpiel – literally, 'salt penis': derogatory term for English South Africans who, because they metaphorically have one foot in Britain and one in South Africa, allow their penises to dangle in the sea.

speel-speel – literally, 'play-play': pretend.

stoep – porch, verandah.

Swapo – South West African People's Organization.

tannie – auntie.

Tassies – abbreviation of Tassenberg: an exceptionally cheap red wine, commonly drunk by students.

toyi-toyi – dance typically performed in protest marches and demonstrations.

Transvaler – someone from the Transvaal province, often scathingly referred to by people from the Cape Province; both are provincial divisions from the Old South Africa.

troepie – one of the troops, the armed forces, a soldier; familiar term used at the time when all young white men were conscripted.

troupand – literally, 'wedding ring'; bird name.

UDF – United Democratic Front: anti-apartheid movement.

vaderland – fatherland.

velskoene – hand-crafted leather shoes.

Verwoerd – Hendrik Verwoerd: assassinated Prime Minister of South Africa and one of the early architects of apartheid.

volk – the nation, the people (specifically Afrikaners).

Voortrekkers – Dutch settlers who moved inland away from British rule in the nineteenth century.

Vrye Afrikaan – newspaper name: '*Free African*'.

waterblommetjies – literally, 'little water flowers': a type of water lily used in a traditional lamb stew, especially in the Western Cape.

wit wolf – 'white wolf.'

wragtag – truly, indeed.

Permissions

The publishers wish to thank the copyright holders of the following song lyrics for permission to reprint them.

'Dancing in the Dark' copyright © Bruce Springsteen (ASCAP). Admin: By Zomba Music Publishers in UK & Eire Only

'Why I Sing the Blues' copyright © King/Clark by kind permission of Universal Music Publishing Limited

'Suburban Hum' published by Janifa Songs, copyright © Jennifer Ferguson, email: jennifer.ferguson@utryck.se

'Homeward Bound' copyright © 1966 Paul Simon (BMI) Pattern Music Ltd

'Tango Till They're Sore' words and music by Tom Waits, copyright © 1986 Jalma Music, USA Warner/Chappell Music Ltd, London w6 8bs. Reproduced by permission of IMP Ltd

'Graceland' copyright © 1986 Paul Simon (BMI) Pattern Music Ltd

'This Be the Verse' by Philip Larkin by kind permission of Faber and Faber

'The Boy in the Bubble' copyright © 1986 Paul Simon (BMI) Pattern Music Ltd

'Vuur' words and music by Stef Bos, copyright © Hans Kusters Music, Belgium, 1994

Every effort has been made to contact copyright holders of material in this book. The publishers apologize if any material has been included without permission and would be glad to be told of anyone who has not been consulted.